CW00869942

Echoes and Shadows

BY THE SAME AUTHOR

My Love, My Land
Who Was Sylvia?
Miss Gathercole's Girls

ECHOES AND SHADOWS

Judy Gardiner

C

CENTURY

LONDON MELBOURNE AUCKLAND JOHANNESBURG

I acknowledge with grateful thanks the use of the Bircher Library during the preparation of this book.

Copyright © Judy Gardiner 1988

All rights reserved

First published in Great Britain in 1988 by
Century Hutchinson Ltd
Brookmount House, 62–65 Chandos Place
London WC2N 4NW

Century Hutchinson South Africa (Pty) Ltd
PO Box 337, Bergvlei, 2012 South Africa

Century Hutchinson Australia Pty Ltd
PO Box 496, 16–22 Church Street, Hawthorn
Victoria 3122, Australia

Century Hutchinson New Zealand Ltd
PO Box 40–086, Glenfield, Auckland 10
New Zealand

ISBN 0 7126 1944 5

Photoset by Deltatype Ltd, Ellesmere Port, Cheshire
Printed in Great Britain by
Anchor Brendon Ltd, Tiptree, Essex

Book One
Shadows

There were one or two who said it wasn't right to hang Bessie Hinton, what with her being a woman and in her particular state. But justice is justice, and as the judge said as he looked along the row of prisoners in the dock, if I go letting one of them off after they've been declared guilty I'll be guilty of interfering with the proper workings of the law. And that's a wicked crime, too.

The legal man who was representing Bessie did make a special plea on her behalf, and although her face had been deadly pale it went red as an Ely sunset when the judge made her stand up so that he could look at her figure.

'When is your child due to be born, woman?'

'Any day now, your honour,' the legal man said, on behalf of Bessie.

'In that case,' said the judge, 'sentence will be delayed until after the event.'

She stumbled a bit as they took her down to the cells because of her being so heavy, and some of the spectators jeered. It was only some of the older ones who felt sorry for her; the young lads didn't because they were at the stage in life when a carrying woman is just something to make jokes about. Hurry up and drop your bolster, Bessie, so they can drop you. . . .

In her cell there was nothing but a three-legged stool and a pile of straw in one corner by way of a bed. The walls were stone and the barred window was too high to see out of.

They brought her a piece of bread and a bowl of gruel but she didn't feel like eating. All she wanted was a cup of water because it was June and the weather was hot. She sat down on the stool but couldn't get comfortable, so she lowered herself down on the straw. She sat with her back against the wall and her legs bowed out in front of her, and all she could think was how much more she had to endure than the rest of them.

3

In the first hours of waiting she wanted nothing so much as to get it all over and done with; to tear the child out of her body and then say to them well, here I am; get on with it and the sooner it's all finished the better. In some ways she felt half-dead already; killed by the weight of shame and scandal and the dread of all the pain that lay before her.

She hoped the travail would start in the night, but it didn't. She dozed in fits and starts, with the straw tickling her neck and her big warm belly pulsing with life. Towards first light she was awoken by the tramp of feet and the sound of voices outside in the street. The noise grew louder, and she knew it was people arriving early for a good view of the executions. The din increased, shouts and laughing and somebody blowing a trumpet, and all the time she lay there listening and trying not to picture it all. Trying not to feel helpless as a rat in a boxtrap.

They brought her some more gruel, which she still didn't want, and asked if there was any sign of the pains starting. No, not yet, she said, and felt guilty. Even more guilty, I mean.

The sun came up from behind the cathedral, but couldn't find its way into her cell. The noise outside got worse, laughing and singing and street vendors shouting and above it all the sound of hammering on wood, and it was the hammering that made her feel worst of all. It was the sound of the scaffolds going up.

She got up off the straw and did what nature required in the bucket they had left behind the door. Then she drank a little more water and then knelt down, very slowly and clumsily, and prayed the Lord's Prayer and asked God's forgiveness for her sins.

Then outside it went quiet. No more shouting or laughing or hammering. No more silly tootling from the trumpet. But she knew they were still there, all the people who had come to see the hangings. She could sense them breathing and rustling and fidgeting, like vultures waiting in a tree.

Then the sound of hooves. The slow heavy hooves of dray horses and the grating of cart wheels over cobbles. She put her hands over her ears but the blood roared in them like the sound of the sea, so she took them away again. The wheels and the hooves had stopped. The silence was broken by the crash of the tailboard being let down and she knew it was the cart in which

4

the men had been driven round the town for everyone to see their wickedness and their shame, before taking them to the gallows.

She tried not to listen, not to think. She didn't want to go through it all twice; once with them in her thoughts, and then with herself and it really happening to her.

She got up off her knees and started walking up and down, wishing again that she was with them so that it would all be over and done with. She hated the child because it was to blame for her not being out there with the others, getting it over and done with.

She heard a man's voice breaking the quiet outside. A high singsong parson's voice; she couldn't hear the words, only the singsong like they always used in church. Then there was a silence followed by a great deep gasp from the people watching, and she clasped her hands tight over her belly, but whether to protect the child or try to squeeze it out of her she didn't know. She started praying again, in the hope that speaking to her Maker would ease her mind.

She prayed a lot during that long hot day, in between rearranging the straw in the corner by teazling it up and then stroking the stalks down flat, then brushing the wisps of it from her calico dress and trying to tidy her hair. Her boots were dusty and she wiped them clean on the underside of her kerchief. When the gaoler came in she asked if she could have some water to wash herself, but it was late afternoon before it came, and by then she was so thirsty that she drank it instead.

And the spectators outside began shuffling away because there was nothing new to see. Just a row of men dangling from the gibbets. There was no more sport to be had because they were all dead; dead as a row of nails held in a blacksmith's teeth.

The gaoler came in again and asked her if her travail had started, and she said no. Beggin' your pardon it hasn't, not yet.

It didn't start for two more days, and because it was her first she didn't straightway recognise it for what it was. She thought it was hunger pangs because she hadn't touched a morsel since before she was sentenced.

When the gaoler came in and saw the nature of things, he told her that they would send for a midwife. A proper midwife from the town. She'd be all right, he said, with a proper midwife to see after things.

5

She nodded, sweating with the pain, and asked will she be here soon? I'm feared to go through it all alone.

The midwife came shortly before dark, her bonnet askew and her breath fumy with gin. She put her hand up Bessie's skirt and said you've got a lot more suffering to go yet. You're nowhere near.

Talk to me, Bessie cried, please talk to me to keep my mind off it, but the midwife slumped down on the straw with her back against the wall and her bonnet cocked over her eyes and went to sleep.

She woke up when the gaoler came back, bringing a lantern to see by and a cup of milk for Bessie. And when he held the lantern up and beheld Bessie lying there running with sweat like a pig in farrow, he went back for a bucket of water and a rag to wipe her face with. Poor creature, he said, bearing a child in a place like this.

Let's pray it's born dead, said the midwife, to spare it all the shame and misery.

She went back to sleep, the gaoler went away, and when the time came that Bessie knew the child was about to be delivered into the world she suddenly sat up, her eyes mad with terror because she didn't want to die by the rope as the others had done. The childbirth pain roared all round her but she tried to hold it back, to stop her baby getting born by sitting hard and tight on the place where she knew it had to come out from, but her moans woke the midwife, who saw what she was up to and dragged her hands away and made her lie back on the straw with her legs wide open.

Bessie swooned, and when she came to again it was to find her son lying beside her wrapped in the kerchief she had used to clean her boots with.

Her first feeling was to hold him, to suckle him at her breast like any ordinary woman, then out of the shadows of her swoon she remembered that she wasn't any ordinary woman. She had committed a dreadful wicked crime, and was feared that some of her wickedness might pass to him through her milk or through her kisses, so she gave him to the midwife and said take him away. I don't want to see him no more.

A cold grey dawn came creeping into her cell and she waited,

*like a poor cornered animal, to hear the first tramping of feet and
the first sounds of cruel jollity in the street outside.*
  I can picture it all now.

Sitting in the hen-run with her hair screwed up in curl-
papers, Lizzie Hinton aged fourteen thought about the
coming visit to Aunt Netta's. She didn't want to go. She
didn't like Aunt Netta, she didn't like going to Wisbech and
she didn't like being dressed up.
  I wish I was a hen.
  If I was a hen I wouldn't have to do anything I didn't want
to. I'd just scratch for worms, go to roost and lay eggs when
I felt like it. And when I got old, Pa would just wring my
neck nice and quick and I'd go in the pot. Boiled chicken
and parsley sauce.
  Preparations for the annual visit to Aunt Netta had begun
last night, when Edwina Hinton removed the tin bath from
its hook on the outside wall of the privy and lugged it into
the farmhouse kitchen.
  'You first, Lizzie.'
  'Just let me finish this.'
  'You've bin reading that book all afternoon. Get your
things off before the water goes cold.'
  'Suppose Pa comes in and sees me?'
  'Pa's gone over the fen to see Willy Stow's cow. Any case,
you can't show him anything he ain't seen before.'
  I dare say not, Lizzie thought. Except that mine are new.
  She closed her book with a sigh and began to undress.
Although it was sultry mid-August she wore a sleeveless
cotton pinafore over a blue serge skirt and high-necked
blouse, a woollen vest, cotton drawers, black cotton
stockings and black button boots. Turning to face her
mother she pulled her shoulders back and squinted down at
herself.
  'How much bigger d'you reckon they'll get?'
  'Wait and see, same as other girls.'
  With its two panfuls of hot water and one of cold, the
bath water came just halfway up Lizzie's rump when she sat
down.

7

'Now bend your head while I do your hair.'

Lizzie complied, her arms clasped round her knees, and Edwina untied the ribbon that held her daughter's long auburn hair back from her face. Slowly she poured a jugful of warm water over it, squeezed it out a little and then began to rub it with a tablet of Sunlight soap.

'I'm not having it in corkscrews, am I?'

'Yes.'

'Oh, Ma – *why?*'

'You know you always have corkscrews to go and see Aunt Netta.'

'It's not fair – '

'As soon as you're sixteen you can wear it done up.'

'Why've I got to wait 'til I'm – ow, it's going in my *eyes* – '

'Hold this in front of them.' Edwina placed a wrung-out square of flannel in her hands and then continued to rub at the mass of hair, lather creaming between her fingers.

'There, that'll do. Now hold still while I rinse.'

Lizzie did so and another jugful of water descended, slowly at first and then gathering momentum until the streaming torrent made her gasp for breath.

'Right. Now wash the rest of yourself while I put some more water on for me and your pa.'

With her hair skewered up in a dripping knot, Lizzie obeyed, then stepped out of the bath on to the brick floor and began to towel herself dry.

'I look like Fanny Stott in corkscrews.'

'I like you ladylike when we go to Aunt Netta's. I hope your white stockings don't need darning.'

'What are you going to wear?'

'The bombazine. She's seen it before, but I can't help that.'

Detecting a faint hint of fellow resentment, Lizzie tried to fan it into flame. 'I don't think it's fair the way we all have to pretend to be different just because it's Aunt Netta. I mean, she's only Pa's sister, isn't she?'

'Aunt Netta's got class. It just seems to come natural.' Edwina arranged another pan of water to heat on top of the black iron range.

'You're much better looking than she is,' Lizzie encouraged.

'I'm getting stout.'

'Well, she's like a bit of chewed twine. I'd much rather be like you than her.'

Edwina smiled; the smile lit up her eyes and illuminated her wide, generous country features, but it didn't prevent her from going to the cupboard under the stairs for a wad of newspapers. Sitting down at the kitchen table she began to tear them into strips.

'Don't rub your hair too dry,' she said. 'It curls best when it's still damp.'

So here was Lizzie on the following morning, sitting in the hen-run, which from earliest years she had regarded as a place of solace in times of trouble. Although it was not yet seven o'clock, they had already breakfasted and the day promised to be hot. The weather had been hot for over a week, draining the Cambridgeshire fens of colour and absorbing every hidden drop of moisture.

The curl-papers in which Lizzie had slept rustled whenever she moved her head, and one of the hens paused to look at her with its red comb flopping over one inquisitive eye like a tam-o'-shanter.

'Aunt Netta always brings out the worst in people,' Lizzie told it. 'She makes everyone else feel wrong. That's why nobody likes going to visit, although nobody admits it except me.'

The hen came closer and began to croon very quietly. It knew Lizzie well, and remained unperturbed when she put both hands round it and lifted it on to her lap.

'Dear ole henny girl . . . who's a good girl then, eh? Love your ole Lizzie, do you?'

After a preliminary fluffing of feathers the hen settled down, its body warm and heavy beneath the layers of petticoat plumage.

'Lizzeee! Come in and get dressed!'

Lizzie sighed, and buried her face in the hen's neck.

'Lizzeee!' Edwina's voice floated through the orchard, its urgency diluted by distance and the inertia of the summer morning. Reluctantly Lizzie removed the bird from her lap, flicked at the wet little mess it had made on her pinafore and went indoors.

Edwina was already dressed, her country plumpness confined beneath Sunday stays which showed a pattern of whalebone busks through her black bombazine. As soon as her daughter was attired in flowered cotton dress, white stockings and well-polished boots, she began to remove the curl-papers. Each lock of glowing auburn hair sprang from its rustling bondage and tumbled in thick ringlets over Lizzie's shoulders and down to her waist. Edwina brushed each one and curled it round her finger while Lizzie shifted and sighed with impatience.

'And when we get there, remember you speak right and don't bolt your food.'

'Yes, Ma.'

'Because I won't have Netta looking down on us, just because she lives in Wisbech. After all, she's only a farmer's daughter like the rest of us.'

'Yes, Ma. Have you nearly finished?'

'Only a couple more. And listen, if she asks to hear you recite, don't do *The Blind Beggar's Lament*. It goes on too long.'

'No, Ma.'

'Do the one about the little girl who lost her dolly.'

'Yes, Ma.'

Finally released, Lizzie went downstairs. Her father, Walter Hinton, was in the kitchen, sitting in the rocking-chair and breathing stertorously while he leaned to lace his new boots. He was wearing a stiff collar and his best suit.

'You look a real dandy-man, Pa.'

'Weather in the eighties and me got up like a dog's dinner. Blooming ole collar's got a real stranglehold.'

He was a square, slow-moving man whose eyes seemed filled with the immeasurable distance of the fens. Both he and Edwina came of farming stock and Lizzie was their only surviving child, the first one, a boy, having died when he was three days old. The desire for a son had resulted in two miscarriages for Edwina, and now Walter was resigned to

10

second best; but the girl he had sired seemed in tune with the land, and appeared quick as any lad at picking up farming skills. If Lizzie kept on the way she was now, Damperdown Farm could do worse than end up in her hands.

With his bootlaces tied in bows round the back of his ankles, Walter straightened up. He sat looking at his daughter with his hands on his knees.

'And you look above average too, my gel.'

'Thank you, Pa.' Lizzie simpered briefly. 'Can I help harness Polly?'

'Polly's already done and waiting. Reuben saw to that.'

'So there's nothing left to do?'

'No,' Walter said heavily. 'Except to git on with it. The sooner we git there the sooner we can come back.'

'I couldn't stand to live in a town.'

'No more could anyone with sense. Towns squeeze the breath out of you.'

Edwina came downstairs, looked sharply at them both, then ordered Lizzie to put her hat on. Lizzie did so; it was a wide-brimmed straw hat with blue ribbon streamers tied round the brim and hanging down the back.

'Where's your gloves?'

'Here, Ma.' White cotton ones with a pearl button at the wrist. She had had them since she was twelve and they were too tight.

'Got your posy?'

'Yes, Ma.' A little bunch of roses and pansies encircled by a lace paper doily.

'Dare say we're ready, then.'

Edwina took up the basket of plums she had picked, then the three Hintons, each bracing themselves a little, filed out through the back kitchen door.

Old Reuben had brushed the mare's tail and mane, and she stood patiently waiting between the shafts of the wagonette. Her nosebag hung from its back axle and the floor had been swept clean and then carpeted with two new sacks.

Nothing more could be done in deference to Wisbech and

11

Aunt Netta, and as Walter gathered up the reins and called *Hup away*, they trundled out of the farmyard and down the long rutted track towards the gate.

Aunt Netta was tall, thin and etiolated, and wore a white lace cap in the house and hid the legs of her parlour piano beneath black twill stockings of her own design. She had never married, having decided at the age of fifteen that men were rude, crude and not to be trusted.

A modest allowance from her father, and upon his death an equally modest legacy, enabled her to live in a state of decorous cheeseparing in the better part of Wisbech. The house was tall and narrow and Georgian, and she lived with the aid of only one domestic. Keziah occupied the basement and spent all her waking hours scrubbing and scouring, cooking and carrying trays. Keziah was small, squat and damp like a toad, and always followed six paces behind the missus when they attended divine service at St Peter and St Paul, the parish church. She had been retrieved by Aunt Netta from the Union Workhouse at the age of twelve, and had remained touchingly grateful ever since.

Aunt Netta thought a great deal about God, and often wondered what God in His infinite wisdom thought about her. It could only be flattering. The opinion of her neighbours was equally important, and while quick to discourage those of a pushful nature, she rejoiced in the friendship of Mrs Plumptre, who lived round the corner by the museum. Mrs Plumptre was a large and otiose widow, rich and lazily powerful in local society, and her father had helped to found Singapore.

But it was devoutly hoped that Mrs Plumptre would not choose to call today, because brother Walter had driven his family over from Damperdown Farm to luncheon. To Aunt Netta's irritation, he had left their old farm wagonette outside the house where everyone could see it.

The small gifts had been dutifully presented and Aunt Netta had graciously admired the posy and then rung for Keziah to take the fruit to the kitchen in case there might be insects in it.

They had then partaken of a little careful conversation. 'How is your harvest, Walter?'

'Not doing too bad, I reckon. And how's Wisbech?'

'I have no information concerning the lower strata, but Miss Wilkins – an acquaintance of my very close friend Mrs Plumptre – has been to a soirée at Buckingham Palace. Her uncle was recently involved in a series of experiments concerning the earth's magnetic field.'

'What's that, then?'

'I should have thought it more a subject for gentlemen than for ladies. But I dare say you have little time for things of the mind, Walter.'

'That's it,' Walter agreed. 'When I'm not working I drop down dead as a hammer in me bed.'

'And how is Lizzie?' enquired Aunt Netta, quietly savouring her sister-in-law's discomfiture at Walter's reference to bed.

'Nicely, thank you, Aunt,' chirped Lizzie from the horsehair sofa.

'And you, Edwina dear?'

'Very nicely too, thank you,' mumbled Edwina, choking on her own social incompetence. Each time she met Netta she vowed it would be different and each time it was the same – the red-faced, stiff-fingered farmer's wife from the fens hopelessly outmanoeuvred by this thin stick of celery with her mincing ways and house full of knick-knacks.

As for Walter, he thought little of his sister Netta one way or the other. They had had nothing in common even as children at Damperdown Farm, when Walter took a boy's delight in chasing the older Netta with a live eel, in shocking her with descriptions of the bull's prowess at its work and sickening her with the sight of partially dead rooks crucified by wings and feet to the barn door. And Netta had aroused comfortable contempt in her brother because she preferred to remain clean and sweet-smelling, because she couldn't stand heights or noise or pain, and because she tattle-taled to Mother about various misdeeds which would otherwise have passed unnoticed.

Adulthood had brought with it a certain understanding

13

and a certain magnanimity, but little in the way of genuine affection. Family duty was as far as it went, and standing stiff-collared and stifling-suited in Netta's parlour, Walter wondered why he always agreed to come. Standing opposite him in full grey skirt, tightly fitting bodice and immaculate white lace cap, Netta was inclined to wonder why she always invited him. And his wife and child.

She smiled and said, 'Perhaps you would be kind enough to assist Edwina in to luncheon, Walter. My cook has everything ready in the dining room.'

They proceeded to the room at the rear of the house. As in the parlour, the windows were tightly closed, the lace curtains closely draped. The darkly papered walls were hung with large engravings, mostly of a religious nature, and on the bobbled overmantel stood a stuffed owl in a glass case.

The table was laid with a green baize cloth over which had been placed a starched white one with fancy edging, and Edwina suffered a reluctant stab of envy at the carefully arranged cutlery, the dainty china (every piece of which matched), and the highly polished glasses and water jug. The covered vegetable dishes were already in place, the leg of mutton steaming on its dish, and after directing her guests to their places Aunt Netta began to carve.

She carved slowly and fussily, little thin slices that ended almost before they began, and the amount of meat on Walter's and Edwina's plates, when eventually she passed them, barely covered the sprig of forget-me-nots with which they were decorated in the centre. To Lizzie she allotted a half portion.

Constraint made Edwina accept one potato only, and then half a carrot when the dish was passed. Reminding Lizzie to tuck her table napkin in the neck of her frock, she missed the cabbage altogether, but was able to cohere what she had with a little thin gravy.

'For this Thy bounteous gift we give humble thanks to Thee, O Lord,' said Aunt Netta, with bowed head and the carving knife at rest.

'Amen,' her guests obediently intoned.

They began to eat, and Edwina frowned across at Walter for shovelling. He always shovelled at home, huge fork-loads of good fen vegetables mixed with great chunks of meat, and as he chewed he hummed; a soft deep humming like that of some large and smoothly running machine. He began to hum now.

'Walter,' Edwina said warningly.

'Dear?'

He looked across at her, still chewing, still humming. Apart from that there was no sound in the room.

'Pass the salt, please.'

'Perhaps you would pass your mama the condiments, Lizzie,' said Aunt Netta. 'Polite people always try to pass things without being asked.'

It was very hot in the dining room. Airless, sultry and uncomfortably constrained. To Edwina's added dis-comfiture her stays began to creak.

Yet somehow the conversation perked up a little, and although Walter thought longingly of home-brewed beer as he eyed the crystal-clear water in his glass, he had a kindliness which sprang from the heart and not from the love of etiquette.

'A very nice dinner, Netta,' he said. 'And very nice of you to ask us over.'

'I often think it strange that we meet only once a year,' Aunt Netta said. 'It can only be that our paths have diverged.'

'We both come off the same rootstock and you could have bin a farmer's wife two or three times over, only you didn't seem to fancy it. Even as a young gel, you didn't fancy the land.'

'Town life is more to my taste.'

'Reckon I'd smother in a town,' Edwina said, 'although I wouldn't mind the shops.'

'And what about you, Lizzie?' asked Aunt Netta, inclining with great deliberation towards her niece. 'What are your plans, now that you are growing up?'

Suddenly aware of being the focal point, Lizzie turned pink. 'I want to stay at home and keep chickens, Aunt.'

15

Aunt Netta gave a benevolent little chuckle, then raised her table napkin to her lips and patted them. 'And is that all?'

'Well, I wouldn't mind a few ducks as well.'

'Lizzie,' Edwina admonished nervously. 'Finish your dinner before you get left behind.'

'Speaking of dinner,' put in Walter, 'I could manage another couple of potatoes, Netta, along with some greens and a chunk more meat.' He passed his plate.

Frowning slightly, Aunt Netta raised the lid of the nearest vegetable dish, and then said a mute goodbye to Keziah's main meal for tomorrow. She served him as requested, and a bead of perspiration rolled from Edwina's hairline towards her eyebrow. The room was far too hot and her stays were far too tight. Declining a second helping, she accepted a little more water.

'Your dear grandparents – on your father's side, that is – were both born in Australia,' pursued Aunt Netta, replacing the lid of the vegetable dish with one small carrot still mercifully intact. '*Their* parents, who were your father's and my *grandparents*, emigrated there in order to teach the natives something of our own farming skills.'

'Yes, Aunt, I know.'

'But your grandfather Harry, after he married Miss Mildred Pew from Adelaide in 1836, brought her back to the old country as a bride. They came back to the Cambridgeshire fens and bought a farm and raised a family. Your father and I, in other words.'

'Yes, Aunt,' repeated Lizzie dutifully.

She had been able to find Australia on the atlas at home since she was six, and had boasted liberally to schoolfriends about having exotic forebears, and was familiar with her grandparents' grave in Upwell churchyard. But her personal recollection of them was no more than a comfortable blur since they had died, within two months of one another, when she was three. The farmhouse she lived in had once been theirs, and her parents now slept in their bed.

Aunt Netta rang the little silver bell at the side of her

16

plate and after a short interval Keziah sidled in carrying a large tray, her freshly starched cap speared remorselessly to her knob of dank hair. In heavy silence she collected the dishes and plodded from the room. She returned with a cabinet pudding and a prune shape.

Walter hummed his way through a helping of both, the two ladies contented themselves with a tiny portion of prune shape, and Lizzie was told that she ought to choose prunes because they were good for growing girls. With her gaze on the cabinet pudding, Lizzie did as she was told.

'We thank Thee, O Lord, for this Thy bounteous repast. Amen,' said Aunt Netta and rose from the table. The others followed her into the front parlour.

Creaking audibly, Edwina sank down on to the horsehair sofa next to Lizzie; Walter went out to the street to give the mare her nosebag, and on returning settled his neck a little more comfortably into his collar and his behind into the button-backed chair, while Aunt Netta seated herself in the window and proceeded to get out her needlework. Glazed with boredom and half-stupefied by the heat, the three visitors prepared, each in their different ways, to endure the next three hours before Keziah brought in the tea.

'What's that you're sewing, Netta?' ventured Edwina.

'Garments for the poor,' said Aunt Netta, threading her needle. 'I belong to the Dorcas Society, which meets every Monday.'

'Oh.'

Interest died. Conversation died. There was no sound but the occasional rustle of material and the rhythmic soughing of Edwina's rigging. Lizzie, counting the roses in the carpet, suddenly cleared her throat and her father's eyelids flew open for a moment, fluttered helplessly and then closed again.

Two more hours and fifty-one minutes of stultifying boredom, so thick that you could crawl into it and expire; asphyxiate, like a fly trapped in the folds of a blanket. There never has been, and there never will be again, a boredom quite as dense and all-embracing as a Victorian boredom. Convention piled upon stifling convention had seen to that.

17

Close the windows. Abhor the sunlight and fear the moonlight. Denounce all laughter and innocent happiness, dwell only upon the tragic, the retributional and the incurable diseases. Rejoice in the smirk of righteousness; cover the ankles, and disinfect the soul three times daily with prayer.

Why did we come – why do we ever come to Netta's? wondered Edwina, perspiration trickling from armpit, upper lip and nape of neck. Why does she ask us? Just to preen? To make us feel rough and unrefined? There's no pleasure in meeting when we've nothing to talk about. I spent two whole days getting us up for this – starching and ironing and mending and polishing. . . . Then there was getting us ready to leave the farm for the day – Reuben, remember to shut the chickens up by after-tea, scald the milk in case it turns, and don't forget to water the pumpkins and feed the dog with the scraps I left ready in the meatsafe. . . . It's not worth it, except as a duty.

And Aunt Netta, stitching a neat French seam, thought why do I ask them except that Walter's my brother and she's my sister-in-law. They're so rough and unrefined and we've nothing to talk about. It's a duty, that's all. It's everyone's duty to preserve family ties. . . .

Duty, repeated the marble clock on the chiffonier. Duty – duty – duty. . . .

Then something totally unexpected happened. Shattering not only in its immediate consequences – a pin running into Aunt Netta's hand, Walter choking on an arrested snore – but shattering in a much deeper sense.

They all sat rigid, and it was as if some premonition told them that the sudden loud knocking on the front door would reverberate down the ensuing generations with all the dark insistence of a family curse.

Hastily Aunt Netta rose from her chair as the visitor entered the room, and her immediate reaction was one of relief that it wasn't Mrs Plumptre.

He was tall and lean, with black hair and mutton-chop whiskers and a pointed nose that twitched slightly as he

18

breathed, and his mere presence seemed to obliterate the little creeping Keziah who had ushered him in.

'My dear Netta,' he said, and produced a bunch of marguerites from behind his back. 'I was passing your way and thought I'd call.'

'Vernon Seagrave!' Aunt Netta looked extraordinarily flustered. 'I – I was not expecting you.'

'Of course you weren't,' agreed Vernon Seagrave. 'As I just said, I was passing your way and decided to call and give you a look-see.' He seized her hand and shook it heartily, then gave her the flowers. 'Beg pardon for the lack of wrapping paper but it was late, and the florist's shop almost closed.'

'Most kind,' said Aunt Netta, beginning to recover. She handed the flowers to Keziah. 'Place these in water – in the old *brown* vase.'

Keziah retreated, and Aunt Netta indicated her other guests. 'I'm not sure whether you are acquainted with my brother Walter, and his wife Edw – '

'Charmed, I'm sure.' Vernon Seagrave smiled and shook hands vigorously.

' – and his wife Edwina and their daughter Lizzie,' Aunt Netta concluded, ignoring the interruption. 'They live some way out of Wisbech, on the farm where we were brought up as children. Mr Seagrave' – she turned to her brother's family – 'is a very distant relative on our mother's side. There were some English Pews, I believe.'

'The Pew side, eh?' said Walter. He smoothed his hair with his hands and endeavoured to sound both affable and interested. 'I may have heard your name spoke, but don't exactly recollect – '

'Mr Seagrave visited the farm several times when we were children,' Aunt Netta said to him, 'but I dare say you were too young to remember.' It was becoming very apparent that she viewed this latest visit with a marked lack of enthusiasm, but as yet no one had had time to wonder why.

'I travel all over the place in my particular line.' Cheerfully Vernon Seagrave seated himself. 'Which is wholesale ironmongery. I'm a partner in an establishment in Rotherhithe – look, I'll leave you my card – and once every few years it's my duty to visit our East Anglian customers. I go round each and every shop personally to make sure that our goods satisfy and that our prices remain keenly competitive. Saffron Walden I go, Littleport, Downham Market, Wisbech, King's Lynn – '

'You've left out Ely,' Lizzie said, and was shushed for interrupting.

A small silence fell.

'Ah yes, indeed,' said Vernon Seagrave. 'Ely. We'll come to that later.'

Reseating herself, Aunt Netta rang for Keziah to bring in the tea, somewhat in advance of its usual time.

'So you're from the Pew side?' Walter subjected Vernon Seagrave to a long and thoughtful stare.

'The eldest son of Mary Pew, who was an English cousin of Mildred – your late mother, that is – which makes me some kind of uncle so far as I can work out.'

His black whiskers and jolly laughter made him seem far too young to be any kind of uncle to Netta and Walter. He turned to Lizzie and pinched her knee. 'And how about you, young lady? Getting to learn a few things down on the farm, are you?'

He pinched her knee again and Lizzie squirmed confusedly.

'How long are you planning to stay in Wisbech?' There was no hint of persuading him to dally in Aunt Netta's voice.

'I've a pony and trap waiting at the Duke's Head. I'm going over to Peterborough tomorrow, so aim to put up at Thorney tonight.'

'I see.' She sounded relieved, and when Keziah sidled in with the marguerites bunched to attention in the old brown vase, told her to place it on top of the piano. And to bring in the tea as soon as possible.

'Peterborough's a tidy step,' observed Walter. 'I've bin there but the once.'

'I was taken there for an outing when I was a child, but I don't remember it,' Edwina said, striving to dispel the strange tension of which they were all conscious.

'And how about you, my dear?' Vernon Seagrave resumed his attack on Lizzie's knee. 'Do you like big cities, hey? Big shops full of cream cakes and smart clothes – I wager you wouldn't say no to a visit if your new uncle was to take you, would you?'

He had a nice way with him; hearty, jolly, vigorous, and it was only the twitching of his pointed nose that somehow gave a hint of the predator. Lizzie's confusion increased, but while her parents sat smiling politely, Aunt Netta picked up her sewing and carried on with her French seam, thimble flashing and eyebrows raised.

Keziah brought in the tea as Vernon Seagrave was talking to Walter about the current state of agriculture. She set the folding table close against the missus' skirts and laid out the cups and saucers, the plates and the silver-handled tea knives, the milk and sugar, the tea-strainer and basin for the dregs.

She departed, and returned in due course with a plate containing buttered scones, a glass dish of strawberry jam, and on another plate a small cake dotted here and there with a sultana, and upon the top of which lay, like an offering upon an altar, a thin strip of crystallised lemon peel. All conversation had ceased as Keziah left the room once more and then came back with the teapot, a large majolica brute with gilt sprigs and twirls decorating its fat and self-satisfied belly.

'That will be all, Keziah,' said Aunt Netta, still stitching.

'Thank you, Mm.' A rustle of apron, a bob of the head, and then Keziah finally withdrew.

Very slowly and deliberately, as if the effort were almost beyond her physical strength, Aunt Netta laid aside her needlework, slipped off her thimble and turned her attention to the tea-table. She frowned, and reached for the bell.

'Yes, Mm?'

'The sugar-tongs, if you please.'

A pause, its duration bombastically measured by the marble clock, then the reappearance of Keziah, now

21

sweating almost as heavily as Edwina, with the sugar-tongs.

'Thank you, Keziah. That will be all.'

'Thank you, Mm.'

The ritual began. Tiredly, Aunt Netta poured each guest a small ration of milk and then, holding the tea-strainer between finger and thumb, applied the teapot spout to each cup in turn with the other hand.

'Walter, perhaps you would care to hand round?'

With a squeaking of best boots Walter did so, and his huge farmer's thumbs squeezing hard on the rim of each little saucer made his daughter want to laugh.

'Lizzie, will you pray follow with the sugar, please?'

Lizzie did so, mincing after her father round the square of rose-strewn carpet.

'A scone, anyone? Edwina, would you be so good as to hand the knives and plates?'

'Allow me.' Vernon Seagrave sprang gallantly to his feet, and for a moment or two it was like a decorous drawing room dance, with everyone crossing and criss-crossing as they passed each other with tea and sugar, scones and spoonfuls of jam. Only Aunt Netta remained seated, primly in charge.

There was one scone for everyone, plus a small dollop of jam, and the first cups of tea had been sipped but not drained to the dregs when Vernon Seagrave dusted a crumb from his cravat, drew a deep breath and said: 'I fear the time has come, dear friends, when I must take it upon myself to acquaint you with news of a disagreeable nature.'

Teaspoons stopped tinkling. Walter stopped humming, a little smear of jam remaining like a bloodstain at the corner of his mouth. Only Aunt Netta sat staring into her lap as if she hadn't heard.

'I might begin by saying that I have cogitated long and ardently upon the decision of whether to speak or not,' Vernon Seagrave went on after a pause, 'and I have finally reached the conclusion that it is my painful duty to tell you what I know now to be the true facts concerning a hitherto highly respected member of our family.'

His tone was one of quiet sorrow, the dignity of his words

22

only slightly impaired by his sharp London accent.

No one said anything. They waited for him to continue.

'I will come straight to the point,' he said, 'and acquaint you with the brutal and scandalous facts as I have learned them, which is to say that Bessie Hinton – her who we thought emigrated to Australia along with her husband and infant son in the year 1816, was in fact hanged at Ely as a political agitator and common felon.'

The words fell like a series of heavy stones in the airless room.

'That's nothing but a black lie –'

Dazedly Walter put his hand out to Edwina, who had given a searing gasp. He said no more, and neither did Vernon Seagrave. Attention in that confused and terrible moment seemed automatically to become centred upon Aunt Netta, who had risen to her feet.

'Bessie Hinton,' she said finally, and with difficulty, 'was my grandmother. Lizzie – I think you had better leave the room. . . .'

She stood staring at them all blankly for a moment, then with a little sigh collapsed in a dead faint among the tea things.

They restored her to her chair with some difficulty, and during the process a teacup was shattered. Lizzie burst into tears and was immediately despatched to ask Keziah for the smelling salts.

'Hold up there, Netta,' Walter said, chafing her hands. 'Hold up now, gel.'

'Can't we open a window?' asked Edwina, fanning Netta with her handkerchief.

Vernon Seagrave hastened to obey, struggled briefly beneath the layers of lace and velvet curtaining and then had to admit defeat. The bolts were rusted and the windows sealed with successive layers of varnish.

Lizzie returned with Keziah, who gave a moan and collapsed on her knees by the side of her mistress. Someone suggested burning feathers beneath Aunt Netta's nose, but Walter snatched the smelling salts from Lizzie, uncorked them and then rammed the bottle hard up against each nostril in turn. Aunt Netta gave a high screaming sneeze and opened her eyes.

Her gaze fell upon Vernon Seagrave. 'Why . . .' she tried to say. 'Why . . .?'

'Forgive me, Netta,' he said, taking one of her hands. He pressed it tenderly. 'I made the wrong decision. I must own to that. I shouldn't have told you. It would have been far, far better to leave you all in ignorance of the dreadful facts. So let's say no more, eh? Let's all forget I ever spoke.'

'Reckon it's too late to do that,' Walter said, relinquishing Aunt Netta's other hand. 'What you've started you'd better finish.'

'No, no, I'm not saying another word. Least said, soonest mended.'

'But it can't be true what you said!' Edwina suddenly cried, and burst into tears. 'Not Grannie Hinton –'

'Don't cry, Ma.' Worriedly Lizzie put her arms round her.

'My brother's quite right,' Aunt Netta said. Now restored to her chair, she spoke in a stronger voice. 'You cannot unsay what has just been said. We must steel ourselves to listen to these wicked lies so that we can denounce them for what they are – but not in the presence of servants and children. Keziah, get up and go back to your kitchen. Lizzie, go for a walk round the garden and don't come in until you're told.'

Keziah rose from her knees and began confusedly collecting the scattered tea things.

'*Leave*,' commanded Aunt Netta, as if speaking to a dog.

Keziah slunk away, followed reluctantly by Lizzie. And somehow, those who remained contrived to calm themselves, to restore themselves to some sort of order. Walter eased his collar a little and then reseated himself next to Edwina, while Vernon Seagrave, after giving Aunt Netta's hand another reassuring pat, left her side and went to sit on the piano stool.

'Now then,' said Walter. 'What's all this about Grannie Hinton?'

24

Vernon Seagrave sat staring at the carpet, as if deep in thought. At last he raised his head and looked at them all in turn, and his expression was one of remorse blended with grief. He suddenly seemed older.

'I'd better begin,' he said, 'by telling you my sources of information. A friend of mine of very long standing, namely a fellow called Ned Taylor, is employed at the Criminal Law Reporting Institute, a learned and highly respected body that has its premises close by Lincolns Inn Fields, which as you may know, is situated at the heart of London's legal profession.

'Well, as I say, Ned and I have known each other for a number of years and so it stands to reason that we are to a certain extent acquainted with each other's family background. I know for instance that he comes from the Bethnal Green area and has a wife and three children, he knows that I am a bachelor and hail originally from the Cambridgeshire area. It must have been some time last winter when I called to meet him coming from his place of work – I'm in his area once a week, you see, and we like to take a glass and have a bit of a jaw before setting off to our separate abodes – but on this occasion of which I speak, Ned asked me in to his office as all the rest had already gone and there was nobody but us two.

'He was putting his papers away and tidying his desk when he suddenly asked me what part of Cambridgeshire did I come from. Near Ely I was born, I said, and then he said well, old fellow, you may be interested to take a squint at this, and he gave me a sheet of paper to read which contained the official report of what became known as the Ely Bread Riots of 1816.

'Well, I looked it over, not all that interested to tell the truth, until my eye chanced to fall on the name Bessie Hinton. There were Hintons in my family, that I knew, and after a bit I recollected that Bessie Hinton was the name of poor Netta and her brother Walter's grandmother. So I read it again, with great care this time, and there it was in black and white. One of the chief planners and motivators in the Ely Bread Riots was of all shameful things a woman

25

called Bessie Hinton, who not only incited men to riot, burn and pillage the surrounding farms, but helped them to terrorize the innocent and rob the weak. It was said that she did her work at night, slipping from her husband's bed in order to meet the insurrectionists, to drink and – beg your pardon, Netta – fornicate with them, and plan further acts of violence.

'The Royston Volunteer Cavalry was sent for and several people were shot dead. It took over a week to restore order and people were afraid to come out of their houses. The ringleaders of the affray were all caught and taken into custody and tried at a special assize at Ely. The judge told the prisoners that their behaviour had not been caused by any form of financial hardship – with bread at a ha'penny a loaf there was plenty for all – but merely by greed and avarice inflamed by drink. Bessie was condemned to death along with the others and there was no reprieve.'

The stuffy heat of Aunt Netta's parlour seemed to have increased during the last five minutes. No one spoke, and no one moved except for Walter wiping the back of his neck with his handkerchief. Edwina was trying not to cry, and Aunt Netta was sitting white as a ghost with her eyes closed.

'You can picture how I felt,' Vernon Seagrave resumed in a low voice. 'Thunderstruck. I didn't believe it. I didn't believe a word of it, even though it was written officially and with the royal cipher on. I couldn't rest until I had further proof, so without saying anything to Ned about it I went straight back home. I couldn't sleep that night, not a wink. I tossed and turned and kept thinking it can't be true – not a woman of our family, not *Netta's grandmother* – and next day I took the morning off work and went to *The Times* newspaper office and asked to see their files for the year 1816. I had a job to find it, but finally there it was. Bessie Hinton hanged at Ely in public, four days after her partners in crime.'

No one seemed capable of saying anything. Even the room itself seemed like something dead.

'And the reason why she was not hanged until four days after the others was because – and this is the hardest part to tell – because of her being just about full term in the family way. Her child was born in Ely Gaol and she was executed just a few hours after.'

Aunt Netta gave a little shuddering moan, her handkerchief pressed tightly to her lips.

'Wait on – wait on a minute,' Walter said with an effort. 'Bessie Hinton's son – and she only had the one, mind – was Harry. And Harry was mine and Netta's father. And it can't be right what you're saying because Harry come over from Australia with his bride, our mother . . . he was born in Australia, not here.'

'That was the story put about,' Vernon Seagrave said gently. 'What really happened was that poor Bessie's young husband took up the baby and emigrated to Australia to escape the shame. It's all a long time ago now, of course, and I dare say all's forgotten, but . . .'

His voice faded, and the word *but* hung on the air. *But there are bound to be those who know. Those who have had the real facts handed down to them through the years. Those who point at us behind our backs.*

'I asked God for His guidance about whether to tell you or not.' Vernon Seagrave broke the stunned silence. 'In some ways I thought it better to let sleeping dogs lie, but the risk of you finding out through some spiteful neighbour or idle gossip was more than my sense of duty would allow. At least with me, I'm a blood relation.'

He looked round at their frozen faces and smiled sadly, wistfully, but the marble clock took up the refrain once more: duty . . . duty . . . duty. . . .

No one seemed to know how to break the spell; how to speak, stand up, move about. Even Vernon Seagrave remained motionless, leaning forward on the piano stool with his hands hanging between his knees, his demeanour one of abject wretchedness.

In the event it was Lizzie who brought the terrible, trancelike state to an abrupt conclusion. Crouching outside the parlour door with her ear to the crack she shifted her position slightly and her elbow bumped against one of the lower panels. It made a thud. Galvanized into action,

Walter strode across and flung the door wide open. Lizzie fell in on her hands and knees, and the tension snapped in a storm of furious recrimination from both parents and aunt. Even Vernon Seagrave shook his head in sorrow.

'Lizzie – you wicked girl! – '

'You were listening at that door! – '

'You were told to go in the garden! – '

'Wicked, wicked girl! And in your aunt's house! – '

'Straight home to bed and no supper! – '

Hands clammy with sweat and trembling with shock seized her, slapped her, shook her, and the room whirled violently before her eyes.

'*Deceitful* girl! – '

'Nothing worse than low cunning in the young! – '

'Straight home – '

'No supper – '

Lizzie bawled, reduced from budding womanhood to the level of a ten-year-old. Helplessly she allowed the straw hat to be crushed down on the hated corkscrew curls. Choking and sobbing, she was hauled from the room, and when Vernon Seagrave winked at her and silently slipped a shilling piece into her hand, her tears flowed faster than ever.

Climbing back into the wagonette, the three Hintons were far too confused and upset to notice that the sun had gone in.

Down in her damp underground cell of a bedroom Keziah knelt, nightgown-clad, and ended her prayers with God bless the missus and keep her safe from the shades of night to come. Amen.

She then rose, pressed the meagre hair back over her scalp with cupped hands, and prepared to climb into bed.

Although the room was allowed no more than a dull smear of light through the pavement window, it was not yet quite dark. But upstairs the tea things had been washed and put away, the crumbs swept, the remainder of the day's milk scalded, and the front and rear doors securely chained and bolted. Out in the garden, the saucer of water for the birds had been replenished and the missus' note for the baker (*one small only*), left in its accustomed place.

The missus had already gone to bed with the curtains tight drawn and the door locked ('Leave me, Keziah. I've a thundery headache and wish to sleep.'), so there were no more duties to perform. No more listening for the bell. No more fetching and carrying, soothing and smoothing and trying to express humble adoration without benefit of words. Normally when there was no more work to do, Keziah slept; in her world, working and sleeping were the only alternatives.

But this evening she was restless. Tired as a dog, yes, but reluctant to creep between the foetid blankets and lose herself in healing, annihilating slumber.

She was worried about the missus. Uncertain whether she was ill or cross, and if the latter, what had made her so.

It could only be her family. Mr Walter and Mrs Edwina were kindly meant, but not as genteel as the missus. Despite being family, they were not her class; Keziah could see that they prickled her like a rough wool vest on a tender skin.

And then there was the other gentleman. What about him? Who was he and what had he come for, all uninvited and unannounced?

There was something going on, Keziah decided. Something was not quite right upstairs. Not only had the missus fainted dead away but all the company had left in a hurry after tea, with Miss Lizzie being given a proper what-for and the rest of them in a rare to-do which they had not even tried to hide.

She lay on her bed, covered only by her calico nightgown, and the damp heat of the basement raised blisters of sweat on her forehead. It was a long while before she slept, and when she did so it was to dream that a rat had got into the larder.

Upstairs in the best bedroom, Aunt Netta was finding sleep equally elusive. She lay in the stifling darkness with a handkerchief sprinkled with eau-de-Cologne folded flat

29

across her forehead, like a label. Through the heavy, drawn curtains came the muffled striking of the parish church clock.

Only seven. It felt like midnight. I am ill, she thought, dreadfully ill. Keziah must get up and go for Dr Bantam. But she seemed incapable even of moving her hand towards the bell.

Again and again her thoughts returned to the appalling disclosures made by Vernon Seagrave, and it was part of the agony that they should have been made by him, of all people.

She had never forgotten meeting him when she was a little girl of six or so, proudly pushing her baby brother Walter round the orchard in his bassinet. He was a tall, lounging youth on a visit with his parents, and she remembered him leaning against a sunlit wall in a wide-awake hat and a black string tie, paring his fingernails with a penknife.

He hadn't spoken to her. Neither had she spoken to him, but a thin mist of mutual dislike arose between them and she walked on with her little-girl's nose in the air.

He had visited several times, always with his parents, and never once did he deign to speak to her. At least, not until the last of the childhood visits, and then it was less a matter of what he said than of what he did. He came upon her alone in the dining room and put his hands on her person. And when she gasped with horror and struck out at him he said in his sullen adolescent's voice: 'Whassermatter? Don't you like . . .?'

She failed to catch the last word, but knew that he meant something essentially dark and dreadful. Something to do with what animals did. She rushed from the room and refused to appear until after he had gone.

Soon afterwards his parents moved to London, and to her great relief he went with them. She forgot about him, and applied herself to embroidery, pressing flowers and studying *Mrs Titterton's Hints on Etiquette*. Already she was planning to leave the fens in favour of a town life.

She was rising twenty-seven and already installed in the

house in Wisbech when he called, suddenly and un-expectedly, as on this last and terrible day. He had grown handsome and self-assured, with a twinkle in his eye and a dog-rose in his buttonhole, and although his reappearance brought back the memory of their last meeting, she was able to control her feelings.

She offered him tea and they conversed pleasantly, exchanging snippets of family news, and he admired the house and the way she had set herself up on her own. 'One day,' he said, 'you must come down to London and let me show you the sights. My landlady would chaperon us but we could still have a real gay time of it.'

Then just before taking his leave he said, 'Look here, Netta, I'm sorry if I offended that last time. I didn't mean to, you must know that. . . .' And even before the colour had time to flare up in her cheeks, he put both his arms round her and kissed her on the mouth.

It was like someone trying to kill her by suffocation. The strength of his arms drove the breath from her body, and when she tried to breathe her nostrils were crushed by his own powerful pointed nose. She struggled, half-crazy with fear and disgust, and he opened his mouth and tried to prize her clenched lips apart with his tongue.

Her struggles increased and a bowl of pot-pourri crashed to the floor. He released her and stood back, smiling.

'Poor little Netta, you don't know what you're missing,' he said, and then picked up his hat. 'Don't trouble, I'll see myself out.'

And now, after eighteen years, he had come back again, this time with the news that Bessie Hinton, her paternal grandmother, had been publicly hanged at Ely. The words rang in her head like the throbbing strokes of a great bell.

It couldn't be true. So far as she knew, the Hintons had never taken any part in the sordid skirmishings associated with political passions, and Bessie in particular had always been spoken of as a modest God-fearing young woman who had loyally accompanied her husband on the hazardous voyage to Australia, where she had died, shortly after arrival, in giving birth to her son.

But had she in fact ever gone to Australia? What proof was there? Aunt Netta scoured her brains for any recollection of letters or other forms of communication about Bessie after her departure from England, but was unable to do so. The davenport down in the parlour was full of family papers, photographs and mementoes that she had inherited from her parents, and which she kept carefully annotated in ribbon-tied bundles, but she was certain that none of them referred to Bessie, apart from the notification of her death from puerperal fever in the late autumn of 1816.

And of course that was what had happened. She had died in Australia as, some thirty years later, had her husband John. And yet . . .

Doubts, the perfidy of which sickened her, kept crowding in. Why should Vernon Seagrave invent such a wicked story? In what way could he expect to benefit? How could it be to *anyone's* benefit?

She removed the eau-de-Cologne-dampened handker-chief from her forehead and thrust it under the pillow. Then after a moment or two drew it out again and wiped her face with it. She wiped under her chin, then unbuttoned the high neck of her nightgown and passed the cool pad of cambric down over her breasts.

She lay massaging them gently, and out of the hot darkness came the face of Vernon Seagrave smiling at her sadly, wistfully, yet with such exciting manliness, and she remembered that he was still a bachelor. Why? Was it because there had only been one love in his life, and she had not responded? Moaning softly, she knew that she would believe anything he told her.

Clouds purple as damsons were massing in the wide East Anglian sky, building layer upon layer against the pale blue as Walter unbuckled the mare from the shafts of the wagonette and led her over to the water trough that stood by the granary wall. Slowly she lowered her head and touched the dark green surface with her lips. She wrinkled them and then shook her head before settling down to drink in slow unhurried silence. Walter stood leaning against her side, filling his pipe with Nosegay shag.

He had been longing for a smoke since the first moment they set foot in Netta's house, and had looked forward to lighting up the moment they set off for home in the cool of the evening. But when the time came, he had had other things on his mind. They all had. Lizzie crying like a watercart, Edwina shouting at her to hold her noise, but above everything else there was the news to consider.

The news of old Grannie Hinton being hanged for a criminal instead of passing away lawfully, if somewhat prematurely, in her bed. He couldn't get over it.

Bessie Hinton. He lit his pipe, and the smoke rose lazily between his fingers. He had heard tell of her, of course, but she was no more to him than a name. No more than a family milestone as the young wife who emigrated to Australia at the time of the unrest. Funny to think she hadn't gone after all; that it was just a story put about to save the family from gossip. Bugger me, thought Walter. Well, I dunno, bugger me.

Standing quietly in his own farmyard away from the women, he was now able to contemplate the idea with reasonable equanimity. Poor little gel, but there, she shouldn't have gone meddling in things that didn't concern her. Everyone had heard tell of the Bread Riots over Ely and Littleport way some seventy years ago, and of the hard times that had caused them. But folks who took the law into their own hands and looted and burned their neighbours' property were against the law, and being against the law had to be paid for. Poor Bessie should have stopped at home where she belonged and got on with her own business, which was that of child-rearing and seeing after her husband.

The mare had finished drinking. Pipe in mouth, Walter unbuckled the heavy harness and stood for a moment with the bridle and the big collar over his arm and looked up at the sky. The clouds had turned black now, and were piled like great soft-shouldered mountains. A drop of rain fell on the sleeve of his Sunday jacket. Instead of turning the mare out in the meadow he led her into the stable.

33

Standing at the kitchen range frying strips of home-cured bacon, Edwina was also in the process of assimilating the news, and if Walter's reaction was ultimately to prove one of tolerance laced with pity, Edwina's was at present showing every sign of unholy glee; not because of what had happened to Bessie Hinton but because it was one in the eye for Netta.

As she stabbed at the bacon with a two-pronged fork, it seemed as if the long-smouldering dislike of her sister-in-law had at last burst into flame; Netta with her smug ladylike airs, her finicking, mincing ways that tried to make ordinary folk look stupid, had long been a splinter under the fingernail for Edwina. In the early days she had tried to emulate her; had made Walter take his boots off at the door and had strewn the farmhouse parlour with knick-knacks. Almost ten years Netta's junior, she had been humbly admiring, and Netta had thrown away the chance of making a warm lifelong friend by looking with disdain upon all these efforts.

She had kept her distance in every sense of the word, and with the passing years Edwina's desire to imitate her shrivelled and died. She enjoyed helping with farmwork more than reading a book or hemming handkerchiefs; she also enjoyed being a wife and mother, which was one of the reasons why Netta's patronizing attitude was so hard to bear. It was Edwina who should have patronized the pernickety old spinster who knew nothing about what mattered yet thought she knew it all.

When the bacon was crisp she tipped it into a dish that was keeping warm in the oven. She cut slices of bread and fried them in the fat. Eggs, and then slices of tomato, went in next, and when the whole lot was cooked she wiped her hot forehead on her sleeve. And then, because there was no one in the kitchen, lifted her skirts, lowered her drawers a little, and began to unlace her stays.

Oh, the bliss. Oh, the relief from intolerable pressure. And oh, the knowledge that even further relief was within a hair's breadth. With the laces now dangling below her

34

knees she unclipped the hooks and eyes, each of which had left its own deep indentation in her skin, and let the stiff white garment fall to the floor. Luxuriously she began to scratch the tormented flesh that had lain packed beneath whalebone and calico for so many hours.

Scratch-scratch. Rub-rub. Slower now, with closed eyes. Her flesh began to sing. Waist, buttocks and thighs, all singing an anthem to freedom, all of them settling back in their proper places in the shape and proportion designed by the loving God who designed us all.

Another pair of hands met her own, somewhere in the region of her private part.

'Walter!'

'Only come to help. . . .'

'*Walter!*' A quick giggle. 'Stop it – suppose Lizzie comes in?'

'Lizzie,' said Walter, breathing down the back of her neck, 'has got to learn, same as the rest of us, hasn't she?'

As for Lizzie, she was sitting up in her bedroom window looking at the turbulent silver-black light falling over Latches Fen and thinking how much she hated everyone. Her face was still stiff with dried tears and one of these days she was going to leave home and go and live somewhere else. Somewhere better, kinder, more understanding.

She had only listened at the parlour door to see if they had stopped talking. She had already walked round the garden three times – Aunt Netta's nasty stiff little garden – and it wasn't her fault if they were still going on when she got back.

In any case, their secrets didn't interest her. If they thought she had been listening at the door because she wanted to eavesdrop they were quite wrong. She wouldn't demean herself to do a thing like that. Not at her age. She hated them all, and their secrets were as silly as they were. Even if they were awful enough to make Aunt Netta faint.

She even hated the man who had given her the shilling piece. She hated the way his pointed nose twitched, the way he had pinched her knee. She had almost thrown the shilling piece away, because of how she felt, but instead she put it in the little tin box that contained her treasures: a kingfisher's wing feather, an onyx button, some shells from the beach at Hunstanton, a white silk tassel from the prayer book her mother had carried at her wedding. All small humble things really, and Lizzie's gloom increased when she remembered how important she had once thought them. Now, they were poor childish things, and she had half a mind to throw them all away along with the shilling piece. That would show them all. Them and their silly secrets.

But it was too soon. She recognized that they still had a dwindling power to comfort and please, and besides, she had nothing to put in their place.

'Want some supper, Lizzie?' Her mother's voice drifted upstairs.

Lizzie remained mute. Being offered supper meant that she had been forgiven her trespasses. She would have liked to ignore the offer but hunger forbade it, so she put the tin box back in its hiding-place and went down to the kitchen. Her parents were already sitting at the table, and moths were dancing round the lamp.

'There's not a breath of air,' Edwina was saying. 'I wish it would rain, or do something.'

'Rain's coming all right,' Walter said. 'I felt the first drop outside.'

While Edwina put out the supper he poured himself a pint of beer and drank deeply, unhurriedly, as the mare had done out in the yard.

'Well, Lizzikin, you a good gel now, hey?' He put down the empty glass with a sigh.

'Yes, Pa.'

'You could have tidied yourself before coming down,' Edwina said, but her tone was mild. Her cross, red-faced heavy-handedness had now faded, and Lizzie found her own sense of injury melting. She began to attack her bacon with zest.

'This is better than Aunt Netta's.'

'Your Aunt Netta doesn't do her own cooking.'

36

'I know. Keziah does it. But Aunt Netta measures it all out and never gives anyone enough.'

'People who live in towns never eat much,' Walter observed, humming. 'They don't need their victuals like country folk.'

A distant rumble of thunder rolled through the open window. A hot little gust of wind blew the curtain.

'It's coming, all right,' Edwina said. 'Is the barn door latched?'

'Reckon so. What about the upstairs windows?'

'All closed tight – unless Lizzie's opened hers. Have you, Lizzie?'

'No, Ma.'

'We'll have to close this one when the rain starts.'

'But not till then. There's no air to be had anywhere.'

A moth heavy with gold dust alighted on the back of Lizzie's hand. It had large black eyes beneath busily twitching antennae.

'Moths know when there's going to be a storm,' she said, tilting it this way and that.

'All living things do,' said Edwina.

Despite the heat she now seemed comfortably at ease, with her thick auburn hair loosened from its bun and the neck of her blouse unfastened. She looked strangely beautiful, and so altogether different from the stiff, awkward woman at Aunt Netta's that it puzzled Lizzie. Conscious of her daughter's wondering stare, Edwina turned pink.

Abruptly, Lizzie didn't hate her any more. She didn't hate anyone, and with the passing of rancour became filled instead with a lovely fierce gladness that they were here, the three of them together, waiting for the storm to hurl its might against their closed windows and outer walls. Nothing and no one could touch the safety of their closeness.

'Ma,' Lizzie said, watching the moth's trembling wings, 'why did they hang Bessie Hinton?'

'So you *were* listening at the door – '

'Oh no,' said Lizzie with all the shining charm of the

37

innocent, 'the gentleman told us she was hanged before I got sent out of the room, didn't he?'

When Vernon Seagrave stood up to leave the saloon of the Duke's Head in Wisbech he found himself staggering slightly. Waving a general goodnight, he went out to the yard, then paused as it became suddenly illuminated by a flash of lightning.

'It's coming,' one of the stablehands said. 'Someone's just come in with the news that Black Ditch Level's already a foot under water.'

Without replying, Seagrave loosed his horse, lit the two lamps and drove off. The town was deserted, gaslight gleaming fitfully along the North Brink that ran close beside the river Nene. Thunder rolled intermittently and a small wind moaned.

He should have left sooner, stayed for no more than a couple of nips and then set off for Thorney well before the weather broke. But once adjusted to the fresh air, his head cleared and he began to look forward to the coming battle with the elements. He had driven all over the country in all kinds of weather and had overturned only once in twenty-five years, and that had been when he was drunk. He was not drunk now.

Keeping to the road that ran by the Nene, the horse settled to a brisk trot, and after a while they passed the garden from which Seagrave had stolen the flowers for Netta. With the whip held at a jaunty angle he gave himself up to relishing the memory of his meeting with her.

Bessie Hinton. Her name had become an obsession, and so had the story. From its casual beginning, it had bitten so deeply into his mind that he had passed far beyond the dry facts and entered the world where it belonged. The world where it had happened. Ely in 1816, with the flitting midnight figures silently applying burning torches to haystacks, barns and houses, lighting the blackness with flames and whirling sparks. And then looting. Looting, ransacking and pillaging; stealthy, secretive fenmen creeping out of the low-hanging mists like rats, crawling out of the stinking spongy peat-bog like maggots. Animals slaughtered. Women raped. Plump women, ripe as plums, screaming and struggling and then lying still, while . . . Children sobbing, the Ely Constabulary sending for the militia. It had happened, it had all happened. And the young Bessie Hinton, newly wed and carrying her first child, drawn ever closer into the wickedness by what had begun as mere sympathy in time of hardship and which ended as a rage for excitement, a lust for violence. He could picture it all.

A streak of lightning flashed, died, and then flashed again, illuminating for a moment the blank face of the fens. No trees, no hedges, no buildings. Even the Nene was no more than a brackish residue lying supine on its muddy bed. But the crack of thunder that followed brought the rain, an abrupt downfall that had Seagrave reaching hurriedly for the old mackintosh cape under the seat. He flapped it open with one hand and draped it round his shoulders. He urged the horse to a faster pace and there was exhilaration in his voice.

Lust for excitement, a rage for violence. Bessie would have had it, and he had always had it, too. And after Bessie was caught and tried, the lust had been transferred to her captors, her judges and all the people of Ely who had turned out to witness the shame. He could imagine it all so clearly.

The pictures passed through his mind; not in the slow, disciplined procession that had absorbed and entranced his journey to Wisbech, but in a series of flashes, brilliant and exciting as the lightning itself. Bessie giving birth. Lying back on the straw with the drunken midwife gripping the child by its head and pulling – pulling so that Bessie couldn't swallow it back in order to stop herself being hanged. The moans and the blood and the gaoler coming in to watch. Then Bessie on the scaffold. Oh yes, let's see Bessie on the scaffold, her belly empty now and hanging loose; the rope round her neck, her hands tied behind her back and the terrible silence as everyone waited for it to happen. Then the swinging, the dancing, the marionette jerkings as the life was strangled out of her and the blood

39

from her womb ran down her legs and into her boots. The boots that kept on chattering together for a long time.

The pictures danced as he could imagine Bessie dancing; shining-eyed, Seagrave laid the whip hard across the horse. It broke into a gallop, its hooves thudding on the dusty road that the rain was now turning to a thick sullage. He began to sing in a wild voice cracking with triumph and the horse flattened its ears and dashed on, pursued by the bark of thunder and the dark demons that were beginning to fill its own vision.

It bolted. In a fury of flying mane and pounding hooves it tore through the darkness, the gig lamps flickering and Seagrave's mackintosh cape billowing like an ill-secured mainsail. The trap rattled, creaking and groaning, and bounding painfully over the stones. Puddles were forming now, and the water from them splashed to the top of the grinding wheels. Still singing, Seagrave hauled on the reins. He stood up, bracing himself against the wind. Rain beat against the brim of his billycock hat and poured in a small torrent at his feet when he bent his head. A raindrop bounced on the end of his pointed, predator's nose. He laughed, swaying, and because he was so happy, suddenly flung the reins free. They flew through the air over the back of the horse and then over its head.

The madness had to end very soon. The reins lay slithering on the animal's neck, swinging in a loop against its front legs. One pounding piston of a foot caught it and snapped the leather as if it had been a thread of cotton. The horse stumbled, almost recovered, then crashed down in a tangle of harness. The lamps were extinguished, and Seagrave seemed to float through the storm, borne on the wings of the wind with his cape outspread.

He lay on the bank of the river, broken as a discarded toy, and his last conscious thought was serve you right, Netta. Serve you bloody well right for what you were and for how you still are.

The rain hammered down, and the Nene had risen and was lapping close to him before his body was discovered late the following day.

*

In some ways the scandal concerning Bessie Hinton should not have been all that surprising, for in spite of an inclination towards secrecy and solitude, fen people have always had a fighting reputation.

Isolated from the rest of mankind by vast tracks of watery bog and silty marshland, the early settlers were quick to adapt to a semi-aquatic life. Fish swarmed in the shallow rivers and duck and wild geese were in abundant supply; they had reeds for thatching, clay for brick-making and peat for their fires, and when all of this came under threat in the reign of James the First they were not slow to rebel.

Noisily they resisted the Earl of Bedford's grand scheme to convert trackless bog into fertile farmland, and sabotaged the drainage system designed and executed by Cornelius Vermuyden, the renowned engineer from Holland. Each new channel cut straight as a die through the squelching peat by imported workers was greeted with riots, and it was not until the restoration of Charles the Second that the work was finally completed. The Fen Tigers had lost their battle, but not their reputation.

Yet long before the latter part of the nineteenth century the fenland of Vermuyden had regained much of the old remote and secretive atmosphere. The new waterways, the lodes, rivers, drains and channels, moved sluggishly between their reed-fringed banks, silt-laden, eel-infested, and in the summer months hummed with insect life. Wild honey-bees, dragonflies big as a man's hand, spiders patterned with yellow crosses, and butterflies by the thousand: chalkhill blues and little blues, greylings and crimson burnets, all of them dancing among the knapweed and bellflowers, meadowrue and milfoil.

But the greatest glory of all was (and still is) the sky: a huge ever-changing spectacle of piled cumulus, rain-filled nimbo-stratus and wind-streaked cirrus filling the hours between blood-red sunrise and sunsets splashed with apple green and bishop purple. Few areas can boast more immense displays of stars, and nowhere can seem more malevolent on moonless winter nights.

As if they prefer living closer to the elements than to their own species, fen people have always tended to inhabit small lonely farms that stand bleak against the skyline, and yellow brick cottages that lean over and eventually split apart because of subsidence caused by the spongy ground beneath them. The only buildings of any size are windmills and churches, although sometimes a barge will sail like a large and drowsy brown-winged moth along one of Vermuyden's drains on its way up to the Wash.

Walter Hinton's farm stood close to the Sixteen Foot Drain on Upwell Fen, no more than half a mile from the railway line that passed Stonea on its way from Peterborough. A tangled orchard stood between the house and the level that ran alongside the drain, and at the back of it, beyond two of his fields, was a short stretch of water called Paxton's Lode. Sheltered by willows, alders and poplars, it was the undisturbed haunt of bunting, sedge and reed warblers. And if Damperdown Farm was considerably less impressive than Walter's sister would have liked her friend Mrs Plumptre to believe, the dwelling that stood on the diminutive island in the middle of Paxton's Lode barely scraped into the category of human habitation.

Built by a turf-cutter, it was scarcely larger than a toolshed, yet had an upper floor with two dormer windows perched high in the pantiled roof. The sole door opened into the living room and there was an iron cooking stove in one corner. The island was just large enough for the house, the privy and a few rows of cabbages.

After the turf-cutter died, the place remained empty for years, the house, garlanded now with ivy, wild rose and traveller's joy, sinking drunkenly into the boggy peat. The turf-cutter's boat rotted and sank, and its grave became lost in an encroaching army of irises. It was possible to walk along the track that ran close beside Paxton's Lode and not notice that there was a building there at all. It was not until Johnnie Moon appeared early one morning in that same August of 1893 that the place was rescued from total oblivion and brought alive again.

He came loping out of the mist, with all his worldly

42

possessions tied up in a small gunny sack, and when he reached the Hintons' gateway he stood looking at the place for a minute or so before walking up through the front orchard to the door.

He knocked, and asked Walter very politely if he had any casual harvest work.

Eyeing the stranger warily, Walter said no.

'It's a busy time of the year.'

'Reckon.'

'And I'm strong and willing.'

'Wherebouts you from?'

'Bury St Edmunds. But Cambridge is my birthplace.'

Walter's eyes travelled over the dusty boots and trousers and the crumpled shirt with the sleeves rolled up. But the face under the broad-brimmed straw hat was that of a sensitive man – a scholar, Walter thought, with an added twinge of suspicion.

'There's twenty-one comb of wheat ready for the cutting. Use a scythe, can you?'

'Give me half an hour and I'll learn.'

Walter's lip curled slightly. 'Otherwise it's women's work. Fruit-picking.'

'I'll do both.'

Casual labour at harvest time was important to small farmers who were unable to afford permanent workers during slack seasons, but a large number of those who tramped the roads in August were no more than drunken vagrants. It was necessary to be cautious.

'You can take a day's trial,' Walter said. 'And I pay minimum rate, with bread and beer thrown in.'

The mist was clearing, the sun coming through warm and strong and flooding the fields with light. They walked in silence, and it was obvious by looking at him that the young chap had never handled a scythe before. But he watched Walter's brief demonstration with care and then copied him, and within a short while he had mastered the swing of the movement and the wheat began to fall.

'Take it steady,' Walter advised, 'or you'll have your feet off an' all.'

43

Old Reuben appeared, sharpened his scythe with slow deliberation and began to swing on the other side of Walter. They worked in total silence until Lizzie appeared at half past eleven with the osier basket containing dinner.

'Dockey-time. . . .' She stared at the newcomer from under her sun-bonnet.

Walter stopped swinging and eased his back. 'Dunno what name you go by.'

'John Edward Moon.' The new hand wiped his forehead. 'Most people call me Johnnie.'

'Done up, eh?'

'Every hour'll make it easier.'

Walter smiled, then nodded across at Lizzie. 'Fetch another dinner.'

They worked on until sunset; until the dew began to spoil the crisp snap of the hollow wheatstalks. Old Reuben shouldered his scythe and trudged off with a grunted goodnight.

'Where you reckon on sleeping tonight?'

'Oh, anywhere. In a barn would do.'

'You'll take no harm this weather.'

So Johnnie Moon bedded down in the hayloft, watching the moonlight filter through the cobwebbed window and listening to the stamping of the mare in the stable below until he fell asleep.

He stayed until the end of harvest; until the fields were bare stubble, the fruit trees stripped and the apples and plums crated and loaded into the wagonette ready for Wisbech market.

Walter asked what his plans were, and Johnnie smiled and said that he had none in particular.

'Be a pity to see you go.'

'I could stay if you like. I've a small allowance from my people and I could work for you whenever you wanted me.'

The idea appealed to Walter: casual labour on hand whenever it was needed, and in the form of a nice quiet pleasant-spoken young chap who wasn't afraid of work but who kept himself to himself. He didn't smoke, didn't drink more than normal to slake a working thirst, and so far

44

Walter hadn't even heard him cuss at anything. He wondered if he might be on the holy side.

But he couldn't go on living in the barn, not permanently. Walter and Edwina discussed giving him the attic room in the house, but were reluctant to have a stranger sitting at table with them every day. It was Lizzie who said, 'Why can't he have the little house on Paxton's Lode?'

They looked it over that same afternoon, approaching it by rowing boat because the wooden bridge connecting the island with the bank had disintegrated long ago. The front door rasped on its hinges and the slow process of subsidence had finally wrenched a wide jagged fissure down one of the walls from roof to ground level. There was a hole in the upstairs floor and a cluster of snails lay in the cool damp darkness of the food cupboard.

'Nothing a hammer and a few nails won't put right,' Walter said. 'Then a bucket of hot water to swill it down a bit.'

'It's not much.' Edwina looked round doubtfully. 'From how he speaks he's used to much better than this.'

'Take it or leave it – I reckon he hasn't got much else in mind.'

'Oh Pa, do make him come and live here!' cried Lizzie. 'It could be a proper little house again with someone living in it and everything!'

Grown out of a casual suggestion, the idea of Johnnie Moon living in the turf-cutter's house was now suddenly of paramount importance to her. She could see it all very clearly; a glowing fire and nice red wallpaper and a rocking-chair with a patchwork cushion and a table laid with willow-patterned china, and then Johnnie Moon in his carpet slippers going upstairs to bed and, before he drew the curtains, looking out across the strip of dark water to the sleeping fields and Damperdown Farm, and he would see the golden candlelight shining from Ma and Pa's bedroom window and think those are my friends over there. My friends whose little friendly light is saying goodnight, Johnnie Moon. Goodnight, sleep tight. . . .

'Oh, make him come!' Lizzie persisted.

45

They told her to keep quiet and not act silly, but were mildly taken aback by Johnnie's reaction to the place when he saw it. Polite refusal they were prepared for, but when he leaned against the drunken door frame and roared with laughter they were momentarily discomfited.

'It isn't real,' he said finally. 'It's an illustration from Hans Andersen.'

'Ole Harry Clay lived here for years and years.'

'Who was Harry Clay – a hedgehog?' He wiped his eyes, and having done so encountered the puzzled, slightly hurt gaze of Walter and Edwina. Instantly contrite, he walked further into the small damp room and said with obvious sincerity: 'It's charming. And I think I could be very happy here.'

'Needs fixing up a bit,' Walter admitted, 'but a few days' work and we'd have you snug as a flea in a cat's ear.'

'And it could have red wallpaper,' Lizzie said, 'and pictures of birds in gold frames.'

'I've got some old curtains put by,' Edwina said. 'There's nothing wrong but a bit of fading down the edges, and I dare say they'd do all the windows here and a door curtain too.'

Because work on the farm was slack for a week or so, they started on the place the following day. A closer survey indicated either slow and painstaking resetting and re-pointing of each brick in turn, or else demolition and complete rebuilding. Pondering the alternatives, Walter came to the conclusion that there was a workable third choice. Purchasing a dozen large sheets of corrugated iron, he refaced the outside, tailoring them neatly round the door and windows and then bolting each one securely in place. When the job was done he and Johnnie Moon painted them a dark glistening green.

They straightened the chimney, cleared the birds' nests from the flue, repaired the hole in the bedroom floor and nailed an oak board across the bottom of the door to keep out the draught. But when the place was finished it bore no relation to Lizzie's ideal. Instead of red wallpaper there was a single coat of limewash which emphasized the defects in the brickwork and the rough fillings-in with cement. And there was no rocking-chair, patchwork cushion or willow-patterned china; just a white tin mug and a couple of plates on the rough old table that had stood abandoned in the granary for years, and an old armchair with the springs gone in the seat. His bed was a narrow black iron one with a flock mattress, and two hooks behind the door were sufficient for his meagre wardrobe. The one thing he did insist upon, and which puzzled Lizzie, was a bookshelf. It was of modest proportions, and the row of books standing on it looked dull and unexciting, but somehow they had the air of books carefully chosen and well loved. And they made a modest contribution towards dispelling the rather chill simplicity that she found so disappointing. To help dispel it a little more she presented him with a black and white kitten which he called the Fat Boy.

He repaired the roof of the privy, built a new wooden footbridge to span the gap between the lode bank and the island, and when he had cleaned the old pathway that led up to the door, Lizzie spent an afternoon on her hands and knees lining the sides of it with bits of broken tiles interspersed with sea shells.

He thanked her warmly for all her trouble while taking care to admire her decorative sense, and when in response she suddenly blurted out in a mortifyingly childish way, 'Please will you be my friend?' he smiled at her with great gentleness and replied: 'I already am.'

So far as Aunt Netta was concerned, the effect of Vernon Seagrave's calamitous news showed no sign of lessening. On the contrary, it seemed to grow both in magnitude and in horror with every day, every hour.

It occupied her mind to the exclusion of everything else, and the more she fought against believing it the more certain she became of its truth.

In braver moments she made plans to seek official corroboration – from the offices of the *Eastern Daily Times* perhaps – but when the moment came to lay pen to paper she could never find the right words. And she could certainly not sign her own name, Henrietta Hinton; it would have to be Yours faithfully, Merely Curious, or something to that effect. And supposing they sent a reporter down to discover why Merely Curious was so curious? Newspaper proprietors were certainly not above that sort of thing.

The only alternative she could think of was to go to Ely itself, but that was quite out of the question. The mere mention of the word Ely made her soul recoil, and she knew that she would never again be able to set foot within its boundaries for any reason. It had now become a place of mortal shame for her, whether or not Vernon Seagrave had spoken the truth.

So she did nothing, but one morning when the August storms had subsided she chanced to meet Dr Barrington, who was a retired friend of the redoubtable Mrs Plumptre. Dr Barrington also happened to be a local historian of some repute, and Aunt Netta plucked up sufficient courage to ask whether he had ever heard of such a thing as the Ely Bread Riots. She had heard someone mention it the other day.

'Oh yes, indeed,' he said, 'a most shameful episode which took place, let me see now, about 1816 or so.'

'And the wrongdoers.' She hesitated. 'Were all . . .?'

'Executed,' said Dr Barrington. 'That is my recollection.'

They began to walk along the quiet street together, and Aunt Netta's soul cried out to her to change the subject. But she forced herself to continue.

'I believe I also heard it mentioned that one of them was a woman?'

Dr Barrington squinted hard at the pavement. 'Yes,' he said finally, 'you are quite right. One of the condemned *was* a woman. A shameful, *shameful* business.'

She managed to agree, and when they reached the corner of York Row held out a trembling gloved hand and said goodbye.

'Goodbye, my dear Miss Hinton.' Dr Barrington shook her hand, then raised his hat. 'Such a pleasure.'

She hastened away, but not before she had seen the

change of expression in his eyes as he pronounced her name. Hinton, Hinton; now why was it suddenly familiar? She knew that he would go straight home and consult his books and papers.

In which case there was no point in stopping now. Why not ask him to let her know the name of the woman who was hanged, after he had looked it up, and then say good gracious me what an extraordinary coincidence. It would at least put an end to the misery of uncertainty.

But she couldn't. The mere thought of it froze her tongue in her head.

And there was an additional torment to Aunt Netta's days and nights, and that concerned Vernon Seagrave himself. It was because of his rude assault on her person as a child that she had reached the early decision never to marry. Men were untrustworthy; they were crude and unpleasant and she wanted nothing to do with them. His first visit to her house in Wisbech may have begun well enough, but once again he had been unable to restrain himself from committing an act of gross misconduct. The memory of it had flooded back with painful clarity the moment he entered the room on this second and last occasion. Her whole demeanour must have shown him that she had not forgotten, and the twinkle in his eyes as he presented the bunch of flowers told her that he too remembered. And was unrepentant.

She disliked and despised him as much as ever, but sitting behind the lace curtains in the parlour she kept watch for his return. Something convinced her that he would return on his way back from Peterborough; she had no desire whatever to set eyes on him again but common sense made it obvious that he was the one person she could approach for additional information. And although she would have died sooner than admit it, in a strange and upsetting way he was the only person who would be able to offer her comfort. It was strange to think that he had remained a bachelor all these years.

Since the storms the weather had cooled. The days had become grey and listless, and Mrs Plumptre, calling on her one afternoon, informed her that she was looking distinctly dolorous.

Mrs Plumptre had a large bosom, round blue eyes, and frizzed grey curls through which daylight could be seen. Her husband had died some years ago, leaving her relieved in spirit and rich in worldly goods, and as an indication of her background – her father had been made a baronet – she tended to address people in a slow drawl, with her head thrown back and her eyes closed. She was vain, autocratic, yet surprisingly kind, and as she was a pillar of the Wisbech establishment, Aunt Netta was greatly flattered by her friendship.

'In fact,' went on Mrs Plumptre, 'now I come to look at you, my deah Nettah, I see that you do not look at all well. Have you been indisposed?'

'No,' said Aunt Netta quickly. 'Oh, no. It must be the heat.'

'But the heat has now gone.' Mrs Plumptre flicked at a frill on her black watered silk. 'Perhaps you have had bad news. Someone has passed away.'

'No, it is nothing, I swear.' To mark her discomfiture Aunt Netta reached for the bell. 'I will ring for tea.'

'Pray don't trouble. I must be wending. I merely called to pass the time of day.'

'As you wish, Mrs Plumptre.' Aunt Netta subsided.

'I noticed an unusual conveyance outside your door several Sundays ago.' Mrs Plumptre gave no sign of departing. 'And I thought to myself, ah, deah Nettah is entertaining company.'

'It was my brother and his wife and their daughter. My brother, as I may have mentioned before, inherited Damperdown, our old family place, and he has a perfect passion for farming life. Merely supervising the men does not suit him at all, for nothing will content him except that he himself must take an active part.' The desire to make much out of little was always paramount in the company of Mrs Plumptre.

'Setting one's hand to the plough is a noble thing, particularly the plough that has been in one's family for generations. As, I take it, yours has?'

'Yes, indeed.' Aware of a sudden desire to change the subject, Aunt Netta asked Mrs Plumptre for her opinion of the sermon delivered by last week's visiting clergyman.

'The church was full, but I feah that he did not rise to the occasion. I for one was left unmoved.'

'Miss Daintry said she couldn't hear.'

'It is doubtful whether Miss Daintry will hear Gabriel's horn when it heralds the dawning of Judgement Day,' commented Mrs Plumptre. 'Miss Daintry is as deaf as a beetle but refuses to admit it.'

Finally she rose to depart. At the door of the parlour she took Aunt Netta's hands in both her own and looked searchingly into her face.

'A small glass of port wine before luncheon,' she said, 'will do you nothing but good, Nettah my deah. Send your woman to purchase a bottle without furthah delay.'

Aunt Netta smiled palely and pressed her friend's hands. Watching her stately progress down the street, she wondered what Mrs Plumptre would say if she even suspected that dear Netta's grandmother had been hanged for a common felon. The idea made her head swim, and drove her back to the endless torment of longing for Vernon Seagrave to return.

Unexpectedly, the next person to call on her was Lizzie.

Ushered into the parlour by Keziah, the girl spun round on her heel when Aunt Netta entered the room, and said beamingly, 'Hullo, Aunt Netta!' Aunt Netta's immediate reaction, apart from astonishment, was one of dismay. For Lizzie's cheerfully untidy appearance (unpolished boots, thick auburn hair carelessly tied back in a crumpled ribbon) was matched by a casual, outgoing friendliness that could only be described as *common*. In the short space of time since the annual family luncheon, she seemed to have grown not only larger (which presumably was natural), but somehow bolder, coarser and more blatantly rustic. She is becoming a hoyden, thought Aunt Netta, but what else can you expect?

'Dear Lizzie, how nice to see you. Where are your parents?'

'I came without them. At least, I came with Johnnie Moon, who sort of works for Pa, and while he was loading up at the mill I thought I'd nip round and see you.'

Nip . . . thought Aunt Netta.

'So here I am,' went on Lizzie. 'Ma and Pa are doing nicely, and now I've left school it's been decided that I'm to have two score of hens all me own, and then come next spring we're going to take in a bit of land off Paxton's Field and dam a few yards of the lode so I can start some ducks. . . .' She bubbled on, beaming, shiny, untidy, and Aunt Netta produced a faintly sorrowful smile and suggested that they should both sit down.

She then said she presumed that Johnnie Moon must be a man.

'That's right,' Lizzie agreed. 'He arrived out of nowhere during harvest and he's stayed along ever since. He lives in the ole turf-cutter's place and I go and see him there – '

'Alone?'

'Oh, yes. He doesn't mind.'

'And you came here to Wisbech with him – alone?'

'Oh yes, Aunt. He knows much more than Reuben does – in fact he's got Pa beat when it comes to book learning.'

'In my day, young girls were not encouraged to be alone with persons of the opposite sex, no matter how learned,' Aunt Netta said. 'But I dare say ideas change. Would you like a glass of lemon barley-water? I believe Keziah made a fresh jugful this morning.'

Lizzie said she would, so Aunt Netta rang the bell. They waited, listening to the stern tick of the clock, for Keziah to answer, and then when the order had been given waited again for it to be fulfilled. Lizzie sat twiddling the thick rope of hair that hung over one shoulder.

'Mrs Stacey over at Swallow Farm's gone all yellow. Her sons reckon she's going to die.'

'Really? How dreadful.'

Keziah entered with the lemon barley-water on a tray. Netta poured a little into each glass before nodding dismissal.

'Keziah goes on much the same, doesn't she? Never got much to say.'

'Keziah is a servant and knows her place.'

'Yes. I s'pose so.'

Lizzie waited for Aunt Netta to say something more, to introduce a new topic of conversation, but none seemed to be forthcoming. So she took a gulp from her glass and rashly embarked on the story that had kept the sprinkling of neighbours along the Sixteen Foot Drain convulsed for a week.

'Shorty Webster found a ferret in his privy just before Harvest Festival. Leastwise, the ferret found him, because it grabbed the tail of his shirt and the poor ole boy went sprinting up the garden calling Milly! Milly! to his wife, with the ferret clinging on behind and his best trousers round his ankles.'

Aunt Netta coughed into a small lace handkerchief.

'Ferret bites can often take bad ways. Best thing's a poultice of cowpat and honey.'

'Really.'

'Some people haven't got much time for ferrets, but as Reuben says, they got their uses.'

'Evidently.' Aunt Netta put away her handkerchief and took a restorative sip of lemon barley. 'And does this person who brought you to Wisbech also keep ferrets?'

'Who – Johnnie Moon? Oh, jolly Moses, no! He's just got a little cat called Fat Boy and he spoils him something wicked. Our cats all live out in the barn along with the rats and mice – at least, they're *supposed* to – but Fat Boy sleeps on Johnnie's bed and sometimes sits on his shoulder when he's reading a book. He's got lots of books – well, he hadn't when he first came, but after he got settled in he bought some more. He had to put some more shelves up and I went over and helped him. I like doing things like that.'

Aunt Netta nodded without speaking, then carefully replaced her glass on the tray by her side.

'Well, I reckon I'll have to be going now, Aunt.' Lizzie stood up. 'Thank you very much for having me, and I was glad to find you hale and hearty.'

Aunt Netta also rose. 'Do come again, dear,' she said.

They had reached the front door and Aunt Netta was on the point of opening it when Lizzie suddenly said: 'By the way, I do think it was a rotten shame about yours and Pa's grandma being hanged.'

The words, spoken by a child, but with all the rough kindliness of a farm labourer to his mate, came like a blow in the face to Aunt Netta. She drew in her breath with a sharp hiss.

'It must have been awful having that strange man come here – I didn't somehow take to him, did you? – and none of us could blame you for fainting the way you did. I'm sure I'd have done the same.'

Aunt Netta tried to reply; tried to silence the staggering impertinence of her niece, but the words refused to form. White-faced, she opened the door on to the street.

'But don't worry,' Lizzie went on, 'I haven't told anyone and I wouldn't – ever. In fact, I wouldn't even have mentioned it now except I wanted you to know how sorry I felt.'

'Thank you. Goodbye,' Aunt Netta finally managed to say, and seeing Mrs Plumptre's lady's-maid passing on the opposite pavement, all but pushed Lizzie out on to the front step and closed the door firmly behind her.

Back in the seclusion of her parlour, she sat drumming her fingers on her knee and telling herself over and over again that she could no longer endure Bessie Hinton forever crouching in a corner of her mind like a macabre and vengeful ghost.

Tomorrow she would take the train to London, and to the address printed on the business card Vernon Seagrave had given her.

'I tried real hard, but I don't think she likes me.'

'What makes you say that?'

'Dunno, really. Just her manner. Ma says she's a stuffy ole piece but I sort of wanted to find out for myself.'

'And what conclusion did you come to?'

54

'Well, she didn't laugh about Shorty's ferret when I told her, but maybe she's just a bit shy.'

'Yes, it's possible.'

'Anyhow, she left me to do all the talking. She only said things like *Really* and then asked if I'd like some lemonade stuff. And then she just seemed to get crosser and crosser while I was trying to be nicer and nicer, and in the end she more or less shoved me out of the door and slammed it shut.'

'Perhaps she wasn't feeling well.'

'Yes. But she could have said, couldn't she?'

Lizzie and Johnnie Moon were sitting side by side on the box seat of the farm wagonette. The mare knew her way home and proceeded at her own pace. Although it was still quite early, the first stars were pricking through the plum-coloured sky and there was a faint hint of frost in the air.

'I can smell winter coming.'

'And I'm going to take advantage of the long dark nights and write a book.'

'*Write* one? Jolly Moses, what'll it be about?'

'A man called Aristotle. He was born three hundred and eighty-four years before Christ and he was a teacher and philosopher.'

'I know what teachers are, but what's a philosopher?'

'Broadly speaking, someone who's interested in ideas. Particularly ideas about religion or politics or science.'

Lizzie digested this in silence. Finally she said: 'Johnnie, what were you before you came here?'

'A schoolmaster. Most of my family were in the teaching world, and I looked forward to carrying on in the tradition, but after a few years of it I became – '

'Fed up?'

'I suppose you could put it like that. Teaching's an enormous responsibility.'

'Miss Cross at our Board School used to say the young are sent to try us. But you can't help being young, can you?'

'It's a condition that time invariably solves.'

'A girl called Mildred Diggin died just before she left our school. She'd already been promised a place as under-parlourmaid at the Rectory but she got the fen ague and was dead in five days. Mrs Diggin said the doctor told her he'd never set eyes on a more beautiful corpse.'

'I don't call dying a satisfactory cure for being young.'

They sat in silence, listening to the steady clop of the mare's hooves and the soothing scrunch of the cart wheels. The twilight was deepening and a last cloud of starlings flew in to roost in the reeds of Euximoor Fen. Soon the winter birds would be arriving: plover, dunlin, redshank, and huge flocks of shovelers and pochard from Northern Europe.

Lizzie sat thinking about her companion. He was still quite young. At least, he hadn't got wrinkles and grey hair, although he was sometimes quiet and rather sad like an old person.

'How old are you, Johnnie?'

'Twenty-seven.'

'I'm coming up to fifteen.'

'Yes, I know.'

'Have you got any sisters?'

'Two.'

'D'you like them?'

'Not as much as I used to when we were children. We've grown apart.'

'I wish I had a brother.'

'We invariably want what we haven't got.'

Something prompted Lizzie to turn to him and say: 'Is that philosophy?'

'More of a cliché. A trite, worn-out phrase of the kind used by lazy writers and bad speakers.'

'I think you speak lovely. As good as the vicar any day.'

'Thank you, Lizzie.'

An eerie rippling cry made Johnnie Moon turn his head sharply.

'What on earth was that?'

'Sounds like a whimbrel, though we don't get many of their sort, especially at this time of the year. They fly south when it gets cold.'

'You know a lot about birds, don't you?'

'Not as much as Reuben. But I like them – I like all living things.'

'Which is exactly how a country girl ought to be.'

'Reckon so.'

They settled back into companionable silence for the remainder of the journey, and Lizzie returned to thinking about Aunt Netta. She wondered what Johnnie Moon would say if he knew about Bessie Hinton being hanged, but had no intention of telling him in order to find out. For one thing, it was a family secret.

She glanced at him in the last gleam of daylight; a nice nose, firm mouth, and chin unadorned by whiskers, and eyes sheltered by the brim of his old straw hat. For all its friendliness it was a sad face, and for the first time it occurred to her that he too might have a family secret too awful to share. Why else would he hole himself up, shy as a badger, in the middle of Paxton's Lode?

Aunt Netta had never been to London before, and had never even heard of Rotherhithe.

Wearing her best coat and a small flat bonnet with a veil, she arrived at Liverpool Street Station on the afternoon following Lizzie's visit, and her fragile self-confidence suffered its first setback at the hugeness, the blackness and the noise of it all. The station was a sour-smelling, soot-encrusted cavern echoing with explosions of steam and the hoarse cries of porters.

One of them rushed up to her, rapacious as a hunting terrier, and Aunt Netta recoiled from the sight of the gaping hole where his left eye should have been.

'Where to, Missus?'

She asked whether he could direct her to the cab rank, but her words were lost in the banging of carriage doors, the shriek of a departing train. Seeing that she had no baggage to be carried, he darted past her, intent on larger prey.

She managed to find the cab rank for herself, and with Vernon Seagrave's visiting card clutched in gloved fingers, asked to be conveyed to 47 Paradise Lane.

The hansom seemed to proceed at the same breakneck

speed as everything else in London, and Aunt Netta clung to the seat and closed her eyes. But it was impossible to shut out the noise: the grinding roar of cartwheels over cobblestones, the hollow clopping of hundreds of hooves, the raucous shouts of carters and cabbies, the scream of women selling fruit and vegetables from coster barrows, bells ringing in churches, factory steam whistles blowing, children howling and, elusive as a summer breeze, the jubilant jingling of a barrel organ.

They rattled over London Bridge and along Tooley Street and then down into Jamaica Road. Aunt Netta held the visiting card against her nostrils in an effort to shut out the damp straw smell of the cab and the more piercing smells that came through the ill-fitting windows. She remained with her eyes closed until they came to a halt.

47 Paradise Lane was a large double-fronted shop in a small slimy street, and over the doorway was written *Mayrick & Seagrave, Wholesale & Retail Ironmongers.* Alighting, she paid the driver sixpence, and he looked at her contemptuously before putting the coin in his pocket and driving off.

The idea of seeing Vernon Seagrave brought a spot of bright colour to either cheek, and for a moment she hesitated; but a man inside the shop was already looking at her curiously, so fumbling a little with the latch she opened the door and went in.

'Can I be of service, Ma'am?' He had a black moustache stiff and dense as a yard broom, and a brown apron attached to the middle button of his waistcoat.

'I am enquiring about a Mr Vernon Seagrave,' Aunt Netta said in a high voice. 'I understand that he is a partner in your establishment.'

'Mr Seagrave? Vernon?' The man looked at her strangely. 'Might I ask who's enquiring?'

'I – he is a distant relative of mine.' Aunt Netta's heart increased its pace.

'I see, Ma'am.' He appeared to hesitate before committing himself further.

The place was full of ironmonger's wares: saws of all

shapes and variety hung from the ceiling, an armoury of hammers was arranged on one wall, together with knives and choppers, pincers and plumber's wrenches. Nails, carefully sorted and all laid heads together, filled boxes stacked on the counter, and there was a smell of paraffin and naphtha.

'So could you please tell me . . .?'

'It grieves me very deeply,' the man said finally, 'to have to tell you that Mr Seagrave passed away very unexpectedly, Ma'am. It was a great shock to us all.'

Aunt Netta gave a little cry and pressed her fingers to her lips.

'When did you last see him, Ma'am, if I may ask?'

'At the beginning of August, at my home in Wisbech. He called unexpectedly. . . .' She couldn't go on.

'Would that be the night of the storm?'

She nodded.

'That was when poor Vernon perished, in the storm. About five miles out of Wisbech it appears that his horse bolted. Took fright, I don't wonder, and he was thrown out and must have died almost instantly. It took some time to identify him and we only heard the news ourselves two weeks ago.'

Shattered, she began to weep. Then, turning away, groped in her reticule for her handkerchief.

'Here now, Ma'am, please to take a seat.' Hurriedly the man came from behind the counter and placed a wooden chair at her disposal. She sank down on to it while he stood by solicitously.

'Vernon,' he said, 'was a dear fellow greatly loved by us all. Straight as a plumb-line and honest as the day. And work – I've never known a fellow work like Vernon did; he had a real zest for it and yet he was always ready to crack a joke and have a bit of a laugh. Always smiling, always full of sunshine. . . .' He passed his hand across his eyes.

'I don't know what to do,' Aunt Netta whispered. 'He was the only hope I had.'

'In some sort of trouble are you, Ma'am?' His voice was heavy with sympathy.

'Yes, I . . . I wanted to talk to him about a family matter and now I don't know what to do.'

Her own words *I don't know what to do* seemed to fill her with increasing confusion and despair. Over and above the shock of the news she had just received was the sudden realization that she was in London. Alone, and with no one to turn to. She should never have come.

'Perhaps the wife and I can help in some way – she's in the back room.' He indicated a door behind the counter, its glass panes obscured by brown and red wallpaper.

'I don't know – I don't know what to do now. . . .'

'Best sit still for a spell and get your strength back, Ma'am.'

'But I don't know what to do – why am I here?' She was becoming increasingly agitated.

'You came to see poor Vernon, and I'm deeply sorry I had to be the one to – '

'Thank you, thank you. It doesn't matter. I must go now.'

Vernon was dead. She had come all the way to London to find him, to ask for his help, and he was dead. He had died after leaving her house. She sat huddled on the chair, her lips working, her fingers unconsciously shredding the visiting card that carried his name.

'You stay right where you are, Ma'am, and we'll get the wife to make you a cup of something hot. You just rest quiet now.'

He patted her shoulder before disappearing through the door behind the counter, and Aunt Netta was left alone with the hammers and chisels, the axes and hatchets, saws with jagged shark teeth ready to bite and tear and maim. All of them cruel and vindictive and smiling their terrible shining smiles in the gaslight. With a huge effort she averted her eyes, then gave a little shriek at the sight of a length of new rope dangling from an iron hook in the ceiling. One end of it had come free and hung down in the shape of a noose.

The sight of it seemed to drain all the blood out of her, for quite suddenly its message was crystal clear.

We know all about Bessie Hinton in this shop. We know all about the lewd and wicked things she did, and we've been waiting for you to call. Vernon's told us all about you, and many's the laugh we've had – always ready for a laugh was Vernon. Always smiling, always full of sunshine . . . so I've just gone to summon the wife so that she can come and take a look at you. At the woman whose grandmother was publicly hanged at Ely. . . .

Snatching up her reticule, and in a little flurry of torn-up pasteboard, Aunt Netta bounded from the shop with all the speed of a terrified hare.

Evening was approaching. The gas lamps of Rotherhithe were gleaming through the blue mist coming up from the river. But the roar of horsedrawn traffic coming from Jamaica Road was as loud as ever; and when, above it, she heard the voice of the ironmonger shouting to her to stop she merely increased her pace. He only wanted to catch her in order to point to her, and to tell everyone in London that she was the granddaughter of Bessie Hinton who was hanged.

It took a long while to find a cab, partly because they were scarce in that area, and partly because Aunt Netta's inexperience prevented her from recognizing them in time. Twice she hailed a private conveyance which jingled unconcernedly past, and blundering in the path of a ragged man and woman pushing a handcart, heard one say to the other: 'Look at 'er, she's orf 'er 'ead. 'er eyes is all wild. . . .'

With her mind fragmented by noise and turmoil and its own incoherent emotions, it seemed when she finally sank into the third-class railway carriage that she had reached a haven of security. Even Liverpool Street Station, when she peered through the window, seemed less hostile than on first acquaintance. The train pulled away from the platform and, having replaced her return ticket in her purse, she leaned back and closed her eyes.

She was tired. Deadly tired. Her legs twitched, her back ached and one of her shoes was pinching cruelly. But she was safe now. She was on her way home. All she had to do in

61

the meanwhile was to soothe and smooth away the jumbled terrors and lead herself towards coming to terms with the fact of Vernon Seagrave's death. She must calm herself, and put her trust in God.

She opened her eyes, and encountered the curious stare of the couple sitting opposite. They were staring at her quite openly; the woman with a beaver hat and tippet to match, the man in a Norfolk jacket and breeches tucked into thick stockings. Colour flooded Aunt Netta's face and she turned her head to look out of the window. There was nothing to see but her own reflection; huge-eyed, it stared back at her like a ghost.

She closed her eyes again, trying to still the increasing pounding of her heart. The train had settled into a steady rhythm and she allowed her body to sway in unison. Rickety-rack, rickety-rack. Mind blank. God the Father will take care of you.

Her eyes opened a crack and they were still watching her, the couple sitting opposite. Eating sweets, holding hands and watching her as if she were a spectacle of the utmost fascination. And the words of the ragged woman with the handcart came back to her: *Look at her, she's off her head. Her eyes are all wild.*

My eyes are not wild and I am not mad. So why are they staring at me? Staring, and smiling.

In a desperate attempt to portray normality – their sort of normality – Aunt Netta sat up straight, twitched at her bonnet and said what nice weather for the time of year. They went on staring, crunching boiled sweets and staring with eyes sharp with curiosity, greedy for something shocking to happen. For they were sharing a railway carriage with a woman who was off her head. And as if to prove it, a sudden handful of raindrops flung themselves noisily at the window.

'Yes,' the man said gently, placatingly, 'we're having *very* nice weather.'

Unable to bear their scrutiny any longer, Aunt Netta got up from her seat and huddled herself in the corner furthest away from them. With her back half-turned and her shoulders bowed, she looked like a small lost animal behind the bars of a cage.

She dozed fitfully, uneasily, then woke herself by crying out when the image of the coil of rope in the ironmonger's shop suddenly reimposed itself on her mind's eye. She crouched lower, as if to shield herself from a blow, then saw through the reflection of the window that apart from herself, the compartment was empty. The man and woman had gone.

She straightened up slowly, relief fighting a losing battle with disbelief. How could they have gone? She had not heard the train stop. But gone they certainly had – unless they had never been there in the first place.

Dull-eyed and hopeless, she remained in the corner, the train's rackety-rack eating into her like some kind of palsy, and when finally they came to a halt and she saw station lights through the rain-blurred window she summoned what seemed like the last of her strength and alighted.

Shivering in the damp cold, she hurried to the far end of the platform then paused to search for her ticket. She handed it to the ticket collector, who scrutinized it in the flickering lamplight.

'It says Wisbech.'

'Yes, I know. I – '

He turned his attention from the ticket to Aunt Netta. He sat on his tall stool, looking at her in the same way as the man and woman in the railway compartment.

'This here is Ely,' he said.

The last train to Wisbech had gone. She had not enough money to put up for the night, not even in a modest temperance hotel. And it seemed in those first moments of fresh confusion that Ely had come to her, not she to it. Ely, the one place on earth she most sought to avoid, had, through some strange and dreadful alchemy, substituted itself for Wisbech.

Sobbing quietly, she hurried through the glistening streets. The rain was falling steadily, but lifting now and then in a sudden gust of wind that banged window shutters and swung gates to and fro. There was no one about, yet she knew that she was being watched. The shadows were full of eyes, and behind the hiss of rain she could hear the whisper of voices. They had all known that fate would bring her to Ely sooner or later.

With no clear idea of where she was going, she hastened up one street and down another; the aching tiredness seemed to have left her and she was no longer conscious of her pinching shoe. She no longer seemed to have any physical feeling at all; she was weightless, bodiless – a grey ghost compelled to flicker silently and perhaps for ever through the streets that had witnessed the shame of Bessie Hinton.

An open space appeared, rain-lashed and smelling of grass and dying leaves. The path that traversed it was no more than a faint glimmer but she fixed her eyes on a point of light shining ahead. As the massive black of a great building loomed up at her, it became obvious that the same remorseless magic had brought her to the gaol. She found herself impelled towards it, and she stumbled through the massive porch lit by the glow of a single lantern and knocked timidly on the door. No one answered. Turning the handle with both hands she crept inside.

The silence in the cathedral seemed to contain a quality all of its own. Chill, vast and infinitely mysterious, it drew her forward between the soaring arches of the dimly lit nave. Tears began to stream from her eyes with the sudden, glorious, mind-bursting revelation that God had brought her here in all His loving wisdom so that He might hold her hand while she spoke aloud the words that had echoed in her brain and given her no rest, day or night, from their torment: *My name is Henrietta Hinton and I am the granddaughter of Bessie Hinton who was hanged.* She would say the words aloud and bravely and He would hold her hand. And then she would be at rest.

Blindly she groped for her reticule, but it was no longer dangling from the crook of her arm. She had dropped it somewhere in the maze of streets between the cathedral and the railway station. But its loss was of no account. God had

64

willed that she should come to Him through suffering: naked, humbled and untrammelled by worldly possessions. Losing her reticule and the purse and handkerchief it contained was no more than a part of the preparation necessary for this moment.

I am Henrietta Hinton and all my life I have been proud and vain, foolish and unloving. I have cared only for the pomp and vanity of this world and I have never opened my heart to anyone. Least of all have I opened it to You. I am Henrietta Hinton, the granddaughter of Bessie Hinton who was hanged, and I feel love and pity for her and ask humbly that You will forgive her and grant her everlasting peace.

She wiped the tears with her fingers but they continued to flow, and she stumbled into a pew. Collapsing on her knees, she lay half-sprawled with her face buried in her hands, waiting for God to touch her with His loving hand.

She was found by the verger, who had come to turn out the lights. Startled, he took a step backwards, and his first impression was that she was a vagrant. She was soaked with rain and her thin grey hair was coming loose from beneath her small sodden bonnet; even Keziah would have had difficulty in recognizing her. Then Aunt Netta opened her swollen eyes and gave him a smile of extraordinary radiance.

'My name is . . .'

'Yes?' He waited, then added as she said no more: 'I must ask you to leave now as I have come to turn out the lamps.'

She remained silent. Only the radiant smile continued to shine up at him from out of the shadows of her tumbled dark clothes, a terrible mixture of the grotesque and the sublime.

'Are you in some sort of trouble? Have you come to seek spiritual guidance? Who are you?'

'I am . . .' said Aunt Netta, and again fell silent. For a moment her smile faltered, then seemed to increase in brilliance. The verger had never seen a smile like it before; the sweetness and clarity of it seemed now to illuminate his own features in turn.

Fascinated and uneasy, he said: 'Don't be afraid to tell me your name.'

'I am no longer afraid,' Aunt Netta said in a little faraway voice. 'I have merely forgotten what it is.'

It was a cold bright morning with a pale blue sky arched over the empty brown of the fens when a pony and trap containing an ostler and Mrs Plumptre trotted smartly along the level of the Sixteen Foot Drain.

It turned in to the track that led to Damperdown Farm, and Mrs Plumptre alighted and knocked on the front door, which caused perturbation within as the front door had not been opened for years. Like most country people, the Hintons always used the kitchen entrance.

Hurrying round the corner to the farmyard she collided with Walter, who was coming to investigate.

'Mr ah – Hinton?'

'That's me.'

'I am Mrs Plumptre of Wisbech and I have called upon a mattah of some urgency. Nettah – your sistah, and a deah friend of mine – has disappeared.'

'Well, I never.'

It seemed a mild expression to use in the circumstances, and Mrs Plumptre hastened to acquaint him with further details.

'Her maidservant arrived at my house in a state of considerable alarm last evening, having spent the entire day waiting for her mistress to arrive back from a visit to London, which she had apparently made the previous day.'

'That would be Tuesday.'

'Exactly so. And now today is Thursday, and the foolish creature waited for twenty-four hours before notifying anyone. She insists that Nettah had made no provision for staying overnight in London; on the contrary, she stressed the fact that she would be home in time for a cold suppah on a tray.'

'And she hasn't come home?'

'That's what I'm telling you. Her maid has not seen her, neither has she received a telegram or any sort of communication telling her of Nettah's whereabouts.'

'Blow me, fancy ole Netta going to London,' said Walter.

Then added after reflection: 'We haven't heard nothin' neither.'

'So what are you proposing to do?' demanded Mrs Plumptre. The crisp cold was making her eyes water. 'Something must be done to find her immediately. Some misfortune may have befallen her, and the constabulary must be notified.'

Before Walter had time to agree, Lizzie appeared round the corner. She was wearing an old coat and a tam-o'-shanter made of rabbit fur, and she stared at Mrs Plumptre with undisguised curiosity.

''morning, Ma'am.'

'I think you must be Lizzie.'

'Yes, Ma'am.'

'This lady,' said Walter, 'has kindly come all the way from Wisbech to tell us that your aunt Netta's gorn and disappeared.'

'Jolly Moses! Where?'

'If we knew, she could hardly be described as having disappeared,' said Mrs Plumptre with a tight smile. She drew a handkerchief from her pocket and wiped her eyes.

'Come in the house,' suggested Walter, 'the ole wind's got a bit of a nip to it.'

He led the way through the scullery to the kitchen, and Edwina raised startled eyes to the majestic figure of Mrs Plumptre.

'This lady's kindly come to tell us – ' began Walter, and was supplanted by Lizzie.

'That Aunt Netta's lost.'

'Lost?' Edwina regarded them blankly.

'Pooah Nettah,' said Mrs Plumptre with her head thrown back and her eyes closed, 'apparently went to London for the day on Tuesday and has not returned. And her maid saw fit not to report the mattah until last night, by which time she had worked herself into a considerable state, and it was as much as I could do to prize from her the address of Nettah's next of kin. Nettah has, in fact, spoken of you many times, and has told me of the old family home. . . .'

Mrs Plumptre opened her eyes, readjusted the tilt of her

head and looked round the warm, shabby, over-cluttered kitchen. Every available surface seemed to be stacked with boxes and papers, plant pots, clothes waiting to be ironed, stubs of candle and bits of farm implements. A two-year-old calendar hung askew on the wall. But a crock of bread was rising on the hob and six stone jars of plum wine were fermenting close by. A subdued murmuring sound came from beneath the dresser on the far wall and Edwina turned sharply to her daughter.

'Lizzie – you've got that hen under there again! Fetch it out.'

Scowling, Lizzie removed the drowsing bantam from the depths of Edwina's mending basket and carried it slowly towards the door.

'There is nothing more soothing than a hen,' observed Mrs Plumptre, touching the top of its head with a kindly finger. 'When I was a child I had a pet one called Cissie, who followed me everywheah.'

The fact that Damperdown Farm and its occupants were not entirely as Netta had described them left Mrs Plumptre both unsurprised and undismayed. Not only was she a shrewd judge of character, she was accustomed to forming her own opinions – and they were not always of an orthodox nature.

'If you have the time to spare,' she said, smiling across at Edwina, 'I do feel that a cup of hot strong tea would be of inestimable benefit to us all.'

Spurning the Hintons' rather flustered attempts to usher her into the parlour, she sat at the kitchen table with them, eating home-made biscuits and watching the bread slowly rise under its covering of blanket. They returned to the subject of Netta.

'Why was she going to London? Don't reckon she's ever bin there in her life before,' said Walter.

'Precisely,' said Mrs Plumptre. 'In all the years I have known her she has nevah travelled beyond the confines of Wisbech. She even declined to accompany me for a few days' holiday in Southwold last year.'

'Perhaps it was just a sudden whim – ' Edwina began,

but Mrs Plumptre told her crisply that Nettah was not given to sudden whims.

They had to admit the truth of her observation. Then Lizzie, who had now returned minus the hen, helped herself to a biscuit and said thoughtlessly: 'Suppose it was something to do with Bessie Hinton?'

'Oh, I shouldn't think so,' Edwina said hurriedly.

'Bessie Hinton?' queried Mrs Plumptre. 'I don't believe that – '

'A distant relative,' Walter said. 'Couldn't be anything to do with her as she's bin dead long since.'

An uneasy little silence ensued, which Mrs Plumptre was too tactful to interrupt. But she stored the name away in her mind for future reference.

'I do hope she's all right,' Edwina said finally. 'I wouldn't want anything to happen to her.'

'Lizzie saw her last.' Walter dipped a biscuit in his tea. 'Seemed right enough to you then, did she?'

Conscious that all eyes were upon her, Lizzie creased her forehead in thought. 'Now you come to mention it I'm not too sure that she *was* all right.'

'You never told us – '

'In what way?'

'She was pale and cross. I know she's always a bit like that, but this time she seemed paler and crosser than usual. And her eyes' – Lizzie was beginning to enjoy herself – 'looked haunted, somehow.'

'Haunted?' They all stared at her. 'How?'

'I don't know. But it crossed my mind that she looked like someone with a secret sorrow.'

'Hmm.' Mrs Plumptre appeared sceptical. 'She has been looking a little under the weathah recently, but secret sorrow. . . . Whatever the cause, Nettah must be found and with all speed. Something must also be done to comfort the maidservant, who appears half off her head with worry.'

'I'll come back with you,' Walter began to say, but Edwina interrupted him.

'No, I will.' Standing up, she removed her apron and smoothed back her hair. 'Lizzie, fetch my brown shoes from under the bed and my coat out of the cupboard. And look after the bread while I'm gone.'

As if the urgency of the situation had at last dawned upon them, the Hintons began to busy themselves, and Lizzie rushed upstairs, followed by Edwina, who had now decided that she would probably stay in Wisbech for the night.

Left alone in the kitchen with Mrs Plumptre, Walter began to fill his pipe with Nosegay shag. 'Reckon the winter's settled in early this year.'

'Has it?' She spoke with a touch of impatience. 'I confess I hadn't noticed.'

'They say we're in for a spate of hard winters. Reckon it's nature's way of cleaning the earth.'

'I take it that I have your permission to inform the constabulary of Nettah's disappearance?' Mrs Plumptre began to pull on her gloves. 'And that if – *when* – she is found, she needs looking aftah in any way, you and your wife will be prepared to assume responsibility?'

'We'll do what we can. Naturally,' said Walter, his expression obscured by a cloud of smoke.

Stupid, lugubrious man, thought Mrs Plumptre, and when the mother and daughter returned to the kitchen – Edwina now dressed in coat and bonnet and carrying a small straw case packed with nightgown and slippers – she began to move towards the door.

Walter and Lizzie saw them off from the farmyard, then in a sudden surge of high spirits because of the unexpected drama, Lizzie ran alongside the trap until it reached the gateway. Panting, she stood watching it bowl away down the Sixteen Foot Level, the only living, moving thing between her and the horizon. A few thin flakes of snow began to fall and she ran back to the warmth of the kitchen, remembering that she was now in charge of the bread-making.

Edwina and Mrs Plumptre went together to the police station to enquire about Aunt Netta. The constabulary apparently had no information concerning her disappearance, but after a little prodding from Mrs Plumptre promised to make enquiries in the London area via the electric telegraph system.

After receiving equally blank looks at the local hospital, they drove to Aunt Netta's house, where Mrs Plumptre dismissed the pony and trap and Keziah covered her poor blotched face with her apron and sobbed unrestrainedly.

'And you have still heard nothing?' demanded Mrs Plumptre. 'There has been no news of any sort whatevah?'

Dumbly Keziah shook her head and Mrs Plumptre informed her that she would be taking Edwina back to her own house for a meal, and that in the meanwhile Keziah must pull herself together and prepare the guest room for when she returned.

'I sometimes feah she is a pooah reward for Nettah's kindness in rescuing her from the workhouse,' commented Mrs Plumptre as she and Edwina walked round the corner.

'She got her cheap,' replied Edwina. Then in case she had sounded rather callous towards someone who might even at this moment be lying dead or dying in some unknown part of London, added: 'But I dare say ole Keziah *is* uphill work.'

Mrs Plumptre's house was opposite the museum, and it became rapidly apparent to Edwina that her maid was of a vastly superior breed. Immaculately attired in starched white cap and apron, she took their coats and bonnets, opened the door into the drawing room, where a comforting fire was burning, and betrayed no surprise at being asked to provide dinner for two at an hour earlier than usual.

'And in the meanwhile,' Mrs Plumptre told her, 'we will both take a glass of sherry.'

'Certainly, Madam.' A quiet withdrawal, and a speedy return with decanter and two glasses on a small silver tray.

'Will that be all, Madam?'

'Yes, thank you, Porter.'

Porter, noted Edwina, not Mary or Maggie or Mabel. This Mrs Plumptre was evidently the real thing, and she began to see with a gleam of amusement from whence Netta had acquired some of her own la-di-da ways.

And sitting on the opposite side of the fireplace Mrs

71

Plumptre considered Netta's sister-in-law over the rim of her sherry glass and thought: A farmer's wife without guile or pretension, and she has a most beautiful head of hair which I see the daughter has inherited. All the same, I cannot believe that she and Nettah would have anything in common. . . .

She asked Edwina casual, friendly questions about the farm, and any restraint Edwina may have felt thawed in the warmth of the fire and the sherry and Mrs Plumptre's ease of manner.

'And your little daughter Lizzie, what are the plans for her aftah leaving school?'

'She left last July, and says she wants to stay on the farm. I'd quite like her to have been a children's nurse with a good family, but she says she'd sooner have animals than humans.'

Mrs Plumptre chuckled. 'Hence the chicken in the kitchen.'

'She's a real terror,' agreed Edwina, laughing. 'A rabbit in her bedroom, kittens in her wardrobe, and she sobs her heart out when it comes time to kill one of the pigs. She'd have the whole house stuffed full of birds and animals if I didn't watch her.'

'It may be the lessah creatures now, but soonah or latah she will turn to human beings. She evidently has a great deal of affection to give.'

'She's a heart as big as herself,' Edwina concurred, and under the influence of her second sherry vowed that in future she would try harder not to lose her temper over Lizzie's shortcomings.

'My deah husband and I were denied the pleasure of children, a fact which caused us both great sadness. Ah, here is Porter to tell us that dinnah is served. . . .'

They went into the dining room, and it was warm and cosy, effortless and graceful. Mrs Plumptre offered Edwina a glass of Madeira with her lamb cutlet, and Edwina accepted in order to find out what it tasted like. It tasted very nice.

Over the apple charlotte and cream they returned to the

72

subject of Aunt Netta, and Edwina said she couldn't get over her going off to London like that, and all on her own, too.

'That is the trouble,' agreed Mrs Plumptre. 'London is such a large place. But find her we must.'

'Perhaps we could put an advert in the paper. *Wisbech woman missing*, or something to that effect.'

'A good ideah. We must leave no stone unturned. In fact, if we have no news during the course of the next few days, I wonder if we should considah employing a private detective.'

'I don't know.' Edwina sat thinking. 'I mean, we want her back and everything, but she's such a respectable person that she might have a fit if she thought some man was following her and prying into her affairs. If she's still all right, that is.'

'It's to be devoutly hoped that she is. Could you manage a little more pudding, Edwinah? If I may call you Edwinah?'

'Yes, of course,' responded Edwina, liking Mrs Plumptre more and more. 'I mean, do please call me Edwina, and well, yes – if there is just a touch more to spare. . . .'

'The nice crunchy part from the outside,' murmured Mrs Plumptre, busy with the spoon, 'together with a little of the soft buttery apple from the middle.' She passed the cream jug.

And then said: 'You were perfectly right to express surprise at the ideah of Nettah going off to London on her own and without consulting anyone. I too was greatly surprised, and like you I feel that the key to the conundrum must lie in the reason for her going. Did I not heah Lizzie mention a name – what was it now? *Bessie* Hinton, would it be?'

Mrs Plumptre's expression was one of total artlessness but Edwina was instantly on her guard; not necessarily from loyalty to Netta, but because Mrs Plumptre was showing signs of poking her nose into a private family matter.

'I don't know, I'm sure.'

'Obviously I misheard,' Mrs Plumptre said generously.

'And fondly concerned as I am for Nettah, it is no business of mine.'

Adroitly a new subject was introduced, and when the time came for Edwina to leave, it was suggested that Porter should accompany her, for although it was only a short distance to Netta's house the street was rather dark.

Touched and amused, Edwina said that the dark held no terrors for her and they parted, shaking hands and promising to communicate instantly should either receive news of Netta.

But she slept badly that night, dozing a little, then waking with a start and wondering where she was. She felt unexpectedly vulnerable without the reassuring bulk of Walter beside her, and lay with wide-open eyes listening to the small alien creaks and sighs of Netta's house. Once she thought she heard a footstep and the sound of breathing outside her door, and sat up.

'Keziah?'

No answer. Nothing but the old bones of the house relaxing in sleep, yet the feeling persisted that she was not alone. Turning on her side, she hauled the chill sheet up to her chin and resolved to think of Walter and Lizzie, but the crouched, cringing figure of a woman persistently filled her vision – a woman in a torn, bulging skirt and a big-brimmed old-fashioned bonnet that obscured her face. It was no one she knew – certainly not Netta – on account of her being pregnant. It could only be Bessie Hinton.

Although normally unimaginative, Edwina became increasingly convinced that Bessie Hinton was in the house. That her poor restless ghost was passing through the rooms, upstairs and down, sighing and creaking and lamenting the dreadful fate that had befallen her. And that her presence was the answer to Netta's disappearance; poor Netta with her nervous finicking ladylike ways had been driven to leave home by the presence of a ghostly grandmother who had put herself against the law like any loose-ended baggage and then paid the extreme penalty for doing so.

She lay awake until the reluctant winter dawn rattled her window with a gust of wind and a handful of cold rain.

Keziah, with swollen downcast eyes and crumpled apron, served her with a boiled egg and two triangles of bread and butter in the unheated dining room, where the plum-coloured bloom of damp covered the furniture and her breath hung like a melancholy fog on the air long after she had left the room.

Encountering her in the hall shortly before she was due to leave, Edwina took her arm and said firmly: 'Keziah, stop crying and tell me everything you can remember about my sister-in-law going to London.'

'She just said she was going, Mm, and then she went.'

'But did she tell you *why?*'

'No, Mm.'

'And you didn't think to ask?'

'No, Mm. It wasn't my place.'

Useless, thought Edwina. She's as rum in her ways as Netta. But the spirit or ghost or whatever it was of Bessie Hinton, while causing Edwina personal disquiet, also had the effect of causing her concern for Keziah.

'Listen,' she said with rough kindness, 'stop being so mawkish and try to help those that want to help you. Are you sure you can tell me nothing about her going, or why she went?'

'No, Mm.'

'Did she take nothing with her? And did she look nothing unusual when she left?'

No, Mm.' A fresh rivulet of tears coursed down the red-rimmed channel between eye and nose. 'But then the missus had looked something unusual for a week or two past. She was pale and off her victuals and I couldn't coax her to nothin'.'

'Do you reckon it was anything to do with that day we all come over here? That day the man from London called?'

Watching Keziah with the utmost care, she saw the tears halt and a stony, beady expression fill the watery pink-washed eyes.

'I don't know, Mm, I'm sure.'

The same reply that she herself had given to Mrs

Plumptre. The reply that meant mind your own business; it's nothing to do with you.

Edwina sighed, conscious that her offer to come over to Wisbech in place of Walter had borne little fruit. Taking a sovereign from her purse she pressed it into the forlorn damp depths of Keziah's hand and said, 'Here – this'll keep you going for a while, and mind you send word the minute she arrives back home.'

Keziah nodded, with a fresh burst of tears.

'Because she *will* come back,' Edwina said with an optimism that was entirely false. 'I know she will.'

She had arranged for Walter to meet her on the road out of Wisbech, but because he was late she had walked almost as far as Oxburgh Hall before she saw the mare and the familiar figure sitting strong and square on the box seat behind. Her heart warmed and seemed to swell at the sight, but she said nothing. He halted, and reached down a hand to help her up beside him.

'All right, then?'

'Yes, all right.'

'Hear anything?'

'No, nothing.'

There was no need to say more. Not merely because there was nothing for her to tell, but because the strength of the bond between them made additional chatter unnecessary. But all the way home she sat with her arm in his and hugged him close, a thing she hadn't done for years.

'My aunt Netta's gorn and disappeared,' Lizzie said to Johnnie Moon. 'She went to London and she hasn't come back.'

'Is that your aunt from Wisbech?'

'Yes, the prim, catty ole one.'

'Surely someone must know where she is.'

'If they do,' said Lizzie, 'they haven't seen fit to tell us.'

They were sitting in front of the small black iron range in Johnnie's living room; the fire-door was open and letting out a fierce red glow, into the heart of which Lizzie was thrusting chestnuts threaded on a long skewer. Those that didn't fall off were mostly incinerated, but one or two she managed to salvage and peel, with jumping, agonized fingers, from their burning skins. Johnnie was sitting with Fat Boy on his lap.

'There's one.' She laid it on the arm of his chair. 'Look, it's nearly whole.'

'Clever girl.'

'Yes, aren't I?' She spoke jauntily, but couldn't help thinking how nice it would be if he really thought she was clever. But bookish clever, not just good at peeling hot chestnuts or being able to tell a sedge-warbler from a reed-warbler by its song.

She liked Johnnie Moon very much because he was different from everyone else, gentler, quieter, so unlike ordinary people in the things that interested him or made him laugh. He was a great one for words and books, thoughts and ideas, and he liked poetry so much that when he read it aloud to her he made her like it too.

But it wasn't only words and books and things with Johnnie Moon; sometimes he was in a lively, boyish mood and his rather sad eyes would light up with happy mischief, like the time she dropped a live eel in his lap and he leaped up and chased her round and round the little island on which his hut stood until she finally slipped and fell into the lode and he pulled her out, choking, laughing and covered in water crowsfoot.

He never touched her normally; even when he handed her a book or a wild flower or a cup of cocoa, their fingers never met. But on the day he laughingly pulled her out of the lode she was strangely aware of the grip of his hands on her arms long after the contact had ceased. It had given her a tingling sensation, more unpleasant than pleasant, and she hoped it wouldn't happen again. But she couldn't help thinking about it, any more than she could help liking him.

'What we can't understand,' said Lizzie, returning to the subject of Aunt Netta, 'is what made her go to London. Pa says it must have bin something real urgent as she's never bin there before in her life.'

77

'She may have had some sudden bad news. A friend in trouble, perhaps.'

'She's only got one friend so far as we know, and that's the prinky ole gel who came to tell us she'd gorn missing. Kept on about deah Nettah, but she made Ma ever so welcome at her house, with sherry wine and everything.'

'How splendid. I do hope they find your aunt soon.'

'Yes. But with all the terrible things you hear, I just hope she's not bin murdered or something.'

Lizzie peeled the last of the chestnuts and ate it with relish. Although she didn't care for Aunt Netta, she wished her no harm; the idea of her violent and dramatic death was attractive merely because it would serve to make the family a little more interesting in the eyes of Johnnie Moon, for instinct told her that his own background was probably strange and impressive to a degree.

But she wouldn't mind betting it was nothing like so strange and impressive as what happened to Bessie Hinton.

Aunt Netta, meanwhile, was lying in a narrow iron bed in Ely hospital, gazing at the ceiling with a mind as blank as the sheet that covered her.

'Who are you? What is your name?'

Everyone continually asked the same questions; nurses in rustling aprons and frilly caps tied under the chin, and the doctor in a tailcoat and pince-nez. 'Who are you? Tell us your name.'

She couldn't tell them her name because she no longer knew it; her name, her address and all the other prosaic but necessary facts had floated gracefully away on that evening last autumn when God had touched her with His loving hand and lifted all the bitter anguish from her heart.

She didn't know her name because she no longer needed to; God had taken away her name at the same moment that He had taken away all the mysterious troubles that had apparently led her, finally and by some uncanny round-about route, to this quiet place of refuge. God had touched her with His hand and performed a miracle of healing, and that was sufficient.

Occasionally at night, when the ward was sleeping and the big round stove threw red shadows on the ceiling, she would try, with strangely detached interest, to probe the mystery of her own past.

Other people have visitors on Sunday afternoons, but you have none. Supposing you did have a visitor, who would it be? A man or a woman? Close your eyes and try to imagine footsteps halting at your bedside, a face appearing round the side of your screen. . . . She could only visualize the nurses or the doctor.

Try to remember being a child. Your first memory. (But what is memory?) Try to remember places. Other buildings, other beds; other meals brought to you by other pairs of hands.

But the interest was never strong enough to withstand the lethargy that overwhelmed her. It enfolded her like a soft warm blanket and increasingly she surrendered to it, trusting and unresisting as a child within its embrace.

'What were you doing in the cathedral that night? Have you no home? Surely you are not a vagrant?' they persisted.

Once, she roused herself sufficiently to ask which cathedral, and when they told her Ely – she was still in Ely *now* – the name meant nothing.

'Who are you?'

'What is your name?'

She didn't know. Sometimes it was too much trouble even to tell them that, so she would just smile at them; a thin vague smile from which they could deduce nothing.

They discussed her case in Matron's office, listing again and again the meagre clues afforded by her appearance. Neat and clean home-sewn underwear; stockings carefully darned; coat and skirt of good quality; hands well tended and hair devoid of vermin. A spinster of reasonably good class and careful habits, they decided, and could get no further.

'You must tell us your name. It is very important to try and remember what it is because there must be family and friends who are very anxious to know your whereabouts.'

A faint shake of the head, a closing of the eyes. I don't

know. And it doesn't matter that I don't know.

'The Board of Governors won't allow her to stay here indefinitely,' Matron said. 'If the mystery remains unsolved much longer I fear she will have to go to the workhouse.'

In the meanwhile they gave her the name of Mary Brown, but Aunt Netta refused to answer it, having succumbed completely to the quiet satisfaction of being a non-person.

By the following February Walter and Edwina were convinced that Aunt Netta was dead. The turn of the year had brought snow and heavy rain, and now the fen waterways were swollen with sullen grey-brown water. Several of the Damperdown fields were flooded, and the lode had risen to cover all but the handrail of the little bridge that connected Johnnie Moon's island with the mainland.

'Reckon she drowned,' Walter said, staring across the flat waste.

'How could she, when she went to London?'

'Could have fell in the Thames, couldn't she?'

The Ely Constabulary had made dutiful enquiries of the Metropolitan Police Force, and an advertisement had been placed in a London evening paper, but neither had borne fruit, and when March brought the roaring winds that drove the drainage windmills into action, Walter went to Aunt Netta's house in Wisbech and told Keziah as gently as possible that he would have to close the house up.

Even to his uncritical eye the place appeared forlorn and unkempt, and Keziah herself had passed from red-faced weeping to a state of pale and pitiful thinness. She no longer wore her uniform, but a strange and motley collection of aprons and shawls that gave her an odd, gypsy look totally at odds with her humble servant mien.

'So – have you got anyone you can go to, Keziah?'

Keziah shook her head, and twisted a finger in the hole of one of her shawls.

'Only until the missus comes back, I mean.'

Another shake of the head.

'Do you reckon you can get another place, then? If I ask around for you, maybe. . . .'

Keziah's eyes beginning to turn pink; the first suspicion of a tearful hiccough.

'It'd have to be somewhere nice, mind. I mean, we couldn't have you going to just any ole place, could we?' An attempt at heartiness every bit as false as the wavering smile produced by Keziah.

'What about that nice Mrs Whatsername – Plumptre? Might she take you on, you reckon?'

'Wouldn't work for '*er*.'

'Well, we got to find you a nice place, Keziah, because you can't stay on here. I'm having to close the house up because of the expense, but as soon as we hear about the missus one way or the other – '

Keziah raised piteous eyes. Walter tried to meet them, failed, half-turned away, and then said: 'If anything's happened to her, like she's passed away or something, the house'll have to be sold. There's nothing else for it.'

She remained standing in front of him, her head bent and her toes turned in, and Walter thought, Gor dear, I wouldn't give her a second look if she was going at a knockdown price in the cattle market.

Sighing, he said: 'All right then, listen here. I'm making a call at the saddler's to pick up a bit of mended harness and I'll be back here in half an hour sharp. You git your box packed ready by then and you can stay along of us.'

The front door banged behind him and Keziah collapsed against the wall. Her eyes went pink again, but remained dry. It was as if the past four months had permanently drained her of every tear; as if she had frittered in one extravagant emotional spree all those intended to last her for the rest of her life.

She didn't want to go and live with Mr and Mrs Hinton. She didn't want to be anywhere else but here, waiting for the missus to come home. Dully she considered the possibility of running away before Walter returned, or of hiding down in the blackness of the coal cellar until he had gone away again, but she had no faith in her own initiative. She had never been taught how to use it, and it was too late to begin learning now.

As if bowed beneath the weight of an intolerable burden, she went slowly down to her damp basement bedroom and began rather hopelessly to gather her few possessions together in a little heap on the bed. By the time Walter returned she had packed them in a small wooden box and tied it round with string; she had also scalded the milk jug, given the bread remaining in the bread crock to the birds, and then gone up to Aunt Netta's bedroom to smooth the already smooth counterpane and twitch at the lace curtains and make sure that everything was in place. She blew a cloud of breath on the dressing-table mirror and then polished it with a corner of her apron, and although she told herself that the missus would be home any day now, the mournful face looking back at her was saying it's no use, she's gone for good, she'll never come back no more, not now.

It occurred to her that she would take comfort from a small personal memento, but didn't know what to choose from the collection of little china ornaments arranged on the mantelshelf. She put out her hand towards Aunt Netta's tortoiseshell shoehorn, then drew it back again; to take something that didn't belong to her, on whatever pretext, was stealing. And stealing was a wicked sin.

So she took no more than her patched calico underthings, her darned black stockings, her caps and aprons, her working boots and her Bible and prayer book. She wore her best black coat and bonnet, and the black stuff dress that Aunt Netta had bought her at the church sale of work six years ago. And she sat perched beside Walter, pinched with despair and chilled by the relentless east wind as they trundled away from everything she loved and knew.

Edwina was very kind to her, and so was Lizzie. She was given the small back bedroom papered with roses that overlooked the new hen-run. It had a truckle bed with a patchwork quilt, a rag rug and a chest of drawers, and on the bamboo table by her bedside stood a blue and white candlestick, a bunch of primroses and a little tin of fruit pastilles. Compared to her old room it was frankly luxurious but, accustomed to the dingy semi-dark of the

82

basement, it took her a long while to come to terms with the brilliant fen light flooding in through a window uncluttered by venetian blinds and lace curtains. It made her feel naked, and afraid.

But she presented herself downstairs each morning at six, and stood meekly awaiting orders to sweep and scrub, burnish and polish.

'I wish she'd git out from under my feet,' Edwina would mutter, but on the whole forbore to criticize.

'She's like a lamb that's lost its mother,' Lizzie said.

'What a lamb,' said Walter.

And what a mother, thought Edwina, but didn't say the words aloud because of poor ole Netta most likely being dead.

Weeks passed, and Walter and Johnnie Moon were about to begin cutting the meadow hay when Walter looked up to see a lone figure bicycling along the level. It was the boy from Wimblington Post Office with a telegram.

Come at once. Netta believed found. And it was signed *Florence Plumptre.*

In the 1890s there were almost as many workhouses as there were pubs, and their standards of hospitality varied as greatly.

Whether grimly entrenched behind arrowslit windows and portcullis gateways or locked behind florid red brick with a florid-faced matron, the inmates' lot, generally speaking, was not a happy one. No laughing, no singing, no gossiping, and a long day's labour in the laundry, the kitchens, the workshop or the fields was the only hope of expiation from the shame of pauperism. Bread and cheese every day, fish on Fridays, and on Sundays mutton stew and half a pint of small beer.

But Aunt Netta was more fortunate; she had been sent to Blessing Hall, a small converted manor-house that stood halfway between Ely and Littleport, and it was run on humanitarian lines by a Mr and Mrs Witherspoon. There were only twelve inmates, most of them elderly, and they were never allotted tasks in excess of their ability. A little hoeing in the kitchen garden, the shelling of peas in the shade of a tree, and in the short dark days of December the snipping and gluing of coloured paper for Christmas garlands. Aunt Netta was given some mending to do, but no one chided her if she left it untouched for several days at a time. Her memory had not returned, but neither had she any cause to mourn its absence for never in her life had she experienced such sweet and untroubled serenity.

'I found her through the Choir Festival!' Jubilantly Mrs Plumptre repeated the story as she and the two elder Hintons drove swiftly towards Littleport. 'I am a membah of our parish church choir – not as a performah but purely in an advisory capacity – which is why I went with them to Ely Cathedral, and aftah the performance I happened to overheah someone speaking of a pooah spinstah being found weeping in a pew late at night, alone and distraught, no longer young and evidently genteel, and that she had been taken to the hospital. Just supposing it were Nettah, I thought, and telegraphed to the matron, whose reply informed me that Mary Brown – a name given until her rightful one could be established – had been transferred to Blessing Hall. I then telegraphed to them, and the description of Mary Brown fits pooah deah Nettah *exactly*, and the loss of memory could certainly explain her absence all this time!'

'But Keziah said she went to London,' Edwina said. 'So what was she doing in Ely?'

'I have no ideah, and neither apparently has Nettah, supposing it is she. And if it is, I feel perfectly certain that the moment she sets eyes on us her memory will return and she will be able to explain all.'

Edwina made no reply, but for the rest of the journey her mind played uneasily with the thought of Ely. The Ely of Bessie Hinton, that poor ghost who had been woken up from the past and couldn't seem to lie at rest.

They arrived at Blessing Hall during the afternoon and waited rather apprehensively to be admitted. The front of the house was thickly clad in ivy, and wood-pigeons purred in the high trees. An old woman in a sun-bonnet appeared with a basket of gooseberries on her arm. She smiled, and bobbed a little curtsey. 'Still warm from the sun, they are,' she told them, and wandered away again.

The door was opened by Mrs Witherspoon herself, a corpulent woman with thick grey hair and a broad smile.

'Good afternoon,' said Mrs Plumptre, stepping forward and assuming control. 'We have called, as arranged, in order to ascertain whethah or not – '

'We've been expecting you, Ma'am.' Mrs Witherspoon held open the door and they stepped inside. 'What a good thing it will be if the poor soul really does turn out to be your friend!'

She led the way across the hall hung with bonnets and cloaks and walking sticks, and up the wide creaking staircase to the first floor.

'What beautiful weather we're having.'

'Really splendid. . . .'

'Wouldn't say no to a drop of rain, meself,' mumbled Walter, clumping along behind.

They were led down a corridor and Mrs Witherspoon paused outside a door at the far end of it.

'She's not been one whit of trouble to us,' she said in a low voice, 'but we do find that she prefers her own company. Of course, in my experience a lot of older folk are like that, whether their minds are clouded or not.'

She opened the door and went in, while Mrs Plumptre, Walter and Edwina stood peering a little apprehensively from the threshold. Afternoon sunshine streamed across the bare scrubbed floor and whitewashed walls, and caught, like a twinkling eye, the coloured print of Jesus holding a bunch of lilies and surrounded by a crowd of dimpled children. There were three black iron bedsteads in a row opposite the door, and in the end one sat Aunt Netta.

With a glad little cry Mrs Plumptre hurried across to the bedside. She clasped Aunt Netta's hand in both her own. 'Nettah, my *deah* – it really is you!'

With audible sighs of relief Edwina and Walter hastened to join her, and stood smiling and red-faced at the foot of the bed.

'Hullo, Netta gel! Remember your ole bor, do you then?'

'Hullo, Netta.'

And Aunt Netta, dressed in regulation workhouse night-shift, smiled vaguely, politely, emptily, without replying.

'Nettah,' said Mrs Plumptre, massaging Aunt Netta's hand. 'Look at me, deah. Now tell me – who am I?'

The same smile, blank as a piece of paper.

'I am Florence Plumptre, your friend. I live opposite the museum and you just live round the cornah – '

'In Wisbech,' put in Walter.

'You remember your nice house in Wisbech,' contributed Edwina. 'And Keziah.'

'Keziah is completely lost without you, deah.'

'Poor ole gel don't hardly know what to do.'

'She's living along with us for the time being, Netta.'

'And Lizzie – you 'member Lizzie, don't you? – she's got some chickens all her own now. They come in to lay lovely last March.'

'I had suppah with the vicar last Wednesday and he was most anxious for news of you.'

'Aren't you going to say anything to us, Netta?'

'You do recognize who we are, don't you?'

'Now, see here, gel.' Walter leaned over the bedrail and stared hard into her face. 'Just tell us one thing. What's your full name? Your proper name?'

She looked from one to the other of them, a little half-smile dodging in and out between flickering frowns.

'What's your name, then? You can tell us, can't you?'

They continued beseeching, cajoling, patting her hands and smiling bright smiles until finally Walter turned away.

'No use. I reckon she's unsensed.'

Mrs Witherspoon came back. 'Having a nice time with your visitors, are you, Mary?'

'*Mary.* . . .' choked Mrs Plumptre.

'I really thought she'd remember who she was when she saw us,' Edwina said.

'She'll remember all right soon as she gits back home,' Walter said with an effort. 'Once she leaves here and gits among her own things.'

The little smiles and frowns that had been ruffling the surface of Aunt Netta's face disappeared, abruptly replaced by an expression of violent alarm.

'This is my home! I live here!' Her voice was rough and hoarse, as if it were insufficiently used.

The Hintons and Mrs Plumptre began to expostulate, but Mrs Witherspoon held up a warning hand. 'Yes, dear, of course you do. Now there's nothing to get upset about, is there?'

But her alarm persisted. Removing her hands from her visitors' well-meaning grasp, she seized the woollen blanket that covered her and hugged it close to her breast. She began to rock to and fro, and watching this shocking travesty of the primly restrained Netta, Edwina began to sob convulsively.

Mrs Witherspoon made a sign that they should leave the room and they did so, Walter with his arm round Edwina's shoulders. Through the closed door they heard Aunt Netta's rough voice shouting '*This* is my home! *This* is my home!' and the calm tones of Mrs Witherspoon saying 'Yes, dear, of course it is – don't you fret yourself now. . . .'

She rejoined the three of them down in the hall a little while later, smoothing her cuffs and smiling a reassuring, professional smile.

'Does she really believe that this is her home?' Mrs Plumptre's voice quivered.

'It would seem so, Ma'am. And it's my opinion that something's frightened her. It's frightened her so badly that it's knocked her brain right off balance. But I'm sure it's only temporary.'

'So what shall we do about taking her home?'

'I think it best to leave her for a day or two. But if you were to come regularly to see her, and talk to her about her old life, I'm sure it would help to bring things back to her.'

'And now you know what her real name is, you will call her by it?' said Mrs Plumptre. 'It's most upsetting to see that she refuses to answer to it.'

'She doesn't really answer to Mary Brown either,' replied Mrs Witherspoon. 'Hers is a very funny case.'

They parted at the front door, and in order to help jog Aunt Netta's memory it was arranged that Walter should call again on the following afternoon and take Keziah with him.

Clutching a bunch of sweet-williams, she trotted in behind him to where Aunt Netta was languidly mending a pillowcase, then fell on her knees with a loud wail of anguish. Seizing Aunt Netta's hand, she began kissing it with a terrible fervour. Aunt Netta drew her hand away and looked down at her with a squeamish expression in which there was not the slightest hint of recognition.

Sweating and upset, Walter commanded Keziah to get up and behave herself, but the sight of the person sitting up in the black iron bed, so dear and familiar, yet again so totally strange and unknowing, appeared to drive Keziah to a state bordering on hysteria. Wailing and gasping, she began beating her forehead against the side of the mattress and calling on the Holy Shepherd to bring back the missus to her rightful ways. . . .

Mr Witherspoon appeared in belt and braces, and helped to carry the convulsively sobbing Keziah from the room. They took her down to the kitchen and gave her a cup of tea while Mrs Witherspoon arranged the sweet-williams in a jug and told Aunt Netta how lucky she was to be loved so much.

'Won't it be nice to go home and live among all the people who love you, dear?'

'This is my home,' Aunt Netta said. 'I live here.'

And that was how the situation remained: Aunt Netta rousing herself from her tranquil, trancelike state only when it became necessary to ward off any possible threat to her continued sojourn in the workhouse, while all those nearest to her continued in their efforts to prize her away from Blessing Hall and back to her rightful niche.

They plied her with tempting personal mementoes: the pincushion made for her by Lizzie during her first year at school; Edwina and Walter's wedding photograph, and the sampler that Netta herself had embroidered at the age of ten. Lizzie sent her a nice letter tucked inside a moss-lined basket containing a dozen pullets' eggs, the Wisbech branch of the Churchwomen's Guild sent her a copy of *Prayers for Everyday Use*, and old Dr Barrington the amateur historian sent a bunch of Gloire de Dijon roses and a note telling her that she was sadly missed by himself and other gentlefolk of Wisbech.

But whatever the blandishments, the kindly, well-meant attempts to coax her back to normality, Aunt Netta persisted in her avowal that Blessing Hall was her home and that she had no intention of being moved from it into a world of total strangers.

So they waited, with Mr and Mrs Witherspoon's agreement, for her memory to return and her mood of inexplicable stubbornness to pass, and fearful of the outcome of removing her bodily and against her will back to the house in Wisbech, continued delaying tactics as one summer week followed another.

In the meanwhile, Keziah's health began to fail. Always pale and humid-looking, she now began to exhibit signs of positive illness. Unable to eat more than a morsel at any one meal, she grew hunched and thin, with lips that folded inwards and hands that became ever more like bent claws. She spoke even less, and at times seemed to have no more grasp of the realities of life than Aunt Netta.

'She's going unsensed the same way,' Walter said one evening when Keziah had crept off to bed without supper. 'Reckon she's pining, and it's taking extreme ways.'

'I fear she'll die if we don't do something,' Edwina said.

'Such as what, then?'

'I only wish I knew.'

The problem was finally solved by the Witherspoons, after a last concerted attempt to persuade Aunt Netta to return to her house in Wisbech, if only for a night. Less convinced now that one glance at the old familiar place would instantly restore her to sanity, they nevertheless persisted until Mrs Witherspoon said finally that to harry the poor creature any more would result in her doing herself a mischief. Instinctively Edwina glanced at the open window, and Mrs Witherspoon nodded, without saying any more.

When, exhausted and dejected, Walter and Edwina left Aunt Netta to sob herself to sleep and went downstairs, the kindly Witherspoons took them both into their private parlour and offered them a glass of barley wine.

'There's only one answer,' Mr Witherspoon said. 'My good lady and I have already talked the matter over and come to the conclusion that whether or not her case fulfils the statutory requirements, she had better be admitted here on a permanent basis. And furthermore, that the poor old soul that comes with you had better be admitted and all. The widow Clay died last Thursday night, so she could have her bed.'

It took a bit of getting used to, the idea that a workhouse, of all places, was prepared to unbend the rules and accept Aunt Netta, of all people, as a permanent inmate; but, accepting another glass of barley wine, Walter and Edwina decided that there was nothing else for it. And any lingering misgivings were dispelled by Keziah's expression turning slowly from wintry grey to incredulous rapture when they broke the news to her.

She was given the bed next to Aunt Netta, who displayed a polite indifference to her presence, which caused no particular grief to Keziah as she had never been privileged to experience warmer sentiments. It seemed as if nothing would ever grieve Keziah again, for not only had she returned to the slow, ordered, institutional world in which her life had begun, but she had been allowed to retain the greatest gift her Saviour had to offer: the gift of someone to love and care for.

*

Unwatched, the garden bough shall sway,
The tender blossom flutter down,
Unloved that beech will gather brown,
This maple burn itself away. . . .

Johnnie Moon met Lizzie coming through the orchard. He was on his way back to the cottage after the day's work, while she was mooching through the trees as if without purpose.

'What's that? Browning?'

'No, Tennyson. It's in the book I lent you.'

'Oh.'

He fell into step beside her, their footsteps rustling in the leaves that had fallen.

'Haven't set eyes on you for days, Lizzie. Been hard at work?'

'Just the usual.'

'Come over and have some cocoa with me later on. I've got something to show you.'

'Oh? What?'

'Wait and see.' He swung off towards the footpath that led to the lode.

Lizzie stood watching him go, leaning against a greengage tree with her arms folded tightly against her chest. There were times when the new misery trapped inside her was almost more than she could stand. This was one of the times, and she wished she could understand what brought it on. It was like an illness, but most illnesses were caused by something like germs or catching cold or being breathed on by the dying.

And the misery was manifesting itself in different ways. Sometimes it flared up and became a furious anger at being asked to perform some ordinary everyday task like laying the table or polishing her boots or feeding the pigs; tasks that she had quite enjoyed in the past, or that at worst she had regarded as inevitable. But now she was angry a lot of the time. Angry with her hair because it was thick and obdurate and got full of tangles; angry with her thick woollen stockings when they sprouted another hole at the side of the bit she had just darned; and, most of all, angry with her parents. Her mother had become a martinet for ever chasing her, criticizing her, blaming her; and her father had metamorphosed from an endearing and enduring loved one to a thick, stupid block of fenland peat for ever stinking of Nosegay shag and for ever saying nothing that didn't begin with I reckon.

And after the furious anger, the furious tears. She had never cried like it before. There had never been reason to.

Tears, up until now, had meant the shocked pain of falling over and grazing her knee, or the fearfulness of a nightmare soothed in the darkness by loving-mother arms, but now the tears were secret and inexplicable. A huge new abyss seemed to have opened up before her, swallowing all the old familiar childish things and offering in exchange such worrying abstractions as self-doubt, self-reproach, and a dull hopeless feeling that there was no way ahead – that this was all there was, and after all it wasn't very much. All the early promise had fled.

The fifty chickens that Walter had bought her that spring were no more than a tedious chore – is this all I'm going to do for the rest of my life? Mix corn, sweep droppings, collect eggs and finally wring necks? She didn't want to cuddle them any more, yet the mere fact of not wanting to cuddle them left an aching void in her life.

Someone she might well have talked to was Johnnie Moon, yet conversely he was now the last person she felt inclined to approach. Last winter she had spent many hours in his company, marvelling at all the things he knew, revelling in his gentle jokes and easy conversation, but now it was different. Yet as one instinct compelled her to avoid him and to ignore his existence as much as possible, so another one, equally perverse, insisted that she should brood about him endlessly. And the brooding led to dreaming about him: restless, disturbing dreams about him stroking her hair as he would occasionally stroke the old mare's rough forelock, and on one occasion a dream in which he rose up out of the sea without any clothes on and she saw his dicky bird. This particular dream haunted her for days and made it impossible to speak to him, even to look at him, without blushing scarlet.

Like most country children she had had no need for coy instruction on the facts of life; there had been no need because the facts of life were all around her, but now they had begun to assume a new and somehow threatening aspect. And they were coming too close. The new misery was gradually extinguishing her childhood and she now spent most of her time in brooding solitude.

Either that, or indulging in her new secret pastime of spying on Johnnie Moon; perhaps not spying so much as watching him when he wasn't looking. Watching and noting the way he walked (loosely, lankily, with his hands in his pockets), the way he talked and smiled and thrust back the thin lock of hair from his forehead with a long thin hand. Working on the farm had broadened his shoulders and ripened his skin to a russety-gold, but he still didn't look like a farm labourer. Nothing like Pa or Willy Stow over at Latches Fen.

She liked watching him secretly, silently, from windows, from behind trees, from the shadows of the granary doors, much more than she liked being in his company. Sometimes she thought she was going unsensed like Aunt Netta, and during bouts of deepest pessimism suspected that she had evolved into this new unpleasant person on account of having inherited some of Bessie Hinton's bad blood.

For although Bessie Hinton's name was never mentioned at home, there seemed to be a tacit agreement that Aunt Netta's lapse into insanity was somehow connected with her grandmother's diabolical carryings-on; Keziah, in a rare talkative mood, had once volunteered the information that the missus had never been the same since that hot afternoon when the strange man came, and although Walter and Edwina agreed that it might well be so, they refrained from confiding in her the purpose of his visit.

But there must have been something diabolical about Bessie Hinton; and the fact that she had been hanged – far from exculpating her and cleansing her of sin – had merely imbued her with additional horror. Why else would her shadow still seem to hang over them like a fen ague, like a giant bat crouching in a church belfry?

On that particular evening when Johnnie Moon invited Lizzie over to his cottage for cocoa and the prospect of something surprising for her to see, she made a great effort to smooth herself into a mood of equanimity. She even put on her new woollen winter frock and brushed her hair. Less than a year ago she had been avid for the day when she could wear her hair coiled on top of her head, but already the plaiting and winding round and skewering with hairpins had become a tedious bore. She wished women could have short hair, like men.

It was dark early now, with an eerie wind moaning over the fens. She lit a hurricane lamp, and with the volume of Tennyson under her arm, made for the door.

'You going to visit Johnnie?'

'Yes, Ma.'

'Ask him over for a bit of dinner on Sunday. Twelve o'clock time, tell him.'

'All right.'

'Doesn't hang around him like she used to, does she?' Walter commented when Lizzie had departed.

'She's at a funny age for girls,' replied Edwina. 'And sometimes I confess I clean forget it.'

Johnnie Moon had a fire glowing in the range and the tin kettle singing on the hob. Golden lamplight cast trembling shadows on the walls and played among the piles of books.

'Hullo, Lizzie, nice to see you.'

'Hullo.'

'Let me take your coat.'

He did so neatly, courteously, and without touching her. She laid the book down unobtrusively.

'You're looking very smart this evening. Is that a new frock?'

Lizzie said that it was, then warmed sufficiently to ask whether he liked it. He said that he did, very much, to which Lizzie replied well, that's all right then.

Motioning to her to sit down, he folded his long graceful frame into the old armchair.

'I gather you found Tennyson a bit of a dud?'

A sudden return of the old pleasure at being in his company prompted Lizzie to gush. 'Oh no – it's very beautiful! Even more beautiful than the *Bible*. . . .' Then sickened by her own fulsomeness, she turned a deep pink. 'But the way he talks about nature hasn't got much to do with the fens.'

'I believe he came from Lincolnshire, which isn't all that far away.'

'Well, it must have more trees and things up there.'

'Yes, I take your point. But, on the other hand, it's surely the essence of a poet's genius to be able to describe things in such vivid and exciting terms that we can actually see them, whether in fact we're familiar with them or not. It's this wonderful knack of making us open not only our eyes but our hearts as well.'

'Reckon even he couldn't find a lot to say about the Sixteen Foot Drain except it's long and narrow and wet.'

'Lizzie dear, you're an incorrigible individualist!' He laughed, leaning back in the chair.

'What's that?' demanded Lizzie suspiciously.

'Don't worry, it's a compliment.'

'Oh.'

Johnnie began to make the cocoa, measuring a cup of milk into a pan and then setting it on top of the stove to heat. He mixed the cocoa powder with sugar and a little cold water, and Lizzie watched, noting the neat unhurriedness of each movement.

'By the way, how's your aunt?'

'Still much the same. We don't go all that often now because she never seems to want to see us much. I dare say it's because she can't remember who we are.'

'Loss of memory is sometimes nature's way of protecting us from something too painful to remember.'

'Yes, that's what we think. And on that last time we went to see her in Wisbech something awful *did* happen, but it's a family secret.'

Suddenly she wanted to tell him, just to see what he would say. Even more, she wanted to ask him whether he thought it possible that she could have inherited some of her great-grandmother's bad blood. It would have been so easy, and such a relief, to confide in him here in this funny cosy room, with him bending over the pan of milk with his face in shadow.

But she didn't. She had promised not to tell and – with another swift flip of her mood – it was no business of his anyhow.

He added a cup of hot water to the milk then carefully

mixed it into the cocoa. Returning it all to the pan, he put it back on the stove and gently began to stir it.

'You make your cocoa like custard.'

'It's the proper way. I became proficient when I was a schoolboy old enough to share a study with another chap, and I perfected the technique when I began my career as a schoolmaster. Sitting over the fire marking Latin grammar and sipping hot, milky, impeccably made cocoa. Nothing like it.'

Lizzie sat smoothing the skirt of her new frock and picturing what it must have been like. All those young gents obsessed with the making of perfect cocoa in the middle of all their books and pens and papers.

'Did all the schoolmasters always make cocoa?'

'Oh, no. Some of them preferred a glass of port.'

'Johnnie, why did you stop being a schoolmaster and come down here?'

He began to pour the cocoa, rich, steaming and frothy, into the cups. He passed hers, without their fingers touching.

'Oh, I just felt like a change. And as I told you before, I wanted to write a book.'

It made sense. And yet it didn't. She thought how funny it would be if he was here because, like Aunt Netta, he had lost his memory. And like Aunt Netta, he didn't realize that he had lost it. Jolly Moses, suppose he was really a runaway prince or something?

'What are you smiling at, Lizzie?'

'Oh, I dunno. Nothing, really.'

'I know I haven't seen you much, but I've a feeling you haven't been smiling much lately. Is that right?'

'I get fed up sometimes. Sometimes I really hate myself and everybody and every blessed thing.'

'I suffer the same way,' he said. 'But it passes.'

They sipped in silence, and something still prevented Lizzie from looking him openly in the face, from feeling the old sense of natural ease.

He didn't seem to mind looking at her, though. Glimpsed through her lowered lashes, his expression was half-smiling, half-sad; gentle, loving, yet with a hint of teasing. She had never realized before what a lovely face he had, and her wild idea that he might be a prince or something seemed wild no longer. For some reason her heart began to thud, as if she had been running.

'It's time I went home.'

'I haven't shown you the surprise yet.'

'What is it?'

Without answering he motioned her to the far corner of the room, away from the lamplight. She tiptoed towards it, and in a deep wooden box lined with straw lay Fat Boy.

'I've changed his name to Fata Morgana,' Johnnie said, and lifted out a kitten no larger than a well-grown mouse. It lay sprawled, blind, toothless and earless, on the palm of his hand. Crouching on her knees, Lizzie drew a long soft breath.

'Three of the little beggars, born yesterday.'

'Did you really think she was a tom?'

'Yes, until she began making a nest.'

Very gently Lizzie took the kitten from him and held it close against her cheek while its mother lay watching intently.

'I never get over baby things. How little they are, yet you know that there's a whole complete person folded up inside.'

'Humans of that age must be even more extraordinary.'

'Oh no, they're horrible! Mrs Langdon who keeps the shop let me hold hers, but it was all white and bald and slimy like a slug. I couldn't give it back to her quick enough.'

She didn't want to give the kitten back. She wanted to go on looking at it, stroking it with her forefinger and then holding it close against her lips. And neither did she want to go home any more. She just wanted to stay like this, kneeling close to Johnnie Moon and sharing with him the shadowed intimacy of the cat and her young.

The spell was broken when the kitten gave a shrill squeak and its mother began to show signs of alarm. With a last tender stroke of her finger, Lizzie laid it back in the box, where it was thoroughly washed before being allowed to settle down to suckle.

'I must go now. I can hear the last train coming.'

They remained motionless, listening. To begin with, its distant huffling was no more than a stirring of the wind in the reed beds, its whistle no more than the high lament of a bird flying over the fens.

'How lonely it sounds.'

'When I was little I used to lie in the dark listening for it. I used to try and stay awake so I wouldn't miss it. I think I got it mixed up with saying prayers and thought it was Gentle Jesus on his way to watch over me 'til morning light, amen. Even now, it's like a sort of friend.'

'Have you ever been on a train?'

She shook her head. 'I think it'd spoil it if I did.'

'Oh, Lizzie, Lizzie. . . .'

He said it like a sigh, and her heart pounded against her ribs like the heavy chuff-chuff-chuff coming across Horse Moor to Stonea crossing.

'I've really got to go now.'

'Want to take another book? I think perhaps it's time you tried some Jane Austen.'

She accepted a copy of *Pride and Prejudice* without undue enthusiasm, and was halfway through the door before remembering to deliver her mother's invitation to Sunday dinner.

He said that he would be pleased to come, and going back over the bridge she wished that Pa didn't have to hum whenever he ate. Other girls' fathers didn't, and it made her look stupid.

Left in solitude, Johnnie Moon washed the cups and saucers and stoked the fire. The volume of Tennyson lay on the table where Lizzie had left it. He took it over to the bookshelf, then as if against his better judgement, opened it and turned to *In Memoriam*:

Sphere all your lights around, above;
Sleep gentle heavens, before the prow;

Sleep gentle winds, as he sleeps now,
My friend, the brother of my love.

He closed the book sharply, and put it away.

With the turn of the year came the hard frost; harder than
they had known for several years. After the first week of
searing winds alternating with icy stillness, Walter took
down the three pairs of skates hanging in the granary and
had the blades reground. He then oiled the straps with
Russian tallow, rubbing them until they were as supple as
satin ribbon, and Lizzie felt a glow of the old childish
excitement at the prospect of skating.

By the tenth day the Sixteen Foot Drain was considered
sufficiently frozen to bear Walter's weight and he ventured
on to it, red-faced and a little stertorous, as Edwina and
Lizzie watched from the bank. He began to glide up and
down, then finally nodded permission for them to join him.
They did so, wobbling to begin with and then striking out
boldly as the old skills returned, until they were swooping
and skimming with cries of delight.

Everyone who lived in the fens skated in those days;
when the hard weather set in it was the best way of getting
about, but the skating season was also the time for
socializing. Apart from seeing to the livestock, there was no
farming to be done in the dead of winter and the time
dragged, short bitter days yielding to endless-seeming
evenings spent huddled round the stove. The whole world
shrank to the size of a farmhouse kitchen that smelt of
paraffin and peat, candlesmoke and camphor, where
conversation was desultory and winter's aches and pains,
coughs and colds were drearily soothed by sixpenny bottles
of Godfrey's Cordial. Like the lifeless fields, the cows
munching and steaming in the barn and the lop-eared pigs
burrowing ever deeper in the straw, fen families were
waiting for the warmth and the light to return.

In the meanwhile, there was skating, and when Lizzie
came in on the afternoon of January the twenty-fourth with
the news that Ezekiel Stacey from Swallow Farm was

roasting an ox and there was to be mulled elderberry wine to go with it, Edwina put on her apron, pulled out the dampers on the stove and began to make a dough cake. Invitations to socializings were never issued formally; there was never time in case the thaw set in, but it was understood that all were welcome and that everyone should contribute to the refreshments.

Swallow Farm was less than a mile from Damperdown, and Ezekiel had the ox set up on the bank of the Sixteen Foot. It had taken four men to hoist the carcass into position and it hung by the legs over a slow, carefully constructed fire of penetrating heat. Local boys volunteered to take turns with the basting, and by early evening the first huge fen potatoes were being shoved into the white-hot ashes to bake.

There was no fear of a thaw; the frost had been holding all day, and now with the coming of night its presence could be felt like tingling fingers tightening their grip. It made the air dry and sharp-scented, and a small full moon rode high behind black fragments of cloud.

The lanterns began moving towards the scene in clusters, their pinpoint lights merging and then separating as those carrying them stumbled across a cart-wheel rut or slipped on a frozen puddle. Voices called out of the wintry silence and a peal of laughter roused a moorhen to a sharp pluck-pluck of alarm. Folk were coming from miles around, over Boots Bridge from Wimblington, in from Manea, from Tips End, even one or two suburbanites from March; but mostly they were from the small isolated farms, ghostly in layers of coats and shawls and scarves and with their skates slung over their shoulders. They came along the frosted droves and across the open fens – Nightlayer's Fen, Benson's Fen, the big Langwood Fen, and further north from Upwell, Binnimoor and even Euximoor, where the dead grasses crackled underfoot like slivers of glass in the bobbing light of the lanterns.

Some were able to skate all the way, along Vermuyden's Drain or along Popham's Eau to where it joined the Sixteen Foot at Three Holes, and Billy Freeman came flying

100

through the stinging cold, bent low and with his hands clasped behind his back. Two days ago he had skated one mile in three minutes twelve seconds and was hoping for a place in the fen team that had raced against the Dutch.

An old door had been laid across trestles and the women began unpacking their osier baskets and setting out loaves of bread, cold vegetable pies, cakes and bottles of ale. They laughed and bantered in the lurid fireglow while the men stood appraising the glistening ox and sniffing the steam rising from the cauldron of elderberry wine.

The three Hintons arrived on skates just as Sam Kitchin was taking his concertina out of its box, and the first wheezing chords of 'The Blue Danube' waltz seemed to complete the carnival mood. Walter took Edwina's hands and swirled her away into the crowd. A farmboy Lizzie had known at school seized her in a boisterous embrace, but she shook him off and skated away by herself with her arms folded across her chest. Rejoicing, she swept past the others and out of the range of fire and lamplight, her blades singing, then turned in a wide arc and swept like a bird back towards the sound of the waltz and the smell of roasting.

Everyone except Ezekiel Stacey and his helpers had taken to the ice, laughing and shouting, swooping and swinging to the first decent bit of music they had heard since last Michaelmas Fair. An excited little dog frisked on to the ice, lost its footing and slid on its chin towards a voluminous woman in a large hat who tried to avoid it, and in failing to do so, sat down heavily. With a whoop of delight, two men hauled her up and brushed her down and the little dog floundered merrily away, delighted to be part of the fun.

Panting, Lizzie sat down on the bank, and a dark figure stopped in front of her and bent close to peer at her.

'Lizzie – '

'Oh, Johnnie, it's you!'

For the first time for months her pleasure in seeing him was unspoilt by deeper and more complicated feelings. The clean cold and the jovial music had brought back the simplicity of childhood, and she sprang to her feet and held out her gloved hands to him.

'You'll have to be patient with me,' he laughed. 'I'm nowhere near your standard.'

'Come on, come *on*!' she cried. 'Don't let's waste time.'

They linked hands and glided away from the bank, and she sensed at once that he was only a beginner. But any disappointment immediately melted into a kindly desire to help and encourage him. Steering him between the other groups of skaters, she told him to move more slowly, more smoothly, and after a while his gawky lungings settled down. He began to fall into the same easy rhythm.

'Good ole boy, you're going a treat.'

'Am I really?'

At that moment the moon disentangled itself from the last wisps of cloud that clung to it and sailed clear. Small, white and remote, its light was astonishingly brilliant and it transformed the bleak waste of winter into a sparkling Aladdin's cave. As if for the first time, they saw the hoar frost looped like strings of diamonds from the tall spires of last summer's loosestrife and twinkling its blue sparks among the frozen sedges. The world that had been drab as a dun cow, listless as an old patched petticoat, had sprung alive with a million pinpoints of scintillating colour; the ice beneath their flying skates passed from silver to amethyst to emerald, and even their laughing breath turned to a pearly radiance on the snapping cold air.

They had left most of the other skaters behind now, and Sam Kitchin's concertina was no more than a plaintive voice carrying some faint unheeded message when Lizzie became aware that she and Johnnie were now holding one another closely round the waist. She could feel the muscles of his long thin leg moving in easy unison with her own. They had slackened speed to a slow swinging rhythm, and when she looked up at his smiling face patterned with moonlight she knew that she loved him the way women loved men when they got married to them and made love with them and gave birth to their children.

She couldn't understand why she hadn't realized it before, now that it was so obvious; but the sudden marvellous tumult of feeling brought with it an explanation of all the things that had so tormented her, and she reckoned that it was worth going through a certain amount of misery before reaching this highest possible peak of happiness.

In a passion of joy she pressed even closer to him and he laughed down at her.

'We ought to turn back now.'

'I want this to go on for ever and ever.'

'If it does, we'll end up in the sea.'

'Oh, Johnnie. . . .' She nearly said it; nearly said, Oh, Johnnie, I love you, but something stopped her just in time. Probably the instinctive knowledge that no matter what the circumstances, all the way down the centuries it had always been the man's place to do the declaring.

So they turned, and picking up speed swept back towards the lanterns and the sound of the concertina.

The heat from the fire had melted the frost in a wide circle that had now been trampled to mud. Ezekiel Stacey, a sweating hobgoblin in the smoky firelight, was slicing hot thick slices from the blackened ox while boys equipped with long iron spikes speared potatoes from the ashes.

Willy Stow was in charge of the mulled wine, and tarpaulins had been spread for people to sit on. They came up, laughing and glowing from the sparkling ice, and Edwina asked Walter if he had seen Lizzie.

'Reckon she's about somewhere.' He craned to look, then turned his attention to the food set out on the table. Everyone had come to the socializing armed with a plate, a knife and fork and some sort of receptacle for the liquid refreshment.

'Want me to help you, gel?'

'Yes, do,' Edwina said, sinking gratefully on to a corner of a tarpaulin and rubbing her calves. 'I'll have a slice of meat, a bit of Nellie's leek and carrot pie, and perhaps a mite of the pease pudd'n Emma Finch made – and a taste of Mrs Crabb's sweet pickle – oh, and anything else you reckon I'd fancy. I'm starving to death after all that gallivanting.' She laughed up at him, warm and plump and pulsing with life, and Walter thought hang me if she ain't still the handsomest piece this side of Wisbech.

By the time Lizzie appeared they were halfway through a second helping of wine, but the closeness with which she was standing to Johnnie Moon was immediately evident to Edwina. She sensed that they must be holding hands.

'Get stuck in afore it all goes,' advised Walter, humming. 'You got a plate, have you, Johnnie?'

'He can share mine,' Lizzie said quickly.

They moved away through the crowd and Edwina nudged Walter with the handle of her knife and said, 'Our daughter's courting with Johnnie Moon.'

'You reckon so?'

'I know so.'

'Well, she could do worse, though we don't know much about him save he's a gentleman.'

'Trouble is there's not a lot of choice for a young gel living in these ole parts.'

'You done all right though, didn't you?'

The affectionate teasing in his voice was obscured by a mouthful of meat and Edwina turned her head away in sudden irritation: 'Did all right, not done.'

He accepted the rebuke placidly, and hummed his way through another baked potato as big as his fist.

The noise of the socializing was increasing steadily, the clatter of plates and the chatter of voices rising and splintering in the brittle cold. Only a handful of children were skating now; everyone else was eating and drinking, and the little dog stole up behind Martha Waskett and removed the rib bone from the plate of her over-attentive swain.

There were quite a lot of girls with swains, some of them girls Lizzie had been at school with; Midge Morton and Phyllis Beck, and stuck-up Rosie Harris, who was officially engaged to a greengrocer from March. They were all there, all gleaming enticement and all made mysteriously beautiful by the moonlight.

And love itself was there. Love creeping among the muffled figures that leaned against each other on the tarpaulins while they ate and drank and giggled and glanced, and the power of its magic drove young Lizzie half-wild with a helpless excitement that made her cheeks scarlet and her eyes like stars. She was in love, in love, in love; not like Midge and Phyllis and stuck-up Rosie, but in love in a rare, wholly wonderful way with a wonderful handsome chap who was in love with her and who would declare himself to her before long.

She had drunk half a mugful of the hot fruity wine, swigging it down as if it were lemon barley, but she couldn't be bothered to eat.

'Come on, let's go back on the ice while we can have it all to ourselves!' She dragged at Johnnie's arm and he took a last bite from his slice of Grannie Parsons' seed cake before obeying.

No one noticed their departure and they held one another closely round the waist before setting off. Tilting her face, Lizzie smiled up at him without speaking and he gravely bent his head and kissed the shaft of moonlight that lay across her cheek.

Diamonds were still sparkling from the motionless spires of loosestrife but the ice had turned to a deep green laced with silver. Their skates sang in unison over the frozen world below them, and away from the noise of the socializing Lizzie's quick ears caught the mournful cry of a hunting owl from somewhere over Euximoor Drove.

Poor ole thing was hungry. From the richness of her new and blinding happiness she pitied it. But she also pitied the fieldmouse, awoken from its sleep by hunger and driven forth into the bright moonlight in search of a grain of seed.

I love them all because they're part of the world I love and because I love Johnnie and Johnnie loves me. . . . She began to skate faster, pulling him along with her, and the words burst out of her although she knew they shouldn't because it was always the man's place to make the declaration.

'I love you Johnnie – I love you – I love you – '

'I love you, too.'

She accelerated, bending forward and driving her skates in a shorter, more rapid stroke which he did his best to

105

follow. Dizzyingly the banks sped by as they flew faster and faster, eating up the shadows and penetrating the tunnel of winter darkness that lay ahead.

'I love you – I love you – I love you!' She no longer knew whether she was shouting the words aloud or whether they were merely ringing round in her head, but the wildness seemed to grow and grow until it exploded. She halted abruptly, far too abruptly, and it felt as if Johnnie were being torn from her grasp. He fell forward and smacked on to the ice, sliding a little way and then remaining still. He attempted to rise, then fell back with a groan.

'What is it? What's up?' She knelt by him with her arms round his shoulders, peering into his face, but it was in shadow.

'Oh my God, my leg – my foot. . . .'

'Which one? This one, or that one?'

He stifled a yell, but the sound seemed to alert a hundred small creatures from sleep. The reeds rustled, and a bird gave a startled cry.

She repeated her attempt to help him up but he gasped to her to leave him, so she snatched off her woollen cap and placed it under his head. Dismay, coupled with the wine she had drunk, made her unsteady and she almost slipped when she stood up. Dragging her cuff across her eyes she promised to return in a few minutes, and then skated back towards the sound of the socializing.

They all stopped whatever they were doing and they all looked at her; hatless, and with her hair beginning to tumble down, it was all she could do to stop the tears at the way they went on looking at her, even when she kept saying, 'Come quick, Johnnie's hurt!'

Her father and Billy Freeman were the first to respond, and then another young chap whose name she didn't know set aside his bottle of beer and came to join them. In silence she led the way to the darkly huddled shadow lying on the ice, and between them they lifted Johnnie Moon and glided slowly back to the lamplight and the dying fire and the interested gaze of all the others, while Lizzie skated alongside holding his hand and tenderly observing each ripple of pain passing over his moonlit face.

As well as being the fastest skater, Billy Freeman also knew a bit about first aid because he had worked for two years with a horse doctor, and when they laid Johnnie on to one of the tarpaulins he carefully removed the boot from his rapidly swelling foot and diagnosed that the ankle bone was broken.

Sweeping the last remains of food from the improvised table, they laid him on it and carried him back to Paxton's Lode, and Edwina suddenly lost patience with Lizzie and told her sharply to put her hat back on and stop snivelling because she was making a spectacle of herself.

She had no faintest inkling of the numbing shock, of the cruel depth of calamity that had reduced her daughter's radiant world to a handful of ashes.

It was all my fault. I made him go too fast when I shouldn't have, and now he's got all that pain and suffering all on account of me. How can he feel like loving me now? He must hate me for being so bold and for acting so lummoxy.

I wish we hadn't gone to ole Stacey's socializing; I wish we'd just stayed at home as usual, staring into the stove and waiting for bedtime. I wish I didn't love him, I wish he'd never come here in the first place. But I do love him – like a pain, like having ate too much – and I can't stop. Yet just supposing he does still love me? After all, he did say he did, but that was before I made him fall over and hurt himself. . . .

The doctor from Wimblington had set Johnnie's ankle, and he lay back in his old chair with his leg propped on a stool padded with a cushion. It took courage for Lizzie to tap on his door and go in, and her cheeks flushed crimson when he looked up and said gently: 'Hullo, Lizzie dear.'

'Are you cross?' Her eyes filled with tears.

'What about?'

'Me being so bold and lummoxy. I lugged you over and made you break your ankle.'

'Rubbish, it was an accident. Of course I'm not cross, you silly girl.'

107

'And do you still . . .?' But she couldn't say the word love, not here in this room in the ordinary daylight.

'Everything's just the same as it was,' he said. 'Now, what's that you're carrying?'

'Some soup Ma sent over.' She put the lidded enamel can down on the table, then went to the cupboard to find a bowl. 'You must have it while it's hot.'

She watched solicitously as he spooned it up and crumbled the hunk of bread in his fingers. Then she restoked the fire and cleaned out the ashes, tidied the room and washed the bowl and spoon in a little hot water drawn from the kettle.

'You don't have to go to all this trouble, you know.' He looked so pale and wistful that it made her heart start its old thumping tricks again.

'I know I don't. But I'd better fill the lamp while I'm here. Where's the paraffin?'

'In the tin down by the bucket.'

She filled the lamp's container carefully, without spilling any, then trimmed the wick and set the glass chimney and the globe back in place. 'I'll be over to light it before it's dark.'

'You really mustn't bother. I can manage perfectly.'

'Mustn't bother?' She stood with her hands on her hips, in unconscious imitation of her mother. 'Seems to me someone's got to bother or you'll starve!'

The misery of guilt had now given way to the fierce joy of proprietorship; to the practical housewife who had at last struggled free from the dreaming ineptitude of adolescence.

For everything was just the same; he had only this minute told her so, and one of these days she would be cooking and cleaning and running his home because she would be his wife. She would be Lizzie Moon. . . .

Lizzie and Johnnie Moon, it would be.

Her cheeks flushed crimson again, and she hurried back to Damperdown too inarticulate with bliss even to say that she would be back again within the hour.

Yet within the space of a few days it became apparent that

108

things were not as they should be; with the shock of the accident now over, she had expected Johnnie to refer to their newly developed feelings for one another, but he didn't. He was still gentle and kind, and his reluctance to ask for her help touched her immeasurably, not only as an indication of his unselfishness but because it also proved that he was a gentleman. Ordinary men that she knew – her father included – had no qualms about ordering their women to do this and that, but Johnnie was far too refined and sensitive.

She had been going over to the turf-cutter's dwelling four and five times a day for a whole week before the suspicion dawned that he didn't actually want her help, that he preferred to do for himself what he could, and leave the rest.

The suspicion hurt dreadfully, but she made herself miss out one or two of her by now regular visits to see whether he expressed concern about her absence. He didn't. He did however look at her a little more enthusiastically after the second four-hour period of deprivation had ended, and asked if she would like him to read some Longfellow. She said yes, and sitting on the end of the stool that supported his ankle, listened to his voice as if she were listening to music; enjoying the sound without worrying too much about the meaning.

When he had finished she made them both some cocoa, scrupulous in her attention to the mixing of the powder, the warming of the milk and the cooking of it over the fire like custard.

As they drank she talked about the spring: 'Not far off now, Johnnie. The hazel's all yellow catkins down the drove and a thrush was whistling fit to bust this morning.'

He smiled, without replying.

'Soon's the days get longer and the sun gets a bit more spark in it you'll be getting about again. I'll help you.'

He looked at her, his head resting back on the cushion she had brought over from the parlour at Damperdown, and she wanted to ask if he remembered the night of the socializing, and what it had been like before he fell and

109

broke his ankle. Did he remember the glitter, the clear stinging cold and the moon admiring its reflection in the ice? And did he remember them skating close, like one person, and her saying Johnnie I love you, and him saying I love you too . . .?

But she couldn't ask, because it was always the man's place to ask that sort of thing, not the girl's; his place to do the courting, not hers.

So the days passed; a slow milky-blue thaw set in that turned the drove roads to slime, and lumps of ice, clumsy and discoloured, hung suspended in the turgid water of the Sixteen Foot Drain. One afternoon she walked all the way to the spot where Ezekiel Stacey had roasted the ox; the stakes and the crossbar were still in place but the fire was long since cold, and one or two bones picked clean and white by ravenous birds still littered the grass. It was possible to trace a rough circle where the tarpaulins had been spread, and the sight of it all, forlorn as a deserted children's playground, filled her with melancholy.

She hurried back to Paxton's Lode, and found Johnnie hopping round the room on one leg with the aid of a broomstick.

'Here, let me help.'

'No, leave me, I can manage.'

'But the doctor said you've got to keep your leg up for three weeks.'

'Damn the doctor.'

'Oh, Johnnie . . . whatever it is you want, I'll get it.'

She put her arm round his waist so that her shoulder fitted like a crutch beneath his unsupported armpit. He gave another hop, then pushed her away.

'Do go away and leave me, there's a good girl.'

She recoiled as if he had hit her. 'You really mean that?'

'Yes. No.' He hung on to the back of the chair. 'Look, Lizzie dear, I know you're trying to help and it's all my fault – I'm just a rotten patient, that's all. But I can't stand being helped and – and touched. . . .'

'I'm sorry.' She stood there humbly, rather clumsy-looking in her old coat and mud-streaked country boots.

110

'Do you mean you want me to go now?'

'Yes,' he said gently, and his sad smile was a torture to her.

'What about your supper?'

'I've still some eggs left, and I can cook them quite easily.'

She went on looking at him, searching his face for the slightest crumb of a hint that he loved her and was soon going to declare.

'Please,' he said.

She turned away, blinded by tears and without saying goodbye.

She went home and up to her bedroom, but it was cold and cheerless up there. She crossed the landing and opened the door of the room that had once been allotted to Keziah. It too was cold and cheerless, and now bore no trace of Keziah's presence. The passing of time had blotted her out, just as it would blot everyone out sooner or later.

Edwina called upstairs from the kitchen, and when Lizzie appeared told her crossly that she had called her five times. Why didn't she answer?

'Because I didn't hear.'

'Didn't want to hear, more like.'

She told Lizzie to set the table and to take whatsisname's supper over to him and to come straight back because she was sick of cooking good food and having it go cold.

'If you mean Johnnie, he doesn't want any.'

Edwina eyed her sharply. 'Had a tiff, have you?'

'No.' Back now to the sullen adolescent; to the scowling pout that hid the torment and the harrowing uncertainty of being in love for the first time.

'Well, look sharp and set the table, I can hear Pa coming.'

Glowering, Lizzie flapped open the tablecloth and set it down askew. She flung two knives and two forks down and slapped a plate between each of them.

'Where's yours?'

'I don't want any.'

'You *have* had a tiff!'

'Oh, for God's sake stop *crazing* me, Ma!'

111

'Li-*zzeeee!*'

The slam of the door that led to the stairs, followed by Lizzie's boots pounding up. With a quick snatch she drew her bedroom curtains closed, then, fully clad, crept under the quilt and pulled it tight over her head in a vain attempt to shut everyone out.

But at this particular time Edwina had miseries of her own, and if Lizzie's anguish was about the onset of sexual maturity, her mother's asperity was pointing to the sad but inevitable decline of it.

Desirable plumpness had given way to stoutness, which in turn was exhibiting every sign of giving way to fatness. Fat women were still esteemed among men of an earthy disposition, but such fashion guidance as filtered down to her via the ladies' column of the *Eastern Farmers' Weekly* implied that women should have neat busts, tiny waists and not be a day above twenty-five.

No mention was ever made of greying hair, a less than full set of teeth, hot flushes or varicose veins. Walter still loved her – and proved it about once a week – but what had once been a time of delight was now an absurd and ungainly chore ('Oh, git on with it Walter – do!') that left her both unmoved and unsatisfied.

And although she loved her daughter as deeply as ever, the knowledge that she was now courting seemed merely to increase her profound sense of gloom. She should have rejoiced with Lizzie, should have offered sympathy and wise counsel and seized the chance of enjoying, if only vicariously, the joys and fears, ups and downs of first love. But she couldn't. She could only nag and censure and then hate herself bitterly when she saw the hurt look in Lizzie's eyes.

To be fair, she was also uneasy about Lizzie's choice being Johnnie Moon. Johnnie was a nice enough chap – quiet and well-mannered and a good worker – but what was he doing here? Why had he come? What lay behind his being content to bury himself away in an old turf-cutter's cottage? No one ever went to see him and he never spoke of his family.

There was something funny about him and she didn't want Lizzie to be harmed in any way, yet when she tried to talk to Walter about it he merely told her that there was nothing wrong with Johnnie and that Lizzie's feelings for him were no more than the first trial flutterings of any young mawther.

'You keep saying that,' Edwina complained. 'And one of these days it'll be too late.'

She didn't know exactly what she meant, but worry about Lizzie on top of the aches and pains and the long dreariness of winter did nothing to sweeten her temper.

As for Lizzie, things had progressed no further and she was now turning over in her mind the best way in which she could make her feelings for Johnnie abundantly clear to him without actually doing the declaring.

Instinct told her that it was not a matter of simpering and fluttering her eyelashes; something more tangible was needed, like a special present or a keepsake that would speak the words for her, but she didn't know what it could be. Girls didn't give men bunches of flowers (even if there were any to be had in February); in any case flowers died, and the present she had in mind was to be a permanent one.

If she had been any good at drawing she would have done him a nice picture of a horse of something and put it in a frame; but she wasn't, any more than she was good at knitting socks or embroidering slippers. In despair she even got out the old tin of childhood treasures, but she could hardly give him an onyx button or a kingfisher's wing feather. She had nothing to give except herself, and it was common knowledge that girls who offered their virtue before their wedding night were regarded with scorn, and quite rightly so, by honourable men like Johnnie.

And then it came to her that the most rare and precious thing she had to offer at this delicate stage of the proceedings was the family secret about Bessie Hinton.

Admittedly, the fact of being sworn to secrecy had always impressed Lizzie far more than the fact that her great-grandmother had been hanged, and for a moment or two

113

she wondered whether God might not smite her in twain for breaking her word, before coming to the conclusion that it was a risk she would have to take. A gift of the significance she had in mind could not be given without risking something, and she was prepared to gamble the entire world to ensure that Johnnie would make his declaration.

So she told him, sitting on the floor in front of the stove with her arms linked round her knees and a long thick curl of dark red hair hanging over her forehead.

'I wouldn't tell anyone else this but you, Johnnie, because you're someone special and because it's been weighing on my mind for so long. It's a terrible thing I have to tell you – I suppose some people might say *burden* you with – but all these years of carrying this secret has sometimes been more than I could stand; so lonely, and oh, how I've longed for someone kind and wise to share it with – and now I've found someone, although a voice within me says stop, you mustn't burden him, it isn't honourable and it isn't fair – I can't help myself. Things will never be the same between us after this, I know, yet I'm helpless – '

'What have you been doing, Lizzie?' Johnnie asked from the depths of the armchair. 'Stealing the jam?'

'My great-grandmother Hinton was hanged at Ely for causing a riot.'

'Good Lord. What about?'

'What about?' She turned tragic eyes in his direction. 'Does it matter what about? Isn't it enough to have to confess that she was just plain hanged?'

'No, of course it isn't. It's the cause, not the effect, that counts.'

'I don't follow.' Her underlip jutted; peeved adolescence threatened to return.

At the end of a long day of boredom and discomfort he tried hard to be patient. 'Very well then, your great-grandmother was hanged, which was a shame and a scandal and a cause for family consternation. I quite see that, but nevertheless you must understand that the matter of prime concern to any outsider must be the motive. Did she swing because of a *crime passionnel*, or because of stealing two

114

penn'orth of cats' meat from a barrow or because of some loftier ideal concerning morals, duty, accountability, or – and here's another interesting possibility – because of the helpless, craven love she felt for another human being? For we are all mortal, my dear Lizzie, and another person's downfall always interests and intrigues us, at least between tea and supper.'

This wasn't how it should be. And this wasn't Johnnie, this rather high voice and stabbing forefinger elongated to frightening length by the gentle lamplight. She didn't know what he meant by cream pashunell or even the word accountability, but along with being cowed and subdued by his educated words came the healthy desire to hit back. She had given her all, in the emotive sense at any rate, and the practical parsimony of the born fen-dweller forbade her to fritter anything lightly.

'I've just told you something that's the most important thing in my whole life, and if all you want to do is scoff and be clever, well, it just proves that you aren't the chap I thought you were.'

'Oh, Lizzie, Lizzie. . . .' He said the words half-teasingly, yet with an undercurrent of exasperation. 'What a child you are.'

'I'm not a child, I'm a grown woman! I'm old enough to be loved and married and that's what I want and what I thought I was going to be – ' She tried to stem the torrent of words, knowing that they were all wrong and stupid and that she was throwing away the carefully laid plan to bring him to the point of declaration, but it was no use. The words went on pouring out and wouldn't stop, even when she began to cry.

'It was so lovely being in love because I thought I was being loved back, but now I know I'm not it's just awful and horrible and I feel such an ole *fool* . . . I was a fool to tell you our family secret because it doesn't mean anything to you and it doesn't bind us together like I thought – or maybe it *does* mean something to you but not what I thought – and you're just being clever and scoffy because you're shocked that the great-grandmother of any girl you – you thought you – '

115

'Lizzie.' He leaned forward from the chair and took her arm. 'Lizzie, please listen.'

'It's no use Lizzying me – it's too late.' She wrenched her arm away and dragged her fist angrily across her cheeks. 'You said you loved me but you don't. That night didn't mean anything to you – '

'I do love you, and that night did mean a lot to me, but not in quite the same way – '

'There's only one way.'

'Oh, if only that were true.'

His sad, rueful words seemed to goad her to fury, and the fury increased her mortifying inability to express herself. 'There's only one way that men love women and it ends in them declaring – with the men declaring to the women that they love them and the women shouldn't have to do the declaring and if they do it's a sign the man's a poor ole thing and not all that worth having anyway but by the time the woman's heart's broke because she thought – '

'For Christ Almighty's sake, girl, will you stop your miserable maundering and listen?'

The extraordinary roughness of his voice silenced her abruptly. She dropped her hands from her tear-stained face and stared at him. During the brief silence that followed they could hear Fata Morgana purring in her box.

'I do love you, and the night you refer to did mean a great deal to me. But there are shades and degrees of meaning, just as there are sorts and types of love. That night on the ice meant a lot because of its beauty and friendship and sense of acceptance, and when I said I loved you I meant it – I did, and do – but unfortunately it's not the kind of love you have in mind. I'm not the sort of man who should be married, Lizzie.'

She continued to stare at him helplessly. 'That's the only sort of man I know.'

'Which is greatly to your credit.'

There was a finality about his words which indicated that the scene should end there. But it couldn't, because she didn't know what he meant, and because she loved him it was imperative to find out.

116

'Do you mean you've got a girl somewhere else?'

'No.' He sounded infinitely weary. 'A boy.'

'A little boy? You mean you're already married?'

'No, I'm not married. Nor ever likely to be. Oh Lizzie, you dear sweet girl of the birds and bees, do try to understand without too much attention to detail that for some people the supposedly fixed rules of the game don't apply. I'm – well, my needs are . . . different.'

'How?' Her stare was unblinking.

'The question should be why, not how. And I don't know why. It's an abnormality, or, if one's a believer, a sin.'

Sin? Abnormality? Dazedly she remembered hearing of a gypsy woman on Upwell Fen who gave birth to a baby with twelve toes and everyone said it was abnormal. So was Mrs Crabb's goat that had a double set of teats, but . . .

'But what's this got to do with us? With you declaring, and Pa consenting?'

'Lizzie, I love you as a sister and a dear friend, and I suggest we leave the matter there before either of us becomes overwrought and inadvertently hurts the other.'

His supposition that neither, at this point, had yet been hurt, was more than she could stand. Her fragile calm deserted her and she started shouting: 'You say we mustn't hurt each other, well, we already have – at least, you've hurt *me*! You've hurt me worse than I ever thought anybody could hurt anybody, but I'll even put up with that if you'll just tell me *why*. You keep saying you love me, but only like a sister – well, you can't do because I'm not your sister, am I? Any more than I'm your aunt or your grandmother.'

'Lizzie, go away. Just go away.'

'No, I won't. Not till you tell me what's at the back of all this.'

'Please go away, Lizzie, I'm tired.'

'You're married, that's what it is! That's why you're here – because you've run away from your wife!'

'*I am not married*!' He seemed to scream the words at her. 'And I never will be because I can't stand women! I can't stand the touch of them, the feel of them or the smell of them. The touch of their flesh makes my skin creep.'

117

'You're horrible – you're a pig – I hate you!' The wild grief of childhood became merged with the lacerating pain of first love. 'All right then, I'll go and I'll never come back – not even when you beg me on your knees I won't!'

She flung herself out and the door crashed behind her. Running across the bridge she slipped on a dollop of mud and clutched at the handrail to save herself – *Serve him right if I fell in and drowned.* . . .

She kept running until she reached home, and desperate to avoid parental curiosity, made a bolt for that soothing old refuge of the past, the hen-run.

It was a couple of hours before Johnnie Moon could pick up the shattered fragments of his interview with Lizzie; to do so seemed at first to require more courage than he could command.

Sunk deep in the chair, he forced himself to a state of relative calm while he examined the things he had said to her. Evasions and half-truths to begin with, and there was very little comfort in the knowledge that he had tried very hard to protect her from hurt. (Had he been protecting her, or himself?) And then the loss of control, the burst of violent hatred that had sent her flying white-faced away from him.

Good. With the onset of defiance he felt cleaner, rejuvenated. No more lies, or at least sub-lies, because of kindness or compassion. She was young and she would recover. Lizzie, the bouncing tumble-haired farmer's daughter, would soon find herself tumbling happily with a local swain wise in the ways of the fens and content to live in close proximity to dear old Mother Nature who fashioned us all.

Or nearly all.

Did she fashion me? Make me what I am? I wonder how many of us there are, we sad, nervous shadows hugging our secrets and picking our way through the dangerous quick-sands of moral rectitude. I should have been safe here, God knows. Free from temptation, free from the beautiful demeaning lusts that twist and shame us. And so I was, until Lizzie.

Little Miss Lizzie with her bright eyes and insouciant rustic charm, who made me see the possibility of escape. Could I marry her, beget children by her? Would she make me whole, make me clean? How would one know, unless one tried? I wanted to, and was almost ready to, but with the increasing threat of physical proximity I lost courage. I knew that I couldn't. And the poor quivering inner being shrieked out like a washerwoman confronted by a mouse – to be freed from fear and torment and disgust.

So here we are. I must have made clear what I am, even to Lizzie's turnip intelligence, and she will tell her parents that they have a sodomite in their midst. What will they do? Send for the constabulary? Or regard me as a manageable freak, and double my work and halve my pay?

I can't stay here. I can't face their embarrassment, their fear and their prurience. They will be angry with me for trying (and almost succeeding) to love their daughter. . . . If I don't go they'll serve me with notice to quit anyway. The idyll is over.

He got up from the chair, struggling until he had the broomstick under his armpit for support. The stove was burning low, only the occasional clink of a falling cinder to remind him of its presence. The kettle's song had died and it was an effort to light the lamp that stood on the table.

He remained motionless, looking at the room with its pockets of shadows and soft pool of light. He would soon be leaving, his book not only unwritten but unstarted, his pathetic half-pledge to Lizzie abandoned and dishonoured. With nothing to give, he could accept nothing, not even the shelter of a turf-cutter's hut fast sinking into the fen peat.

Fata Morgana was curled asleep with her kittens as he stooped awkwardly to stroke her before hopping on one foot to the chest of drawers. From under a layer of clothing he took out an unframed photograph and carried it over to the table.

The lamplight fell on the school group, on the sixty or seventy boys sitting cross-legged in rows wearing knicker-bockers and shiny Eton collars. They stared at the camera, unsmiling, unblinking, with hair greased down and arms folded, and they were alike as peas except that one of them was Drummond.

Unerringly his eye found the boy third from right in the second row and his heart kicked as the memory of wicked joy came flooding back. The joy of watching and loving behind a schoolmaster's rigid mask and waiting for another chance to touch him; a fleeting contact between fingers as an exercise book was returned and the occasional *Well done, Drummond* pat on the head. And Drummond with downcast eyes (the sweep of dark lashes on soft unweathered cheek), would murmur, *Thank you, Sir*. And a whole world filled with graceful images and magical love would unlock its doors and admit Mr Moon, housemaster at St Athelstan's Preparatory School for Boys. But only as a spectator; never, it would seem, as a participant.

One day in autumn term shortly before Christmas, Drummond was caught cribbing in a Latin test and referred to his housemaster, as was the custom, for a beating.

Aghast, yet hideously elated, Mr Moon paced his study hearthrug. If he had any desire to lash Drummond's tender flesh with a cane it was only that he might afterwards alleviate the hurt for both of them by taking Drummond in his arms and tenderly kissing away his tears. Aware of the floorboard creaking outside the door he wiped his forehead and then seated himself behind his desk. Several minutes passed before the timid tap-tap.

'Come in.'

Another pause, then Drummond standing small and irresolute in the doorway.

'Come in and close the door.' The tick of the clock. 'Well, what is it?' (Oh, the feigned testiness of a man in love.)

'I've come to be beaten, please Sir.'

Was it any wonder that men were driven to all kinds of violent depravity, whether real or imagined, locked away with beautiful little boys in such a system? It was invited, encouraged, in some schools a matter of proud compulsion, that males of all ages should take part in ritualized forms of sado-masochism.

'Come here, Drummond.'

Drummond came, and stood before the desk, head bent and hands clasped behind him as if already preparing to protect his buttocks.

'Now – what have you been up to?' Hard to look at him without melting, without a smile of tender indulgence.

'Cribbing, Sir.'

'Cribbing? That's bad. . . . Not in an exam, I hope?'

'Yes, Sir.'

'Which one?' Lips contriving to remain severe.

'Latin, Sir.'

'That's bad. Very, very bad. What made you do it, Drummond?'

And Drummond raising eyes of angelic blue: 'I did it because I didn't know the answer, Sir.'

'I see.' A pause, during which Drummond fidgeted slightly and a distant bell rang for prayers.

'I'm afraid I'll have to beat you.'

'Yes, Sir. I know.'

'Very well, then. Trousers down.'

The pushing back of his chair and the manly stride towards the cupboard where the cane was kept. So far, he had managed never to use it. He took it out, swished it experimentally, and tried hard to avert his eyes from the small white-faced figure with its knickerbockers and under-drawers round its ankles.

'I'm sorry about this, Drummond, but . . .' *I'm doing it for your good. It hurts me more than it hurts you.* . . . The sickening clichés passed through his mind but remained unuttered.

'Bend over, and let's get it finished and done with.'

The poor little behind proffered so piteously. White as marble. Skinny as a rabbit's. He heard Drummond draw a deep breath that was half a sob. With closed eyes and gritted teeth he raised the cane, and startled by the sudden opening of the door, brought it down far harder than he had intended.

It was Follett, the senior maths teacher.

'Oh – sorry, Moon. Didn't realize . . . I'll come back later.'

121

The door closed swiftly and he heard Drummond give another little sob; he looked down, forcing himself to see the damage he had done: a single red weal crossing the buttocks from left to right. He flung the cane back in the cupboard and strode over to the window. He remained there with his back turned.

'You may go now, Drummond.'

Drummond was crying openly now, partly because of pain and partly because of relief at having been let off so lightly. He dragged his clothing back into place. 'Thank you, Sir.'

'And don't let me hear of you cribbing again.'

'No, Sir.'

The quiet closing of the door, and even as a cloud of treble voices rose from the chapel (*The da-ay Thou ga-avest Lord, is ended* . . .) he could see nothing but the friendly, knowing leer in Follett's eyes as he backed out of the room.

Did he know? Did he guess? Was he, himself . . .?

Three terms passed; Drummond playing Puck in the school's annual Shakespeare production, with bare legs and gauzy tunic and a new tormenting roguishness; Drummond swimming, lithe as a silver eel; Drummond with a white mouse confiscated in a divinity lesson; and Drummond coming back from the summer hols suddenly taller and with his hair brushed to one side instead of covering his forehead in a little-boy fringe. Every stage, every situation watched with love, with hunger, and with tormented self-control.

There were one or two narrow escapes, of course. Drummond being knocked out by a cricket ball at the nets, and Mr Moon, who happened to be passing, dropping his books and sprinting forward to raise Drummond's head and shoulders in passionate arms, unaware for a dangerous moment or two of the other boys clustering round. Dudley, the sports master, came over, and anguish gave Mr Moon the power to say harshly: 'I'll see to him – he's in my house.'

Unassisted and unaccompanied, he carried the unconscious boy across the wide playing field to the main school buildings and the sanatorium. He must have weighed well over seven stone and Mr Moon's thin arms began to ache, but like Christ carrying the symbol of His suffering, he staggered on his way to Golgotha. Matron met him at the entrance and cried: 'Good gracious, Mr Moon, what have we here?'

Although the idyll was due to end with Drummond's elevation to Rugby, the situation was in fact resolved before then, for shortly after the Whitsun break Drummond's mother was washed overboard from the family yacht and drowned.

The news was delivered to the headmaster by telegram, and he passed it on in tones of throbbing sorrow; the weeping boy was referred to his housemaster for comfort.

The days were still chilly, and they drank cocoa by Mr Moon's study fire during the period of officially approved intimacy.

'Tell me about your mother, if it helps.'

'She was . . . she was jolly decent, Sir.'

'I'm sure. But even though this has – has happened, Drummond, one needn't think of her as . . . dead in the conventional sense. Those whom we have loved can never be truly dead to us.'

'No, Sir.'

The bowed head and childlike hollow at the nape of the neck, and on the cheek a tiny blemish never noticed before (surely not the first puberty pimple?); an inkstain on the wretchedly clasped fingers; and around the sleeve of his regulation Norfolk jacket a broad band of ribbon in deepest black.

'We all get the strength from somewhere to bear these burdens, Drummond.'

'Do we, Sir?' Wet blue eyes lifted momentarily, as if the magical wherewithal might be lurking in a fold of the curtains.

'Yes, of course we do. I remember when my own Mater died – ' You remember nothing of the sort. Your mother died when you were three, and so you had to make do with your own private myth of a wise and womanly image in

123

Parma violet singing hushed lullabies in a firelit nursery. . . .

He poured more cocoa, and covertly watched the pink tip of Drummond's tongue remove a fragment of milk skin from his top lip.

'But in the meanwhile it's worth remembering that we still have good friends ready to stand by us, to show sympathy and, it goes without saying – without any sort of namby-pambyism – you understand what I mean, Drummond?'

'Yes, Sir.'

And so the evening would end. But only as a prelude to the next one. And the next, and the next. Drummond, excused chapel and excused prep on account of his bereavement, tapping on his housemaster's study door; the cocoa simmered on the hob and the pale, gentle face would be raised with carefully assumed reluctance from a pile of housemasterly papers. 'Ah, Drummond, yes. Come in.'

And oh, the rhapsodic beauty, the ridiculous beguilement of a blue-eyed boy with neatly parted hair above an Eton collar and the memory of the little proffered buttocks and the strangled sob. Gentle probing of the personality (as opposed to gentle probing of the person) elicited a certain amount of humdrum insight into Drummond's homelife, all of it eagerly seized and swallowed by the hungry Mr Moon. Papa was a stockbroker, the late Mama third daughter of Sir George Mount, a fierce old gentleman who mocked the wearing of flannel next the skin and the love of small animals . . . three elder sisters, one pitted by smallpox and all of them devoted to needlework and The Poor. They were all pretty decent on the whole, but none of them anywhere near as decent as the Mater had been.

The tears flowed again and, aching with love and pity, Drummond's housemaster opened his arms and Drummond crept into them.

The idyll lasted for a week, ending with a summons from the headmaster, who sat back with his thumbs in his armpits and said that he had a matter of the utmost gravity to discuss.

There was no point in trying to explain the difference between molestation and harmless cuddling; not only was it sickening and demeaning, it was in all honesty very difficult to ascertain the dividing line between the two. So he said nothing, except to protest, overheatedly, at the word debauch. Which was a mistake, for it allowed the headmaster to flourish in triumph the small notebook found hidden beneath Mr Moon's blotting pad.

'*Cool as starlight, my child-limbed love/Fills my heart with incredulous joy*. . . . Did you write those words, Mr Moon?'

Senseless to deny it. And hopeless to try to protect the frail yearnings that had prompted that and other equally bad scraps of verse, all of them now dragged into the daylight and the dirt by the headmaster's fruity drawl.

He packed his box that same afternoon and left the school without seeing Drummond. He never learned what had happened; whether someone had spied on them, or whether Drummond had either deliberately or unintentionally peached to the authorities. It was of no consequence. In an effort to heal the sense of unutterable loss, he sold his box and most of its contents and tramped the white summery roads until he reached the Cambridgeshire fens.

And the present predicament in which he found himself.

Standing in the pool of lamplight in the turf-cutter's cottage he slowly tore the school photograph in two. He tore it again, detaching Drummond's head from his body, then hobbled over to the stove and put the pieces inside. They would be found because the fire was out, but it no longer mattered.

Everywhere was clean and bachelor-tidy, but he plumped up the cushion in the armchair, then washed his cup and saucer and poured the last drops of milk from the jug into Fata Morgana's bowl before arranging the details of his final departure.

Walter found him: suspended motionless from a hook in the ceiling with lolling tongue and mournfully staring eyes.

White-faced and shaking, he and Reuben cut him down and covered the body with a blanket. In a confused attempt

125

to spare both Lizzie and Edwina, Walter broke the news by saying that Johnnie had died, most likely of a heart attack, and even tried to persuade the Wimblington doctor to corroborate the story, at least to the womenfolk. But he forgot to remove the bit of rope still tied to the hook, and when Edwina saw it she screamed so loudly that Lizzie, still dazed with shock, came running.

Then he had to tell them. And Edwina turned hysterically on Lizzie and said that it must have been her fault for saying something, doing something, that had upset him. Walter tried to calm her, and forced her to sit down in the armchair, at which Lizzie broke out of her daze and tried to drag her upright again: *'You can't sit in that chair! Nobody must sit in it – it was his!'*

The doctor issued Edwina with a sleeping draught and, without fully comprehending the situation, instructed Lizzie rather sternly to pull herself together and see after her parents. They were her responsibility now she was a grown girl.

And while all this was going on, Reuben on his rickety boneshaker was hastening along the Sixteen Foot level to spread the news.

Within a few hours everyone knew: all those who knew the Hintons and all those who had been at Ezekiel Stacey's socializing, and plans were made to attend the coroner's inquest by all those who had transport and nothing better to do with their time.

With evening now advanced and Edwina asleep upstairs, Walter tried rather fumblingly to comfort Lizzie. Stroking her hair with his rough farmer's hand, he said he always reckoned Johnnie wasn't robust in his health, and that that was always bound to affect the way a chap was in his head. As for doing away with hisself, well, he reckoned that everyone had a right to do as they thought fit, and heavy-hearted though it might leave them as were left, it wouldn't be any sort of kindness to wish them back.

Lizzie nodded, dry-eyed. 'You could do with going to bed, Pa. You look tired enough to drop.'

'Wouldn't say no.' He tried to smile but it was a failure. 'You coming up too, Lizzie gel?'

'Yes,' she said.

'Reckon you'll sleep?'

'I'll try.'

She went up to her room and lay on the bed, fully dressed and with the quilt drawn up to her chin. She listened, motionless, to the familiar sounds indicative of retirement. Muffled coughing, the thud of his boots – one, two – on to the bare boards, then the creak of bedsprings as he sank down into his accustomed place beside Ma. She lay counting the minutes, listening sharp-eared as a cat for the first sound of snoring. There had never been a disaster yet that could keep Pa from eating and sleeping.

By the light of one candle she rolled a few clothes and her best pair of boots in an old coat and tied it securely. Then she drew the old tin treasure box from its hiding-place and removed the two pounds four shillings and one penny ha'penny which she had been saving for her trousseau from her hen money. Then she put on her coat and woollen cap and tiptoed downstairs.

She looked round the shadowed kitchen for the last time, where Johnnie's cat and her kittens had now been installed and where the scent of Pa's Nosegay shag still hung on the air. She said goodbye silently, tearlessly, then let herself out of the door and began to hurry away down the farm track to the Sixteen Foot level.

It was a still, surprisingly mild night, and from far away over Horse Moor she could hear the sound of the last train coming.

Dorothy Paynim was short, plump and jolly, aged forty-five and unmarried.

She had received comparatively little education but all necessary instruction on the dos and don'ts, the right ways and wrong ways of conducting herself as the only daughter of a wealthy furniture manufacturer and his purring wife. By the age of sixteen she had reached the conclusion that such tiresome spuriosity was not for her, yet its absence

127

would create an undeniable void.

Briefly she toyed with various ideas, all of them childish, passionate and useless: running away to live in the Sahara, marrying a Balkan prince, or espousing the Fenian Risings (of which she had heard a garbled account from Mrs O'Hare, the Paynims' cook). None of them satisfied her, and it was not until her German governess, Fräulein Scheel, went down with scarlet fever that her future was made clear. 'Dear God,' she prayed to the Heavenly Father who was no more to her than a kind of superannuated vicar, 'if you let her die I'll believe in you properly and for ever, and do whatever you say, amen.'

That night she had a dream (vision?) in which she and God were sitting alone together in a beautiful garden eating strawberry ices at a little bamboo table. Although He was dressed in striped trousers, a swallowtail coat and a high cravat like Papa, she knew it was God because there was a sort of luminous mist round Him that other men didn't have. He asked her whether she believed in Him, *really* believed, and she said yes she did, now. She could scarcely help it, could she?

So God said: 'In that case, Dorothy my dear, I am prepared to grant your wish if in return you promise to dedicate your life to a project that is particularly dear to My heart.'

And He told her what it was. It was to go out and succour all the other poor thwarted young girls who, like herself, were expected to conform to whatever kind of life their parents had in mind as right and proper.

She asked where she was supposed to find them, all these poor thwarted young girls like herself, and God said: 'You will find them everywhere. Rich girls, poor girls, pretty girls, plain girls, all of them forced to conform to a role decreed by someone else. You must help them, protect them, educate them, so that they will have the knowledge and the self-confidence to rise up, proud in their young womanhood and say, No more: from now on we choose our own destiny, tread our own path. You are to bring them all, in other words, to Me.'

Then God finished His strawberry ice and disappeared, taking His luminous mist with Him.

That same evening Fräulein Scheel rallied, and appeared on the point of recovery. But during the night she slumped dramatically and by breakfast time was no more, leaving Dorothy relieved, amazed and converted to a kind of bubblingly thankful Christianity which never throughout her long life deserted her.

And she kept her promise. It was difficult at first, haranguing other daughters within her parents' social circle on the importance of being freed from the vain trammels of sitting about waiting for a husband to appear. Most of them were rather surprised and disconcerted – they quite liked sitting about; few took her seriously, and only one took her literally, shinning trouserclad down a drainpipe and running away with the under-gardener.

Still, it was a beginning, and because of her innately cheerful disposition Dorothy was able to detach herself from her parents slowly and without causing pain, until they were able to accept her preference for two rooms in Paddington rather than a mansion in Reigate. Occasionally she went home for weekends, and her papa increased her allowance by five pounds on the first of January every year.

In the meanwhile she discovered that the world in general and London in particular treated its young working women abominably. Factory, sweatshop or domestic service, there was little to choose between any of them when it came to humane conditions and adequate pay, and it became clear to Dorothy that for those out of work, a bowl of soup or fourpence for a night's lodging took precedence over any form of spiritual aid.

The sheer weight of human wretchedness appalled her, and standing inconspicuously in the shadow of factory gates or the narrow stairways that led to sweatshop workrooms, she watched the arrival, and then the departure after a fourteen-hour day, of the pale threadbare girls with hollow chests and hacking coughs, too tired and too indifferent to notice her presence. Servant girls were rarely seen as they were rarely allowed their freedom; perhaps one half-day a

129

month, and by the time it came round they were too weary to go out, unless it was summertime and there was a park nearby where they could sit on the grass and listen in a state of dull wonderment to the chirping of London sparrows.

It was difficult to know how to begin the work that God had called her to; she wondered if He meant her to join one of the larger organizations such as the Salvation Army or the Church of England Temperance Society. She watched them at their work, uniformed, earnest and portentous, huffing on their trombones and extolling the virtues of total abstinence to girls whose sole aspiration was a twopenny mutton pie for supper. She watched them and admired them, but was unable to commit herself. She asked God about it in her prayers but He made no reply. Either He was engaged elsewhere, or preferred that she should work it out for herself.

Then she met Annie Dawkins – or tripped over her, more accurately, as Annie was exploring the contents of a box of kitchen refuse outside a restaurant.

'Why don't you look where you're bleedin' well goin'?'

Dorothy apologized, and when her companion drew a lump of mouldy bread from beneath a pile of potato peelings and showed every sign that she was about to eat it, it seemed as if Dorothy found her crusading voice at last.

'Put it down, dear,' she commanded. 'It is extremely dirty and no doubt covered in disease. If you are hungry, come home with me.'

Too surprised to argue, Annie Dawkins did so, and Dorothy took her firmly by the arm and led her off to Paddington. Without bothering to remove her hat, Annie wolfed down the remains of Dorothy's shin of beef stew, four slices of bread and a hunk of cake, then leaned back in the chair and belched thunderously.

Then she straightened her hat and regarded Dorothy through suspicious little eyes.

''oo are you?'

'I'm Dorothy.'

'Dorothy 'oo?'

'Dorothy Paynim. Now tell me who you are.'

Annie did so. Then thanked her for the victuals and stood up. 'Well, I'd best be gettin' orf 'ome.'

'Have you got a home, Annie?'

'Wot's it to you?'

'There's a spare bed here, if you want it.'

Annie stayed. And so it began. Annie was the first of the girls who cottoned on to Miss Paynim and the crisp, breezy hospitality she offered. There was no sermonizing, no pi-jaw, but on the other hand no crookery, thievery or loose talk was allowed. Girls down on their luck for whatever the cause were welcomed into the circle, and those cynically or casually prepared to lie, cheat or steal, quickly discouraged. Within a couple of months five of them were kipping in the room Miss Paynim had previously used as a sitting room. After Annie there was Lucy (whose parents were in gaol); Dot, who was halfwitted and sometimes wet the bed; the Weldon sisters, who had been sacked from domestic service without references for refusing to take a cut in wages; and then poor Lily Peek, who had worked in the yellow phosphorus fumes of a match factory until phossy jaw rendered her both incapacitated and hideous to look at.

After a swift and lucrative trip home to her parents, Dorothy was able to rent the floor above her own, and eventually the floor beneath as well. By 1894 she had the entire house at her disposal and had filled it with young women, all of whom had been buffeted by fate, or the system, to such an extent that they frequently needed coaxing to grasp the helping hand extended to them.

She fed them, sheltered them, steered them towards the rudiments of hygiene – 'If you sleep in your boots you will get foot rot like our poor lads in the Crimea,' – and instilled into them something of her own artless but wonderfully intelligible relationship with God. There was no kneeling, no bowing or scraping. God was addressed with the affectionate courtesy one might reserve for an older brother, a jovial uncle, or for that rare phenomenon, a papa who refused to adorn his status with all the customary trappings of majesty and fear. And lo, the air was filled with the voices of the young girls counting their blessings and praising Him loudly and ardently because He had brought them in His loving wisdom to safe harbour at number 67 Gossett Street and to the genial commonsense of dear Miss Paynim.

They didn't all stay permanently; in fact, the level of arrival and departure remained remarkably constant. Some were birds of passage resting after a particularly bad patch of weather before flying forth again; for others the lure of the West End proved too strong; and in the case of poor Lily Peek, a merciful death after her lower jaw had finally disintegrated in a suppurating puddle.

When the average number of residents reached twenty, Miss Paynim decided that the time had come when both she and they might assume some kind of official status. She therefore dressed them all, at her own expense, in a pleasant but serviceable shade of green and decided that they should be called The Girls' League of Fellowship, although one of the brighter ones said she didn't see how girls could be fellows, and people in the vicinity, intrigued by the green uniforms, christened them Paynim's Pixies.

Miss Paynim laughed when she heard this and said never mind, we are now a corporate body, and, anticipating Baden-Powell and his sister Agnes by almost twenty years, devised a series of little ribands and badges, all of which could be earned by simple acts of courtesy and kindness and worn with modest pride by their recipients.

They ran the house efficiently and well: sweeping the bare wooden floors and keeping the rows of small iron beds tidily aligned. They took it in turns to prepare the simple meals while Miss Paynim took charge of the family purse and saw to all the shopping. But the main purpose of The Girls' League of Fellowship was to succour those in need of support and compassion, as they themselves had once been.

'It's not enough to sit here and wait for them to come to us,' declared Miss Paynim. 'It's our job to go out and find them. God has called us to do His work and we must strive our utmost to obey.'

So she led them on briskly efficient little forays through-out London, taking in the false allure of the West End, the pubs, the music halls, the theatres, and then the dreadful temptations of the murky river sliding along the Embankment.

In many ways time was more important than place, for during the hours of darkness an estimated ten thousand young women roamed the streets for want of anywhere better; no vagrant of whatever age or sex was allowed to sleep in public places and a zealous police force kept them constantly on the move. Green Park was the first to open its gates, shortly after four in the morning, and the first inside was always a ragbag miscellany of the homeless making for the nearest bench and merciful oblivion. The dead hours of night belonged to the dispossessed: to the hapless and homeless, to the drunks and the dying, and to the poor young girls, vulnerable as March blossom, who struggled to survive the dirt and the poverty, the wickedness and the cynical contempt of the world that bred them.

It was an uphill task that would have daunted many, but Miss Paynim seemed to reach ever new heights of responsiveness. She never tired. She never lost her temper or her appetite or her sense of humour.

'God,' she would cry, 'is our universal Provider. With His aid we can perform miracles, and without it we are sunk.'

The only thing she found difficult to deal with was sin. Naturally she had become conversant with it at an early stage in her career, and as a robust and contented spinster her reaction to sexual delinquency had always been one of instinctive aversion. But she learned to conquer it, and to treat the impure, the pregnant and the poxy with a sort of gusty familiarity that blew away the shame, the secrecy and any lingering hint of agreeable notoriety.

Those who were pregnant were briskly referred to the Foundlings' Hospital and those with venereal disease to the nearest general practitioner. They could not stay at the house in Gossett Street, although they were invited with great sincerity to keep in touch.

'What we must do,' she declared with a wisdom far ahead of her time, 'is to stop the rot at its source. We must catch

133

these girls while they are still young and untried, before they have a chance to fall victim to debauchery and beastliness in general.'

With this in mind she switched her attention to the main-line railway stations: to Euston and King's Cross, Paddington and Waterloo, where young girls arrived from the country ripe as peaches and innocent as buttercups, and all of them secure in the knowledge that they could make their way, that this twinkling gaslit city would recognize them, love them and shower its wealth upon them.

Thus it came to pass that Miss Paynim, flanked by two attendant Pixies, was on Liverpool Street Station on the night of February the fourth, 1895. Business had been unusually poor and they had been on duty for a number of hours, scanning the muffled, hurrying figures while the raw London fog ate into their bones.

They were on the point of going home when the last train from Peterborough and the Cambridgeshire fens steamed in and deposited a young auburn-haired girl with her belongings tied up in a bundle.

'*Ha!*' cried Miss Paynim, preparing to pounce. 'I do believe we're in luck at last!'

'Pore little bleeder,' whispered one of the Pixies compassionately, 'she's cryin' her bleedin' eyes out.'

They took her back to Gossett Street in a four-wheel cab and she made no resistance; just sat in a corner wiping her eyes and sniffing.

They gave her some supper in the little firelit room used as a kind of private sanctum, but all she did was crumble a bit of bread and drink a mouthful or two of soup. It had been obvious from the start that she was not in the category of girls who ran away *to*, but in the rarer and more difficult group of those who ran away *from*. A brutal father, perhaps. A tiff with her young man, or any one of the hundred situations that could make family life appear unendurable. Miss Paynim had heard most of them in her time, but was unprepared for this particular girl's reply to her questioning.

134

'I ran away because the chap I loved hanged himself and it was all my fault.'

'Mercy on us.' Then quickly recovering, Miss Paynim added: 'What makes you believe it was all your fault?'

'I put the idea into his head when I told him our family secret – which I'd no business to have – about my great-grandmother Hinton being hanged outside Ely Gaol. He would never have done it otherwise.'

'But my dear girl, supposing I put my hand in the fire – I wouldn't take it for granted that you would do likewise. He must have had a better reason than that, poor fellow.'

'Yes, he had.' Her tears flowed. 'He found out he didn't really love me. He only thought he did and hoped it would be all right.'

'Well, well,' Miss Paynim said, with a helplessness unusual for her. Then she pulled herself together. 'So what are you going to do now?'

'I don't know. Find work somewhere, I reckon.'

'It may not be easy. Do you know London at all?'

'No.'

'And what about your parents? Do they know where you are?'

'No.'

'You really ought to let them know. Or failing that, give me their address and I'll write to them for you.'

'No, I don't want – '

'Only to tell them you're safe. I won't give them your address if you prefer me not to.'

'Please yourself.'

She had seen it so many times before: the grumpy, tearful shrug, the mutinous underlip of the girl who feels herself ill-used.

'In the meanwhile,' went on Miss Paynim, 'we'll look after you. You can have a bed in room four – it overlooks a nice big tree so you won't feel too homesick – and such rules and regs that we have are easy to pick up as you go along. I'll drop a note to your parents to tell them you are safe, but nothing more – and in a day or two we'll have you right as rain and smiling again. By the way, you do smile, don't you?'

135

'I don't know. I can't remember.'

'Never mind. But trot along now – Gertie will show you the ropes. I'm sure we're all very tired and a sound night's sleep will do us all a power of good.'

She beamed cheerily, then as the girl reached the door, added: 'By the way, dear, are you by any chance expecting?'

'No, I'm not expecting anything,' Lizzie said, and escaped from the room just before a fresh gush of tears.

London meant nothing to her, to begin with. She might have been in Timbuctoo for all she noticed. And it was the same with the other occupants of the house; they were no more than a vague cabbage-coloured blur, and she moved through those first days seeing only Johnnie.

Johnnie's face and Johnnie's smile. The long graceful length of him in the old armchair, the lock of brown hair falling across his forehead as he bent over a book. Johnnie in his old straw hat picking plums and packing them for market. Laughing down at her from the box seat of the farm wagon, and the dear lovely gentleness of his hands as he cradled Fata Morgana's kittens. And then the final picture that still seared her: Johnnie lying motionless on the floor of the turf-cutter's cottage beneath a hastily improvised shroud.

Mercifully she had been spared the first dreadful sight of him, but the image of that long thin form so unbelievably motionless beneath the calico sheet haunted her more powerfully and more painfully even than the moonlit magic of Ezekiel Stacey's socializing. She could scarcely deal with the fact of his death, and the additional burden of knowing that she had caused it was a torment akin to physical agony.

He would still have been alive but for her pestering and importuning, and he would never have thought of hanging himself from a hook in the ceiling if she hadn't told him about great-grandmother Hinton simply because she wanted to appear important in his eyes. It would serve her right if the old girl came back and haunted her for making wicked use of her secret.

Bowed by grief and the weight of miserable guilt, she

trailed numbly, dumbly through the days, oblivious of the watchful care and muted sympathy extended by Miss Paynim and her Pixies. Yet she had no regrets about running away; on the contrary, she knew that time would only harden her resolve never to return. Even from this distance she could scarcely bear to contemplate the memory of old days and old places; everything – home, the farm, the fen country lying with its face upturned on the vast ever-changing skies – was poisoned for ever more by the horror of what had happened.

And equally, her mind shied away from her parents. Somehow they could have helped more; could have made it clear to Johnnie how much they would welcome him as a son-in-law; could have been nicer to *her* too, while they were about it. But now they knew what she really thought of them. Running away would have shown them that. And they would never forgive her, any more than she would ever forgive them, although she had finally relented sufficiently to allow Miss Paynim to write a brief anonymous note to say that she was safe and well.

It was March before she began to return to life; to look about her, to contemplate and consider, and the first thing she noticed was the swelling buds on the tree outside the house. She noticed the house itself; bare and ramshackle yet filled most of the time with cheerful voices and the energetic patter of feet. Everyone seemed to be constantly busy although no orders were given: girls sweeping, preparing meals, washing dishes, washing and ironing clothes, and setting off in groups of two or three to seek out and bring home to God and Miss Paynim the poor lost ewes that had strayed from His flock.

Although the place had a strong religious atmosphere, it was of the jolly and slightly haphazard variety as practised by Miss Paynim herself; there were no holy pictures, no particular corner set aside for services or even private devotions. There was no need, because everyone prayed wherever they were and whenever they felt like it. Perhaps it wasn't praying so much as having a one-sided conversation, and Lizzie was silently astonished by the casual but

137

affectionate mateyness with which the Creator was frequently addressed. He was called upon to advise, admire,
laugh at and laugh with, and it took a while to become
accustomed to living among people who suddenly paused in
whatever they were doing, raised their eyes to the ceiling
and invited God's honest opinion of their efforts.

And with the return of awareness came the first tentative
desire to decide what to do next. There appeared to be no
coercion to stay or to leave the house in Gossett Street –
quite a few girls had already arrived and departed during
the course of her stay – but a strange kind of inertia
prevented her from making up her mind. She still felt
tearful and debilitated, as if she were convalescing after a
serious illness.

Despite the prevailing custom of chatting to God, she felt
too shy and awkward to do likewise, so in the end she went
to Miss Paynim, who advised her to stay where she was until
she received a definite call to do otherwise.

'You really think I'll get a call?' she asked dubiously.

'Of course you will, dear. Everyone does, if only they'd
keep their ears pricked.'

Perhaps not surprisingly, it arrived on the day she first
put on the strange and rather baggy green dress that had
been made for her by Kate and Bertha, and from which she
had been allowed to remove the tacking threads when it was
finished. She might have been putting on the dress uniform
of a colonel in the Household Cavalry, or conversely, the
hairshirt as worn by some exclusive band of zealots, for
even before the buttons were fastened and the limp belt was
tied she had a sudden rapturous feeling that at last she
belonged, that this was the outward proclamation of her
new, true self.

'When can I go?'

'Go where, dear?'

'Go to start rescuing poor girls.'

They treated her gently and told her that she must first
earn her badges. Badges? Yes, hadn't she noticed? Badges
for Helpfulness, for Cheerfulness and Tidiness, and then
badges for Cooking and Sewing, and finally the most senior

and most coveted badge of all – God's Badge for All-Round Fellowship.

She looked at them for the first time, those neat little embroidered squares stitched above the left bosom of the cabbage green dresses. And to possess them, as Alice and Winnie, Kate and Bertha possessed them, tore her convalescent heart with fierce new yearnings.

She swept and dusted, scoured the sink and unblocked the privy; she cleaned obstinate London soot from the windows and ran round in circles after a vociferous new inmate called Mavis, who, it was later discovered, was suffering from advanced delirium tremens. One by one she earned her badges and the loyal applause of the other Pixies, but on the only occasion she tried to chat with God in front of them all she made a hash of it and vowed never to do so again. God was with her, she felt it quite powerfully, but she could only speak to Him at night, in the dark silence of room four with her face buried in the pillow.

Dear God, I didn't mean to put the idea for doing what he did into Johnnie's head. I loved him much too much for that, and as You can see into my heart and read my thoughts, You'll know I'm telling the truth. I loved him very much, and I still do. I love everyone – my new life here has taught me how to – even my mother and father, but I don't want to go back there because there's so much of Your work to do here. Thank You for making me so happy and for teaching me that other people's happiness comes before my own. I do like it here very much, although I miss the fresh air sometimes. . . .

Finally, she earned the right to go out on patrol with the other seniors. They generally went in groups of three, and instead of standing mutely watchful as before, Miss Paynim now decided that they should vary the monotony with a little hymn-singing.

Hymn-singing in public was easier than might be supposed, firstly because it came naturally to young hearts swelling with joy on His account, and secondly because in late-Victorian London the streets rang with the sound of voices uplifted in song. Beggars, drunks, children singing a roundelay and the hoarse sing-song chant of the rag-and-

139

bone man, the cats'-meat man and the knife-grinder. All the street vendors had their own identifying cry, from the milkman's cheerful yodel to the sepulchral growling of the coal-carter; and the trios of Paynim's Pixies were not alone in their hymn-singing – all too often they found themselves singing in direct opposition to the Salvation Army, the London City Mission, the Open-Air Mission, not to mention such impassioned groups as Baptists, Methodists, Congregationalists and sometimes the dulcet tinkle of representatives from the United Temperance Society. They all spoke, propounded, harangued and sang their messages, hopefully launching them upon the grimy air already loaded with the roar of hooves on cobbles and the grating of iron wheels.

To begin with, the noise of it all had filled young Lizzie with animal terror. Accustomed to a world where the churring of a reed-warbler might be the only sound to break an hour's silence, she was both confused and deafened, and she had clung to her companion's hand like a small child afraid of the dark.

But it got better. Gradually she gave up trying to unravel the complex tangle of sounds and learned eventually to conquer the habit, so natural in a country-dweller, of nodding and smiling good-day at anyone who might be approaching. Soon she was bawling hymns with the best of them, and Miss Paynim said how nice it was that God had really got inside her. He knew a good thing when He saw it and had never been One to let the grass grow under His feet.

As early spring blustered and sulked and eventually smiled its way towards summer, Lizzie's confidence in her proficiency as a Londoner increased. She knew her way from Gossett Street to all the main-line railway stations, to Piccadilly and Leicester Square. She knew about Hyde Park, and of the dangers that lurked within its tree-shadowed glades, and one of her first night-time hymn-singing assignments was outside the Metropolitan Music Hall in the Edgware Road. Dan Leno was appearing there, so was Marie Lloyd, and she never forgot the night when the Pixie trio's brave rendering of 'Through the Night of

Doubt and Sorrow Onward Goes the Christian Band'
collided with and became totally extinguished by the loyal
roar of 'Knocked 'em in the Old Kent Road' as the great
Albert Chevalier emerged from the stage door.

She grew accustomed to the smell of London (soot, horse
muck, cigar smoke and bad drainage), and learned to
cherish the odd whiffs of wallflower, chestnut and lime-tree
blossom. Sometimes it seemed as if she were on the verge of
homesickness, but a few words with God invariably put
things right.

Then came the day when she met Peg, and perhaps
things would have turned out differently if she had been in
the usual Pixie trio. But she had volunteered to slip round to
the printer's to collect the new leaflets Miss Paynim had
ordered (*God loves YOU as well as me!*) – and she almost
collided with this poor ragged girl peering hopefully into
the faces of passers-by as she proffered a bunch of violets.
She had spots and steel-rimmed spectacles and the sweetest
expression that Lizzie had ever seen.

She smiled at her. 'What a lovely day God has sent us!'

The girl did her best to smile back, and Lizzie saw that
there was only twopence in the small container at her feet.

'Having a bad day, dear?'

The girl nodded.

'Had any dinner?'

A reluctant shake of the head.

'Come with me,' Lizzie said, 'and we'll soon fix you up
with something.'

The girl looked dubious, even scared, but Lizzie told her
to pick up the twopence she had earned, then took her arm
and guided her towards Praed Street. Still holding her arm,
she escorted her into the printer's office. The packet of
leaflets was only a small one, and cost one-and-sixpence.
Lizzie paid with a florin, pocketed the change and began to
tell the girl about the work of the Girls' Fellowship as she
propelled her in the direction of Gossett Street.

'By the way, what's your name?'

'Peg.'

'Peg what?'

'Peg Honeyball.'

'It suits you,' Lizzie said impulsively. 'You've got such a sweet sort of look.'

But Peg had to be persuaded to stay, and to avail herself of the free hospitality so willingly offered.

'I can't,' she kept saying. 'I've done nothing to earn it.'

'God doesn't expect payment from those down on their luck,' Miss Paynim told her. 'When did you last eat, dear?'

'Tuesday morning.'

'But today is Thursday.'

The girl blinked myopically through her spectacles and said, 'Yes, I suppose it must be about Thursday by now.'

Little by little they extracted her story, and it was even more piteous than most. Father a sailor drowned at sea. Mother carried off by consumption. Four little brothers and sisters boarded out with an aunt near Tunbridge Wells, while Peg remained in London, trying to earn a little money to provide for their keep. But work was difficult because of her deteriorating sight. 'Bad sight runs in our family and they've told me I'll be blind before long. I don't mind for myself but I worry about the little ones. Auntie can't afford to feed four extra mouths, but' – she began to weep – 'but my greatest fear is that I'll never see them again.'

In the positive tones of those on familiar ground with the Almighty, they assured Peg that she had no need to worry. God, through the agency of the Girls' League of Fellowship, would show tender mercy not only towards her but towards the four children and Auntie as well; and the fervent Lizzie, who had found her, went a step further and suggested that He might also feel inclined to make a real job of it and restore Peg's failing sight while He was at it.

You never knew. That was the wonderful thing about God.

So they fed her and gave her the spare bed in room two, and Miss Paynim sent for a small jar of Frisby's Wonder Ointment to rub on her spots. And in all the usual pleasant bustle of making a new arrival feel welcome, Lizzie forgot about the sixpence change from the printer's that she had

142

put in her pocket. When she remembered it next morning it was no longer there.

'God dear, this is the first time I've ever seriously challenged Your decision, but why did You send us Peg? Was it in order to try our belief and our durability in the face of disaster, or was it because You too are really human and not always competent to spot a wrong 'un when You see one?'

Detaching her gaze from the ceiling, Miss Paynim looked round once again at the room that served as office and sanctuary for new arrivals. The curtains hung askew and a windowpane was broken. The drawers of the cheap mahogany desk had been wrenched open, where they remained like so many mouths in the act of spewing; papers and envelopes, notebooks and account books, sheets of pink blotting paper and spare copies of *I Love Him as a Friend*, all of them cascaded in their individual pools on to the bare floor. The tin cash box had been rifled, and that holiest of holies, the worn leather concertina purse, had been emptied of its careful housekeeping pennies, six-pences, shillings, florins and half-crowns and left con-temptuously in the grate. Nothing else had been stolen except a loaf of bread, four herrings and half a seed cake from the larder. Her bed in room two had been planted with that hoariest of deceivers, a bolster down the middle, but the jar of Frisby's Wonder Ointment remained open and already an unhealthy crust was forming on top.

'If You were taken in by her as we were, well, I'll say no more. After all, we're only human. But if You deliberately sent her to rob us of practically all we've got, then I must say I think You've gone a bit too far. Money doesn't grow on trees, and as I've already told You, I've got other worries at the moment. . . .'

God didn't answer. He remained inscrutable. Sighing, Miss Paynim took up an account book, wrenched off the back cover and forced it into the aperture where the windowpane had been. It didn't fit very well, but it stopped the draught. Then she sat down with her little fat legs outstretched on top of the ravaged desk, linked her hands behind her head and gave herself up to serious consideration of the facts.

Unknown to the Pixies, they were extremely grim, for Miss Paynim's contentedly purring mother had died suddenly and unexpectedly three months ago, and her father, that hitherto loving and uncomplicated provider of funds for little Dorothy's Fellowship thing, had already fallen victim to the machinations of a young lady bookkeeper from his office. They had been married at Marylebone Register Office four days ago, and Father had written to ask for her blessing and to warn her that the provision made for her in his will would naturally have to be adjusted, particularly in view of his earnest wish that his dear one might well present him with a son. (Was she already in the family way? Miss Paynim wondered, aghast.) And the solicitor's letter which arrived yesterday informed her that his esteemed client Mr R. F. E. Paynim had instructed him to advise her that the monthly allowance made to her would henceforth be reduced by one half.

'I can only repeat,' Miss Paynim said to the ceiling, 'that in all honesty I think You've gone a bit too far.'

Receiving no answer, she sighed and set about restoring the room to order, and as she did so began to devise various schemes for saving money.

The Pixies were surprised and a little mutinous when told that from now on they would have to rattle collecting boxes on their hymn-singing, girl-saving forays, and when reminded that the Salvation Army had always done so, muttered that they had understood The Girls' League of Fellowship to be a superior kind of organization.

As inmates were strictly non-paying, there was no point in trying to cram more beds into the already closely packed bedrooms as a conventional landlady might have done, so economies had to be made in food, in the mending of boots – 'I suggest that in His name we all try to take longer *strides*!' – and in the general maintenance of 67 Gossett Street. It was all very harassing, and if it hadn't been for her loving but jocular relationship with the Almighty, Miss Paynim might

144

well have succumbed to despair and the temptation to pack the whole lot in.

So far as Lizzie was concerned, her reactions were complicated by the bitter knowledge that she alone had been responsible for introducing Peg Honeyball to the Fellowship, and as she had no more inkling of Miss Paynim's financial dilemma than anyone else, she could only imagine that the theft of the family purse had brought them all to this depressing state of penury.

It was her fault. As Johnnie's death had been her fault. And at the back of it all lurked the fear that it was because of some sort of curse laid on her by Bessie Hinton – her that had been hanged at Ely.

And with the return of the old anxiety came a sense of disillusion with the new life she had made for herself. It was fine being able to talk to God as if He were some kind of jolly, ragging elder brother, but the fact that He had exhibited such a cynical reaction to her amateurish espousal of Peg Honeyball's case was both hurtful and hard to comprehend. He might have realized that she was only a beginner in the saving business, and made allowances accordingly. She would have done if she had been Him.

Looking back in later years, she was always to remain convinced that the first real hint of the new and crucial direction her life was to take came on that Tuesday morning in the June of 1895 when she and two other Pixies were dutifully singing and rattling their boxes in the vicinity of Marble Arch.

Hot sunshine sparkled from a cloudless sky as the sound of cheering and whistling came from further along Oxford Street. They paused and looked at each other questioningly when the sound grew louder, and the traffic slowed almost to a halt, as an open landau, crested and glittering and drawn by two superlative bays, made its proud way down the centre of the street. Against the pearl-grey cushions in the back of it reclined a woman in a tight-fitting gown of azure lace. A matching parasol partly shaded her face, but Lizzie caught a glimpse of queenly, damask features beneath a small flowered toque, and one of her companion

Pixies, forgetting all religious scruples, suddenly flung her collecting box high in the air and screamed: 'Ow Christ, look – it's Lillie Langtry!'

Never having heard of Lillie Langtry, Lizzie felt no more than a mild interest; it was certainly not enough for her to join her colleagues in their darting, dodging attempts to secure another glimpse of the languid vision as it reached Marble Arch and bowled through the great gates of the park.

'Who's Lillie Langtry?' she asked when they rejoined her, panting and perspiring.

'Don't you know?' They looked amazed. 'She's the famous actress, and people say that she and the Prince of Wales . . .'

'People say what?' The noise and the heat were making Lizzie's head ache and she made her way across the street to the drinking fountain. The iron mug on its heavy chain looked greasy and unpleasant, so she drank out of her cupped hands. 'That's better.'

'Feel like singing some more?' They had caught up with her.

'Can't say I do. It's too hot.'

'How much have you got in your box?'

'Dunno, but it's not very heavy.'

'Neither's mine.'

'Oh well, soon be dinner-time.'

'Cold mutton and mash.'

'That's all we ever seem to get, these days.'

'Ow Christ, I wish I was Lillie Langtry.'

'Don't keep on saying "Christ" like that,' admonished the senior Pixie. 'You know He doesn't like it.'

Wearily they plodded back to Gossett Street.

It was the girl who slept in the next bed who further enlightened Lizzie about Lillie Langtry. Although she was married to Mr Langtry and was only a commoner, the whole world knew that she was Teddy's fancy piece. But apart from that, the whole world also knew that she had had lots of men friends who had given her beautiful jewels, houses, racehorses and of course thousands and thousands of pounds in money. She was the toast of London, and more than one man who had seen her on the stage had gone off and shot himself while in the grip of uncontrollable desire for her.

'She baths herself every day in a solid-silver bath filled with champagne, and she once put an ice cream down poor ole Teddy's back at a party in front of everyone. Anybody else who'd have done that would have been put in the Tower for treason, but he forgave her because he was so potty about her.'

Lizzie was fascinated. She had heard of actresses, but only in the way that one might have heard of Gay Paree or a four-leafed clover. Yet even as her thoughts were busy with Lillie Langtry she raised her head from the pillow, nostrils dilating.

'I can smell a storm brewing.'

'How?' asked her companion with all the direct simplicity of a city-dweller.

'I don't know.' Useless to try to describe the animal sense of unease and oppression, of waiting for something to explode in a demonstration of primitive wrath.

But she could sense it. Just as the horses and cows and cats and dogs back on the farm had always sensed it. And her chickens had always known too; they would stop their lazy scratching and crooning and fall silent, heads tilted, eyes cocked brightly heavenwards until they heard the first thunder, felt the first heavy drops of rain fall. They they would file unobtrusively into the wooden hen-houses like people who understood the workings of fate and had no desire whatever to meddle with them.

Through the layers of London smells – soot and horse muck, old stuffy clothes and carbolic soap – came the scent of thunder and lightning, wind and rain. Perhaps it was coming down from the open fenlands of Cambridgeshire and would bring with it the mingled scents of mint and bedstraw, wild orchid and parsley, comfrey, willowherb and loosestrife. The thought of it suddenly brought Damperdown very close and she buried her head under the blanket in sudden anguish.

147

The storm broke in the early hours of the morning, the first prolonged flare of lightning flickering across the beds and over the bare floor, the crack of thunder shaking the old house and dislodging a chimney pot with a crash. One or two Pixies moaned with fear, but Lizzie lay awake, silently resigned now to the crowding memories of home: summer storms that brought a roaring wind racing eastwards across Ranson Moor, over Wimblington and across Latches Fen until it leaped the Sixteen Foot Drain and took Hinton's farm into its fierce embrace, rocking it and shaking it so that the windows rattled and tiles slid from the granary roof. 'Please, God, look after them and tell them I'm all right. . . .'

By 3.15 a.m. torrential rain had burst through the roof and flooded one of the attics. It found its way under the door and began to drip down the staircase. By the wobbling light of candles, they managed to mop up the worst, and then placed a tin bath beneath the hole.

'In the beginning God created heaven and earth!' cried Miss Paynim in a flannel dressing gown and bare feet. 'He made the sun to shine and the rain to fall, and if sometimes He seems to be overdoing it we must all remember that He's got a lot on His hands quite apart from 67 Gossett Street. Bertha dear, fetch another bucket from the cellar. . . .'

Next morning as they gathered to survey the damage, a girl called Fanny rushed in to say that a lump of ceiling had fallen on Fat Flo and knocked her out cold. There was no going out singing that day, and all they had for dinner was cold bacon between slices of bread. But they thanked God for it warmly and affectionately, and when the odd-job man arrived to patch up the roof he charged Miss Paynim far less than she had feared. She insisted that he should stay for a cup of tea.

Life returned to normal and the streets smelt fresh and clean for an hour or two. But, for Lizzie, the initial gratification that had come from being a Paynim's Pixie was fading. There was nothing dramatic about it, just a rather dull sense of plodding along the well-worn path of an unremarkable routine, while life – like the glittering

148

carriages of the rich – bowled merrily past. She tried to describe how she felt to God; then, as He didn't answer, to Kate in the next bed. And Kate reckoned that nightly sessions of singing-and-saving in the sooty gloom of St Pancras Station was probably getting her down. If she liked, she would swop duties with her, so that Lizzie could be cheered up by the twinkling lights of the Strand, although she must always bear in mind that it was a *false* twinkle and that its one purpose was to snatch the unwary and drag them down into a life of sin.

Lizzie thanked her, and set off rather glumly on the following evening with Winnie and the bandaged Fat Flo. It was the time of year when darkness never seems to fall completely, and although the West End streets were full of the heady excitement associated with night hours, the theatre lights bore a gentler, less strident invitation in the grey and violet dusk.

The London season was at its height; the great houses of Park Lane beckoned their guests from behind flowering window-boxes and gaily striped awnings, and the gleam of chandeliers only seemed to fade with the morning sun. The theatres were full, the restaurants crowded, and beautiful women and handsome men were all magnificently accoutred in diamonds and feathers, silks and tailcoats and opera hats, uniforms and medals – medals so much more colourful and splendid than the poor little Pixie badges for Cheerfulness and Tidiness and General Helpfulness.

None of this lot seemed to need any General Helpfulness. Laughing, elegant and brilliant, they drove in their open carriages from one splendid red-carpeted function to another, occasionally lifting a languid hand in acknow-ledgement of the common herd's recognition – 'Crikey, that's Lady Curzon! Aow, there she goes – the Princess of *Wiles*!' And occasionally there was the shadow of a bearded face and the flash of a diamond cuff-link as Teddy himself drove past in company with some rare and heavenly body the like of Mrs Langtry.

Yet it was not the great London mansions, not even Marlborough House itself, that seemed to epitomize the spirit of the nineties; for the majority of people able to look back on that brief golden age of beauty, wealth and raffishness it would always be the Gaiety Theatre in the Strand.

Outside which Lizzie, in company with Winnie and Fat Flo, was now spending her evenings singing cheerful hymns, rattling her collecting box and staring fixedly at the ladies of the chorus as they arrived at the stage door.

They were very different from the rowdy, raucous chorus girls at the Met in the Edgware Road. Beautiful, graceful and (outwardly, at least) refined, they adorned the Gaiety musicals with all the charming appeal of roses round the door, and it seemed as if half the male population of London was in love with them.

They danced competently and sang delightfully, but their main purpose was to bewitch and bedazzle with their silks and laces, frills and furbelows; their white shoulders that gleamed beneath large flowered hats and waists that could be encompassed by the span of two male hands, and with the occasional glimpse of a slender ankle from beneath layers of gaily swishing frou-frou. They smiled and teased and decorously flirted, and they were the brainchildren of an Irish impresario called George Edwardes, who hired them, fired them and taught them all they knew. Like a domineering father, he loved them and bullied them, made them laugh and made them cry. He took some of them to his bed, and always figured prominently at the wedding ceremony of those who married into the peerage. It seemed as if everyone knew about George Edwardes and the Gaiety Girls except for the few dim-witted clods who lived out on the Cambridgeshire fens.

As if determined to make up for lost time, Lizzie watched them arriving by hansom cab for the evening performance, and it was difficult not to compare their lot with that of Paynim's Pixies. Exquisitely gowned, they wafted across the pavement on a cloud of French perfume, to be greeted with touched forelock by the stage door-keeper. Other people standing nearby would raise a cheer, but Lizzie,

Winnie and Fat Flo were there to sing hymns and to save poor girls from the miseries of ill-use and degradation.

They kept at it, but for the first time Lizzie began to wonder whether living in a state of chronic Cheerfulness, Tidiness and General Helpfulness etc., etc., need go hand in hand with looking so dowdy, not to say downright comic in their cabbage-green dresses and flat hats that tied under the chin. She had been so proud of the uniform to start with and, sickened by these first suspicions of disloyalty, sang louder than ever:

> Ye servants of the Lord,
> Each in his office wait,
> Observant of His heavenly word,
> And watchful at His gate. . . .

A four-wheeled growler drew up at the kerb and an elderly man with a square face and small eyes got out. With lips pursed beneath a heavy moustache, he paused to stare at Lizzie.

> Let all your lamps be bright
> And trim the golden flame:
> Gird up your loins as in His sight,
> For aweful is His name. . . .

Singing defiantly, she stared back at him, and after his glance had swept over Winnie and the bandaged Fat Flo, he turned on his heel and marched through the stage door.

'That was Arthur Roberts,' whispered Winnie. 'He's the tenor and always sings the hero's part.'

If I couldn't look a better hero than that, I wouldn't bother, thought Lizzie. They sang another hymn, passing along the queue for the gallery with their collecting boxes and enduring the usual harmless taunts about their uniforms.

Because the Gaiety Theatre and its girls were beginning to get on Lizzie's nerves in a strange sort of way, she asked Miss Paynim if she could transfer back to St Pancras Station

151

again, but Miss Paynim was more concerned with two new arrivals who had both developed rashes and high temperatures.

'For heaven's sake, dear, stay where you are and stop fussing. As it is, I fear we're all in for a good old bout of spotted fever. . . .'

Spotted fever, thought Lizzie dolefully. It'll look nice with dresses the colour of boiled greens. . . .

To prevent the spread of contagion, Miss Paynim decided that they must all go round to the public bath-house in the Harrow Road and take advantage of its facilities for disinfecting both clothes and person.

'We have all come to be sterilized!' she cried joyously as they filed inside, and was the only one to remain resolutely cheerful throughout the long and humiliating procedure that included being scrubbed in carbolic and almost boiling water by grim-faced matrons built like all-in wrestlers; being searched for head and body lice; and then having to wait in a long stone corridor for over two hours dressed in workhouse calico until their own clothes were returned to them. And it was when they discovered that the process of fumigation had not only stiffened them like boards but also shrunk them to half their previous size that it finally dawned upon Lizzie that she didn't want to be a Paynim's Pixie any more.

Having come to love God as a dear and trusted friend, she couldn't see why He should treat her with such lack of consideration in return; with such meanness, and such grey lack of imagination. She felt her faith sliding from her as she struggled into the grey matted vest that had now assumed the texture of a medieval hairshirt, and then tried to wriggle into the cotton drawers that might have fitted a child of seven.

'What is the chief end of man and woman?' demanded Miss Paynim, hauling energetically at her now three-quarter-length sleeves. 'To glorify God and praise Him for ever!'

You can if you like, thought Lizzie. Me, I'm finished.

But this was to be no precipitate departure choked with

tears and racked with bitterness and grief like the last one. She was older now, and wiser. Above all, she had become a Londoner.

So she said nothing, but went through the next day's routine of sweeping, helping to wash dishes, being nice to the others and praying in the conversational Paynim manner to the God in whom she no longer believed, and at half past six set off for the Strand with Winnie and Fat Flo for the evening session.

They began in the usual manner with a brisk and professional inspection of Charing Cross Railway Station and its purlieus, their experienced eyes taking in the ticket barriers and the third-class ladies' waiting room before singing two hymns outside the Lyceum Theatre and then moving on to the Gaiety across the way. They sang as usual to the cloth-capped swells and their giggling girls (total result between three collecting boxes one shilling and fourpence ha'penny), then went round to the stage door, but they were a little later than usual and most of the ladies of the chorus had already arrived.

'But the main ones haven't,' Lizzie said. 'So you go on over to the Strand Theatre and I'll catch you up after I've nobbled Miss Ada Reeve and her mates.'

They obeyed, and when they were lost in the crowds Lizzie marched up to the Gaiety stage door, opened it and all but fell into the arms of the stage door-keeper.

He asked her what she wanted, one hand outstretched to grab her by the arm and propel her back into the street, but she said that her name was Miss Hinton and that she had an appointment with Mr Arthur Roberts, who had expressed a desire to hear her sing.

'Mr Roberts hain't arrived – '

'No matter, I can wait.'

'Sorry, miss, but my hinstructions – '

'Look – there he is!'

Evading his grasp, Lizzie sped towards the man who had appeared behind him: an elderly man with a square face and small eyes above a heavy moustache. The stage door-keeper spun round.

153

'That hain't Mr Roberts, that's Mr George Hedwardes.'

'Oh . . . who's he?'

Disappointed, Lizzie's perky self-confidence faded. Her cheeks flared bright pink as she confusedly prepared to make a bolt for it, then Mr Edwardes gave a brief nod to the door man and said: 'It's all right, Jupp. The young lady and I have already met.'

Twitching a thimble-length of ash from his cigar, he motioned Lizzie to follow him.

She did so, along corridors, up a staircase and along more corridors, and every now and then muffled bursts of music and the trill of voices would sound very near, and her heart would begin to pound with fright in case she should suddenly find herself standing in the middle of the stage in front of the audience. But Mr Edwardes led her into an office furnished with a large desk, a lot of photographs and papers, and an open tantalus containing cut-glass decanters filled with liquids in varying shades of golden brown. The room was very warm and smelt of cigars.

Seating himself behind the desk, he left her standing alone in the middle of the room. She didn't know what to do with her collecting box, so hid it behind her back while she waited for him to say something; to tick her off for trespassing or whatever.

She was disconcerted when instead of speaking he began to laugh. Her cheeks turned deep pink again and she looked down at her boots. Then she looked up, and in spite of her embarrassment found it difficult to suppress an answering giggle.

He went on laughing; great hearty gusts of it bursting from under the thicket of dark moustache, while his little eyes disappeared in a series of pudgy creases. She had never heard a man laugh so hard or so long.

In the end she managed to straighten her expression and to ask him in the pert cockney tones she had only recently acquired: 'What's up with you, then?'

He sobered immediately. His laughter ceased and the room fell uncomfortably silent.

'Dear God,' he said, 'they're all the same. Lovely until

they open their mouths.' He continued to stare at her moodily. 'Every sign of a beautiful girl with a piquant face, a high bosom, a tiny waist and exciting hips, and she hides it all beneath a hat like a pancake and some sort of garment the colour of a slimy pond. 'pon my soul, I've seen a better colour than that on an Irish midden.'

'In that case – ' She made for the door.

'Case, not *kise*. Come back here.'

Unwillingly she did so.

'Can you sing?'

'I never seem to do anything else these days.'

'Let me hear you. Properly this time.'

Rather grumpily she sang the first verse of 'I Need Thee, Precious Jesu'.

'You're sharp.'

'I know. I generally came second from top at school.'

'Can you dance?'

'Only country dancing, like the "Black Nag" and – '

'Spare me that.'

'Well, I could hardly dance it all by myself, could I?'

'Hmm.'

It had begun to dawn on her that he was someone important, and although she had every intention of saying something like I must be going now, sorry to have troubled you, she heard herself confessing in a parched and desperate little voice: 'I'd give anything to be a Gaiety Girl now I don't believe in God any more.'

'What's God got to do with it?' He sat back in his chair.

'Well, I'm in The Girls' League of Fellowship and I've been helping to save poor girls from destitution and bring them to see that God's not just some lordly ole gent sitting up on a cloud but a kind and loving friend who helps all them that helps themselves – '

'And in what way is He helping you?'

'He seems to have stopped. I mean, it was wonderful at first having somewhere to go to and call home, and Miss Paynim's a dear ole soul, but it's all singing hymns and peeling spuds and scrubbing floors and having our clothes shrunk just because two soppy girls were supposed to have

155

spotted fever. Nothing nice or beautiful ever happens, it's all work, work, work, and Miss Paynim gets fed up if you don't keep cheerful and praise His Nibs all the time.'

'You'd have to work very hard indeed if you worked for me.'

'But you wouldn't expect me to sing hymns all the time, would you?'

'No,' he said. 'Not hymns.'

He sat smoking in silence for a moment or two, then rang the bell on his desk.

'Take this young lady down to Mrs Porter and ask her to dress her in one of the *pas de quatre* costumes we used in *Cinder Ellen*. Then bring her back here and let me see.'

Lizzie returned within twenty minutes, and the change effected by the wardrobe mistress seemed even to surprise George Edwardes. She was wearing a long, tight-fitting dress of shot silk that appeared to caress rather than cover her, and a large black feathered hat from beneath which her auburn hair seemed to blaze with light; long black gloves, black stockings and narrow buckled shoes with a Louis heel completed the picture.

'Turn around.'

She did so, flushed with incredulous delight.

'Now walk up and down.' He watched intently, squinting through a haze of cigar smoke. 'Shoulders back – hold your head up.'

Pertly she tilted her chin, and swishing grandly towards his desk, kicked over the collecting box which she had left on the floor. It rattled hollowly into a corner.

'Doesn't sound as if there's much in it,' he said dryly. 'And when you come here you won't earn all that much more to start with.'

'You mean, you – '

'I mean that I'm prepared to give you a chance, but it'll mean a lot of hard work on your part.'

'Oh yes, I'm – '

'Now, tell me your name.'

'Elizabeth Hinton, but everyone calls me Lizzie.'

'They won't here,' George Edwardes said, pulling a sheet

156

of paper towards him. He picked up a gold fountain pen. 'From now on you'll be known as Liza.'

He wrote down the name Liza Hinton, then sat back and studied it almost as carefully as he had studied her. Then he said: 'Very well, Liza Hinton, go back to Mrs Porter and return to your slimy pond outfit. Then report to the stage door tomorrow morning at 9 a.m. sharp, and, here' – he bent, breathing stertorously – 'take your moneybox and tell Miss Whatsername that this is the last she's likely to get from you.'

Removing two sovereigns from a black leather purse, he dropped them in before handing it back to her. Crimson and incoherent, Lizzie thanked him and rushed from the room.

She had missed supper and some of the girls had gone to bed by the time she returned, but a light shone under Miss Paynim's door.

She knocked and went in, laid the collecting box gently on the table and said: 'I've come to give in my notice, Miss Paynim.'

Lizzie's arrival at the Gaiety coincided with a curious patch in its history.

Sensing a decline in the popularity of old-style burlesque, George Edwardes, presiding genius, had been pondering a new style of entertainment to take its place. Instinct told him that the time had come for a gentler, more lyrical approach: a story told perhaps in both words and music, and in such a way that the result would be lighter than opera, yet have greater visual appeal than a straight play. Most of all it must be a vehicle for that supreme artistic creation of his, the Gaiety Girl.

A man of boundless energy and indestructible optimism he commissioned a new author to construct the plot and a new composer-conductor to write the music, and then he engaged an almost unknown actress named Ada Reeve to play the lead. The first night was on 24 December 1894, and with its catchy songs, its sumptuous sets and costumes, and its coherent storyline, *The Shop Girl* was an instant

157

success. And with its creation, George Edwardes had invented musical comedy.

The show ran to packed houses for a record 546 performances and, still intent on the Gaiety Girl image, Edwardes devised a second musical comedy, again with 'Girl' in the title. This was *My Girl*, another brilliantly cast and opulent production, and it flopped.

After the triumph of *The Shop Girl*, its failure was doubly distressing and Edwardes was advised to play safe and return to burlesque; he refused, preferring like all good betting men to back his own judgement. So with *My Girl* playing to a fast-dwindling box office, he began to search for a replacement, and had reached the point of auditioning for the cast of *The Circus Girl* when young Lizzie walked in.

It would have been pleasant to record that upon taking one look at her youthful beauty and glowing auburn hair he offered her the leading role, thereby projecting her to instant stardom, but he did no such thing. He didn't even offer her a part in the chorus. And Lizzie, fresh from a world where theatres were considered at best morally dubious and at worst heartless exploiters of poor young girls, had no idea that a new show was in the process of creation. She thus expected even less than she received.

What she received, in fact, was a very great deal. Arriving at the stage door on the following morning as instructed, she found herself despatched with a note of introduction and a shilling for her cab fare to a house in Notting Hill Gate where a large elderly lady studied her thoughtfully, presented her with a black woollen practice dress then led her down to a cold bare dance studio. Here she proceeded to teach her the art of graceful carriage.

'Shoulders back – point your toes – watch your derrière – now float . . . *float*. . . .'

With a Bartholomew's atlas balanced on her head, Lizzie did her best to comply. Never having heard of a derrière, she ignored that part of the instructions and concentrated fiercely on shoulders and toes, only to receive a sharp slap in the appropriate region: 'That's your derrière, dear. In other words, your bum!'

During the weeks that followed she was taught to dance, to glide and sway graceful as a long-stemmed lily to the demands of an out-of-tune piano. Music had always found a ready response in her and she had no difficulty in moving in sympathy with its rhythms and moods. She was then given singing lessons by an Italian who lived above a corn merchant's shop in Soho. He too was elderly, but not as large as the dancing teacher, and he bullied her out of the bawling voice she had developed in competition with the rattle and roar of London's thoroughfares and replaced it – slowly and painstakingly – with a sweet and ladylike bel canto.

She was then sent, ostensibly to tea, with a dear old lady with faded eyes who lived in St John's Wood.

'When taking drawingroom tea, the cup and saucer should be held poised halfway between lap and bosom and the cup should never be raised more than three inches above the saucer when you sip. Sip, dear, not *drink*. The teaspoon must of course remain in the saucer at all times once it has performed the act of stirring – three quiet and unostentatious revolutions should be sufficient to melt even the most *obdurate* knob of sugar. . . .'

And while all this was going on she was being given board and lodgings off the Pentonville Road by a lady called Emmie Weston who worked in the Gaiety's wardrobe department. Emmie had skimped grey hair and a tooth missing in front and was in the habit of telling stories of theatrical life with a sibilant hiss. During Sunday lunch was her favourite time, and with the roast mutton finished and the baked jam roll to come, she would take another sip of brown ale, lean back in her chair and say: 'Ah, I could tell you some real tales if I'd a mind to. Tales as'd make your lovely hair stand upright on your head!'

'Go on then,' Lizzie would prompt.

The table stood in the window, and the sun shining through Emmie's Nottingham lace curtains made patterns on the tablecloth. Dreamily Lizzie traced them with her finger as she learned that Florence St John had had four husbands and that Connie Gilchrist – *lovely* dancer, dear –

had married a lord. She learned their names: Kate Vaughan, Sylvia Grey, Mabel Love, Kate James, Letty Lind and dozens more; some who faded too soon, others who stayed the course to become famous.

'A lot of them get carried away and fall by the wayside, stupid little things,' Emmie said. 'And between you and me, I know more than one who's given way to the demon drink. But it's a wonderful life for a girl if only she keeps her head and plays her cards right.'

'When you say "fell by the wayside", do you mean . . .?'

'Yes, dearie. There's never any scandal; Mr Edwardes would never stand for that. But I believe that quite a lot of the gentlemen concerned – the *real* gentlemen, that is – are quite generous in seeing the girl over her trouble, and when all's said and done it's generally her fault for behaving loose and egging him on.'

'Do they ever come back, after they're over their trouble?'

'Oh Lor, no. The Gov'nor wouldn't stand for that either. A very moral gentleman he is, although I'm not saying he's always been above indulging his fancy, mind, because he hasn't. He's only human, like the rest of us.'

'Yes,' agreed Lizzie, deep in thought.

Sometimes when Emmie was at the theatre and she was in the house on her own, Lizzie would sit at the table in the window and look at the collection of picture postcards kept in a shoe-box on the chiffonier, studying the pretty faces beneath the elaborate coiffures, the smiles that were half saucy and half demure, and the beautiful tight-fitting dresses with their cascades of frills and ribbons. Then she would leave her chair and go to the mirror set in the overmantel above the fireplace and compare her face with theirs. She couldn't help seeing that it compared very favourably. Large velvet brown eyes beneath well-defined eyebrows, a neat little nose, and if her mouth was a trace larger than the fashionable rosebud variety, her teeth were good and her lips full. But her best feature of all was her hair: what seemed like yards of rich gleaming copper that appeared to have taken on a life of its own since being

160

released from the confines of poor Miss Paynim's ridiculous headgear.

To be a Gaiety Girl was the one desire that consumed her now, and the world of Paynim's Pixies was as remote as poor old Damperdown Farm out on the Cambridgeshire fens.

In the meanwhile the cast had been assembled for the Gov'nor's new show that was due to open later in the year, and as the final stage in her theatrical education Lizzie was commanded to attend some of the rehearsals. From the first row of the dust-sheeted balcony she looked down upon a small world of total chaos. Dancers in practice bloomers and with their hair tied up in voluminous scarves forgot their steps and bumped into one another. Ethel Hayden dried up on the words of her song ('Oh happy little circus girl, so proud and gay – come take your place in pleasure's whirl and dance awaaay. . . .') A backdrop from the circus ring scene fell on Percy Ward and almost killed him. Upon first hearing that he was the father of twins, a member of the orchestra became deliriously drunk and had to be removed from his place in the pit. The white horse that was part of the cast refused to go on stage, and when remonstrated with, expressed its contempt in the obvious way. Quarrels broke out loudly and interminably; people gave in their notice and others were fired. The rage and the fury of it all astounded and appalled the solitary watcher up in the balcony, and when Emmie, drawn and exhausted after sixteen hours a day of cutting, pinning, fitting and sewing in the costume department, said it was a well-known fact that any show dealing with a circus was bound to fail, Lizzie succumbed to sleepless nights with the rest of them.

The only person who appeared to remain calm was George Edwardes, the Gov'nor.

Cool and impeccable in high stiff collar and elastic-sided boots, he moved among his fretful, nerve-torn flock – soothing, smoothing, coaxing and, if the tantrums were proving severe, exploding in a spectacular display of thunderous wrath which reduced everyone to instant silence. And gradually, very gradually, all the disjointed

161

bits and pieces, the wearisome little fragments that had been rehearsed and repeated again and again ad infinitum, came together in a coherent way; the story emerged, that of a schoolgirl miss who went to Paris to meet her parents and instead met a handsome young man she understood to be a circus performer whose speciality was being fired from a cannon. At a time when all heroes were compelled to be English, wealthy and well-born, the plot depended on a series of misconceptions and misunderstandings which reached their climax in the final scene when the man fired from the cannon on this occasion proved to be none other than the heroine's papa, who had sought refuge in the circus from the strident hectoring of her mama.

The dress rehearsal went tolerably well, apart from one minor disaster when one of the girls who formed the Serpentine Quartet was abruptly and violently sick in a fire bucket, and food poisoning was diagnosed after she had confessed to eating shellfish the night before.

'Sometimes I think you see the working of God's hand in the theatre more than you ever do in church,' Emmie said to Lizzie. 'Her waist was only half an inch bigger than yours and you're both the same height – hold still dearie, while I hook you up. . . .'

Quivering with nerves, Lizzie said, 'But it's only for this last rehearsal, isn't it? I mean, she'll be back for tomorrow's opening, won't she?'

'I expect so, dearie,' Emmie soothed, 'although shellfish poisoning can lay some people low for a week or more, I'm told.'

After the effortless success of *The Shop Girl* and the subsequent failure of *My Girl*, it was of paramount importance to score another hit.

Half an hour before curtain up on that first night, Lizzie was sitting on a costume basket with her head bowed and her hands dangling between her knees, torn between hope and dread that the girl whose place she had taken was still indisposed. Heralded by a whiff of cigar smoke, the

162

Gov'nor bustled up to her and asked why she wasn't in the dressing room with the others.

'You mean I'm to . . .?'

'Of course that's what I mean. I haven't spent all that time and money on you for nothing.' Then his little eyes softened, and he winked at her. 'And don't forget – no hymns, there's a good girl.'

Apart from Emmie, there was one other person who made a point of wishing her luck, and Lizzie cherished the memory of it until the end of her life. She was standing in the wings when a dainty little figure touched her lightly on the cheek and whispered: 'You look lovely, my dear. All the very best.' It was Ellaline Terriss, the star of the show.

Then the house lights dimmed, the overture began and the curtain rose on the first act, set outside the Café de la Régence on a Parisian boulevard, and the change in the atmosphere backstage was astonishing. In place of bickering, gossiping and apparent lack of concentration was a company of people bonded together by a sense of allegiance and a tough proud professionalism.

They bounded on to the stage and into the dazzling light, and it was more than remembering their cues, their lines, their songs and dances; they were giving themselves, offering all their skill, their charm and their energy to the world out there beyond the footlights. They were generous people, alight and alive with a strange and marvellous force that Lizzie had never encountered before. And the moment they came panting off stage they switched the light off in order to conserve it, and she smelt the hot sweat and saw the made-up eyes already intent and focusing on the next entrance. Beneath all the beauty and the laughing exhilaration they were as tightly disciplined as soldiers in combat.

'Remember the steps, ducky?'

'Yes. Well – I think I do. . . .'

No time left for uncertainty, no time even to be aware of the great dark audience. They swept on stage, skirts rustling, and the orchestra surged into the charming music of the Serpentine Quartet that she had heard hammered out on rehearsal pianos for so many weeks. After being a

163

passionate spectator for so long, the dress rehearsal had been the only one she needed. Now, she found herself dancing because she wanted to, not because she had been taught and would henceforth presumably be paid for doing so. She danced with the same childish happiness of the little auburn-haired girl taking part in the 'Black Nag' and Sir Roger de Coverley at Stonea Board School, and of the older girl intoxicated by first-love waltzing on skates to the sound of Sam Kitchin's concertina.

In and out . . . weaving the complicated figures with little dainty steps (*shoulders back – point your toes – now float . . . float . . .*) and every now and then sheer high spirits compelling her to sparkle a smile at the mysterious unseen audience beyond the footlights. She danced because she was young and pretty and because she wasn't a Paynim Pixie any more – what was God's opinion of this, then? Could the poor old Boy see her twitching aside the frou-frou of her skirt to display a silken ankle and a little pointed Louis-heeled shoe that rightly belonged to the girl who'd got food poisoning? What did He think of her bare shoulders and the soft teasing frills that covered those two important Things she had once been so afraid of Pa seeing when she was in the bath? God knew all about Things because He was supposed to have designed them in the first place, but she didn't believe in God any more, she only believed in being happy and beautiful and loving people.

As if aware that she loved them, the audience began to make reciprocal sounds before the quartet had ended; soft little sounds to start with, sighs and rustlings and little low murmurings that burst into a storm of applause, and then lusty male cries of Bravo! Bravo! as the four girls swept in a low curtsey, holding hands. They were compelled to dance an encore, and the cries and the clapping were then joined by the violent pounding of feet.

Sweating with the best of them, they danced off stage, and Lizzie's auto-intoxication was no more than lightly dented when the nice girl who had called her 'ducky' told her sharply to stop hogging the limelight on future occasions.

That night the curtain fell on one of George Edwardes' greatest triumphs; not only was *The Circus Girl* a critical and box office success, she was also the final proof that musical comedy with all its sparkling charm was here to stay.

There was a party afterwards, and Lizzie was hardly aware of Emmie squeezing her hands and saying 'Don't hurry home, dearie, I'll wait up for you' because at that moment the chap who had played the hero came up and said: 'Well done, Liza – you're a real trouper!'

It took a second or two to remember that she was now Liza and not Lizzie, and another one or two to remember that the hero's real name was Seymour Hicks.

He was smiling and charming and very, very handsome, and all the instincts reawoken by this new heady atmosphere urged her to fall instantly in love with him. She did so, until she remembered that he was already married to Ellaline Terriss and that their marriage, along with their unusually lovable, generous characters was one of the few things regarded as sacrosanct in the theatrical world of the nineties.

She drank champagne for the very first time, and a young man in immaculate evening dress kissed her hand, presented his card and asked if she would do him the honour of dining with him on the following evening after the show.

She went home to Emmie's in a hansom cab, the smell of grease-paint and hot lights and cigar smoke still strong in her nostrils, and she knew that something wonderful and beautiful and magnificently happy was about to happen. That life, in other words, was at last beginning.

But it proved a false start, for on the following day the girl who had been suffering from food poisoning came back, pale but determined to reclaim her rightful place in the quartet.

Having forgotten her existence, Lizzie removed the girl's costume slowly and silently, laid it over the back of her chair and then put on her own frock. She buttoned her shoes and then reached for her coat unaware that the dressing room had fallen silent. Everyone was watching the sad little drama.

'I'm sorry,' the other girl said.

'There's really no need, thank you.'

The girl held out her hand. Lizzie shook it briefly, eyes averted and jaws clenched. She put on her hat, fumbled for the gloves in her coat pocket, and after a whispered goodbye to the room in general, slipped out of the door.

The tears started in the corridor outside. It was impossible to stop them, and she hurried towards the stage door, brushing past scene-shifters, dressers, and Harry Monkhouse, who was playing Ellaline Terriss's father in the show.

'Hullo – what's up?' Concernedly he took her arm. She wrenched it away and bolted past the stage door-keeper's cubby-hole and out into the street. She cried all the way back to Emmie's house, and Emmie made her drink a cup of rum and hot milk, then warmed a brick in the oven for her to put her feet on.

'You're shivery because you're all upset.'

'I'm finished, Emmie! It's all over even before it got started.'

'Don't talk so silly.'

'It is, it *is*! If I'd really been any good he'd have kept me on instead of her.'

'That wouldn't be fair, dearie, and say what you like, the Gov'nor's always fair. After all, she got the part before you did.'

'But why did she have to get so ill and then get better again so blooming quickly?'

Emmie began to laugh, hissing through the gap in her front teeth. 'That's what life's all about, dearie. Good patches and bad patches, and if you can't take the bad along with the good you'll never make a real trouper. Best to try your hand at something else, otherwise the theatre'll break your heart.'

Lizzie sipped in tear-streaked and mutinous silence.

'And what about this young toff who's asked you out to dine?'

'He won't want me now.'

'Why ever not?'

'Because I'm not a Gaiety Girl any more. . . .' A fresh burst of tears and a mouthful of rum and milk that went down the wrong way. Coughing and choking, she allowed herself to be led up to bed, where she cried herself to sleep, well satisfied with her role of piteous martyr.

Three days later she received an irritated telegram from the Gov'nor demanding her instant reappearance at the theatre. Nervous and unwilling, she went, and discovered that an extra part had been written into the show for her benefit, and that a song had been specially composed for her by the up-and-coming Lionel Monckton.

The new character's name was Fifine, and she had two appearances; the first was in the circus ring scene, where she wore pink and silver and performed a dance with a skipping rope, and the second was in the grand finale; the artists' ball scene was continuing to draw cries of admiring wonder from the audience, and Fifine, in an emerald green gown and a large black hat that set off her brilliant hair to perfection, sang the new waltz:

> *Come, let us dance the night away*
> *And take our pleasures where we may;*
> *For youth is fleeting and youth is sweet*
> *And Cupid guides our happy feet. . . .*

The ladylike voice she had recently acquired was admirably suited to the honeyed tune and cloying words, but every now and then a stronger, slightly hoarser note would creep in, a legacy from the old hymn-bawling days, and it reached to the back of the stalls and to the top of the gallery with gratifying ease.

The show settled down for a long run, and each day taught her something new; along with the artless act of performing, of wooing an audience, she learned that Gaiety Girls were not always the models of feminine refinement that the Gov'nor strove to produce. With some, the winsome smiles and dainty deportment were no more than

167

the thinnest veneer, the *Ai don't maind if Ai dooo* drowned by a cockney deluge of damning and blasting when the customers were out of earshot. The girl who sat next to her in the dressing room, delicate as a wild rose, regularly sent out for a cup of gin; then there was the girl called Polly who boasted of being kept by three separate gentlemen in three separate Mayfair establishments all at one and the same time, and the girl who dared Lizzie to perform the skipping dance without her drawers on. (Lizzie giggled and was tempted, but refused.)

They were young, saucy and high-spirited, and the dressing room would be filled with bouquets of orchids and roses in the centre of which might be hidden a ten-pound note or a gold bracelet. The Maharajah of Cooch Behar offered Cissie Gibson a villa in the South of France, and another besotted potentate offered to buy the entire chorus for his harem. Both offers were gracefully declined.

Although she was now earning six pounds a week, Lizzie continued to live with Emmie; part of her was eager to try her wings, to get fixed up with one of the young toffs who crowded the stage door and then whirl away with him to the land of love and romance, but she hesitated. Not for want of offers – a young Guards officer had sent her a diamond brooch concealed in a basket of hothouse carnations and propositioned her most strenuously – but because of a lingering reluctance to commit herself. She had done so once, with poor old Johnnie Moon, and the pain that had resulted from it still seared her when she thought about it. She was equally wary about entering into any form of relationship as a business arrangement. Apart from Polly, a number of other girls were quite open about their profitable liaisons, but when it came to it she felt squeamish about pandering to old men in their forties for the sake of a few extra bits and bobs.

So she remained in Emmie's front bedroom, alone and relatively satisfied with what she had, and committing herself to no more than the occasional supper party at Romano's or the Savoy, where she learned how to eat oysters and asparagus and to remain smilingly at ease when

168

people stared and whispered: 'See that gorgeous creature over there? She's a Gaiety Girl. . . .'

Then she met the Honourable Fairford Polperro. He was young, tall, fair and good-looking, and he doffed his opera hat outside the stage door and said: 'Miss Liza Hinton, may I have the pleasure of escorting you?'

'Where had you got in mind?' She had already learned the art of pert repartee.

'I thought perhaps the Café Royal. There's a secluded little table they keep for me.'

'Where, at the foot of the bed?'

His laughter was loud and appreciative. 'I say, you're a quick 'un! No, as a matter of fact the table I have reserved is behind a potted palm.'

'That's more like it.' Although his laughter was infectious she permitted herself no more than a twinkling smile.

She had planned to go straight home to Emmie's for an early night, but something about him made her change her mind. So he took her arm and guided her through the gaslit crowd jostling outside the Gaiety and handed her into a private brougham. They set off towards Piccadilly.

As they sat side by side in the flickering darkness, he said: 'I greatly admire your singing and dancing, Miss Hinton.'

'Thank you.'

'And I think you're one of the jolliest girls I've ever seen.'

'Thank you again.'

He made no attempt to hold her hand; just squeezed it gently and smilingly as he alighted outside the restaurant.

The table was, as he had said, secluded. And it was laid for two, with a single white rose lying by her plate.

'Thank you, Mr er. . . .'

'Fairford will do, Liza.'

He ordered *bisque d'écrevisses*, followed by *filet de boeuf Richelieu*, and when the champagne had been poured he leaned across the table, smiled into her eyes and said: 'Now, tell me about yourself, Liza. Where do you come from, apart from heaven?'

'Cambridgeshire.'

'Ah, Cambridgeshire. I was up at Trinity with dear old Dully and the rest of the crowd. Got sent down for being a bad boy, I'm afraid.'

'I'm afraid I don't know anything about the university. I come from the fens.'

'Really?' He looked quite passionately interested, and he really was very handsome. 'Whereabouts, exactly?'

'You wouldn't know it. The Sixteen Foot Drain.'

'The . . .?' He began to laugh, corrected himself and then laughed more than ever. 'Do you actually mean down a – '

'No, silly, *on* it.' She too began to laugh. 'My pa's got a farm alongside this long stretch of water called the Sixteen Foot Drain, which was dug by some chap who was brought over from Holland or somewhere to drain the marshes ooh, simply ages ago. It's very lonely and quiet out there, but it's quite nice, really.'

'I've got an idea that Dully's family place is somewhere out there. No, Suffolk, I think.'

'There's a lot of difference,' she said primly, 'between Suffolk and Cambridgeshire.'

'I'm sure there is. You must tell me more.'

The *bisque* arrived, and Lizzie demolished hers hungrily.

'Now, how about telling me where you come from?'

'Our main place is down in Dorset.'

'Main place? How many have you got, then?'

'Don't know exactly. About four, I think. My favourite is – '

'If your family's got about four different places they must be very important. Your father a duke or something?'

'Alas no,' he said humbly. 'Only a lord.'

They began to laugh again, because of the champagne and because of his father only being a lord. He picked up the white rose that lay by her hand and gently and very deferentially tucked the stalk of it down her *décolleté*.

'Ow, it tickles.'

'Oh Liza, you glorious being – '

'Now then, Mr Son-of-a-lord. . . .'

Through the frond of the potted palm, an orchestra was

playing, and although it was winter now the restaurant was as warm as summer, the air tinted with cigar smoke and richly cooked out-of-season luxuries. Bending her head to inhale the scent of the white rose, Lizzie thought: This is what money does for you. It makes summer last all the year round.

But outside, it was winter all right. Frost sparkled on the pavement and on the motionless, heavily shrouded figures of waiting cabbies, while their horses' breath hung white as fog. A girl selling matches moved timidly out of the shadows towards them as they hurried towards the brougham, and Fairford Polperro dropped a coin in her hand without looking at her, and without taking the box of matches. She melted away, a cold wraith in broken boots and a tattered shawl.

They drove out to Emmie's house without saying much. An abundance of good food and wine and the lateness of the hour discouraged animated conversation but the silences between them were comfortable and companionable. They sat close together, ostensibly because of the cold, and he held her gloved hand lightly between both his own.

'Will you join me at a supper party tomorrow night after the show, Liza?'

She said that she would.

'I can't wait to see you again.'

'I'm afraid you'll have to, Mr Son-of-a-lord.'

They arrived at the house, and the moon, cold and remote, touched the closed and tightly curtained windows with silver.

'May I kiss you goodnight, Liza?'

It was nice of him to ask. She said that he could.

He folded his arms round her tightly, and beneath the front of her coat she could feel the soft petals of the white rose pressing against her skin.

'No more . . . that's enough.'

'Oh, Liza, Liza – you *delicious* girl. . . .'

She crept hurriedly up to her room, undressed and climbed into bed. Lying down in the darkness, while the room seemed to be revolving giddily, she thought: I think I'm in love. I also think I may be a bit tiddly. . . .

Resolutely she closed her eyes, and sleep came almost instantly.

★

Come, let us dance the night away
And take our pleasures where we may. . . .

Her voice rose, lilting and soaring up to the box where he had said he would be sitting with his friends. The waltz, her own special waltz, seemed to reach out and touch everyone in the house with its magic, and behind her the Gaiety chorus held out their full frou-frou skirts and swayed enticingly to the rhythm. The theatre was packed, and it was one of those evenings when everyone seemed to be giving a little extra something to their performance. Edmund Payne and Arthur Hope had drawn continuous roars of laughter in the wrestling scene, and Harry Monkhouse had contrived an extra depth to the henpecked husband Sir Titus Wemyss, making him memorable as something more than a mere figure of fun. Even the superlative Ellaline Terriss and Seymour Hicks seemed charged with a greater luminosity, and played the heroine and hero with a special tenderness, knowing that she was soon to make a temporary retirement from the stage in order to become a mama.

The curtain swept down for the last time and the assembled company trooped off stage, but the clapping and cheering continued after the house lights had gone up and the exit doors were opened. It was as if some composite and monumental love affair existed between the Gaiety Theatre and its devotees, and the Gov'nor removed himself from his inconspicuous seat in the balcony and went across to his office, well pleased. Supper parties and fashionable routs were not for him, but like the rest of the cast he felt in need of a little pleasurable relaxation after such an evening. Sending Jupp the stage door-keeper out for some sandwiches he invited three old friends in for a card party which broke up at five a.m.

When Lizzie left the stage door, Fairford Polperro took her arm and propelled her towards the brougham. They were kissing even before the door was closed, and when they arrived at the Savoy Lizzie gently slapped his arm for making her look disarrayed.

'I haven't made you look disarrayed, my darling – I'm reserving that for another occasion. . . .'

The supper party was held in a private room. They entered, Lizzie radiant in green chiffon with her arm through that of her escort, and three paces inside the door a tall young man with dark hair took Fairford Polperro's other arm and said in a low, urgent voice: 'Martha's here.'

'She *can't* be.' Fairford's voice was equally low and urgent, and listening confusedly, Lizzie had a sudden premonition that something extremely unpleasant was about to happen.

But London's society was adept at side-stepping unpleasantness, and she found her arm smoothly removed from that of Fairford and transferred with equal smoothness to that of the young man with the dark hair. At the same moment, an extremely beautiful young woman with china blue eyes set in a heart-shaped face came up to them, kissed Fairford lightly on his cheek and said, 'Dearest, I had to come up to town, I was missing you so!' She had an accent that Lizzie was unable to place.

'Miss Hinton,' said Fairford with a gallantry that flabbergasted her, 'may I present my fiancée, Miss Martha Bogbice from the United States.'

With pale faces and set smiles, the two young women shook hands.

'Miss Hinton is a close friend of my dear old chum Dully,' went on Fairford, indicating Lizzie's new escort, and Lizzie, recovering a little, stared hard at her adversary and said: 'Bogbice. What a funny name.'

'After the violet,' said Miss Bogbice, smiling sweetly. 'Which is the state flower of New Jersey.'

'It was named after her, of course,' added Fairford with fervour. 'A dear little purple thing. . . .'

'I can think of a flower that would suit your lady friend

much better than a violet – ' Lizzie began to say, then found herself being propelled gently but very firmly out of earshot. A glass of champagne was removed from a nearby salver and presented to her.

'Drink this.'

'Why?'

'Because I say so.'

'That's no reason – '

'Under the circumstances, it's the best one I can think of.'

Her indignation died. She seemed to dwindle and fade. After a small obedient sip she handed the glass back.

'I don't understand the sort of games you play. Anyone else would think they're mean and despicable.'

'I'm truly sorry,' he said, and looked her straight in the eyes as he said it. He had quite a nice face, but it wasn't as nice as Fairford's. And what was his name supposed to be – Dully? Well, it was even sillier than Bogbice.

'Don't mention it,' she said. 'Please call me a cab, I'm going home now.'

'Oh no, do please stay. I would be delighted to – '

'I said call me a cab.'

'Very well. You're a cab.'

He said it very gravely and deferentially, and in spite of being torn between anger and misery she found it difficult to suppress a giggle. Nevertheless, she had no intention of giving way.

'You only want me to stay so that your friend and Miss whatsername won't be embarrassed. If she sees me leaving she'll know for certain there's something funny going on.'

'Please listen,' he said, and replaced the glass of champagne in her hand. 'I'm asking you to stay because I want you to. Because I like you. And most of all perhaps, because I respect you.'

'But I'm not going to be treated like a parcel – just handed over from one man to another.'

'I admit that it may have begun like that. My first instinct was to save a close friend from embarrassment, but you behaved so graciously, with such tremendous courtesy – '

174

'Do you really think I did?' Taken off-guard, she took a sizeable swig of champagne. And then another. Then handed him the empty glass and said: 'Well, I didn't mean to.'

Smilingly he took her arm. 'Come along, let's go in to supper.'

'No.' Hastily she drew back. 'What if I have to sit next to *her*?'

'You won't. Didn't you know that separate tables are *à la mode* this season?'

The whole room seemed to twinkle in the light from the chandeliers, and a string trio was playing unobtrusively. Each table was set for four people and garlanded with mimosa entwined with smilax. Her new escort guided her to one where an elderly gentleman was sitting on his own.

'Good evening, Sir. May we join you?'

'Whatsay? Ah, yes – do, m'boy.'

'And may I introduce Miss Liza Hinton? Miss Hinton, this is Brigadier Mainstay.'

The old boy half-rose, half-bowed, and then subsided.

He must be the oldest man in the room, Lizzie thought disconsolately.

'How d'you do,' she said. Then, mindful of her reputation for extreme courtesy, added: 'Awful weather we're having, aren't we? Still, spring's not all that far off.'

He stared back at her, red-faced and glassy-eyed, and her escort bent a little closer to her and said: 'Save your breath. The old buffer's deaf as a beetle.'

'Well, I will say one thing, your class of people certainly knows how to manoeuvre things. And how did you know my name?'

'I manoeuvred my way into Fairford's box this evening.'

'Oh. Did you enjoy it?'

'Every single minute of it. But most of all when you were on.'

She might have been tempted to parry the compliment coquettishly but something about his demeanour made her respond seriously: 'Yes, there was something special about this evening. We all felt it, and didn't really understand what it was.'

'Perhaps it was the gods preparing the world for our first meeting.'

'Huh – God,' she said. 'I used to believe in Him at one time.'

They were eating foie gras now, and drinking more champagne. The Brigadier patted his lips with his napkin then suddenly bawled: 'Awful weather we're havin', eh? Still, spring's not all that far orf.'

With unnecessary fervour they agreed. Lizzie suppressed a rising desire to giggle and pressed her companion's foot under the table. He pressed back.

'By the way,' she said, 'what's your real name?'

'Henry Dullingham-Reve. But my friends call me Dully.'

'Like your friend over there.' She indicated Fairford and his fiancée sitting a few tables away. 'Is he really engaged to her?'

'Yes, I fear so. By the way, what was the name of the alternative flower you had in mind?'

'Cow itch. It grows by stagnant water.'

'I see.' But instead of laughing (as Fairford would have laughed), he looked at her very attentively and said: 'I take it you're a country girl.'

'Yes,' she said, and sighed when she remembered last night. 'I used to live down a drain.'

'The only drains I know are the Cambridgeshire drains. But one lives by the side of them, surely, not down them.'

It wasn't fair to expect him to laugh because he didn't know the joke. In any case it didn't matter, because suddenly it was very nice to have someone to talk to about the lodes and rivers, the levels and drains and cuts. He didn't know the Sixteen Foot, although he had once been to Wisbech and of course knew Cambridge well.

'Martha Cow itch,' he said thoughtfully. 'Ye-es. . . .'

'I still think that what he did was awful, considering that your class is free to come and go and do everything as it pleases.'

'It certainly isn't. Fairford, for instance, is under heavy obligation to marry an heiress.'

'Marry money?'

'To put it bluntly. He has the breeding and the broad acres to offer. She has the money.'

'I call that downright shameful – '

'I seem to remember a Gaiety Girl marrying into the peerage not long ago. It was in all the newspapers.'

She wanted to say yes, but that's different. Instead, she sat looking at his hand resting on the table not far from her own. It was well-shaped, well-manicured, and there was a gold signet ring on the little finger.

'Are you a peer?'

'Afraid not. Most I can claim is to be the nephew of one.'

'In that case, you'd be free to marry me if you felt like it, wouldn't you?'

He raised his head to smile at her, and she noticed for the first time that his dark blue eyes had an attractive upward slant at the outer corners.

'Oh, yes,' he said. 'If I felt like it.'

Although the supper party was at separate tables, guests strolled from one to the other during the lengthy intervals between courses. They were all animated, richly attired and wonderfully self-confident, and between the *petits soufflés à l'ananas* and the *bombe glacée* Fairford leaned over between their shoulders and whispered: 'Thank you again, Dully. You saved my life.'

'You also did me a very good turn,' Lizzie exclaimed, stung. 'I like your friend very much better than you, so there.'

She pushed back her chair, and saw the blonde American girl standing motionless behind Fairford. She held out her hand to her, and said with a radiant smile: 'I'm *so* happy to hear of your engagement to dear old Fairford and I *do* hope you'll be as happy as I know I'm going to be with darling Dully. *Such* exciting times, aren't they?'

'Well, I did think you were different, but now I see you're not. Silly as the rest of them. So mark my words, if you don't pull your socks up and learn to say no, you'll end up same as most of them have done – a Jermyn Street whore!'

Harsh words, and whistled through the gap in Emmie's front teeth they sounded bitter as the east wind outside.

'No, I won't. You don't understand how it really was.'

'So how was it? Promised you a carriage and pair if you'd let him take your drawers off?'

Emmie seemed extraordinarily angry, and her anger had the effect of making Lizzie's own temper rise. 'No, I took them off myself!'

'Then you're a fast thing, Lizzie Hinton, and if I was you I'd be ashamed!'

'Well, you're not me, so you can hold your tongue. You're my landlady; I pay you good money for second-rate lodgings, and that doesn't give you any right – '

'Don't start talking to me about rights, my girl, or I'll ask you to pack your things and go.'

'Then leave me alone and mind your own business!'

Lizzie stormed out and went up to her bedroom, slamming the door behind her. She flung herself on the bed and lay back, ankles crossed and arms linked behind her head.

Last night she had gone back to Dully's rooms in Charles Street, where she had lost her maidenhead to a man she didn't love. She had only done it to spite Fairford Polperro. Which, she could now see, was very stupid. Emmie would be even more scandalized if she realized just how stupid she had been.

And she hadn't enjoyed it all that much, either. She had thought she was going to – all the kissing and fondling and the strangeness of being so close to another human being had excited her to the point of feeling hot and desperate and not able to breathe properly. But the final part had been so rapid – no sooner begun than apparently finished – that she was left feeling disconcerted and embarrassed and not knowing what to say.

Neither, apparently, did he. And Lizzie lay turned away from him on the rumpled shadowy bed and wished it had been Fairford; with naughty old Fairford it would have been quite different.

He made love to her again the next morning, and this

178

time she refused to let herself become hot and bothered; instead, she concentrated on trying to look dignified and ladylike and left all the panting to him.

The most enjoyable part of the entire affair was breakfast. Served by a stately gentleman's gentleman with eyelids discreetly lowered, he set out porridge topped with cream and melted butter, followed by smoked haddock kedgeree that contained shrimps and hardboiled eggs, and then toast and marmalade, and coffee in a silver pot – all on a folding table drawn up by the fire. Lizzie, with her hair loose and wearing Dully's dressing gown, smiled graciously and said good morning, because it was useless to pretend that she wasn't there. Or that what had taken place (twice) hadn't.

I am a woman of the world, her smile was meant to imply; beautiful, poised, and highly experienced in the ways of society. And I can well afford to appear charming and unflustered because I have behind me a wealth of experience, and am well versed in the art – among all the other multitudinous arts at my disposal – of dealing with even the slightest hint of sly insolence from a common or garden servant such as yourself.

'Does madam prefer salted or fresh butter on her porridge?'

'Oh – I don't really mind. Whichever comes handy. . . .'

She left shortly before midday. She would have stayed longer had she been pressed to do so, but although kind and courteous, Dully offered little in the way of conversation. She couldn't think of much to say either.

She wandered round the room, glancing at the shelves of books and studying the pictures. There were some watercolours and quite a lot of photographs. Rows of schoolboys sitting with crossed legs and folded arms and silly little hats with tassels; groups of people standing in gardens, sitting in gardens, out riding horses, and they all stared back at her with enigmatic calm.

'Who's that man there?' Not that she really wanted to know; it was just for something to say.

'That was my father.'

'Was? Is he dead, then?'

'Yes.'

She was about to say what a pity, then drew a sharp breath. 'Oh look, there's the Queen! Is she a relation of yours?'

'No. A friend of my grandmother's.'

She wouldn't have minded asking more about that, but his lack of response discouraged her. She remembered then that it was unladylike to be nosey.

So she sat down by the bright fire burning in the brightly polished grate and asked if he fancied a game of ha'penny nap.

'What's that?'

'A card game. The girls play it in the dressing room sometimes.'

'Maxton,' he called, 'have we a pack of cards?'

Maxton, who had been making subdued chinking sounds somewhere out of sight, stepped from behind a Japanese screen. He had removed his black jacket and was wearing a pair of elasticated cotton sleeves drawn over his white shirt cuffs.

'I fear not, Sir. But I will send the porter's boy to purchase some.'

'No, don't bother. Thank you, Maxton.'

'Thank you, Sir.'

Maxton disappeared, but his presence remained hovering in the air like some kind of vengeful ghost.

'Was he here all last night?' Lizzie mouthed.

'No, Maxton goes off at eight and returns in the morning.'

'Oh well, that's a good thing.'

For some reason he reached forward then and took her hand. He kissed it, smiling up at her with those dark blue eyes that slanted at the corners. He had a long straight aristocratic nose, and a nice mouth.

'You really are a splendid girl, Liza.'

'Thank you kindly. And you're not so bad yourself.'

If Maxton hadn't been there they might have made love again then, and it might have been better. She felt the tingle of wanting to, and was on the point of whispering *Can't you send him out for a walk?* but Maxton forestalled her. He

180

reappeared from behind the screen and stood with his toes turned out and his hands clasped together.

'Will the young lady be staying to luncheon, Sir?'

'No, I won't thank you, if it's all the same to you. I've an appointment with the Prince of Wales in half an hour.'

'I see, Miss.' He looked at her for the first time, and his eyelids seemed to flutter with distaste.

So she left, and went back to the Pentonville Road, where Emmie as good as called her a whore.

He sent a bouquet to the stage door that evening. There was no expensive present hidden among the freesias and early tulips; no reward for services rendered – for which she was secretly gratified – just a card saying *Yours always, Dully*.

Meagre enough, measured by the average flowery standard of twaddle, but it filled her with surprising pleasure. After all, if someone really meant that they were yours, always, there wasn't much left to say, was there?

But he was not at the stage door after the show. He wasn't there the next night, or the night after that, and on the fourth night who should move forward out of the throng and gallantly take her arm but Fairford.

'Beloved Liza, I've booked a table at Rules – '

'Well, you can share it with your fiancée.'

'My what?' Even in the subdued gaslight he looked staggeringly innocent. 'Oh – you mean Martha. But my dear old darling, Martha's returned from whence she came.'

'Where's that?' Not that she gave a damn.

'Down in Dorset, with my people.'

'But she *is* your fiancée?'

'Well. . . .' Fairford looked momentarily wretched. 'Only sort of on and off.'

'That's quite enough for me.'

'Look, Liza, do be a sport.'

'No fear, I've got my reputation to think of.'

'You can trust it with me.'

'Like I'd trust it with ole Nick.'

'Just this once, Liza. Just a quiet little supper *à deux*. . . .'

They were walking further and further from the jostling crowd. His private brougham was waiting round the corner in Wellington Street, and with his hand under her arm she mounted the step and climbed inside.

They drove to Rules. They ate supper, and again she found it difficult not to warm to his good looks and bubbling humour, but he was a cad and a bounder and she began to feel sorry for his fiancée.

'I'm staying at a little hotel in Dover Street. Would you care to come back with me and partake of some additional refreshment?'

She wanted to. No doubt about it. 'No, thank you. I've had all I want.'

'I'd like to show you my room.'

'I bet you would.'

'Because there are some particularly nice etchings – '

'I know. On the wall above the bed.'

'Oh, Liza, how *could* you?'

'Very easily. I'm getting to know you and your sort.'

So he drove back to Emmie's house with her, and although she longed for him to kiss her goodnight like the last time, when he attempted to do so she turned her head away.

'Goodnight then, dearest Liza.'

'Goodnight.' She walked towards the house, then paused. 'By the way, what happened to your friend Dully? Gone away, has he?'

He looked at her in surprise. 'Yes, didn't he tell you? He's in Venice.'

'Oh? What's he gone there for?' She tried to sound light and casual.

'Search me. Felt the need of a sudden change, I dare say.'

She nodded, without saying any more, and from the shadow of Emmie's front porch watched the brougham drive off into the shadows.

They are all the same, she thought. Come up and see my etchings, then next morning the bed's empty and he's skipped off to Venice for a bit of a change.

For the first time she began to feel a certain sympathy for

those girls who made a virtue of rapacity – *Do the bleeder down, dearie, before he leaves you high and dry*. There was a small clique of them, and sometimes she used to listen to them comparing acquisitions as they made up before the show; smoothing the wet-white over arms, neck and bosom with a sponge; melting the eyeblack on the end of a matchstick in a candleflame and then applying it – blinking and grimacing – to each separate eyelash. Teazling and back-combing their hair and then frizzing the little forehead curls with curling irons. Seen close to, they looked ugly, coarse and stupid as they compared diamonds and sables and love nests in St John's Wood, but as soon as they were on stage the old magic was back; the lights and the lilting music, the bewitching costumes and the roguish charm of their smiles and glances up at the boxes where the toffs were. They were all George Edwardes' Gaiety Girls, and the cold acquisitive ones blended in harmony with the simpler sort like Lizzie Hinton, who sang and danced and smiled because it came naturally to her.

The show had settled down for a long run, yet so far as Lizzie herself was concerned she had begun to feel strangely lethargic and out of sorts. The winter had been long and cold, and Emmie provided her with a bottle of Dr Wilkins' Wonder Tonic, which made her sick. She went on being sick, and the girl who was understudying Lucille nudged her in the ribs and said, 'Looks to me as if you're in the family way, ducky. Know who to go to, do you?'

She didn't, but an instinctive pride made her say, 'You're quite wrong, but thanks all the same . . .' while she endeavoured to come to terms with this new doleful situation.

As a farmer's daughter she was naturally familiar with the facts of conception and birth among animals, but that was all. Human beings were another matter, although admittedly the technicalities were of small importance compared to the social problems involved in bearing a bastard.

She would have to leave the Gaiety, and there would be no sympathy, either in theory or practice, from the

183

Gov'nor. Girls were warned of that before he engaged them.

Emmie, kind as she was, had also made her views on the subject of immorality very clear, and there was no one else to help her. Going back to Damperdown Farm was somehow as impossible as throwing herself on the mercy of Miss Paynim (*God and I have had a jolly old chinwag dear, and He suggests the Foundlings Hospital*). And now that the baby's father had prudently skipped off to Venice, she was well and truly on her own.

For a while she carried on, confiding in no one and hoping that somehow a solution would present itself. Perhaps she would miscarry – perhaps a tidal wave would surge up the Thames and engulf London and herself with it – and in the meanwhile she had to lace her corsets ever tighter in order to fasten the hooks and eyes on her costume, and then when she got back to the Pentonville Road exhausted and drained, remember not to stand sideways-on to Emmie, who being a dressmaker had sharp eyes for people who bulged where they had no business to.

London's flower girls were proffering the first bunches of daffodils, brought by express train from the West country, and although the wind still had a nip, the sunshine brought the promise of warmth. But it didn't do her any good, and one evening before the show she swallowed her pride and asked Lucille's understudy if she knew an address she could go to.

'Cost you two guineas, ducky, but she's very reliable.'

'Thank you.' She pocketed the address without looking at it. 'You're very kind.'

'You look a bit peaky. Want me to come with you?'

'No, thanks. I'm fine.'

And she felt fine when she woke up that morning because at last she had screwed up the courage to do what other girls did. By evening it would be all over, and from then on there would be no bedding, no hanky-panky, without a wedding ring.

Telling Emmie that she was going to see one of the girls whose mother had died, she set off early after breakfast, wearing a black velvet cloak over a dark blue skirt and jacket. The address she had been given was that of a house at the back of Dalston Junction, and her courage began to falter when she looked up at the dirty windows and torn curtains, the dilapidated front door and broken railings, around which a group of children was clustered, mean-eyed and bare-footed. Dismissing the hansom, she picked her way between them, and it was obvious from their expressions that they knew what she had come for. Even the smallest had an air of hideous knowing.

A middle-aged woman with the swollen neck and protruding eyes of the goitrous let her in. The house was poorly furnished and smelt of mice and rancid fat, and Lizzie's nausea, never far away, threatened to return. With her hands gripped tightly beneath her cloak she followed the woman upstairs into a bedroom.

The woman told Lizzie to loosen her corsets and remove her drawers, and then to lie down on the bed. She then asked, quite politely, for the money, and Lizzie took the coins out of her purse with shaking fingers.

'Mother'll be up shortly,' the woman promised. 'Just as soon as you're ready.'

She left the room, and trying not to look at the rust-coloured stains on the blanket that covered the bed, Lizzie removed her cloak. Raising her skirts she untied the tapes of her drawers and took them off, careful not to let them touch the dirty floor. She loosened her corsets and then very gingerly lay down on the bed.

From over at the junction came the whistle of a train, the ting-tang-tang-tang of shunting trucks, and she tried to draw comfort from the woman's assurance that Mother would be appearing shortly; the very word 'Mother' was a comfort, suggesting someone cosy and kind, practical and very wise in the ways of women and their misfortunes.

The reality could not have been in greater contrast, for the woman who appeared round the door was old as a witch and dreadful as a death's head. She stood looking at Lizzie through small sunken eyes in which there was no pity; and there was no pity in the hard, grimy old hand that prodded her flinching belly.

185

'How far gone?'

'It happened about the middle of February.'

'Know who the father is?'

Her immediate reaction was to say mind your own business, but Lizzie contented herself with a curt nod. In her present situation it seemed wise to remain meek.

The old woman crept across the room and began to ferret in a cupboard by the window. Lizzie closed her eyes and tried to regulate the uneven thumping of her heart. She heard a match strike. (Soon be over. Soon be over now. . . .)

'Will it hurt much?'

'Hurts some more than others. You can rest here for ten minutes after I've done it and I'll give you a drink of something, but after that you'll have to be off the premises. I don't want any trouble.'

The ting-tang-tang-tang over on the railway sidings; the foetid smell of the room and then the creak and sag of the bed as the old woman sat down on the edge of it.

'Pull your skirt up – higher. Now open your legs – come on. Gawd, I bet you opened them wider than this for '*im*.'

A bony hand thrust under her buttocks, tilting her pelvis upwards. The old woman's breath on her bare belly, and then the warmth and the smell of melting wax. Lizzie's eyes flew open and saw the steel knitting needle being heated in the candleflame.

She screamed, and kicked out, and the candle leaped out of the old woman's hand, its flame extinguished. The knitting needle clattered on the bare floor. Mad with horror, she half rolled and half fell off the bed, barely conscious that the old woman was gripping her by the arm and swearing at her.

'Let me go – let *go* of me!'

'Git back on the bleedin' bed, you silly cow, you – '

'Get *off*!'

They struggled briefly, clumsily, and the old woman wrenched a hand free and dealt Lizzie a stinging blow on the cheek. Then she stood back, adjusted a hairpin in her greasy bun and left the room without another word.

186

Panting and sobbing, Lizzie plunged back into her drawers, and with her corsets still untied flung her cloak round her shoulders and rushed headlong from the house. The children were still grouped by the railings and they burst into derisive chanting as she fled past. They knew, they all knew about what went on, and they stared after her as if hoping to see a trail of blood between her flying feet.

There were no cabs in that area but it didn't matter. The macabre and horrifying scene in the bedroom had had the effect of filling her with a wild nervous energy, and only after she had turned into the Kingsland Road and begun to walk south towards Shoreditch was she able to breathe deeply and to look about her at the ordinary everyday things: the carts and drays crackling over the cobbles, the dingy houses and shops, the street singers and blind beggars hobbling in the murky gutters. The sky above the patched and tumbling roofs was a tender springtime blue but the day's chimney-smoke was already bleaching it to a dull grey-white. She looked at it all, but it registered no more than the lens of a camera that has no film.

She paused outside the old Standard Theatre on the corner of Great Eastern Street, but the photographs outside failed to rouse her interest. She crossed into Curtain Street, and at the top of it came to the high plane trees of Finsbury Square. She sat down on a seat and a pigeon, iridescent in new spring plumage, tapped its beak on the toe of her shoe. She had nothing to give it. She continued to sit there like someone in a dream; unaware of time, or hunger or thirst. London rolled past her in all its grandeur and its grime, and she had nothing to give to it, either. It had already taken all she had.

All except the baby. And it was the thought of the baby that finally stirred her into action.

She arrived at Liverpool Street Station with twenty minutes to spare, which gave her time for a cup of tea from a station urn, and to send two telegrams; one to Emmie and one to the Gov'nor, and they both said the same thing: *Please forgive and forget me, Liza.*

Then she bought a single third-class ticket and sat in a

corner seat, watching without joy or sorrow the blackened slums of Bethnal Green sliding past. She was going home, not only for the sake of the baby but for another, darker reason.

The spectre of Bessie Hinton, her that had been hanged, had reawoken and was beckoning to her.

Walter saw her first, a woman in a dark cloak with her hair blowing free, walking along the level from the direction of Stonea. Silhouetted against the wide expanse of sky, there was something both strange and familiar about her. He remained motionless, leaning on his spade while he watched her graceful swaying walk. She drew closer, and he saw that she had auburn hair.

'Lizzie?'

'Yes, Pa, it's me.' She paused a little way off, as if unsure of her welcome. He dropped the spade and hurried towards her.

'Gor, Lizzie gel, where you bin, eh? What you bin up to?'

She ran to him then, and he put his strong fatherly arms round her and held her close. They didn't speak – didn't need to; just stood there motionless, the only human creatures in a vast and empty landscape.

'Where you bin, you bad gel? Your ma an' me's bin in a rare ole state all this time . . . got you dead an' buried an' not even knowing where.'

'I'm sorry, Pa.'

'You don't have to be. Reckon it was all on account of that poor ole Johnnie Moon, eh? Oh, it was a bleak time that, an' you so young an' giddy. . . .'

With his arm round her shoulders, he turned her gently in the direction of the farm and began to lead her home.

Edwina was in the kitchen, stirring a pan of soup on the range.

'Guess who's come to see us, Mother.'

She spun round, and her hand flew to her mouth.

'It's me, Ma. Come to say I'm sorry.'

Edwina tried to speak, uttered a kind of croak, then burst into a flood of tears. Lizzie cried as well then, and brushing

188

his eyes with his hand, Walter hurried to the corner cupboard for the bottle of brandy kept for medicinal purposes. Edwina clung to Lizzie as if she would never let go; she seized rough handfuls of her – hair, arms, face, hands, any part anywhere to prove to herself again and again that her child had come back.

Then with staggering speed the feverish kisses and cries of joy switched to rage: 'Well, what've you got to say for yourself, hey? Where you been while we've walked the floor night after night?'

'Oh now, Ma – wait.'

'I won't wait. I waited well over a year and I reckon that's long enough.'

'Well, I'm back now, aren't I?'

'And I hope you didn't come back just because of me! Didn't drag yourself away from some fine place where – '

'Oh, shut up, Ma dearie, and listen.'

'Don't you start "Ma-dearying" me!'

Then they fell into one another's arms again, their tears flowed and Walter said, 'Look, I've poured three tots of the best French physic – what say we all settle down nice and gentle and drink it, eh?'

They did so, and Lizzie's eyes misted over again when a striped cat with large ears and round eyes stepped towards the hearth and they told her that it was, or rather had been, one of poor Johnnie Moon's litter.

'And the others? The mother?'

'They're all about, 'cept for the one we gave to Reuben.'

'How *is* ole Reuben?'

'Oh, cunnin' as ever. Had a bad nose bleed last Thursday. . . .'

Somehow they managed to steer the conversation into calmer waters, and in between sips of brandy Lizzie looked round the kitchen and saw that nothing had changed. Except that it all looked smaller. But the old homely country smells were still the same: paraffin and spices; beeswax and turpentine; and thick vegetable soup on the simmer. A row of Walter's farm boots stood against the wall, and on the table among the preparations for supper was a small osier basket containing a chick with a damaged leg.

'Do you ever hear anything about Aunt Netta?'

'We went over to see her last Christmas before the roads got bad. She keeps quite nicely considering, but she's still wandering in her senses. She doesn't even seem to know who Keziah is.'

The time was approaching when she would have to tell them about herself. They were looking at her now, hungry to hear tell of where she had been, yet even Ma not quite liking to ask outright. Pushing back her chair, Lizzie stood up with her hands at her sides and said: 'Before we go any further, I'd better tell you straight out. I'm in the family way.'

They digested the information in silence, Walter's features obscured by a cloud of Nosegay shag.

'I tried to get rid of it, but when it came to it I couldn't. And as it meant I couldn't go on working and doing what I enjoyed doing, I thought it best to come home.'

She had put it very badly, very bluntly, but perhaps under the circumstances that was the best way. She stood listening to the tick of the clock.

'What were you working at? In service, were you?'

'I was on the stage in London. I dare say you've heard of the Gaiety Girls, haven't you?' Even now it was impossible to keep the little quiver of pride out of her voice.

'On the stage? In London? You mean you danced about and showed your legs?'

'Oh no, they only do that in burlesque – and then they wear tights, of course.'

'But people must have been looking at you.'

'That's what you go on the stage for, Ma.'

'Well, I never,' Walter said heavily. 'Stone me if I never.'

They seemed far more upset about her being on the stage than about being pregnant, and torn between despair and a hopeless desire to laugh, Lizzie said: 'So I thought I'd come home and see if I could give a hand around the farm until such time as I – well, I'm – '

'And what are you going to do with it when you get it?'

190

'Well, I don't exactly know.' The desire to laugh increased, although she was close to tears. 'I mean there's not a lot you *can* do with a baby, is there, except feed it and wash it.'

Her parents sat in silence, then Edwina heaved a sigh. 'Ah well, you're not the first and I don't reckon you'll be the last. No chance of marrying the chap?'

'No.'

'Has he asked you?'

'No. But I wouldn't even if he did.'

They didn't probe, for which Lizzie was grateful. The spring evening faded quickly; they closed the door and lit the lamp, and while Walter hacked hunks of home-made bread Edwina poured the soup.

'That's a nice jacket and skirt you're wearing,' she said to Lizzie as they sat down. 'Mind you don't spill on it.'

'It's getting a bit tight.'

'I dare say. But that's all the fashion now, isn't it – waists that nearly cut you in half.'

'Did you leave your box at the station?' Walter asked, humming between mouthfuls of soup.

'I didn't bring anything with me, just came as I am. I'll tell you more about it later.'

They nodded, and she thought, how kind they are; good manners with them just comes natural, unlike some people. . . .

In the meanwhile she told them a bit about the theatre, about Mr Edwardes and what a stickler he was, and about Emmie who worked so hard and had such a lot of responsibility. They listened, wide-eyed and receptive, but they had never heard of the Gaiety or *The Circus Girl*; they had never heard of Seymour Hicks or Ellaline Terriss even. The Cambridgeshire fens began to seem frighteningly remote.

She went to bed in her old room that night, touched that the bed was still made up in readiness for her return and that her childhood treasures remained as she had left them. By candlelight she re-read the titles of the books on top of the cupboard: *Improving Tales for Little Folk*, *The Parable*

191

of Our Lord Jesus, *Butterflies of the British Isles* and *The Girls'
Adventure Book*. Even her treasure box was still in its hiding-
place, its contents intact, and she took out the kingfisher's
feather, the shells and the onyx button, together with the
shilling piece that the man with the sharp twitching nose
had given her. The man who had told them about Bessie
Hinton, and about her being hanged.

She sat for a long time with the shilling piece in her hand,
thinking that Bessie Hinton had called to her from beyond
the grave because with a ghost's supernatural powers she
had divined that she and Lizzie were the same kind of
creature: headstrong, immoral and prone to disaster. It
almost felt as if Bessie was in the room, trying to warn her,
trying to help her.

Bessie had been pregnant and had kept the hangman
waiting until her child was born; she had gone through the
awful unknown of childbirth, only to be led away a few
hours later and hoisted up on the gallows while her baby lay
crying in the prison straw, lonely and cold and hungry. She
could picture how it must have been.

She would never forget kneeling outside Aunt Netta's
parlour door and listening through the keyhole to the man's
voice telling them how it had been with Bessie. And the
shock and the horror and Aunt Netta fainting dead away
because of the wickedness of their ancestor. . . . Am I like
her? Are there really ghosts, and was she really calling to
me? I suppose I'm what you might call wanton, like her, but
I don't know that I'd ever want to kill anybody. Or maybe I
would, if I believed in anything hard enough. . . .

'You all right, Lizzie?' The soft whisper at the door made
her jump violently. Instinctively she threw the shilling
piece back in the treasure box and shoved it hastily under
the bed.

'Yes, Ma. Fine.'

Edwina came in, nightgowned and carrying her bedroom
candle. Its soft light dealt kindly with the encroaching signs
of age and she looked beautiful in the way Lizzie
remembered from childhood.

'I'm glad you're back.'

'You're not really angry?'

'No, dear. Well, I have to own feeling a bit disappointed – I reckon all mothers have fine plans for their daughters and it's not likely anyone'll ask for you now.'

'Who did you used to have in mind?'

'I quite fancied Billy Freeman for you. He's a nice young chap and he'll inherit three hundred acres or more – anyway, I hear he's courting a girl from over Langwood Fen.'

Billy Freeman, that oaf. Couldn't put more than three words together without choking over them. Only thing he was good at was skating. . . .

'I shouldn't want to be married now, Ma. I don't think much of men.'

Edwina sighed. 'It's a sad thing when a girl gets let down.'

'I don't really feel sad. It'll be nice living with you and Pa in the way we used to, and when Reuben gets too old I can take over his work.'

'Don't forget the baby's going to keep you busy. Wonder if it'll be a boy or a girl?'

'I hope it's not a girl in case it's another Bessie Hinton.'

'What makes you start thinking about her?'

'Ma, am I like Bessie Hinton?' She waited with painful anxiety for the reply.

Edwina gazed thoughtfully into her candleflame for a long moment. 'No,' she said, suddenly brisk. 'To all accounts she was wicked – you, you're just daft.'

They said goodnight, and as Edwina departed Lizzie climbed into bed. The calico sheets smelt of wild herbs and grasses, and she lay listening to the old, subdued sounds of the night. The rustling of the reeds and the small splash of a water vole. The shivering cry of an owl, and then from far away over Horse Moor the huffling of the last train coming.

She put her head under the bedclothes and wept as if her heart would break.

Despite the isolation of Damperdown Farm, the news that the Hinton girl had turned up again, pregnant and unwed, was common knowledge within forty-eight hours. Everyone knew from Stonea to Wimblington, and contrary to Victorian fondness for moral rectitude, there was little or no condemnation. Bastards were accepted philosophically in a loose-knit community where some of the worthiest were unable to produce a completed birth certificate.

But it was less easy for Lizzie to accept the consequences of what Edwina called her daftness. Sometimes she felt overwhelmingly happy to be back where she belonged; for the first few days she could hardly bear to be indoors because the wind felt so clean and the air smelt so fresh. She walked along with her face tilted to the sun, and when she was tired she lay down among the cowslips and forget-me-nots, her cloak bunched under her head for a pillow. She lay watching the sky, the great lazy clouds moving over the face of the sun and then sliding away, leaving the fens re-bathed in golden light, and she wanted no other life.

Then quite abruptly her mood would change and despair seemed to eat into her very bones like the fen ague. It wouldn't be so bad being here if I hadn't known anywhere else, she thought, and memories of the theatre would come rushing back. She was young, and in love with Fairford Polperro, and in spite of being pregnant and unwed, she still wanted to dance. She wanted the music and the excitement and the other girls – even Miss Paynim's Pixies would have been better than this great green flat nothingness.

She wished she hadn't left all her clothes behind; with the money she had earned and with Emmie's help she had amassed quite a wardrobe of frocks and skirts and blouses, all of them pin-tucked, ruched or frilled. She had left four pairs of pure silk stockings in her dressing table drawer and, hanging behind the door, a lace parasol that had come from Paris. What a fool!

She sorted through the garments that still hung in her bedroom cupboard, turning each one aside with a grimace of distaste. Rough tweed skirts and flannel blouses like working men's shirts; black woollen stockings with holes in the toes, and a couple of faded gingham frocks that no self-respecting milkmaid would be seen dead in.

But there was no point in mourning her stupidity because none of her clothes would fit her now. Although Edwina offered to help make some loose smocks, she declined the suggestion, preferring to cling to the skirt she had arrived in and pinning it together as the gap between the hooks and eyes became ever wider. She began to look strange and forbidding and gypsylike, and she didn't care.

She had now revisited all the old haunts – the pool where the otters used to play, the rushy bit of meadow where the yellowshank had nested – but she had not visited Johnnie Moon's cottage. She had only once walked along Paxton's Lode, and even then she had kept her eyes carefully averted from the marshy little island upon which it stood. After the first few weeks in London his memory had dimmed, but now he was back again, painfully alive in her mind's eye, and she would be overwhelmed by a return of the old gawky schoolgirl love. And with the return of love came the return of guilt and the certainty that he had only hanged himself because of her burdening him with the story of Bessie Hinton. How could any man love a girl whose great-grandmother had been hanged as a common felon? All the other things he had said had just been excuses.

She loved Johnnie Moon, she loved Fairford Polperro, and yet deep down she loved no one at all. Men were horrible – cruel and calculating, careless and cynical.

Her state of confusion sometimes made her difficult to live with, and Edwina, never the most tolerant of women, found it increasingly hard to remain patient.

'Look, I made you a nice baked custard for your dinner.'

'No thanks, Ma.'

'But you've had nothing since yesterday, bar a bit of cheese.'

'I only fancy cheese.'

'So what d'you reckon on giving birth to – a litter of mice? Lawks sake, it's no use giving way to fancies now you've got the baby to think of. How's it going to grow healthy and strong on a bit of ole cheese? If you take my advice, Lizzie, you'll stop mooning about and start sewing some baby clothes and eating proper.'

'Yes, Ma.'

'Well, then. There's a spoon and fork – now get on with it like I say.'

At times like this, Walter found her equally trying.

'What happened to all my hens, Pa?'

'I sold 'em.'

'Oh, *why*?'

''cos I didn't know if you was coming back or not, did I?'

'But my hens meant a lot to me. Bella and Snowball and Dilly. . . .' Her eyes would fill with tears and Walter would clumsily pat her shoulder.

'Don't fret now, my little queen. Pa'll git you some new ones at the Friday market.'

'I don't want any more . . . I don't want to be a poultry-keeper for the rest of my days.'

A period of rain set in, darkening the fresh young foliage and draining the light from the fens. They went to bed with it drumming against the windows and awoke to it falling in a thin, debilitating drizzle. Reuben suffered a sharp attack of rheumatism, known locally as 'the screws', and Edwina made him a new pair of moleskin garters to help ease the pain in his knee joints.

'And you shouldn't be wandering about in the wet either,' she told Lizzie. 'That baby'll be born with webbed feet, if you don't die of pneumonia first.'

Heedless of her advice, Lizzie continued her solitary ramblings, the rain teasing her hair to little springy curls round her face and loosening the heavy coil of it pinned at the back of her head. And one afternoon, as she was idly kicking a pebble along the Sixteen Foot level, she looked up and saw someone walking towards her from the opposite direction.

It was the figure of a man, blurred against the skyline. He was walking quickly and purposefully, and something about him made her heart begin to beat painfully fast.

She walked on; the distance between them lessened sufficiently for her to recognize London clothes, London fashion, and a tall young man with long legs and shoulders unbowed by manual work.

196

She stood still. He did the same. The rain had almost stopped, and a weak gleam of sunlight illuminated the puddles.

'Liza?'

'Yes?' Then she gave a huge dry sob and ran clumsily towards his open arms.

'Fairford – oh, *Fairford*!'

But it wasn't Fairford, and she realized with a sudden shock that during the past weeks she had forgotten all about the baby's father.

'I didn't desert you – you deserted me! Skipping off to Venice or wherever it was.'

'I had to go, Liza.'

'And I'm Lizzie now I'm back home.'

'I had to go suddenly, Lizzie, on family business.'

'That's what they all say.'

'But surely the fact that I'm here now speaks for itself?'

'Yes. Well. . . .'

'So why did you rush off like that? No one knew where you'd gone or for what reason.'

'There's the reason.' She unwrapped the velvet cloak and held it open. 'And it's your reason, as a matter of interest.'

'Oh Liza . . . Lizzie. . . .'

'Don't you Liza-Lizzie me.'

But all the time she was watching his face in the watery gleam of sunlight. Watching it, and already bitterly prepared for disbelief or anger or repugnance. But his blue eyes slanted up at the corners in the smile she suddenly remembered now, and he took her hands.

'Oh, my word – d'you mean we're having a baby?'

'Well, *I* am, I don't know about you.' The gruffness in her voice strove to conceal emotions she preferred to ignore. 'Which is why I left the Gaiety and Emmie and everything . . . no sense in hanging on, was there?'

'You could have waited for me.'

'But I didn't know where you'd *gone*, did I? Or whether I meant – it meant . . . or whether you'd ever come back. . . .' She wrenched her hands away from his and began to walk hastily and distractedly away. He caught up with her and put his arm round her.

'Let's go for a walk.'

'It's raining.'

'I love walking in country rain.'

'Walking in the rain's all I ever do.' She burst into tears then, and stood sobbing like a small hurt child. 'I walk down the level and over Boots Bridge to Honey Bridge, then I walk over the fen to Darcey Lode and cross over to Manea and then back home by the Dams, then other times I go up to Stonea and watch for the train, and then . . .' She broke down utterly, but he said nothing; just held her a little more tightly as the mizzling rain once more obliterated each weak gleam of sunlight. 'But I still can't bear to go down Paxton's Lode and past the cottage where – where . . . It's only a little lode and it runs out before it gets to Cow Common, which is on the edge of where – '

He took a white handkerchief out of his pocket and dried her eyes.

'Now blow.'

She blew. 'Which is on the edge of where . . .'

'That was a first-class geography lesson, but I don't think I'd be capable of assimilating any more in one go. So could we talk about something else now?' He put his arm round her again and they went on walking.

'Such as?'

'Such as getting married.'

'Married? You mean, me to you?' She had to stop again, in order to peer at him through tear-washed eyes.

'That's what I had in mind.'

'What – make an honest woman of me?'

'Hadn't really thought of it that way.'

'Then why?'

'Because I love you, you silly ass.'

Lizzie gave a long high wail that disturbed a nesting moorhen. It swam away from the reeds with a little shriek of alarm.

'You can't . . . you don't . . . you're just doing the decent thing. . . .'

198

'I love you, Liza-Lizzie.' Holding her face very tenderly between his hands he kissed her mouth. Then he drew back, searching her eyes with great intentness. 'Do you by any chance love me?'

She looked at him, then looked away.

'Do you, Lizzie?'

'Yes,' she said finally. 'I think perhaps I do, a bit.'

When they were within sight of Damperdown they turned and walked back the way they had come. There was a lot to think about, a lot to get used to, and with their arms closely entwined they remained unaware that the rain had become heavier.

'Where'll we live? In your little place in London?'

'We'll keep it on for the time being, yes.'

'I'd sooner live in the country, really.'

'I think we'll be doing that too.'

For the first time he struck her as being a little evasive. She turned to look at him sharply. 'What'll your family think? Will they make you feel ashamed of me?'

'No, of course not, you silly.'

'One of our girls at the Gaiety got married to some high-up gent and none of his lot would have anything to do with her. She lived most of the time on her own and the only person who called once a week was the vicar.'

'Poor soul.'

'We won't be like that, will we?'

'I should say not! But what are your parents going to think of me? They'll call me a cad and a bounder.'

'They don't know words like that.' She began to giggle, then sobered. 'I think they'll just be too struck all of a heap to say anything.'

'The sooner we find out, the better. Let's turn back now and go and face them.'

By the time they reached Damperdown Farm the rain had ceased and the sun was making some headway, but the arrival of Henry Dullingham-Reve, soaking wet, smiling and supremely courteous, took some assimilating.

Edwina remained silent but her eyes missed nothing, while Walter, dazed behind a hastily erected cloud of

Nosegay, asked him how he had found his way. Which way had he come? Why had he walked all the way from March when he could have come on to Stonea?

Fearful of another geography lesson, Dully replied that he would certainly take the train to Stonea next time as Mr Hinton advised, but really the walk had been very pleasant, and in the meanwhile could he possibly ask for his daughter's hand in marriage?

'What – Lizzie's?' Walter's confusion seemed to increase.

'Are you its father?' Edwina spoke for the first time.

'Yes, isn't it stupendous? The only sad thing is that I was away when Lizzie needed me.'

'Lizzie,' said Walter, standing up and removing his pipe from his mouth.

'Yes, Pa.'

'Now, take careful heed. Do you want to get fixed up with this young chap?'

'Yes, Pa.'

'You don't have to, on account of being in the family way. Your ma an' me'll always see you through an' give you a good home.'

'Yes, Pa. I know.'

'But if you really want to get fixed up with him, and he can swear to me that he'll provide you with a home as good as this, and take care of you – '

'I can swear to that, Sir,' Dully said.

'And you really know your mind, Lizzie gel?'

'Yes, Pa. I do.'

'Then I reckon there's no more to be said.'

'Except,' Edwina said to Lizzie and Dully, 'that you'd best get out of your wet things while I make us all a cup of tea.'

It seemed the only thing to do, to concentrate on ordinary sensible things while striving to grow accustomed to Lizzie being married to the young gent who had put her in the family way, and although Walter and Edwina were gratified that he had decided to turn up and do the right thing, they remained wary.

Edwina gave Dully the little room that had once been slept in by Keziah and warned Lizzie in an undertone that there was to be no goings-on; there had been more than enough of that already.

Two evenings later Lizzie took Dully to Paxton's Lode. They had crossed the little footbridge to the island where the tin-clad cottage was sinking deep in new luxuriant summer growth when she turned to him and said: 'I've got something to tell you.'

She told him about Johnnie Moon; about being in love with him and hoping that he loved her too, and then about him killing himself after she had confided the secret about Bessie Hinton. 'He hanged himself like she was hanged, and it was all my fault.'

He didn't say anything; just opened his arms wide and laid his cheek against hers with a subtle caressing gesture that seemed to stroke away all the old dark shadows, all the pain and the horror. She could look at the cottage now, at its small blind windows and leaning doorway, and at the little row of shells half obscured by weeds that lined the path, and it was as if it had all happened to someone else a long, long while ago. Now, and for the first time, she was able to think of Johnnie Moon with an adult's wisdom and the affectionate pity of a true friend.

Then Dully moved away towards the bridge, leaned over the handrail with his back to her and said: 'I've got something to confess to you, too.'

'Oh?' She stood motionless.

'The reason why I went to Venice was a message to say that my uncle and his son, my cousin, were both down with typhoid. I hadn't seen either of them for years and the whole thing was pretty grisly. My cousin died the morning after I arrived and Uncle Berry on the following day. Somehow it seemed rather pointless to have them brought home so I arranged for the burials out there. The British Ambassador was extraordinarily kind.'

'Oh Dully, you poor thing.'

'But what I've rather put off telling you is this.' He

turned to look at her, smiling ruefully. 'As a direct result of it all, I've just become an earl.'

The marriage had already been planned to take place on the following morning, but now Dully's news stopped everyone dead in their tracks.

'A *nerl*?' Edwina repeated blankly. 'How d'you mean?'

'My uncle was the eighth Earl Dullingham, and his son, who was born Viscount Reve, should normally have inherited the title. Failing Rollo, it would have been taken by my father, who was my uncle's younger brother, but my father died some years ago.'

They stood staring at him, striving to assimilate the sense of his words.

'So supposing what you say is true, what would this do to Lizzie?'

'Nothing, except make her a countess.'

'A countess? What – Lizzie?'

'Did you say Lizzie a *countess*?'

'You could have told us before,' Edwina said, unreasonably cross. 'I mean, if you are what you say you are, you won't want a wedding like the one we just done our best to arrange – that is, supposing you really want to marry Lizzie at *all*.'

'I want to marry Lizzie, and I came down here for the express purpose.'

'Why didn't you let on about being a nerl before you asked her?' demanded Walter.

'Finding her and proposing to her came before any other consideration,' Dully said. 'I also have to admit that I was afraid it might put her off, for some reason.'

'Ha – there you are! So what you really did was try to trap her.'

It was strange how no one seemed to view Lizzie's imminent elevation with anything other than crossness and suspicion, and, on Dully's part, with a kind of weary contrition. It went on and on.

'Doesn't a nerl have to get married in London and invite the Queen?'

'And what about your family – if there's any left? What'll they think?'

'They'll want it down there, not up here. And how can we go down there – not knowing what to wear, what to say?'

It was Lizzie who finally put an end to the prevarication by saying flatly: 'I don't care a damn whether people want it up here or down there. I'm the one who's getting married, and unless I get married from here, which is where I *know*, I won't get married at all – so there!'

Worried, wearied and curiously aggrieved, the four of them went to bed early that night.

'I don't believe he *is* a nerl,' Walter said in the darkness.

'I do. And he's not telling his family until it's all over because he's ashamed.'

'But he hasn't *got* to marry her, has he?'

'I suppose he feels he has. At least that shows he's a gent in the ole-fashioned proper way.'

'P'raps it'll be all right. . . .'

'I don't want her going off just anywhere. I know she's been silly, but I want to see her happy.'

'You were two months gorn with the first one when we got wed.'

'Whose fault was that?' A sharp rustle of bedclothes.

'Both of us, I reckon.'

'Oh, Walter. . . .'

'Don't cry, gel. Come to ole Pa, now.'

Listening to the low murmur of voices on the other side of the wall, Dully lay wishing that he could be with Lizzie.

She's confused and unhappy, and no wonder. She's no idea what's ahead of her, and her parents seeing me as some kind of wicked squire doesn't help.

I wish tomorrow were over. I don't care about the ceremony any more than she does; I just want us to be married and together. I want to take care of her, I want to love and cherish her. . . .

Restlessly he turned on his side and the loud twang of bedsprings arrested the conversation in the next room.

I wish I could go back to how I was, thought Lizzie, across the landing. Back to when I was at the Gaiety and before I was in the family way. Before I ever met him or Fairford or anybody. I wish I could be like I was then, but knowing what I know now.

I wish I loved him. Loved him properly like I loved Johnnie and like I love Fairford. I've been trying to, but it won't come. Oh, I like him well enough – it's hard not to. He's kind and gentle and nice-looking and an earl and everything – what more could anyone want? I want to be in love, that's what I want. In love, and soppy with happiness the way I would be with naughty old Fairford. . . .

None of them slept well that night, and on the following morning no one felt like eating anything. Lizzie, pale and obdurate, was able to give the bridegroom no more than a chill peck on the cheek by way of greeting, before insisting upon going out to feed Walter's new pig.

'There's no need to go messing about with pigs on your wedding day – you'll never get rid of the smell!' Edwina's temper was already rising.

'It's the last chance I'll have!'

'In an hour's time from now,' Walter said, 'she's going to be a countess. Best let her make the most of being plain Lizzie Hinton.'

'She hasn't even cleaned her shoes yet.'

'I'll clean them,' Dully volunteered. 'In fact, I could do everyone's.'

'I already did mine last night,' Edwina said repressively.

Finally they set out, and it was a strange and constrained little wedding, organized so hastily and conducted by the Reverend Pool, who couldn't pronounce his r's and who kept his eyes virtuously averted from the bride's figure.

With no time in which to purchase new finery, Edwina was wearing her old bombazine with the bonnet she had bought for last year's harvest festival; Walter was dressed in the suit he always wore for special occasions, which in the old days had meant visits to Netta in Wisbech before she became unsensed; Dully was in the clothes in which he had arrived – impeccably tailored, but curling at the edges because of being soaked by rain and then dried in front of the kitchen range; and Lizzie, still in a tumult of conflicting emotions, had insisted upon going as she was. So she proceeded to the altar on her father's arm (no choir, no congregation), wearing the once smart blue skirt now gaping conspicuously down one side, and over her shoulders and trailing behind her the once luxurious velvet cloak that was now rumpled and smelt of wet earth. Even so, she had a marvellous air about her; her rich auburn hair gleamed in the miserable light and she walked in defiantly unpolished shoes with all the proud, graceful, upright carriage of one of the Gov'nor's Gaiety Girls.

A *nerl*, Edwina thought with fresh incredulity. I still don't know whether I believe him or not, but supposing he is – what does it make me and Walter?

And standing grimly to attention by the chancel steps, Walter thought: I wish I'd put a stop to it. It's not natural. Lizzie's a good little gel and she doesn't deserve getting messed about with by some young turk who now tells us he's a nerl. She's bin messed about with enough already and it's my place to put a stop to it before it's too late.

He opened his mouth in readiness, then closed it when he heard his daughter say in a scratchy little whisper: 'I will.'

Then, as if anticipating Walter's increasing desire to interfere, the Reverend Pool turned to him with what seemed like sudden aggression and demanded: 'Who giveth this woman to be mawwied to this man?' and Walter turned a dull red and muttered, 'Me.'

'I do,' corrected the Reverend Pool, and the service proceeded to its close. The vows were exchanged, the ring was placed upon Lizzie's finger, and when they reached the final solemn command *Those whom God hath joined together let no man put asunder*, Edwina was overcome by audible sobs.

Reuben and Willy Stow had been pressed into service as witnesses, and as Lizzie walked out of the church on Dully's arm, Reuben grinned at her and touched his cap. 'Well now, Missus, how's it feel to be a wedded woman, hey?'

'I haven't had time to find out yet.' Lizzie took her place in the wagonette and they all drove back to Damperdown

Farm for the hurriedly concocted wedding breakfast.

I'm a countess, thought Lizzie. All I did was make a few promises and sign my name in a book and it's changed me from Lizzie Hinton, spinster of this parish, into Elizabeth, Countess Dullingham. At least, that's what Dully says I'll be known as. I don't know how it makes me feel; how I should expect it to make me feel. And I don't know what I'm supposed to do, how I'm supposed to behave. . . .

Dully's hand found her own buried deep in the folds of her cloak. He pressed it gently.

'I love you, Liza-Lizzie.'

'Do you?' Bleakly she searched his face; his smiling eyes and long straight nose. He really was handsome in his own quiet way and he had a lovely way of speaking.

'Do you love me, too?'

'Yes,' she said, 'of course I do.'

She damn well ought to have done, but she didn't. She knew she didn't. She only liked him, and the thought of having to be married to him and having to be a blooming countess for the rest of her days filled her with deep, impenetrable gloom.

They had just jolted over Boots Bridge and were about to turn left along the Sixteen Foot level when the baby, as if tired of being ignored, burst gloriously into life with a sudden vigorous kicking.

Henry Porteous Dullingham-Reve, alias Dully, had been the only child born to the Honourable William and his wife Constance.

He had had a restless, unsettling infancy, sailing for India before he was one year old and subsequently taking up residence in a variety of nurseries in charge of a variety of attendants from Simla to Somerset, from the Northern Transvaal to Southern Ireland, and once, after a quarrel of spectacular fury between his parents, to his mother's home in Argyllshire, secreted in a laundry basket.

Upon resigning his commission in the Brigade of Guards, his father tried the diplomatic service followed by politics, gold-mining and dairy farming, and met a violent and premature end by sticking his head out of the window of the London to Brighton express a second before it passed the slow train from Reigate. The head was retrieved, dusty and snarling, on a long-handled shovel, and upon being taken to kiss Papa goodbye in his coffin, little Henry was greatly intrigued by the white pierrot frill that concealed the dreadful severance.

And if his father had been a man of limited intelligence and irascible temper, his mother had no more control over her moods than a small boat has over the waves that toss it hither and thither.

Weeks of sombre brooding would suddenly yield to fits of hectic vivacity, and if her son had learned with difficulty to endure her neglect and the long lonely hours in the darkness of the night nursery waiting in vain for the rustle of her gown and her bless-you-my-darling kiss, he found the bouts of excessive maternal attention even harder to bear. Now it was he who would endeavour to avoid her; to hide from the lacy clutching arms and the passionate kisses and questions: Do you love Mama? Do you *truly* love her? How *much* do you love her? He learned the art of polite evasion, became an expert dissembler, and his governess was overheard to say that he was the dullest child she had ever encountered.

From a very early age he had known that his parents were unhappy together, and was content when storms raged to be sent to stay with various relations. His Scottish grandparents were as dour and unyielding as the granite castle walls that enclosed them, but at least the atmosphere remained at a constant temperature, then three years after his father's death he spent several months at Reve, seat of the Dullingham family.

Although he was well accustomed to cavernous castles and large foreign establishments, the enormous proportions of Reve overwhelmed him. Designed by Flitcroft in the early eighteenth century, the Palladian grandeur of its main frontage seemed to his anxious child's eye to extend into infinity – pediments and columns, triumphal arches, and a portico at either end lavishly decorated with stone goddesses and cherubs blowing trumpets. And once inside, the echoing marble of the great hall caused him to walk on tiptoe.

Yet despite its size, Reve appeared to be only sparsely populated by resident Dullinghams, each one administered to by an average of three personal servants: a footman, a lady's maid or valet, and a message-running page.

Except for the pages and one or two visiting children, everyone seemed to the ten-year-old Henry to be rather elderly, and although they were kind to him they tended to stare at him with a frank interest that disconcerted him. He knew that they referred to him as poor William's boy, and discussed the more flagrant examples of his mother's instability in tones of hushed tut-tuttery.

Already an expert in the art of avoiding people, it was simplicity itself to escape through the glowing gardens and out into the surrounding parkland after such necessary courtesies as 'Good morning, did you sleep well?' followed by 'Good morning. I slept very well, thank you. Did you?'

He fell increasingly under the spell of the soporific countryside; of the gentle folds and lazy green of mid-Suffolk that seemed to offer a quiet, healing friendship that made no demands, exacted no promises. He surrendered to it, lost himself in the woods and coverts, winding lanes and secret poacher's tracks, and during the course of those shimmering summer weeks began taking the first slow steps towards self-discovery.

He discovered first of all that he was a person in his own right, and not a mere adjunct to other and more powerful beings. He had his own likes and dislikes, and lying in the sun-spangled shadows of an oak tree, rib-stockinged, tweed-breeched and Norfolk-jacketed, he listed them slowly and thoughtfully on his fingers.

I like the country better than the town. I like birds and animals and plants and the weather. I like apple charlotte and *Robinson Crusoe* and being alone. I don't like Mama, or medicine, or saying prayers or learning Greek. I don't like any lessons at all except biology and history.

Two days before he was due to leave, his uncle Berry

arrived home from Venice with his only son, who was introduced as Cousin Rollo. Uncle Berry was an older and less choleric version of Henry's father; he had the same eyes that slanted up at the corners, but his were of a cheerful blue rather than a thunderous grey, and shaking hands with great cordiality he said: ''pon my word, m'boy, why go everywhere on foot? Mean to say no one's fixed you up with a mount?'

Having been taught to ride at the age of six, Henry was proficient if not particularly keen, and on his last morning at Reve waited with his cousin Rollo for their ponies to be brought round from the stable block. Rollo was fifteen, and Henry was impressed to note the beginnings of a faint down on his upper lip. He wore a billycock hat, and stood swishing at his boots with his riding crop.

'Where d'you hunt?'

'Nowhere,' said Henry. 'At least, I haven't yet.'

'Lived abroad a lot, haven't you?'

'Yes.'

'My father says your father was a bit of an ass and that your mother drinks.'

Saved from the necessity of a reply by the arrival of the ponies, Henry placed the toe of his boot in the cupped hands of the groom allotted to him and took his seat. They rode out on to the soft turf of the park, and there was sudden exhilaration in galloping, in feeling the prick of early autumn wind on his face and in watching the ground flying beneath him. They raced side by side, scattering sheep and startling a heron from the lakeside; then down a steep curving incline and up the other side until they drew rein, neck-and-neck and panting. They sat looking back at Reve.

'One day all that will belong to me,' Rollo said, when he had regained his breath. 'I shall be the ninth Earl Dullingham.'

'Will you like that?'

'I dare say I shall.' Rollo turned in the saddle to look at his cousin. 'Funny, but you don't seem like one of the Dullinghams, somehow. Still, you ride pretty well for a young shaver.'

They might have become friends if Henry had remained at Reve for more than a few days, but the tenuous thread was broken with an abrupt summons from Mama. Three years were to pass before they met again, and this time things went badly. Although he had longed to return to Reve and to recapture the quiet golden beauty of the place, this visit took place during the Christmas holidays from Eton, and the five-year gap between him and his cousin seemed to have widened immeasurably. Rollo at eighteen was fashionably attired in a black slouch hat and a long jacket with narrow lapels. He smoked cigars and drank port, and greeted Henry with a lordly affability that was next of kin to insolence.

And the cold. After the benevolent warmth of summer, the foggy cold of the corridors, the chill of the water in the bedroom ewers and the low sobbing of the wind outside, all combined to change the atmosphere he had loved from that of open-handed plenitude to one of drained and cheerless discomfort. Although huge fires burned in the great saloon and in the library, their heat was lost in the mystic heights, and what seemed like flocks of blue-tinged uncles and aunts precluded any hope of a chilled thirteen-year-old creeping close to the hearths.

Outside, the change was even more depressing: the glowing rose bushes reduced now to handfuls of spindly brown twigs, trees in the park naked and forlorn, and the white breath of sheep hanging on the air like the steam from miniature railway engines.

But on Boxing morning the hunt met outside the main south wing. Uncle Berry was Master, and the servants were allowed to watch the ceremony of the stirrup cup from the windows. Henry had never hunted before, and clad in borrowed pink was uncertain of his role.

'Just keep well to the back with the other youngsters and the girls,' Rollo advised. 'You'll be all right.'

They moved off, and ran the first fox for an exhilarating twenty minutes before they lost him, and Henry glowed when a whipper-in nodded, 'Well done, Sir,' for the way he took his first jump. He had forgotten Rollo's advice and was well to the fore when the hounds roused a second fox. He caught a glimpse of Uncle Berry's cheeks suffused with excitement and the intense cold, as they wheeled and doubled and then spread out at a headlong gallop after the small brown speck zigzagging across the fields and then over the road and into the front garden in one of the Dullingham farm cottages. They cornered him, and Henry had a quick glimpse of a small animal frantically at bay before the hounds closed in. The shouts and yelpings almost deafened him, and suddenly for Henry there was no more excitement or exhilaration – merely a churning mass of reeking horseflesh surmounted by a mob of men and women crazy for the kill. They whooped and cheered; the man who was Field Master sloshed Henry's cheeks with a lump of the hot bloody flesh, and the cheers and the turmoil increased.

Shocked and nauseated, the boy wrenched his mount away from them and spurred hard for the quiet fields, where an early mist was already rising in the hollows. He rode furiously and heedlessly until he had left the laughter and the yelpings far behind, and he came to the curve of the river that fed the lake at Reve. He flung himself from the saddle and, crouching on his knees, filled his cupped hands with the ice cold water and tried, shuddering and sobbing, to wash away the blood that stained him.

It was a long while before he felt able to return to Reve, to hack alone up the endless avenue and through the triumphal archway that led into the huge stableyard. Grooms and ostlers came running to meet him ('Are you hurt, Sir? 'Had a bit of a spill, Sir?'). He shook his head, and sliding to the ground handed them the reins and walked away.

He bathed and changed, then rang for tea to be brought to his room, and the parlourmaid gave him a telegram that had arrived for him that afternoon. It was from his mother, demanding his return to London in order to meet his new stepfather, the Baron Josef von Kassel.

The Baron was handsome and corseted, with scarred cheeks and a waxed moustache, and he swept out an arm to indicate that his stepson should be seated. Seated, but not at ease. Studying him covertly, Henry reached the conclusion that he was certainly no better, but probably no worse than his father had been, and so returned to the old tactic of polite evasiveness. He spoke only when spoken to, and counted the days until his return to Eton.

He had already made up his mind that he would never go back to Reve again.

The Baron made jokes about Dull Little Dullingham and laughed heartily, displaying strong yellow teeth. Then they closed up the London house and went first to Paris, followed by a lengthy spell in Baden-Baden. Henry spent the majority of his remaining school holidays with the family of a clergyman who augmented a meagre stipend by taking in the occasional schoolboy whose parents were unavoidably detained abroad. He had only been allowed to visit Reve on the two previous occasions because his Dullingham family had requested it, but now no more invitations seemed to be forthcoming, and he was glad. For the first time in his life he had ventured to become emotionally involved, and could only look back on the fox-killing incident as some kind of callous betrayal. He remained firm in his resolve never to see Reve again.

It was Cambridge that saved him. Sceptical of the notion that university would be any more interesting than school, he nevertheless presented himself as a freshman up at Trinity on 14 October 1889 and almost immediately began to enjoy himself. The casual freedom and the easy friendships amazed him. He met Fairford Polperro and other lively-minded young men, joined several societies, and the terms sped by. But the best freedom of all was the freedom of the holidays. Regarded now as old enough to look after himself, his mother and stepfather relinquished whatever token interest they had felt in him, her bouts of sticky maternal maunderings having now been channelled into a new shrill coquetry. His Scottish grandparents died, Reve remained silent, and he was free to join Fairford and other friends in walking expeditions in France and Switzerland, to take part in reading holidays and to accept invitations

212

from people he liked and whose company he enjoyed.

He renewed the process of self-discovery begun during that far-off summer at Reve. He found pleasure in ordering his own clothes from a London tailor, and although he was not as spectacularly handsome as Fairford, remained content with his own verdict of middling-average. The news that he had gained a First in the second part of the History Tripos surprised and gratified him, and he spent part of his grandparents' inheritance in setting himself up in the chambers in Charles Street.

But what came next? He didn't know. At times he felt the lure of taking up a profession – one in the legal world seemed to be most congenial – but apart from making a few preliminary enquiries he did nothing.

Fairford had always been disarmingly honest about the directions in which his own interests lay: expensive living and beautiful girls. He enjoyed being in the swim, and despite family exhortations to think of the future, thought only on a day-to-day basis. Sometimes he was flush (he was lucky at cards and had a couple of maiden aunts who thought of him fondly), but from whatever the source the money never lasted, and on more than one occasion he sought refuge from creditors in Henry's rooms.

'Good old Dully, what a marvellous pal you are!'

And Dully would smile his quiet, eye-slanting smile and think, Dully – meaning dull. Dull, unimaginative and boring as the deuce.

There were times when he envied Fairford his easy self-assurance if not his chaotic way of living. He had met no girls at Cambridge, yet long before the end of their first year Fairford was conducting a passionate liaison with a barmaid from the Blue Boar while making overtures to a doctor's widow in Trumpington. It must have been splendid indeed to have the admiring attention of every woman in the room, but Dully contented himself with dutifully escorting such unattached females as were given into his care – lumpish daughters from the shires, giggling younger sisters, and girls little older than he who already bore the seal of spinsterhood stamped on their colourless features. He was kind and courteous to them all, squiring them at social functions of impeccable propriety and earning a reputation among mothers for decency and dependability; for a quiet charm that betrayed no hint of dangerous undercurrents.

And so his life, pleasant but carefully uncommitted, might have continued indefinitely if Fairford – now the mutinous and somewhat harassed fiancé of an American heiress – hadn't introduced him to the world of the Gaiety Theatre. He had almost decided to refuse the invitation to share Fairford's box that night and was unenthusiastic about the supper party to follow.

'I don't think I will. I'd planned to turn in early.'

'Ridiculous. I'm going to show you some of the most beautiful girls in the world.'

'I can't be bothered to change.'

'Yes, you can.'

Fairford propelled him towards the bathroom, and while Dully bathed and shaved, removed a set of picture post-cards from his pocket and propped them in a row along the marble shelf below the mirror.

'There you are, just to whet your appetite. . . .'

Dully glanced at them, his chin white with shaving lather, while Fairford introduced each one with a loving flourish: 'Miss Ellaline Terriss, Miss Kate Vaughan, Miss Ethel Hayden, and my own particular fancy, Miss Liza Hinton.'

'Yes. But you'd better move them in case I get soap on them.'

'My word, Dully, you're a crusty old codger!'

But the Gaiety worked its spell, and he came away dazed by its unique atmosphere.

He had been to plenty of theatres, but never to one that seemed to welcome him with a friendly embrace, to make him part of its own special radiance, and when Fairford handed him the opera glasses he had to agree that the girl who played Fifine was an absolute stunner.

'Look at the colour of her hair, Dully, and can you see her smile? It's the smile of a girl who's young and glorious and glad to be alive . . . but don't forget that I have prior claim.'

214

Dully left him at the stage door, the old reticence preventing him from joining the ecstatic mob waiting for the girls to appear. He drove to the Savoy, wondering whether Fairford would introduce him to this latest paragon of womanhood or whether, like a dog with a new bone, he would keep her all for himself.

Totally unprepared for the appearance of Martha Bogbice, he found himself obliged to offer his arm to the paragon in question. Concerned only with protecting Fairford, he remained largely unaware of her until they were safely seated at the supper table, when her large velvet brown eyes, charming little nose and warm generous mouth beneath the piled auburn hair made him realize that she was in fact quite the most beautiful girl he had ever seen.

He began to admire her for the way she had behaved in a difficult situation – he could only describe it as being a kind of spirited dignity – and when towards the end of the meal she gave a sigh and told him that she used to live down a drain, he fell hopelessly and irretrievably in love with her.

It was a love that would last unswervingly for the rest of his life.

They left for London on the evening of the wedding day, and Edwina and Lizzie dived abruptly into one another's arms as the train approached the platform at Stonea.

They stood motionless, tears streaming, then Lizzie flung herself at Walter and sobbed against his shoulder while he patted her back with his clumsy farmer's hand.

'Hup back, now . . . hup back there, gel. . . .'

Moved, Dully shook hands with his parents-in-law and then handed Lizzie up into the first-class carriage, where she collapsed in the corner with her face buried in her handkerchief; he stood at the window, dutifully waving on behalf of both of them. Walter and Edwina were the only two people on the platform and he watched them dwindle to fly-specks as the train ate its way further and further south across the flatness of the fens.

'I'm sorry.' Lizzie gave her eyes a final wipe then put her handkerchief away.

'There's no need to be. And I do understand.'

'Do you?'

'It must be an awful wrench leaving them.'

'But it's not the first time. Don't forget I've already run away once.'

'Did you cry then?'

'Not until I got near to London, and then I wasn't really crying about them, I was crying about – '

She almost said his name: Johnnie Moon. Then realized in the nick of time that it wouldn't be right to talk about him any more now. At least, not to her husband and on their wedding day.

'I don't know what made ole Ma and I take on that way,' she said finally. 'I mean, we don't really get on all that well.'

'Something to do with blood being thicker than water, no doubt.'

'Yes.' She sat watching the countryside pass. 'Tell me about your mother.'

'We don't get on very well, either. In fact we seldom meet, particularly now she's remarried.'

'I suppose I'll have to meet her, will I?'

'Not necessarily.'

Still unused to his manner of speaking, the clipped words sounded to her cool and indifferent and reawoke the suspicion that he was ashamed of her. He would never have married her if she hadn't been in the family way with his child.

And looking at her bent head and tightly clasped hands Dully thought of course it's not necessary to meet my mother if she doesn't want to. I don't want her to do any mortal thing she doesn't want to. . . . But it never occurred to him to say it. So the conversation remained both intermittent and impersonal until they reached London, and sitting side by side in the cab on their way to Charles Street Lizzie asked, as off-handedly as possible, whether his butler chap would be there.

'Maxton? No, there'll only be us.'

'Oh. Well, that's a good thing.'

The street lamps flickered across the cab's dark interior

216

and something about the lovely old jingle of London seemed to bring a certain reassurance to them both. It was all around them, the clip-clopping hooves, the hoarse street cries, the theatres and restaurants, the laughter and whiffs of cigar smoke. He put his arm round her and kissed her. She responded, and the tentativeness of this new relationship seemed to melt a little more.

In the Charles Street chambers a small bright fire awaited them, with a cold supper set out on a small table in front of it.

'Who did all this?' She looked round anxiously.

'Don't worry, he's not here,' Dully laughed. 'It's just part of the service.'

It seemed strange to be going to bed together again, and even stranger to think that they were married. He made love to her very gently because of the baby, and when afterwards she guided his hand to where he could feel its movement he suddenly buried his face in her hair and the words poured out of him as if they would never stop.

He loved her, loved her. And he had never known that love would be anything like this: the beauty, the tenderness, the happiness, and above all, the desire to cherish and protect. He would never let anything harm her or hurt her, and he longed for the baby to be born because it would be part of her and part of him; it would unite them even more. . . . And she lay there listening in silent wonderment to the passionate outpourings of a lonely child who had grown to manhood without even a dog to love.

'Oh Dully,' she said, 'I will try very hard not to let you down.'

On the following morning a lady arrived from Derry & Toms with a selection of coats and frocks and lingerie suitable for an expectant mother, and for the first time Lizzie heard herself addressed as Your Ladyship.

Attired in pale blue lace and with a matching hat, she lunched with Dully at a quiet restaurant nearby, then they went for a drive through Hyde Park.

'I'll never get used to this – never.'

'Of course you will.'

217

'But it feels so funny just to be sitting here doing nothing. Not working at anything, I mean.'

'I don't believe anyone works on their honeymoon.'

'Yes, I keep forgetting it's a honeymoon. . . .'

They spent a week in the rooms in Charles Street, living quietly and companionably. On the afternoon Dully had an appointment with his lawyers, Lizzie decided to go for a walk. With no particular destination in mind, she wandered down the Haymarket and crossed Trafalgar Square, then her footsteps quickened as she reached the Strand, and it seemed as if she had known where she was going from the very start.

She reached the Gaiety Theatre and stood looking at the posters outside. At three o'clock in the afternoon the place was deserted and she lingered by the stage door thinking I used to belong here. This was my world. Oh, how happy I was then. . . .

The sight of the place brought back the memory of Fairford, and she knew that if by some miracle he should appear round the corner and ask her to go away with him, she would do so. She would be unable to help herself.

A policeman stood eyeing her from the opposite corner. 'Everything all right, Madam?'

'Yes, thank you.' She moved away, and began to walk back to Charles Street.

She felt tired when she reached Dully's chambers; he had already arrived back from his lawyer's office and he smiled with relief when he saw her.

'Lord, I was worried in case something had happened.'

'Did you think I'd run off with another man?' A silly thing to say, but she couldn't help it.

'Don't know what I thought.' He drew her inside and removed her hat before kissing her. 'I only know that I don't want to lose you.'

He made her sit with her feet up, and grateful that he had not demanded to know where she had been, she told him that she had walked all the way to the dear old Gaiety.

'Do you miss it dreadfully?'

'Not really. It's just being in London that made me think

of it. But I wouldn't mind going back to see the show just once.' (If I did I might see Fairford. Just to catch a glimpse of him would be enough. . . .)

'I think,' Dully said, 'that before much longer we'll have to present ourselves at Reve.'

'Your family's place? Oh Dully, can't we stop here?'

'We'll come back to London, of course. But I think we've got to resign ourselves to living mainly at Reve.'

'Will there be lots of other people there? Relations and servants and things? Oh, I don't want to go – it's all so new to me.'

'It's pretty new to me, too. Remember I only became an earl a couple of weeks before you became a countess.'

'Yes, I know, but . . .'

He meant to say don't worry, everything will be all right, but instead heard himself saying something entirely different.

'I didn't want to succeed to the title, you know. Actually, I've never been much of a family chap up until now.'

Lizzie sat looking at him gravely and without blinking. 'Why don't you tell me?' she said finally.

'Not a lot to tell, really. My parents were unhappy together, and as an only child I suppose I got bundled round quite a bit. Well, they say travel broadens the mind. But I never stayed anywhere long enough to become fond of anyone. The closest I came to it, funnily enough, was at Reve. But it wasn't a person, it was the whole place. It had a sort of magic for me that summer when I must have been about ten. I didn't take much notice of grown-ups – I'd become awfully good at escaping from people by then. I didn't need them and they didn't need me. But as I say, I loved Reve in a way I'd never loved anywhere else and I couldn't wait to be asked back there again – and to be allowed to go, because my mother was antagonistic towards my father's people – but when I did, it all went wrong. It was winter, and I hadn't realized that winter's a very cruel time in the country.'

'Yes, I know.' She sat thinking of birds frozen on the ice of the Sixteen Foot. 'Haven't you been back to Reve since?'

'No, never.' Then he smiled, his eyes tilting up at the corners. 'So you see, we've got to hold hands and protect one another, haven't we?'

She agreed, and it eased her mind a little.

As they were preparing for bed that night, she suddenly said: 'It was my first time, you know, that night I stayed here.'

'It was mine, too.'

'Go *on*!' She looked astonished, then began to laugh.

'What's so amusing?'

'I dunno – I suppose I didn't realize that men ever had a first time.'

He began to laugh too. They kissed, then he ran his hand tenderly across her belly and said: 'And I don't think we did too badly for a couple of beginners, do you?'

It was the end of July and the roads were white with dust as they drove through Bury St Edmunds and out into the country beyond. They arrived as the afternoon heat was cooling a little, and Lizzie said, 'Oh – fancy putting such a beautiful big house so close to the road!'

'I'm afraid it's only one of the lodges,' Dully replied, and nodded to the old woman who bobbed a respectful curtsey from the open doorway.

Lined on either side with giant chestnut trees, the south avenue seemed interminably long, and with each minute that passed Lizzie's nervousness increased.

'What shall I say? Will I have to curtsey to anyone?'

'No, of course not.' He held her hand, but she sensed that he too was apprehensive.

The arrival surpassed her worst fears. Reaching the end of the tunnel of trees, they drove between acres of smooth grass, and there spread before them was the vast rambling presence of Reve itself. It was far bigger than Liverpool Street Station, bigger than St Paul's Cathedral, and as they drew closer she became aware that the entrance to the central block of the building was adorned by a motionless guard of honour: maids in caps and starched aprons, men in black tailcoats and, even more alarming, men wearing yellow coats and black knee-breeches, white stockings and white wigs. All told, there must have been close on a hundred people in various sorts of costume, each one of them staring impassively in the direction of the approaching carriage.

'Dully, for God's sake let's turn back!'

'Sshhh, it'll be all right. . . .'

So they alighted, and passed between the double row of bowing, curtseying, forelock-touching figures and a large man, sombrely clad and portentous as a prime minister, stepped forward and wished them long life and every happiness on behalf of the household staff and estate workers and tenants. Dully smiled and said a few appropriate words in reply; and, clutching his arm, Lizzie found herself face to face with the family drawn up in readiness in the great marble hall.

The soaring pillars, the statues – some of them of life-sized men on horseback – and the groups of big faded flags hanging from a balcony, all added to the sense of unreality, and it was the sudden desperate decision to treat the whole thing like the big scene from a Gaiety production that saved her. Her shoulders went back, her head went up, and she glided forward in the Gov'nor's approved manner, and seizing the hand nearest to her said: 'How do you dooo? Charmed, I'm sure-ah.'

The hand belonged to a small and rather tubby lady dressed, like the other females, in mourning. She smiled, murmured something, then reached up and touched Lizzie's cheek with her own as a sort of token kiss.

Lizzie moved on, gracious, charming, sparkling: 'How do you dooo? And how do *you* dooo?' There didn't seem to be anyone of her own age, and they all regarded her with a grave dignity which was at least better than the freezing contempt she had feared. She heard Dully, just behind her, saying, 'Hullo, Aunt Minna – yes, of course I remember . . . Uncle Badger, jolly nice to see you again. . . .'

When every hand had been shaken, the small tubby lady suggested that Lizzie might care to withdraw in order to rest and refresh herself from the dust and fatigue of the journey. Obediently she allowed herself to be led through to the staircase hall – oak-panelled, but almost equally vast – and along the upper balcony to a broad corridor where one of the massive doors opened into what had been designated her own private suite.

Although the sun was still warm, a bright fire burned in the sitting room grate, and a silver bowl of roses and carnations stood on the writing table in the window. An open doorway disclosed the bedroom, and the four-poster hung with pale blue watered silk. Her trunks had been unpacked and the pink-cheeked young woman in attendance dropped a curtsey and said that she had the honour of being Her Ladyship's new personal maid. If Her Ladyship required anything, would she please ring?

In a stifled voice Lizzie agreed to do so, and as soon as the door had closed cast herself down in an armchair and lay back, with her legs stuck out in front and her hands cupped over the baby.

'Oh Ma,' she said aloud. 'I just wish you could see me now.'

Then someone tapped on the door. It was Dully, and she held out her arms.

'Did I do all right?'

'You were splendid!'

'But I can't get over the size of everything – as if it was all built for a family of giants.'

'Yes, I'd forgotten what a wandering old pile it is.'

'And where's your room? Oh Dully, I don't want – '

'Don't worry, I'm only next door.' He kissed her.

'But you will sleep here with me, won't you?'

'I've a feeling my bed won't be slept in very often.'

A maid brought tea on a silver tray and set it down on the table by Lizzie's side. Beaming with delight, she fell upon the tiny watercress sandwiches, then with her mouth full began to pour the tea. She handed a cup and saucer to Dully, then nipped up a couple more sandwiches.

'I get so hungry these days.'

'Don't eat too much now, I gather we're in for a full-blown banquet this evening. I'd no idea they kept up the style like this.'

222

'But they're quite nice, aren't they? Much nicer than I expected them to be.'

'Quite honestly, I don't remember half of them.'

'And it will be all right, won't it, Dully? Us being here, and everything?'

'It's going to be wonderful.' He smiled at her fondly. 'Anywhere's wonderful, where you are.'

Wearing a loosely fitting black frock with a low square neckline, Lizzie sailed down to dinner on her husband's arm, prepared for another Gaiety performance. Most of the family was gathered in the saloon, and the murmur of voices seemed to float through the enormous space and lose itself in the misty heights of the painted ceiling.

She became detached from Dully, and an old girl with faded eyes and a parchment skin drew her to one side and said: 'What a dear boy Henry is! We so look forward to him being head of the family.'

'How kaind of you to say so!'

'And I'm perfectly certain that we shall all love you, too.'

Her friendliness melted Lizzie's grandeur a little. 'I don't mind letting on we've both been a bit nervous. Me, especially.'

'That is because you are sensitive. I am a poetess, and can always tell these things.'

'Really? I beg pardon, I didn't quite catch your name.'

'I am Henry's second cousin and my name is Lavinia,' she said. 'But the family always calls me Lavvy.'

It went on for while, the smiles and pleasant expressions of cordiality, while the great house lay all around them, splendid and echoing. *Lavvy*, thought Lizzie. Only someone very high-bred would let themselves be called that.

When dinner was announced, she and Dully were smilingly accorded the honour of leading the procession into the dining room. The table shone with silver and twinkled with eighteenth-century glass, and the light from a hundred candles illuminated the Claudes and Géricaults lining the walls and brought them disconcertingly to life. At least, the people in them looked more alive than the footmen posted at intervals behind the diners' chairs.

They were all seated and the consommé was being served when a small, furtive-looking man sidled rapidly into the room and slid into the one vacant chair, which happened to be nearest the doors. His appearance was greeted with expressions of surprised approval, and he half-raised his hand in acknowledgement. He had thick dark hair and a blue chin, and Lizzie was interested to see that he kept his head lowered and spoke to no one. He seemed totally set apart.

'That is Merton, the brother of Woodstock and Badger,' said the lady on Lizzie's right. 'We didn't imagine he would come, as he is a recluse.'

'Oh? Fancy!' (What on earth's a recluse?)

'He lives in a tree.'

'Oh, I say. Doesn't he ever fall out?'

'If he does, I feel sure he would never tell us. He seldom feels the need to communicate with anyone, but for all that he has a kindly disposition.'

'And nobody interferes with him?'

'Gracious, no. Why should they?'

Lizzie had now established that the lady to whom she was talking was the Dowager Countess. She had been the proper Countess until Lizzie's appearance, and it seemed awful to think that she had been demoted, particularly by a stranger. And it was even more dreadful to think that she had so recently suffered a double bereavement – to lose your husband and your son must be really awful – and Lizzie wanted to offer her condolences, but hesitated for fear of appearing presumptuous.

So she finished her soup in silence, and under the table Dully patted her knee and whispered: 'See the old boy sitting next to Cousin Lavvy? That's Uncle Woodstock, and I remember him telling me when I was a boy that he was the only male Florence Nightingale ever kissed.'

'Florence Nightingale – the *nurse*?'

'Yes. She was his godmother and he was only a few weeks old. I don't know the lady in purple, sitting next to him. . . .'

'Do they all live here? I know it's big enough, but – '

224

'Search me. But I rather imagine they mustered all ranks for this special occasion.'

'I'll never learn all their names, Dully – never!'

'Don't worry, you won't be the only one.'

As the meal progressed the conversation became increasingly animated. Dazedly watching from behind a gracious smile, Lizzie thought, Even the Gov'nor couldn't have dreamed this up; even this room alone would take up most of the auditorium, let alone the stage. . . .

There were only two ways in which the Gaiety could have shown itself superior; one was in the music (here, there was none), and the other was in the physical beauty of the performers, and Lizzie studied them all afresh from over the pineapple russe. All the Dullingham profiles had long straight noses, high cheekbones and eyes that slanted up at the outer corners when they smiled. Some slanted more than others, but apart from Dully, none of them could be called very good-looking, mainly because they were all getting on. Practically every head was at least lightly tinged with grey – Uncle Merton, the tree-dweller, was the only startling exception, apart from Dully and herself. Oh yes, they were all getting on, all right. In their forties at least.

With the arrival of the port and brandy, the ladies showed no sign of retiring. On the contrary, the Dowager Countess ('*Do* call me Minna, my dear,') banged loudly on the polished table with a silver sugar castor and cried: 'We will have silence now, as I believe Badger wishes to propose a toast!'

'Badger,' Lizzie whispered to Dully. 'How did he get to be called that?'

'A nickname, probably. He's the brother of Woodstock and Merton.'

Cigar smoke was drifting now, and by this stage in the proceedings Lizzie was no more than mildly surprised to see a high-bosomed, ringleted lady puffing away with the rest of them.

Then Badger clambered to his feet, cleared his throat and began to address them all.

'Family,' he said, 'we are gathered together in this

225

particular room and on this particular evening for two reasons. One joyous and one melancholy, and I suggest we take the melancholy one first. A bare six months ago we suffered a grievous blow in the form of a double bereavement. A blow from which we have scarcely recovered. Our dear Berry George Edward Henry, eighth Earl Dullingham, passed from us in what might be termed the very prime of his sunset. A loving friend, a boon companion and a wise and responsible patriach. And as if his loss alone were not sufficient for us to bear, his dear and only son Rollo passed from us almost simultaneously. Poor young Rollo! His life stretched before him, rosy with promise, and alas we will never know to what heights of achievement and happiness he might have risen. Our hearts continue to overflow with sympathy for dear Minna, so cruelly deprived. . . .'

He paused, and everyone murmured a wordless agreement. Beneath the loose folds of her skirt Lizzie could feel the baby kicking.

'But now to the joyous reason for our presence here together,' went on Badger, his tone lighter, his face brightening. 'In the midst of death we are in life – *ne cede malis*, as Virgil so rightly said – and it is time now to put away our grief and to welcome the new head of our family, dear old William's boy Henry, as the ninth Earl Dullingham. Let us raise our glasses.'

They did so, the Dullingham smiles tilting their eyes as they all turned towards him. 'To dear Henry,' they said.

'And furthermore,' went on Badger, now well into his stride, 'we have an additional cause for celebration in the form – in the *divine* form, if I may say so – of Henry's recently wedded wife. Too engrossed in our own sorrows, I dare say, we had no inkling that such a lovely young lady was about to be presented as a new member of our family, and I ask you to join with me in welcoming her as the new Countess Dullingham. May her radiance never dim, her beauty never fade!'

The glasses were raised again and Lizzie, blushing deeply, saw the strange, furtive-looking Merton take a hasty sip. Their eyes met briefly, then she became aware of Dully releasing her hand as he rose to his feet.

He thanked them for the warmth of their welcome, touched briefly on the double bereavement and on the sad part he had had to play in it, and ended by admitting a little ruefully that he had never envisaged himself as the head of any sort of family, let alone this one. 'But with my wife by my side and warmed by the affection of you all, I promise to do my very best.'

They applauded, and with the coming of darkness the candlelight became brilliantly reflected in the huge windows. It was like watching a separate but identical performance of the proceedings. Her Gaiety smile flagging a little with fatigue, Lizzie noticed the dark and rather crabbed form of Uncle Merton slide unobtrusively from his chair and depart.

There were speeches of an informal nature, some rather rambling and others more to the point, but the sentiments were all roughly similar: poor old Berry, poor young Rollo, but now welcome to Henry and his bride. Gratifying though it was, it struck Lizzie as rather hasty and certainly a bit heartless. If she had been the Dowager Countess (Aunt Minna, that is), she would have been in floods of tears about her husband and son. If she had been *any* of the others she would have been, but wherever she looked their expressions betrayed no more than a relaxed geniality. She could only suppose that that was how it was with the bon ton.

They left the table after midnight, and she noticed how the slightly younger ones helped the older ones as they slowly left the dining room. Even one of the footmen was stifling a yawn behind his gloved hand.

They stood in small groups in the saloon, saying goodnight, and almost faint with tiredness, Lizzie whispered to Dully not to be late up to bed. He was talking to the lady who had smoked a cigar, but he nodded and smiled and kissed his fingers to her.

She was accompanied up the staircase by Cousin Lavvy, the poetess, who said what a splendid evening it had been and kissed her goodnight at her door.

Her personal maid was waiting up for her and came forward to help her undress, but Lizzie dismissed her, mumbling that they would start doing things the proper way tomorrow. Within five minutes she was in bed and asleep.

*

Dear Ma and Pa,

Just a line to let you know I'm getting on all right here. It's the biggest place you ever saw and Dully really is an earl. In fact he's other things as well but I can't remember the names. There's a lot of family here, all Dullinghams, and I have a job trying to remember who's Sir or Lady or Honourable. But at least they're all very nice to me – even the woman who was the Countess until Dully and I got married. Although she's now called Dowager Countess it's not the same, and I wouldn't have blamed her for being fed up with me coming here and pinching her title but she wasn't. We had a chat about it the other day and she said that rules that people have kept to for five hundred years or so were quite good enough for her. She's very nice, and we call her Aunt Minna.

There's also a nice old boy called Basil George, I think he's an Honourable, but everyone calls him Badger. He's got a spaniel called Eulalie and it sometimes chases Cousin Lavvy's ginger cat when they meet, which isn't all that often because the place is so big. Cousin Lavvy writes poems and I think she's only staying here – a lot of the others have gone home already – but I still can't get over them calling her Lavvy without laughing. But she's very nice to me too and so is Uncle Woodstock who likes playing the piano.

They all seem to have a lot of hobbies which I dare say is a result of never having to work, and some of them take a bit of getting used to. I've never seen a man doing embroidery before but an old chap called Wilfred who was here was doing a set of chair seats. There's also an aunt who's got a parrot that sits on her shoulder and she smokes cigars – not the parrot, ha ha – but the funniest one is Uncle Merton who lives up a tree. I didn't believe it at first, but it's true! It's a great big old beech tree that was planted by somebody famous and it's got a dear little wooden house wedged tight between the branches and he climbs up to it on a ladder. He's very shy and a bit strange – stranger than the others, I mean. I haven't seen him again since the night I arrived.

I still get lost in the house sometimes. We all live in what they call the south wing, which in itself is bigger than any railway

228

station, and then there's still all the rest of it. Whole big areas enough to house an army and doors leading into more and more rooms until you lose count. Really I've never known anything like it.

As for me and Dully we're both well and happy, and judging by the way the baby kicks it's feeling ditto. It's getting a bit heavy to lug around now and I shan't be sorry when it's born. It's due about the middle of November and everybody's very nice about me obviously having it long before I should have. Things like that don't seem to worry them at all – I often wonder what Aunt Netta would make of them all and the way that nothing ever seems to shock them.

Hope the harvest is going well and that you're both in the pink, as this letter leaves me. Please write soon.

Ever your loving daughter
the Countess Lizzie (ha ha!)

It was very nice sitting at her little desk writing letters in her best schoolgirl script and pausing every now and then to look out of the window at the rose garden still massed with colour. She wrote other letters too, but always tore them up into small fragments: 'Dear Mr Edwardes, I'm sorry I left the Gaiety like that. I know I let you down and I really am very sorry but I had to go and I just couldn't face telling anybody why. Thank you for all you did for me and I bet you'll be surprised when I tell you that I am now Countess Dullingham! I still remember all the things you taught me and they have come in very useful. I often think of you and the theatre and the other girls and wish I was back although it is very nice here and I am happily married. Yours sincerely, Liza.

And then, the one she wanted to write most of all: 'My dearest Fairford, I know you are a bounder and that you treated me very badly but I love you and miss you and I would give anything to be with you although I know it would be very painful knowing that I am now married and that you are shortly to be. If only things had turned out different how happy I would be! I am happy in a way with Dully and everyone here is very kind and nice but I would rather be living with you in a cottage or even a tent because I love you and can't forget you. . . .'

229

Then when the letters had been torn up and fed to the small sleepy fire, she would wander downstairs, the silence of the great house sometimes broken by the sound of music or a faraway murmur of voices. Perhaps a lone footman would cross her path and she would unthinkingly smile hullo and be rewarded by a dignified obeisance.

Very gradually she began to learn her way about Reve, passing slowly through one room into the next and occasionally coming upon a small family group sitting together. Smilingly they would invite her to join them and she would do so, and as the conversation invariably reverted to people and places unknown to her she would be free to follow her own thoughts. Living in such a huge house, she wondered whether they made appointments to meet in a certain place at a certain time or whether they came upon one another by happy accident.

Those early weeks constituted a strange interim period in her life; with Dully now involved in mastering the rudiments of estate management, they met only at mealtimes or in the evenings, and she sensed from his preoccupation that the running of Reve was a vast and complicated affair. She found her own interest in the place deepening, and out of her haphazard ramblings developed planned expeditions to various parts of the house. She studied documents in the muniments room, family portraits in the long gallery and marble tombs in the church, but during the early stage of acquaintanceship it was the bricks and stone, the actual fabric of the place that first stirred her affection: the subtle curve of an archway, the silken sweep of a banister beneath her hand, a shaft of sunlight illuminating the beauty of a painted ceiling. The sense of quiet, untroubled infinity that came from the long vistas reminded her of the Cambridgeshire fens.

On one occasion Dully unexpectedly came upon her sitting in the deep window embrasure of what was known as the admiral's room.

'Good *afternoon*.' She spread out her skirts and dipped her head in mock deference. 'Fancy seeing you!'

'What a delightful surprise!' His rather careworn

expression melted into a smile. 'I say, do you come here often?'

'It used to be by accident, because I got lost. But now I come because I like it.'

'You're not too bored here, with nothing to do?'

She shook her head. 'This room is called after Admiral Charles Henry Dullingham, who fell at the Siege of Gibraltar.'

'I know,' he said, and sighed. 'There's an awful lot of them.'

'Admirals?'

'No, Dullinghams. And now here I am in charge of them all, past and present.'

'Oh dear.' She looked at him in wonderment. 'Are they getting you down a bit?'

'In a way. I suppose it takes a bit of getting used to, suddenly finding yourself head of a large establishment.'

'I think Reve is a beautiful place.'

'So do I. But apart from the London house, I've discovered that we own three other places as well – a mouldering old pile on the Yorkshire moors plus fifty thousand acres; there's a fortified manor house let to a shipping magnate down in Dorset; and another place going to rack and ruin somewhere in Ireland. We're going to sell them, if only we can find a buyer. Oh yes, and I'm told that we also have some kind of manorial rights in France. The family's supposed to have strong connections with the old Ducs du Berry.'

'Is that why your uncle was called Berry?'

'Seems so. A lot of the Dullingham earls were given that name.'

'It sounds nice. . . . If the baby's a boy shall we call him that?'

'Might as well.' He kissed the line of rich coppery hair on her temple. 'Looks as if he'll be saddled with an earldom too, one of these days.'

'You hate all this, don't you?'

'No, of course not.' He spoke with an effort. 'There's just

231

so much to learn and so much to do, if one's to take it seriously.'

It was at moments like that that she wished she loved him; only love, she sensed, could help him and give him the support he needed.

'It'll all come right,' she said. 'In the meantime, Cousin Lavvy's sent a little matinee jacket for the baby. Come, and I'll show you.'

'I can't just now.' He snapped open his pocket watch. 'I promised to meet Briggs in half an hour.'

'Who's Briggs?'

'The estate manager. I'm going round the farms with him.'

'See you at dinner, then.' She eased herself off the window seat and began to walk away. Quickly he came after her and put his arms round her waist. 'I love you, Liza-Lizzie.'

'I love you too,' she replied, wishing that she meant it.

The late Earl Dullingham had been a fair-minded and conscientious man, a guardian of his tenants and a worthy custodian of his acres, and studying the massive leather-bound account books which detailed income and expenditure to the last farthing, Dully noted that every completed page had been duly initialled by His Lordship. The care and attention to detail was both impressive and oddly dispiriting to one of his rootless, loveless upbringing, and as Briggs, in starched collar and leather gaiters, brought forth more and more documents containing leases, tenures, easements, freeholds and copyholds, his depression increased.

Two hundred estate workers at Reve alone, plus seventy-five indoor staff if one counted boot-boys and laundry-maids, all of them now dependent upon his care; the burden appalled him, and more than once he was secretly tempted to sell off his entire inheritance and buy a small house of, say, no more than ten bedrooms, where he could live for the rest of his life in carefree seclusion with Liza-Lizzie.

But there was no point in making any sort of decision until he had at last mastered the system employed in running the estate, and he dutifully fought down boredom (The View of General Court Earl Thomas Henry John Berry Dullingham Viscount Reve Baron Fylmore, Lord of the Manor of Reve Magna in the County of Suffolk as Grantee of our Sovereign King Lord George the Fourth there Holden for the same Manor . . .) and repugnance (Three score sucking pigs slaughtered this Day . . .) and finally, a stealthily growing resentment of Briggs' constant and loving reiteration of Uncle Berry's virtues.

Not only had His Lordship the late Earl been kind, firm, generous, honourable and nobody's fool, he had been, perhaps most important of all, a good sportsman. A crack shot, a fearless huntsman, a skilled fisherman, he had also been a champion oarsman, a strong swimmer and an intrepid mountaineer. Yet there was nothing he enjoyed so much as books and poetry (very strong on the classics was His Lordship), and many a time he had been observed to shed a tear over a particularly touching performance of a special song by Schubert (doubtless Your Lordship has heard of the gentleman concerned?) which had something to do with a miller's daughter. . . .

'I fear His Lordship will be missed for many a long year, My Lord,' Briggs would sigh. 'In the meantime we had better get back to the list of estate cottages at present occupied by retired members of His – I beg pardon – of Your Lordship's staff. . . .'

No wonder he felt a usurper, a miserable sheep in lion's clothing.

But the student ability to learn and assimilate had not deserted him, and within a few weeks he was familiar with the broad outline of Reve's financial and administrative history. He knew most of the rules and rituals appertaining to the running of it, and if there were any facts of which he was unsure he at least knew where to look them up.

Driving round with Briggs in a dogcart, he met the tenant farmers and their families, the farm labourers, the woodsmen, gardeners and gamekeepers. It became a matter of pride to memorize their names, and he was quick to realize that they were even more anxious to create a good impression than he was; as the occupants of tied cottages they had far more to lose, poor devils.

Very gradually the place began to cast its old spell over him. Hazy late summer sun turned the parkland to dreaming gold, twinkled through morning-misted cobwebs and sank in a blaze of glory that silhouetted the stone goddesses adorning the roofs of the south front. It came to him that instead of selling Reve he need only dismiss Briggs, and he began to feel better, but it was the morning that they drove to the foxhound kennels that marked his true debut as the new Earl Dullingham.

The head kennelman released the dogs for His Lordship's inspection and they swarmed round his legs, a panting jostling mass of liver-brown on white. Loose-limbed and clumsy-footed, they leered up at him, whining, yelping, wagging their tails and wiping their salivating jaws across his breeches.

'Down, Chester! Get away, Frippence! They're getting ready for the season, M'Lord. . . .' The kennelman caressed the bobbing heads with rough affection. He too seemed to leer.

'I'm afraid they've seen their last season at Reve,' Dully said. 'I'm putting the pack up for sale.'

Briggs and the kennelman appeared to think he was joking. He looked from one startled, disbelieving face to the other and said: 'There will be no more meets at Reve and I shall not allow any hunt to intrude anywhere on my property. See to it, Briggs.'

Speechlessly Briggs nodded, then indicated that they should return to the dogcart.

'You may drive back. I prefer to walk,' Dully said, and nodding good day, disentangled himself from the swirling hounds and marched blithely down the lane. Not only had he laid some miserable kind of ghost to rest, he had wiped away the painful memory of a shocked and sobbing boy trying to wash away the daubs of animal blood from his face.

Walking back to the house along the side of the lake, he paused to watch a pair of mute swans gliding in midstream with their three grey-clad young. The cob was in the lead, wings slightly arched, magnificent in his watchful pride, while his mate paddled silently in the rear of the last cygnet. The airy grace and strength, and the palpable sense of family unity, moved him very much. He told himself that he too would have three children and that they would grow up in the steadfast arms of a home where they would know nothing of loneliness or fear. Everything was possible on that triumphant sun-dappled morning with the loosestrife in bloom and the three young swans with all their lives before them. Everything was possible; even that Liza-Lizzie would one day come to him and say she loved him, and looking into her eyes he would know for the first time that it was really true.

Like his late uncle Berry, Dully was nobody's fool.

'I believe the village doctor to be quite competent, but our family physician is in Harley Street in London, and he will be sent for in good time,' said the Dowager Countess Dullingham, in other words Aunt Minna. 'I should think two nurses on loan from the cottage hospital plus our own staff should prove sufficient for the accouchement, and then it is merely a matter of taking our time over the appointment of a suitable and experienced children's nurse to take control of the nursery staff.'

'Yes,' said Lizzie.

They were taking a turn along the broad gravelled path that led through a series of yew arches into a sequence of gardens, each one enclosed in dark green hedging like the walls of a room. They had traversed the knot garden and were halfway through the rose garden, where the last of the summer's blooms tilted their faces to the dying sun. Baronne Prévost, Boule de Neige, Louise Odier, all of them filling the air with their incomparable sweetness.

'*Never sure, since high in Paradise, by the four rivers the first roses blew,*' quoted Aunt Minna. Then taking Lizzie's arm with a fond little gesture, she added: 'But my dear child,

235

you must not think that I am trying to take charge of the proceedings. First and foremost the baby's arrival concerns you and dear Henry, and I am perfectly certain that the one person whom you will need close at hand will be your own mama.'

Lizzie had already thought of this. Heavy now, and plagued by cramp in the calves and a desire to pass water every half-hour, she had longed spasmodically for the rough country comfort of Edwina. Oh Ma, I'm so sick of lugging this great ole lump around, but I'm not all that keen on getting shot of it, either. What's it really like, Ma? How bad was it when you had me?

Then at other times she felt that the task of introducing her mother to the slow, sumptuous world of Reve was more than she could tackle. Let her come down and view the baby when it was all over and its mother back on form. Perhaps she and Pa could come for Christmas or something.

'I don't really know,' Lizzie said finally. 'I'm in a funny sort of state and I don't really know what I want.'

'Perfectly understandable,' sympathized Aunt Minna. 'I felt much the same when my own child was due.'

'You only had the one?' Lizzie skirted round the delicate subject of Rollo.

'Alas, yes. He was my sole chick.' There was a thread of sadness in Aunt Minna's voice, but no self-pity. Aware that this was a good opportunity to express her sympathy and possibly draw closer to her, Lizzie nevertheless remained silent. Because of the wilful, unpredictable nature of her moods she felt fairly certain that she, if not Aunt Minna, would start to cry.

'My parents had a son older than me, but he died at three days,' she said finally. 'Which luckily didn't give them time to get fond of him.'

'Your arrival must have been a great solace.'

'I think they wanted another boy because of the farm, but we got along pretty well on the whole.'

'I look forward to meeting them,' Aunt Minna said. 'And now I think we should turn back before you become overtired.'

236

They did so, and passing through the final archway saw, across the expanse of lawn, members of the family with rugs and shawls grouped on the terrace for afternoon tea.

The pains began on the morning of November the thirteenth, and for several hours they were no more obtrusive than the distant rumble of thunder.

Sir James Royle had arrived from Harley Street the day before, and a nursing sister from the cottage hospital sat knitting close by the bedroom window. Dully had been with Lizzie since first light, swallowing no more than a cup of tea for breakfast, but when the pains suddenly sharpened he was abruptly banished from the room.

Clinging, bent double, to the back of a chair, Lizzie cried out that she wanted her mother's presence after all. The words were relayed to Dully, waiting in her private sitting room; grateful to be of use, he gave orders that a carriage was to be instantly despatched to Damperdown Farm.

Sir James, in grey frock-coat and spats, made Lizzie lie on the bed while he applied a small silver ear trumpet to her drum-tight belly. He listened intently, then a slow smile lit up his features.

'Aha! I do declare our young viscount is on the move, My Lady!'

'It's a girl,' Lizzie said crossly. 'I'm the one who's having it and I can feel it's a girl.'

'Whichever it may be, I declare the time of arrival' – the physician clicked open his watch – 'to be approximately that of late teatime. In the meanwhile, I suggest that nurse should administer a series of hot towels to the abdomen.'

He went away and Lizzie, who had risen restlessly from the bed, was persuaded back to it. The hot towels appeared to increase the severity of the pains and sweat seemed to burst from the roots of her hair. She tried to wrench the towels away, but the nurse held them firmly in place. Her hands smelt of carbolic and her breath of peppermint.

'Try to go *with* the pains, My Lady,' she advised. 'Try not to fight them.'

It's gone wrong, thought Lizzie, lying temporarily at

237

rest. It shouldn't take all this time and all this pain. The cord's got round its neck and it can't shift either way. That's what happened to our cow once and there's no gainsaying it can't happen to humans as well. They'll have to cut it out. . . .

She braced herself for the next bout of pain as it came rolling in, gathering strength and then hitting her like a giant wave.

Gaspingly she asked the time.

'Twenty-five minutes past two, My Lady.'

'What time's tea when it's late?'

'That I couldn't say, My Lady. But the second stage should be starting before long.'

'Jesus, how many stages are there?'

'Only the two, My Lady. Once you start bearing down it will be much easier.'

Tea's generally at four, she thought. So let's say late tea is four-thirty. Can I last out until then? What's it now? Must be getting on for three. . . .

'Can I have a drink?'

'Only a sip, My Lady, otherwise you will be sick.'

Greedily Lizzie seized the glass in both hands and drained it. She vomited and, rolling the soiled sheet from under her, the nurse said, 'There, there. Young mothers never really know what's best for them, the poor little dears.'

'I've got to go,' Edwina said to Walter at ten to four that afternoon. 'It's no use, I've got to go. I can hear her calling me.'

'It'll all be over be time you get there.'

'I can't help that. I know she's in trouble and it must be the baby, and I've got to go to her.'

'I'd better harness up, then,' Walter said, and began to replace his boots. 'What time train you reckon on getting?'

'There's the four-thirty. I'd best catch that.'

'And where's their nearest station?'

'It must be Bury St Edmunds. I'll most likely get a station fly from there.'

Hurriedly she packed cambric nightgown, slippers and flannel dressing gown, added washing sponge, brush and comb and a handful of spare hairpins. She changed into her black bombazine and the straw hat that had seen service at Lizzie's wedding, and then she was ready. Walter helped her up beside him, and with a flap of the reins across the mare's back they drove off towards Stonea.

'Shouldn't you have let them know?' Walter asked as they were halfway there. 'They might be struck all of a heap.'

'I can't help it if they are,' Edwina said, grim-faced. 'It's Lizzie I'm worried about.'

'I can smell rain on the wind. Hope you don't get a wetting.'

'Don't reckon I'll shrink. Listen, there's half a rabbit pie in the larder and some stewed apples in a basin. You've enough bread to last you, but don't forget to scald the milk if it looks thundery while I'm gone.'

He left her at Stonea Station, and tucking her ticket inside her glove, she watched him drive slowly back down the flat expanse of the Sixteen Foot level. By the time the train arrived he was no more than a dot on the empty skyline.

The latest possible time for afternoon tea had come and gone, and the pains had merely tightened their grip. Hollow-eyed and soaked with sweat, Lizzie lay between sleeping and waking, between living and dying, as she waited for the next onslaught. Sir James took her pulse, checked her heartbeat and applied the silver ear trumpet to her tortured belly every fifteen minutes, while both the nurse and her assistant remained constant in their attention, soothing, smoothing, and applying cologne-soaked pads to Lizzie's forehead.

'Whasstime?'

'Half-past five, My Lady.'

'Howmushlonger?'

'The second stage is almost here and then we can give you something to help the pain. Try to sleep a little now.'

Sleep. Tattered fragments of it. Swimming into un-
consciousness, grasping at the shadows, basking in the
intermittent silence, then the first slow griping of the pain
again, its gathering strength and its remorseless surging
through her body. She hit out at the nurse, and the nurse
caught her fists in her own cool carbolic hands and held
them tight – tight – tight as Lizzie rose to the crest of a new
and even higher wave. She remained poised, every nerve at
snapping point, then collapsed shuddering and sobbing
down the other side. The nurse wiped her tears and stroked
back the lumps of wet hair from her forehead.

'That's one more of the old nasties out of the way, isn't it,
My Lady? Soon be over now.'

But this time there was no peace even in the trough of the
wave. Nightmare visions of wreathing shapes, tormented
limbs and screaming faces filled the hot blank space behind
her closed eyes. Hatred and bestiality flickered blood red
and Bible black, and she saw Bessie Hinton – she *was* Bessie
Hinton – lying racked on the prison straw at Ely, torn apart
in childbirth and then strangled on the end of a rope for
everyone to see.

The monstrous cruelty of death and dying and the barren
loneliness of suffering were suddenly so real and so dreadful
to her that they blotted out the next gathering wave in a long
high animal scream, and outside in the corridor Uncle
Badger took the ashen-faced Dully firmly by the arm and
marched him away.

'At last – at last,' murmured Sir James, and removing his
grey frock-coat and turning back his shirt cuffs, prepared to
administer chloroform.

While the Reve carriage horses were resting and Walter was
entertaining the cockaded coachman to rabbit pie and
farm-brewed beer in the kitchen, Edwina was pacing the
railway station at Ely, waiting for the next train to Bury St
Edmunds.

The discovery that the train from Stonea would not take
her all the way to Bury St Edmunds came as an unpleasant
shock, for there was something daunting and distinctly

hazardous about changing trains for someone who had never been on one before.

And of course it would have to be Ely, she thought. Of all places to choose they would have to set me down at Ely, wouldn't they, where poor old Bessie Hinton met her Maker.

Bessie Hinton. She hadn't seriously thought about her for years, and now, in her heightened state of emotion, a prickle of superstitious fear ruffled the back of her neck. She wondered whether the gaol was anywhere near the station; she wondered what it looked like, and for the first time her mind switched from its agitated niggling about Lizzie and began to picture in heightened detail the last hours of poor Bessie.

Poor Bessie, a strumpet and a troublemaker no doubt, but no woman on this earth deserved to suffer as she had. Giving birth on a heap of straw in a prison cell then being torn away from her baby and strung up on a gibbet outside in the street for all the world to see. It was horrible – horrible – and she tried to calm herself with visions of Lizzie having her own baby in a rich and beautiful place filled with loving sympathy and clever doctors and, once this damn-blasted train arrived, the solace of a mother who understood her with a deep painful love that even now was forcing tears to the surface.

She accosted a meandering porter and asked him roughly when the Bury train was due.

'Twelve minutes.'

'And how long does it take to get there?'

'Depends' – he removed his cap and scratched his head before replacing it again – 'if you have to change at Snailwell Heath. Sometimes you do and sometimes you don't.'

'How'll I know if I do?'

'Reckon the guard'll shout it out.'

'If he's as spolk-witted as you, I doubt he will.' Edwina continued her pacing, and when the train steamed in climbed hastily into an empty compartment and sat with her eyes closed until they left Ely and its evil associations well behind.

It was dark by the time she arrived at Bury and she hastened towards the cab rank outside the station.

'I want to go to a big house called Reve,' she said. 'It's somewhere hereabouts and I want to get there quick.'

The cab driver glanced at her curiously in the wan light, and when finally they arrived he set her down outside the main servants' entrance because of her carpet bag and country boots.

Tired, confused and dreadfully anxious, it seemed to take an unnecessarily long while to explain who she was. They too were looking somewhat anxious and strained, and kept saying that Her Ladyship was indisposed and not receiving.

'Her Ladyship as you call her is my daughter!' Edwina finally exploded. 'And she's not indisposed – she's bearing a child!'

They conducted her via passages and back staircases to the south front, and crossing the great marble hall she glanced through open doorways and saw one or two small groups of people who looked as if they were waiting for something.

Up the enormous staircase and along the broad corridor with its rows of doors – wondering however do they find their way about? – and then finally she was shown into a charming room with comfortable chairs and a fire and great bowls of autumn flowers spicing the air.

She wasn't sure whether she was meant to sit down or not, so, tired as she was, remained standing. She heard the low murmur of voices, then a door opened and a uniformed nurse appeared. She began to say something quiet and polite, but over her shoulder in the room beyond Edwina caught sight of Lizzie. She rushed forward, shoving the nurse aside, and Lizzie looked up and saw her and cried: 'Ma! Oh Ma, come and see what I've just got!'

Unaware of Sir James and the two nurses, unaware even of Dully, who was sitting on the side of the bed, she collapsed on her knees between the two new parents and peered with streaming eyes into the depths of the white shawl Lizzie was holding. He was a big, strong baby, with a cheerful thatch of bright red hair and, even at two hours old, eyes that seemed to tilt up at the corners in a smile.

Recollected in later years, the occasion of young Berry's birth seemed surprisingly out of keeping with conventional late-Victorian behaviour – no relish of recent suffering, no pious maunderings or pompous medical edicts – but perhaps the Dullinghams had always been a law unto themselves.

Glowing like a June rose, Lizzie received the family at her bedside, and Edwina, tired, bemused, and somewhat out of her depth, shook hands with what seemed like dozens of them while Dully and Uncle Woodstock (who had been kissed by Florence Nightingale) opened bottles of champagne, filled and refilled glasses, and Sir James Royle, offering yet another toast, described his patient as an angel of fortitude and the mother of fighting men.

'Who's he supposed to fight with?' Lizzie's fingers caressed the baby's soft red hair.

'A mere figure of speech, My Lady,' amended Sir James. 'The mother of peaceable men.'

'That's better. My son's not going to fight with anyone – and I mean son, not sons.'

'Don't declare your intentions too soon, my dear,' smiled Uncle Badger, then turning to Dully murmured: 'I think this is an appropriate time to signal the breaching of a barrel down in the servants' hall.'

A bonfire was lit on the crest of Chanter's Way, the highest point on the Reve estate, and its ruddy glare illuminated the startled sheep and then the human figures dancing to the sound of fiddle and concertina. The vicar of Reve Magna was alerted, and under his direction the bellringers rang a tumbling tumult of joy that could be heard from Barrow to Great Barton, from Fornham to Horningsheath.

'It's a boy! It's a boy!'

It was also the new Viscount Reve, and the moment came when Lizzie instinctively opened her arms to the Dowager Countess, and with equal lack of predeliberation the

Dowager Countess raised Lizzie's shoulders from the pillow and embraced her in return. There was no need for words when each shared the other's feelings, and the spontaneous gesture lasted them for the rest of their lives.

'She looks quite a nice woman,' Edwina said to Lizzie on the following day. 'Not the uppity sort like your poor aunt Netta was.'

'She's been through hard times, poor soul, what with losing her husband and son so quick, and then me prancing in and even taking her title away from her. But she never lets it show.'

'I suppose it's their dignity. I mean, the ole Queen never lets anything show either, does she?'

'Don't reckon I'll ever get like that.'

'Maybe not, but you're getting a little bit like them already.'

'How? You mean I'm getting hoity-toity?'

'No. . . .' Edwina gazed at the organdie-draped cradle standing at the opposite side of the bed. 'It's hard to say what I mean, but of course all of this is bound to change you, isn't it?'

'I don't feel any different, except that I've had *him*.' She too looked towards the cradle.

'I don't mind telling you neither your pa nor me believed he was really a nerl. Not really. And then when we found out that he really was, we still couldn't help worrying because it didn't seem natural somehow. I mean, not and him marrying our daughter.'

'He didn't just marry me because he got me into trouble.'

'Anyone can see that. The poor chap dotes on you, and I only hope' – Edwina looked suddenly severe – 'that you dote on him a bit in return.'

'Oh I do, Ma – I do!' Lizzie said with more fervour than truth. 'I've got the very best husband in the world!'

'That's all right, then.' Edwina stood up and jabbed a loose hairpin back in place. 'And now I must go and pack my bag and get back to your Pa. Gawd knows what he'll get up to without me behind him.'

'Oh Ma, must you? You only came last night.'

'I know, but there's things to see to.'

'What things? He's got Reuben.'

'Yes, but . . .' Edwina turned away. 'I mean, I can't go on staying here because I haven't got the right clothes and things, have I? It's been all right so far because I've just stayed up here with you, but if I went downstairs among all them I wouldn't be wearing the right things and I wouldn't know any of the right things to say and do. I can't frame about like that at my age.'

'But I *want* you here, Ma.'

'There you go. That's what I say. You're changing into being someone who only has to ring a little bell and someone else'll come and answer it and do exactly what you want. Well, I'm happy I've seen you and the baby – I do wish you'd called him Arthur – and I'm glad everything's so nice, I really am, but Pa will have finished up all the food I left him, and besides' – she turned round and impulsively tweaked a lock of Lizzie's hair – 'he'll be in a rare ole state to hear all the news.'

'Yes. I s'pose so. . . .'

'And you've got to rest and get strong again. You must have had a bad time with a baby that size.'

'If I did, I've forgotten it. Oh Ma, isn't he delectable?'

Delectable. What sort of a word's that? thought Edwina, going over to the cradle. Then her eyes softened. 'He's just about the finest boy I've ever seen and I'm proud as paint to be his granma.'

She went home by carriage, enjoying the comfort and perplexed by the problem of whether she should tip the coachman. When they finally arrived at Damperdown Farm she decided to compromise and offer him a jar of tomato chutney.

'Thank you kindly, Madam,' he said, touching his hat with his whip, 'but the gentleman very kindly gave me one yesterday.'

Walter and Edwina were nevertheless persuaded to attend their grandson's christening. It was held in the private chapel at Reve and the Bishop of St Edmundsbury and Ipswich officiated, assisted by the Vicar of Reve Magna.

245

It was a day of brilliant sunshine with a gusty wind making the red and gold leaves swirl and eddy in a mad, dying dance. The first snap of autumn's fingers had already touched the heliotrope and the late lilies, but the sheltered rose garden was still starred with the poised and trusting faces of late summer blooms. Having intimated that the new viscount's christening should mark the end of full mourning, the Dowager Countess duly appeared in parma violet adorned with black braid, while the other ladies wore lavender or grey. Lizzie, in a small feathered bonnet and a dark blue costume with a nipped-in waist, looked pale and preoccupied and Aunt Miriam, the one who smoked cigars, touched her arm and said, 'My dear, I do hope you are not up and about too soon.'

Lizzie smiled and shook her head, then busied herself with making Edwina and Walter feel at home. Everything was wonderful, everything was fine, except that Fairford was to be one of the godfathers.

To begin with, she had wildly resisted the idea when Dully suggested it.

'But Fairford's my oldest friend.'

'I don't care – I don't want him here!'

'I thought you liked him.'

'Well I don't, and I never did.'

Dully remained silent for a moment or two, then said quietly: 'He's married now, you know.'

'Oh?' She kept her head bent in an effort to hide her scarlet cheeks. 'What's that got to do with me?'

'Nothing in particular. I just thought you might be interested.'

'Did he marry that whatsername girl – Bugbice, or something?'

'Martha Bogbice. Yes, the wedding was in Boston – no end of a splash, so I hear.'

'Well, I don't want him splashing round my baby.'

'He's my baby too, Liza-Lizzie.'

Unnerved by the idea of seeing Fairford again and suffering from the emotional turmoil now diagnosed as post-natal depression, Lizzie cried. Appalled by what seemed to be his own callousness, Dully stroked her eyes dry, held her in his arms and promised that Fairford should not after all be godfather.

Sniffing, Lizzie said: 'No, I think you're right. He ought to be.'

'Oh, come now, surely we can think of someone else?'

Stubbornly she persisted. She had been horrible and selfish and flighty, and he was quite right to say that the baby was half his because it *was*, wasn't it? 'And that's how I always want it to be. Something that you and I will always share and that will always hold us together, no matter what happens.'

Touched by her earnestness, he agreed, and Lizzie began to laugh a shade hysterically. 'Let's have his wife as one of the godmothers, and make a proper job of it!'

Dully agreed with enthusiasm, and after no more than a startled flick of the eyebrows agreed with equal enthusiasm that Mr George Edwardes should be approached to fulfil the role of second godfather.

'After all, I do owe him a lot,' Lizzie said. 'If it hadn't been for him I wouldn't have met you.' (Or Fairford either. . . .)

So the invitations were issued, and to Lizzie's gratified delight the Gov'nor also accepted the formal request to join the houseparty at Reve for the weekend of the christening.

Lizzie was resting when Fairford and his wife arrived, and in a sudden agony of nerves buried her face in the cushions and thought I can't . . . I *can't* . . . I'll only have to look at him and I'll give the game away. Everyone'll see me blushing, or going pale and fainting or something.

But the play-acting had to begin from the moment her maid came in to help her dress, and she sailed downstairs wearing green chiffon and the Dullingham tiara crowning her dark red hair.

'Oh, my *word*,' said a warm fruity voice, and the Gov'nor, in immaculate evening dress, was standing close by. He took her hand and raised it to his lips, even as his eyes noted and approved every detail of her appearance.

'Are you proud of me?'

247

'Very proud, and very admiring, Countess.'

'I'm still Liza, Mr Edwardes.'

'You are also the mother of a very fine son, so I hear.'

'Yes.' Her radiance seemed to increase, and impulsively she laid her hand on his arm. 'Would you like to see him?'

He nodded, beaming at her, and like a couple of conspirators they tiptoed hurriedly upstairs and she led the way to the night nursery.

Dismissing the nursemaid, she led him over to the cradle and they both peered inside, their heads almost touching.

'Isn't he a beauty?'

'A most singular creation, my dear Liza. I offer my heartfelt congratulations.'

The baby was awake, and lay contemplating them at leisure in the soft lamplight.

'I make so many plans for him,' confided Lizzie in a whisper. 'I want him to see things and do things and to be well educated and well travelled and to be a real man of the world.'

'In that case, I trust that part of his education will take place in a box at the Gaiety.'

'Not to mention the stage door.' She touched her son's cheek with a loving finger. 'Look, he knows his mama already.'

'May I hold him?'

Surprised and touched, she gently turned back the covers. She held the baby close to her for a moment or two, then placed him in the Gov'nor's arms. It suddenly struck her what strong sheltering arms they were.

'I'm very sorry I let you down the way I did,' she said, without looking at him. 'I kept trying to write and apologize, but I always tore it up.'

'The final result is well worth any interim vexation on my part,' he replied. 'And now, in the somewhat unfamiliar role of fairy godfather on this private opening night, may I wish your first-born goodness and wisdom, long life and the gift of laughter.'

The baby stared at him solemnly and without blinking. He handed him back, and his mother returned him to the

248

warmth of his cradle, and when the tucking in was completed to her satisfaction she straightened up.

'It's funny,' she said with a smile, 'how frightened of you I used to be.'

'But you're not afraid of anyone now, are you?'

She wanted to say no – just afraid of seeing someone.

'I'm a bit afraid of one of Dully's uncles,' she told him instead. 'He lives in a little house up in a tree.'

The Gov'nor chuckled. 'One of the minor disadvantages in marrying aristocracy is the possibility of having to deal with eccentricity. But one old man who merely has a preference for outdoor life I would call a very minor disadvantage indeed. Is he coming to the christening?'

'He's been asked, of course, but I don't know whether he'll turn up.'

'Now that is very serious.' He shook his head, his heavy moustache trembling with mock sorrow. 'No matter what the circumstances and no matter how profound the eccentricity, I would never tolerate slacking in my company when it comes to an important debut.'

'I know.' She looked at him fondly. 'You taught me such a lot, and it saved me on my first night here. It was all so big and magnificent and I felt so silly and lost that I just pretended I was back at the theatre and it was curtain-up.'

'No one could ever improve on that as a game of let's pretend. Whatever you get thrown at you, catch it and throw it back, but with a grace and style that makes them sick with envy.'

The sound of his resonant, authoritarian voice with its hint of Irish brogue brought the old Gaiety life very close; the hot smell of grease-paint and sweat, the costumes like bunches of brightly-coloured fruit hanging from the dressing room ceiling; the mateyness, the bitchiness. . . .

'Don't become too sentimental about the old life,' he said, as if he read her thoughts. 'The chorus is fine to begin with, but now you have a starring role and you are going to continue playing it with all the charm and panache we have learned to expect from you. And I know you will never let me down.'

'What I do still matters to you?'

'You are one of my children.'

There seemed nothing more to add, and they returned to the staircase hall, where Fairford stepped quickly forward from a knot of people and held out both hands to her.

'Liza – my dear, what a pleasure!'

For a moment his smile almost wrecked her self-command. She felt her lips tremble, her heart thump painfully.

'Fairford, how nice to see you.' Bravely she gave him her hand and smiled, then turned with a regal little gesture to the Gov'nor by her side. 'May I present Fairford Polperro? This is my friend, Mr George Edwardes.'

They shook hands, murmured a few conventional words, then Fairford said: 'May I introduce my wife Martha?'

She had dreaded this moment more than any other, but she managed to get through it. Shaking the tips of the American girl's fingers, Lizzie remarked that they had already met, she seemed to remember . . . and the American girl, equally constrained, said yes, she believed they had. . . .

Lizzie remembered the china blue eyes in the beautiful heart-shaped face and thought it wouldn't be so bad if she was ugly; if she had cross-eyes or a wooden leg or something, I'd be able to be ever so nice to her. . . .

Then other people intervened, and Lizzie steered a graciously smiling course between groups of Dullinghams and house guests to where Walter and Edwina were sitting blankly to attention on a vast marble bench of classical design.

'Ah, here you are!' She gave them a brilliant smile, then leaned closer. 'Whatever are you sitting on that ole thing for – you'll get piles.'

Walter's unguarded guffaw was snapped off by a violent dig from Edwina's elbow. 'Remember where you *are*!'

'You're both in my home, where I can talk about piles and Pa can laugh if he wants to. Come on now, get off this awful cold seat and come and meet people.'

She led them round the saloon, introducing them with a

250

bright, loving gaiety, and when Walter said, 'Who's that pretty young mawther standing on her own over there?' she took him across to her.

'This is my father,' Lizzie said. 'Walter Hinton, and this is Miss – I mean, Mrs Polperro.'

They shook hands and Lizzie glided rapidly away as she caught a glimpse of Fairford approaching. She didn't want to speak to him. Didn't dare to speak to him or even look at him, and she sighed with relief when the head footman announced in suitably ringing tones that dinner was served.

That was on Friday night, and her adept manoeuvrings ensured that they exchanged no more than a couple of general pleasantries before the formal goodnight.

Saturday was easier. The ladies and the elder Dullinghams mostly breakfasted in their own rooms, while mounts were ordered for those who wished to ride. Dully and Fairford were in the party, but sent a note back with a groom to say that they wished to extend their ride and would take pot luck at an inn. They returned as everyone else was lingering over a cold luncheon set out in the orangery, and Lizzie spent most of the afternoon conducting her parents round the home farm, where Walter felt secure for the first time since leaving Damperdown and Edwina couldn't get over the size of the cream pans in the dairy.

'Lizzie, it's all too big. It's too much to take in, and it gives me a headache.'

'That's how I felt at first, but you get used to it. I suppose people can get used to anything if they try, bad things as well as good.'

'All I can say is' – Walter suddenly looked resolute and very serious – 'that you'd better be a credit to it all, my gel. You'd better make sure and play your part and do what's right for somebody who's now a lady in your position, otherwise it'll all . . .' He seemed incapable of expressing the powerful thoughts that appeared to overcome him.

'In case it strikes midnight and I get home from the ball too late, and I'm back at Damperdown in my old pinafore, feeding the chickens?'

'There's nothing wrong with Damperdown,' Edwina started to say. Then added: 'No. Your pa's trying to say mind you don't pay a heavy price for all this, that's all.'

Lizzie perched herself on the edge of the white scrubbed table that stood in the middle of the dairy. The walls were covered in blue and white Delft tiles, the brick floor was still damp from its daily scrubbing and the faint clean smell of milk still lingered.

'Funny,' she said, 'I kept seeing poor ole Bessie Hinton all the time I was in labour, but she was all mixed up with the pain and the fright and in the end I really thought I *was* her.'

Edwina began to say something, then stopped. Any strange feelings of coincidence about them both thinking of Bessie at about the same time were best kept to herself.

'Poor little ole gel's bin dead all these years but she goes on like a sort of echo.' Walter fumbled in his pocket for pipe and tobacco.

'An echo of violence,' Lizzie said.

'Life's full of echoes and shadows,' Walter ruminated, striking a light.

The wind blew a scutter of dead leaves against the window and the sudden banging of the door made them jump.

'Walter,' Edwina said sharply, 'if you want to smoke, go outside.'

They walked back to the house, and at dinner that evening Walter told the new Mrs Polperro about last spring's fen blow, the force six southerly wind that had whipped away both topsoil and newly set seed, and she responded with cautious interest. Dully, at the head of the table, paid gallant attention to his mother-in-law, and Lizzie, a safe distance from Fairford, chatted busily about embroidery to Uncle Wilfred. The Gov'nor, at the opposite side of the table, did his best to discover a common interest with Cousin Lavvy and agreed, with sinking heart, to read some of her poems.

The christening took place on the following morning, and Lizzie found herself standing disturbingly close to

252

Fairford as parents and godparents grouped about the font. Determinedly she fixed her gaze on her son (a fizz of red hair protruding from one end of a sumptuous froth of Lyons silk and Brussels lace), and when Fairford shifted his position very slightly and their arms touched she closed her eyes in a spasm of mingled rapture and pain. When she opened them again she found herself transfixed by the wide blue stare of Martha Polperro. It was an effort to smile at her, and distractedly she wondered whether the answering smile she received cost as much. She looks very pale, Lizzie thought. I wonder if she knows?

'Henry Berry Albert George. . . .' The baby's names, enunciated with heavy grandeur by the Bishop, rolled round the painted walls of the chapel and drifted, dying, towards the gilded ceiling.

I wish you goodness and wisdom, long life and the gift of laughter, the Gov'nor had said. Lizzie glanced across at him, portly and immaculate and standing to attention, and caught the ghost of a wink from one heavy-lidded, button-bright eye.

I want everything for my son but nothing for myself except the man who's standing next to me. I love him and want him, want him. . . .

The brief service ended and the Dowager Countess carried her godson at the head of the procession across the great marble hall, and it was Lizzie, now resolutely calm, who noticed Martha Polperro falter slightly. Swiftly she moved across to her, then put her arm round her waist and led her out through the great double doors to the terrace. She helped her down the steps, then held her without flinching as she vomited harshly and convulsively. She recovered, and Lizzie wiped her sweating forehead and waited until the gasping and panting had ceased.

'I'm so sorry.'

'Don't be.'

'I don't want to . . . I just can't face . . .'

'No, of course you can't,' agreed Lizzie. 'Come on, we'll go through another way and you can go upstairs without seeing anyone.'

On impulse she led the girl to her own sitting room, removed her bonnet and placed her in an armchair close to the fire. She rang for her maid and ordered sal volatile, a hot-water bottle and, to follow in ten minutes' time, a pot of weak tea and some dry toast.

'I feel such a fool,' the girl said, leaning back. 'And so far from my folks.'

'Is it a baby?' Lizzie removed her own bonnet and tossed it aside.

'I guess so.'

'I'm so happy for you and Fairford.' The words were easier to say than she would ever have guessed. 'The early stages are awful, but it gets better and better.'

'Does it really?'

Lizzie grinned, and held her arms wide. 'See for yourself.'

'I know. But it's all over for you, isn't it?'

'Not for long, I hope. I want another one to match Berry.'

She supervised the exact placing of the hot-water bottle when it arrived, and the sipping of the sal volatile. A little colour began to return to Martha's cheeks, and she raised both hands to her head to adjust a hairpin or two.

'Try not to worry,' Lizzie said impulsively. 'Once the sickness wears off you'll feel fit as a flea.'

Conscious of a pleasant glow of seniority and reminding herself that this was Fairford's wife, Lizzie was moment-arily tempted to describe her own recent experiences in the fullest and most lurid detail, but charity prevailed.

'I wish I knew more about it,' Martha said in a small bleak voice, 'but Marma always said it's not ladylike to show curiosity about things like that. So I try not to, but I can't help wondering how it's going to get out.'

'You mean you don't know?' Lizzie looked incredulous.

'Marma said I'd just fall asleep and wake up when it's all over, but I still want to know where it comes out.'

'It comes out of your fan, of course.'

'My – fan?'

'Next to where you piddle. In other words, it'll come out from where it went in.'

'Oh, *Lord*. . . .' Again the colour fled from Martha's lovely face. Acute apprehension coupled with the ever present sense of lonely abandonment fought with and finally overrode the long training in decorum. 'But mine's too small!' She began to weep.

'Don't reckon it's any smaller than anyone else's,' Lizzie said, then added 'Come in' as a parlourmaid arrived with a tray of toast and tea.

She set it down on the table beside Lizzie, bobbed a curtsey and then withdrew.

'Silver teapots are all right but they burn your blinking fingers,' Lizzie said, wincing as she poured.

'Put my handkerchief round the handle.' Martha passed the small damp object with which she had dried her tears.

Touched, Lizzie gave her a sudden glowing smile and said: 'Cheer up, duck, it's not nearly as bad as it sounds. Just think of our babies growing up to be friends and getting up to high jinks together!'

'And we'll be friends too, won't we?'

'You bet your life we will. Now drink your tea while it's hot and have a bit of toast to stay you until you feel like a proper meal.'

She left the girl drowsing by the fireside and went down to take her place at the photographic session in the saloon. I didn't mean to tell her we'd be friends, she thought, but I suppose it's too late now.

Despite Lizzie's evasive tactics, she came face to face with Fairford on her way back from delivering a finger of christening cake to Uncle Merton.

He had attended neither the ceremony nor the luncheon, and exasperation with him was only exceeded by the desire for a solitary walk in the fresh air before darkness fell. The beech that cradled the small wooden building in venerable branches stood in a belt of trees that curved in a protective sweep round the north side of the house, and Lizzie called his name from the foot of the ladder. There was no reply; only a chink of light gleamed like a watchful eye through the thinning foliage.

Leaving her offering on the small rustic table that stood to one side of the ladder, she turned away and, walking back along the edge of the trees, jumped violently as a figure stepped out of the shadows at her side. He was wearing a tweed coat with a cape, but no hat.

'Liza!'

'Oh! It's you.'

'Is that all you can say?'

'What else were you expecting?'

He stood very close to her, and the last flush of sunset silhouetted his head and shoulders against the sky.

'I've been trying to have a private word with you all weekend.'

Her heart quickened its beat but she managed to keep her voice steady. 'What about?'

'What do you imagine? Oh my God, Liza, how I've missed you.'

He put his arms round her and held her against his shoulder, and she closed her eyes and thought this is all I've dreamed about. This is all I've ever wanted.

She allowed him to kiss her on the mouth, the nose, the eyes, but when he drew her closer into the shadow of the trees she began to resist.

'No, we mustn't. It's wrong.'

'Why is it wrong? Oh, my lovely Liza, I've waited for such an eternity.'

'I said *no*!' The word sounded like a small explosion in the silence and a small animal scuttled away through the leaves.

'Liza darling, what's wrong?' He tried to kiss her again but this time she pushed him away.

'What's wrong is that you and I are married. And both of us to different people.'

'Is that all? Oh come on, be a sport.'

'A sport?' Her temper flared. 'So that's what you call it? In other words, all you want's a bit of slap and tickle on the side.'

'Of course I don't, you silly girl.' He nuzzled her ear, pushing her little fur bonnet askew. She jerked it straight.

'Well what, then?'

'I just want you and me to go on being special pals as we used to be . . . no need to be too desperately naughty, but there's nothing wrong with the odd little cuddle for old time's sake, is there?'

Wrenching herself free, she began to walk rapidly away, striking out across the dew-soaked grass towards the house.

'Darling, listen.' He hurried after her and grabbed her arm.

She shook him off, breaking into a run. He ran after her, and when she stopped abruptly and turned to face him he collided with her. Their noses crashed together.

'No,' she said, taking a deep, steadying breath, 'you listen to me instead. Over there in that house there's a girl who's been made to marry you because she's rich and you're noble – huh, *noble*! – and she's eating her heart out with loneliness and longing for her own family and friends and her own country and everything, and not only that, she's being sick something rotten with your baby and what's more – what's bloody well more, Mr Honourable bloody Polperro – because of being reared so rich and polite she didn't even know where it was going to come out of! It could be going to come out of her ear for all she knew – but you, having done your noble bit by marrying a girl you don't love and then dutifully getting her in pod, you see no reason why you shouldn't carry on where you left off with somebody else! Well, all I can say is, it's not going to be *me*!'

The wet turf squeaked beneath her feet as she turned and marched off, and this time he made no attempt to follow.

It was all over. All over and done with. The last of the helpless, hopeless, fervent infatuations of adolescence had just shrivelled and died and she felt clean as a new pin, clear as a silver bell. The crisp air of autumn stung her cheeks, and suddenly filled with a marvellous immeasurable joy, she picked up her skirts and ran towards the twinkling lights and the wide welcoming arms of Reve.

Book Two
Echoes

'Tickle your arse with a feather?'

'Beg pardon?'

'I said, particularly nasty weather.'

The Honourable Basil George Dullingham-Reve, first cousin to the late Earl and alias Uncle Badger, seated himself next to Lizzie and fanned himself with his panama hat. Flawless sunlight covered the park and the drowsy tail-swishing cattle, and fell in a twinkling shower down through the leaves of the tree beneath which steamer chairs and a garden table were arranged.

Lizzie, in a white frock and a wide-brimmed hat trimmed with marguerites, turned to smile at him.

'I wouldn't call this particularly nasty.'

'A mere figure of speech, plus a shameful desire to bring a blush to your modest young cheek.'

'Take more than that to make me blush.'

'A brazen hussy? Oh, *never.* . . .'

They lapsed into companionable silence.

Badger and Woodstock were brothers and had spent long periods of their lives at Reve, having completed the normal cultural forays and necessary terms of colonial service – Badger in India, Woodstock in South Africa – in the minimum time possible. Neither had married, although Woodstock was known to have an eye for a pretty woman and Badger had once been engaged to a comely young lady (her portrait still hung in his dressing room) who had died shortly before the wedding ceremony. Sorrow, mingled with natural lassitude, prevented the search for a replacement and he returned to Reve, convinced by the age of thirty-four that he had done everything in life that could possibly be expected of him.

The two brothers sank gratefully into a premature middle-aged calm, and allowed Reve to wrap them in its timeless, motionless splendour. Badger acquired a succession of spaniels, all of them called Eulalie after a girl in a play, while Woodstock was the current owner of a pug called Scotus. They rose, each in their separate rooms along separate corridors, every morning at eight, were shaved and served tea by their valets before descending for breakfast, crisply refreshed and dressed, to either the winter parlour or the garden room, depending on the time of year.

Newspapers were read, but with no more than an amused tolerance, letters were written and diaries were kept up to date: *Early rain cleared by noon. Noted green woodpecker busy on mulberry. Euly's paw improved.* Then a walk before luncheon either alone or in company with another member of the family. An afternoon nap ('Wake me at three, Saunders'), and the rest of the slow tranquil day spent in reading, strolling, conversing, and drinking a glass or two of claret before retirement to the large and sombre four-posters which stood like galleons in full sail beneath soaring, richly decorated ceilings.

The beds themselves were a world of privacy – large enough to encompass man, dog, books and boxes of comfits – and these personal worlds were encompassed in turn by the stately protection of Reve. The world outside was no more than a muffled drum.

Although there had seemed to be dozens of Dullinghams drawn up in serried ranks to greet the arrival of Lizzie, in fact the permanent residents amounted to no more than five, if one included Merton. Aunt Minna, the Dowager Countess, spent three weeks away each year (one week in Bournemouth in the spring and two weeks at her old family home near Bath). The other resident was Aunt Miriam, a cigar-smoking childless widow. She too had been born a Dullingham, had travelled extensively during her marriage, and now clung to Reve with the same serene tenacity as that exhibited by Badger and Woodstock.

All five got on remarkably well together and, apart from Merton, enjoyed one another's company when they met for meals or strolls or a game of cribbage. But in a place the size of Reve, it was as easy to escape from tedium as it was simple to invite friends or other members of the family to stay for a week or so, and once when Lizzie impulsively exclaimed how nice all the Dullinghams were, Uncle Woodstock replied that when people had everything they could possibly want there was no reason why they should be anything else.

Naturally they had been shocked and saddened by the unexpected deaths of the late Earl and his son – the place seemed so quiet without the jolly booming laughter of poor old Berry – but there again, awareness of the brief human span was not only inevitable but somehow rendered quite acceptable by living in a venerable house whose every stone breathed history, whose every family portrait hanging in the long gallery spoke of the transience of life, along with the fashion in ringlets.

To begin with, they accepted Lizzie in the same philosophical vein. The second Earl had married a high-class harlot, the fourth had married an apothecary's daughter, so the sudden arrival of the newly created peer in company with a farmer's daughter turned actress was greeted without censure. And the arrival of the new heir within a few weeks of his parents' marriage was accepted with equal calm by a family in whom bastards, actual and potential, were no particular novelty.

That was how the relationship began, but within a short space of time they found Lizzie possessed of qualities that delighted and entranced them. They appreciated her youthful good looks and had noted with benevolent sympathy her game attempt on that first evening to disguise her nervousness at so much grandeur. They knew they were grand, it was one of the immutable facts of life, and without her noticing, Dullingham eyes had slanted in smiles of kindly amusement at each carefully drawled *How doo you dooo?*

The eyes also took note of young Henry's adoration of her, and they began looking forward to the birth of the baby in the way that one looks forward to the first new springtime

263

bud on an old familiar tree. In the midst of death we are in life, as Uncle Badger was fond of saying, and sitting beside Lizzie on that golden afternoon he laid aside his panama and cocked an enquiring eye at the book she was reading.

'Rather a large tome for a hot day . . . not?'

'It's Alfred, Lord Tennyson.'

'Oh, *awful* fella. What made you choose him?'

'A friend of mine who lived in a little cottage near us and who was very well educated liked Tennyson's poems. He said he had a wonderful knack of making us open our eyes and our hearts as well.'

'He stayed here once back in the seventies, on the way from visiting his two sons who were up at Cambridge, I seem to remember. Dirty, unkempt beggar, reeked of tobacco and had no manners. Insisted on reading aloud the whole of *Maud* after dinner. Took over two hours and annihilated everyone with boredom.'

'I'm trying to get through the *Idyll of the Kings*.'

'Ha! "*And ever and anon the wolf would steal/The children and devour, but now and then,/Her own brood lost or dead, lent her fierce teat/To human sucklings; and the children housed/In her foul den, thus at their meat would growl*" . . . lot of portentous twaddle. You'd be much better off with Macaulay if you must go in for that sort of stuff. His *Lays of Ancient Rome* have at least got a bit of bounce to them.'

Lizzie dropped the book down by her chair and sighed. 'I can't help wishing I was a bit more educated.'

'Reading and writing and a little elementary arithmetic are all you need, my dear. Experience will see to the rest.'

'It's all so easy and comfortable here, and I'm getting more and more used to not having to work or struggle for things.'

'What's wrong with that?'

'I don't know.' She looked uneasy. 'Nothing, I suppose.'

'So stop feeling guilty, there's a dear child.'

He took out his pocket watch, and Lizzie looked up to see a distant footman marching towards them with a large silver tray containing afternoon tea.

'There you are,' she said. 'If we'd been sitting on the

264

terrace the poor man wouldn't have had nearly such a long walk. From here to the house must be almost quarter of a mile.'

'But that's what footmen are for.' He leaned back in his chair and watched the approaching servant through half-closed eyes. 'In my grandfather's time we had running footmen. Astonishing chaps, some of them. There was one called Ned who always ran by the side of the old boy's carriage when he drove over to Newmarket for the Cesarewitch. Marvellous sight.'

'Pity they didn't put him in for the race.'

'No need to, they had their own. The fifth Earl used to race his against the Harveys' – used to bet very heavily on their favourites too, so I've heard.'

The footman drew nearer. Near enough for them to catch the first faint jingle of teaspoons.

'What would he do if I went to meet him and offered to carry it?'

'Drop dead with shock. So don't try it.'

They lapsed into dreamy silence, mesmerized by the warmth and by the steady approach of the figure in white stockings, dark knee-breeches and jacket, and white cravat tied high under the chin. A few yards nearer and they recognized him as John, the second footman.

'I hope he's remembered an oatcake for Eulalie.'

'Sir, M'Lady. . . .' John arrived at the table and set down the tray. Small beads of sweat glistened on his forehead. Eulalie crawled from beneath the shade of Badger's chair and examined his ankles with interest.

'Have you seen His Lordship anywhere about, John?' Lizzie asked.

'No, My Lady. But I will have enquiries made.'

'Oh, please don't bother. I expect he's busy.' She watched the twinkling light playing over John's hands as he deftly set out cups and saucers, milk and sugar, lemon slices, hot-water jug and teapot.

'Ah,' murmured Badger. 'Marchpane slices instead of boring old pound cake.'

'And Eulalie's oatcake on a plate all of its own.'

265

John retreated with a bow, the tray under his arm, and they had finished their second cup of tea before he finally disappeared from sight.

'Oh, I do so love it here,' Lizzie sighed, licking a crumb of pastry from her top lip. 'And I can't help hoping it'll stay exactly the same for ever and ever.'

Dully was also under the spell of Reve, for the old remembered delights of that first boyhood visit had now become deepened and intensified by his new familiarity with the running of the place. He had mastered the administration and could put a name to every face on the estate, and was now beginning to feel that he had passed from apprentice to craftsman as trustee and guardian for future generations. The family's kindly attitude had helped to establish him in this new role, and before long he had begun to plan new improvements. There was no electric light, so he set about having it installed, then helped to design the circuit of a steam heating system to run through all the major corridors and rooms. The same method had been used in the orangery and the hothouses for years, and when Badger murmured lazily about expense, Dully asked why peaches should be given priority over people.

He installed more water closets, more bathrooms, and turned what had once been a little-used ante-room into a billiard room with red flock wallpaper and a full-sized table set beneath green-shaded lamps. The Dullingham uncles took to the game with the gleefulness of schoolboys.

For despite the grandeur of Reve and the huge staff of servants at their command, the occupants were curiously unspoilt when it came to the smaller luxuries of life; whist and bezique and cribbage were often played after dinner, but with packs of cards so antiquated that it was sometimes difficult to distinguish a club from a spade, and the Hopkinson piano in the library, although still used a good deal, was so internally ravaged by damp and moth that its voice was little more than a graveyard whisper. Dully had it replaced by a Broadwood concert grand and Lizzie taught

Woodstock, who was good at playing by ear, the accompaniment to some of the old Gaiety songs.

They all loved music. Mendelssohn and Schubert and Miss Lehmann's delicious song cycle *In a Persian Garden*, which Aunt Miriam would sometimes sing in a rolling contralto with Benbow her parrot perched motionless on her shoulder and her cigar sending up a thin plume of smoke from its temporary resting place on the edge of the piano.

Then Dully would whisper to Lizzie: 'How about singing your waltz for us? We don't hear it nearly often enough,' and Woodstock would play his own improvised introduction while Lizzie shook out her skirts and patted her hair into position before beginning.

The world of the Gaiety seemed very far away now, but the lilting charm of Fifine's waltz invariably brought the memories close. She still loved to perform. The high spirits were still there, the old happy love of music and movement, and sometimes she would dance as well as sing, kicking off her shoes, holding out her arms and twirling like a lovely copper-tinted autumn leaf up and down the library and in and out of the furniture – smiling, twinkling, flirting – and the joy of it all shone in her cheeks and sparkled in her eyes, and their hearts went out to her and waltzed with her, and they loved and admired her with all the simple generosity of the blessed.

They loved her for being what she was, and they also loved her because she was the mother of young Berry.

The Viscount Reve had learned to crawl, and now, like a young plant struggling up to reach the sun, hauled himself on to his feet by the aid of the nursery fender. He stood there, swaying precariously, and the smile that disclosed four teeth also disclosed a glowing sense of achievement.

He was achieving new things every day, and the waking hours were filled with wonderment at the feel of things, the look and the taste, the scent and the sound of them; the desire to capture them and explore them, to shake them, bite them and pull them apart, while a large bead of saliva

267

hung from his lower lip because he was too busy to swallow. He wore frocks and socks and tiny buttoned boots, and Nurse brushed his hair in a curly red halo round his beaming face.

Unlike most children of his class, he was not permanently confined to the nursery. To one of Lizzie's background it was a funny idea to have children and never see them, and for Dully it was a matter of passionate importance that there should be no repetition of his own lonely, loveless childhood. So Berry was taken downstairs and allowed to toddle around the family's feet, to sit on his mother's lap and watch while Uncle Badger made rabbits out of his handkerchief, and to play among the skeins of silk that Aunt Minna used for her embroidery. They talked and sang to him; told him stories and took him for slow patient walks on the south terrace or across the marble waste of the great hall. Aunt Miriam took him for a ride on a horse, sitting side-saddle and holding him close with one strong protective arm while he squealed with joy.

He discovered the outdoors, the sun and the breeze, the cawing of rooks and the haunting cry of the peacocks. He discovered the scent of flowers and dug his fingers into the soil with a child's ecstasy, and when they thoughtfully replaced soil with nice clean sand he pointedly ignored it and made off for the nearest herbaceous border.

He was constantly absorbing new impressions, and when they took him to his mama's room to be introduced to his new brother Thomas, he stared at the small whickering thing and wondered wordlessly what it was for.

'Baby,' they said. 'Love baby.'

'Ahhh,' he replied, and laid his cheek against the soft shawl.

His protective instincts were immediately aroused by this small red-haired replica of himself, and although he waited impatiently for the time when Tommy would be able to play with him, he assumed the role of responsible elder brother with touching pride.

He was four years old and Tommy a little over two, when Papa took them both on his knee one winter's morning and told them with a very grave face that the Queen had died.

'Oh. Is she pleased?'

'No one is ever pleased to die, but I dare say that when we are very old we become resigned.'

'And now,' put in Mama, 'we've got a king for a change. His name's Edward the Seventh.'

No one in the house could remember a reign other than Victoria's; she had seemed immovable as an oak, immutable as the Sphinx, and the news of her passing caused a momentary tremor of insecurity. As distinct from wars and political upheaval, the death of Victoria was somehow a domestic affair. Sensing this, Dully ordered that the staff should wear a black ribbon and that a Union Jack should be flown at half-mast. The parish church bell was tolled, and the villagers stopped work and drew their blinds as a mark of respect.

He also told Lizzie that they had received an invitation to attend the funeral.

The Queen had died at Osborne on the Isle of Wight during the early evening of Tuesday 22 January 1901, and the body lay in semi-state while the news was telegraphed round the world. Foreign royalty and diplomatic representatives had already gathered when her coffin was taken to Cowes on a gun-carriage and put aboard the royal yacht *Alberta*. She spent the night in an improvised mortuary chapel on the quarter deck, and the next day's progress was marked by thunderous gun salutes from accompanying warships. The unrolling of the great pageant had begun.

On the following morning, Saturday 2 February, the coffin was taken by train to London and met at Victoria Station by the full splendour of a military funeral. The arrival platform was covered with crimson carpet, and purple and white draperies tactfully concealed advertisements for Stephens' Ink and Pears' Soap. There were potted palm trees and massed white flowers, and massed bands played Beethoven's Funeral March with a hoarse and terrible poignancy.

The King and his late mother were met by the German Emperor, the King of Portugal and Prince Henry of

269

Prussia, by Franz Ferdinand of Austria and the Hereditary Grand Duke Michael of Russia. There were Hohenzollerns and Mecklenburg-Strelitzs, Tecks and Saxe-Coburgs and Schaumburg-Lippes, the women muffled in black and heavily veiled, the men strutting proud as prize gamebirds in cloaks and plumed helmets. The Lord Mayor and the Sheriffs of London were wearing state robes and the court officials wore gold-laced hats.

The procession formed outside the station, the Queen's coffin placed on a gun-carriage drawn by eight cream-coloured horses and draped in a cream-embroidered pall with the Royal Standard laid over it. The orbs, sceptre and crown were placed on top. The King rode directly behind it, accompanied by the German Emperor and the Duke of Connaught, out into the London streets lined with silent spectators. Pale sunlight struggling through the mist touched bare heads and black clothes, and glinted on the drawn swords and polished helmets as the cortège passed on its way to Paddington Station and the royal train to Windsor.

Dully and Lizzie had put up at an hotel there the evening before, and they drove slowly through the seething, mourning-clad crowds on Castle Hill towards the Great Gateway that led to St George's Chapel. Every lamp post had been hung with a laurel wreath and every building festooned with purple hangings.

Dully was wearing morning dress and a silk hat and Lizzie was obscured behind the almost impenetrable folds of regulation black veiling. Her tightly fitting black coat touched her black buckled shoes, and inside the black fur muff her fingers gripped a large black-edged handkerchief.

'I hope I don't cry.'

'I think it'll be difficult not to.'

'I know. We've had her for so long.'

They alighted where the precincts of the Chapel were heaped with wreaths and flowers that had been brought from almost every corner of the Empire, and then joined the mourners being admitted through the north door. A man in levee dress and black gloves glided up to them and shook Dully's hand.

'Dullingham-Reve, isn't it?'

Dully murmured that it was, then introduced Lizzie to Sir Spencer Ponsonby Fane, who showed them to their seats in the nave.

There was a long wait before the arrival of the cortège, and Dully passed the time by pointing out some of the notables he recognized seated over in the choir: the Marquis of Salisbury, Austen Chamberlain, Sir Henry Campbell-Bannerman and Dr Hornby, the Provost of Eton – 'He'll be taking charge of our sons in a few years' time . . .'

'Oh damn this veil, Dully, I can't see properly.'

But when the subdued murmuring and rustling ceased as the clergy began to take their places, her heart started to thump. They moved slowly past, their long dark mantles adorned with a knot of white mourning ribbon, the Bishop of Oxford robed in crimson.

The silence intensified until it seemed to beat on the waiting eardrums, then the great west doors were opened and the Chapel was instantly flooded with music and light.

Preceded by heralds, the Queen's coffin was carried by Grenadier guardsmen, and craning desperately to look at it – 'Is that her *real* crown on top?' – Lizzie almost missed the King, who was walking directly behind. He looked pale and very remote.

'He's wearing field marshal's uniform, and that's the Kaiser with him,' Dully whispered.

She could only watch them passing the end of the row where she was standing, but the long, slow-moving procession seemed endless. Now that the cloaks had been laid aside, it was all scarlet and gold, silver and blue, highlighted by the glitter of orders and decorations and touched by the majestic ray of sunshine coming through the west window. Even viewed from behind black veiling, the magnificence was unparalleled and her eyes filled with tears.

'You and I look like a couple of ole black crows compared to all this,' she whispered shakily. 'Where's the Queen and the Princesses?'

'Not sure. Probably secluded from public gaze,' he whispered back.

271

The service began with Psalm 90, its beautiful and terrible words soaring higher and higher above their heads, and when they were seated she slipped her hand from her muff and sought the reassurance of Dully's warm clasp.

It was because of him that she was here, sharing in this marvellous awesome moment in the history of kings and queens, and she stole a grateful look at his profile: the straight, rather long nose, the firm chin and well-formed lips unadorned by whiskers, and her fingers tightened on his when she remembered how he had come to find her that day at Damperdown because he loved her and wanted to marry her. His fingers returned her pressure.

The congregation rose to its feet and sang Wesley's setting of 'Man that is Born of Woman' and it made her think of Berry and Tommy, who had been born of her. They too belonged in this setting and among all these high-born aristocrats. The King and the Kaiser, and everyone. Berry was a viscount and Tommy was an honourable, but only because of Dully coming back that day to marry her because he loved her. She stole another look at him.

The service was conducted by the Bishop of Winchester and the aged Archbishop of Canterbury, and although she could see little of the proceedings, the soaring music and sad, sonorous rhetoric continued to sharpen her sense of passionate awareness.

She belonged here. To England, to the dead Queen and to the new King and his wife, to the Empire and its farflung outposts, and to Reve and to Dullinghams past and present, but most of all she realized now that she belonged to Dully. She always had and she always would.

She found his hand again and pressed it tenderly. Tenderly he pressed back. Slowly and stealthily she wove her fingers through his, and she couldn't understand how it was that the touch of his hand had never made her feel like this before. She seemed to be melting inside, dissolving into some kind of rich creamlike substance that had no will of its own.

Dully, she thought. Oh Dully, Dully, Dully. . . .

She continued the subtle weaving movement. Their two

thumbs met and began to circle with caution, as if they were meeting for the first time, and only began to touch deliberately as the Anthem by Tchaikovsky swelled to heightened anguish. Still revolving they pressed closer, polished nail slipping against warm, soft thumb pad. Their fingers gripped, intertwined again and pressed tighter and tighter, imprisoning and enslaving. Lizzie gasped quietly.

The Anthem sank to a whisper and their fingers relaxed their brutal hold. They touched again, shyly and tentatively, and she sensed that Dully was glancing down at her from the corner of his eye. She felt herself blushing furiously, and for the first time was glad of the veil's protective folds. If it was anyone else but Dully I'd think I was falling for him. . . .

Their hands fell apart as they stood with the rest of the congregation to hear the Proclamation delivered by the Norroy King-at-Arms. The clear well-modulated voice floated through the Chapel, which was silent now, save for suppressed sobs.

'For as much as it hath pleased Almighty God to take out of this transitory life unto His divine mercy the late most high, most mighty, the most excellent Monarch Victoria, by the grace of God of the United Kingdom of Great Britain and Ireland . . .'

Their hands met again, as if by accident, and clung together in the shelter of her coat. Gently Lizzie closed her hand round Dully's index finger. Her palm was warm and moist, and she sensed rather than heard him breathing heavily.

'Defender of the Faith, Empress of India and Sovereign of the most noble Order of the Garter . . .'

To the sonorous enumeration of the late Queen's many titles she began to move her hand very slowly and rhythmically, still gripping Dully's finger. Almost faint with emotion, she felt the strength of it, the strong hard bone that stiffened and held rigid the silk-soft flesh, and thought, I've no right to be feeling like this and to be doing this . . . not with the Queen lying up there and everything that's going on.

273

But she went on with what she was doing, and so did the Norroy King-at-Arms: 'Let us humbly beseech Almighty God to bless with long life, health and honour and all worldly happiness the most high, most mighty and most excellent Monarch our Sovereign Lord Edward, now by the grace of God of the United Kingdom of Great Britain and Ireland . . .'

The final cry of 'God save the King!' rang through the Chapel and fled away through the stone arches to lose itself in echoes and re-echoes, and Lizzie dropped Dully's index finger and leaned heavily against him. It seemed to her as if the warmth of their arms was burning through both their coat sleeves. Dully, oh, Dully. . . .

The service ended with 'Blessed are the Departed', and a solemn benediction by the Archbishop of Canterbury, who spoke in a surprisingly strong voice considering his age.

Then it was over, and as they stood waiting for their turn to file from the Chapel, Lizzie told herself that she would feel normal again once she got outside in the fresh air.

She didn't. The February cold stung her cheeks but failed to chill the miraculous glow of Dully's hand on her arm as he steered her towards their carriage.

They drove back to the hotel in silence, and now she took a perverse pleasure in sitting apart from him. Not even their coats were touching. She stared through the window at the crowds who had waited so patiently for so many hours to say a mute goodbye to the old Queen. Tomorrow she was to be interred at Frogmore in Windsor Great Park, in the giant mausoleum she had had built for Prince Albert. Tomorrow she would be lying by his side.

The hotel manager greeted them reverently, bowing from the waist and repeating that he was at their service. Would they care to order a pot of tea? Or perhaps something a little stronger for His Lordship?

They said no thank you, and hurried towards the lift. Last evening the place had been filled with mourners arriving in readiness for the funeral but now most of them were departing for the railway station. Maids and porters hurried about with dressing cases and Gladstone bags, and under a large potted palm sat a chubby old lady weeping bitterly into a black silk handkerchief.

'We have just witnessed the end of our world,' she kept saying to anyone who paused to listen. 'This is the end of all we hold dear to our hearts. . . .'

For some of us it's more like the beginning, thought Lizzie, and grabbing hold of her husband hurried with him along the first floor corridor to their room. She turned to him, snatching off her hat and veil and flinging them on the floor.

'Dully,' she said. 'Do you know what I want?'

'You've already given me a pretty good hint.' He drew her close and stood looking down at her, his dark blue eyes tilting in a smile. A smile that melted her insides.

Very slowly and deliberately she put her arms round his neck and kissed his mouth, and the contact seemed to drive them both wild. Still clinging together, they undressed, tearing at buttons and hooks and eyes until they looked like two pale statues risen from a lake of black water.

He picked her up and laid her on the bed, but hers was no longer the passive role. She couldn't stay still. She was all hands and mouth, hungrily exploring, tasting, teasing, kissing, and all long slender limbs twining and binding like a rapacious plant. She couldn't get enough of him, of any part of him. With closed eyes she explored with her nose the line of his hair, tracing its tendency to curl behind his ears, then travelling up to his forehead and down to his well-defined eyebrows. She kissed his eyes, those beautiful honest, gravely smiling eyes with the upward tilt at the corners, then his arms tightened round her again and he rolled her over, laughing, sobbing and gasping.

He needed no guiding. He had been there many times before, and he sank deep into her, and it was lovely the way everything was both so reassuringly familiar and so newly, wickedly exciting. She heard herself moaning to him to make her pregnant again – she wanted to be pregnant with a new baby of his that would always remind her of this time, in this hotel. . . .

They rolled apart, their bodies sticky and replete. It was

almost dark in the room, and out in the corridor they heard a voice saying: 'Elsie dear, did you remember to tip the chambermaid?' They giggled silently, and Dully leaned over his wife and buried his face in her hair. They slept a little, and the gaslight from the street outside filled their room with a soft golden gleam that seemed to lie like a loving spirit on the velvet dark shadows.

'The poor ole Queen's dead.'

'Yes, my darling.'

'Tomorrow she'll be lying with Prince Albert.'

'But not, alas, doing this. . . .'

Soft kisses; soft lips on soft flesh; the sighs and little whispered words of love. Then her hands exploring him again; the body that had given her two children but which she had never examined in careful detail. Her peering eyes could just distinguish a small mole above his left nipple, and her fingers traced a thin white scar on his shoulder.

'How did you get that?' She retraced it with her lips.

'Think it was when I fell out of a tree.'

'What were you doing up a tree? Having tea with Uncle Merton?'

'No, bird's-nesting . . . must have been about seven or eight.'

'Oh, my poor darling.'

She made love to him, this time by kissing him; kissing the blossoming red flesh that she was holding between her hands until he turned on his side with a groan and gathered her into his arms. They lay mouth to mouth and thigh to thigh, almost senseless with the power of tenderness.

It could never have been like this with poor Johnnie. Or with that silly ass Fairford Polperro. It could only ever have been Dully, and even then, it seemed, not until they had been married for over four years. Perhaps we all have to break through some sort of barrier, she thought, like sheep suddenly finding their way into a beautiful new green meadow.

She wondered whether the Queen had felt like this about the Prince Consort. He must have meant a lot to her, the way she went into mourning all those years ago and never

276

really came out of it. They said that hardly anybody ever saw her. She just hid herself away with his photograph and her black widow's weeds and could hardly be bothered to rule the Empire any more. . . .

Lizzie dozed, her face hidden deep in Dully's neck, and downstairs the weeping matron was persuaded to take a glass of port wine to calm her nerves, and the gong sounded for dinner.

They dined alone in their room, much later, Dully in a silk dressing gown and Lizzie softly rumpled in a white peignoir, and both of them tucking into game pie and a bottle of claret followed by a good ripe Stilton and a basket of fresh fruit. A maid knocked on the door to ask if she could tidy the room for the night. She cleared away the remains of the meal, heaped the fire with fresh coals and after one swift glance at the bed decided that it was her tactful duty to ignore it. She drew the curtains and departed.

When she had gone, Dully turned out the lamps and spread a blanket down on the hearthrug. They stood on it in their bare feet, kissing slowly and voluptuously. Still kissing her, he slipped her arms out of her peignoir.

'You too.' With closed eyes she untied the fringed sash of his dressing gown. They lay down, lazily watching the play of firelight on their coupled flesh, and they might have been the first two people on earth tasting for the first time the sweet subtle joy of one another.

They moved slowly and gently together, and when at last he slipped out of her she gave a tired little sigh and lay back with her forearm across her eyes to conceal the tears.

'I nearly forgot to tell you, Dully. I love you.'

Now, at last, she had everything. There was nothing left that anyone could possibly wish for, and in rare moments of introspection she would wonder, Why me? What have I done to deserve it all? Heaps of girls are better and wiser and nicer-looking than me, yet they end up their lives in a furnished room with only a cat to love. . . .

She didn't know why it should be. She only knew that Dully was the heart and soul of all her happiness.

277

The new warmth of love also brought with it a kind of divine restlessness, an instinctive urge to share this great explosion of happiness with everyone (without necessarily explaining the reason for it), and impulsively she invited her parents to Reve for a holiday. They had already paid several previous visits, and now that the cold damp of winter had receded, she wanted them to see Reve in the springtime, the ground golden with daffodils and the green stars of chestnut buds sweeping down to meet them.

She overlooked the fact that springtime is one of the busiest seasons on the farm.

Your Pa and I would be pleased to accept, wrote Edwina at the kitchen table, *but because the weather's been so slow to mend he's all behind. He hasn't got all his seed in yet and he's got a pig due to farrow any time now. Reuben's been poorly, he won't eat more than a hen's noseful, but we hope with the better weather coming he'll start to pick up. I hope this finds you and yours all doing nicely. Ever your loving Mother.*

The stolid phrases inscribed with the dip pen and penny bottle of ink always kept next to Pa's tobacco jar filled her with a sudden passion to see them. On the spur of the moment she ordered a telegram to be sent stating the time of her arrival, and kissing Dully and the boys a quick yet semi-tearful goodbye, wrenched herself away from Reve. It was the first time she had left it on her own, and she turned back to look into the soaring tunnel of trees that lined the south avenue, and when a lone woodman respectfully touched his forelock she answered him with a dazzling smile that left him transfixed.

Damperdown was exactly the same, but smaller. She realized for the first time that standing on tiptoe she could touch the ceilings with her hand, and for the first hour she seemed to do nothing but collide with the furniture. But she laughed and chattered and rushed round the house to see everything, and no one could ever have accused her of having changed, either. She evinced no la-di-da ways, no hint of the grand lady, and when Edwina told her to put on an apron before helping with the supper things, she did so with suitable meekness.

They too were conscious of the happiness that seemed to glow all about her, and agreed in the privacy of their bedroom that it didn't merely stem from material gain.

'It's not the money or being a nerl's wife, I'll lay a bet,' whispered Edwina, 'but I never seen her so well set-up, even after her boys were born.'

'Lizzie's always bin a good little gel.'

'I worked hard to bring her up the right way.'

'Reckon you succeeded.'

She was up early the following morning, hurrying down the rough track that led to the Sixteen Foot level. The quiet music of the fens filled her ears: the lap of water against the reeds, the quick tumbling song of a newly arrived sedge-warbler, and the wind sighing over the freshly green surface of Latches Fen. She stood there with her head thrown back and her eyes closed, and she remembered the day when she had seen Dully's tall figure coming towards her in the drizzling rain. The picture of him in her mind's eye quickened her pulses and made her heart thud. What a lovely love it was to have, after the other two dismal failures; exciting, exhilarating, and yet comfortable, safe and warm as a big feather bed. She decided that she must return home first thing tomorrow.

A stray whiff of Nosegay shag made her open her eyes.

'Ole sow farrowed in the night. Eleven of 'em all doing nicely save one little runt.' Walter came up to her in a collarless shirt and shapeless trousers. There was a grey stubble on his chin but his eyes were bright, and she knew he wanted her to see them.

'You still go in for Large Blacks, Pa?'

'Best breed for these parts. Always have bin.'

'Can I come and see her?'

He tried to appear doubtful. 'Well, I dunno. Spoil your shoes in there.'

She took his arm, and walked in step with him back to the farmyard.

The sow lay on her side in the straw, with her flop ears over her eyes and a piglet clinging leechlike to every teat.

'She's *beautiful*, Pa.'

Walter picked up a bit of stick and caressed the sow's bristles with it. She grunted with pleasure. Then he burrowed his hand in the straw and brought out the little runt. It gave a feeble squeal and tried to nestle against him.

'Oh, let me!'

'You muck your clothes up and Ma'll shout.'

Lizzie made no reply, but held the piglet close to her braid-trimmed jacket. Half-heartedly it tried to suck her fingers.

'Don't reckon it'll last above a few days – hasn't got the strength to fight for its grub.'

'Can I have it, Pa? Oh, please can I have it?'

'Won't do you much good.' He tried to remain unaffected by the old eagerness, the old wheedling of a child passionate to keep hens and ducks, rabbits and kittens.

'I could take it home and bring it up on the bottle. It's a good little pig really, Pa. It's just a bit small, that's all that's wrong, and it'll catch up in no time.'

Of course he let her have it. And Edwina shook her head at the idea of a countess taking the runt from a litter of pigs home with her.

'All living things deserve a chance,' Lizzie said. 'And it's up to us to look after the ones that can't look after themselves.'

After breakfast she called on Reuben to ask how he was, and to show him the photograph of her two boys. The sight of her seemed to cheer him up and they talked about the old times.

'Remember when I fell in the pond and came up covered in duckweed?'

'You come up covered in worse'n that. You didn't half get wrong by your ma.'

'I got pretty wrong by you too, didn't I? The way you told me off.'

'Don't reckon I could tell you off these days, could I?' He looked at her with sly affection.

'I'm not any different, Reuben,' she said. 'Honest I'm not.'

After midday dinner, she went over the rest of the farm

280

with Walter, and then sat with Edwina in a sheltered patch of sunlight by the back door. They gossiped, and Lizzie talked about Dully and the boys and tried hard to explain how marvellous they were.

'They must be,' Edwina commented dryly. 'Not only by what you say but how often you keep saying it.'

The Reve coachman had put up at Wimblington for the two nights of Lizzie's stay, and early next morning she and her parents watched the slender curve of the carriage turn on to the level at Boots Bridge. The two greys were fresh and eager and the clip of their hooves beat a brisk tattoo on the still air.

''morning, M'Lady. 'morning, Sir . . . Madam. . . .'

Lizzie's dressing case was stowed away and he offered her a deferential arm up the step; at her request he placed the piglet, wrapped in a bit of old blanket, in her arms, and Walter and Edwina stood waving until they were out of sight. Slowly they returned to the kitchen.

'Seems dark in here, doesn't it?'

'The sun's gone in,' Edwina said.

They were approaching Littleport when it suddenly occurred to Lizzie that the one person she had forgotten to ask about was Aunt Netta. She knew that her parents still paid an occasional duty visit, and she knew also that the place where she lived was somewhere in the vicinity. It took her a moment or two to remember the name of it.

Blessing Hall. That was it, and on impulse she ordered the coachman to stop and enquire its whereabouts. They found the old, ivy-clad house, and after instructing him to look after the piglet, Lizzie knocked on the front door.

A pale-eyed skivvy in a print frock opened it, and Lizzie asked to see her aunt, Miss Hinton. The skivvy beckoned her inside and wordlessly departed. Another woman appeared, hatchet-faced and ratchet-jawed.

'Mrs Witherspoon?' She had recalled the matron's name along with the name of the house.

'The Witherspoons left six months ago. I'm in charge now.'

'Oh. So may I see my aunt?'

'The name's Mrs Hardcastle.'

If time spent among the aristocracy hadn't changed Lizzie, it had at least given her the ability to deliver the delicate snub when necessary.

'Thank you, Hardcastle. And now perhaps you will conduct me to my aunt.'

When the door opened she gave an involuntary cry and the colour left her cheeks.

The room stank, and every bed seemed to be occupied by a grey-haired, grey-clad wraith. Thin-faced and hollow-eyed, they stared at her apathetically, and her eyes travelled from one haunted, ghostlike apparition to another, desperately seeking for some sign of the prim, neat-and-tidy Aunt Netta.

They came to rest on a small figure crouching lopsidedly over a motionless mound in one of the beds, and something about the way it was crooning and patting the sour-smelling coverlet made her catch her breath.

'Keziah?'

The figure made no response, and Lizzie picked her way across to it, stepping round the beds and over the brimming chamberpots that littered the floor.

'Keziah. It *is* you. . . .'

Keziah looked up at her then. Her face had the same ghastly pallor as all the others, and her hair, never exactly plentiful, had now fallen out completely. She gave a faltering, rather empty little smile and said: 'Poor Missus is sick.'

Coming closer, Lizzie extended a shaking hand and turned back the coverlet. Aunt Netta was lying beneath it, curled in a foetal position with her fingers clasped under her chin. Her eyes were closed.

'Poor Missus been sick a long while.'

Lizzie nodded, unable to take her eyes from the motionless, marble-white profile. Then with an effort she slipped her hand inside the torn and stinking nightshift and felt the feeble beat of Aunt Netta's heart. The knowledge that she was still alive drove her to instant action. Replacing the coverlet with a quick gesture, she ran downstairs and out through the front door to where the coachman was waiting with folded arms.

Hoarsely she ordered him to follow her, and pushing past the woman called Hardcastle hurried with him back to the women's dormitory. Aware of his shocked repugnance, she heard him gulp convulsively as he followed her through the minefield of chamberpots to where Keziah was crouched over Aunt Netta.

'Help me wrap her in the coverlet and then carry her downstairs. We're taking her home.'

The other inmates watched impassively as Aunt Netta was lifted from the bed and laid over the coachman's shoulder like a sleeping child. Only Keziah began to whimper distractedly.

'And you're coming too,' Lizzie panted, tugging the cover from the next bed. She draped it round Keziah, pushed her bare feet into a pair of bast slippers that caught her eye, then holding her tightly and protectively, led her downstairs.

In the hall, Mrs Hardcastle attempted to bar the way through the front door. 'Who are you? What d'you mean coming in here and upsetting my inmates? Where d'you think you're taking them?'

Lizzie drew herself up to her full height. 'I am taking these two inmates, as you call them, away from here because it's the most horrible, wicked place I've ever seen in my life. That lady there' – she indicated the motionless form of Aunt Netta – 'is my aunt, and this is her personal maid. And since you haven't recognized who I am, I will tell you: I am the Countess Dullingham of Reve.'

There was no further opposition, but as she half-lugged Keziah through the open door, Lizzie delivered a final shot: 'Furthermore, you will shortly be hearing from the authorities about the state of this place. I now bid you good day.'

It was not an easy journey back to Reve. Aunt Netta lay in the corner, supported by rugs and cushions and with her legs propped across Keziah's lap, while Lizzie, remembering that she had omitted to feed the piglet, sat squashed in the other corner with it clasped against her breast as she coaxed it to suck from its improvised baby's bottle.

At one point she turned her head and caught Keziah looking at her; a nervous, puzzled, pitiful look that affected her profoundly.

'Do you remember me, Keziah? Do you recognize me after all this time?'

Keziah went on looking at her, her poor bald head nodding in time to the horses' trot.

'You're Miss Lizzie,' she said finally. 'You must be.'

'Two old ladies, one bald and the other at death's door, and one small ailing pig. No, of course not, my darling. No trouble at all.'

'Well you see she *is* my aunt, and I couldn't leave Keziah because she'd pine, and as for the pig – '

'I'm sure it'll be a very nice pig. Eventually.'

'But you really don't mind?'

'No, my darling, anything for you.'

'Do you really mean that?'

'Yes. I do.'

'In that case there *is* something else, Dully. Something a bit bigger.'

'An Indian elephant.'

'No, be serious.' Lizzie drew a deep breath. 'I want us to buy a workhouse.'

'Good God!'

'It's only a small one – as workhouses go. But oh, Dully, if you could have seen inside it and seen that awful woman who runs it and all those poor old souls crouching there like ghosts . . . if we bought it, and I'm sure it wouldn't cost much, we could clean it up and paint it nice colours and find a nice kind matron to run it and I could visit it once a week to make sure that everything was all right – oh, please Dully, *do* let's!'

Amused and touched by her earnestness, he promised to think it over.

In the meanwhile, Aunt Netta had been installed in a room overlooking the south terrace. Sunlight streamed through the windows, and Lizzie had two small beds moved in in place of the big four-poster. She filled the place with daffodils and pots of early tulips and engaged a hospital nurse to work in conjunction with the local doctor.

Aunt Netta's condition was diagnosed as malnutrition accompanied by acute melancholia. The doctor prescribed beef tea and junket for the first few days and stressed the importance of a warm blanket-bath twice daily. She was also to be discouraged from lying in the foetal position, and so began the process that became known as uncurling Aunt Netta. At regular intervals throughout the day, Lizzie and the nurse would gently coax her thin white limbs out straight while they talked to her and softly called her name. And Aunt Netta would moan a little at being disturbed, and curl herself up again the moment they had left her. She kept her eyes closed because she was too weak to keep them open, the nurse said, but Lizzie suspected that it was because she was still afraid of what she might see.

Keziah, being in better shape, was allowed to potter about the room, dressed in a new grey skirt and flannel blouse, and one morning Lizzie impulsively sent for one of the white wigs that were part of the Reve footmen's ceremonial dress. Rather to her surprise it fitted, and she was even more surprised by Keziah's reaction, which was one of unmitigated joy.

'You shall have a nice wig of your own then, Keziah,' Lizzie announced, but for the first time in her life the meek and lowly Keziah asserted herself in an astonishing display of force and defied anyone to remove it from her head. They were not even allowed to touch it.

'There is no reason why the poor woman should not wear a footman's wig if it pleases her,' Aunt Minna said placidly. 'Let her keep it, and we will send to London for a replacement.'

In an attempt to coax Aunt Netta back to life, Lizzie brought Berry and Tommy to see her one afternoon. After shaking hands with Keziah, they stood very close together by the bed, staring in silence at the white marble features and closed eyes.

'I think we prefer the little pig,' Berry said finally.

It was the sense of closeness coupled with his kindly desire to assume responsibility for a younger brother that prompted Berry to use the regal-sounding *we*.

'We do not like rice pudding,' was frequently heard, even when Tommy was spooning his portion up with relish, but the natural empathy between them was very real. If one was not well, the other languished, and if a misdemeanour had been committed, even Mama and Papa had difficulty in discovering the culprit.

Yet it was becoming apparent that their characters would be as different as their physical appearance. They both had bright red hair and brown eyes that tilted at the corners – Tommy's a little more markedly than Berry's – but whereas Berry was tall and broad-shouldered for his age, Tommy was of a lighter build, with slender hands and feet and a rather pointed face. They played together without quarrelling, and although Berry preferred games of physical skill with a competitive element, Tommy invariably opted for the world of make-believe. For him, there was always the possibility of a dragon under the bed.

'If there is, I'll chop its head off!' Berry would cry, brandishing a wooden sword, and already there was something strangely impressive about him; something strong and brave and magnificent that would draw people to him.

The plight of the Damperdown piglet filled them both with equal solicitude and they begged to be allowed to look after it. Upon Lizzie's instructions, it had been placed in a small improvised run in a corner of the orangery, and they took turns to give it its bottle and to change the straw bedding heaped close to the hot-water pipes. It throve, and learned to recognize them, and they called it Glycerine because Tommy thought it was a very beautiful word.

Spring merged into the stately pageantry of summer, and the long weeks devoted to uncurling Aunt Netta at last began to compensate Lizzie and the nurse for their pains.

She now lay straight of her own volition, and one day

286

opened her eyes. She evinced signs of pleasure when they propped her up with pillows, and when they brought her a fresh home-grown peach served with a little cream from the dairy she wielded the spoon herself.

Fragile as tissue paper, she took her first tottering steps supported by Lizzie on one side and Dully on the other.

'Come on, old lady, you're doing splendidly.'

'Just two more little steps, Aunt Netta,' promised Lizzie, and they guided her towards the chair by the window where Keziah was hovering with cushions and a shawl.

But there was still no sign of returning memory; in fact, she seemed at times to betray far less awareness than that which twinkled in the small eyes of Glycerine.

'It's gone on for too long,' Lizzie sighed. 'Her mind's all rusted up, but at least we know she's not unhappy, don't we?'

There had been one or two minor obstacles of a legal nature to be overcome before the Littleport workhouse became Dullingham property, and on the day Lizzie took Dully to see it, the Hardcastle woman had already been replaced by a temporary substitute from the village.

They wandered among the inmates sitting in the warm overgrown garden, and then she led him round the house, which had now been cleansed of its worst filth.

'What a dreadful place!' He held a handkerchief to his nose as they explored the foetid sculleries.

'But it's going to be beautiful, Dully, you mark my words! It's all going to be cleaned and scrubbed properly and the builder's going to colour-wash all the walls inside, and I've ordered some nice cretonne curtains and some padded chairs and I want to get some nice cheerful pictures – '

'My word, Matron, how you rattle on.' He drew her close and kissed the tip of her nose.

'Not here, darling, someone might come in. And listen, they're not going to wear paupers' uniforms.'

'Very right and proper.'

'They're going to wear whatever they fancy. Or failing that, we'll persuade them to wear nice bright colours and no miserable old widows' caps unless they really want to.'

'We? Am I really included in all this?' He looked at her comically.

'Naturally you are.' She traced his name on the dusty windows. 'Otherwise it wouldn't mean anything.'

'That's jolly civil of you, Liza-Lizzie.' He drew a plus sign, then added her name to his.

'Uncle Badger once said it's easy to be nice to people when you've got everything in life you want, but it's more than that with me. I keep on wanting them to be as happy as I am – I want to share it all, somehow.'

'That's because you're such a darling.'

'No, it isn't. It's something more, something deeper. . . .'

'What, then?'

She stood thinking, then slowly drew a heart shape round their two names. 'I don't know. Love, I suppose.'

Uncle Merton descended the ladder from his tree house and sidled into the belt of woodland that protected the north side of Reve. Sunlight flickered through the leaves of birch and oak, and he trod noiseless as a small hunting animal.

He knew every step of the great park, every tree, every rise and fall of the ground; moving into the open, he crossed the wooden footbridge spanning the two-mile stretch of river that fed the lake. Red deer were grazing in a cluster and they made no attempt to move off when he passed close. They all knew him. So did the sheep and the longhorn cattle. Only a heron rose lazily from the river's edge and settled a little further up water away from the disturbance.

Rough grass gave way to smooth lawns, and Uncle Merton continued his circuitous route towards the south front, bending towards the earth and slipping between groups of trees whenever possible. He heard the sound of voices; a slow murmur of conversation from the shade of a tree where steamer chairs were grouped, then the squeal of children's voices and the splashing of water. Young Berry and Tommy were in a rowing boat on the lake, Berry straining manfully at the oars while their mother and father watched from an ornamental stone seat nearby.

As he drew closer to the terrace he caught the sound of piano music, a ripple of notes, cool as a shower of raindrops, spilling from the open library window. All the windows were open; in some, the cream holland blinds were partly drawn, and in others the heavy curtains hung motionless and becalmed.

In the centre of the terrace was a flight of steps, its stone balustrade laced with blue wisteria. He mounted quietly, and saw that the terrace was deserted save for the occupant of a hooded Bath chair. Its back was turned towards him, but he could see the occupant's white hand lying limply on the armrest. The piano music stopped, then started again, and he heard the rich blackbird notes of a woman singing. Miriam, he supposed.

Taking small rapid steps, Uncle Merton reached the side of the Bath chair, coughed politely, then peered cautiously round the edge of the hood. Aunt Netta opened her eyes and smiled.

'Good afternoon.'

'Good afternoon.'

'I hope you are feeling better?'

Aunt Netta's smile faltered a little, then returned. 'I can walk quite well now, but I tire easily.' Her voice was like a little silver thread.

'That is understandable.'

They remained silent for a moment or two, listening to Aunt Miriam singing, then Aunt Netta said: 'Why don't you draw up a chair? I'm sure Matron wouldn't mind.'

The request that he should sit down perturbed Uncle Merton far more than the reference to Matron.

'I'm not sure. . . .' His glance darted nervously.

'There's an empty one over there.'

Something about her impelled him to obey. He hurried to fetch it, but set it down at a safe distance.

'Have you lived here long?' Aunt Netta asked presently.

'All my life.'

'How sad.' She looked at him wonderingly. 'Were you a foundling?'

'I was subject to fits as a child.'

'You remind me of someone, but I can't remember who.'

'Did they suffer the same disability?'

'Fits? I can't remember, it all seems so far away.'

The stilted, rather disjointed conversation seemed to satisfy them both and they sat thinking. Faint screams drifted up from the lake and mingled with Aunt Miriam's song.

'My memory is not very good these days,' Aunt Netta said eventually.

'I rarely make use of mine. There is no need, as my life is very simple and repetitive.'

'How pleasant.'

'Are you enjoying your stay here?'

'Oh, yes. Matron is very kind.'

The screams were coming nearer; near enough to hear that they were of a happy nature, but Uncle Merton rose hastily.

'I will have to leave you now.'

'Oh, must you go?' She looked up at him with large faded eyes. 'I do hope you will call again.'

'I will – I would like to.' He was backing away nervously, and his face had a tight, clenched look. Dully and Lizzie were coming across the lawn, Dully carrying Tommy pickaback while Berry pranced in front crying, 'We both fell in! We both fell in and we're *fearfully* wet!'

'Goodbye.' Uncle Merton dabbed rapidly and inconclusively at Aunt Netta's hand, then turned and hurried away.

'Uncle Merton! Uncle Merton!' The children caught sight of him and he waved his hand fleetingly, before setting off at a dogtrot back to the north side and the river that led towards his sanctuary.

He had never met anyone who impressed him as Aunt Netta had done. He had first come upon her three weeks ago, lying on the terrace in her Bath chair, shrouded in shawls and with her face partly obscured by a white veil to keep off the insects. He had crept up to her, curious as a cat.

She had looked like a dead bride. Like a woman who had pined away painlessly and romantically, and been painted by Mr Burne-Jones before the onset of decay.

He had no idea who she was, and it never occurred to him to enquire; partly because there were often transitory guests at the house, but mainly because of his reluctance to communicate with anyone. So he had said nothing, done nothing to further his acquaintance with her, but instead had filled his waking hours with thoughts of her strange, fragile appearance.

As the summer settled into its stride, her Bath chair began to appear on the terrace with greater regularity. Afternoons only to begin with, then any morning after eleven he would see from across the head of the lake her Bath chair being wheeled through the great double doors by a uniformed nurse. He found himself irresistibly drawn towards it, even to the extent of allowing himself to be greeted by Woodstock or Badger as they took a pre-prandial saunter with pet dog close at heel.

'Good morning, Merton! All well in the woods . . . not?'

A kindly, typically incurious greeting, and Merton would duck his head in acknowledgement and hurry past, only pausing for an instant to flick a glance into the interior of the Bath chair where the strange woman lay.

One morning he muttered good morning as he scuttled past; her eyes were open and she was no longer wearing the white veil, but she made no sign of having heard; possibly he had not given her time.

But Aunt Netta had noticed him, and his appearance teased at her blank memory with a pleasant insistence. Matron she had learned to recognize, for she was younger and kinder in her ways than the last one, but all the rest were a mere blur of faces and voices. This place was much larger than the last one and it was more comfortable, but she had no desire to pursue comparisons further. She was content to accept things as they were, without question and without quibble, and only the dark intensity of the strange man's glance prickled at her mind. Once upon a time she had known him very well.

Now, for the first time, he had spoken to her. Although they had not been introduced, his soft voice and deferential manner led her to believe that he was a gentleman, and she wondered vaguely what had brought him to this place. Then she remembered that he had had fits as a child. No doubt they had left their mark on him.

The renewed sound of laughter scattered her thoughts. Just below the terrace, Berry was chasing his mother round and round the base of a statue; craning, she watched them dodging this way and that, panting and giggling. Berry's wet hair was plastered over his forehead and his clothes flapped heavily with water. Then Dully charged towards them with Tommy on his back, and with a scream Lizzie made a dash for the terrace steps. In doing so she collided heavily with Uncle Badger, who was about to descend them with Eulalie at his heels.

'Save me! Save me!'

He put out his arms and lifted the pursuing Berry high in the air and held him there, dripping and shrieking, and as Dully galloped up to them with the equally dripping Tommy, a small dark object hurtled towards them from the direction of the orangery and flung itself upon Eulalie.

'Oh Lord, who let the pig out!'

'It's Glycerine – it's *Glycerine*!'

Struggling from his father's back, Tommy seized the pig and crouched down with it but Eulalie, excited by the tumult, flew at it and nipped the bit of curly tail that protruded from beneath Tommy's elbow. With a shrill squeal the pig leaped from his grasp and crashed into Lizzie, who sat down heavily on her behind. Helpless with laughter, everyone rushed to pick her up, and when Aunt Miriam appeared and mildly enquired whether there had been a contretemps, they all laughed harder than ever.

It took several minutes to restore order, and when the children had been despatched to the nursery for baths and clean clothes and Eulalie and the pig had been separated, Lizzie repinned her hair, straightened her dress and went across to Aunt Netta's Bath chair.

'What a dreadful family I've got!' she said, and reached for her aunt's hand. 'I do hope the noise didn't upset you.'

'Oh no, Matron,' said Aunt Netta. 'It was a nice noise.'

★

The glory of summer deepened to a final splendour before the onset of autumn and the arrival of Miss Trout, the nursery governess.

Miss Trout was a large woman balanced upon small feet, and a large gold locket dangled in space off the richly curved salient of her bust.

'Miss Trout,' murmured Dully, out of earshot, 'is very stout.'

'Which is better,' added Lizzie, 'than being like Aunt Netta. . . .'

The two little boys mastered the alphabet, chanted multiplication tables and were told that all the areas coloured pink on Miss Trout's map of the world were part of the British Empire. There was an awful lot of them, and she informed her pupils that when they attained manhood they might well be expected to help rule the Empire as Governors or even Viceroys because they were sons of the nobility.

'What's that?' Berry asked blankly.

'My dear boy, your papa is an earl,' Miss Trout reproved. 'Surely you are aware of that?'

They were not aware. They knew nothing of genealogy or social privilege, and to begin with were frankly baffled when Miss Trout sought to explain what made their position in life different from that of most other people. She also told them that as members of the aristocracy the world would expect them to behave not only with decorum ('Sit up straight, Thomas, don't droop . . .') but with courage and dignity, loyalty and honour. These vital qualities would have to be observed at all times if they were not to let the side down. The side being their family name and the country of their birth.

They listened politely, and ten minutes later Tommy had forgotten what an earl was, and returned to drawing mice on the back cover of his copybook. He was growing into a docile, dreamy child, content to spend long periods in the world of his imagination, where small animals and birds predominated.

Miss Trout's discourse made a far greater impression

293

upon Berry, possibly because he was older, and when lessons were concluded for the day he disappeared in the direction of the long gallery.

It was deserted, and he stole quietly down the length of white drugget that protected the floor, looking at each portrait in turn. They were all Dullinghams, all family, and he tried hard to draw a sense of pleased recognition from the eyes that seemed to follow his every movement. He found the calm enigmatic stares a little unnerving, but remembering Miss Trout's edict about courage and dignity, loyalty and honour, he paused in the middle of the long row.

'I'm a Dullingham too,' he said, 'and I promise that I'll always be very nice to everyone.'

They continued to stare at him, almost as if they were expecting him to elaborate a little, so he clasped his hands behind his back and added: 'What I mean is, I promise on my honour not to let the side down.'

As a Christmas present that year, he and Tommy were each given a pony, and although both learned to ride with facility, Berry was the one who begged to be allowed to gallop before they were officially off the leading-rein. In him, lack of fear seemed coupled with a practical common sense unusual in a child of his age. He took a couple of tumbles and got up laughing, and galloping side by side with his father through the crisp frozen park was the most wonderful thing in his world.

It was wonderful for Dully too, and he would glance down at the small sturdy figure sitting so firm and competent, and at the merry face and flying red curls, and feel a surge of tenderness. There was still no hunting at Reve, but when Tommy joined them his imagination supplied all the drama they could wish for. They chased dragons and goblins and wolves-who-had-stolen-little-children, and although it was natural that they should take their father's loving indulgence for granted, he occasionally overstepped the mark by interrupting the game with a sudden fierce and wordless embrace to which they submitted with ill-concealed impatience.

The Polperros came to stay early in the new year. With

the passing of time the friendship between the two couples had become easy and comfortable; Martha had found her place and no longer wept secret tears over old family photographs, while Lizzie's wrath towards Fairford had long ago cooled to the same temperature as that of her passion for him. And little Felix Polperro, with his mother's good looks and his father's charm, was a play-fellow of the Dullingham boys.

Sprawled on the rug before the schoolroom fire, he told them that one day he was going to join the Royal Navy and become an Admirable like his great-grandfather Polperro. 'What'll you be, Berry?'

'Me?' Berry looked at him in surprise. 'I'll just go on being what I am.'

'But when you're grown up you've got to be something else as well.'

'No. I'll just be the same thing, only bigger.'

Dissatisfied, Felix turned his attention to Tommy, who was lying on his back with his eyes closed. Firelight gleamed on his red hair and touched the handful of freckles on his nose. 'What about you? What'll you be?'

'He's gone to sleep.'

'No, he hasn't. Tom – what are you going to be?'

'I'm going to be' – Tommy's voice seemed to come from a long way off – 'someone who watches things and then writes it down, but I don't know what it's called.'

'It's not called anything because it *isn't* anything.'

'Yes, it is.'

They tussled, like young animals testing their strength, and Berry flung himself on top of them. They rolled off the hearthrug and under the table, three small boys in knicker-bockers and nurse-knitted jerseys, and years later Felix remembered that day and thought how Berry had spoken with a child's clarity of vision. He had known instinctively even then that he was one of those rare creatures whose personal lustre outshines the most dazzling achievements. There was no need for him to be anything, because he already *was*; he was more real, more vivid and more splendid than anyone around him.

Yet he was far from invulnerable, and his arrival at preparatory school that autumn was a total disaster. He had looked forward to going, had zestfully counted the days to his departure, but he had been unable to foresee the effect of leaving home. Without the family and Reve, he seemed to dwindle and die. He was not the only new arrival to spend the first night in tears, but his tears continued; he couldn't eat, and like a small lost animal, seemed helplessly resigned to the long dark misery which was all he could envisage ahead of him.

The headmaster and his wife were very kind, the matron tried to comfort him on her large bosom and other little boys regarded him with an awe which was their nearest approach to sympathy, but no one seemed able to break through the wall of sorrow that imprisoned him. He just lay or sat or stood wherever they told him and continued to pine for home, his golden-brown eyes awash with tears, his chin perpetually aquiver.

After seven days the headmaster telephoned to his parents, and when they arrived to take him home that afternoon, he rushed to them and clung to them both, speechless, and soggy with crying.

Lizzie cried too, and Dully had to refuse the tray of tea and hot buttered scones and lead his wife and son away, after it had been arranged that Berry should return the following September when Tommy would be old enough to accompany him.

'We've got a surprise to show you,' he said to Berry when the front door had closed behind them. 'Something special.'

Berry sobbed, still incapable of speech.

'Something *very* special.'

'Papa only bought it yesterday,' said Lizzie, and bent to wipe her son's eyes so that he could see the Panhard that stood glinting in the driveway. 'And he drove it here all by himself.'

A maid stowed Berry's trunk and tuckbox on the back seat, bobbed a curtsey and withdrew. He sat on his mother's lap with his arms round her neck as she adjusted her motoring veil and his father put on his new white motoring gloves and fur-trimmed goggles.

They set off, a little convulsively, and Berry clung to his mother and hated the new motorcar because it wasn't one of the Reve carriages that smelt of Reve with a pair of the fat Reve carriage horses between the shafts. He felt betrayed, but by the time they reached the outskirts of Bury St Edmunds he was dry-eyed and shaken by the implosion of only an occasional huge dry sob. He loosened his arms from his mother's neck and began to take note of his father's new acquisition. He disliked the smell of oil and petrol but found the soft chug-chug of the engine curiously exciting.

'Want to steer?' They had turned through the gates of the south avenue.

'Oh yes – please!'

He scrambled on to his father's lap and held the steering wheel between his small capable hands.

'Mind how you go – whoops, nearly had us in the ditch!'

'I was just going round something.'

They arrived, their clothes white with dust and Lizzie with her hat tilted over her nose, and everyone hugged Berry lovingly and forbore to comment on the salt tearmarks that still stained his joyous face.

'One cannot detach a fruit from the tree until it is ready,' observed Miss Trout, and Aunt Minna patted her shoulder and said how wise she was.

'I have always found wood more amenable than brick or stone,' Uncle Merton said to Aunt Netta. 'And I prefer living wood above all else.'

'You have a point, I'm sure,' Aunt Netta replied, and looked with mild surprise at the way her hand was lying at rest in the crook of his arm.

It had taken a long while to reach this stage in their relationship. During the winter months their meetings had been sporadic, for it was too cold for Aunt Netta to venture outside, and Uncle Merton was unable to overcome his deeply rooted dislike of human assemblage. The best he could do was to send her, via a waylaid footman, little gifts of winter-berried twigs, and on one occasion a bunch of early snowdrops which he had picked and tied with a small piece of faded ribbon.

She accepted these gifts with dreamy pleasure although she was not always certain of the donor's identity; her memory had returned to a certain extent, but remained patchy, and these days seemed to prefer to register impressions rather than facts. She still thought of Reve as some kind of institution of which Lizzie was the matron, and had no desire to question matters further. She was happy to drift with the tide, and if fate had robbed her of independence it had also shown mercy by smoothing all the fretful captiousness and petty pretensions of the old days. What was left of her was plain and clear as springwater.

Now that her physical strength seemed to have returned hand in hand with the warm weather, she was walking arm in arm with Uncle Merton. They had crossed the wooden footbridge over the river, and Aunt Netta exclaimed with pleased surprise when a rabbit bounded from the sheltering trees on their right, noted their nearness with alarm and bounded back again.

'The two little boys keep rabbits. They are allowed to bring them indoors.'

'I had a pet hare when I was a boy. Found him half-strangled by a poacher's snare, and he lived in my wardrobe for years. Very sensitive creatures, hares.'

'It is very sad if the two little boys are orphans.'

'They are also very clean. Only ever used one corner for its droppings.'

'But Matron is very kind. . . .'

They walked on, pursuing their own thoughts yet each very aware of the other. They came to the large beech tree that spread its shade out to their feet, and Aunt Netta's attention was caught by the little rustic table that stood close to it.

'Oh, I wonder who left it there?'

'It's mine.'

She paused, slipping her hand from his arm. Then she noticed the ladder. Slowly her gaze travelled its length and

298

she saw the wooden house wedged between the giant branches and half hidden by trembling leaves.

'That is also mine. It is where I live.'

Like a wondering child, she moved closer and touched the ladder with her thin white fingers while he stood watching from beneath bushy black eyebrows. He had planned this moment many months ago but had always postponed its final commitment for fear that she might find the whole thing rather strange. No one else had ever visited the house by invitation, and now that the moment had finally come when she herself was about to be welcomed to his private world, he was a little surprised that he should feel so calmly happy.

'Would you care to mount?' He gave a stiff little bow and stood aside, but when she placed one foot on the bottom rung of the ladder and then hesitated, he moved forward.

'Perhaps it would be better if I led the way.'

Aunt Netta had never climbed a ladder before – had never felt the slightest inclination to do so – but in this new state of gentle acquiescence there was no reason why she should not at least try. So she followed behind him slowly and carefully, brushing her skirt aside before attempting each new step.

He was waiting for her at the top, standing on the little wooden platform that spanned the gap between door and ladder.

'Don't look down.' He took her hand and she stood motionless, lost in silent contemplation.

The miniature Gothic house, hexagonal in shape, was cradled in the tree's smooth grey embrace and almost entirely obscured by leaves. To begin with, it was the leaves that impressed her most; she had never been so close to so many living breathing leaves before, and had never been aware that they could whisper and shiver and pulse with vitality. There must have been hundreds and thousands of them, brushing her cheek and touching her hair, and all of them glowing with animation and twinkling with needle-points of sunlight. She had entered a new secret world of green luxuriance poised high above all human affairs, and she put out her free hand to touch a spray of foliage that seemed to seethe and dance with life.

'So many,' she whispered. 'So *many*. . . .'

Without replying, Uncle Merton led her inside. Although his house was small, something about its unusual situation made it appear quite spacious. And it was made entirely of wood. The average summerhouse has a wooden floor, wooden walls and roof, and most houses contain wooden furniture, but there was something totally different about this place. It was dominated by the living strength of the beech tree in whose capacious arms it lay.

The wooden chairs and table, the swept, rug-strewn floorboards and tongue-and-groove walls all seemed to irradiate the power that had come from an acorn, a seed, a winged fruit blown on the wind. Aunt Netta stood with her hands clasped against her breast. The place glowed with cleanliness, with a sweet, quiet, old-maid's pride, and outside the two leaded windows and the open door the young green leaves bobbed and beckoned and cast patterns on the floor.

'Pray, do be seated.' Uncle Merton indicated a chair and Aunt Netta sank into it. 'Would you care for some tea?'

The question was largely rhetorical, for he had made his preparations in advance, and with much care.

The teacups and saucers, and a dish of petits fours, were set on the low table in front of Aunt Netta, and a silver kettle simmered on its matching spirit stove. A small silver knife and a lace-edged table napkin were set by each plate.

'It is all very tasteful,' she murmured.

He made the tea, and she noticed the sprinkling of black hairs on the backs of his hands. He seated himself opposite, and they began to eat and drink.

'Do you entertain often?' Aunt Netta asked eventually.

He shook his head. 'I have never liked anyone sufficiently.'

She thought over his words, and was on the point of saying what a pity, when the vague stirring of memory prompted her to admit that she too had never greatly cared for other people.

300

'Although I believe there was someone once, I seem to remember. . . .'

He looked across at her with his head on one side. 'A gentleman friend?'

'It may have been.' Her voice sounded faint, as if it too had retreated into the past.

'I have no wish to pry.'

They sipped their tea in silence for a moment or two, then Aunt Netta indicated the petit four on her plate. 'Did Matron make these?'

'No, my man fetches them from Bury St Edmunds.'

'The food here is very good,' Aunt Netta commented, nibbling daintily. Then touching her lips with the lace-edged napkin, added: 'I believe I had a servant at one time.'

'Is that the woman in a white wig?'

'The one I have in mind has white hair, yes, but whether it is a wig I have no knowledge.'

For the first time for many months Aunt Netta tried hard to prize open the door of her memory. The woman with the white hair slept in a small room that communicated with her own and was constantly fussing over her, and because of her obviously loving devotion it had become increasingly difficult to ask her who she was. She supposed she should have done so ages ago, when whatever had happened had first happened.

'The trouble is,' said Aunt Netta with a rare burst of confidence, 'I don't know what happened.'

'The past is of little consequence, particularly when one lives an uneventful life,' replied Uncle Merton, pouring more tea. 'The hours merge into days and the days into years, but the seasons are the only measurement of time that matters. The rhythm of the seasons dominates our lives.'

'It must look very different in here when the tree is bare.'

'Beautiful and rather stark, yes. But you will see for yourself.'

'Does that mean that you will invite me again?' Her ivory cheeks acquired a touch of colour.

'I would like you to come often.'

When it was time to go, he escorted her across the

301

footbridge and along the lakeside to where the formal gardens began. They heard the stables clock striking six, and the sound mingled with the echoing cry of a peacock.

'I must hurry,' she said, 'in case Matron is cross.'

Briefly and timidly they shook hands. Now within sight of the house, his old furtiveness had returned, and he hurried away towards the safety of the trees.

'Oh, Missus dear, wherever you been?' cried Keziah, hastening towards her.

'I have been with a friend,' replied Aunt Netta, with something of her old self-confidence. 'As for the details, they need not concern you.'

By the year 1906 Lizzie and Dully had become immutably set in the pattern of life at Reve, and the knowledge that it would last forever was like a safe and loving presence in the background of each day.

True, they made a brief sortie into the outside world shortly after Berry and Tommy went off to school, and servants were sent ahead to open the London house in readiness for their arrival. Shutters were opened on to the dusty birdsong of Park Lane, chandeliers were debagged, dustcovers were removed and windowboxes burst into miraculous flower in time for the reception given by the Earl and Countess Dullingham.

It was a grand reception in a very grand house, and Lizzie and Dully stood at the top of the staircase to receive Argylls and Asquiths, Balfours and Battenbergs, Gloucesters and Grevilles, Legges, Lascelleses and Londonderrys, all of whom were charming and gracious and – as Dully whispered in his wife's ear – paltry as twopenn'orth of pins.

'Some of it's our fault,' Lizzie said later. 'We're not in the swim.'

'What's that got to do with it?'

'We don't follow politics or the social calendar. We don't hunt and shoot and go to Marienbad – you haven't met any of them for years and I've not met any of them before in my life.'

'Oh Liza-Lizzie, I've been selfish, haven't I?'

She cradled his rueful face between her hands, then slowly leaned forward to kiss his mouth. 'What time's the next train home?'

With the departure of the last guests, the house already had an air of abandonment. Servants were clearing away the champagne glasses and the remains of caviar and smoked salmon; they were removing the carnations and tuber roses and the long green garlands of smilax; they were dimming the lights and bolting the doors while firelight flickered sleepily in the master bedroom and the Earl was unhurriedly pleasuring his wife.

They stayed in London for three days and bought presents for all the family, and when they arrived home Lizzie flung her hat and gloves high in the air and cried: 'That's it, old boy! We're never going away again!'

Reve was everything, and because she was still restlessly impelled to share happiness with other people, Lizzie pestered Dully to humanize another workhouse. The one that caught her attention was a larger and less prepossessing building than Blessing Hall, with bars at the windows and iron-studded doors that crashed shut every evening at six.

Most of the inmates were married couples who had been turned out of their tied farm cottages because they were too old to work. Their goods had been sold and they had been trundled off by horse and cart to the Union Workhouse, where they were ruthlessly separated. Males and females were allowed to meet on Sunday afternoons after a dinner of meat pudding and small beer, and the senseless bigotry of it appalled Lizzie.

'Dully, we've got to buy it and make it like Blessing Hall.'

'This one's not so simple. To begin with it's Town Council property and we'd be up against all sorts of local bigwigs.'

'But we're far bigger wigs than they are.'

'I'm not sure we can pull rank like that. Try to be patient while I make enquiries.'

He was told that the appropriate committee would be graciously pleased to accept an endowment, should he care

303

to make one, and would also be prepared to include his name on the Board of Governors, but as for the rest . . . They shook their heads regretfully.

Lizzie heard the news in silence, then said: 'Did you know that two of the inmates are people from Reve? An old gardener and his wife, and their name's Dawkins. I only found out about them this afternoon.'

'They should be in one of our almshouses.'

'*Should* be. Seems we haven't enough to go round.'

'Which suddenly simplifies everything. We'll build our own place on our own land, and those who wish to transfer to it may do so.'

The project took six months to accomplish, and Dully insisted upon having *The Elizabeth Dullingham Sanctuary* inscribed over the main door. It stood back from the road, yet close to the village shop, the church and the Dullingham Arms, and the ex-nurse and her husband engaged to run it were told that there was to be no segregation of the sexes.

The arrival of the two Dawkins was followed by a migratory flock of other old souls, and to begin with Lizzie drove to the sanctuary daily in a pony-chaise to superintend the running of the kitchen and the planting of the garden with fruit and vegetables, and became violently embarrassed when a gnarled old East Anglian tried to kiss her hand in gratitude.

'It's all wrong, Dully, when all I'm trying to do is share a tiny bit of what I've got.'

Dully smiled, and arranged that Lizzie's birthday should be celebrated by a sit-down dinner and a garden fête for all those, both working and retired, who were in their care. It became an annual event, and one year her photograph appeared in the paper with the caption *Countess with the Common Touch*, which also embarrassed her greatly.

The only person who seemed unable to find her rightful place in the happy scheme of things was Keziah.

Unaccustomed to any form of consideration, she still had no idea how to respond to the casual geniality of Reve. Perplexed and bothered, she curtseyed to footmen and once snatched a small silk cushion away from Aunt Minna because she fancied that it belonged to the missus. Like some poor old workhorse finally released into a green field, she found it difficult to adapt to a new life without the jerk of the reins and the crack of the whip, and for her, the long days were filled with frustration and unease. She knew Miss Lizzie, and recognized that she must have married into the gentry, but was unable to grasp the sheer magnitude of Reve itself; it frightened her, and having mastered the shortest route from bedroom to bathroom to the ground-floor rooms most generally in use, she left it at that. Shadowed archways and rambling corridors intrigued her not, and she scuttled from one recognizable landmark to another as if pursued by an alien power.

But it was Aunt Netta's recent behaviour that lay at the heart of her distress; she felt comfortably at home with a sharp-tongued mistress, and a mistress returning from death's door via a long and silent convalescence she could also understand with loving patience, but this new, un-characteristic habit of going off with a strange man and sitting up in a tree with him was beyond her powers of comprehension. She was left in a state of total bewilder-ment.

And as the weeks passed, bewilderment became darkened with suspicion. Who was this man? He couldn't be gentry if he lived like some sort of squirrel – and suspicion was only one step away from the jealousy that now tormented her days and racked her nights.

Vainly she tried to steer Aunt Netta away from his sinister and pernicious influence – 'Don't go out there, Missus, it's going to rain and if you get wet it'll take bad ways. . . .' And Aunt Netta would give her a smile of vague forbearance and proceed as planned.

She was spending more and more time with her fancy man and, prowling in the vicinity of the beech tree, Keziah would listen hungrily to the low murmur of voices floating down through the leaves. Sometimes she could smell cooking and hear the subdued clinking of china and cutlery, and she would lean against the tree's great smooth trunk and weep for the old days in Wisbech, when she had been

305

happy in the dank fastness of her basement and the missus had been correctly ensconced in the best bedroom behind Nottingham lace and concertina blinds.

She had endured a great deal since those days, but no amount of worry or misery could equal the terrible sense of no longer being needed.

I might as well die, she thought. Just curl up and die and be done with it.

Uncle Woodstock, with Scotus at his heels, came upon her one day trailing disconsolately by the river. Spied even from a distance, her squat black-clad form appeared bent beneath a weight of intolerable sorrow. He overtook her, and falling into step, remarked on the beauty of the day.

Keziah nodded, and surreptitiously applied a handkerchief to her eyes.

'Oh, my poor creature, is something wrong?'

Pausing only to bob a brief and confused curtsey, she shook her head and hurried on.

'Are you indisposed? Have you a pain?' He took her arm and turned her gently to face him. Beneath the tousled white wig her face was blotched with tears.

'Come now, tell me.'

'It's the missus, Sir. She's gone funny.'

'In what way?'

Keziah squirmed in his grasp, her face averted. 'Don't rightly know, Sir. But somebody's to blame for the way she's carrying on – she's never bin like it before.'

'In what way has she become funny?'

Formed by a world in which criticism of one's betters was akin to blasphemy, Keziah struggled hard to contain her feelings, but the words burst out, staccato with sobs and then torrential with tears. Little by little, Uncle Woodstock learned that Aunt Netta had always been a lady of pride and gentility – a lady who always observed the niceties and the proprieties suitable to her station in life – she had always been as fussy about her food and delicate in her habits as any other lady, but now . . . since meeting up with this man who lived in the woods and never spoke, she'd lost all her rightful ways and gone funny. 'It's not right to go climbing up trees with strange men and sitting there heedless as a pigeon.'

'Come, come,' said Uncle Woodstock, and lent her his handkerchief. 'We must try to remember that the more bizarre examples of human behaviour are often caused by a rush of emotion, and I venture to suggest that in your mistress's case the emotion is merely one of sudden harmless delight. She and Merton seem to get on un-commonly well – we have all observed the budding friendship – and surely it would not be right to begrudge either of them their happiness.'

'But up trees,' wept Keziah.

'Up *a* tree,' amended Uncle Woodstock. 'And a very special tree at that. It was planted to commemorate the visit of William Pitt at the time of his elevation.'

Keziah looked at him helplessly from above the snowy mass of his handkerchief.

'His elevation to the peerage – he became Earl of Chatham, did he not?' Uncle Woodstock took her arm and they continued pacing along the river bank while Scotus bounded ahead. 'But let us be clear about one thing: your present state of dolour is caused by self-pity rather than anxiety for your mistress. She has at last recovered her health and is now in the throes of belatedly chucking her bonnet over the windmill. To stop her would be wrong, for she is harming no one. It would be selfish and meagre-minded, and I am perfectly sure that you are neither. Merton is a dear chap, and his tragedy has always been his inability to chum up with other fellow beings. None of the rest of us has ever experienced the slightest difficulty in that direction, so we can only surmise the loneliness and sense of alienation he has suffered all these years. And now he has met your mistress, someone else who has obviously suffered long years of imprisonment from self-restraint. Can we honestly deny them the pleasure they seem to find in one another? Surely not. So dry your eyes, my good woman, and reflect on the words of Goldsmith; man wants but little here below, nor wants that little long.'

'Yes, Sir,' mumbled Keziah, who had understood about one word in six. 'Thank you kindly.'

She bolted away, while Uncle Woodstock stared thoughtfully after her. Then whistling to Scotus, he strolled back to the house in search of Lizzie.

Because he never entertained, no one in the family realized that Uncle Merton was an exceptionally good cook.

The manservant who cleaned his house and saw to his linen also purchased provisions for him twice weekly, and years of leisured solitude had given his master ample opportunity for experiment in the culinary arts; he learned by a slow process of trial and error, which he conducted in secret and sampled with analytical care, and he built up a store of practical knowledge almost equal to that of the French chef who presided over the kitchens at Reve.

His equipment was modest, but so was the quantity of food he normally prepared; for roasting and baking he used the small iron cooker with its built-in bain-marie that also heated the place, and for more rapid cooking he had a single-burner Primus stove. His kitchen was no more than a tiny galley, but it was maintained with an exemplary neatness (not to say an old-maid fussiness) that in her heyday would have rivalled Aunt Netta's own.

It took some time for her to accept the idea that a man should cook, and it seemed doubly extraordinary that a man who was presumably some kind of gentleman should turn back his cuffs and peel a potato and hash an onion. To begin with she tried to ignore – then watched with reluctance – his neat hands with their sprinkling of black hairs dealing competently with sauces and soufflés, with puddings and pastry so light that they almost blew away.

'Try a little more,' he would say, slipping the knife beneath another slice of Pithiviers cake, 'it is excellent with this apple wine.'

He made all his own wines from fruits and flowers, leaves and hedgerow herbs, most of them garnered from unfrequented corners of the estate. Each retained its own special quality, and after a little hesitation Aunt Netta took pleasure in joining him for an aperitif in the form of a carefully decanted young 1907 elderflower, before proceeding on to its senior and more stately cousins during the course of the meal.

And they would sit there in the long summer evenings, sipping the last of their wine as the light dwindled and the last bird settled fearlessly to roost on a level with the open window. Sometimes they would pursue their gentle and characteristically disjoined conversations – to an outsider it would have sounded more like two monologues running side by side – then at other times they spoke very little. As the spirit of harmony strengthened between them there became less and less need.

At ten o'clock, Uncle Merton would rise quietly from his chair and light the lantern that hung by the door, and then fold Aunt Netta's cashmere shawl carefully about her shoulders before escorting her back through the park to the big house. Gravely they would shake hands and say goodnight outside the doors that led on to the terrace, and Aunt Netta would smile vaguely at anyone she met as she drifted up to her room, where Keziah would be warming her nightgown on the bedroom fender.

Uncle Merton always extinguished the lamp before making the return journey because he knew every step of the way; even on moonless, starless nights his feet trod as unerringly as those of the wild creatures. Sometimes he went straight home, but quite often he roamed far into the night, hearing the owls call and watching the silver-grey shapes of badgers moving through the woods. And all the while he would be thinking of Aunt Netta; thinking of her with an awed delight that nevertheless contained an element of torment.

He had never had a friend before. Had never wanted one. Even as a small child he had disliked physical contact – warm, hearty nursemaids who washed him and dressed him, lavender ladies who kissed him, and tobacco-scented gentlemen who clapped him on the back with hands hard as iron. He had never had the slightest need of any of them. And as he grew older it became apparent that he was equally

309

deficient in any form of emotional warmth. He remembered once, many years ago, one of his brothers complaining that he never shared secrets.

'I haven't got any to share.'

'Oh, yes you have. Your whole bally life's a secret.'

They let him go his own way. School, and the cult of the strong silent male, did little to encourage him socially, until even the smallest doses of enforced camaraderie filled him with a panic-stricken desire to flee. He had nothing to say. And could think of nothing to do that would be acceptable, let alone excite their admiration.

On the day he overheard them discussing him and commenting a little sadly on his growing eccentricity ('Still, he's not as bad as the second Earl, who used to *chase* people . . .') he decided that it would be far better to give up even trying to live in normal juxtaposition to the rest of them.

He thought he had better emigrate, and chose Central Africa, but the one night spent in a London hotel before proceeding to Tilbury Docks filled him with such horror that he cancelled his passage and returned home. And he discovered with a curious sense of relief that his life depended on Reve, the place; on its parkland, its sweeping woods, its meadows and stretches of sky-reflecting water. It was his own defined territory, and he knew that he would never leave it again.

Patiently the family offered him various small houses on the estate and even offered to build him one on Charles Pasture, which lay over towards Reve hamlet, but in each case he was hesitant and evasive. Most were too large, some too close to other people, and about others he merely remained silent – unable to explain that for him they were still uncomfortably full of the atmosphere engendered by their previous occupants.

'So where do you want to live?' they asked. 'Up a tree?'

'That would be splendid,' he muttered, and purely as a joke Badger and Woodstock had the tree-house constructed by an estate carpenter for his thirtieth birthday. They were disconcerted when he thanked them and moved in, but

310

after a few months had passed, no one saw anything particularly remarkable about Merton's choice of dwelling-place. It had merely become part of the history of Reve, and the great beech tree dedicated to William Pitt, statesman and orator, continued to cradle its burden protectively.

Aunt Netta had been accepting his hospitality all summer, the first hesitant invitation to afternoon tea becoming gradually extended to luncheon and then to dinner. By August she was spending almost every day with him, and on Thursday the twenty-fourth of that month their relationship tumbled unexpectedly into its final stage.

Early sunshine had become hazed with light cloud and the air was still and hot as she set off through the formal gardens. A gardener's boy in a straw hat was dead-heading roses, and stepped aside respectfully as she passed. Another inmate, thought Aunt Netta; this must be one of the largest infirmaries in the county. . . .

Uncle Merton met her at the far end of the lake, and shook hands with her before carefully placing her arm in his. As usual, he was dressed in black.

'The weather has broken.'

'Oh, dear.' Aunt Netta glanced about her, as if for some visible sign of damage.

'August is frequently turbulent.'

'There was a spider in my tooth glass this morning.'

'The birds always know. They seem uneasy.'

'It was not a very big one, which was a mercy, for I have never felt comfortable in their presence.'

'There's little birdsong at the moment, save for a few robins tuning up for the autumn.'

'I don't care for autumn,' said Aunt Netta, straying briefly on to Uncle Merton's subject-matter. 'It is too cold and sad.'

'But necessary. Otherwise there would be no berries.'

'Berry. That is the name of one of the little boys staying at the home. There are two of them, and they both go away for long periods.'

'Like the swallows.'

311

He had prepared luncheon in readiness for their return, and they ate fresh salmon that he had poached in the bain-marie, and drank a little sparkling wine. It was one of the days when conversation languished, and after the meal they sat by the window, contemplating the becalmed leaves and feeling the hours pass silently.

Almost imperceptibly, the light was draining from the sky. The room took on a dull, bruised look, and in spite of the stifling heat, Aunt Netta gave an involuntary shiver.

'August storms,' she said, suddenly breaking the long silence. The words seemed to have a strange effect on her for she repeated them. 'August storms. . . .'

'They pass.'

A gust of wind rattled the beech leaves with a tinny sound. Thunder rumbled, and Aunt Netta sprang hastily to her feet. 'I must leave here.'

'No, you will get wet. Stay until it is over.' He put his hand on the arm of her chair and she cowered back into it again, her eyes huge.

'It happened in Ely.'

'What happened in Ely?'

'And he was drowned.'

The thunder sounded another drum-roll, louder now, and the hot wind blew in through the window. There was a scurry of birds in the tree.

'Who was drowned?'

She sprang up again without answering, then suddenly spun round in a mad little circle as if impelled by some terrible vision. She found the door only by blundering into it, and before he could prevent her had thrown it open and stumbled hastily and clumsily down the ladder. With her skirts bunched in her hand, she began to run along the edge of the wood. A zigzag of lightning streaked the sky. The thunder that followed was like the deep roar of cannon fire, and it released the rain; driven by the wind in a slanting silver curtain, it whipped Aunt Netta's frail hurrying figure, plastering her clothes against her body and her grey hair flat against her skull.

He caught up with her and seized hold of her while she

312

struggled frenziedly, half-demented by the torment of returning memory. It was like the agonizing return to life of a frozen limb; it seared her nerve ends and she screamed for it to go away again, but it beat against her brain with all the savagery of the storm. It would not be silenced.

'He was drowned in the storm! And I loved him! I loved him! He was wicked and cruel and I loved him all my life!'

Grimly Uncle Merton tightened his arms round her in an attempt to curb her wilder movements. Her head rolled back, and through the lashing rain he saw that her eyes were filled with madness. He tried to propel her towards the beech tree and shelter.

'No, no – I must go home!'

'You're going in the opposite direction – Reve is over *there*!' He gestured with a wet hand and she all but slipped from his grasp.

'Pity – oh, have *pity*!'

Another flash of lightning cast its dazzling flare over the bowed woods and trembling earth; half-deafened by the bark of thunder, he now hauled her roughly away from the trees and made her stand with him in the open meadow. It was impossible that they could become any wetter, and there was nothing more he could do than remain there with her and try to keep her safe from the fury of the lightning and from the paroxysms that seemed to be tearing her apart.

Looking over her shoulder, through rain-streaked eyes he saw a group of cattle standing heads down and motionless, and fleetingly he thought, we are like them; two animals waiting for the turmoil to cease so that we may continue with the interrupted pattern of our lives. . . .

He had never held anyone in his arms before, let alone a woman, and it was surprising how natural it seemed. He would have expected to feel squeamish embarrassment if not outright aversion, but his only reaction seemed to be pity, coupled with an unflurried desire to restore her to some kind of disciplined harmony.

She had stopped struggling now, and hung loosely against his shoulder. She was crying, and he continued to hold her in silence until a primrose-coloured shaft of light streamed weakly from a gap in the leaden clouds. The wind dropped and the rain slackened to a weary drizzle.

'The weather is trying to smile,' he said at last. 'And you must try to do the same.'

She returned with him to the tree-house, silent and docile as a child as she tried to deal with this sudden and calamitous remembrance of things past. It was almost as if an enormous book full of loose, unnumbered pages had been held open over her head to shower down upon her their closely written and unrelated facts.

Fragments of people – hands, faces, voices; things they had said. And places – the old family farm, and brother Walter when he was a boy.

Then other places. Vague, fleeting glimpses of neat grey streets running down towards a river – *Wisbech*, her mind pounced upon the word. And then – she stopped at the foot of the ladder and put her head in her hands – the dark-haired man reappearing one sultry August day and once again disturbing her careful calm with his forceful masculinity, and then telling her about – about –

She was hanged at Ely. But who was she – what was her name? Her newly awakened memory ached and throbbed as she forced it to fill in the blank spaces. . . . Then she felt someone touch her arm.

'Come along,' Uncle Merton said, 'we must dry ourselves and then make some tea.'

He gave her a bath towel and then a long green dressing gown in return for her wet clothes. He changed his own things in the far corner with his back to her, and outside the window a blackbird shook out its wet plumage and then swelled into the rich beauty of full song.

They drank tea and listened to the raindrops falling off the leaves on to the wooden roof, and if she sat very still and breathed very slowly her mind seemed to calm itself. She concentrated on the blackbird's song; it was sitting so close to the window that she could see the yellow circle of its fierce round eye and into the dark cavern of its open beak.

'Would you care for another tartlet?'

She shook her head and managed a smile. I was worrying

about something, she thought. What was it? Cautiously she allowed her mind to return to the events of the past hour, but the pictures were already fading. With the passing of the storm, the terrifying kaleidoscope of faces and places with their attendant emotions of fear and yearning were creeping back into their box and closing the lid behind them.

'I do apologize.'

'For what?'

'I think I became a little distraught.'

Without replying, he carefully refilled their teacups, and a ray of sunlight twinkling through the diamond drops of rain touched his bent head. Such black hair he had, and not a sign of grey, she thought.

'What happened at Ely?'

'Ely?' She frowned. 'I don't know . . . I think I went there once, perhaps when I was a child. Why do you ask?'

'Don't worry,' he said. 'It can't possibly matter, can it?'

She raised her head, and his image, dark-haired and dark-eyed, sparkled through her tears.

'I don't know. I don't understand what happened to make everything different.' She dabbed her eyes.

'Everything is exactly the same as before. It was merely the effect of the weather.'

'Are you quite sure?' She wanted to believe him.

'Of course. It's common knowledge that sensitive people are particularly susceptible to the electrical currents released during a thunderstorm. One merely needs rest and quiet, and – '

She leaned forward, staring into his face. 'And?'

He remained silent, and when the words finally came, he said them so quietly that she almost missed them.

'A loving friend.'

'Ah, yes.' She sighed.

They didn't embrace. The need to hold and be held had passed, out in the meadow along with the storm.

'I'm rather old,' Aunt Netta said reflectively.

'I am no longer young.'

'And I don't think my memory is very good. For instance

315

– and it must sound very silly – I don't know where I am or what I'm doing here.'

He smiled across at her. The blackbird finished its singing and began to preen its feathers now that they had dried. It wiped its beak to and fro across a twig, as if it were sharpening a knife.

'Look, the gnats are dancing. It's going to be a fine evening.'

'But who am I? What is my name?'

'Your name is Netta. Now, can you tell me who I am?'

She looked at him for a long time, openly and without embarrassment or any trace of the old prudish fear. Then the smile she gave him seemed to illuminate the room with its radiance.

'Of course I know who you are! You are Vernon Seagrave.'

'Papa, may I have a gun for Christmas?'

'What makes you think you need one?'

'I want to learn to shoot.'

'Why not leave it to the gamekeepers?'

Berry and his father were walking back from the home farm; harvest was almost finished and the golden stubble fields stood waiting for the plough.

'All the other chaps at school know how to shoot. Mountjoy's people had the King to stay last autumn and they bagged a hundred and fifty brace.'

'Is that what you want to do?'

'Not necessarily, Sir. I just think it would be fun to be a good shot.'

Aged twelve, Berry's head now reached his father's shoulder and he was finding it easier to fall in with his long strides. His hair, cut short now, gleamed a brilliant copper red and his warm brown eyes slanted up at the corners in the Dullingham smile.

'We'll see.'

They walked in silence, each aware that there was more to be said before the matter could be considered closed.

'I was about your age when I once rode to hounds. I was

staying here, and didn't realize what it entailed. Beneath all the swagger, it was a beastly business and I wanted no more of it.' It had never faded, that brief glimpse of the cornered beast with the foreknowledge of death in its eyes. 'Creatures have to be killed for various reasons, but man's amusement needn't be one of them.'

Dully stalked on, and Berry lengthened his stride accordingly.

'I don't think I'd like to kill anything, either – at least, not unless it was dangerous or something.'

'We'll see,' repeated his father, and resolutely changed the subject.

But the desire to own a gun remained; he tried to talk to Tommy about it, but his brother's interest in firearms was minimal, and when he mentioned it to Uncle Badger with conspicuous offhandedness, Uncle Badger, equally off-hand, asked what was wrong with a bow and arrow.

There was a gunroom at Reve but it was kept locked, and so the last weeks of the summer hols were spent in playing tennis and croquet and going for picnics; in sailing and riding and swimming, often with Tommy but sometimes on his own. It was during a lone ramble through the bluebell woods that stretched on either side of the little-used west avenue that he came upon the old man sitting with his back propped against a tree and his head bowed in sleep. Flies clustered around the crumbs of bread and cheese clinging to his moleskin waistcoat and buzzed round the mouth of the empty beer bottle close at hand. Berry stood poised, looking at him, then his gaze slowly transferred to the rifle that was also resting against the tree.

Shafts of mellow sunlight struck its polished wood, and he took a noiseless step forward. What he was about to do was extremely wicked. He took another step, and held his breath as a twig snapped sharply beneath his foot. The old man remained motionless. Close enough now to hear the purring snores, Berry continued to advance, then reaching forward, snatched up the rifle and silently and rapidly retreated.

Stealing was wicked, and stealing a rifle was even

wickeder, but his conscience was soothed when he told himself that he was, in fact, merely borrowing. He was only borrowing the rifle for ten minutes or so, and then he would return it and no one would be any the wiser.

On one side, the bluebell woods ended in a rough and uncultivated stretch of meadowland. It was a wild place, with strong bramble clothing bushes and old tree stumps and transforming them into dense rounded shelters for wildlife.

Panting, Berry crawled between two of them, and half-concealed by the thick tussocky grass began to examine his prize.

It didn't look particularly lethal, as guns went; the butt was polished and faded with age, and the trigger was shaped in a pleasing little curl. Very gingerly he placed it against his shoulder and squinted along the barrel. It felt right. It felt good. It felt as if he were taking his place in the ranks of men who had used guns to defend freedom and protect the weak.

'I promise on my honour not to let the side down,' he said to the drowsing world around him.

Still squinting, he rolled gently backwards, pointing the barrel at the sky. His finger found the trigger and squeezed it, just a little bit.

Nothing happened. In a way, he didn't want it to. Yet he squeezed again, a little harder, and instantly the rifle seemed to spring to life in his hands and the shot cracked out, sudden, deadly and invisible. Profoundly shaken, he all but dropped it, then struggled to a sitting position just as a rabbit darted in alarm from the thicket of bramble nearest to him.

Instinctively Berry pointed the rifle at it and fired, and the rabbit leaped in the air with a little squeal and then fell on its side. With his heart thumping tumultuously, he sat watching and waiting for it to move. It remained quite still, and the light had faded from its eyes before he dared to pick it up.

It was dead. Soft and limp and warm. There were fleas on its ears, and between the fingers of its narrow little front paws were beads of rolled earth, as if it had been digging a

318

burrow only recently. Berry's eyes filled with tears. It probably had a wife and children . . . and now it was dead. He had killed it. He had stolen its life, as well as the gun.

Very gently and carefully he laid it in the shelter of the bushes from which it had emerged. He stroked its fur down flat and placed its paws neatly together, then, shouldering the rifle, went back into the woods to find the old man.

He had thought it would be easy but he couldn't remember which was the right tree. It had been a larch tree, but there were a lot of larches in the wood. He thought that the old man would have been roused by the sound of the two shots and would be looking for him, angry and shocked that a Dullingham of all people would have stolen from him while he slept. But the place was silent. There was no sign of anyone. And when he came upon the beer bottle, lonely and abandoned, he propped the rifle against the tree nearest to it and shouted: 'I say! Is there anyone here?'

No one answered. Only a bird shrilled in alarm. He stood irresolute, then after a moment or two shouldered the rifle again and began the long walk home.

They would be angry. Very angry indeed. Already he could see his father's face, hear his mother say 'Oh, *Berry*, fancy stealing from a poor ole *man*!' while the uncles and aunts made coughing noises of disapproval. But if he didn't take the gun home, he needn't tell them. No one need ever know. Even if the old man was a gamekeeper and not a poacher, he probably wouldn't dare to admit that his gun had been stolen while he slept.

It was tempting. All he need do was throw the beastly thing into a clump of bushes and no one would ever find it. But he didn't. He marched on with it propped against his shoulder, and when he finally turned the corner of the house and began the long walk across the terrace he saw that a strange motor car was standing on the sweep of gravel below it.

He walked towards the family clustered round lace-draped teatables – long skirts, flower-strewn hats, linen suits and panamas, and Uncle Badger's Eulalie yapping idly at Aunt Miriam's parrot . . . and he swallowed hard in preparation for the confession.

319

Mama was the first to notice him. She said 'Berry' and then stopped, but it wasn't because of the rifle. It was because of Papa, who rose unsmilingly from his chair and said: 'You had better come and meet my mother and your paternal grandmother, the Baroness von Kassel.'

Papa's mother was a large woman, tall and tightly laced, and she looked down on Berry from beneath a hard straw boater trimmed with a striped ribbon.

'So you are the older boy,' she said, taking his politely proffered hand. 'Which is why they have named you Berry, I suppose.'

He said yes, it was.

'Well, well, nothing like family tradition.'

Aware that the family – Tommy he now saw was half-obscured behind Aunt Minna – was watching with a strange intentness, Berry laid down the rifle as unobtrusively as possible and said: 'Have you come to stay with us? I do hope so.'

He hoped nothing of the sort, but conscience forced him to a display of extra good manners.

'Only for two or three days. My husband and I are on a motoring tour – we live in Germany, as you probably know.'

He didn't know. He couldn't recall ever hearing Papa speak of his mother and had concluded that she must be dead.

'How jolly,' he said, and was about to move away, when the Baroness indicated a portly gentleman with a vehemently waxed moustache and said: 'This is my husband, the Baron von Kassel. He is your father's step-papa.'

They shook hands, and the Baron indicated the rifle with a lift of his eyebrows. 'You like shooting – yes?'

Berry gave him a reticent smile.

'Come and have some tea, dear,' called Cousin Lavvy, who had been staying at Reve for some weeks, and the family relaxed its rather taut watchfulness and made room for him. He sidled in next to his father, and was gratified

320

when he put his hand on his shoulder and gave it a squeeze. He looked a bit pale, Berry thought, but not angry.

'The same old place,' drawled the Baroness, looking up at the looming mass of the house. 'Same old statues and fountains – same old family faces.'

'We are all growing older,' said Aunt Minna, and Uncle Badger raised mournful eyes and sang: ' "When I am *dy-y-ing* . . ." '

'Are you acquainted with *The Indian Love Lyrics*?' Aunt Miriam leaned towards Baron von Kassel. 'Amy Woodforde-Finden, such a *sensitive* composer.'

'I prefer music that uplifts to that which enervates.'

'But Miss Woodforde-Finden is not in the least enervating!'

'Aha.' The Baron wagged a playful forefinger. 'The trouble with the English is that they are in love with the idea of slow decay.'

'I suppose it's preferable to fast decay,' put in Uncle Woodford.

'I find that rather an extraordinary statement,' Aunt Minna said mildly. 'I am perfectly sure that we enjoy life quite as much as any other race. Possibly more.'

'You are a beautiful race, and I salute you. But you are running down like a big grandfather clock. It is not good to live in the past and to sing songs about dying. You need someone to come along and wind you up.'

'You?' Lizzie gave him a charming smile.

'I would be prepared to assist.'

The air of slight tension returned, and Berry was conscious that his father's hand still lay across his shoulder. It felt firm and protective.

'And I would begin,' went on the Baron, 'with that young gentleman with the gun.' Instinctively everyone looked at Berry, who turned pink. 'Now, that young gentleman – he is the Viscount, yes? – has the old spirit that made the British Empire. I could see it in his fearless eyes, in the way he carried his gun and walked head up and shoulders straight. That young gentleman, I told myself – and I am never wrong – has the heart of a young lion. You will never hear him sing songs about dy-y-ing.'

321

It was an extremely awkward situation for Berry, but he reacted instinctively. Still pink in the face and with everyone watching, he put his hand on top of his father's and said: 'It's not my gun. I sto – borrowed it from someone and I meant to give it back to him but he'd gone, so I brought it home. And' – the final confession was of such gravity that he stood up – 'I shot a rabbit and killed it.'

He felt his father's hand slip from his shoulder, and was sorry. But he continued to stand there, looking round at them all and feeling miserable because of his sins and proud because he had just been compared to a lion.

He looked down at his father and whispered: 'I'm sorry.'

But Papa's eyes were fixed on his mother, the Baroness, who was eating an éclair on a fork. His face bore an expression that Berry had never seen before.

'Even better!' cried the Baron. 'A young gentleman who seizes his opportunities – yes?' He laid the same busy forefinger against his nose and winked: 'And I wager they will not let you have a gun yet? They say you are too young, and must wait a little, and so you tell yourself God helps those who help themselves – yes? Is that not so?'

Humour sparkled in his eyes; he was laughing and jolly, but some newly developed instinct told Berry that he was intent on making mischief.

'I beg your pardon, Sir, but I'm allowed to have a gun whenever I like,' he said. 'Although my father and I don't agree with killing things for pleasure, of course.'

It might have sounded very precocious, very priggish, but that special quality of his took away all suspicion of the spoilt young milord. The family contemplated him across the teacups and the last flakes of *pâte millefeuille* and didn't give him away. He had handled the situation adroitly, and the fib, considered harmless, was forgiven.

A footman appeared with the offer of fresh hot water for the teapots, but Lizzie waved him aside. 'I think,' she said, nodding at Aunt Minna, 'that it's getting rather chilly. Shall we go in?'

'Did you really shoot a rabbit?'

322

'Yes. I said I did.'

'Don't believe you.'

'I'll take you and show it you tomorrow, if you like.'

'It'll stink by then.'

Berry and Tommy still slept in the old night nursery, in two white iron bedsteads side by side. It was getting dark earlier now and they lay listening to the cry of a tawny owl.

'Did you like doing it – shooting it?'

'Didn't really have time to tell. But afterwards I felt half pleased and half fed-up, I suppose.'

'That old German chap said you'd got the heart of a lion.'

'Lot of bosh. He was just buttering me up.'

'That's what they call Germans – bosh.'

'Is it? Well, no wonder.'

'Why was he buttering you up?'

'Probably because he wants to get into our family. He wants to be a Dullingham.'

'But he can't be, can he?' Tommy sounded anxious.

'No, of course not. You've got to be born one.'

The owl's cry grew fainter. It faded into silence.

'Mama wasn't born one.'

'Mama's different,' Berry said, and fell asleep.

Uncle Badger leaned back on his pillows, sipping a nightcap and turning the pages of the *Illustrated London News*. The curtains of his massive bed were cosily drawn and Eulalie was asleep close by his feet. He sensed rather than heard the great house settling down for the night, and was mildly surprised to hear a tap on his door.

Uncle Woodstock, in nightshift and dressing gown, appeared through an aperture in the bedcurtains and sat down on the other side of Eulalie.

'What d'you make of her turning up again like this?' There was no need to ask who.

'Bad business. Rather like a bird of ill omen.'

'Seems Dully and Liza received a telegram no more than two hours before she arrived. *And* bringing that German fella with her.'

'She must have been married to him for years. . . .'

'Which makes it all the more singular. Why has she suddenly turned up now?'

Badger gazed at the hump made by his feet. 'Probably no more than a spontaneous decision – you heard her say they're touring over here. I suppose we must give her the benefit of the doubt.'

Woodstock made a growling sound, which woke Eulalie. Seeing him, she thumped her tail and went back to sleep. 'What's that you're drinking?'

'Brandy – warm yourself a drop. There's a spare glass here somewhere.'

Badger leaned over and rummaged in his bedside cupboard while his brother poured a tot into the upturned silver ladle. He waved it over the little blue flame of the spirit stove that stood between the clock and a photograph of Aunt Minna in a tiara.

'Settle your stomach.'

'It's not my stomach that needs settling. I always abhorred that woman; she's a born troublemaker – '

'Her husband – Henry's father, I mean – wasn't an easy man either.'

'Granted. But she made him worse with her moods and her tantrums.'

'Remember the time she threw a whole charlotte russe at him and it exploded? Cream and stuff everywhere.'

Woodstock chuckled unwillingly. Brandy fumes rose from the ladle and he carefully transferred the contents into the waiting glass.

'Your health.'

'Tickle your arse with a feather.'

They sipped meditatively, each roaming back over the past and reliving the years of poor old Berry, the eighth Earl Dullingham. Minna had borne up wonderfully after the loss of both husband and son. Seemed like only yesterday. . . .

'The young shaver spoke up well for himself over tea,' Badger said, returning to the present.

'Young Berry? Yes, he has the makings.'

'Even the Hun said something about lion-hearted.'

'No business to have taken the gun, though. Hope he'll get a dressing-down for it later.'

'Dully will see to it. Good chap, Dully.'

'By the by, who christened him that? Real name's Henry – not?'

Their gruff murmurings faded. Woodstock shifted his back to a more comfortable position. 'Must go. . . .'

'Stay,' said Badger, without opening his eyes. 'Plenty of room.'

'No. Scotus'll worry.'

'Damn Scotus.'

'You've never told me much about your mother.'

'Not much to tell, really. Didn't see a great deal of her.'

'Oh, Dully, how cold that sounds!'

'I *was* cold until you came along to warm me up.'

He gathered her into his arms in the dark. The sheets rustled softly.

'Fancy Berry taking someone's gun and shooting a rabbit. But at least he did own up.'

'I must have a serious word with him in the morning.'

'But don't be cross with him, Dully.'

'Am I ever?'

Silence, except for the soft sound of kisses.

'But I'm glad nobody said anything when he told your stepfather he was allowed to have a gun. It would have let him down dreadfully.'

'It would have let us all down. That's why the young rascal said it – some sort of tribal instinct he's inherited.'

'Us Dullinghams must stick together!'

'Absolutely.'

'Oh, it's all so happy . . . and I promise to be *very* nice to your mother.'

The visitors stayed for two days. On the first morning, the Baroness came upon her daughter-in-law crossing the great hall and wished her good morning.

Lizzie replied suitably and they both paused, irresolute.

It was an odd situation – two total strangers tied by such a powerful (and notoriously difficult) relationship.

'You are quite beautiful,' the Baroness admitted after looking her over. 'And I gather that you were some sort of actress.'

'I belonged to the Gaiety Theatre. You may have heard of it.'

The Baroness gave a small, ambivalent smile. 'How very interesting, you must tell me all about it some time.'

This was the kind of treatment Lizzie had expected when she first arrived at Reve; then, she would have had little defence against uppercrust put-down, but instead she had been welcomed and befriended and had responded to their geniality by unfolding like a sparkling midsummer rose. And now, armed with something of their own unruffled courtesy and unflurried way of speaking, she was proof against most aggressors, covert or otherwise.

'One day, perhaps.' She inclined her head graciously. 'But I would sooner hear about my husband's boyhood. He speaks of it so seldom that I sometimes wonder if it was entirely happy.'

'We had better walk outside,' replied the Baroness. 'Voices echo so stupidly in this place.'

They did so, and Lizzie stifled a grin as Uncle Badger raised his old panama with exaggerated deference as he passed.

They talked neither of Dully nor of the Gaiety; pacing the box-edged paths of the knot garden – the Baroness shielded by a lace parasol – they spoke in general terms of the weather, of her mountain home near Koblenz, and when Tommy appeared and politely offered them both a piece of barleysugar, the Baroness smiled briefly and said: 'You must learn not to interrupt your elders when they are speaking.'

But he's your grandson, Lizzie thought, quietly aghast. You've missed almost the first eleven years of his life and all you can say is don't interrupt.

Tommy melted away, and as the day passed Lizzie watched for signs of any rapport between Dully and his mother. Shortly after luncheon she overheard the Baroness commenting on the improved lighting and heating at Reve, and adding that German methods were considerably in advance of the English. Dully smiled, and offered her more coffee, which she declined.

She seemed to have no rapport with anyone. The aunts each took a turn in making a little suitable conversation, while it became increasingly obvious that both Badger and Woodstock were keeping sedulously out of her way. Dully spent part of the day dutifully escorting the Baron round the estate, but by the evening of the second day his mother was exhibiting increasing signs of nervous irritability. To those who knew her, her drumming fingers and twitching lips had always been a sign of approaching bad weather, but the storm, when it finally arrived, was not entirely of her making.

With the exception of Aunt Minna, who had excused herself and retired early, they were all in the billiard room after dinner that evening. The dark green lampshades cast a rich light over the table and left the rest of the room in shadow. Decanters twinkled dimly on a side table and the air was plumed with cigar smoke.

Four of them were playing; Dully and Woodstock against Aunt Miriam and the Baron, while the rest of them watched from the sofas nearby.

Idly Lizzie asked the Baroness whether they played billiards in Germany, but before she could reply the Baron straightened up from potting the red. 'Very rarely. We have better things to do.'

He said it while smiling expansively, but the discourtesy of the remark seemed to mingle and hang in the air with the cigar smoke. Removing the red ball from the pocket, he replaced it on the table for further play, but missed the obvious cannon.

Uncle Woodstock cleared his throat and studied the latest turn of events before deciding upon retaliatory measures.

'Perhaps we do things a little more efficiently, which gives us time for the harmless pleasures.' Squinting along his cue, he hit the ball for an in off stroke. It missed the pocket and he stood back.

'Like your Francis Drake and his game of bowls?' The Baron's smile remained expansive.

'Nothing wrong with Sir Francis Drake,' drawled Aunt Miriam. From his perch on her shoulder, Benbow leaned forward and appeared to study the lay of the balls intently.

'He's wondering if they're edible,' Lizzie murmured to her mother-in-law, who gave a token flick of the lips in reply.

'Oh, well played!' The Baron applauded Aunt Miriam with what seemed like genuine admiration, then added: 'Sir Francis Drake would have been proud of you.'

It could so easily have been a harmless, affectionate joke – the Dullinghams themselves were well versed in the art of teasing – but spoken in the Baron's precise and faintly guttural accent, there was more than a hint of derision. Or even worse, of patronage.

It was Dully's turn. He stood rubbing chalk on the end of his cue while he considered the benefit of going in off either the top or middle pocket. The shot he attempted was a difficult one and it failed; he hit his stepfather's white ball and potted it.

'He was foolish to attempt it,' said his mother, loud enough for him to hear.

'Well tried!' Lizzie's cry sounded defiant, and Cousin Lavvy, sitting on her other side, squeezed her arm.

For a while the game proceeded in silence. No one was playing particularly well and the atmosphere remained slightly tense. A footman appeared with fresh coffee, but no one wanted any.

'I noticed an extraordinary old crone wandering about wearing what looked like a footman's wig,' said the Baroness. 'Does anyone know who she is?'

'She's my aunt's maid,' replied Lizzie. 'We let her have it because the poor ole thing's gone bald.'

The Baroness said nothing, but her expression spoke volumes.

'If she is old and bald, surely she should be dismissed?'

328

said the Baron, coming round to their side of the table.

'Keziah is retired, and has the freedom of the house,' said Dully.

'We don't dismiss anyone from Reve because they're old,' added Lizzie, 'not even our horses. Come to think of it, we've got a pig that's eight years old.'

'And I dare say it lives in the house with you?'

'Not officially, although it has been known to scuttle through the hall.'

The Baron studied the layout of the table, then turned towards Lizzie. Lamplight caught the two scars on his cheeks and etched them white.

'I fear you are all doomed,' he said, slowly shaking his head. 'All you nice kind sentimental English with your animals in the bedrooms and servants sitting with their feet up. Once you were great; you conquered other lands and built an empire and we all respected you, but now you are letting it all disintegrate and die. You even sing songs about dying. You no longer believe in fighting and you no longer care about supremacy.'

Uncle Woodstock cleared his throat, then said heavily: 'I for one have never regarded aggression as a virtue.'

'That was not the viewpoint of your ancestors who built this house, I think.'

The Baron was still smiling his good-humoured and expansive smile, but Lizzie was not the only one to sense the temperature in the room dropping a further degree or so.

'I'm not aware that any of them were unduly aggressive, considering the times in which they lived,' boomed Aunt Miriam. 'The second son of our third Viscount – Mad Harry, they called him – died at Tyburn for supporting Charles at the Battle of Worcester, but he merely fought for what he believed was right: in this case, the monarchy. And this house, incidentally, is the third to have been built on this site by our forebears.'

Her voice roused Benbow, who had been drowsing, and he nuzzled her earlobe with a harsh kissing sound.

'Exactly!' cried the Baron, flourishing his billiard cue as if it were a sword. 'He was strong in his belief, in his faith – '

'You make it sound like a non-conformist religion, Sir,' Dully remarked.

'These days, we are more inclined to pride ourselves on being civilized,' piped up Cousin Lavvy.

'Quite so, dear Madame. And the brand of civilization you have in mind – be kind to dogs and the old and useless – is the first sign of weakness. And one cannot afford to be weak if one merely wishes to preserve one's place, let alone improve upon it.'

He turned back to the table. Bending low over his cue, he cradled the tip of it between his fingers and gently nudged the ball. He made a cannon. Silently they watched him follow with an in off the red. Dully moved over to the scoreboard. Still smiling, the Baron retrieved his ball from the pocket and replaced it on the table. For someone who seldom played, he showed considerable skill. He continued playing and scoring, while his wife watched twitchily and the Dullinghams eyed one another uneasily.

The good manners which the Baron appeared to regard as a sign of weakness prevented them from arguing with him; to disagree with a guest – and in the process probably to lose one's temper – went deeply against the grain, so they remained silent. Yet their very silence, however aloof and dignified, seemed even to them somehow to corroborate the Baron's charge of moral degeneracy.

It was deeply offensive to Woodstock in particular that the man who criticized them should be winning a game of billiards at their own table almost single-handedly.

Old fat bum, thought Lizzie, gazing stonily at the rounded derrière and rather short ramrod legs in front of her. She yawned as openly as she dared without letting the side down.

'For instance,' went on the Baron, dreamily potting the red, 'your lack of economic growth is a source of bewilderment and sorrow to your friends in Germany. You are not investing your money in your own industries any more. Your mills and your coalmines are run with mediaeval brutality, but what is far worse, with gross inefficiency. And your agricultural policy is equally backward. You are suspicious of new labour-saving devices because of your worship of the past, and so you can no longer compete. You are now importing about sixty per cent of your wheat from other countries, which is sad. Very, very sad.'

'No doubt it will be a relief to you to return home, Sir,' Dully remarked.

'Where no doubt the country is run more to your liking,' put in Aunt Miriam.

Once again her voice woke Benbow, who had been asleep on her shoulder. With no more than a token flutter of wings, he transferred himself to the edge of the billiard table, and after a moment's consideration proceeded to walk across it. He then perched opposite the Baroness, and subjected her to a long hard scrutiny before suddenly flying up at her and attacking her elaborately piled hair.

The Baroness screamed. Lizzie gave a yelp and batted him off. He nipped her finger, and the Baroness, whose composure had been slowly disintegrating during the last half-hour, leaped to her feet and continued to scream hysterically.

The loud noise caused Benbow to panic. He half rose in the air in a violent agitation of feathers, and it was Dully who strode over and captured him. Benbow applied his iron-hard beak to his hand and bit it.

'*Bloody* bird!' He released him, and Benbow fell to the floor like a brilliantly coloured shuttlecock.

'My *treasure!*' cried Aunt Miriam, scooping him up.

'It blinded me – it tried to blind me!' shrieked Dully's mother, and Lizzie, catching Uncle Woodstock's eye, began to laugh helplessly. Cousin Lavvy caught the infection and hid behind her handkerchief.

Only the Baron appeared to maintain his composure. He continued to play, stroking one ball against another and scoring cannon after cannon until the uproar subsided a little. Then he turned round.

'It is said that an effete society tends to lose emotional control on the slightest pretext.'

'Your wife,' said Dully with emphasis, 'is having the vapours. Perhaps, Sir, you should attend to her in whatever way you think fit.'

A hint of genuine amicability warmed the Baron's smile. He looked at Dully, and at all of them, as if he very nearly loved them, then laying aside his cue led his wife from the room. Her cries echoed behind her for several minutes and Uncle Badger glanced significantly at Aunt Miriam.

'Remember?'

'Only too well.'

'In the meantime, my poor husband is bleeding to death,' said Lizzie, binding her handkerchief round Dully's hand.

'My own poor bird,' murmured Aunt Miriam, stroking the parrot, who had now returned to his place on her shoulder. Tenderly her hand moulded the soft curved shape of him: 'Mama's poor *darling* bird.'

'My God.' Uncle Woodstock approached the table that held the decanters. 'Perhaps we really are going down the drain a bit. . . .'

The guests left after breakfast on the following morning, the Baron wearing a cape and a hat with a feather, his wife concealed behind motoring veils. The family stood at the top of the terrace steps, dutifully waving goodbye.

'What were those lines on his cheeks?' asked Berry.

'Duelling scars.'

'You mean, he got them fighting a duel? He must be awfully brave!' His eyes glowed.

Dully made no reply, but put his arms round him and Tommy and walked slowly with them into the house.

They joined the others, and the sense of relief put them all in holiday mood. They ordered a luncheon hamper, and an hour later set off in two open carriages for a picnic. The golden beauty of the day filled Cousin Lavvy's head with garlands of poetry, and sitting next to her, young Tommy looked across the park at the motionless splendour of the chestnut trees and searched through his vocabulary for the right words to fit them. The need to match words and objects continually preoccupied him, although he never told anyone. He didn't want to write poetry; he didn't particularly want to put the words down on paper at all – he merely wanted to get them right in his own head.

332

Their destination was a sheltered spot, on a bend of the river, that was known as the dell. The two boys helped the coachmen to unpack the rugs, the sunshades, the walking sticks, the cricket bag, the fishing rods, Dully's camera and its tripod and all the other interminable paraphernalia essential on a bona fide Edwardian picnic. Scotus and Eulalie yapped and chased in and out of the trees, and while the ladies spread the tablecloth and unpacked the hamper, Berry helped to unbuckle the horses and set them free to graze. The coachmen retired a little way off with their own basket of food, and Tommy listened to the low slow sound of their Suffolk voices and thought *murmurling . . . burmberling . . .?*

Cold beef, cold chicken, and a huge pork pie with battlements like a castle; salads and fruit – home-grown peaches and nectarines, early grapes and a *tarte* of late strawberries. Claret for the gentlemen, a light Sauternes for the ladies and gingerpop for the boys. The mellow sunlight caressed the glasses and willow-patterned picnic plates, the rose-strewn hats and genial Dullingham faces with its own brand of loving magic; perhaps on that day it really did love the Dullinghams slightly more than other people.

While Dully arranged his camera on its tripod, Uncle Woodstock captured a Bath White butterfly. It clung to his index finger, and the family clustered round to see.

'A very rare chap, this. Comes from the Mediterranean and the Near East and only occasionally finds his way over here. Just look at those *splendid* black markings on the white, boys.'

The butterfly closed its wings and then slowly opened them again. It seemed in no hurry to depart.

'He likes you,' Berry exclaimed, still peering closely. 'Can we take him home with us?'

Uncle Woodstock shook his head. 'No use in trying to argue with what's inevitable.'

'But he'll die when it gets cold.'

'So will we all.'

Dully took photographs while everyone lay back, replete. The uncles lit cigars, and from the coachmen's direction came the homely scent of pipe tobacco. Lazily Aunt Minna cut a slice of beef, divided it and fed it to the dogs, and Lizzie removed her hat and lay back again with her eyes closed.

'My dear, you will freckle.'

'Mmm,' replied Lizzie, and thought, I'm not a person; I'm just a plant drinking in the last of the sun and the warmth before winter cuts me down and I get raked up for stable fodder. Or else the harvest mice build nests in what's left of me. . . .

Only the boys remained active. Hidden by trees, they were fighting a duel with sticks.

'Bags I be the Baron!'

'Who'll I be?'

'You be the Black Prince or someone.'

And then the grown-ups roused themselves to play cricket and rounders, the ladies hitching up their skirts and running in a laughing pitter-patter of hairpins, while the uncles rolled up their shirtsleeves and played majestically; the two coachmen were persuaded to join in, and they laid aside their brass-buttoned livery jackets and exposed the tattoos on their arms.

'Good old Jenkins! *Run*, Jenkins!'

'Mama – you're *out*!'

'No, I'm not!'

'Yes, you are!'

Their voices floated in the air; laughter and shrill cries and the reverberating boom of the uncles.

'Papa, may we bathe?'

'Oh *please*, Papa . . . Mama. . . .'

The hasty shedding of shirts and breeches and stockings, then slender white bodies and small male parts twinkled as they ran. They leaped, and the lazy water closed over their gleaming red heads and then rose in an arc of glittering spray.

They both swam well; Berry churning the water energetically as he pounded to the far bank ahead of Tommy.

'Race you back.'

'Bet you won't.'

'Bet I will.'

The grown-ups watched from the bank, proud, loving and approving. Climbing out of the water, Berry remembered that the Baron had likened him to a young lion. The idea still pleased him, and he wondered whether anyone had noticed the three or four pubic hairs that now adorned his person. He hoped so, but didn't want to swank by drawing attention to them.

The sun was setting earlier now, and on the ride back Uncle Badger looked across at the year's assemblage of haystacks gleaming in its dying rays as they passed the home farm; they seemed to speak comfortably enough of the farming methods used on the estate, and he dismissed the Baron's criticisms from his mind; he was, after all, a foreigner.

At the top of the long ride, where a lone elm, shaggy and monumental, stood close to the sandy road, Aunt Minna stopped the carriages. It was a favourite viewpoint, and they looked down in silence on the great house lying below them, like a jewel on a bed of green silk. The heraldic statuary along the balustraded roofline seemed to pierce the calm sky, and a thread of smoke rose from an invisible chimney. The sad cry of a peacock echoed up to them.

'It never fails to touch one's heart,' murmured Aunt Miriam.

'Drive on now,' Aunt Minna ordered finally. 'The air is growing chill.'

The day had been perfect, almost too perfect, and the simple pleasures of the family picnic had temporarily erased all memory of the two uncongenial and uninvited guests. But in the library after dinner, the previous evening's scene in the billiard room returned.

'He seemed to know a great deal about our economic affairs, that German fella,' observed Woodstock.

'Most of it inaccurate . . . not?' Badger helped himself to a little more port.

'How do we stand, in the long-term scheme of things?' Woodstock asked Dully. 'Everything pretty well shipshape?'

335

'The barns looked nicely full when we drove past the home farm,' Badger said hopefully, and topped up his brother's glass. Then he too looked across at Dully.

'Everything's fine,' Dully replied, after a slight hesitation. 'All the farms are doing well and our beef cattle made a good profit last year. But we've got a certain amount to make up still; Harcourt's Reformed Death Duties were very hard on Uncle Berry's estate, and we've spent a certain amount on repairs and bringing the place a little more up to date, but – '

'But everything's all right?' Uncle Woodstock persisted, and Aunt Minna paused in the act of playing patience to listen.

'Everything's all right,' Dully said. 'But I must take care not to die for a long while because we couldn't easily bear another set of death duties like the last.'

A small chill seemed to creep through the room, then Lizzie snatched up a discarded shawl that belonged to Cousin Lavvy and draped it laughingly round Dully's shoulders. She asked if he would like a little calf's foot jelly, or perhaps a cup of hot milk, and her light-hearted solicitude warmed them all to laughter.

'Let's have some music, Miriam.'

'Yes, come along – let Liza do her waltz for us.'

'Only if you all join in.'

They did so, some more stiffly than others, after playing cricket and rounders, but the happy sounds were too far away to penetrate Tommy's dark and troubling dreams about the German gentleman with the scars on his cheeks.

He crept shivering into Berry's bed, and Berry put his arms round him and held him tightly and protectively without waking up.

On the day that Aunt Netta and Uncle Merton were married, Keziah woke up feeling very strange and rather ill. Her limbs seemed heavy and her head light, and she peered at the new frock hanging against the front of the wardrobe and wondered whose it was and why they had left it there.

Then she remembered that Miss Lizzie had driven with

her to Bury St Edmunds and bought it for her, so that she would look nice for . . .

For?

She stood with her hands pressed against her eyes, and when she remembered gave a little cry and hastily knelt down by her bed to say her morning prayers.

'Our Father which art in heaven . . . thank you, dear Lord Jesus, for keeping me safe 'til morning light . . . bless all those around me, Miss Lizzie and My Lord and their little ones, and bless the missus today in particular – and her gentleman. . . .'

Having already been numbed into a state of inchoate misery by Aunt Netta's gradual transfer of herself and her small possessions to the house in the beech tree, the news that she and Uncle Merton were to marry came, in some ways, as no more than an official seal on Keziah's painful sense of desertion.

Her vague fear and dislike of men had been nurtured by Aunt Netta herself, and so she had long ago adapted to a life in which they played no part; yet now, here was the missus at the age of sixty-two getting married to one of them. Not only that, she was going to live with him up a tree.

The Wisbech days had become no more than a faraway dream, but sometimes when Keziah's sense of outrage was even deeper than her grief, she would wonder what Mrs Plumptre would say if she knew even the half of it; in moments such as these she would dream of herself cushioned on Mrs Plumptre's kindly bosom while she raged and wept and spilled out all the pent-up emotions that had racked her for so long.

But today she felt so strange, so tired and so unreal. When she looked at herself in the dressing-table mirror, the bald-headed apparition who looked back at her bore no hint of recognition in its eyes. Please Lord, she thought, take me away.

A housemaid brought her a tray of tea and bread and butter. Her manner was civil, but Keziah always read a hint of resentment in her eyes: Why should I have to wait on you? You're no better than I am.

'My Lady says please will you be in the saloon at eleven-thirty.'

'All right.'

'Remember where it is, do you?'

Keziah nodded, and the housemaid withdrew.

She drank some of the tea but left the bread and butter because she wasn't hungry. It was only nine o'clock and she had nothing to do until eleven-thirty, apart from getting dressed. So she crept back to bed and pulled the covers close up to her chin. It was October now, and an autumn mist breathed against the window.

At ten-thirty she began to get dressed. The can of hot water left outside her door had cooled, but even tepid water was a novelty to someone of Keziah's station. The missus' room had a basin and water coming out of taps, and she was going to give it all up to live in a tree.

She washed slowly, breathing heavily, and sat down to rest before putting on the new frock that Miss Lizzie had bought. She put on her wig and laced her shoes, and because it was still only five past eleven, went for a little walk down the corridor. Statues and pictures and rows of closed doors. She had no idea what lay behind any of them. A footman passed her, whistling under his breath, and Keziah dropped him an involuntary curtsey.

She thought she knew where the saloon was, but got it wrong because she started off down the wrong staircase. She wandered across a hall she had never seen before, then the gentleman called Woodstock came upon her from the opposite direction. He was looking very smart in a black suit and a high cravat secured with a ruby pin, and to Keziah's confused embarrassment he smiled and offered her his arm.

He escorted her into the saloon, where the family was already gathered, and Miss Lizzie came forward with both hands outstretched and said: 'Oh Keziah dear, you do look a treat!' She embraced her and kissed her cheek, a thing she had never done before, and Keziah, already feeling strange, swooningly closed her eyes among the frills and scent of eau de chypre.

They were all dressed up, and everyone admired her new frock, then My Lord and Miss Lizzie led the way across the great hall to the chapel. The lady who wrote poetry walked in with her, but when it came to deciding where to sit, Miss Lizzie took her hand and said: 'Keziah's going to sit next to me, aren't you, Keziah?'

They were in the front pew, and Keziah's tired, reverent eyes took in the beautiful paintings on the walls and ceiling before coming to rest upon the black-haired, black-suited man standing by the chancel steps.

It was him. She continued to stare at him in silent agitation, but in spite of her antagonism became aware of a reluctant sense of kinship. Beneath the rigid and indomitable stance she recognized a fellow-creature nervously at bay on alien ground.

A trickle of music came from the hidden voice of the organ as the vicar of Reve Magna moved smoothly to his place at the head of the chancel steps, and as the music swelled a little and the family rustled to its feet, Lizzie took Keziah's hand.

The progress up the aisle seemed to take a very long time, and Keziah gave one deep and terrible sob as she saw the missus, in a dove-grey costume and a small flowered toque, on the arm of His Lordship. She looked rather pale, and Keziah saw how she moved like someone in a dream towards the man who could scarcely raise his eyes to look at her. She saw His Lordship gently pat the missus' gloved hand in the crook of his arm.

The service proceeded, and Miss Lizzie slipped a dry handkerchief to Keziah as the vows were exchanged in voices that were almost inaudible. Through streaming eyes she watched the gold ring being carefully placed on the missus' finger, and when they all knelt to pray she could only whisper, 'Make him take care of her – see that he takes care of her – ' against the folds of Miss Lizzie's handkerchief.

The return journey down the aisle was conducted at a somewhat brisker pace; the bridegroom wore a painfully constrained smile, while the missus had a patch of pink on either cheek, and Miss Lizzie bent solicitously to dry the last tears from Keziah's eyes before they left the shelter of the pew.

To comply with the wishes of the bride and groom, the reception was neither lengthy nor elaborate. They all returned to the saloon for champagne and foie gras. His Lordship made a short and affectionate speech, to which the groom dutifully and painfully replied. Watching him, Keziah thought: Out of all the people in this place, him and me are the only ones that don't belong. He's not in his right-feeling place any more than I am.

But Keziah was not left unattended. Sensitive to her probable feelings, the ladies took turns to chat to her; and after the wedding cake had been cut, the gentleman called Badger clapped her on the shoulder and said something about tickling something or other with some feathers, to which she agreed numbly, dumbly, cheered nevertheless by two glasses of champagne.

'And listen, Keziah,' Miss Lizzie said. 'Just because Aunt Netta's got married, it doesn't mean that we don't need you any more, because we do. We couldn't be without you, Keziah.'

She was very beautiful, Miss Lizzie. She had lovely rich auburn hair like her mother, and beautiful features and a beautiful tall graceful figure, but the most beautiful thing of all was her smile. It warmed and embraced, and Keziah mumbled and fumbled because she wanted to warm and embrace her back, but she didn't know the words. She was just like the gentleman who had married the missus.

At the end of the brief celebration, they all moved slowly through to the great hall, where the booming voice of Woodstock reverberated round the statues and up past the noble, threadbare flags and the balustraded balcony to the high curved roof, and as two footmen opened the great double doors on to the outside world, Aunt Netta moved across to Keziah and held out her hand.

'Thank you,' she said. 'You have been my dear friend.'

Keziah gave a great gasp. She seized the outstretched hand, then hurriedly released it because of the old impulse to wipe her own on her apron before proffering it to her betters.

'Give me your hand, Keziah,' said the missus, and Keziah held it out; it was the first time that the two hands had ever touched except by accident.

'And I would like you to shake hands with my husband.'

He was standing there beside her, the gentleman who had stolen her, and in the small dry strength of his hand Keziah again sensed the feel of a fellow alien. His rather small, deep-set eyes stared into hers, and it was obvious that he recognized her, too.

'Come and visit us,' he said.

A carriage had been adorned with white ribbons, and the smiling coachman had dressed up in full livery and with a white cockade in his top hat. The mist had cleared now, and a shaft of pale autumn sunshine touched the tight satin rumps of the two horses as the bridegroom handed his wife into the carriage and then climbed in beside her.

The family stood at the top of the steps, waving and smiling. They watched the carriage take the broad sweep of raked gravel and then bowl away across the park towards the belt of trees where the beech tree stood.

Goodbye, thought Keziah. I won't see you no more.

They took her back into the house with them and they offered her tea, but she declined. The tiredness had returned, and with it the strange sense of hollowness. She said she would like to go and lie down for a little while if there were no tasks for her to do.

No, they said gently, there were no more tasks that needed doing, and Miss Lizzie walked with her to the foot of the staircase – the one she was familiar with – and stood watching as she slowly ascended.

She found her way to her room without taking a single wrong turning. A small fire glowed in the grate and her bed had been neatly made during her absence. The room was dusted and tidied, and there was nothing left to do.

Very slowly she undressed and laid her clothes carefully over the back of the chair. She removed the wig, and after stroking its silky white hairs down flat, placed it on top. She drew the curtains and crept into bed, and with her hands folded on her breast and her eyes closed, she was like a small boat withdrawing slowly and effortlessly from the shore. Jealousy, loneliness, uncertainty, even love itself, were being left behind like tedious old friends, and she surrendered with tired gratitude to the endless song of the sea.

They went to her room as the day itself was dying, and already it was too late to send for a doctor. Keziah had departed as unobtrusively as she had lived.

Having attained seniority at prep school, it was a little disheartening when Berry realized that he would have to begin the long upward climb all over again.

He appeared very small indeed during his first term at Eton, while members of the sixth form appeared almost preposterously large. Both the uncles and his father had prepared him for some of the more idiosyncratic customs he was likely to encounter, and Uncle Badger spoke with a certain nostalgia of the organized rat hunts after winter floods had invaded the cellars. His father warned him of the fagging system.

'Do you think I'll get beaten much?'

'With a bit of luck you might escape – I gather they're far more humane these days. But if you do, you'll have to grit your teeth and bear it, like the rest of us. Chances are you'll have deserved it.'

He slept on a small fold-up bed in a cubicle known as a stall, and his appointed fag-master was a blond and drawling sixth former called Pentworth-Haigh, who issued orders from the open doorway of his room down sixth form passage.

Early mornings were the worst time; a cold hip-bath in his stall at seven a.m. before a hasty dash to supply Pentworth-Haigh with hot water for his own more splendid ablutions, which included shaving. Then early school at seven-thirty and back to breakfast in chamber, but only after Pentworth-Haigh had been supplied with hot buttered toast from the kitchen.

The kitchen fireplace was not particularly large, and his first sight of six other fags armed with slices of bread impaled on toasting forks was a little unnerving. It became apparent that he would have to shove his way in, and when he politely extended his toasting fork to the heat, another more experienced fork deflected it, and Pentworth-Haigh's bread fell off. Worriedly Berry retrieved it, blew on it and then re-impaled it.

A boy with a pugnacious jaw was hogging the best position (an area of smooth red glow), and defying with fierce jabs of the elbow any hint of encroachment; the next best place (a raggedly leaping flame) was being jostled by another four hopeful offerings, which left a small area of dead coal to a shortsighted boy whose bread was obviously destined to become stale before it became toast.

By dint of careful manoeuvring enforced by unobtrusive muscle power, Berry managed to prepare three reasonable slices for Pentworth-Haigh. He buttered them lavishly then sped back along the cold corridors, and upon rushing into his fag-master's room tripped over the mat and catapulted his offering into Pentworth-Haigh's lap, butter side down.

Triumph died. Pentworth-Haigh remained motionless, and his expression of patrician abhorrence had a fatal effect; in spite of the seriousness of the situation, Berry tried to suppress a grin, failed, and then broke into a fit of uncontrollable giggles.

It was the kind of thing everyone laughed at at home, and in a hasty attempt to retrieve the situation, he went over to Pentworth-Haigh and began reverently to remove the grease-soaked offerings from his striped trousers.

'Leave it.'

Berry did so, and in stepping backwards collided with a small table and knocked it over. A pile of books crashed to the floor.

'For . . . God's . . . *sake*. . . .' Pentworth-Haigh said the words very slowly and quietly, while Berry waited with bowed head for the inevitable beating. He heard Pentworth-Haigh take a deep breath and then order him to return at five-thirty that evening. In the meanwhile he was

343

to remove his putrid carrot-headed carcass as far away as possible.

Berry did so, and spent the rest of the day wondering how he would acquit himself on the flogging block, but when he returned to Pentworth-Haigh's room at the appointed time, he wasn't there. There was only a note pinned to the offending pair of trousers telling him to get them cleaned as good as new – or else.

And it was a sign of the good luck that would attend him during his entire school days.

Prowess at games has always ensured popularity at school, and Berry's innate love of action had already been successfully channelled into a love of sport. He loved competition, and threw himself with joyous ferocity into whatever the struggle; big, glowing and beaming, he began to build a reputation for zest and natural skill, for courage and unswerving loyalty that was to linger on long after he left Eton. He seemed to be the natural material from which heroes are fashioned; and when illustrious awards were made, endeared himself even more by tripping up the dais steps on the way to receive them.

At the early age of sixteen he was elected a member of Pop, that most prestigious of all Eton societies, and sported the glorious privilege of check trousers, fancy waistcoat and tailcoat trimmed with braid. He was as genial with fellow members as he was magnanimous towards the small boys who fagged for him, and was far too preoccupied with the day-to-day business of life to consider himself a fine figure.

His brother Tommy shone with a gentler light. At sport he was an adequate if unambitious performer, and although people liked him, they were made aware that for him it was essential to alternate spells of conviviality with periods of solitude. He often walked along the towpath to where the wet-bobs were training below Windsor lock. He would watch the flash of blue blades in the sunlight, yet remain apart from the other boys from Lower School who sprinted along the bank in an effort to keep up with their heroes. He would walk as far as Bargeman's Bush, and words would wind through his head like a lovely garland that paled and withered the moment he tried to commit it to paper.

He told no one of his attempts at poetry, but once confided to Berry the wish that they could study less Latin and Greek and more of their own language. Virgil's *Georgics* were stilted and tedious, and he was equally fed up with the Peloponnesian War and the endless campaigns of Hannibal. Why couldn't they read modern writers?

'I suppose one must begin at the beginning,' Berry said vaguely. 'Anyway, no one seems to know who the modern chaps are until they've been dead for ages.'

Tommy made no reply, but continued to doubt the benefits of a classical education.

Yet for both boys Eton was a blithe time, and the culminating glory of each school year was the fourth of June, when the river Thames was crowded with decorated boats and rafts, and the bank was crowded with equally decorative parents and sisters who had come down for the day. The sun always shone and there was always strawberries and cream, and as night fell there was the splendour of the firework display on the darkening river. Rockets soared and exploded over Brocas Clump, and showers of golden rain illuminated the castle. When the thunder was particularly loud, Berry and Tommy stood protectively close to Lizzie in case she should feel nervous.

The realization that their mother was a good-looker, and thus a cut above other mothers, came early on in their school years, and they also became more clearly aware of their father's earldom. But in the world of privilege, it was not only unnecessary to swank – it was also revolting badform; so they were careful never to refer to it.

But the world outside school and Reve was less halcyon, if anyone bothered to notice.

A strange sense of irritability had set in among the European nations, and state visits from one royal household to another, however assiduously conducted, were now seldom free from calumny. Great importance was attached to the presentation of decorations, and failure to pin the right one upon the right chest resulted in diplomatic discord. As far back as 1904 there had been injured feelings at King Edward's apparent niggardliness in this respect when he visited the German Emperor at Kiel. Prince Ferdinand of Bulgaria became equally incensed when the Emperor refused to bestow the Golden Fleece upon him in Vienna.

Peevish and petulant, the beautiful peacocks who had strutted at Queen Victoria's funeral were becoming tired of mere display, yet to the comfortable British observer the assassination at Sarajevo on 28 June 1914 was no more than a tiresome fluttering of foreign feathers. They heard with mild interest that Austria had declared war on Serbia, and tut-tutted when Germany declared war on Russia. The sense of alarm began when Germany declared war on France on 3 August, and only deepened to astonishment when it was realized that the chain of events had somehow led Great Britain to declare war on Germany.

We were at war. The long golden summer was over, and idiots rejoiced.

'Ah well, make a change from Hannibal, won't it?' Berry squinted slyly at his brother.

'No. I think it'll be Hannibal all over again.'

'Rubbish. Be over by Christmas.'

'You sound sorry. Are you?'

'No. At least . . .'

They were lying side by side on the grass after a game of tennis, racquets flung down and their eyes closed.

At least, thought Berry, I wouldn't mind having a crack at them. His thoughts roamed back to the day he shot the rabbit, which was the day his paternal grandmother introduced her German husband (who had said that he was like a young lion). It would be rather a joke to fight against one's step-grandfather. . . .

'At least?' prompted Tommy.

'At least, one's got to be prepared to bestir oneself if the need arises.'

'If it really arises.'

'What about poor old Belgium? The cockpit of Europe, they call it.'

'All be over by Christmas, as you said.'

Reve was so safe, so remote. The September sun was warm on their freckled, upturned faces, and Berry, at seventeen, was about to embark on his final year at Eton before going up to Cambridge. Tommy had two more years of school and was planning to become editor of a new college magazine.

There was plenty of time, plenty of choice, and if the time and the choice had already run out for some people, it took a little while longer for such innocent sybarites as the Dullingham-Reves.

For the British Expeditionary Force the war began at Mons, and it also began with a crushing defeat. Within seven days the Army had been reduced from 90,000 men to a little over 22,000.

People at home were aghast, and when the first hospital trains arrived at Victoria, hundreds of them were lining the platforms with flowers and chocolates and cigarettes. Tea urns steamed and small children waved Union Jacks, and the sight of the pallid, pain-racked men on their stretchers filled everyone with a new and bitter hatred of the Boche.

At Reve, John the second footman was the first to enlist in the new Kitchener's Army, and was followed by three men from the stables and four under-gardeners. The bootboys both joined the Navy, and old Harry the kitchen porter returned dolefully from the recruiting office with the news that his age group was not required. Everyone who joined the colours received a warm handshake from Dully and the present of a sovereign; they were also assured that their old jobs would be waiting for them when they returned and that their wives and children would be looked after in their absence.

The first War Office telegram arrived only four months later, and Lizzie had to break the news to Frank Birtles' widow, whose third pregnancy was well advanced. He died at Ypres, and although he had been a farm labourer of only moderate efficiency, he had belonged to Reve, and the realization that he would never return suddenly made clear

347

the true nature of war. It also made clear the fact that the magic of Reve was not, after all, sacrosanct.

Lizzie joined a branch of the Red Cross and learned to apply splints and tourniquets, while the older Dullingham ladies sat in the winter parlour, rolling bandages and knitting socks. Dully applied himself to increasing farm production, but with a steadily dwindling work force it was far from easy. The gardening staff was drastically cut, and in the early summer of 1915 everyone dutifully said how much prettier the lawns looked now that they were sprinkled with daisies.

But it was not enough. Whatever they did they were left with a feeling of impotence; Neuve Chapelle, Festubert and the Second Battle of Ypres, and the length of the casualty lists in each morning's paper made the extent of the carnage only too clear.

The decision to turn the west front of Reve into an auxiliary hospital was taken in September. Wounded from the Battle of Loos choked the casualty clearing stations and the field hospitals of Northern France, and even those who would normally be considered too sick to move were compelled to endure long hours of jolting over shell-pitted roads, often without food or drink, on their way to the ports. Doctors and nurses toiled almost in their sleep, but the relentless tide of shattered, blood-soaked bodies continued to arrive at Calais, Dieppe or Le Havre, and it was not unknown for men to be packed on to the boats for Blighty still covered in Flanders mud.

Reve was not the only stately home to open its doors to the sick and wounded in an effort to relieve the pressure on military and general hospitals. With an impresario's delight, Lizzie helped to throw open the shutters in the huge disused rooms, and supervised the replacement of Italian gilded furniture and ghostly ormolu mirrors with white iron bedsteads and a big scrubbed table to stand in the centre of each ward. One room at the end of a corridor was transformed into an operating theatre; very bare and very scrubbed it looked too, although a particularly lovely Reynolds portrait was allowed to remain facing the table in the hope that it might soothe the apprehensions of whoever was about to undergo surgery.

Lizzie wore the Red Cross uniform to which she was now entitled, and after Dully had formally inspected the Reve Auxiliary Hospital for Wounded Servicemen, he smiled fondly at her and said that she reminded him of a little girl with a new dolls' house.

'Oh – what a horrid thing to say!'

'Not horrid, merely stupid.' He was instantly contrite. 'And love makes us say very stupid things sometimes.'

She took his arm and showed him the cupboards full of linen, the new kitchen with its big cooking stove and the larders already stocked with tempting nourishing food. He saw the medical supplies, the trolleys set out with dressings, and he remarked on her thoughtfulness in providing boxes of dominoes and packs of playing cards for the con-valescent.

'They'll get better as soon as they get to Reve,' she assured him. 'They won't be able to help it.'

'You're right,' he said and, leaning against the doorway of the last ward, gazed at the double row of beds with their snow-white pillows and blood-red blankets. There was not a wrinkle, not a crease, but he turned away, unable to face their air of silent waiting.

The medical staff arrived in a charabanc: three sisters, ten Red Cross nurses and six VADs, several of whom had already seen active service in France. They settled into their quarters with a rustle of starched aprons, and Aunt Minna, who now walked with a stick, came round to welcome them all in person.

Everything was ready, everyone was poised for the first ambulances which were due to arrive at mid-afternoon, when Berry came home and broke the news that he had joined the Suffolk Light Infantry.

Lizzie's first reaction was one of extreme crossness.

'But you're too young! You're still only seventeen.'

'Eighteen in November.'

'But this is only October!'

Suddenly the war was closer now than it had ever been; as

349

close as the few paltry days that remained of his official childhood. He put his arms round her, but she gently pushed him away and stood looking at him in silence.

He was very tall and broad-shouldered, with brilliant red hair that curled behind the ears in the same way as his father's; he had big, wide, generous features and golden brown eyes that tilted up at the corner in the Dullingham smile. He was warm and vigorous and glowingly alive, and for the first time for many years her mind returned to that terrible room in the house at Dalston Junction and to the old harridan with the knitting needle.

'There was no need to hurry,' she said. 'I haven't had you all that long.'

'I won't be far away.'

She let him hold her, then. His arms were very strong, very gentle, and she closed her eyes against his shoulder.

'When?'

'The day after tomorrow.'

I love you because you're part of me, and part of your father, she thought. Oh, what a trap love is. . . .

A young VAD hurried towards them, then stopped abruptly.

'Oh – I beg your pardon, My Lady. The first ambulance has just arrived.'

'Coming,' said Lizzie, and wrenched herself away.

'Why the Suffolk Light Infantry?' demanded Dully. 'Why not the Brigade of Guards, if that's how you feel?'

'Because we live in Suffolk,' Berry said. 'It's where I belong.'

'Let the boy make his own decisions,' rumbled Uncle Badger. 'If he's old enough to fight, he's old enough to choose his weapons.'

'But he should have consulted me! I admit that my knowledge of military affairs is hardly impressive, but everyone knows that the poor bloody infantry has the thin end of the wedge. A chap who's rowed at Henley and been a good player at the Wall *and* a member of Pop, not to mention an excellent record in the Officers' Training

350

Corps . . . Furthermore, he'd no business to lie about his age.' Dully seemed deeply distressed.

'He has volunteered to serve his country,' put in Aunt Minna, 'and I for one am very proud of him. He is a Dullingham through and through.'

'I agree with his father,' said Uncle Woodstock. 'While no one is disputing his courage or his sense of duty, I can't help thinking that a chap of his calibre would do far better in the cavalry.'

'Berry will be a credit wherever and however he serves.'

'Agreed. But there are distinctions in the way.'

'Stop it – stop it!' Aunt Miriam cried, and abruptly burst into tears. No one had ever known her cry before, and her harsh sobs quietened them.

Then the door opened and Lizzie appeared. She looked pale, and the red cross on the front of her apron gleamed in the fading autumn light.

'We've just had our first death,' she said. 'From something they call gas gangrene.'

The one person who remained somewhat outside the family's new preoccupations was young Tommy.

Although the brotherly relationship with Berry had never been marred by jealousy, he couldn't help brooding on the difference engendered by the fifteen months' gap between their ages. The difference had always been there, but Berry, with one typically fearless leap, seemed to have bridged the abyss between boyhood and manhood, and left Tommy stranded and disconsolate.

Berry was now in soldier's khaki, and would in the briefest possible time pass from private to second lieutenant. He had enrolled in a typically careless, magnanimous Berry-type gesture as an ordinary ranker in an ordinary regiment, leaving the future to take care of itself; and it was already in the process of doing so, for no English viscount, however eccentric, had ever served his country other than as officer and gentleman.

And Tommy was still at Eton; bored by the narrow schoolboy world yet unable to precipitate himself into the

351

barking officiousness of the Officers' Training Corps. Sport meant little, and even the new poetry magazine seemed to be withdrawing its charm. He was in limbo; passing ghostlike through the days that were still coloured by the memory of Dullingham Major – his charm, his popularity, his name engraved on so many honours boards. . . .

He went home for the Christmas hols, and found it difficult to be hearty with the blue-clad soldiers in the west wing. He was ready to like them and had no difficulty in admiring them, but it was impossible not to feel an unlicked cub in their presence. And the only way to overcome this sense of inferiority, of bored and helpless lassitude, was to do what Berry had done and become one of them.

He waited, like a fly trapped in amber, for his eighteenth birthday.

'Wonder how she feels now?'

'Pretty cock-a-hoop, shouldn't wonder.'

'Beats me how she could have married a Hun.'

'What about the old Queen's eldest girl? She married the German Emperor.'

'The higher up you are, the less choice you have. That certainly didn't apply to *her*.' Uncle Woodstock swung his walking stick at a clump of groundsel in a rose-bed. 'Anyhow, the wretched woman had already been married once.'

'Which ought to be enough for anyone,' agreed Badger.

The two brothers were back on the old topic of Dully's mother. They had never liked her, having believed that any woman worth her salt would have made a better fist of being married to William than she had. William had had his faults, irascibility being not the least of them, but a woman's job was to soothe tempers, not ruffle them even more. And in the light of subsequent events, they could only view her last, unexpected visit as some sort of presage of the wickedness about to be unleashed upon an unsuspecting world. So far as they were concerned, Dully's mother was little short of a witch.

'Young Berry's off tomorrow.'

352

'His mother'll take it hard.'

'But she's plucky.'

'Oh, yes. Deuced plucky.'

Woodstock's walking stick thwacked at another weed. 'Splendid chap, young Berry.'

'Puts me in mind of Great-grandfather.'

'*Great*-grandfather? Oh, come now, I should have said more like the sixth Earl – '

'Old Thomas George? No end of a womanizer – '

'I fancy young Berry could prove the same, given the chance.'

'And chance is everything, these days.'

Melancholy settled like a heavy cloak upon their shoulders. There was no fun any more. No lightness, no joy. The war news was seldom good, the stock of claret in the cellars was not being replaced and this morning the bathwater had been cold. They needed so much hot water for the hospital – both brothers' minds grappled briefly with the idea of new and rapacious plumbing sucking every teacup of hot water from the south front (not that they begrudged it, of course) – and now young Berry was off to France.

'Remember Liza when she first came?'

'*Lovely* creature.'

'Remember how she used to sing and dance for us in the library?'

'Best-turned ankle in London. And now she's dressed herself up like a kitchenmaid.'

'A *nurse*.'

'Nurse – kitchenmaid – they're all the same. All jolly dreary.'

'But she's plucky.'

'Oh yes, I grant you.'

Their attitude towards the soldiers in the west wing was a complicated mixture of admiration, pity, embarrassment and squeamishness, which finally resulted in much the same kind of shyness as that suffered by Tommy.

They would have liked to visit them, to help cheer and amuse them, but doubted their capacity to do so. They had never come into contact with such persons before, except as servants, and had no idea of the correct approach. Fear that they might inadvertently say or do the wrong thing, or might appear pompous or patronizing, troubled them deeply, and therefore prevented them from acknowledging the soldiers' presence by anything more than a jovial wave in passing.

None of the gardens at Reve was out of bounds, so one might occasionally come upon a uniformed figure hauling himself painstakingly along on crutches, and if it was too late to retreat, the cry of "morning, young fella! Getting back on the old pins . . . not?' sounded far too hearty even to their own ears.

They wanted the war to be won and finished with, and all the casualties restored to health and sent home again, so that life could return to normal for everyone.

Instead, they watched Second Lieutenant Berry Dullingham-Reve, smartly accoutred, set off to join the 3rd Battalion of the Suffolk Light Infantry at the embarkation camp at Folkstone.

Although the British press was loyally inclined to present defeats as victories, little of value had in fact been achieved since the beginning of the war and the casualty lists had been enormous. Both German and Allied armies had by now dug themselves into lines of trenches that straggled across the face of Europe from close by Ostend to near the Swiss border, and the troops had resigned themselves to a new dark, dank world down among the earthworms. Dugouts were hollowed in the steep sides for sleeping accommodation and were lit by candles; in winter the trenches flooded and froze, and in summer the clammy heat was asphyxiating.

The British were largely inactive during the early part of 1916 as the Germans had decided to concentrate upon hammering the French sector at Verdun. Heavy bombardment preceded each advance made by the three German Army Corps involved; a few hundred yards of ground would be won, only to be lost the following day as the

French rallied and counter-attacked. There were heavy losses on both sides, and by early summer the exhausted French were complaining ever more bitterly about lack of British support.

Douglas Haig, of the iron moustache and cavalry background, was now commander-in-chief of the British forces on the Western Front, and in consultation with his French counterpart, the equally inflexible Marshal Joffre, drew up plans for a new British offensive. The enemy was to be attacked along an extended front and the German lines broken, once and for all.

They haggled about the finer details and about the date upon which this new big push was to begin, but on one major point they were agreed: exceptionally heavy casualties must be expected. So preparations went ahead (in full view of the German lines), for what was to become one of the most protracted and terrible bloodbaths of all time – the Battle of the Somme.

Berry was one of a small party of young officers who arrived at Albert, a little town not far from Amiens, on 3 June.

The journey from Bologne via Etaples, that huge new city of tents and huts among the sand dunes, had been long and sweltering, and he and another second lieutenant found themselves billeted in an ivy-clad *manoir* outside the town on the bank of the river Ancre.

They were expected. Madame, small, dark-haired and white-skinned, indicated that a meal had been prepared for them and that a servant would deal with their luggage. Berry's companion, an ex-bank clerk called Forrester, worried audibly in case they would be called upon to eat snails. What implements would they use?

'Easy,' replied Berry, whose ignorance was equally profound, 'they give you a straw and you suck 'em out.'

The room they were in was large and sepulchral, with heavy furniture and walls adorned with religious pictures suspended from long cords. A slight whiff of drains mingled with the aroma of fine cooking, then Madame returned and presented them with a bottle of Médoc.

355

It was all very strange, very foreign and exciting, and Berry, who had known Forrester for a mere forty-eight hours, leaned closer across the table.

'I'm jolly glad we're here, aren't you?' His eyes glowed.

'We've been called to serve our King and Country.' Forrester spread his table napkin across his knees. 'And we must be prepared to make the best of it.'

'Yes, quite. But it might be rather a lark too, mightn't it?'

Forrester seemed unwilling to admit the possibility, and the resulting silence between them seemed to deepen slightly as a young woman in a black frock approached them with a large *soupière* clasped in both hands like a chalice. Her eyes were large and dark, and something about the poise of her head and her rather unsmiling smile warned Berry that she was no ordinary waitress.

Assuming command, he thanked her in his best Eton French.

'Not at all, Captain,' she said in English. 'I hope it will be to your liking.'

'I'm afraid I'm only a . . .' Berry turned pink, then raised the lid of the *soupière* and said far too heartily: 'I say, this does look jolly good!'

Her gaze lingered thoughtfully upon him for a moment before she withdrew to the shadows.

It was the best meal either of them had had since joining the Army, and after the *filet de porc en croûte* and three glasses of wine, it seemed even more exhilarating to be in Northern France at last. It also made Berry feel pleasantly speculative.

'Forrester, have you ever – have you ever had a girl?'

'I have a young lady,' Forrester said. 'She is a lady clerk in the Prudential.'

'Oh, how nice. But what I actually meant was, have you ever . . .?'

'No,' said Forrester. 'Neither Mavis nor I believe in it until you're married.'

After the cheese ('Gosh, you don't get stuff like this in Blighty, do you?' 'No, these people don't seem to have heard of Cheddar . . .'), Madame asked if they would like to take their coffee in the garden. Berry accepted, but Forrester said that he was tired and would prefer to turn in early. They said goodnight.

Although it was past ten o'clock it was still not completely dark. A silvery half-light lay over the tangle of trees and gravel paths, and a sweet reedy smell came up from the river. He drank his coffee alone in a small rustic arbour, smoking a cigarette and listening to the occasional bursts of gunfire, like the grumble of distant thunder, coming from the Front. He wondered what it would be like, tomorrow.

Unlike Forrester, he felt wide awake; he felt strong and vigorous and restless with unspent energy. The child's instinct to run and jump had long ago been channelled and disciplined into a love of competitive sport and he wanted the game to start. Now.

He wondered whether he should go for a long walk; if he had had a towel handy he would have taken a dip in the river . . . then through the trees he noticed that the lights of the *manoir* were going out, one by one.

He rose and walked back, and inside the hall Madame glided out from the shadows and bade him goodnight. She took his hand and pressed it with her small cool fingers, and because all his senses seemed to be in the same state of ultra-responsiveness as his body, he felt himself blushing furiously.

'Goodnight, Madame.'

'Goodnight, Captain.' She too spoke English and she too thought he held a senior rank. This time he made no attempt to disillusion her.

He went to bed and lay on top of the rough linen sheets, thinking about Forrester and his young lady in the Prudential. Mavis. He wondered whether moral scruples allowed them to kiss and fondle when they were alone, and he wondered what it would be like to do a bit of spooning with the dark-haired girl who had brought in the soup. It was a long while before he slept.

Instead of going straight to the front-line trenches and pitching in, Berry and Forrester were detailed to attend a course at the Fourth Army School at Flixécourt. Their day

357

was divided between parades, lectures and tactics; they were taught, very briefly, how to deal with the men under their command, and attended a lecture given by a Highland major on The Spirit of the Bayonet that made Forrester feel faint.

Yet there was a magical spirit of bravery and camaraderie, and the old sweats of three months were unable to maintain an air of weary superiority over the young eager beavers like Second Lieutenant Dullingham-Reve who so obviously envied their experience and sought to emulate their skills.

They learned about the new Lewis gun, and Berry was among the first to volunteer to ascend in one of the balloons tethered close behind the line in order to report on enemy movement. It was marvellous up there, with the breeze whispering sweet nothings in the rigging and the June sunlight glinting playfully on faraway guns and bayonets and barbed wire.

General Rawlinson, in charge of the Fourth Army, to which the Suffolk Light Infantry was attached, issued his *Tactical Notes*, which laid down the correct procedure for infantry advance towards the enemy lines, and to Berry, aged eighteen, its glaring deficiencies were merely on a par with the handicapping rules that held sway over the Eton playing fields. He was longing to get into the coming fight, and found it difficult to remain patient with Forrester, who thought he was developing a boil.

Still billeted at the *manoir*, he acquired a second-hand motorbike and roared off each day to Flixécourt, to Albert, or to wherever he was ordered, and on 22 June made his first excursion to the Front to meet the platoon he was to command.

The youngest member was his senior by eighteen months, and they drew themselves up and saluted him with a lackadaisical patience that spoke volumes; all but four had already been in action and several had survived going over the top in previous attacks. Half were conscripts, the other half volunteers largely bereft of illusions; they were competent fighters experienced in the art of living like tunnelling moles and, so far, adept at the art of keeping alive.

They could have told Berry that as a young infantry officer his life-expectancy at the Front was three weeks.

But no one talked about anything except the Big Push which was now expected daily, and because of his school background Berry found no particular difficulty in assuming responsibility for the men who made up the 4th Platoon.

He inspected their sleeping quarters, questioned the adequacy of their diet, and was frankly appalled when a large brown rat suddenly darted over his foot. He promised to see the quartermaster about supplying a trap. His men smiled at him gently, indulgently, and Berry beamed back like a loving father.

Although nothing had been said, even Madame at the *manoir* seemed to sense the coming of a new Allied attack, and when he returned for dinner that evening she invited him to join her for an apéritif. Forrester was still over at Flixécourt.

'Poor Mr Forrester is not made for a soldier, I think.'

'I imagine he feels happier in his bank,' Berry agreed. 'But he's a jolly nice chap.'

'And it is very hard to see all you jolly chaps enduring so much.' Madame laid her head on one side. 'War is bad.'

'It's not much fun for you civilians, either. All of us coming over here and taking everything over.'

'You are very brave.'

'Oh, I wouldn't say that. . . .'

The door opened and the dark-eyed girl came in. He had learned by now that she was Madame's daughter, that her name was Marguerite and that her father, a great Anglophile, had died three years ago. Politely he rose to his feet, unaware that both small, soft-bodied Frenchwomen were covertly appraising his long loose limbs, his powerful shoulders and glowing red hair.

Marguerite helped herself to a little vermouth and sat down next to her mother.

' 'ow hees your mottorbike?' Although she spoke English as well as her mother, her accent was not as good.

359

'Fine, thanks. Don't know what I'd do without it.'

'Hi 'ave never ridden on mottorbike.' Now that she knew him better, her smile had lost its guarded quality; he had realized for the past week that she had dimples in both cheeks.

'Oh, you should! It's tremendous fun.'

'Heet not possible for women, I sink.'

'Of course it's possible! I'll give you a little ride on the pillion, if you like.'

Mother and daughter threw back their heads and laughed delightedly at the idea. Berry drained his glass and set it down.

'Come on, you'll be quite safe with me.'

Their laughter increased, then Madame shook her head. 'There is no time before dinner. But after, perhaps. . . .'

A young moon was lounging in the silvery sky when they set off, Marguerite perched in decorous side-saddle behind him, and Madame laughing from the open doorway.

'Ten minutes! Ten minutes only, or I shall have fear.'

'Ten minutes, I promise.'

The headlamp sliced a golden pathway down the tangled drive where birds rustled and an owl called. Outside on the country road they heard the sound of faraway shelling.

'All right, Marguerite?' He turned his head and the soft tip of her nose met his cheek.

'Hees good. Hi like.'

Her arms were round his waist and she gave him an excited little squeeze. She was nothing like the silent, stand-offish girl of his first evening.

Ahead of them was the main road to Amiens and the throb and grind of Army convoys. It came too soon, and reluctantly he turned in a wide circle and prepared to return, then stopped. He silenced the engine.

'Listen.'

Soaring above the noise of war, the sweet probing voice of a nightingale came from somewhere in the woods on their left.

It brought Reve back – the woods and the park and the soft lapping lake. He gently unclasped Marguerite's hands

360

from his waist and enveloped them within his own very strong and very young ones. He kissed them, and without a word they dismounted and went hand in hand into the shelter of the trees. It happened easily, naturally, and all the time the bird poured its marvellous song over them, and Marguerite, lying beneath him, cupped the back of his head in her hands and whispered to him in French.

All of which took more than ten minutes. Accustomed by now to the lights of the *manoir* being extinguished at an early hour, he rode swiftly back and Marguerite kissed him a lingering goodnight at the foot of the stairs.

'Can't you stay with me?'

'Not posseeble.'

'Oh, my darling!'

'Oh, mon amour!'

The shelling had increased as the moon began to wane. The darkness had lost its silvery quality and became deeper and more mysterious. He woke out of a light sleep to hear his bedsprings squeak and to feel her arms sliding softly beneath his neck.

'Mon amour. . . .'

'Oh, you darling, clever girl!'

This time it was even better, and he lay half-drowned in the magical womanness of her: the soft yielding, the tender words and the dark cloud of hair brushing his naked chest. The scent of her, the –

The scent was different. Stronger, more musky, more imperative.

'Marguerite?'

He ran his hand roughly down her naked flank and her husky laugh of delight told him everything.

'*Madame!*'

'You may call me Geneviève.'

Morning came too soon. He drank scalding black coffee and left the *manoir* in a roar of motorbike exhaust. They waved to him from the door, and he loved them both triumphantly and yet humbly for all that they had taught him. And for all that in their loving generosity they had given him.

As a carefully planned preliminary to the Battle of the Somme, the heavy bombardment of the German lines began at 6 a.m. on 24 June.

The German retaliation was less than expected, and on the night of the 24th, General Rawlinson's Fourth Division followed up the bombing with a gas attack. There was little wind, and it took time to drift over the German lines. The Germans replied with concentrated artillery fire, and from his place with the 4th Platoon Berry listened to the swishing of light shells and the vicious thud of shrapnel. Then the heavies opened up.

'Keep your head down, Sir.'

'Yes, Corporal. Are the men all right?'

'Yessir.' The corporal grinned in the darkness. 'Ready for whatever you say, Sir.'

The noise was deafening, but in all the brutal cacophony he learned to distinguish the different voices coming from the artillery behind the front line: the rise-and-fall whistle of a high-angle shell, the deeper crump-crump of six-inch howitzers and then the earth-shaking boom of the huge gun firing from the railway behind Albert, which had a thirteen-mile range.

The barrage continued at pre-arranged intervals over a period of four days, and its purpose was twofold; firstly to soften the morale of the enemy crouched low in their deep trenches on the other side of no man's land, and secondly to cut through their barbed wire entanglements in preparation for the infantry attack.

And for Berry the game really began on the night of the 29th, when he was detailed to lead a raiding party across that narrow strip of pock-marked land to ascertain the extent of the damage to Fritz's wire. The corporal went with him, and a man called Roberts. They blacked their faces, and as the barrage fell silent, crawled cautiously over the top of the sandbags and squirmed across to the enemy line. The long spell of hot dry weather had broken and a light misty rain was falling.

They froze as a machine gun stuttered out its rat-tat-tat,

362

and Berry, with his face pressed close to the earth, thought how strange if I was killed so soon. . . .

The wire, cautiously examined here and there, seemed to be disappointingly intact, and Berry heard the corporal swear very quietly as it ripped his sleeve. They crawled back and reported to the senior officer from Battalion HQ who was waiting for them. He nodded, acknowledged Berry's salute and departed.

The rain fell faster, and the smell of wet earth and wet hairy uniforms mingled with that coming from the latrine buckets. Private Bird was brewing the inevitable strong tea laced with tinned milk, and from one of the dug-outs came the melancholy wheeze of a mouth-organ.

The next stage was interminable. Rifles were cleaned and re-cleaned as the hours waiting for the assault slipped by; in his own candlelit dug-out, Berry sat on the edge of his bunk and wondered how Forrester, two miles down the line, was getting on. He removed his revolver from its holster and polished it on his sleeve, then replaced it. He paced restlessly, then pushed aside the army blanket that served as a door and walked to the end of his section of trench. Water seeped through the duck-boards and he paused by a man who was on look-out.

'Anything happening, Peldon?'

'No, Sir. Reckon they haven't got over the pasting we gave 'em.'

'Seems quiet without the barrage, doesn't it?'

'Yessir.' Peldon was a grocer's assistant from Sudbury.

'Feeling all right?'

'Yessir,' Peldon repeated automatically. Then added: 'Waiting gets you down a bit though.'

'Won't be long now.'

'You bin over the top before, Sir?'

'No, as a matter of fact.'

'You'll be all right, Sir.'

'Thank you, Peldon.'

Berry walked as far as the traverse that contained the ammunition store and the first-aid post. Muffled sounds from other platoons came through the banked earth. The

network of trenches ran for miles, cross-cutting, inter-
secting, and occasionally coming to an abrupt halt where a
shell had exploded and blown the sides in. He walked back
to his dug-out at the measured pace deemed suitable for
those in command, and sat down at the table improvised
from ammunition boxes and covered over with another
army blanket. He sat tapping his fingers and whistling
softly, then remembered with a little gleam of delight that
he had some toffees by his bed. He still preferred toffees to
tobacco.

'Sir?' There was the slap of boots coming to attention on
the duck-boards outside.

'Enter.'

It was Private Mottram, whose nickname was Stunners.
Berry would have liked to know why, but it was impossible
to ask. He was supposed to be above such childish curiosity.

'Yes, Mottram?'

'Men's letters, Sir.'

'Thank you. Put them down.' The authoritative jerk of
his head was somewhat impaired by a voice blurred by a
lump of Palm toffee.

'That be all, Sir?'

'Yes, thank you, Mottram. At least – ' He parked the
toffee on a back tooth, which made enunciation a little
clearer. 'Any problems?'

'No, not really, Sir.' Mottram showed signs of reluctance
to depart.

'You sound uncertain.' Bored and lonely, Berry was
equally reluctant to dismiss him.

'It's Saunders, Sir. I think he needs watching.'

'Oh? Why?'

'He's sort of turning in on hisself, Sir.'

'You mean he's fed up?'

'Could put it like that, Sir. Won't speak or nothing.'

'This hanging about's nerve-racking for all of us,' Berry
said. Then he drew the pile of letters closer to him. 'Has he
written home?'

'Don't think so, Sir.'

'He's got a wife and children, I believe?'

'Yessir.' The careful woodenness of Mottram's countenance seemed to hint at a great deal.

'Very well, I'll bear it in mind,' Berry said finally. 'Thank you, Mottram.'

Mottram stamped over to the blanketed doorway. The candle flickered and sent up a tail of smoke as he passed.

'By the way, Mottram. Care for a toffee?'

'Oh. Yessir. Thank you, Sir.'

Mottram departed, and Berry was left alone with the little pile of letters he was supposed to censor.

My dear Minnie, I hope you are alright. I am alright. How is Mum? I hope she is alright. The last two days has been wet but now it is quite alright. . . . (The cautious voice of Private Foskitt from Beccles.)

. . . the bloody barrage has never stopped for four bloody days (part of Private Bird's missive to his wife) *and my sodding feets playing old Harry. . . .*

As instructed, Berry deleted the swear words and the reference to military activity, which in this instance seemed to leave no more than a sprinkling of prepositions and a row of kisses.

O my darling girl it seems so long since I —–—– (Berry's fountain pen reluctantly obliterated the word from Lance-Corporal Pollard's letter) *you and in spite of all that goes on here all I can think of is wanting to* —–—– *you again and again. I picture doing it* —–—–—–—– *we haven't ever tried it that way before but O my darling I think you would love it I lie here and dream about kissing your* —–—–.

Dear Ethel, I'm sorry to hear you are laid up with your old trouble. Glands are nasty things. . . .

They went on and on, painstakingly written and painful to read because their homely sentiments had nothing to do with him. However hard he tried to imagine that he was merely a schoolmaster marking prep, the task always left him feeling unpleasantly voyeuristic. But they had to be finished and officially stamped so that they could be sent on their way before the onset of the Big Push. Everything had got to be tidied up and tickety-boo before then.

It was six o'clock when he went in search of Saunders,

whom Mottram suspected of turning in on himself, and that was the time when the signallers from Battalion HQ at last began telephoning the command *Company to parade in battle order* through the waiting trenches. Berry listened to the faint crackling voice and became filled with exultation. This was it. This was the big show, the start of the real action, and he hurried down the trench, passing on the word and relaying instructions.

They all seemed glad, even Saunders. They grinned and joked as they made their preparations, and at eight o'clock soup containers arrived from the field kitchen behind the line. They drank the soup and ate bully beef and biscuits followed by bread and jam but they were all careful not to make jokes about the Last Supper. They exchanged Woodbine cigarettes, and continued to smile.

The weather had cleared, and a light barrage drowned the tell-tale sound of the Fourth Army taking up their positions. They had marched from Albert, even from Amiens, every infantryman loaded with the official sixty-six pounds of battle equipment, and they filed down into the trenches and assembly points. It was not always easy to find their correct positions in the dark and there was a certain amount of exasperation and confusion before every group was assembled in accordance with General Rawlinson's operation order.

The 4th Platoon Suffolk Light Infantry were fortunate that they were already in position, but the additional hours of waiting they endured began to tell on them. Herded closely together and massively accoutred with steel helmet, two gas helmets, rifle, entrenching tool, rolled ground sheet, haversack, water bottle, wire-cutters, field dressing and small-arms ammunition as only a part of it, their shoulders were already sagging and their smiles becoming strained.

'All right, Saunders?' Squeezing through his cluster of men with difficulty, Berry peered closely at him.

'Yessir.'

'Won't be long now.'

'No, Sir.' Saunders gulped suddenly, turned his head

aside and a stream of vomit ran down the sleeve of the man next to him.

'Sorry, I – ' Confusedly, Saunders tried to raise his own arm in an attempt to repair the damage, but they were packed too closely together.

'Don't worry, mate. If it helps, I got the shits.'

The kindly magnanimity touched young Berry deeply, and he knew that men like that – Suffolk men – would come through whatever lay ahead.

At five-thirty he gave the order to stand to. The sun rose over the slopes of the Somme valley and he noted that all his men were wearing their name tags as ordered; their helmets bore the regiment's insignia and their shoulder straps were decorated with the company ribbon. They were ready for the show. Ready for the game.

Someone began to sing very quietly; others followed, humming beneath their breath so that Jerry, listening on the other side of no man's land, wouldn't hear. *There's a long, long trail awinding* . . . The sadness of the tune was inescapable, and Berry wondered fleetingly why they didn't feel disposed towards something a little more bracing at a time like this.

Just as the first ray of sunlight spilled over the rim of the frontline trench, the barrage opened up, as planned. Unobtrusively, Berry consulted his watch. The noise was deafening and the men stopped singing. One or two cheered, but their voices were lost in the thunder. Eight minutes to zero and the mortars began firing, thirty rounds a minute.

Berry looked at his watch again, his heart thumping.

'Fix bayonets.'

He heard the order repeated further down the trench during a second's pause in the noise. He heard the answering clink of steel and saw the hands of Private Saunders fumbling. He caught his eye and nodded to him – a fierce, protective nod that said you are in my care and I will look after you. . . .

Peldon, the grocer's assistant, lunged forward and grabbed at Berry's hand. 'God bless, Sir.'

'You too, Peldon.'

Perhaps it was the strengthening sunlight or perhaps it was what lay ahead, but all the faces beneath the steel helmets seemed suddenly blanched and thin, as if the living blood had already been drawn from them. Berry kept his eyes on his watch.

The barrage stopped. Silence glazed the world for a second or two, and then the whistles blew, shrilling their message along the wavering line of the eighteen-mile Front. Berry leaped, revolver in hand, and he was out in the open. The bright morning met him with a dazzle of blue and gold.

He heard his men behind him, clambering and scrambling, panting and grunting beneath their heavy equipment, and he heard the first scream before he became conscious of the enemy fire. A man called Linton was hit in the chest as he cleared the wire. He tumbled backwards into the trench and disappeared beneath the next row of men precipitating themselves over the top.

And the bright morning had been a myth. The gold was already tarnishing and the blue had faded to funeral grey in the smoking gunfire ahead of them.

Walk, do not run. Remember to keep an arm's distance from the man next to you. Advance steadily towards the enemy and never forget your objective. It is to kill him.

Berry led, and it was nothing like the old Field Game at school. The fierceness was there, the desire to win was singing in the blood, but this time he was walking with his team into the roar of gunfire. The man next to him – he thought it was Private Durrant – flung up his arms and fell headlong. But he couldn't stop. The rules of this new game forbade him to call a halt while the injured player was escorted from the field.

He walked on, and gusts of shrapnel tore great holes in the line of men. They fell, and were trampled on by those advancing from the rear. The noise increased, the bellowing guns providing a furious accompaniment to the savage stuttering of machine guns and the hissing and spitting of rifle bullets.

And there was no mercy, no calling a halt. It went on and

on, the screams and the cries, the bloodstained bodies littering the narrow strip of tortured earth. Bits of khaki, bits of human meat, were blown through the air as the lines of infantry continued to advance through the stinging, blinding smoke, and it became more and more difficult to understand what they were doing, and to grasp what it was all about.

He had no thoughts left in him now. Perhaps he was already dead, for the blow that felled him brought no pain. There was only blackness, and the gradual cessation of tumult. The revolver fell from his hand.

The Big Push had failed, and the attack was halted during the afternoon.

Despite the preliminary bombardments, the Germans had been in control since the first ten minutes, emerging nerve-strained but intact from their deeply constructed shelters in order to mow down the British as they advanced.

When the guns fell silent it seemed as if the dust would never clear. Parties of stretcher-bearers picked a pathway through the dead and briefly examined the wounded to see whether it was worth retrieving them. Too often they set off with a loaded stretcher, only to discover that the occupant had died before they reached the clearing station. There was nothing for it then but to leave him for the burial party. They ran out of stretchers and had to use blankets, and the injured, groaning and weeping, choked the entrances to the hastily organized field operating centres.

The medical services worked in grim and concentrated silence, cleaning, stitching, bandaging, administering chloroform and amputating shattered limbs that piled in grisly mounds outside the tents. A nursing sister supervised the labelling of each man before he joined the queue for the ambulances.

'Is it a Blighty one, Miss?'

'Yes. You'll be going home.'

Clenched jaws relaxing, pain-clouded eyes closing in relief, they waited stoically to begin the crowded, jolting journey that would take two days.

Twilight was falling, and there were not enough ambulances. Ammunition wagons were hastily daubed with red crosses and pressed into service. The narrow road back to the railhead was pitted with shell-holes, and the waiting hospital trains were packed so tightly that it was impossible for the medical orderlies to step between the stretchers.

There should have been nine trains, but there were only two.

There were not enough medical supplies; the clearing stations and the operating centres began to run out of iodine and bandages, and still the wounded poured in. They came hobbling, limping, crawling; a man with no arm tenderly supported another with a leg torn off at the knee. They came out of the evening shadows and the acrid dust, wearing their stunned and ghastly smiles, and when Sir Douglas Haig, twelve miles away at GHQ, received notification that the day's casualties amounted to some sixty thousand men, his reaction was as prompt as it was pitiless: 'Carry on!'

As the clouds of concussion slowly thinned, Berry stretched out his hand. His fingers closed round something hard, rough and oddly shaped. He lay with his eyes shut and tried to concentrate his confused and wavering mind on the object. It was softer at one end than the other and it appeared to have two strings coming from it.

He pushed himself up, then fell back with his cheek against the earth. Slowly the dizziness retreated, and opening one cautious eye he saw that the thing he was holding was a soldier's boot. He wondered whose it was. Private Bird's? Mottram's? Poor old Saunders'? He wondered what could have possessed anyone to lose a boot, like a horse casting a shoe . . . then he remembered.

And with the return of memory came awareness of his surroundings.

The guns had stopped. It was over. Our side had won. A sweet floating peacefulness descended; then he heard the moaning. It came from somewhere close by and it was not the kind of sound a human being would normally make.

370

He sat up again very slowly and carefully, and his eyes took in the terrible litter around him. It took a long while because of the concussion and because of the sheer incredibility of what he saw. Humped, slumped bundles of old khaki – not *men*, surely? – shattered bits of equipment, steel helmets and rifles abandoned and weirdly evocative, and a strange new lunar landscape of smoking craters and bone-white chalk. Close to him – close enough to touch – was a man lying on his back with half his face blown away. Too incredulous even to feel sick, Berry leaned closer; every time the man moaned, a little bubble of blood welled in the glistening mess that had once been a mouth.

He didn't know what to do. But he had to do something.

'Hold on,' he said, 'I'll get help . . .' and staggered drunkenly to his feet.

Unsure of the right direction, he set off through the broken bodies and then paused, suddenly convinced that he was walking in the direction of the German front line. He about-turned and lurched back again, and a medical orderly in bloodstained overalls took his arm.

'Come on, youngster. All over. . . .'

He remembered little more of that first of July 1916.

It was only over for the dead and wounded. The shattered Fourth Army obediently gathered itself together and on the following day took possession of the village of Fricourt, an advance of just over a mile. Fricourt was undefended, but there was nothing left to defend except a pile of rubble.

Suffering no more than bruises and a splitting headache, Berry was advised to return to his billet for twenty-four hours' sick leave, but refused. There was too much to do.

He spent the day trying to trace the remnants of 4th Platoon; poor old Peldon was dead, so were Durrant and Thompson and Linton. Lance-Corporal Pollard was missing and Mottram had a leg wound and was reputed to be on his way to the base hospital at Le Havre. The men who were left – twenty-two out of thirty-six – were repairing the trenches, restacking the sandbags and reinforcing the barbed-wire entanglements. Fresh supplies of ammo were

371

arriving from Albert, and a soldier unpacking tins of bully beef paused to salute him.

"morning, Sir. Nice to see you.' It was Saunders.

Berry grasped his hand and shook it warmly. 'Glad you came through all right, Saunders! Bit of a show, wasn't it?'

Saunders agreed that it was, and returned to his unpacking. Walking back along the trench, Berry pondered on the reason why some men should come through, and some not. This time yesterday he would have considered Saunders an unlikely bet.

His motorbike had also come through unscathed, and he rode over to Albert after lunch, where he learned two items of news. One was that he had been promoted to first lieutenant, and the other was that a visitor was waiting to see him in the officers' mess. He strode over there, and a slim red-haired figure in khaki rose from a window-seat.

'Tom!' Filled with incredulous delight, he pumped his brother's hand up and down. 'My God, you old rogue – what are you doing over here?' He ordered two double brandies.

'Same as you, you fathead.' The delight was mutual.

'What outfit?'

'Royal Field Artillery.'

'What – no Guards regiment?' Berry teased.

'No, I just went for the nearest, same as you. I dare say they're all much the same, really.'

'There speaks an ardent military man!'

'Well, *aren't* they?'

'Yes, in a way.' Berry took a mouthful of brandy to ease away yesterday's memories; death hadn't been very discriminatory then, certainly. 'How's everyone at home?'

'Fine, when I left. They've been getting your letters, but of course they worry.'

'Now they'll have two to worry about.'

They sat looking at one another, and the affection between them seemed to bring Reve very close. A sudden longing for its loving safety assailed Berry like a pain, and he snapped his fingers at the mess waiter and ordered two more brandies.

372

How splendid he is, Tommy thought. How large and brave and magnanimous. Nothing worries him or frightens him, and it's not because he's insensitive. It's just because in some odd way he's naturally greater than the rest of us. . . .

'They say there was heavy action up front yesterday, and we all heard the guns and saw the smoke. It must have been pretty ghastly.'

'Yes.'

'Were you anywhere near?'

'Yes. Not far away.'

Even half an hour ago he would have welcomed telling someone close to him about the advance; it would have relieved him and helped him to face his reactions instead of brushing them aside. Part of him still wanted very badly to describe it all, in all its terrible and unexpected detail, but he couldn't tell Tommy. Tommy was his younger brother and needed protecting.

'Does everyone hit the bottle out here?' Cautiously Tommy eyed his second brandy.

'When they get the chance. Mostly it's stewed tea and condensed milk.'

'Urgh.' Tommy's nose wrinkled in a schoolboy shudder and Berry thought oh God, what a kid you still are. You shouldn't be here because you don't belong. . . .

'Berry.' Impulsively Tommy leaned across the table. 'I say, listen, have you had a chance to meet any girls out here? And have you ever . . .?'

How it brought back that first evening at the *manoir* with Forrester. (What happened to Forrester yesterday? Must find out.) *Forrester, have you ever had a girl*? And Forrester's prim simper to the effect that he had a young lady and didn't believe in premature indulgence. The roistering letter he had censored from Lance-Corporal Pollard swam before Berry's eyes; Pollard certainly believed in cashing in while the going was good, and now he was missing, believed killed, poor sod. . . .

'Berry?'

'Yes?'

373

'We were talking about girls.'

'Yes,' said Berry, as if from a long way off. 'I've got two girls, a mother and a daughter, and I have them both whenever I get the chance.'

That statement, even to his own ears, seemed to mark him off as a hardened, seasoned soldier. He saw Tommy recoil in shock, in amazement, in reluctant admiration.

'I say, you *are* going it.'

He also saw the repugnance.

His crashing headache, the lingering result of concussion, began to hammer against his temples and he was unable to explain, or mollify, or comfort. He ordered a third brandy – Tommy refused – and silence fell between them.

There never used to be silence in the old days. There had been easy confidences, happy bantering, and always laughter. Laughter that echoed round the nursery and the schoolroom with dear old Miss Whatsername – and Mama making everyone laugh with her earthy fenland jokes and then stunning them all her with Gaiety Girl beauty. . . .

Berry downed his brandy and then stood up. 'I must get back.'

'To your mother and daughter?' There was a querulous note in Tommy's voice.

'Oh, shut up,' Berry said briefly, tiredly.

They left the mess together, and outside in the hot and sulphurous light, Tommy noted that his brother's uniform was dusty and creased; it looked as if it had been slept in. Far from diminishing him, it gave him an additional glamour. They were so close, such equal participants in history, yet communication between them was vanishing to needle-point.

Conscious of a desire to retrieve the situation, they shook hands.

'Cheer-ho. Keep in touch.'

'Of course.'

'Best of luck.'

'You too.'

'War affects everything,' Tommy thought, walking away. 'Even brotherly love.'

*

374

It's a long way to Tipperary;
They sing the words in different ways
On different days.
Sometimes jauntily, with rifles slung
And hobnails beating a brisk tattoo.
Other times, like a
Mumbling, grief-stricken dirge for the dead.
It all depends on Brigade HQ, who
Issue the orders.

Tommy pushed the notebook aside and stared into the sunset. It glowed through the violet-grey smoke that still hung over the Somme battlefield, where the fighting had been yesterday.

He had not yet seen a corpse, but he had seen plenty of wounded – bandaged heads, arms in slings and white-faced men with closed eyes lying on stretchers. He had seen bloodstains, and a dead mule still harnessed to a smashed cart. He had seen the patient queues for the hospital trains taking them back to the big coastal hospitals, or better still, to Blighty.

Unlike Berry, he didn't really want to be a part of it. He too had enlisted under-age, but everything about him rejected the pain and the ugliness, and he could see no glory in killing and maiming men whom he had never even met. The only German he had ever known was his grand-mother's second husband, and he had seemed nice enough in his way; there was certainly no need to kill him.

His thoughts returned to Berry, and he wondered whether he had appeared unbearably raw and in-experienced in his eyes. He hoped not, but however much he valued their relationship he still found it difficult not to be just a little shocked by Berry's casual reference to having a mother and daughter. (By *having*, he presumably meant making love to them.)

But shocking or not, it was certainly very impressive; and so was his ability to drink three brandies – the first one a double – and then walk away in a straight line. He would always remember Berry walking away through the hot dusty afternoon towards his parked motorbike; long-legged, broad shoulders swinging. . . . They had made no plans to meet again, but presumably it wasn't the done thing when one was on active service.

He pulled the notebook towards him again and read through the lines of poetry, and their paltry cynicism disgusted him.

The fine weather broke on July; torrential rain flooded the trenches and turned sticky mud to slime. The duck-boards disappeared from view and the soaked puttees tightened painfully on the soldiers' legs. They lived in wet boots for days together and the first signs of trench foot began to appear.

But the attacks had to continue, and the two villages of Ovillers and La Boiselle were pounded again and again, despite the fact that as villages they had already ceased to exist. The orders were to obliterate the deep German strongholds that ran beneath them, and the Germans' orders were to defend them to the death.

Ovillers was finally taken on the 17th, and Berry watched the first Germans as they came slowly up into the daylight. They were bearded and dirty and hollow-eyed with hunger and fatigue, and a sergeant from the Royal Welch Fusiliers marched them away through the smoke and clinging mud.

The following day began in reasonable quiet; 75s growled further north and an occasional shell exploded, sometimes a little too close, but the rain had ceased and Berry's men set about cleaning the dug-outs and restocking the ammo store. Private Bird warmed the regulation meat and veg in an iron pot over a wood fire, and Berry sat on a sandbag writing the regulation officer's report for Brigade HQ. Someone was playing 'Sweet Adeline' on a mouth-organ.

'Shut up,' Bird said suddenly. 'Listen.'

It was the song of a lark. They watched it, shielding their eyes from the sun, and the little brown speck climbed, fluttering and pouring out its melody, higher and higher into the air.

'Well, you cocky little bleeder,' Private Bird said admiringly.

'Sings better than you do, Birdy,' someone commented.

They continued to listen, mouths agape, eyes gazing heavenwards, then a man called Dawkins said very quietly: 'Sir. . . .'

Berry looked at him sharply, and then in the direction he indicated. Private Saunders was staring straight ahead and tears were pouring down his cheeks.

It was a long, strange moment, sitting in the sunshine among the devastation of war while they listened to the song of a lark and watched the helpless weeping of a man driven beyond endurance.

'Saunders.' Berry went over to him. 'You're excused duties until first call tomorrow. I suggest you turn in and have a good sleep.'

It seemed to take a long while for the words to penetrate. The tears continued to roll down his cheeks and Berry stifled the natural desire to offer him a handkerchief.

'Saunders . . . come on, old chap.'

'I'll go with him, Sir.' Private Crisp was new to the platoon. He led the way and Saunders stumbled after him.

The lark stopped singing and plummeted to earth, and everyone continued with what they were doing.

Towards four o'clock, the German guns began to open up; forced to take cover, 4th Platoon swore at the whistling sigh of shells passing overhead.

'They're after the ammo dump at Albert, Sir.'

'Shouldn't be surprised.'

Berry and the look-out turned at the sound of feet stumping briskly round the corner from the traverse. It was Major Pommeroy, with a sergeant in attendance.

'Afternoon, Major.' Berry saluted.

'Arfnoon. All correct?'

'Yes, Sir. I think so.'

'*Think*?'

'Sorry, Sir. All correct.'

No one was ever pleased to see Major Pommeroy. Berry stared with determined deference at the small blue eyes set in the red brick wall of a face and at the clipped moustache set above the small red lips. His visits, invariably without warning, were always conducted with an air of belligerent suspicion, as if he were dealing with the enemy instead of his own men. 4th Platoon referred to him with weary tolerance as the Old Fart.

'Fags out and smarten up,' muttered Bird as the little procession reached the dug-out used as sleeping quarters.

'What is that man doing there?' The Old Fart pointed his swagger stick at one of the improvised bunks. Saunders lay curled in a foetal position with his back to the room and the blanket over his head.

'He's off-duty, Sir.'

'Has he nothing better to do with his time?'

'He took part in the Ovillers show, Sir.'

'I trust he was not the only one.' The Old Fart stepped forward and prodded the motionless form. 'Get up.'

Saunders groaned. With a brief jerk of the head, Berry dismissed Bird and the two others with him.

'I said, "Get up." '

'The man is very tired, Sir. I ordered him to rest.'

'And now I am ordering him to get up. See to it, Sergeant.'

Obediently the sergeant ripped the blanket from Saunders' tightly rolled form. He took him by the arm and jerked him off the bunk. Saunders stood there, white-faced and shivering.

Berry's face reddened with temper. 'Pardon me, Sir.'

'Get dressed,' the Old Fart said to Saunders. 'And you are awarded two days' field punishment for insolence in the presence of a senior officer.'

He stumped out, and Berry followed. A large brown rat fled across their path, and Bird appeared with two mugs of tea and an ingratiating smile.

'We didn't stop for dinner today, Sir,' he said virtuously. 'That's why we got everything so shipshape after fighting so hard yesterday, Sir.'

His complacent smirk defused Berry's temper and he led the way into his own dug-out. Bird laid the tea on the improvised table and withdrew.

'Sugar, Sir?'

'Thanks.' The Old Fart dug the tin spoon hard into the paper bag. He stirred his tea vigorously.

'You're an earl, they tell me,' he said abruptly.

'My father is an earl, Sir.'

'So what does that make you?' There was truculence in the small blue eyes.

'A viscount, Sir.'

The clipped moustache twitched at the first sip of Bird's monumentally strong tea. 'So why aren't you in a Guards regiment?'

'I'm very happy where I am, thank you, Sir.'

'But you're Eton and Harrow and all that?'

'Eton, Sir. I've only played against Harrow at Lord's.'

A commotion outside denoted the enforced removal of Saunders. 'By that I mean cricket, Sir.'

It was difficult to be sure whether or not Berry's voice held a hint of sarcasm, but the signs of strain in his face were unmistakable.

'Quite.'

The Old Fart drank the last of Bird's terrible tea and prepared for departure. 'But I think you must bear in mind that we are not engaged in a game of cricket now. We are fighting the deadliest, most beastly war it is possible to conceive, and we must win. To win is imperative, and we will not do so if we show undue indulgence towards the men under our command. These men are fighting animals; we must always remember that, and to remain in pristine condition they must not be indulged.'

'Sir.'

The dug-out was too low for Berry to stand to attention. He moved aside the blanket that covered the doorway and stepped outside just as the German shell, falling short of its target, hit the ground close to the barbed wire.

It made no more than a soft crumping sound but the trench seemed to shiver with the impact and the light was suddenly extinguished. Earth from the crater outside rose high in the air and then fell in a dense hard-hitting cloud, blocking the entrance to the dug-out.

Knocked sideways, Berry fell out into the trench and lay half buried beneath trickling soil and lumps of chalk. His ears sang and he was filled with the terror of being unable to breathe. As if through cotton wool, he heard the sound of voices and the clatter of boots on duck-boards.

'Hang on, Sir. That you, Sir? All right, Sir?'

Grimly he tugged and strained to free himself, then felt someone grasp him by the shoulders. Daylight reappeared. Coughing and gasping, he gulped in great lungfuls of air.

'Everyone all right? Where's the Old . . .?'

They pointed to the mound of earth that completely obscured the doorway of his dug-out, and protruding from it were two motionless, highly polished boots.

'Oh, God.' He began to scrabble with his bare hands. Gently they dissuaded him.

'S'no use, Sir. . . . No chance.'

'But, Christ, we must try!' Haggard with shock, he fought them off.

'Must be four or five tons of soil there, Sir. At least it was bloody quick.'

Poor Old Fart, what an ignominious end: two riding boots sticking out of a heap of dirt.

On the other side of the wire, the sergeant had been decapitated by the explosion; and there was no sign of Saunders. The shelling increased.

'Poor Mr Forrester ees keeled. They come and take away ees sings yesterday.'

'Four of my chaps copped it last night. There's only Bird left now, out of the original lot.'

Berry was in bed with Marguerite, sipping brandy in a state of post-coital cogitation. 'Perhaps when he and I have gone too, it'll be a signal for the war to end. The Hun will capitulate and everyone'll be able to go home, including my kid brother – who's no business to be out here anyway. He's not cut out for this kind of thing. Why he got himself into the artillery, God alone knows – it's no better than the infantry. Some people can cope with beastliness but he can't. It'll haunt his dreams for ever.'

'Eet will not do that to your dreams?'

'I don't propose to let it. If I come through to tell the tale, that is.'

She smiled without replying, then gently removed the glass from his hand and placed it on the table by the bed. 'In the meantime . . .'

She turned to him, covering his bare breast with a cloud of dark hair. He put his arms round her and held her close, and they floated in a quiet peace unruffled by desire.

They never spoke of love, or of the future, and Berry had been guilty of schoolboy exaggeration when he told Tommy that he slept with mother and daughter indiscriminately. After the glorious confusion that involved his initiation on that first night, Madame had gracefully withdrawn; she treated him easily and affably, like a son, yet a certain smile in her eyes showed that she remembered and saw no reason for regret. The French were really rather splendid about such things.

They were also marvellous cooks. Of course the food had always been marvellous at Reve too, but in a more formal sort of way; now for the first time in his life he could sit in the kitchen and watch Madame prepare a *coq au vin* and savour the first hint of aroma rising from the browning of the bird in home-churned butter; the aroma would strengthen and gain character from the addition of early field mushrooms and the little pearly onions that he helped to peel, and would finally reach full majesty when the ignited brandy – warmed in a ladle of heroic proportions – was dramatically extinguished by a bottle of good Beaujolais. He watched the preparation of the *beurre manié* used to thicken the sauce when the dish was cooked, and he helped to chop the chives and parsley into the butter that was spread over the steaming dish of accompanying potatoes.

Now poor old Forrester had gone and was so far unreplaced, they often dined in the kitchen, with the exhausted stove dying to a twinkle in the corner and the door open on to the starlit, owl-haunted garden. They drank rough local wine and, watching a small trickle of sauce at the corner of Marguerite's lovely mouth and thinking of the joys to come in the big bed upstairs, it was sometimes difficult not to be glad about the war – because otherwise he would never have known all this. Presumably he would have been squiring other chaps' sisters to the theatre and to Henley and Newmarket, and it wouldn't be half such fun.

As it was, he preferred to settle for this happy and loving interval, and would have been resignedly in agreement if he had overheard Madame's occasional homilies directed at Marguerite: 'Love him, but expect nothing. In a war, there is no future. Give him your body, give him your heart, but know that it will end in loneliness. That is inevitable.'

Marguerite, also, was happy to settle for a blank future.

Saunders was not killed by the shell that destroyed Berry's dug-out and provided a buffoon's death for the Old Fart.

He was first spotted on the following morning dodging round the craters of no man's land like a dog that had slipped its collar. They didn't recognize him to begin with, and Corporal Sayer laid the muzzle of his rifle over the parapet and snapped a quick shot at him. He fell, but through binoculars they saw him wriggling quickly into cover. He emerged an hour or so later, greeted this time by the rat-tat-tat of German machine-gun fire.

'Christ, Sir, it's Saunders!' Bird said. '*Saunders, come back here, you stupid bastard*!'

'Keep your head down,' Berry ordered, 'or you'll get it blown off.'

They watched, staring intently at the wavering and irresolute figure as it hurried this way and that.

'What's he doing now, Sir?'

'Dunno, exactly. Think he's gone into another crater.'

'Shall I go out and try and get him in, Sir?'

'No,' Berry said shortly, 'don't be a bloody fool.'

Apart from his other duties, Bird had now casually assumed the role of batman to Lieutenant Dullingham, and woke him next morning with the customary mug of tea and tin bowl of hot water for shaving.

'He's hanging on the wire, Sir.'

'Who is?'

'Saunders, Sir.'

Berry passed a hand over his tousled red hair. 'Whose wire?'

'Jerry's, Sir.'

'Dead?'

'Not sure, Sir. Hard to tell.'

A breeze had arisen during the night, and peering through the binoculars Berry was able to make out a doll-sized shape, khaki-clad, spreadeagled on the outer wire of the German defences. One of its arms appeared to be waving.

'Not much we can do, is there, Sir?'

Berry shook his head. 'I don't know why Jerry doesn't finish him off. If he's alive, that is.'

By midmorning the early sun had disappeared, leaving a grey sky loaded with the heavy fumes of war. Shelling was sporadic on both sides; kept up, it almost seemed, for want of anything better to do. Morning dwindled into afternoon, and 4th Platoon was dominated by the thought of Saunders. No chance of the poor sod being alive after all this time – the breeze had dropped and the flapping arm flapped no more – yet however hardened they had become, the thought of him was curiously upsetting. Saunders had never been strong up top; he should never have been here in the first place. They tried to avert their gaze from the motionless figure but it was impossible to drive away the memory of his white face and anxious, haunted eyes.

Dusk seemed merely a deepening of the day's heavy gloom. It promised to be a dark night.

'I'm going out to get him.'

They looked at Berry in silence. He stared back at them, then without saying anything more, went back to his newly improvised dug-out. He poured a tot of brandy, swallowed it neat, then changed into a pair of light canvas shoes.

'Bit risky, Sir.' Bird was hovering outside.

'Get me some wire-cutters.'

He waited until Bird returned, conscious of his men's

silent presence. Someone whispered good luck as he put one foot on the firestep and then launched himself quietly over the top.

Away from the foetid confines of the trench, exhilaration filled him. The rash decision and all it entailed was suddenly no more than a schoolboy lark. He had always loved taking risks at school.

He began to walk forward, slowly and silently, and the tingling at the back of his neck reminded him of playing hide-and-seek in the dark at Reve. They played it every Christmas.

The stretch of no man's land was very quiet, and he walked on, avoiding obstacles, real or imaginary, and sensing the eyes of his platoon straining after him in the dark. It wasn't all that far now to the German wire – he was tempted to break into a run – then a Verey light soared and hung trembling overhead.

He dropped like a stone, and lay motionless beside a heavy crater. His heart was pounding. The weird cold light illuminated the abandoned rubbish of past battles: twisted metal, lumps of chalk like bleached bone, a rag of uniform that could have been either khaki or German field grey.

The Verey light died and he wriggled forward, every nerve alert. He could see the dim, hedgelike outline of the German wire now, and he lay with his chin on his hand, scanning it for the darker lump that would be Saunders.

The lump was a little to his right, and for the first time he began to consider how he would best carry the body once he had freed it. If he had to crawl back, it would mean dragging it behind him. So be it, he thought. At least it can't hurt him any more.

The German line was incredibly quiet. He lay listening, tense as a cat, then began to wriggle forward again. The wire was very near now, the dark blob that was Saunders almost within reach of his outstretched arm. He wriggled up to it, then very smoothly rose to a standing position. There was little shadow to aid concealment, but the darkness was thickening.

With the wire-cutters poised ready in one hand, he

touched the cold, army-clad bundle that was Saunders with the other.

It was difficult to see exactly where he was caught, and the first snip seemed to reverberate like a pistol shot. He froze. Nothing happened. He took another snip, peering closely and tugging as hard as he dared. He began to wish he had brought a pair of scissors instead of wire-cutters; if he left half of Saunders' uniform dangling on the wire it could scarcely matter to him now.

Snip-snip. God, were they all asleep? They *must* hear. He snipped faster, then in a burst of impatience dropped the wire-cutters and seized the material in both hands. He managed to tear it, and Saunders' body fell on top of him, knocking him to the ground.

He smelt. Christ, how he smelt. Breathing through his mouth, Berry half-dragged and half-carried him away from the wire. Another Verey light suddenly soared, followed this time by the swish of a magnesium flare. Its ghastly light shone without pity, and Berry dropped again and lay in the lee of Saunders' body. A burst of machine-gun fire split the silence. Berry cradled his head in his arms and waited. The stream of bullets thudded into the ground a little ahead of him, then stopped as abruptly as they had begun.

And in the ensuing silence he heard Saunders moan.

Torn between gladness and horror, Berry cautiously put out his hand and explored the man lying beside him. His fingers found Saunders' bare head and thin hair, and then his face. It felt very cold.

'Saunders – listen – can you move?' The whisper sounded like a roar in his own ears. He thought he heard another moan, more like a deep exhalation of breath.

'Listen – I'm going to have to drag you.' Raising himself as little as possible, he grasped Saunders by a handful of clothing and hauled. Although he was not a big man, he was immovable to someone trying to shift him with only one arm and while in a prone position.

Berry rolled over and tried the other arm, but Saunders remained inert as a sack of grain. The light from the flares died, leaving a rusty glow. A small night wind began to rustle among tufts of dead grass. Filled with sudden impatience, Berry stood up and seized Saunders beneath his arms and began to drag him backwards. He completed a distance of six yards, then tripped over something and fell backwards, and once again the machine gun started raking the area with its savage fire. Squatting hastily in front of Saunders, Berry groped for his arms and clasped them round his neck. He staggered to his feet and began to run, carrying Saunders on his back. The machine gun was joined by another and then another. He heard the hiss and smack of rifle fire and felt the bullets lashing the earth like heavy hailstones. Blindly he kept running, and heard answering British gunfire coming from further down the line.

The sound of it helped to guide him back. It was very dark now, but he knew that his own men would hold their fire until he returned. With bursting lungs, he hurled himself and Saunders towards what he hoped was the gap in the wire – and almost shouted with relief when he heard their hoarse whispers and saw the glimmer of a white handkerchief that someone was waving.

'Come on, Sir! Over here!' They caught him as he staggered and fell, precipitating Saunders into the middle of them.

'Careful – he's still alive!' Berry flopped down into the trench, his head between his knees and his chest heaving. He heard them carrying Saunders towards the first-aid post and waited to regain his breath before joining them.

Good old Saunders. This would mean Blighty for him. Wiping his forehead on his sleeve, he began planning the customary recommendation in strong terms: *Despite a great sense of duty and a determination to serve his country, this man is not suited by nature to . . .*

He went down to the first-aid post, and because of his soft shoes they didn't hear him coming. He saw them standing round Saunders, who was now lying on the table, glassy-eyed and open-mouthed. They had stripped aside the remains of his tunic and shirt, and Dawkins was leaning over him with his ear pressed against his heart. He straightened up when he saw Berry.

''fraid he's dead, Sir.'

'Nonsense! He's alive.'

Dawkins shook his head, and a sense of outraged and monumental grief swept Berry like a tidal wave. To his own horror, he burst into tears in full view of the shocked and kindly faces of 4th Platoon. He couldn't stop. Couldn't speak. All he could do was stand there and sob noisily and convulsively until he had the wit to turn on his heel and walk away.

He went back to his dug-out and dropped the curtain over the doorway. A rat leaped from the table and tried to scramble up the glistening, newly dug earth wall. Fumbling for the matches, Berry lit the candle and sat down on the edge of his bunk. For some reason he remembered the evening he had offered Private Mottram a toffee. Mottram was dead too, of course, and he had never learned why they called him Stunners. He only knew that he had died of gas gangrene and that he had had to write and tell his wife.

How long ago it all seemed. Peldon, Durrant, Lance-Corporal Pollard; Linton, Thompson, Anderson, Martin, Bagley . . . all dead. All ghosts in an endless column of ghosts, and although he had just been blubbing like a kid, he knew that a lump of Palm toffee no longer had the power to comfort him.

Wiping his eyes, he reached for the brandy bottle.

★

Dear Mater and Pater,

I meant to drop a line last week but we've had rather a busy spell. Nothing too anxious-making, I hasten to add, just normal routine. The weather still somewhat hot and clammy but a lot of it's due to the clouds of chemical stink from bombs and shells – which someone rather pompously described as the inevitable obfuscation of martial combat! I am now a Section Commander of a Six Gun Battery – how about that? We are stationed quite a long way back from the front line – quite right too, because the racket we make would keep 'em all awake! Big guns are such funny things – ours are 74s – and although they look so big and clumsy they're really quite precise and delicate things. And no two sound quite the same. I saw a captured German howitzer the other day – a simply enormous brute – and all round the breech it was most exquisitely engraved with laurel leaves and doves of peace! Sometimes I think I don't understand human nature *at all*.

Last Thursday evening the Welch Fusiliers gave a concert – oh, it's not all blood and guts, you know – and who should I see there head and shoulders above everyone else but Lieutenant Berry Dullingham! We managed to sit together and he was really splendid the way he roared with laughter and joined in all the singing in that terrible tuneless bray of his! He seems immensely popular – just like he was at school. Anyway, you'll be pleased to have a junior subaltern's report to the effect that he's still in one piece and bursting with vigour. We meet up whenever we can – we're not all that far away – but it's not always easy to get in touch and certainly very difficult to plan time off together.

I'm sitting here writing this on a grassy slope just outside a little village that's been rather knocked about. No one lives here any more but there are rabbits bounding in and out of the church – or what remains of it. Well, they're all God's creatures, I suppose. Will write again very shortly, and by the way, thanks awfully for the marvellous parcel – I was the most popular chap for miles around! Love to everyone and lots to you both, ever your loving son Tommy.

*

They received the letter at Reve two days before the telegram announcing Berry's arrival on a week's leave.

Excitement became laced with perturbation when they realized that he had given no final details.

'He will come to Bury St Edmunds.'

'Let's go and meet him at Liverpool Street!'

'But at what time?'

Lizzie was all in favour of a quick dash to Dover ('No, no, darling, it might be Folkstone or Southampton . . .') and it was Uncle Woodstock who counselled patience until they heard more. 'He will telephone to us from the railway station – mark my words!'

'Can we all fit in the Daimler? I mean, we *do* all want to go, don't we?'

'What about the wagonette, if it's fine? Remember how he always *loved* the old wagonette?'

'How I wish Tommy was coming too. . . .'

'They couldn't possibly spare both of them at the same time,' Dully said, and Lizzie took him seriously. 'No, I suppose you're right.'

But they received no further news, and were consequently unprepared for the dusty figure that scorched up to the south front on a large and ramshackle motorbike. He walked up the terrace steps, slowly removing his gauntlets and leather helmet.

This was how he had dreamed it would be, how he had wanted it to be – the soft evening light, the last song of a thrush and the timeless peace of Reve enfolding him. He walked on, savouring every precious second.

'Anyone at home?'

His mother was the first to see him. She flew to him wordlessly, and as her arms fastened round his neck he held her by the waist and swept her round in dizzying circles of joy. Her feet left the ground and her skirts fluttered.

They all came hurrying, including the servants, and they all looked just the same. He couldn't get over how nothing had changed, and the happy relief shone in his tired dusty face and boomed in his laughter. He laughed at everything, breathlessly, heartily, and when Uncle Woodstock's new puppy (Scotus III) skittered merrily across the great hall with Aunt Miriam's knitting in his mouth, tears of mirth filled his eyes.

Over dinner they asked him about conditions on the Western Front, and he said that they weren't all that bad; there were nasty patches, of course, and he had lost several of his chaps – which was jolly hard really, because they had all been pretty decent. . . . Tommy was fine – he had managed to see him for half an hour before leaving and he sent his love – good old Tom, they would all be very proud if they could see him.

'Does he have any spare time for poetry?'

'Oh, I should think so. He'll probably come back armed with reams of it.'

The talk went on, the ladies remained at table with the gentlemen when the liqueurs were brought in, and then it was his turn.

He wanted to know about Reve in great detail, and they told him that they now had beds for thirty officers and seventy other ranks, and that every bed was full.

'Marvellous,' he said warmly. 'Now tell me about Uncle Merton and Aunt Netta, and how the home farm's doing. I know it's ridiculous but I keep dreaming about the herons down by the river – did the blighters raise a good brood this year? I know they steal the fish, but . . .'

But he remembered herons flying over the river Somme, trailing their long legs and searching for a place away from the roar of guns and the stench of rotting corpses, where they could go about their lives in peace.

He reached for the brandy decanter and refilled his glass, and then looked up to meet his father's eyes.

'Here's to victory!' Berry raised his glass.

'And to both your safe returns,' replied his father, raising his own.

One-thirty seemed far too early for bed (Aunt Minna had unobtrusively retired at eleven), and he leaned out of his window, inhaling the scent of late roses on the mild Suffolk air and listening to the quivering cry of owls in the woods. Reve was all around him – he almost imagined that he could hear the slow beat of its great heart – and although the soft high bed with its crisp, turned-down covers invited him, it seemed a criminal waste of time to spend even a couple of hours in sleep.

Resting his arms a little more comfortably on the stone coping, he decided to go downstairs very quietly and let himself out into the park. Like Uncle Merton, he knew every stick and step of the way, and for once he would be able to walk without fear. No Jerry trenches, no sudden blaze of machine-gun fire. . . . His head drooped on to his arms and he slept, and instead of dreaming about herons he dreamed about Marguerite.

But things had changed; it was inevitable. Next day he allowed himself to be led over the west wing, which was now the Reve Military Hospital. He shook hands with the sisters and nurses, chatted with the wounded and the convalescent and walked quietly past the beds hidden behind screens. His mother still wore her nursing uniform, and her dark auburn hair was coiled gracefully under a little white lace cap; she was still no end of a good-looker, and he watched with amused pride as the eyes followed her progress through the wards.

'We've had a lot of surgical cases,' she said in a low voice as they stood watching a group of men in hospital blue lining up on their crutches beneath a mulberry tree. One of the nursing sisters was with them and her sprightly cry of 'One to be ready – two to be steady – ' came drifting towards them.

' – and three to be *off*!'

The row of men began to lumber forward, swinging their crutches with awkward haste. Most had lost at least part of a leg, and a double-amputee in a wheelchair had been placed in position as the winning post. He was cheering them, and the competitors were laughing.

'Sometimes I can't believe it,' Lizzie said abruptly, and turned away. Berry put his arm round her in silence.

He hadn't realized what an integral part of Reve the hospital had become, and he had never realized before how beautiful Reve was, how many beautiful vistas and corners it had under the slow sailing clouds. He had always loved it, but had never really seen it in the way he was seeing it now.

One afternoon he climbed the long slope where they always used to pause on the way home from picnics in the dell. The big lone elm was still there, and he stood leaning against it and looking down on the great house that would one day be his. Perhaps. If he came through.

Perhaps it might even be his and Marguerite's. They had still never spoken of such things; so far as he was aware she had no idea of his home background – she didn't even know that he had a title.

The week was already half over when his father drew him on one side and asked if he didn't feel like taking a trip up to town. 'London's a very jolly place these days, I'm told.'

Berry demurred, saying that he was quite content to remain where he was for the little time that was left.

'I thought you might like the idea of dinner and a theatre.

Perhaps you could invite your mother – she's had precious little in the way of amusement recently.'

'Of course!' His enthusiasm was immediate. 'Won't you come too?'

Dully hesitated, then smiled. 'No, not this time. I think she'd like to have you all to herself for an hour or two.'

They set off, Berry driving, and beneath the lights that were dimmed in case of zeppelin raids, the West End was seething with wartime gaiety. Theatres and restaurants were crowded with uniformed men and jewelled women, and the only glimpse of an uglier mood came when a young woman handed Berry a white feather, suspicious of his patriotism because he was wearing mufti.

They went to the Russian ballet, and its marvellous savage brilliance intoxicated them. 'There was nothing like this in my day,' Lizzie kept saying. 'We'd never have *dared* to dance like that!'

They supped at Romano's, and the old place brought back all the old memories. She laughed and sparkled and told him all about being one of Miss Paynim's Pixies, and he laughed with her and ordered another bottle of champagne. Someone at the next table said isn't that the Countess Dullingham? And that must be one of her sons with her. . . .

They had reserved rooms at Brown's Hotel for the night and they strolled slowly through the thinning crowds; the air was warm and still, and the late summer moon hung low over the jumble of London roofs.

'I got to know London very well when I was a girl,' Lizzie said. 'But Reve's made me forget I ever lived anywhere else.'

'I'd like to get to know it, one day.'

'You will,' she said.

They walked in silence, arm in arm, and their footsteps echoed lightly.

'Tell me more about being in London when you were young. Tell me about meeting the pater.'

She told him. And because he was so tall and adult and well-educated and soldierly – all of those things and many more – she told him about falling for Polperro and being miffed when she got landed with Dully, and even more miffed when she got landed with his baby.

'That was you.'

'I know.' He squeezed her arm, smiling down on her in the moonlight. 'I *can* add up, Mother dear.'

She told him about Dully coming to find her, about the ill-contrived fenland wedding ('I was flimmocky as a hen on lay') and she told him about the delayed falling in love with Dully. 'I fell for him at the ole Queen's funeral – must have been the lovely music – and it's never changed, except to get more sort of coated over with the years.'

The only thing she didn't tell him about was going to the house at Dalston Junction; about trying to get rid of him that day because she was all alone and the other girls at the Gaiety said it's the only way out for you, dearie.

'And now here we are,' he said, almost as if he hadn't needed to be told, 'you and I strolling down wherever-it-is and happy as a couple of larks.'

'I'll be glad when it's over, Berry. You and Tommy . . .'

'We'll be back.'

'But how much longer's it going *on* for?'

'Not long,' he said. 'I think they're planning another big push for the autumn.'

The war. It hung like a shadow, like a pall of black smoke over the future; however bright the gaiety, however fervent the promises, it was always there, ready to annihilate. Walking in silence, they both thought how little they had spoken about it; Berry determined to remain casually offhand for fear of worrying them even more, and the family deferentially unquestioning for fear of spoiling his leave.

God alone knows what they both face out there, thought Lizzie, silently counting the cracks in the London paving stones, but it's up to us to be cheerful and happy and pretend there's nothing wrong. But please let it end soon. Before he has time to go back out there again, and before anything can happen to Tommy.

They reached the hotel and said goodnight quietly and

soberly. Next morning they motored slowly back to Suffolk, and the one Reve footman too old for military service proffered a silver salver upon which lay a crumpled travel-stained envelope bearing a Field postmark.

'A letter came for you, Sir.'

Opening it, Berry discovered that he had been awarded the Victoria Cross for conspicuous bravery while on active service.

For some reason he didn't at first understand, he stuffed the letter in his pocket and said nothing. Then he realized that it was because he didn't know what he had done to deserve it.

He supposed that it must have been because of Saunders, but any bravery he might possibly have shown had been a waste of effort. Saunders was dead. Perhaps he had been right in believing he detected signs of life when he freed him from the wire, but he had certainly been dead as a doornail on arrival. And what could be more futile than lugging a dead body across no man's land? The memory of it merely sickened him, particularly his own shameful loss of self-control.

It also brought Saunders back with a vivid persistence he could have done without. Poor old Saunders – easy to pity but hard to like. He had seen so many other finer chaps cop it and had managed to conceal his feelings from himself as well as others, but Saunders with his white face and frightened-animal eyes, his involuntary sicking and shitting, was going to be some kind of perpetual symbol. As he had carried his corpse on his back, so he was going to carry him round his neck like the proverbial albatross; the VC would bind them inexorably together, and would ensure Saunders' pallid, ghostlike presence in his mind for ever more.

The letter also brought the Western Front disturbingly close. And with it, the realization that he didn't want to go back.

He had known it for some days – perhaps he had really known it from that first quiet magical evening when he

394

arrived – but now he had to look the fact squarely in the face, and deal with it.

Dread was a new sensation for Berry. Everything about life was so highly enjoyable – even the mere act of breathing sometimes seemed a source of pleasure – and the thought that it might all be snatched away in the very near future had become unendurable. He was well aware that he had outlasted his allotted span, and he wanted to go on living. It didn't seem a lot to ask.

And the last hours were already trickling away. He went to tea with Uncle Merton and Aunt Netta in the tree house, and the glorious profusion of yellowing leaves outside the window made him think with horror of the blighted and piteous stumps on the battlefields of Northern France.

Aunt Netta greeted him with gentle incomprehension and they talked of the weather while Uncle Merton carefully adjusted the shawl round her shoulders and then set about making the tea. Neither of them asked about the war, and he began to realize that this was one fragile corner of the world which it had been unable to touch.

He left them standing gravely side by side on the little wooden platform as he descended the ladder, and walking back across the park he thought, another hour gone. Soon it will be time for dinner.

On his last morning he drove into Bury St Edmunds and bought some new shirts and socks to take back with him, some warm Jaeger underwear and some silk stockings for Marguerite and her mother, then on impulse a dozen ragtime records for the gramophone in the convalescent ward of the Reve hospital.

No one ate much at luncheon, and no one could find much to say. Uncle Badger sighed heavily and repeatedly, and listening to the tick of the clock, Berry looked up and caught the silent agony in his father's eyes.

How to fill the last hours? A stroll round the gardens, now frankly unkempt but exploding in a last glory of asters and chrysanthemums? A wander round the house, through the vast quiet rooms with their soft faded carpets and the portraits in the gallery that looked at him so enigmatically?

He recalled the day when he had stood braced in front of them while he promised not to let the side down. . . . No, he wouldn't go into the long gallery now.

He ought to spend the time with his parents. He wanted to – needed to – but a dry-mouthed, wooden-faced inertia had overtaken him, almost as if he were in the initial stages of becoming anaesthetized. He couldn't break out of it; couldn't laugh or joke any more; he couldn't even clench his big strong hands in a futile effort to stop the minutes from oozing away.

He became aware that his parents were avoiding him, too. That they wanted to be with him but couldn't. From the library came the strains of someone playing the piano – probably Aunt Miriam. She was playing 'Rose of Picardy', then the sound stopped abruptly, as if someone had cried *don't – not now!*

'I must go and pack.'

'Pritchard will see to it. . . . Have you room for some books and a cake for Tommy?'

'Oh yes, of course I have. He'll be delighted. But I'd better see to it myself. . . .'

Stupid, meaningless words left trailing on the air. Then a stiff-limbed soldier's walk across the echoing great hall, a polite nod to a parlourmaid encountered along the corridor (and the look in her eyes as if she too wanted to say something, do something, but didn't know what). She scurried away. He sat on his bed and smoked a cigarette, and the minutes went on ticking past.

With his valise packed and strapped, and wearing his carefully sponged and pressed uniform, he went round the hospital wards to say cheerio. And their eyes all held the same look – because they all knew precisely what he was returning to – You poor young sod, we don't envy you. . . .

Bland, the chauffeur whose knock knees and flat feet had so far eliminated him from the war machine, had spent most of the previous day cleaning and servicing the big BSA, and the time came when he wheeled it reverently round to the south front to await its owner.

The last effort at the last moment wasn't so very terrible

after all. The family walked with him on to the terrace, and his mother and father went down the steps with him. He embraced them both wordlessly, and his mother's facial contortions, prompted by the effort of not crying, were almost funny.

Astride the motorbike, he took one last look at Reve: at the aunts and uncles, and at the maids peeping from upper windows, and he heard the last lonely cry of a peacock before he started the engine. He adjusted his goggles, glanced round to make sure that his valise was properly secured, then waved a last cheerio before accelerating with a roar. He disappeared in a burst of smoke and a spurt of gravel towards the night boat for Boulogne.

He had managed the goodbyes in a manner befitting someone who had just been awarded the Victoria Cross, and even as the schoolboy side of him began to regret having kept it a secret, he also knew with an adult's certainty that he would never come back.

The Allied armies were pushing slowly forward but their progress was hampered by the results of their own heavy barrages, while the Germans were withdrawing to comparatively unspoilt country and uncratered roads.

Autumn rains came, and reduced all military movement to a crawl along roads blasted by shells and littered with dead horses and abandoned wagons. Splintered trees were festooned with fallen telegraph wire and here and there among the debris was the occasional hastily dug grave, with the occupant's name sometimes scrawled on a bit of paper inside a bottle inverted on a stick.

But a grave was a luxury on the Somme. The majority slowly putrefied where they lay.

'Cheer up, Sir, when you've seen one you've seen 'em all,' Tommy's sergeant said as the battery moved further south towards the High Wood ridge. Although Tommy nodded, he was unable to agree.

They were all different. All lying in different positions, all wearing different expressions and all in different stages of decomposition, and their air of mute helplessness

397

appalled him as much as their sweet rotting smell turned his stomach. They racked his very bones with pity, and the horror of their degradation froze any instinct to convert what he saw into words. Poetry was as dead as the men who lay torn and flung down, with open eyes and curly hair and maggots swarming among their entrails. The humble house sparrow was treated with more mercy than this at home.

Home. Sometimes he tried to blot out the present by thinking of the past – to go about his duties with quiet acquiescence while he pulled childhood memories over his head like a soft nursery blanket that would shut out the light. But even Reve seemed to desert him, to withdraw itself with a shudder from an inferno that had no parallel in history.

The front line of Allied trenches was now strung in a wavering seam across the plains to the north of Langueval, and supporting artillery was forced to take up its position on the exposed high chalk ridge behind. They were within full view of the enemy, and only minimum crews of three were kept at each gun, with one officer and one sergeant in command.

The rain continued, drumming relentlessly on the living and the dead, and during spells as duty officer, Tommy would lie in the shadow of the hewn chalk and peer at the infantry entrenched below and wonder if old Berry was there. He had heard nothing from him since his presumed return from leave.

Although they were less conspicuous than the artillery, Berry's crowd was a great deal nearer the enemy, particularly to those ensconced in the Butte de Walencourt. The Butte was a chalk mound some sixty feet high and reputed to be a prehistoric burial site. It looked over the Allied troops like a white and malevolent ghost, and was heavily fortified with German deep mine galleries and machine-gun emplacements.

Time and again they were ordered to attack it, and time and again they were thrown back by the blazing shellfire and yapping machine guns. The mud on the plain between the Butte and the Allied ridge deepened and became churned to thick slime. Swiftly it immobilized Haigh's new toy, the caterpillar steam tractors that became known as tanks. It swallowed horses and suffocated men in their repeated efforts to take the Butte, and in the trenches they had won from the Germans the men of the 3rd Light Suffolks were living knee high in oozing filth.

The days shortened and darkened over a world where bits of trees stood gaunt as gibbets in the weeping mist. Up on the high ridge a cold wind moaned and Tommy's sergeant lit a cigarette between cupped hands. Shelling from both sides had been fairly sporadic for the past hour.

'Easin' off a bit, Sir. They always do about this time.'

'Probably stopped for a brew-up.'

'Na, Sir.' The sergeant looked wise. 'Jerry don't go in for tea, Sir. He drinks snapps.'

'Oh. Well, I could do with a hot cup of something. . . .'

They lapsed into silence while the three men on the nearby gun slewed the big muzzle this way and that as they made adjustments on sights and range drums and shell fuses. They were scarcely older than Tommy, and it went without saying that they too would have welcomed a mug of hot tea.

'My step-grandfather's a Jerry,' Tommy said inconsequentially. He banged his chilled feet together.

'Reely, Sir?'

'Can't say that he struck me as particularly satanic, although I didn't know him very well.'

'I believe there's some very nice ones, Sir. Very fond of music a lot of them are, I'm told.'

'Beethoven was a Jerry. So were Bach and Mozart, I think.'

'An' what about the "Blue Danube", Sir? Strauss was one too, wasn't he?'

'Ah, I forgot Strauss. And they were pretty hot stuff at poetry as well. There was a chap called Schiller we did a bit of at school. . . .'

The German shell took them unawares. It seemed to arrive with no more than a harmless whoosh, and the last thing Tommy saw before the cloud of earth and chalk blotted out the light was the cigarette dropping from the sergeant's lips.

He was dead. Disembodied, he was vaguely annoyed by the cool quiet voice that was asking his name.

'Tommy,' he managed through parched, swollen lips.

'Yes, you are all tommies. But try to tell me your *name*.'

Useless to argue, or to strive for clarification. With most of his uniform in shreds, and the bits that remained discoloured by wet earth and blood, it was impossible to tell whether he was of a comissioned rank or not.

'Thomas Dullingham-Reve.'

'Yes. Good. Now you must go to sleep.'

He sank back behind closed eyelids (always obey a command).

Merciful freedom from cold and worry and responsibility. He dozed, unaware of his surroundings or the occasional jolting of his stretcher. There was no hunger or thirst, no feeling of any kind save a huge inchoate thankfulness that it was over. He was dead, and the thing was finished. Berry, wherever he was, would be thankful on his behalf.

Pain woke him. It roused him gradually, limb by limb, muscle by muscle. Reluctantly he opened his eyes and gradually became aware of the interior of some kind of conveyance. They were in motion, and it was the jolting that caused the pain. Biting his lips, he listened to the low whine of the engine and tried to anticipate each jerk and jounce and to brace himself accordingly, but it was impossible. He tried to shift his position but he seemed stuck to the thin canvas stretcher and the bumping went on. He heard moaning and gasping coming from the dim shapes around him. He lost consciousness again.

They arrived at the casualty clearing station, a collection of tents separated by duck-boards, and the hospital stretcher-bearers broke step to reduce the jolting as they carried the wounded inside. White-clad figures lifted him gently on to a high table, and the pain came roaring back as the same gentle hands tried to prize away the shreds of

uniform burnt into his flesh. He died. Again. Then floated
back in time to feel the gauze mask touch his face while the
drops of ether sent him spinning down into a starry
darkness.

He was lying in a hospital bed when he came to; it had
white sheets and pillows, and he was warm. The smell of
ether still clung, still held him in a queasy mist, but there
was no pain. He closed his eyes, and when he opened them
again a girl's face was close to his and her arm was beneath
his neck.

'Have a little sip,' she said, proffering a cup with a spout.
'It will do you good.'

Clumsily he obeyed, and it was the sweetest nectar he had
ever tasted. With her help he drank it all, and her arm
supported him and then laid him carefully back on the
pillow.

'Better?'

'Yes . . . thanks.' His lips still felt stiff and swollen. It
was an effort to move them.

'Don't talk any more now,' she said, as if she knew, and
he listened tiredly to the crisp rustle of her nurse's uniform
as she hurried away.

Blue eyes and golden eyelashes. Pink cheeks and a rosy
mouth. She was the first female he had seen since leaving
home and he had a good mind to invite her out to
dinner. . . . He floated off to sleep.

They woke him in order to re-dress his wounds; to pull
away the pads and bandages already stuck with drying
blood; to swab with hypochlorous acid and then rebandage,
tightly and securely, while he gasped and tried to conceal
his livid sweating face with his forearm.

He asked if he could be sent back home to the hospital
run by his mother, and they said yes of course, as soon as
you are well enough to be moved. They discovered that he
was an Honourable, and thought it would be nice for him to
meet another young subaltern further down the ward who
was a Sir.

He slept, fitfully and feverishly, and sometimes he was
back at school. But mostly it was Reve, where the great

401

trees held out their lovely unshattered arms wide to him, and the house, lying gracefully at ease, waited to receive him. It was the quiet green unity, unbroken and unbruised, that he dreamed of most.

His sleep became tormented and his body hurt when he moved. They brought him some more of the nectar to drink, but this time he couldn't swallow. Then it was time to dress his wounds again, to destroy the fragile ghost of peace and set the pain roaring as they removed layer after layer. This time they showed the wounds to the medical officer, who muttered fresh instructions before hurrying away. They had to insert drainage tubes into the gaping hole in his groin, and when it was over the gentle nurse wiped his forehead with a piece of cool surgical gauze.

'Was that me, kicking up a fuss?'

'No, no, someone further down the ward.'

'What's your name?'

'Elsie . . . but don't tell Sister I told you. We're not supposed to make friends with the patients.'

Elsie. Perhaps it would be better if he began by taking her out to tea. . . .

It always seemed to be night. He had no means of knowing whether it was all one long night or whether he slept through a succession of daylight hours. But he clung to the knowledge that once back at Reve time would revert to normal.

The limey smell of hypochlorous acid, the giant shadows thrown on the quivering canvas walls as the nurses rustled up and down, the distant boom of guns, the cries and groans and retchings, but – struggling to shine through it all – the beauty of good old Reve.

Yet Reve was receding. Behind closed eyelids he fought to recapture it, to hold it closer, but it was dissolving. He tried to find the words that would bring it back – euphoric . . . harmonious . . . what about pulchritudinous? No good, any of them, all been used before . . . someone ought to invent some new ones.

A man's face bent over him, peering closely through the shadows. The voice was familiar and so were the eyes, the

402

way they tilted up at the corners. Points of lamplight caught his hair in a glowing red.

'What on earth are you doing in here, you silly young sod?'

'Pulchritudinous.' His voice was no more than a weak little gasp. 'Have you ever heard such a ghastly word?'

He seemed to dwindle and fade like one of the shadows on the canvas wall. Like the memory of Reve, there was no substance to him any more. His hand slipped from his brother's, and leaning forward to close his eyes, Berry saw through his grief that the silly young sod had been trying to grow a moustache.

Tommy had gone. The war continued.

Fog tinted yellow by gas and the lingering fumes of high explosive hung over the waste of mud, and the German-held Butte reared its great white skull over the British lines. Shellfire continuously wreathed it in drifts of smoke, but its mocking face was never totally obscured. Its brooding presence dominated their days and haunted their brief periods of sleep, for no matter how many attempts failed and how heavy the resultant losses, Haigh had ordered its capture.

The autumn rains continued, sweeping no man's land in a grey curtain shivered by a bitter wind. The mud deepened, and men already ill and undernourished were too exhausted to continue wading through it. They fell, and were trampled underfoot, and suffocation in the cloying filth seemed no worse a fate than being ripped apart by machine-gun bullets.

In the early weeks on the Somme there had been joking and singing; rough jokes and rude songs – 'Have you ever caught your knackers in a rat trap?' to the tune of 'Colonel Bogey' – and games of pontoon and ha'penny nap, and a good-natured tolerance of the close proximity thrust upon them. They still believed that the war would end one day.

But now they were sinking into an apathy as deep and remorseless as the mud outside the wet and foetid trenches they shared with the rats. Alarmed by reports of dwindling

403

morale, HQ sought to tighten discipline. The commander of one division withdrew the regulation issue of rum, and several young subalterns were shot for cowardice, their gas helmets reversed over their heads.

Because of the ruthless expenditure of life, Berry had been elevated to the rank of captain upon his return from leave. The position brought additional responsibility if no personal benefit, and he was entirely unaware that he had by now become something of a legend. Like everyone else out there, he had lost weight, but although the boyish contours had sharpened and become taut long before their time, he was still growing. He was now six feet two, and the appearance of his looming broad-shouldered figure topped by the ruffled thatch of defiant red hair had become a symbol of security, of affection, even of hope, in a world where hope was in increasingly short supply.

For Captain Berry had survived longer than anyone, apart from his batman. In spite of the risks he took (he had won the VC for dragging a bloke in off the wire even though he was three-parts dead), and in spite of his contempt for his own discomfort (he had lain for two nights and a day in a shell-hole after knocking out a machine-gun emplacement), he was still alive; more than that, he was still colourful, vigorous and smiling, with his battered motorbike and mud-stained uniform, and it was not surprising that lesser men felt a surreptitious desire to touch his sleeve for luck.

But he didn't know any of that, and on the day after Tommy's death he sat in his dug-out with a blank sheet of paper in front of him and tried with a feeling of hopeless ineptitude to break the news to his parents.

He looked round at the bare earth walls, black in the candlelight, and remembered that this was a captured German dug-out. He wondered about the Jerry who had inhabited it before him – probably killed in the hand-to-hand fighting – then returned to the blank sheet of paper. *Dear Mater and Pater* . . .

Bird came in, dingy and unshaven, and bearing a tin mug that steamed in the wan shadows.

'Have it while it's hot, Sir.'

Laying aside his pen, Berry took a cautious sip. The hot tin burned his lip and he swallowed convulsively. 'Christ – why don't you give up trying to make tea?'

'Not tea, Sir,' Bird said reproachfully. 'It's oxtail soup.'

'Ah.' At any rate it was hot. He continued sipping.

'You had any?'

'Me, Sir? Bully, jam and biscuit.'

'It's not enough.' Berry fumed quietly. 'When did you last have something hot?'

'They send a can of tea up the line once a day, Sir. It keeps fairly hot because it's wrapped in straw.'

A rumble of gunfire penetrated the ground.

'Reckon they're warming up, Sir. What time's kick-off?'

'Eighteen-thirty hours after thirty minutes' barrage. Usual thing.'

'You sound a bit down, Sir.' Bird eyed him narrowly.

'My young brother copped it last night.'

'Oh. Sorry to hear that, Sir. Very sorry.'

Bird's face seemed to close in on itself, as if he were in emotional retreat. Apart from muttering the usual condolences, there was nothing he could say or do.

'That be all, Sir?'

'Yes. I'll be along for inspection in ten minutes.'

Bird vanished, and Berry returned to his letter. *Dear Mater and Pater, This letter is very hard to write. Tommy died last evening. . . .*

He couldn't go on. The words wouldn't form. He sat with his head bowed and his eyes closed, but the tears wouldn't form either. Sometimes it seemed as if he had passed for ever beyond the ordinary expressions of emotion.

He pushed his chair back, then buckled on his Sam Browne before going out into the open trench. The last dingy rags of day had faded and it promised to be a starless night. The latest attacks on the Butte had all taken place under cover of darkness, and he glanced over the sand-bagged lip of the trench to where the great mound of it glimmered malevolently across the glistening mud. The rumble of gunfire continued, and an occasional flare hung trembling for a moment or two in the murky sky.

405

Two hours to go before the attack.

His men were crowded into a big crumbling dug-out that had been shored up with planks and fragments of chicken wire. The place stank of sweat, urine and tobacco, and they sat on the hard mud floor with their backs against the wall, waiting.

Seeing Berry, they began lethargically unlacing their mud-caked boots for the routine foot inspection recently ordered by HQ. Trench foot was yet another hideous manifestation of their present way of life. No boots could withstand the remorseless cold and wet, and standing sometimes knee-deep in water for hours on end tightened the regulation puttees and cut off the circulation. By the onset of autumn it was reckoned that one man in eight was suffering from trench foot, and daily rubbing with whale oil was the compulsory form of prevention.

'All well? Any trouble? How about you, Clarke?'

He moved slowly round the dug-out, stooping low while he shone a torch on the cold, grimy, sour-smelling objects obediently offered for his inspection. Beneath the dirt, all the feet were white, but he had learned to detect that other hard, lard-like whiteness that preceded the swelling and loss of sensation.

'Can you feel that, Brewster?' A gentle dig with the pin kept behind his lapel.

'Yes, Sir.'

'Sure? And are you sure you're rubbing them?'

Brewster looked confused, as if he couldn't remember. Perhaps he just didn't care; it was hard to blame men for not bothering to rub their feet in greasy, stinking whale oil when it was more than likely that they would be dead from bullet wounds during the next twenty-four hours.

Yet they bore him no grudge, and their patient acceptance of his authority had a strange and animal-like dignity.

He stayed with them for a while; smoked a cigarette and told them that the Jocks were putting on a concert on Saturday night back at the main depot, all being well. He also told them that a new load of Red Cross parcels had arrived and would be distributed within a couple of days,

406

and that a double rum issue had been ordered for this evening. He didn't tell them that he himself had filched it from the ration store.

And they smiled at him in the foetid flickering candle-light as the time ticked ruthlessly by, and a lot of them wanted to say something respectful but kind about his young brother because Bird had just told them he'd copped it. But they didn't. Couldn't. Death had no real meaning any more because there was so much of it.

So they watched him go; tall and brilliantly red-haired, ducking out of the dug-out while they quietly and resignedly assembled themselves in readiness for the next kick-off. Groundsheet, water bottle, haversack; gas helmet, field dressing, two bandoliers of small-arms ammo, and a rifle. They sat down again, stiff and awkward, and began to pass the time by flipping spent matchsticks into Brewster's upturned tin hat. No one talked. There was nothing worth saying. But they counted the minutes like men awaiting execution.

The barrage opened up. The British guns behind the line began belting out the shells that sped in fast streaks like a chalkline zipped across a blackboard, and the banshee screaming of them passing low overhead rocked the dug-out and set the candles jumping convulsively.

. . . Tommy died last evening. I was with him and there was no pain. He just slipped away in the quiet and gentle fashion that was typical of everything he did. He was a much-loved member of his battery and his Colonel was genuinely very cut up when he heard the news. He will be writing to you personally. . . .

He wrote fast, this time. The words tumbled out beneath the nib of his fountain pen, and when the letter was finished he waved it to and fro before the candle flame because he had no blotting paper, then folded it and placed it in the envelope that he had already addressed to *Reve, Suffolk, England*.

He looked round the dug-out that had once belonged to a Jerry. The bed was neat, his spare uniform was hanging tidily if precariously from a balk of timber and the brandy

407

bottle was empty. The officer's report book was on the blanket-covered table close to a photograph of his mother and father, and the letter home was propped against a little carved statue of the Virgin Mary that Marguerite had given him.

Dear Marguerite. He had nothing left for her, nothing for her to remember him by.

Ripping another sheet of paper from the pad he wrote hastily: *Dear Marguerite, I love you, and my love is all I have to give. Yours, Berry.*

He blew out the candle, and outside the trench the men were already filing into position. He could hear the muffled thump of boots and the clinking of metal as scores of them moved up from the rear, along the miles of winding traverses, ready to take the places of those who would be going over the top ahead of them. They queued silently, resignedly, knowing there was no alternative, but they kept their eyes averted from the looming mass of the Butte that was waiting to spit death at them.

The barrage ceased, and in the moments before the whistles blew, Berry moved among them, unaware that it reassured and comforted them to furtively touch his greatcoat because he was big and strong and magnificent, and because he had managed to stay alive for a record four and a half months of front-line duty.

He waited in front of them, one foot braced on the fire-step, his eyes on his watch. Two minutes to go. And if he lived to tell the tale, tomorrow would be his nineteenth birthday. He looked round and gave them all a beaming smile.

The two War Office telegrams were delivered to Reve within the space of four days. A week later, Berry's letter arrived.

. . . and try not to mourn for young Tom, and I will try my damnedest to follow my own advice. But I don't mind admitting that it's going to be difficult because I will always be left with the feeling that I should somehow and in some way have done more to

408

protect him in a situation that was totally alien to all he believed in, and held dear.

In the meantime, please help me by holding fast to the sure knowledge that whatever happens, life will go on. The trees will blossom and the flowers will bloom and everything will be jolly again. Bless you, and thank you for all your loving care of us both. Ever, Berry. PS. Captain now, I'll have you know!

Time stopped. The world stopped. For however vividly sorrow is imagined, is tried on in secret like a shroud, no amount of pretence can ever make adequate preparation for the agony of the real thing. There can be no rehearsal for the blow that annihilates.

The only glimmer of mercy lay in occasional spells of numbness; they all experienced them, and those temporarily suspended from reality were able in some small measure to comfort those for whom the pain of double loss was at crisis point.

Under Dully's orders, the news of Berry's death was kept from Lizzie for almost a week in the hope that it would allow time for her to recover a little from the blow of losing Tommy. Grey-faced, he told her as they walked through fallen leaves in the still November twilight, but even he, lacerated by grief, was unprepared for the violence of her reaction.

She fell on her knees, screaming, and tearing at her hair. She tried to fling herself face down, clawing at the earth as if she wanted to throw herself into it in some mad attempt to join the bodies of her sons. Her screams disturbed the rooks and they left their late feeding and fled up into the sky, wheeling and cawing in distress.

Weeping, he tried to raise her; to take her in his arms and hold her preciously close because he loved her and wanted to shoulder her poor wild agony as well as his own. She fought him off, ripping at his cheek with her fingernails before scrambling to her feet and lunging clumsily away.

Blindly he ran after her and caught her. She struggled free, her hair flying, and swiftly changing direction began running towards the lake. Her movements were no longer clumsy; she ran fleet as a deer, desperate as a hunted

409

animal, and his horrified pity was suddenly shot through with the memory of the long ago fox cornered by hounds in the farmyard.

He caught her again and they struggled violently, and when he saw the madness in her eyes he smacked her cheek. She collapsed, head drooping, knees folding. He picked her up and slung her across his shoulder and carried her back to the house.

The doctor kept her sedated for several days. Dully sat by her bedside, staring numbly at her white face and rich tumbled hair, and when she awoke she struggled up from the pillows and cried weakly against his neck.

'Not *both* of them . . . it can't be *both*. . . .'

There was nothing he could say.

And there was no comfort anywhere. The aunts and uncles tried separately – and occasionally made touchingly concerted efforts – to resume the normal pattern of life, but invariably one or other would crumple and hasten speech-lessly away. The domestic staff crept about their work with swollen eyes, and no one had the necessary resolve to remind Dully that so far he had omitted to put into effect any of the usual customs associated with bereavements.

There had been no obituaries in *The Times*, no arrangements made for a memorial service in the church at Reve Magna and no reference to the wearing of mourning. The blinds had not even been drawn in the boys' rooms. Pale winter sunshine continued to stream through the windows and touch battered schoolboy treasures with loving fingers.

Lizzie remained in her boudoir. She refused to dress, and huddled by the fire in a fur-trimmed robe, sometimes stony-faced and sometimes with tears trickling unheeded down her cheeks. She found it impossible to eat, to speak, to think, and the hours passed, marked by the silvery *ting* of the clock and the occasional shift of coals in the grate. She seemed indifferent to Dully's presence, yet made no objection when he sat close by and silently took her hand.

The news had to be broken to her parents, and tentatively he asked whether they would come and stay for a little while.

410

They arrived, pale and suddenly old, and Edwina finally persuaded Lizzie to eat a little breast of chicken.

'Remember all your hens? How fussy you were with them when you were a little gel?'

And I remember my sons, Lizzie's silence told her. I was ever so fussy with them too, and now they're gone. Both gone.

'How about another little forkful? Just to please ole Ma, eh?'

She began to obey the family's loving entreaties to eat, to dress, and finally managed to go downstairs to the room they called the winter parlour, where bowls of freesias scented the air and there were no photographs of the boys.

She moved among them, pale and listless as a ghost. She tried to smile because she remembered that she loved them and that they loved her; she remembered with fresh searing pain that they too had loved Berry and Tommy, and sometimes for a little while she could sink her own grief in her sympathy for them. They were getting old now, and it must be bad for them to have loved ones snatched away so brutally. The old were not as resilient as the young.

But she too was old now. Her hair was lifeless, her face grey-white, and there was no future. Her lovely boys had gone – blotted out by a puff of gunsmoke in a land that didn't matter and in a cause that was of no importance to them. Time and again she fought for and almost achieved calmness and rationality, only to have it overturned by the sudden memory of a freckled smile, the chewed elastic of a linen sun hat or the concertina wrinkle in a schoolboy sock.

Little by little she struggled back, learning to smile but dead at the heart of her. She asked for their photographs to be replaced, although she was careful not to glance at them too often. She asked to be left alone to read Berry's final letter, and she held in her hand the crimson ribbon of the Victoria Cross that had been forwarded with his other effects.

The final test came on 24 December, when they suggested that she should go through the west wing hospital wards to wish the soldiers and nursing staff a happy

411

Christmas. Do this, they said, for the sake of Berry and Tommy, and all that they have come to represent.

She said no, wildly and agitatedly. She locked herself in her room and refused to come out, but at five o'clock in the evening she unfastened the door and stood on the threshold, staring in silence at Dully, who was camped patiently in a chair nearby.

Tired, creased and chilled, he stared back at her, then rose and slowly offered her his arm. She had put on a black dinner gown and brushed her hair into some rough semblance of its old gleaming beauty.

'Help me.'

'I'm here.'

'I can't do it on my own.'

'You don't need to, Liza-Lizzie.'

She had fled from the hospital the day the first telegram arrived, and had not been back since. She couldn't bear the thought of it, and had taken elaborate care not to catch the faintest glimpse of blue-clad figures hobbling through the gardens. She hated them because they were alive. She had even bundled her Red Cross uniform into her maid's arms and told her to get rid of it because she never wanted to see it again.

In the early stages, Dully had been at great pains to protect her; he had diverted her attention from the slow whine of ambulances arriving up the west avenue, and had dealt quietly and tactfully with expressions of sympathy from the nursing staff. But now he was helping her to break out of the ice, to confront, one by one, the small innocent reminders of their sons. Sometimes now she could even bring herself to speak their names, and after today he hoped that the hospital would no longer be an object of her hatred and fear.

He walked with her very slowly down to the dark panelled staircase hall, and from the open doorway of the saloon the family watched them cross the echoing great hall, where the faded banners of past wars hung motionless, and then pass through the double doors that led to the west wing.

412

The smell of iodine and ether reached her and she faltered momentarily. He waited, then gave her hand a reassuring little squeeze as Matron approached, bobbed a token curtsey, then silently took her place behind them.

The first ward was occupied by men no longer confined to bed; some sat in wheelchairs, others stood touchingly to attention on crutches. Holly and ivy decorated the walls and a Christmas tree twinkled with colour. The nurses, obediently striving for an appearance of normality, dropped hasty little curtseys before busying themselves smoothing counterpanes that were already smooth.

No one spoke. No one looked at her, and she walked the length of the ward with her fragile composure intact. But only just. Her chin wobbled painfully and Dully held her close as they passed a boy with a thatch of red hair protruding from a bandaged head wound.

They walked through all the wards in turn, each one silent and respectful and heavy with the weight of sympathy. At the end of the final one she managed a smile, but the words 'Merry Christmas' refused to form.

Before they returned to the family's wing, she paused to look at Dully, childishly anticipating his praise because she had come through the ordeal without breaking, then groped hastily in the little jet-beaded bag she carried.

'Oh, darling – here. . . .'

With a handkerchief inadequate as a small cobweb, she dabbed at the tears coursing down his cheeks and falling on to his collar, his shirtfront, the revers of his crumpled jacket. 'Oh, my poor love. . . .'

'Sorry,' he managed finally. 'Rather let the side down . . . not?'

'No, you haven't,' she said very earnestly. 'Because you've just given all your courage to me.'

Christmas morning, 1916. The early rain had stopped and the sky was lightening to a pale and distant blue. Thin twists of smoke rose from the chimneys at Reve, and out in the park the cattle's breath hung silver-white on the still air.

Uncle Merton had decided to roast an Aylesbury duck for

413

luncheon, and set out the necessary preparations after he and Aunt Netta had exchanged their small gifts. (A pair of handknitted gloves for him and a white silk scarf with fringed ends for her.)

The family's double bereavement had affected him deeply, but the old tormenting shyness prevented him from making any overt declaration of sympathy. Instead, he left little gifts for Lizzie; ringing the bell and hurrying away before the servant had time to open the door and take in the little bunch of pink spindleberry threaded with the long green tassels of *Garya elliptica*, or the saucerful of brightly polished Himalayan fir cones, all of them addressed to Elizabeth, Countess Dullingham, in his fine, pointed handwriting.

He told Aunt Netta, and her large eyes opened wide with distress; an hour later and she had forgotten every word. Because they seldom visited the big house, her memory of its inmates had faded almost to vanishing point.

'You remember the two little boys,' he would say patiently, 'with red hair. They used to ride their ponies this way.'

'Yes. Oh yes, I remember them.'

'And they grew into men and went to fight in the war.'

'War . . .?'

'And they were killed.'

'There used to be two little boys,' Aunt Netta said, looking about her. 'What became of them?'

But if she was incapable of offering comfort, he was grateful for her acquiescence, her tranquil acceptance of whatever the days might bring, and he stilled his own sorrow silently and as best he could.

He had made a small plum pudding several weeks ago and he now set it to steam in the bain-marie. With his cuffs turned back, he began to prepare a rich herb stuffing for the duck while the oven warmed. As usual, Aunt Netta asked if there was anything she could do to help, and as usual he said no thank you, my dear.

'Do you think it is a little early for a glass of sherry wine?'

He pretended to consult his watch. 'It is mid-morning,

414

and I think perhaps a small glass for each of us would do very well.'

She poured them, measuring the same height in each glass with great exactitude.

'Your very good health,' she said. And then remembered just in time: 'And a very merry Christmas!'

'A merry Christmas,' he responded, and wrenched his thoughts resolutely from Berry and Tommy's parents up at the house. And also, upon reflection, from the parents of all the poor sick and bleeding travesties of young men lying in the hospital wing.

'Are you sure there is nothing I can do?'

'Nothing whatever,' he assured her. 'Luncheon will be quite a simple affair.'

She left the little galley-like kitchen and wandered round the living area, smoothing the chair covers and removing an invisible speck of dust from the table. She felt restless and strangely ill at ease. Steam from the simmering plum pudding was misting the windows. She rubbed a patch clear with her hand and it clouded over again.

'I think I will go out for a breath of air.'

'Do. But put on your hat and coat.'

She did so. Her coat was of dark alpaca, and it swept in a loose curve from the shoulder to just above the ankle. Her hat was deep-brimmed and of matching velour. She took up the long silk scarf Merton had given her that morning and tied it slowly round her neck. Its creamy whiteness looked very well against the dark of her coat and hat and its touch was soft against her throat.

She stepped outside. The great supporting arms of the beech were shining black and slippery with rain. Large iridescent drops still hung from the naked twigs, and last summer's nests were like small and dishevelled straw hats.

She went to the top of the ladder, then decided against descending. She walked slowly round the narrow wooden platform, which was becoming dilapidated and was now slippery with moss, but all around her stretched the protective beech, cold and gleaming in its winter majesty. She pictured its summer leaves as one might picture a

415

multitudinous throng in the heart of a great city. She peered through the winterbound branches to the cold shining greensward that stretched from the woodland belt to the river, and saw two people walking towards her – two muffled figures walking side by side, a man and a woman, and the woman was carrying what looked like a small parcel in her cupped hands.

Aunt Netta withdrew, unwilling to be seen, then craned a little further because something about the two figures puzzled and intrigued her. They were still a long way off, but her heart began to beat fast. She knew them. At least, she thought she did.

Memory, that painful, tugging old spoilsport, recommenced its nagging tricks. She leaned further out into the tree, squinting anxiously, and the animal awareness she had absorbed from Merton told her that they were coming straight to the tree house that sheltered them both from the outside world.

She panicked, and leaning still further forward felt the handrail suddenly snap. She lost her balance and fell.

She fell with a curious deliberation, feet first through the gleaming branches; past owls' holes and squirrels' snuggeries, while twigs tore at her clothes and stiffly outthrust legs. She was fractionally aware of the fringed ends of her scarf floating before her eyes, and then the fall ended abruptly, with a moment of intense choking pain before the obliterating blackness.

Walter and Edwina broke into a run as they became aware that something strange and terrible had happened. They reached the tree, and gasping for breath and rigid with shock, they saw Aunt Netta hanging by her white silk scarf from the jutting peg of a broken branch. Her body was still swinging gently, but one sickened glance at her face told them that she was already dead. The Christmas present she was carrying dropped from Edwina's hands.

Shaking and still gasping, they looked deep into one another's fenland peasant eyes, and both read the same message.

416

Hanging. Like Johnnie Moon. And like Bessie Hinton, who goes echoing on and on down the years with the curse that she laid on us all.

Book Three
Pax Vobiscum

The Great War dragged to its weary, dingy conclusion, the dying year of 1918 unable to illuminate the shallow rejoicing with anything more than a bruised and sombre light.

The manic celebrations in London failed to penetrate the countryside. The lanes and hedgerows and village greens remained the same, although the occasional cottage bore the hopeful home-made banner WELCOME HOME SID (or Ron or Alf or Bill) beneath its cosy thatch.

Those who were left came limping back, haunted by dreams of unimaginable horror and restlessly ill at ease with soft beds and reproductions of *Lead, Kindly Light* hung over the wash-stand. Readjustment to civilian life was often a sad let-down, and for all those who came home and for all of those waiting with outstretched arms to receive them, the ghosts of slaughtered millions came between them.

At Reve, they were glad that it was over, but that was all. They could not rejoice. And as the weeks passed, the scale of losses was constantly brought home on a personal level. Not only was there no successor to the earldom, there was no John the second (and favourite) footman; of the other three, the first had reached retirement age, the third was now a neurasthenic wreck, and the fourth had come home mentally and physically intact but imbued with the novel idea of leaving service and emigrating to Canada. They saw him off regretfully, bewilderedly, and he promised to write. Both bootboys had died at Gallipoli; the lamp-room boy (a position now largely obsolete anyway) had fallen at the Third Battle of Ypres and Uncle Badger's valet had had both legs blown off during the German offensive on Lys.

A swathe had also been cut through the estate workers; stablemen, gardeners, farm labourers, woodsmen and two

421

out of the three estate carpenters – almost half of them had been either killed or disabled. And those who came back were subtly different from the boys who marched away; they knew more swear-words, and no longer touched their forelocks with quite the same degree of country bumpkin servility.

Although Aunt Netta's death had deeply shocked Lizzie at a time when she was ill-equipped to deal with additional bereavement, she had not shared her mother's appalled certainty that the manner of her dying was somehow connected with Bessie Hinton being hanged outside Ely Gaol. It was an extraordinary coincidence, but no more. Her parents left for Damperdown Farm shortly after the funeral, and the suspicion that they now found Reve a place of superstitious horror half irritated and half grieved her.

She let them go, and tried with equal lack of success to comfort Uncle Merton, who had barricaded himself into the tree house and refused to see anyone.

At the onset of peace they began to dismantle the Reve Auxiliary Hospital, and she wandered past the rows of empty beds as the last ambulance chugged away. These rooms have seen so much pain, she thought. Mine, as well as theirs. It'll go on tainting the air for ever, and people who come after us will shiver and say there's a funny sort of atmosphere in these rooms. . . .

Matron came in, cloaked and stiff-collared and carrying a Gladstone bag. She bobbed her customary token curtsey.

'Goodbye, My Lady. And thank you for all your kindness.'

'Goodbye, Matron. Thank *you*.'

They both gulped, then Matron's bag hit the floor and they were standing with their arms about one another, weeping with gladness that it was all over, and with sorrowful despair because it was over too late.

'Do let's meet again, Matron – we can't just say goodbye after . . . after all that's . . .'

'Thank you, My Lady. And may I say how much I . . . I . . .'

'For God's sake' – Lizzie raised her drenched face from

422

Matron's cloak – 'stop calling me "My Lady". I'm Lizzie.'

'Thank you, My – Lizzie. And I' – with a desperate gush of tears – 'am Lettice. . . .'

It was all ending on a downward note. It was all goodbyes and departures amid winter snow (hateful now, with no snowballing and the two toboggans hanging neglected in a stable tack-room) – and the knowledge that the aunts and uncles were growing older and a little more frail. There was nothing left but old age and old customs whose time and place had been eroded by brutality.

Then in the January of 1919 Lizzie discovered that she was pregnant.

It came as a shock almost equal in intensity to that rendered by the mode of Aunt Netta's death.

In the early years of marriage, the idea of a large family had greatly appealed to both Lizzie and Dully. Their first two children having been such a source of delight, they naturally wanted to repeat the performance. But encores were denied them, and so with the passing of time they learned to be philosophical, and then came finally to believe that two such lovely glowing works of art could not, indeed should not, be repeated. They were content with their lot.

Then with rude abruptness came the heralding of new life: morning sickness that racked and wrenched with its violence, and breasts suddenly plumped and hideously tender with the excitement of their coming function.

'But I'm thirty-nine,' moaned Lizzie, lying back with closed eyes and a pad of eau de Cologne on her forehead. 'By the time it's born I'll be forty.'

The morning sickness passed, and in its wake came swollen ankles, dyspepsia and breathlessness. She became very large and very maladroit, bumping into things and knocking things over, and when someone attempted to sweeten her lot by remarking on nature's extraordinary ability to make good her losses, snapped that the task of single-handedly repopulating the earth after four years' carnage was not her avowed intention.

Sir James Royle, who had been in attendance at both previous confinements, had retired, and she was now in the hands of a pale, bald man who kneaded her grossly distended belly at the onset of labour and murmured that there seemed to be two heads.

'*Attached to one body?*'

Lizzie fainted, and was given twilight sleep; upon coming to, she learned dazedly that she was the mother of identical twin daughters.

Girls. From her tumbled pillows she looked upon the red squalling faces and red, equally enraged-looking little vulvas.

Girls. She had never seriously contemplated having a single girl, let alone two at one fell swoop, and her first reaction was one of baffled distaste.

'I don't like them, Dully. They're all huffy and hostile and I don't know what to call them.'

'How about Hetty and Betty?'

'Don't make jokes, it's serious.'

The girls were finally christened Celia and Pamela, and the newly engaged nursery staff became proud of their prowess at telling them apart. Lizzie tried honestly and conscientiously to do the same, then after a while gave up and decided to wait until they began to exhibit more overt signs of individuality. They had brown hair and round faces, and their eyes showed no sign of tilting at the outer corners in the Dullingham smile. They didn't seem to smile much at all.

She tried to love them with the same old rich glow, but that too failed. It seemed as if the boys had used up all the love she had, and the sights and sounds of a revitalized nursery filled her with resignation rather than elation. She couldn't bear them to use the same cradles and bassinets that had once belonged to Berry and Tommy, and their chewed and faded teddy bears and woolly rabbits she carefully locked away out of sight.

The war's end had brought with it a need for reappraisal, and taking stock of her own situation, Lizzie had to admit that the appearance of two more children at this stage in her life was not going to satisfy the growing restlessness that plagued her. She loved Dully, she loved Reve and the family, but every face and every stick and stone of her surroundings reminded her of the boys.

If some miraculous healer had offered to erase all memory of them for ever more, the answer would have been a passionate refusal, but in those early years of loss the pain of remembrance was sometimes beyond endurance, and roaming through the woods she would smash her fists against the tree trunks in an effort to anaesthetize the torment.

Reve was haunted by them, its ancient beauty a background for endless mental snapshots of red hair ablaze in sunlight and bent over small-boy business, and of smiling young men grown tall and ready for life.

And what a travesty of life – a few ugly, miserable weeks spent in the heartless wickedness of other men's making, and then oblivion. No more laughter, no more games. No more singing and dancing. Time for bed with the curtains drawn tight and not even the comfort of a night-light. Neither had they the comfort of one another; they lay in separate war cemeteries in France.

She remembered the old men who had formed the procession at the old Queen's funeral. How impressed she had been by the theatrical splendour, and how ignorant of the cold aggression behind the display of cocks' feathers and medals like market-stall geegaws, of clanking swords and epaulettes like brass ashtrays. They were the men who had started it all. The men who had taken the lives of her two sons in their hands and snapped them in two and then tossed them away. And given in exchange for one of them another silly bauble dangling on a bit of red ribbon.

She didn't talk to Dully about such things, and now he rarely saw her in tears. There was no point in adding to the burden of pain in his own eyes.

And so she meandered through the days; restless, purposeless, and plagued by guilt at not involving herself more closely with the two little girls ensconced in the new nursery suite.

'Oh darling, let me.'

'No, no, all's well. Don't worry.'

'Let me help.'

'Please. I'm quite *able*. . . .'

Taut with compassion, Martha Polperro stood watching as her son explored his way into the room, stick tapping, smile shining slightly off-target. Involuntarily she stretched out her hand as he walked towards the sofa table, then let it drop as the white stick rattled a warning against it.

'I always forget that thing's there.'

'We'll have it moved.'

'No, don't. I like it.'

'But it's in the *way*.'

She moved towards him then, although she tried not to. Taking his arm, she said: 'Come and sit down here with me. There's a big bowl of sweet peas close by – perhaps you can smell them.'

'I've only lost my sight,' he said.

She recoiled, sickened by her own stupidity.

And it was like that every day. Every day the love and the aching pity trapped her into saying stupid things that hurt him and forced him to acknowledge again and again that he was blind.

It happened at Jutland – a shell splinter deflected in part by a steel helmet. The wounds to his jaw healed rapidly, for teenage flesh is vigorous, but nothing could be done for his sight. It had been like a black shutter coming down over the smoke and the desperation of battle. It had blocked out the ugliness as it had blocked out the sunlight and the faces of pretty girls, and it was for ever. His eyes were to remain sealed shut, the dark lashes pressed down tight and motionless, until the day he died.

He spent several months in a Blighty hospital that specialized in rehabilitating the blind to their new condition, and he learned that he was a good deal better off than the majority. He had no splitting headaches, no violent changes of mood; no trembling, no nausea, no anything except total blackness that was sometimes shot with a fleeting star or two; mostly not even that.

The coming to terms had been hard, the instinct to lie

426

with his face to the wall overwhelming. The world had blinded him, had rejected him, therefore he would reject the world, and all of life, totally.

It was music that tempted him back. Someone had brought a gramophone into the ward and a collection of records as random in condition as they were in content. A comic song called 'The Laughing Policeman'; 'The Dance of the Little Cygnets' played with unsuitable beefiness by a Yorkshire brass band; a Puccini aria sung as if through a dense fog by Madame Patti, and a Glinka waltz that always got stuck in the scratches. But the record that made him take notice was the one they didn't play very often. It was of strange, indeterminate music that wove sleepy patterns in the air, and in order to hear more of it he had to uncover both ears. He rolled over on to his back.

He had no desire to know the name of the music. He merely waited in passive, self-imposed silence for them to play it again, and fumed inwardly when its delicate tracery was obliterated by the rattle of trolleys or the voices of fellow-patients. Then one day a young subaltern suddenly lashed out with his stick in a paroxysm of neurasthenic fury and the record flew from the turntable. They repaired the damage to the gramophone with sticking plaster, but the bits of record were swept up by an orderly and thrown away. The loss was not irredeemable, however, because the music was by then safely stored away in his head and he could hear it whenever he wanted to.

He discovered the power of listening to the language of mere sounds. Squeaks, creaks, tappings and tinklings slowly began to fill his useless eyes with relevant pictures: hospital bedsprings, rubber-soled shoes on polished lino- leum, blinds flapping at an open window. There was melancholy pleasure to be found in the buzzing of a fly.

They coaxed him to leave his bed, and made a jolly game out of learning to dress himself without being able to see what he was doing. He joined in the game because of their kindness, and because there was no viable alternative. He learned to walk through the wards and along the corridors, using a white stick as an antenna; he learned to convey food

427

to his mouth with the minimum of spillage and, when they were finally convinced that his blindness was really permanent, they taught him Braille.

As a cat moves cautiously and haltingly through unfamiliar territory, so he moved through the weeks of subtle acclimatization from daylight to darkness. He fell, and raged because he felt a fool. He fell, and sprained his ankle; fell again, and reopened one of the wounds on his face. But his hearing became steadily sharper and his brain steadily faster at picking up and interpreting the small sounds that sighted people ignore. He learned to distinguish the doctor's footsteps from those of the ward orderly, and he learned to recognize people by their voices instead of their faces.

As things went he was really very lucky, and when he sat listening to 'The Laughing Policeman' and thinking back to the laughter that used to bubble from the two Dullingham boys, he learned that sightless eyes are still capable of tears.

But home was another matter. Instead of the jolliness of hospital there was overwhelming love and sorrow, pride and reverence, and pity clogged the air like a fine powder. They loved him and he needed love, yet all he could feel in return was an irritable impatience. He struggled to attain docility in the face of their monumental solicitude, but he was so alone with it. The hospital had been full of blind men. Here, he was the only one.

His mother was the worst, yet it was not her fault that love made her say and do all the wrong things. She began by planning each day with a care that meticulously excluded any possibility of being left alone. Little strolls, little chats, little drives in the car, and if ever he took a little nap, it was with the knowledge that she was watching over him. He could feel her loving, heartbroken eyes literally boring into his face.

The chats would have been more endurable if she had occasionally allowed him to choose the subject; sometimes he felt an overwhelming urge to talk about the war, to set experience into words, but stressful subjects were taboo.

'Felix darling,' she would say, in the soft voice that still bore traces of a Boston accent, 'all the horrid things are over now. There's no need to remember them.'

He discovered that Berry and Tommy, presumably because they were dead, were also grouped under the heading of horrid things, and the desire to reminisce about them – a sudden thirst to hear their names mentioned – precipitated their first row.

'But darling, there's no point in dwelling on the past! It's time to build a new life.'

'And I totally reject any form of new life that doesn't include my friends just because they had the misfortune to be killed.'

'But I want you to be happy! I love you, and you've been through so much.'

'For Christ's sake, Mother, spare me your love and your pity.'

He heard the sharp intake of breath, then the terrible silence of a body held rigid with grief and shock.

'If you don't want love and pity, then perhaps you could spare a little for *me!*' she cried. 'And perhaps you could explain to me why I mustn't love you or feel sorrow when you're my son. Why is it wrong to feel love and pity? Why have I got to keep hiding my feelings? Are they wicked? Cruel?' Her voice broke and his imagination supplied the sight of her tears.

'I've tried so hard, and I'm still trying to do what you want – to be how you want me to be, but I don't always get it right. . . .'

He got up from his chair and walked over to her. He patted the empty air before his hand found her shoulder.

'Sorry,' he said, and gave it a squeeze. 'I'm an unfeeling brute.'

'No, you're not! It's only natural that – '

Somehow he evaded her arms and left the room after no more than a minor collision with the door. He heard her voice cracked with bitter pain: *'Can't you realize that we're all groping in the dark. Not just you.'*

There was also additional cause for fortitude at Reve.

429

The contraption had arrived, and Badger nodded silently in its direction when Woodstock appeared at his door.

'That it?'

Another nod.

'Odd-looking device . . . not?'

'Dare say it'll work all right.'

'Oh – bound to. What time's zero hour?'

'Fella's due ten o'clock tomorrow morning.'

Woodstock walked round the black iron stand looped with rubber pipes, a dial, and an object like a deflated football. He pointed to the black iron cylinder clamped to the side of it.

'What's that? Looks like some sort of bomb.'

'Suppose it's the gas stuff. Come in and have a tot now you're here.' Badger poured two brandy and sodas from the table by his elbow.

'Nice fella, is he?'

'Who?'

'The tooth-puller.'

Badger winced slightly, then mumbled that he seemed all right. 'Anyway, I won't know, will I? Be knocked out.'

Gazing into the bright heart of the fire, they sipped. Spring was arriving, heralded by howling gales and tempestuous rain. Several big trees had come down in the night. But inside Badger's room the peace of past decades prevailed.

Books, papers, photographs; a relic of schooldays in the form of a banner embroidered with the words *Floreat Etona*, and the latest small dog lay curled in a basket by the brass coal scuttle. In the background loomed the giant four-poster. All was comfort, all was dear old familiarity, save for the contraption standing over by the dressing table.

'This time tomorrow . . .' began Badger.

'It'll all be over . . . not?' finished Woodstock comfortingly.

The wind hurled itself with a harsh cracking sound against the great Cedar of Lebanon on the lawn beyond the window. As if it were trying to prize it out of the ground by its roots, thought Badger. And winced afresh.

He said with an effort: 'Scarcely wise of old Merton to remain perched in the top of Pitt's beech in this weather. Why doesn't the silly blighter come down?'

'He's in mourning.'

'Everyone's in mourning these days.' (And this time tomorrow I'll be in mourning for my teeth. Had 'em upwards of sixty years. . . .)

'Are you getting the fella to make a set of imitation ones?' asked Woodstock, who was evidently brooding on the same subject.

'Haven't planned that far. For all I know I mayn't come through.'

'Balderdash,' said Woodstock, but without total conviction.

Badger replenished their glasses. 'How many have you got left?'

'Teeth? Dunno for sure, haven't counted.'

'Well, for God's sake don't start counting them here!'

'Steady on, old fella. Hadn't the slightest intention of doing so.'

'Sorry,' mumbled Badger. 'Bit on edge. . . .'

The new Eulalie in the basket woke up and floundered over to her master, who bent to caress her.

'Nice little dog, that.'

'Not a patch on the last one.'

'Nothing ever is a patch on the last one.'

Instinctively their thoughts turned to poor young Lizzie and Dully. Their little daughters would probably be very nice too, but no, you could never replace the dead. Foolish to try, really.

And death was all around them. It had ripped away the young and fair, and left the old to mourn while they awaited their turn by whatever mean or bizarre form fate decreed. Death had covered the whole sweet face of the world with its pall.

They parted soon afterwards, and Badger sent a message downstairs to the effect that he would prefer to dine alone in his room that night.

He did so, masticating with gloomy and ritualistic relish a

431

small pink-fleshed trout followed by lambs' kidneys served in a Madeira sauce. He drank a little Pouilly fumée followed by half a bottle of good Burgundy, then ended the meal with a slice of Stilton, a stick of celery and two dry biscuits.

He sat back, wiping his moustache with the large starched napkin and thinking, The last time . . . the last time. That was their swansong. From now on I shall be living on pap.

He retired early, cleaning his teeth – those dear old broken pegs of yellowed ivory – for the very last time. He swilled the water round them, puffing his cheeks in and out and feeling the cascade rush through the crannies and crevices that would all have been swept away by this time tomorrow. Nightshirted, he climbed into bed, and the last thing he saw before extinguishing the light was the contraption standing by the dressing table.

He wished Woodstock hadn't said that the appendage on the side of it looked like a bomb. Damn silly thing to say.

He slept badly, and awoke with haggard eyes. The toothache that had plagued him during the past months had disappeared – not a whisper of it for twenty-four hours – and in a sudden spurt of jubilation he decided to telephone to the fella and cancel the appointment. But he couldn't; not now. Not without looking like a cowardly old fool.

So he drank his morning tea, read a page of Horace Walpole and rang for a housemaid to take Eulalie downstairs for her morning walk, and then, alone and valetless, performed his ablutions with all the calm and hopeless deliberation of a man about to face the firing squad.

He sat down by the window with his back to the contraption. The gale had lessened during the night, but what was left of it hurled flurries of snow among the brilliant green shoots of the daffodils. If it's my lot to go now, he thought, I'm glad it's before roses-and-strawberries time. . . .

The dental surgeon and his assistant arrived from Bury St Edmunds promptly at ten, and made conversation of a pleasantly soothing nature while setting about their preparations. A discreet smell of carbolic filled the air.

'And now, Sir, would you care to be seated?'

'Ah well, tickle your arse with a feather.'

'Pardon me, Sir?'

'I said particularly nasty weather.'

The contraption was now standing close beside the armchair, and it worried Badger by making a slight hissing sound. They covered him with a thick rubber apron, tying it behind his neck and then covering it with a white cotton one so that only his head was visible.

'And now, if you would be good enough to open, Sir.'

He did so, with a child's unwillingness, and the fella inserted a cork between his jaws with all the airy aplomb of a conjurer preparing to perform his most celebrated trick.

'As you were saying, Sir, funny sort of weather for the end of March. Now just breathe deeply and we'll soon have you under.'

From behind the chair, the assistant suddenly seized Badger's arms in a vicelike grip as the hissing filled his head and the sickening stench reached down into the lowest depths of his vitals. He began to spin in a mad circle, drowning in horror and the violent clanging of bells. Death, death, death . . . the dear old days had gone, all of them blotted out by violence and the echoes that reverberated from it.

When I am dy-y-y-y-ing . . . Then the spinning ceased and he floated effortlessly away.

Lizzie unlocked the door, then stood back and said to Martha Polperro: 'You're the only person I've ever allowed to come in here. No one else knows about it.'

'Not even Dully?'

'No.'

They stood side by side in the doorway, and a ray of sunlight lit the small room with a subdued golden light. Half-hidden in an embrasure between Reve's central block and the long wing that extended eastwards, the room appeared designed for discretion rather than display. Lizzie had only come upon it by accident. Empty, dusty and timeless, with panelled walls, a small marble overmantel

433

and a broad window-seat, it was a room to hide in, a secret place in which to nurse bitter sorrow and hopeless longing. During the first months of bereavement she found herself returning again and again down the out-of-the-way corridor that led to it.

Closing the door behind her, she would sit hunched and brooding in the window, the slow empty hours marked by the distant chime of the stables clock. No one knew where she was, and she sometimes pictured with melancholy pleasure the prospect of dying in there and remaining undiscovered for months. She removed the key from the outside and took to locking herself in.

One day she took a photograph of the boys with her and propped it on the overmantel. It was an enlarged snapshot of them sitting bare-legged on a fat white pony, Berry holding the reins while Tommy's arms were linked round his waist. They were tousled and laughing, and she remembered that the picture had been taken on her thirtieth birthday, shortly before everyone had to go and spruce up for the opening of the annual garden fête. Sometimes she stared at it stony-eyed, and at other times it would dissolve in a shimmering haze of tears that rolled unhindered down her cheeks.

The idea of turning the room into a shrine was not a deliberate one. She was in a remote and mindless state when she first began collecting small personal mementos of her sons and storing them in the secret room, but on the day she ordered a table and some bookshelves to be installed, the vague instinct to hoard and protect had hardened into a formulated intent. To fill the room with every object that had once belonged to them now became her sole aim in life.

An essential part of the project was its secrecy – no one must see, no one must intrude – and with a new and taciturn manservant to carry the heavier things, she gradually fashioned a shrine for her sons and a sanctuary for herself out of storybooks and teddy bears, Eton College caps and mudstained letters from the Western Front.

It brought her comfort to touch and rearrange the collection, and it was only on bad days that she would snatch up an empty garment or a small shoe and cry, 'Come back to me! Come back to me!' But no one heard because of the room's remoteness.

'Are you quite sure you want me in here?' Martha Polperro hesitated uneasily.

'Yes. It's to make you feel better about Felix.'

Lizzie led the way, and Martha followed in stunned silence. Every object, every small childish possession had been lovingly and meticulously arranged, and Martha glanced involuntarily over her shoulder, expecting to see two red-headed boys, freckle-nosed and laughing-eyed, standing in the doorway.

'Oh, *Lizzie*. . . .'

'I know.'

'I don't know what to say.'

'Don't say anything. Just be grateful that yours is still alive.'

They sat side by side on the window-seat and the sun caressed their shoulders and touched the fierce flaring nostrils of the old rocking-horse. Felix had ridden on it many a time.

'Does it help . . . this?'

'It's better than nothing.'

Martha burst into tears, covering her eyes with her hand. 'But sometimes it's as if – I mean, since he came back . . . oh, I don't know, I try so hard, but . . .'

'He's still alive,' Lizzie said remorselessly. 'Mine are both dead.'

'But he's not the same! He's alive and breathing but he's a different person! And he hates me, Lizzie.'

'I could put up with hate.'

'Could you?' Martha scrubbed her fist across her eyes. 'Someone who always loved you coming back cruel and bitter and you don't know what to say to them? You ache all over with love and pity, and they reject you? How can you switch it off? How can you pretend indifference – and why do they *want* indifference when surely to God it's time for healing and loving understanding?'

'I don't know. I wasn't given the chance to find out.'

435

'What's more, you don't want to know, do you? You just want to be a goddam martyr –'

'How *dare* you!'

'I dare, all right. And it'd be a good thing if some of the others dared too, instead of pussyfooting around and treating you like some kind of tragic madonna –'

In all the years of friendship it was the first row they had ever had. Breathing hard and flushed with anger, they stared into one another's faces.

'I think you'd better go.'

'Yes. I'm going.'

Neither moved. They remained side by side in the window embrasure, lacerated with pain and held together by shared memories.

'I hope they're satisfied with what they've done,' Lizzie muttered finally. 'All those ole bastards dressed up in scarlet and gold and chickens' feathers. I saw them strutting up the aisle at the Queen's funeral and I should have realized then that they should never have been put in charge of dangerous things like wars.'

'Or our sons' lives. If only they'd let me stay home and marry the way I wanted to' – Martha groped in her sleeve for a handkerchief – 'instead of fixing up with British nobility. I mean, what's *nobility*?'

'Nothing. Except what you make of it.'

'Well, I don't make much, so there.'

'Don't think you're insulting me,' Lizzie said, 'I'm just a farmer's daughter from the Sixteen Foot Drain. What's more, my great-grandmother was hanged as a felon outside Ely Gaol.'

'Mine were pretty rough too, in the beginning.'

Martha sniffled, then put away her handkerchief. In doing so, her hand encountered Lizzie's. The hands flew apart, hesitated, then joined together in a hot and fervent clasp.

'Martha, duck, I *do* worry for you about Felix.'

'But I've no cause to complain compared to you. And gee, I'm sorry that I – '

'You didn't. . . .'

They put their arms around one another, and the small room crowded with its poignant memorabilia drew them closer than they had ever been before.

After Lizzie had carefully locked the door behind them, they joined the family for afternoon tea, and it was not until the shadows had lengthened and it was time to dress for dinner that Lizzie went upstairs to the new nurseries. Her depression returned as she bent over the first neatly brushed bobbed brown head and touched it with her lips.

'Goodnight, Pamela – Celia – whichever you are. . . .'

A couple of weeks later she and Martha decided to open a hat shop in London.

Enough has been written about the birth of the strident Twenties; about the jazz and cocktails, the strap shoes and cigarette holders, the naughty-boy and baby-girl gaiety that gave the decade its curious brittle charm.

Defiantly it attempted to drown the street-singing of unemployed ex-servicemen with its Charlestons and fox-trots, and in a mood of mingled rebellion and despair Lizzie and Martha shortened their skirts, painted their lips and joined the dance. They were both forty-two, and neither of their husbands was particularly enthusiastic about being married to a milliner.

'It's not as if you needed the money,' Fairford pointed out.

'No. I just need to be needed.'

'I need you.'

'Really? I thought I was as indispensable to you as I am to Felix.'

'I've told you before, you must give the boy time.'

'And what about you?'

He returned her challenging stare, then added: 'Trouble with you is that you're too sensitive.'

She shrugged. 'In the meantime, I'll be at 97 New Bond Street selling Paris models.'

'Hats?' Dully repeated blankly. 'What sort of hats?'

'Smart little chapeaux for ladies.'

'But why, in God's name?'

Lizzie didn't answer. He went over to her and tilted her chin up with his forefinger.

'No good running away, you know.'

'I'm not.'

'Sure?'

'Of course. I just want something to occupy me now that . . . and don't tell me that I've got two old folk's sanctuaries and two daughters, because I know I have.'

He turned away, without kissing her. Then paused to smile at her from the doorway, the dear, eye-tilted Dullingham smile that racked her so miserably these days.

'Come back to me, won't you?'

She nodded, her chin wobbling.

Although the uncles were inclined to be censorious when they heard the news ('Liza? A bonnet-maker? Like the female who coughed herself to death in *La Bohème*, you mean?), Aunt Miriam showed a warm sympathy that rather surprised Dully.

He found that he was able to talk to her with unexpected ease, and he needed someone to talk to.

He was now fifty; still lean and long-legged, but with flecks of white in his hair and a deep, sad crease running down either cheek. The loss of both sons had destroyed something in him; increasingly he felt like a broken mechanism, and the knowledge that Lizzie would now be spending so much time in London ('But I'll be down every weekend, of course . . .') increased the drained and lifeless feeling that marked his days.

He had tried very hard to nurse Lizzie through the pain of bereavement; had tried to cosset and protect her, to shield her with his love from the torment of memories and imaginings, and to guide her steps back to a normal path. But something had broken in her too, and he waited with patient solicitude for it to heal.

He watched over her silently and interminably; depressed by her indifference to Celia and Pamela and worried that she might suddenly take it into her head to do something drastic and self-destructive.

He knew about the secret room. He had watched its

438

transformation into a shrine, sneaking in there when she was asleep and tiptoeing like a thief among the treasures. He discovered that she locked herself in there for hours at a time, and took the precaution of having a duplicate key cut.

He watched over her tenderly, helplessly, and tried to deal as best he could with his own desolation.

'You must let her go,' Aunt Miriam said. 'In order that she has somewhere to come back to.'

'It's hard.'

'Of course it is. Everything is hard these days, and one of the things that troubles me most is whether we really appreciated everything to the full when it was given to us. Did we really wring every drop of happiness out of every hour?'

'How can we tell? One lives for the moment, I suppose.'

'We won't any more. After what has happened, we'll be far more careful to hoard any happiness that comes our way.'

'Supposing any should. . . .'

He sounded so sad that she took his arm. 'It will, my dear, it will. Look, there is a little speck of happiness to be going on with.'

In the shade of a philadelphus a cock thrush was patiently prodding a lump of green caterpillar down the gaping gullet of its fledgeling.

In the meantime, please help me by holding fast to the sure knowledge that whatever happens, life will go on, Berry had written in his last letter. *The trees will blossom and the flowers will bloom and everything will be jolly again. . . .*

Enjoy your meal before the cat gets you, thought Dully, and when the insect had finally been disposed of, leaned forward and picked a spray of philadelphus and handed it to Aunt Miriam. She held the white flowers against her cheek.

'Such a delectable scent. . . .'

He looked down at her grey hair, high cheekbones and long Dullingham nose, and the final hastily scrawled words of Berry's letter were still warm in his mind.

'It's a long while since you played the piano and sang to us. Don't you think it's time to start again?'

That was the beginning of their conversations; hesitant and cautious to start with, then gradually deepening and widening beyond the aunt-nephew relationship until they reached a stage when neither age nor sex was of any account. Aunt Miriam still remembered the shy, sensitive boy who had twice stayed at Reve – once happily and once unhappily – and Dully still remembered having heard of the musical aunt who had flung herself youthfully and some-what ridiculously at the feet of the composer Jules Massenet in Paris – but the new easy range of their friendship was merely enriched by such things.

They talked of the boys, and found themselves able to laugh over old memories and old anecdotes. Neither sought false comfort in sentiment; neither, for that matter, had an unswerving belief in an afterlife, but to speak of them openly, even to say aloud the names Berry and Tommy, prevented the wounds from festering. Dully wished that he could have the same sort of conversations with Lizzie, but in the meanwhile loyally maintained silence about the new uneasiness of their relationship.

He was also becoming increasingly troubled about money, and this too he discussed with Aunt Miriam. Although far from poor – each member of the family had a comfortable private income – he was aware that Reve had not been paying its way for many years. Despite careful administration by the last Earl and by Briggs, the now retired estate manager, it was impossible to reverse single-handedly the continuing decline in English agriculture; the decline had begun back in the 1870s with the arrival of cheap American imports of corn from newly developed prairie-lands, and Reve was not alone in being unable to match either quality or price. Frozen meat from Australia and New Zealand was a further blow to farmers who had laid cornland down to grass, but with continuing blind faith in the Free Trade doctrine, there seemed no way of reversing the downward trend. The war had temporarily halted the flood of imports, but almost immediately after the Armistice British farmers were once again left to compete or go under. Hundreds were going under. Tilled

440

fields were returning to bracken and bramble, farmhouses and tied cottages were abandoned as their occupants set off to the cities in search of factory work.

When dry rot was discovered in one of the roof timbers at Reve, Dully decided to sell the London house. He talked over the decision with Aunt Miriam.

'We never use it, it's far too big and unwieldy. Whenever the uncles go up to town they stay at a club, and now the boys are gone it seems to me a frank waste of money in rates and repairs.'

She agreed. Then added a little sadly: 'But it would have been nice to follow tradition and see the girls' coming-out ball given there. It was such a lovely house for the London season.'

'I dare say. But I think it would be foolish to keep the place on for another thirteen years just for that.'

No one in the family offered much resistance, although Aunt Minna was now too frail to care much about anything, and Uncle Merton, when finally persuaded to come out of hiding, muttered that he knew nothing about there still being a London house anyway. As for Lizzie, she and Martha had taken a service flat in Portman Square in which they lived during the week, and she told Dully that he must do whatever he thought best.

So Dullingham House became the Dullingham House Hotel, and a small penthouse suite was reserved in perpetuity for any member of the family who wished to stay there. The roof timbers at Reve were replaced, and in the absence of his wife, Dully engaged a nursery governess for Celia and Pamela from the wanted columns of *The Times*. Her name was Miss Brookes, and she had bright blue eyes and golden hair.

After a prolonged period of trial and error, Badger's dentures had settled down and were behaving well. They chewed competently, remained in place in the upper and lower jaw respectively when not required, and after repeated readjustments by the fella from Bury St Edmunds, finally enabled him to speak without a harsh and distressing sibilance.

441

Yet all was not well. He still missed the old days with a pain that he could not easily communicate, even to Woodstock. He had loved the boys perhaps even more than any of the other elders, either resident or visiting, during the golden years of their childhood, and for him, sunlight and the sound of laughter had died with them. He was also missing Lizzie, and fretted in a low monotone about the stupidity of selling fool bonnets when she should be cheering up Reve with her charm and beauty. They needed her here, and he was concerned by the weariness in Dully's eyes.

Restless and disgruntled, he took to going for long walks through the park, his little dog at his heels. He visited places he had not seen for many years – the old brick kilns and the smaller outlying farms where he had always been welcomed with a curtsey or a deferential touch of the forelock. Not any more. Rosebay Farm, Little Doves, Jackstaffs – all three of them deserted; windows blank and barns empty. It seemed as if the war had killed them too.

Jackstaffs stood on a side road, and after carefully latching the gate behind him, Badger looked up to see a solitary figure approaching. Not having seen a soul all morning, he stood waiting, his eyes narrowed against the dusty summer light.

It was a man. Not very tall but rather square, carrying a small suitcase and marching rather than walking. He drew nearer, and seeing the old man standing by the gate, came to a halt. His face was sun-reddened, his expression gritty and obdurate.

'Arfnoon, Sir. Am I on the right track for a house called Reve?'

Non-committally, Badger allowed that he was. 'Are you looking for anyone in particular?'

'Well.' The man put down his suitcase and stood at ease. 'Not in a manner of speaking. I mean, I used to know someone who used to live there, but he's dead now, Sir.'

Something about the man made Badger's heart begin to thud. He strove to remain calmly polite. 'Oh? May I ask the name?'

'A Captain Dullingham, Sir. Leastways, we always called him Captain Berry.'

Badger turned very pale. 'You were in the war with him?'

'His batman, Sir. Name of Bird.'

'I see.'

'Would you – pardon the asking, Sir – be Captain Berry's father?'

Badger pulled himself together with an effort. 'No. I was . . . not.' For some reason he was unable to say more.

'Did you know him, Sir?'

'Yes. I knew him quite well.'

They remained silent for a moment. Then Bird said 'I see, Sir,' in tones that held a hint of resignation. The summer afternoon lay motionless.

'Have you come a long distance?' Badger surveyed the dusty shoes, the tired creases in the blue serge suit. A thin trickle of sweat was creeping down the inside of Bird's collar.

'From Dagenham, Sir.'

Badger had never heard of Dagenham, but concluded that it must be somewhere in the London area. 'Come up to the house,' he said finally, 'and we will give you some tea.'

They crossed the road and set off through the woods, the old man leading the way in silence. As the trees thinned and they entered the park Badger intimated that they should walk side by side. His limbs felt heavy and his mind seethed with questions too unbearable to ask.

Bird sensed this, and strove with kindness to converse on a light note. He remarked on the cattle grouped in the shade of the big spreading trees and on the soft springiness of the turf. He said how nice it was to get away from the noise and the soot of big cities. He returned to the subject of Berry with caution.

'I believe he had some sort of noble rank, Sir.'

'He was Viscount Reve.'

'I see, Sir.' Bird digested this in silence for several hundred yards. 'Would that be something like a civvy Colonel, Sir?'

'Not too sure. That, or a little higher.'

443

'And he never said a blinkin' word.'

They reached the top of an incline and Reve lay spread below them.

'That's not where he lived?' Bird stood motionless, his suitcase slumped at his feet.

'Yes, that is Reve.' Badger whistled to Eulalie, who had bounded on ahead.

'What – all of it? You mean, it's all one house and that's where he. . . ?' Now it was Bird who was at a loss.

'We will go down by the lime walk,' Badger said. 'It's an easier path.'

'I don't think I can, Sir. Not now.'

'Why not?'

'Well, it takes a bit of swallerin', all this, and . . .'

Badger regarded him pensively. 'Suppose you tell me why you came?'

A fallen tree trunk lay a few paces from where they stood. The bark had disintegrated and the wood beneath it was polished palely smooth by weather. Bird went over to it and sat down.

'He was a wonderful young chap. Everybody thought the world of him, not just me. I never met his brother, but he talked to me about him and worried that he couldn't take care of him more. He wanted to take care of everybody. That was him all over.'

Without speaking, Badger set down beside him. Eulalie bounded back to him and licked his loosely dangling hands.

'There was nothing to go on trying for, after he went. God knows how many poor bu – chaps went the last weeks on the Somme, but he didn't orter have been one of them. Not him. It was like a light gone out.'

'The light has gone out here, too. Not only the boys, but so many of our young men on the estate. They were all part of our world.'

From down in the gardens came the haunting cry of a peacock.

'And this is where Captain Berry and his brother . . . Christ, he never let on what a lot he'd got to lose compared to the rest of us.'

'Which brings us back to the question you haven't yet answered. Why are you here?'

Bird studied the rusted locks of his suitcase.

'Are you looking for work?'

'I haven't got anything in view this partickler moment. No, Sir.'

'And you wish to find employment in this part of the world?' He felt an old man's yearning to draw closer to the past, a ridiculous need to touch Bird's sleeve with patrician fingers humbled by loss. He steadied himself with an effort.

'Tell me a little more about yourself. Have you a family?'

'No children, Sir. And the wife has passed away.'

'How very sad. And you are left with no ties?'

'No ties. No, Sir.'

They sat listening to the hum of insects. A rook flew overhead, lamenting quietly to itself.

'My valet sustained monstrous injuries during the war,' Badger said in a low voice. 'Monstrous injuries. He is now in a Star and Garter Home.'

'Very sorry to hear that, Sir.'

'You might perhaps care to consider. . . ?'

Listening to his own precisely chosen words, Badger thought, could you bear it? Could you seriously contemplate being in daily contact with the man bound to remind you over and over again, inevitably and remorselessly, of dear young Berry and Tommy? Will you not be finally tempted to ask exactly how Berry died? To be furnished with the details that are obviously still burning in this man's mind? They will sear you in turn. They will keep you awake at night and they will haunt your living days with the horrors so carefully excluded from the official notifications – *regret to inform you . . . laid down his life for his country* – so clean and dignified in comparison to what must have been the real thing. This man is still suffering from all he experienced, and even if you do not ask, the day will inevitably come when he will break down and tell you things that will cause you exquisite torment from which there will be no escape.

'I don't know whether you might feel inclined to work for

445

me?' He listened to his voice as if it belonged to someone else.

'You mean here, Sir?'

'This is where I live.'

He looked across at Bird, and met the confused indecision in his hot face.

'My requirements are modest these days. You would have adequate time off and of course your own living accommodation. Since the end of the war, religious observance on Sundays has not been compulsory for household staff and uniform is provided – I suggest something in the nature of a black jacket and trousers. I like to be called at seven-thirty on winter mornings, at seven during the summer. . . .'

Suddenly he knew that it was going to be all right, that despite premonitions of pain he was doing the right thing. He stood up, and the fingers that seized Bird's shoulders were strong and decisive.

'We will discuss wages with the housekeeper, but in the meanwhile consider my offer a firm one, Mr ah – '

'Bird, Sir,' said Bird.

They made their way down towards the lime avenue and Reve.

In civilian life, Bird had been a painter and decorator, a one-man-band hacking his way through the jungle of competition with the aid of two ladders and a handful of paintbrushes pushed round the streets on a handcart. He worked seven days a week, and in a brief fit of orgiastic abandonment married Winnie, who within two years grew fat and blowsy and slummocked around with an old coat over her nightdress. Sometimes she looked at him as if she didn't know who he was, and even when she did appear to recognize him seemed none too delighted by the discovery.

He painted anything from shop-fronts to chicken coops, working busily and swearing constantly, until conscription compelled him to join the war. Removing the paint from his fingers with a turpentine rag, he stored the tools of his trade in the shed at the bottom of the garden and said ta-ta to

446

Winnie. He told her to Keep the Home Fires Burning, like it said in the song.

One of the things he discovered about himself on the Western Front was an aptitude not only for survival but for making the best of things. Swearing monotonously at the rain, the mud, the Germans, the British officers and NCOs, he was nevertheless quicker than most men at learning to adapt – to keep warmer, and dryer, and a little more protected by making good use of whatever came his way. Often he looked across at no man's land and at the clutter of abandoned ironmongery and wished with sorrow that he was a scrap-metal merchant – or even, more gruesomely, a rag-and-bone merchant when the piles of unburied corpses buzzed with flies and stank to high heaven.

He was devoid of patriotic fervour and sceptical of surviving until the final whistle was blown. He wrote a weekly letter full of passionless invective to the house in Dagenham, and Winnie occasionally bestirred herself sufficiently to reply. Sending him a parcel seemed beyond her capabilities.

Then the new subaltern arrived to take the place of the last poor little bugger shredded by mortar fire. He had only lasted for five days, but Bird was also aware that their life expectancy was a bare three weeks. They were mostly pink-faced and weedy and pathetically anxious to appear seasoned warriors, but the new one was different.

Tall, red-haired and strongly built, he had a schoolboy grin and an enthusiasm tempered by charm. He was no more averse to asking for their advice than he was to issuing orders, and once he had been told a man's name he never forgot it. They thought he was all right, but studiously avoided warmer feelings until he had survived the statutory three weeks.

Cautiously they grew to like his magnanimity, and to trust his ability to act quickly and decisively. They also became proud of the fact that young Lieutenant Dullingham was a bit of a dog, with his battered motorbike and carelessly slung on uniform. They reckoned that he was something of a lad with the girls too, and when someone

447

discovered that he was a lord or whatever, they said well, there you are; no wonder.

The story of how Lieutenant Dullingham won the VC by dragging Saunders off the wire became a legend, and Bird became the only man left to have witnessed the tears of rage and grief when he realized that Saunders was dead after all.

They all died, sooner or later; some quickly, some taking their time, but he always managed to be there – a big shadow flung against a mud wall, a gleam of red hair, and a strong hand to hold on to in all the fading noise of battle. He seemed to go right to the very edge with them, and they died comforted that he was close. It was hard to credit he was only a kid of eighteen.

Love has many manifestations. Extinguish sexual longing with fear and pain, hunger and gross discomfort, and what remains can assume an almost ethereal quality. They loved him, the handful of old survivors and the endless stream of young newcomers fed on legend, with a simplicity that could have no place in normal life.

It was Bird, that other survivor, who silently monitored the effects of strain, and after becoming batman to Captain Berry had seen how increasingly the cheerful grin had been boosted by slugs of brandy when the hours of duty were over. He died on the final assault on a lump of stupid bloody chalk called the Butte de Walencourt, and Bird spent the rest of the war in a state of mindless, frozen automation. He returned home in time for Christmas 1918 to find the hearth cold and Winnie gone. Scarpered. His ladders and brushes were still in the shed at the bottom of the garden.

He thawed, little by little. Went round to his old customers and tried to restart the old business of scraping and cleaning, painting and varnishing, but after the first heady months of peace, apathy had set in among the clientele. And the competition was fiercer than ever; ex-servicemen by the thousand, all wanting to set up as painters and decorators, all trundling round the streets with handcarts and all trying to undercut each other by a hungry shilling or two.

Bird carried on. Touting, working, swearing, and going

home each night to a small comfortless house and to dreams of the Western Front that jerked him, sweating and shivering, from sleep. For a long while he was certain there were rats scurrying across the bedroom floor. He slept with a row of old boots within reach and hurled them, one by one, at the phantom shadows that sped towards the far corners; he heard their squeaks and saw their eyes bright with gluttony at the prospect of feasting on human flesh.

But most of all he saw Captain Berry, that tall strong flame moving among his men, and he became increasingly obsessed by the memory of a cheerful schoolboy being hurried by circumstances into the premature role of father. Bird remembered the way they had looked at him; men in their thirties, tired and stubble-chinned, racked with rheumatism and respiratory diseases, hoping to elicit a smile, a nod, a touch on the shoulder, and willing to follow him again and again over the top and into the blistering hail of machine-gun fire. And he remembered the address on the envelope propped against a little carved statue-thing on the night of the final assault. *Reve, Suffolk, England.* He had taken it to the field post office himself.

It was not a quick decision to leave Dagenham. It seemed to come gradually, like a signpost appearing through the darkness, and when the time came he posted the front-door key to the landlord, left the few sticks of furniture – even Winnie's photo – and all the doleful accoutrements of a painter and decorator, and walked out armed with nothing more than a small suitcase packed with one or two items of clothing.

Even then, he had made no conscious plan to go to Reve. He walked as far as Colchester, where he worked for a week or two as a cellarman at the George, and had proceeded as far north as Saxmundham before he learned that Reve lay westwards, in the vicinity of Bury St Edmunds. So he turned left, and carried by a mindless instinct unusual in one of his temperament, found himself ultimately arriving at Captain Berry's old home.

The hugeness of the place astonished him without intimidating him unduly, but it came as a shock when the

449

old gent with the china teeth offered him a job. In all honesty he had not even contemplated such a prospect; there had only been this vague notion of going in search of the Captain, as if it wasn't true after all that he had died. Maybe it was just another form of seeking the comfort of a smile, or a nod, or a fleeting touch on the shoulder. Old habits die hard.

He accepted the job – he would have been a fool not to – and slipped into the new routine with extraordinary ease. Valeting the old gent made him aware how much he had enjoyed being batman to the Captain; perhaps he too had an inbuilt desire to look after people.

And he quickly realized that his position in the household was subtly different from that of the other staff. As he had found his way to Reve because of the young Captain, so members of the family, each in their separate way, regarded him with a certain deferential esteem because he had been with Berry until the end. They were all hungry for details of his life in France, eager to set him against background detail, and each made a point of seeking out Bird in privacy in order to ask whatever questions most haunted them personally. They all wanted to know whether he had met Tommy, and displayed touching disappointment when he had to admit that he had not.

'But I heard a lot about him,' Bird took to assuring them. 'The Captain talked about his brother and all of his family a helluv – an awful lot. He loved his brother, the Captain did, and it's my humble opinion he was never the same after he died.' (Perhaps he wasn't. Who could tell out of all that welter of blood and guts what any poor young sod was really feeling towards the end?)

The Earl sent for him on his second morning, asked him to sit down and offered him a cigarette. He said that he was very glad he had come to Reve, and that both his sons would have been pleased as well. He asked Bird a few questions about his own life, and enquired whether there was a Mrs Bird.

'No, Me Lord,' Bird said, assuming an expression of sorrow. 'My dear wife passed away just before the cessation of hostilities.'

450

Dully murmured his condolences, then after a pause and with gaze averted said: 'And our son. It was . . . fairly merciful?'

Bird was prepared for this too. 'He didn't suffer any pain, Sir,' he said, and watched relief lighten the Earl's sad eyes.

'I'm very glad.'

'He was a fine young gentleman, Me Lord.'

'Yes. Thank you, Bird.'

He didn't meet the Countess until she arrived at Reve shortly before dinner on Friday night, and then she only nodded to him as he was crossing the staircase hall. But she sent for him on the following morning. She turned her head from the window as he entered her sitting room, and Bird drew a sharp breath at the glowing dark red hair touched by sunlight. Although past her first youth, she was a very beautiful woman. She smiled at him – that warm, friendly, familiar smile like the Captain's – then it vanished suddenly and disconcertingly.

'How did he die?' she asked with an abruptness that staggered him.

Bird hesitated, then instinct pounced on the explanation. Like her husband, she was demanding to know the worst in order to come to terms with it, and perhaps find peace through acceptance. She was staring at him intently, her head erect and her hands clasped tightly together in her lap. He repeated his previous account, elaborating slightly.

'It was over very quick, Me Lady. A sudden flash and he just fell. His blokes brought him in and he hadn't got a scratch. He looked untouched, Me Lady, just as if he was asleep. In fact, he looked so natural I couldn't believe it at first.'

He saw her eyes swim with tears, and watched how she clamped her jaws tight together. She blinked hard, then said in a little choked voice: 'Thank you. Thank you for telling me.'

'We all thought the world of him.' He knew the words wouldn't help her self-control, but he had to say them. She nodded speechlessly, then with a little flick of her hand dismissed him.

Shortly before leaving for London on Sunday evening, she sought him out. She was wearing a dark green coat and skirt and lizardskin shoes with pointed toes and a lot of little buttons.

'My husband told me that you have lost your wife,' she said. 'I know what it's like to be bereaved.'

He took her outstretched hand.

'You have my sympathy,' she added.

'Thank you, Me Lady,' said Bird, deeply moved. 'Really most obliged.'

The Bond Street hat shop had been a success from its first inception; both Lizzie and Martha were rapturous as schoolgirls at each satisfied customer.

Their hats were smart, exclusive and very expensive; Martha went to Paris once a month and brought back sketches which their own milliner copied. They placed only one hat at a time in the window, and their clientele consisted of society women and West End leading ladies. They made hats for Sybil Thorndyke, Gladys Cooper, Lady Cunard and the Duchess of Westminster; they met Noël Coward at parties, and drove to lunch at Maidenhead with the entire cast of *On With the Dance*.

Renewing acquaintance with the theatrical world was exciting for Lizzie, and the Gaiety Girl who had become the Countess Dullingham and now co-partner in a chic little hat shop was seen regularly at the smart night-spots. Her photograph appeared in the *Tatler & Bystander* when she attended charity concerts and mannequin parades, while Martha, both separately and in concert, worked equally hard at having a good time.

Both women returned to their families dutifully if not always eagerly each weekend, stimulated and exhausted by this new life that was at once brilliant and brittle, feverish and a little frightening. Both were propositioned; both were old enough to be flattered, and young enough to feel flutters of temptation. There were kisses in taxis and fondlings in alcoves, but both retreated instinctively from what Martha called 'going overboard'. They became aware that London society had a dark substratum of rather menacing disrepute, and although it was fun to gossip about – 'Heavens, if it's not DTs it's VD!' – innate squeamishness prevented them from drawing closer.

For the first twelve months the London cure worked like a charm, stimulating and rejuvenating and all but blotting out the young faces that haunted them. Apart from such moments as the meeting with Bird, Lizzie wanted hectically at this period to forget, while for Martha the problem was one of learning to withdraw fretting concern from a blighted young life struggling to recompose itself.

By tacit agreement they never spoke of their sons, and there were no photographs of them in the Portman Square flat. In that respect they were as childless as the new figure-flattening clothes liked to indicate, and dry-eyed, they refused to conform to the official two minutes' silence at eleven a.m. on each 11 November. In sharp bright voices they discussed instead the latest goings-on at Kate Meyrick's infamous nightclub.

They were busy, glamorous and sought-after in the new fragile world they had created for themselves, and the shop had been open for two years and several months when Lizzie received a telegram from her father that said with fenland economy: *Come. Ma poorly.*

It was inconvenient having to go just then because they had only that day received a new and gorgeous collection of little velvet cloche hats that pulled down low and framed the face like a protective bract around a delicate flower. Their jewel colours and marvellous styling made them unlike any other cloche hats in London.

Lizzie debated briefly whether she should go by train, then decided to drive instead. She sent the shop junior round the corner for flowers and a lavish basket of fruit, drove to the flat for an overnight bag and then set off.

She arrived at seven in the evening. The great East Anglian sky was flooded with dying light that streamed from behind purple pillows of cloud, and the Sixteen Foot Drain was streaked with a wild and dramatic pink and still

453

bubbling with hidden birdsong. The moment she got out of the car she could smell the fens: that sweet, cold, green smell that dominated the flat landscape.

The slam of the car door brought Walter into the yard. He looked gaunt and unshaven.

'Your ma's queer,' he said. 'We treated her for the ague but she ain't responded none too clever.'

The broadness of his vowels and the strangeness of his phraseology disconcerted her at first. Perhaps she had become more overtly sophisticated, and perhaps he in his worry had become deeper fenland.

'Come in,' he said, 'and mind your dainty boots.'

The kitchen looked dirty and unkempt. Dishes half-covered by a puddle of greasy water lay heaped in the brownstone sink, and a black cat sat scowling and sepulchral in the middle of the table. Lizzie hadn't been to the farm since before Aunt Netta died.

'Where is she?' The question was merely rhetorical. She stood at the foot of the stairs, looking over her shoulder with one hand on the banister rail.

'In her bed.'

Echoes of the great sunset splashed the small hot room with colour. It glowed on the walls and painted the white cotton quilt with garnet.

'Hullo, darling. Look, I've brought you some flowers.'

'Oh . . . Lizzie. . . .' Edwina opened her eyes, and Lizzie's immediate thought was that she looked less ill than tired. She looked tired to death.

'Now then, what have you been up to, eh? Overdoing it, you silly-billy.' She laid the flowers on the foot of the bed then set about plumping up the pillows. She put her arms beneath Edwina's shoulders in order to raise her a little, and Edwina winced with pain.

'Where does it hurt? Is it your neck?'

'It hurts everywhere. I'm just one big ache.'

Lizzie drew back and regarded her with increasing concern. 'Has the doctor been?'

Edwina nodded, with closed eyes. 'He give me some physic, but it didn't seem to do n'good.' Like Walter, she

454

too seemed to be sinking deeper into a fenland accent.

'Then we must get a specialist. From London, if necessary.'

'That'll cost a quid or two.' Walter came in, and the sunset touched him with fading red. He too looked very tired.

'We'll telephone – or rather, send a wire for one first thing. In the meanwhile, have you had any supper?'

They looked at one another uneasily, then Edwina indicated by a weary shake of the head that food held little interest, while Walter shuffled his feet and said, 'We took a bit of bait around twelve midday.'

She realized then that her parents had lost their authority, that from now on she would have to be in charge.

She established that Edwina was too weak to stand unaided, but was not incontinent. Together they helped her to the commode, and now that another woman was present, Walter looked away while the more intimate services were rendered. With lightning speed Lizzie remade the hot, rumpled bed, shook up the pillows and helped to assist her mother back between the sheets. She relaxed with a tired little sigh, and seemed barely conscious when Lizzie sponged her hands and face with fresh cool water carried upstairs in a bucket by Walter. She smoothed the thick grey hair back from her temples.

'I'll sleep in here with you tonight, and Pa can have my bed.'

'Oh, no. . . .'

'Oh, yes. He looks fit to drop, and anyway it's more fun with us girls together, isn't it?'

Unused to hints of schoolgirl pranks, Edwina smiled faintly and drifted off to sleep.

Tiptoeing downstairs, Lizzie arranged the bouquet of flowers in water, laid the basket of fruit on the dresser and then swept the cat from the centre of the table. The larder contained little in the way of food – none of Edwina's customary pies and pastries – so she took the hurricane lamp and went out into the yard. The hen-houses that Pa had built for her all those years ago were still standing; more

455

to the point, they had occupants, and Lizzie prowled among the drowsing, billowing bodies that muttered and mumbled with hands that had lost none of their old skill.

She returned with ten eggs and made them into a sort of omelette, mashing them and scraping them together in the old blackened pan she remembered from her childhood. She found a loaf of bread and cut it into rough slices, then spread it with butter. Walter concurred with her suggestion that he should make a pot of tea.

They ate and drank at the kitchen table, and the paraffin lamplight threw his features in wild and knobby caricature on the wall. He hadn't looked anything like this before, and she realized with sorrow that he was an old man now, with all of an old man's wavering indecision.

'We'll soon have her well again. She's got a bit run down, that's all.'

'Sshh.' He cocked his head towards the ceiling and she saw that this was how he must have been living recently – poised and ready for the slightest sound that came from the bedroom upstairs.

'Why didn't you let me know before, Pa?'

'You're too busy about your own ways.'

'I'm never too busy for you and Ma.'

He patted her hand, and smiled for the first time since her arrival. 'You're still a good little gel, Lizzie.'

She slept on the floor by the side of her mother's bed, lying on an old quilt that smelt of dust and naphtha and faraway summer flowers, and tired as she was, she was unable to sleep. New worries wove themselves in and out of old memories. She heard the huffling of the last train coming across Horse Moor, and it brought back the memory of poor Johnnie Moon, whom she now realized had suffered from the same weird thing as Oscar Wilde. Johnnie was long since dead, and so was poor old Reuben. The train also reminded her of Miss Paynim and the house in Gossett Street, and she couldn't understand why she hadn't once been back there in all the time she had been in London. She could at least have donated a few pounds to the poor old Pixies' funds. . . .

A sudden rasping in Edwina's breath made her snatch her head from the pillow. Was she choking? She went on listening, straining every nerve to analyse each little sound, then slowly lay back as the breathing regained an even rhythm.

Her mother was obviously very ill, and tomorrow she would send for a specialist from London. She would order proper treatment in a proper nursing home, and she would remove her father to Reve, where he too would be properly looked after. Everything must be done properly, she thought, and finally fell asleep.

It was less simple than she had imagined. The specialist from London suggested that Edwina should visit him, not the other way around, and when Lizzie informed him that this was out of the question, seemed disposed to argue. She accused him of indifference coupled with incompetence, and left it at that. The local doctor looked at Lizzie as if she were some kind of exotic and colourful bird and said there was either a nursing home in Wisbech or else the county hospital and asylum, but as soon as Lizzie broke the news to her mother that she was to be admitted to a nice nursing home, the comatose Edwina became flushed and agitated and refused to consider leaving her rightful bed at Damperdown Farm.

'In that case,' Lizzie said, 'I'm taking you back to Reve and we'll get a nurse in.'

But the mention of Reve caused Edwina even greater distress. She began to cry, and put up her hands in an attempt to grasp the bedpost as if they were on the point of dragging her forcibly away. Exasperated and deeply worried, Lizzie sought to remind her that Reve was home, her second home, where she was loved and treasured and where everyone would want to help nurse her and make her well again. But Edwina's voice rose to a hoarse shout:

'I said I'd never go back there and I won't! Bessie Hinton laid that curse all them years ago and it's followed you to that house! You took poor ole Netta there, and look what happened. She died – and just look *how* she died! Hanging by the neck, same as Bessie and that poor young gent on

457

Paxton's Lode. I'm not for ending up like that! I'm for dying in my bed, same as any other natural woman.'

'But Ma, you don't believe all that.'

'Then what about your boys? Both of them gorn.'

'They died in the war.' Lizzie turned very pale. 'You know perfectly well they did.'

'Hanged as well, shouldn't wonder.'

'Don't *dare* say that!' Lizzie screamed at her. 'They were made to sacrifice their lives fighting the bloody Germans!'

'Come on, Lizzie – Mother,' Walter intervened, and at the touch of his hand Lizzie crumpled into sobs. Edwina slowly relaxed her hold on the bedpost, then rubbed the cuff of her nightgown across her sweating forehead.

'Now then, Mother, no need to get topsides under.'

'But I'm not going – '

'No, no. You stay here alonga me, same as you always done, hey?'

'Bessie Hinton and her curses she laid on people. . . .'

It took a long while to quieten her, and she only slept after they had administered one of the doctor's sleeping draughts in a cup of warm milk.

'She never used to believe in all that Bessie Hinton stuff,' Lizzie said downstairs in the kitchen. 'Ma was never one for superstition.'

'Reckon it gets you as you get older.' Walter reached for a jar of Nosegay and began to fill his pipe.

'It hasn't got to *you*, has it?'

He looked at her without speaking, and her heart felt as if it were beginning to sag.

'Reckon there's bin a rare ole chapter of accidents, then,' he said finally, and sought refuge from further questioning behind a wall of smoke.

So Lizzie arranged for a private nurse to take care of Edwina, and engaged a daily woman from Upwell to clean the house and do the cooking. She stacked the larder with food, and said goodbye despairingly.

Waving from the car window, she noticed for the first time that her old home was also succumbing to senescence. It too was beginning to lean and tilt as it slowly settled further into the black peaty soil. Most houses died of being swallowed by the fens, and one day it would be the turn of Damperdown.

She had intended to drive straight back to London because poor Martha had been managing the shop single-handed all this time, but when she saw Newmarket on the signpost decided on the spur of the moment to spend the night at Reve. So she headed for Bury St Edmunds, and the thought of Dully and Aunt Miriam and the uncles filled her mind for the first time for weeks. She began to smile in anticipation, and her headlamps cut a golden pathway through the summer twilight and illuminated the dancing moths. She drove up the main south avenue and parked below the terrace. Lamps glowed in the windows and she snatched off her hat as she ran up the steps.

Bird, of all people, met her crossing the great hall. He was carrying a small silver tray, and dimly she remembered that in her early days at Reve no servant below the rank of second footman ever ventured within its majestic precincts.

'Me Lady.' Bird paused. 'Welcome home.'

'Where is everyone?'

'My master (by whom she divined he meant Uncle Badger) is performing his ablutions for dinner, Me Lady, and the Honourable Mr Woodstock – I valet both gentle-men now, as you probably know – is performing likewise. Lady Miriam is attending a musical soirée at Ickworth, so I understand, and – '

'Yes?' She looked at him impatiently.

'And His Lordship' – Bird's small eyes were inscrutable – 'has taken Miss Brookes out to dine.'

'Miss Brookes?' Lizzie searched her memory.

'Miss Brookes, the lady in charge of Their little Ladyships, Me Lady.'

Enjoying the echoing sonority of his voice, Bird dipped his head in obeisance and asked if that would be all. Lizzie nodded curtly and went up to her room.

Dully wasn't there when she needed him. She needed him to hear the news about her mother – about her mother's illness, and her father's inability to manage, and about her

459

own attempts to smooth things and organize things, and how she was tired and distraught and carrying far more of a burden than a woman of her age ought to, what with a huge house to run plus a hat shop and elderly parents who refused to comply with sensible requests that were purely for their own good. . . . Furthermore, what in God's name was he doing taking the governess out to dinner? She felt tired and cross and frankly amazed and understandably resentful that Dully should take it upon himself to entertain the servants the moment her back was turned. Her surprise homecoming had been completely spoilt.

She flung open her bedroom window and leaned out, inhaling the scent of summer darkness – why was the scent so different in Suffolk and Cambridgeshire? – and her personal maid glided into the room and stood with folded hands as if she had been expecting Lizzie's arrival hourly. Impatiently Lizzie dismissed her and then began to undress, snatching at her clothes and then flinging them on the floor before going through to the warm comfort of her bathroom.

The water was running into the fragrant foam of Bond Street bath salts when an urgent tapping on the door halted her. Without waiting for permission to enter, the children's nanny appeared, uniformed and distraught.

'Oh, My Lady, thank heavens you're home. His Lordship is out and I don't know what to do – Lady Celia has disappeared!'

'My daughter?' Lizzie stood there, full-frontal.

'She had her supper with Lady Pamela – they were both in their dressing gowns and we played a last game of ludo before bed. I tucked them both up as normal, My Lady – heard their prayers and everything – then I went down to the servants' hall for my own supper. And when I came back – no more than half an hour later because I had some darning to do – I went into the night nursery as I usually do, and there was Lady Pamela sleeping like an angel but Lady Celia's bed was – it was empty, My Lady!'

The hunt began quietly, Nanny and Lizzie's maid searching the cupboards and corridor of the nursery wing while Lizzie, fractious in a silk negligée, peered about her and called, 'Celia – come out and don't be so *naughty*!'

Off-duty maids were then called in to assist, and the kitchen staff was notified that dinner would be delayed.

The uncles, huffing in perturbation, looked in their cupboards and swished beneath their four-posters with walking sticks, and Aunt Miriam's maid gave a scream that brought everyone running when a mouse plopped out at her from behind a curtain. Although the greater part of the house, including the ex-hospital wing, was now unused and consequently kept locked, there were still enough corridors and stairways among which a mischievous child could dodge would-be captors for hours.

Lizzie went to the night nursery and woke Pamela. Sternly she demanded to know whether she had seen or heard anything unusual recently, and Pamela, blurred with sleep, said no, only Nanny in her bust bodice.

'Did Celia say anything to you about getting out of bed after Nanny had gone down to supper?'

'No, Mummy.'

'And you've no idea where she can be?'

'No, Mummy.'

'Right. You'd better go back to sleep.'

Stoically Pamela reinserted her thumb in her mouth and closed her eyes.

It was time to alert the outdoor staff; they turned out of their cottages and out of the three lodges, pulling on their boots and making their way by lantern and torchlight up to the big house, where Woodstock, in the absence of Dully, organized them into as systematic a search party as possible. Watching the bobbing lights fan out in the darkness, Lizzie cancelled dinner and ordered coffee and sandwiches. She felt drained with anxiety and her head ached.

'She must be *somewhere*,' she fumed, drumming her fingers.

'No use dragging the lake until daylight,' Badger said, and handed her a whisky and soda. 'Drink up. Far more efficacious than coffee at a time like this.'

461

She sipped a little. 'I must go and console Nanny. Poor old thing feels so responsible.'

'I wonder if she's roused Merton?'

'She wouldn't be with him, would she?'

'Who knows what's in the mind of a child?'

'Who knows what's in anyone's mind?' replied Lizzie, thinking of Dully. 'So long as no one's stolen her – I just couldn't stand that,' she added from the doorway.

Upstairs she found Nanny, red-nosed and wet-eyed, sitting in the day nursery in front of a basket of mending.

'Oh, My Lady, I don't know what to say. . . .' She fumbled for her handkerchief.

'None of us do,' Lizzie said tonelessly.

'I can't help feeling it's because I love her so much. I know she's a pickle – I mean, she's not nearly as *good* as Lady Pamela – but I do love her. . . .'

'I love them both,' Lizzie said, more tonelessly than ever. 'Try not to worry, Nanny.'

She left the nursery and returned to her own sitting room, pacing restlessly. Her headache had increased, but when she rang for some sal volatile no one answered. They were all taking part in the search for Celia.

She flung herself on to the chaise longue. Dozing uneasily, she returned in a dream to the Cambridgeshire fens, where the flat green earth was sealed round its outer rim by the sky. There was only one bare tree standing stark against the cloudless blue, but when she drew closer it was not a tree but a gibbet, and the body that swung from it by the neck was that of her mother.

She screamed and woke, and at that instant the door opened and Dully came in. He looked very pale, and for some reason the sight of his dinner jacket reminded her again of where he had been – and with whom. She sprang to her feet.

'Well, I hope you've enjoyed your evening – both of you. Perhaps you've heard the news?'

'What on earth's happened? What's all this about Celia?'

'She's missing. Probably murdered – and it's all your fault!'

462

'Darling, for God's sake!'

'I mean it! You're supposed to be in charge here, and as soon as my back's turned you start taking the damn governess out to dinner while your child's missing – probably dead by now.' She began to sob wildly.

'Liza, you're distraught. Now, try to calm down and tell me exactly what happened. For one thing, I didn't realize that you were coming home.'

'No, of course you didn't! A case of when the cat's away, isn't it?'

'Oh, come on, don't be an idiot.' He went over to her and put his hands on her shoulders, but she jerked herself free, and it was terrible how all the accumulated strain of London, her mother's illness and now the worry of Celia seemed to concentrate itself into a sudden raging hatred that she was powerless to control.

'You just don't *care* about your children!'

'Come to think of it, you haven't been exactly over-concerned about their welfare.'

The change in his voice made her pause momentarily, but she plunged on again, reckless and savage with the desire to hurt.

'I went to London because I wanted to forget. All my happiness was centred on . . . on . . . and when they were taken away from me I had to have something else to stop me from going mad. A madwoman would be no use to you or Reve or anything else. But it's hard work, selling hats. You may like to think that Martha and I just fool about having a good time, but we don't. There's a terrible amount of work and responsibility – buying and selling and hundreds of invoices and bills and things . . . and then, and *then*, on top of it all, it may interest you to know that my mother is dying. I've been nursing her and trying to arrange for doctors and nursing homes and people to take care of her because my father is old and useless and doesn't know what to do. . . . I've had a *terrible* ten days and so I decide to come back here – *home* – just for the night for some peace and quiet, and what do I find? My child is missing from her bed and you out on the tiles with the bloody governess!'

463

For a second or two it almost seemed as if he was on the point of striking her. Then he turned away.

'If you feel so aggrieved and so hard done by, then I suggest you leave now,' he said. 'Go back to London or to your people. Don't come back here, having deserted your husband and your children, with some trumped-up nonsense about having to run a hat shop in order to recover from the pain of losing Berry and Tommy. Above all, don't try to delude yourself that you are the only one to have suffered. Everyone has tried to protect you, look after you, love you, because you are a woman and because you were their mother. But don't expect it to go on and on. There is a limit to what we others can give.'

'You gave me two more children,' she raged, 'when I was still full up with love and longing and heartbreak for the others who got taken away from me.'

'They were my children too.'

'But men don't *feel* things like women!' she cried. 'They don't have them growing inside them all those months . . . oh, they love them in a way, but when something happens to the first crop they say, Right, let's get on with siring some more. I saw it all down on our farm and I know it's true – all men are bastards and you're no exception, and when I think I was away trying to recover *and* nurse my dying mother, all you can think to do is go out to dinner with the governess, presumably with the idea of softening her up so that you can get her in pod with a few more beastly kids. . . .'

'That's all it is to you, isn't it?' he said, very quietly. 'Just a matter of rutting – and now I come to remember, you were not all that unwilling to participate on that particular occasion, or indeed any other. So, by our joint efforts, you gave birth to twin daughters, and you have never given two straws for either of them, have you?'

'Yes, of course I have – I do. . . .' She floundered, then recovered. 'But I needed something else, too. Not just more motherhood.'

'You have everything that any woman could possibly require,' he said. 'Any sense of deprivation can only come from within your own persona.'

'At least I haven't been having affairs.'

'How do I know that?' He looked at her with great intentness, his face bone-white and one eye twitching slightly. 'How do I know that you haven't been going to bed with all and sundry?'

'So you don't trust me?' She spat the words at him, and even in the heat of the moment both sensed that the whole future hung upon his reply. He turned away, propping his arm on the mantelshelf and massaging his forehead wearily.

'Well, go on – do you trust me or don't you?'

'What does it matter?' he began. Then fell silent.

'You've told me all I want to know,' she said. 'And now please go away.'

He left the room without another word.

The hunt for Celia went on. A dark blob was discerned floating in the lake; more lanterns were sent for, and cautious probing from a rowing boat proved that it was a log of wood.

From the fastness of his tree house, Uncle Merton watched the bobbing lights play among the groups of uneasy cattle and thought very perturbing – but after what has recently passed, who can dare set a price on any young life? Make more and more of them, easily and mindlessly, in order to sacrifice them on the altar of Mars the god of war and the guardian of Christianity. . . . He drew the curtains, bolted the door and crept silently to bed.

Two farm labourers, shuffling carefully through the deep ferns bordering the bluebell woods, stumbled upon a courting couple, who rose up and fled in a ghostlike flutter of disarrayed garments.

'Ole Billy Stott and Lily Prickett!'

'Never. He give Lily over last Michaelmas.'

'What I heard was she give *him* over. . . .'

'Well, who was it, then?'

'Reckon it could've bin her sister.'

'What – Gladys? *Never!*'

Owls were silent, foxes alert; all the quiet country world was made watchful and apprehensive by the unusual activities of man. And up in her bedroom, blue-eyed and golden-haired Miss Brookes scrubbed at her cheeks with a handkerchief and wished for the hundredth time that she had refused His Lordship's invitation. It almost seemed as if Her Ladyship's unexpected return and now the awful news of Celia was all her fault. She wondered whether she should pack her bag and steal away like Jane Eyre. Moonlight glanced through the window and touched the single birthday card standing on her dressing table.

The same moonlight, appearing fitfully from behind torn clouds, cast a splintered pattern across Bird's back as he left the bumpy gravel of the north avenue and turned on to the smooth road outside. His bicycle tyres hummed quietly and the eye of his headlamp caught a meandering hedgehog in its stare. Bird cycled round it.

He had ridden for half a mile when he saw the short, rather square shadow in the middle of the road ahead of him. He slowed down, squinting through narrowed eyes, and then increased his speed again.

'Miss Celia?' To one of Bird's temperament it was ludicrous to call a bit of a thing her size 'My Lady'. He rode abreast of her.

'Go away.'

'Going far, are you?'

'London. Go away.'

'Can I come too?'

'No.'

She marched on, her head no higher than his handlebars and her face screened by its dark bob of hair. Bird back-pedalled to keep pace with her.

'S'long way to London.'

'I know.' A disdainful little voice. She walked on.

'Got some biscuits in me pocket.'

'What sort are they?'

'Choclit.'

No reply. Just the quick pad of her feet.

'Want one?'

'No.'

'Where I come from,' Bird said, 'people say no, thank you.'

She paused, then turned to face him. Her self-possession – Bird would have called it cheek – was very unusual. Most kids of seven would have been scared stiff out in the dark on their own.

'I'll have one.'

'Please, Mr Bird.'

She sighed impatiently. 'Please, Mr Bird, give me a biscuit.'

Bird dismounted and wheeled his bicycle in a leisurely arc. 'There's a gate we can sit on, back there.'

Moonlight flitted across her face and he saw alarm in her eyes. 'I'm not going home.'

'No, of course not. We're gonna sit on a gate and eat biscuits and rest up a bit. London's forty miles, and don't forget you've got to walk it all. Me, I'm all right; I've got a bike.'

The biscuits were in a crumpled bag in his pocket. One or two were broken, and he watched the way she crunched them hungrily. He wouldn't have minded having a daughter, but not one like this.

'I didn't say you could come with me, did I?' She licked at a crumb of chocolate.

'S'right, you didn't. And come to think of it, there wouldn't be much point, because I could get there days ahead of you on a bike.'

'Days?'

Sharp as a needle, he thought. Latches on to everything.

'Reckon it'll take you about four and a half days on your little pins. Know where you'll sleep, do you?'

'In houses, of course.'

'Oh. Know people on the way, then? That's handy.'

She grabbed the last biscuit. 'I don't need to know them. I'll just knock on the door and they'll let me in.'

'Easy as that, eh? In the meantime,' Bird said casually, 'your ma and pa are in a fair ole state wondering what you're up to.'

'I'm not going home,' she repeated.

'Why not?' He sat staring across the grey ribbon of road, whistling quietly through his teeth.

'Because I don't like it. It's boring and stupid and there's nothing worth doing.'

'Don't you get on with your sister?'

'No. She's boring too.'

The way she talks, Bird thought, marvelling. Like some bleedin' ole la-di-da of fifty.

Celia screwed the paper bag into a ball and aimed it into the hedge. She clambered down from the gate and stood in front of him with her hands on her hips. Cloud began sliding across the face of the moon.

'Coming, then?'

'No, not with you.'

'Why not?'

Still staring at the road, Bird said: 'Well, for one thing I'd have to go so bloomin' slowly, wouldn't I? And fer another thing, I don't like you much.'

'Oh?' She drew a sharp breath. 'Why not?'

'You're rude and bossy. You're *borin'*.'

She opened her mouth the speak, then thought better of it. She turned away and began to march off into the darkness. Bird sat watching her go.

'Ta-ta, then.'

She halted, a glimmering patch in the middle of the road. 'Pardon me?'

'I said, Ta-ta. Cheerio, chin-chin and all that.'

She continued to walk away. He sensed rather than saw that she was going slower and slower.

'I don't like you either,' she called. 'But you can still come.'

'You come back here.'

'Why?'

'Because I want to talk to you.'

'What about?' He fancied she had returned a step or two.

'About running away.'

'You're going to tell me not to.'

'No, I'm not. Swelp me Bob.'

'What does that mean?'

'It's a serious sorta promise.'

'Oh.' Her voices sounded forlorn now; as if she were suddenly conscious of the dark and the loneliness. Four and a half days was going to be a long time.

She came back, wary as a cat, and stood by the propped-up bicycle. 'Well, go on, then. Talk.'

'When we was at the war, we never done nothink without preparation,' Bird said slowly, and with emphasis. 'Every mortal thing was planned right down to the littlest detail. Nothink was ever forgot. Sometimes it took a lotta work and a lotta patience, especially with them whose nature was just to barge orf and do things in a hurry, without thinkin' and without doin' their plannin'. But that was how we won the war. Not because we was bigger or braver, but because we done our thinkin' and our plannin'. Because we never done *nothink* without preparation. See?'

She nodded.

'And it's the same with runnin' away. You gotta plan. You gotta make your preparations as if you was goin' on a war. You gotta have food and drink, a groundsheet and a blanket – 's no use relyin' on strangers to put you up. You gotta be self-reliant at this game – you needa paira strong boots and a change a socks. . . . Got a first-aid kit, have you? Needles and fred? Know how to pinch your grub when you run out? Fry an egg on a bitta flat stone, can you? Know how to light a fire wivvout matches?'

She shook her head.

'Gor strewth, mate, you'll never make it to London.'

'Yes, I will.'

'Not wivvout plannin', you won't.' He looked at her sorrowfully. 'For one thing, you haven't even gotta map, and for another – well, just look at you. Goin' all the way to London in your nightie, people'll think you're potty.'

She stood with her head bent and he sensed that she was close to tears.

'Will you help me plan it, then?'

'Course I will. But it'll take a long time if you're goin' to make a job of it. You mustn't get impatient.'

'All right.'

He rode back to Reve with her sitting on the crossbar on his folded jacket. He held her with one arm and her bob of hair came just below his chin. She was a right little madam, but she was also Captain Berry's sister.

'I'll tell you a story,' he said, 'about a dragon what ate people. And there was only one person in the whole world brave enough to go out and kill it.'

'Was that St George?'

'Oh, Christ no, not him. No, this was a girl called Nellie – and now I come to think of it, she must've bin about your age.'

'Go on,' she said.

'It was very, very naughty, and you must promise me never, never to do it again,' Lizzie said at the termination of her scolding on the following day.

Celia stood in front of her, small, square and implacable in a red and white check dress (with matching knickers), white socks and brown leather sandals.

'Well, go on,' added Lizzie impatiently. 'I'm waiting to hear you promise.'

'Yes.'

'Yes – you promise never to run away again?'

'Yes.'

'Good. Now you'd better go back to the schoolroom.'

Celia went, and if her mother had entertained any hopes of a decent sort of reconciliation with tears, kisses and loving hugs, they were doomed to disappointment. It was always like that with Celia.

Although Lizzie had been away from home a great deal and had not therefore monitored her daughters' progress as closely as she might, it was no longer possible to mistake one for another. Their characters were quite different, and the difference now seemed to show in their appearances; at any rate, it showed in their expressions.

Pamela, the older by half an hour, had at first seemed rather irritatingly docile. (Puddingish, as Lizzie confided to Martha.) As a baby she remained content wherever she was placed, sleeping a lot and crying little. When she was awake

470

she played with her fingers and toes and seemed largely indifferent to the blandishments of those in charge of her. She didn't smile until she was almost four months old, and then it wasn't *at* anyone; it was merely as if she had been struck with a reasonably pleasant thought.

As she progressed, 'reasonable' was one of the best ways of describing her. She was reasonably bright, reasonably pretty, reasonably everything. She looked nice in Liberty's lawn dresses, and her brown hair showed a slight tendency to wave. When the time came to apply herself to lessons under the supervision of Miss Brookes, she worked obediently at her letters and twice-times tables, and her first composition concerned a la-dy called Poll who fell out of a win-dow and went up to hea-ven where she lived happ-ily ever after. She accepted life philosophically, and by the age of six had begun showing signs of quiet concern for such creatures as kittens and dormice.

She was a calm, sensible little girl, agreeable if not vivacious, and Nanny occasionally confided that if she hadn't known she was the twin of Lady Celia she would never have believed it.

Lady Celia's hair showed no tendency to wave. Cinnamon brown and straight as a bedspread fringe, it framed a round and resolute face that appeared to regard the world with relentless nonapproval.

She was the type of child who automatically refuses to comply with the simplest request. *Why?* was the constant challenge, and if the reason she was given appeared insufficient, no amount of cajolery would change her mind. To begin with, tantrums seemed to denote a vigorous personality denied her twin sister, but as they grew from nursery to schoolroom and Pamela's placidity began warming into affection for small furry animals, Celia's squalls and yells merely solidified into a state of permanent displeasure.

The poor child seems incapable of enjoying herself, Aunt Miriam noted in her diary. I wonder why?

She was far too young to tell them – supposing they had asked – about the curious sense of brooding that seemed to

471

permeate her home. It was like a cloud, a ghostly presence, and it affected her profoundly. To begin with, she associated it with the smell of beeswax and turpentine – because the nurseries were swept and polished every Monday and Friday and the invasion of maidservants seemed to make everyone fidgety and cross. Directly they had gone, everything returned to normal; yet the strange and intangible shadow would still be there. She would sense it on the staircase and in the corridors, and by the time she was five years old she had come to the conclusion that it was in some way connected with the grown-ups. A shadowed expression, a dying footfall, a sudden sense of withdrawal eroded her security and made her feel afraid. She had no name to give it, this underlying sense of melancholy that bruised and baffled her, but it was particularly strong in her mother's presence, and it was there that she first became jealous of it.

'What funny, mousy little things you both are,' her mother once said, and although Celia had no objection to things mouselike, she resented the tone in which the words were spoken. They were critical, and wearily hostile.

So she denied that she was either funny or mousy, and when told not to argue, flew into a rage and hurled a silver cigarette box across the room. Nanny was rung for and told to remove her, and although Mummy came to kiss her at bedtime, Celia was unable to reciprocate.

'You won't see me for another whole week because I shall be in London.'

'Why?'

'Because I help to run a business there.'

'Why?' Without waiting for an answer, Celia buried her face deep in the pillow.

She heard her mother sigh, and then the rustle of her silk frock as she left the bedside. She said goodnight to Pamela, who responded adequately if not over-effusively, then from over by the door Mummy said very quietly and hopelessly: 'Sometimes I feel I just can't stand it. . . .'

The words were full of the strange, ghostly presence that tormented Celia, and they sowed the first seeds of the idea of running away.

★

Edwina didn't die. She remained comatose, yet sufficiently aware of external influences to know that there was help in the house. Walter was being fed and cared for, the place was being kept clean, and there was no need to worry.

Lizzie spend a day with her, and when she left, Walter accompanied her out to the car. He put his hand on the door, but didn't open it; just stood there looking at her thoughtfully. 'What's up?'

'With me? Nothing, Pa.'

'There is,' he said. 'Come on, Lizzikin.'

'I'm a bit tired,' she admitted, then as he went on staring at her, added: 'and things worry me, sometimes.'

'What things?'

'Celia, for one. I can't seem to do anything with her.'

'You're not there to do much, are you?'

'Oh, for heaven's sake, Pa, don't you start. Anyone would think it was the wickedest thing in the world, running a shop and being busy and earning some money – and we *need* it, you know. It costs an awful lot to keep Reve up and there's not much coming in.'

'All the time you bin here today,' he said, 'you ain't once mentioned ole boy Dully. Keeping fit, is he?'

'Yes, he's fine. He sent his love.'

Walter grunted. Then he slowly opened the car door for her. 'Tell him when you see him that I don't hold with wives running away.'

'Are you referring to me?' Lizzie regarded him frostily.

'Reckon.'

'Well, you're wrong.'

'Reckon it's a London habit,' Walter continued. 'When people get hit bad by something, like losing their sons, for instance, all they can think of to do is run away so the pain won't catch up with them. A dog or a cat'll do that – run for miles when it's got a boil in its ear or a maggot in its tail – but it don't do n'good. An' it's the same with you, Lizzie gel. You lost your boys, but you got to stop running some time.'

'I'm not running.'

He closed the car door, then took her arm. 'Come down

473

the Lode and see the ole loosestrife on bloom. It flares something wonderful.'

Stony-faced, she allowed him to lead her down through the old orchard towards the footpath that led to Paxton's Lode. She heard the churring of grasshoppers, and the quiet drone of wasps among the fallen plums. Plums had never been allowed to fall when she was a girl; the best had been picked for market and the rest made into jam or plum wine. Nothing had been wasted, then. But now the place was dying. Reuben had gone, and her father had grown old. Walking through the long dry grass she stared at his bowed shoulders and thin leathery neck.

They walked side by side along the footpath, and she remembered the times she had run along it to see Johnnie Moon – anxious and clumsy in thick boots and black ribbed stockings. Running with a can of hot soup or a couple of new-laid eggs cradled in moss, and all het up and blushing bright pink with fear and trembling, love and longing. . . . Now she was forty-seven years old.

They reached the Lode, where the tall spires of purple-pink loosestrife trembled with late-working bees. A moorhen led her string of chicks hastily out of sight and a water vole dived for cover in a scatter of silver bubbles.

The island was now almost completely obscured by willow and alder; the new footbridge that Johnnie had built had disintegrated like the one before it, and the sagging corrugated iron walls, gingered with rust, could only be glimpsed through ropes of ivy and old man's beard. No one will ever live in it again now, she thought.

' 'member when you brought your boys up here? Two little sprats in knickerbockers?'

'Yes,' she said, but her expression added, I don't want to remember.

'Running and laughing fit to bust. And one of 'em fell in, didn't he? Come up covered in water crowsfoot.'

'Berry.'

'You're right, I 'member now. And young Tommy tried to pull him out and slipped in the mud. Gor dear me, nobody could do nothing for laughing.'

'We don't seem to laugh much these days,' she said in a low voice. 'Not now they're gone.'

'They wouldn't want it, you know.' He turned to look at her, and she suddenly remembered what a real dandy-man he had once been with his crisp curling hair and eyes that always seemed to reflect the fen light. 'They'd like to think of you going on same as always.'

'I'm trying so hard.' She turned her head away.

'Perhaps that's what's wrong. You're trying a sight too hard.' He took her arm and they began to walk back towards the farm. 'There's no cure for loss, Lizzikin, and no amount of running away'll alter it. All you can do is to concentrate your mind on them that's still living.'

'Dully and I had a row,' she said finally. Yellowing grassheads brushed her hands and their seeds clung to her skirt.

'Ain't n'harm in that.'

'But it was a bad one, and we haven't made it up yet. We just don't seem able to, somehow.'

'Your Ma and me didn't speak for a whole week, once. Blessed if I can 'member why, but we got over it soon enough when she got stung on her fanny by a horsefly. Gor dear, I never heard a woman squawk so loud.'

Lizzie gave a brief snort of laughter.

'Wouldn't let me anywhere near it to start off with, but in the end I got it out with a little pair of nippers. It raised a bump the size of a hen's egg, even though I rubbed it over with raw onion for her.'

'She won't die, will she, Pa?'

'No, not yet. But we've all got to go sometime, which is why I reckon we should make the most of each other while there's time.'

They strolled back to the car, arm in arm. The sun, wrapped in an August haze, was resting on the horizon and the fens were releasing the sweet damp smell of evening.

'Goodbye, Pa. Let me know how she gets on.'

'Goodbye, Lizzikin, and bear in mind' – he raised her chin with a forefinger thick as a carrot – 'stop running away. It don't do.'

475

The car's hood was down, and she had driven almost as far as Boots Bridge when she turned to wave. He was still standing there against the skyline, old and undaunted and strong with love.

Being with him had done her good. It had soothed her and calmed her, and put her in a mood to attempt healing the breach with Dully.

The greatest obstacle was her anger over the Miss Brookes episode. Although they had not referred to it since the night of the row – they had barely spoken about anything since then – her sense of outrage remained as strong as ever. She still considered it both hurtful and offensive that he should amuse himself with an employee while his wife's back was turned. And then to have the sauce to ask whether *she* had been unfaithful to *him*. . . . But it was no use going over the old ground yet again.

Even so, if she did go home and make it up with him, it would only be on condition that dear little Miss Brookes was sent packing forthwith.

She was driving down a long lonely stretch of road that lay between Newport and Mildenhall when her front tyre blew. The sound of it made her jump. She braked violently, and the car juddered to a halt, half-slewed across the grass verge.

She climbed out, shaking a little, and surveyed the damage. The inner tube was protruding like a lump of flabby intestine and she hadn't the faintest idea what to do next. Cursing, she climbed back into the driving seat and prepared to wait for help. The sun had set now, but the evening was warm. She sat there for fifteen minutes and the road remained empty. The fens of the South Bedford level stretched around her, half concealed by the trees and rough hedges on either side.

She tried to remember how far she was from the nearest house, and thought that the last little group of cottages had been about three miles back. She continued to sit there, tapping her fingers, then decided that a walk of three miles would be less tedious than sitting doing nothing. Grabbing her handbag, she opened the car door and climbed down.

476

She was only a hundred yards away from it when a man appeared ahead of her in what seemed like a gap in the hedge.

She hastened towards him, waving. 'I say – please can you help?'

He stood looking at her gravely; a man of about her own age wearing grey flannels and a sleeveless pullover, and she noticed that he had a bald patch on the side of his head.

'I've got a puncture – could you help me change the wheel?'

'Certainly.' His voice was quiet and courteous.

'There's a toolbox on the running-board,' Lizzie told him encouragingly 'and the spare wheel's in the dickey. I suppose I ought to be able to do it myself, but some-how . . .'

He opened the dickey, removed the spare wheel and laid it on the roadside. He rummaged in the toolbox and took out the jack and a pair of spanners. He laid them beside the wheel with all the precision of a surgeon laying out his instruments. She noticed that his hands were very white and strong-looking.

'Have you far to go, Madam?'

'Near Bury St Edmunds. I've been spending the day with my – '

'Bury St Edmunds is only about fifteen miles from here.' He straightened up, dusting his fingers together. 'I suggest you walk.'

'Pardon?' She looked at him uncomprehendingly.

'Walk,' he said, still very courteous. 'Do you good.'

'You mean, you. . . ?' Puzzlement gave way to exasperation. 'In that case, perhaps you would be kind enough to replace the tools and the spare wheel.' She indicated them with the toe of her shoe.

'Sorry.' With a regretful smile he turned and began to walk away.

What had she said or done that was wrong? Nothing.

'Why did you say you would help if you didn't mean to?' she shouted after him. 'You must be a crank!'

He continued to walk away with his hands in his pockets,

and when she heard him whistling her temper snapped. She stamped her foot, then on impulse picked up one of the spanners and hurled it at his retreating figure. Even in the heat of the moment she didn't mean to hit him, and was frankly appalled when it struck him on the back of the head. She saw him stagger slightly and put up his hands. He was still nursing the injured place with them as he turned and walked back towards her, and his white-faced intensity made her heart increase its pace. She moistened her lips apprehensively.

Gripping the open door of the car, she said: 'I'm awfully sorry, I really didn't mean to . . .'

He continued to advance, and there was no one to help her. The road was as blank as pre-creation, but she went on standing there, still unable to believe that he intended to harm her. Then her nerve broke, and with a little gasping cry she began to run.

He caught up with her, and put his arm round her shoulders. She struggled, trying to shake it off. 'Leave me *alone!*'

'You shouldn't have done that,' he said in his quiet voice. 'You really shouldn't.'

'I said I'm sorry – it was an accident.' She struggled harder. 'Let me go before I – '

'Call a policeman?'

She kicked at his ankles with her pointed-toe shoe, then swung her handbag up and clouted him hard. It missed his head and struck him harmlessly on the shoulder. She kicked again and began to scream, then managed to tear herself from his grasp.

She ran fast – she was tall and long-legged and terrified – but he had no difficulty in catching up with her again. And the road was still empty of any other living creature. He put his arm round her shoulder again, hugging her close against him and forcing her to walk on. Her hair was flapping loose and she was gasping for breath.

'Why are you so hostile?' he asked perplexedly.

'Will you let me go!' It was beginning to feel as if this nightmare situation had lasted for hours. And as if it were going to last for ever. '*Please!*'

478

The struggling recommenced. His arm slipped upwards from her shoulder until it was round her neck, and terror merged with blinding fury as she kicked and hacked, clawed and bit. He dragged her to the roadside and she lost her balance. She fell, dragging him down with her, and a blackbird started up with a scream of alarm.

His hands were round her throat, encircling it like a hard white collar. 'You really shouldn't have done that,' he said again, and she shut her eyes in an effort to avoid his mad, white-faced stare.

Then his hands relaxed their grip and he suddenly hit her on the jaw with his fist. The pain leaped to the top of her skull. Her senses seemed to ricochet, then she lost consciousness.

She came to slowly, piece by piece. Hearing returned first, with the creaking lament of a lone rook flying home to roost. She wondered why she was lying on the damp grass – childhood days returned briefly – and then she re-membered.

She tried to sit up, gasped with pain and giddiness, and sank back again. With closed eyes she rethreaded the past events and she couldn't believe it. No one had ever been physically cruel to her before. She wondered if she had been sexually assaulted, but had no memory of it. She passed her hands down over her body; her underclothes were intact, her skirt down over her knees. Crying weakly, she climbed to her feet. Standing up brought the giddiness back and her mouth filled. She vomited, and when it was over she wanted badly to lie down again. But she wiped her face on a handful of grass and then saw her handbag lying by the side of the road.

She picked it up and its fastener was still closed, its contents undisturbed. She stood in the gathering dusk, wondering dazedly which way to go. To the right of her was the dim blur of the car. She decided to turn left, back the way she had driven, and after a few tottering steps came to a break in the hedgerow and a signpost that read *Footpath to Penny Green*.

She had gone some way down the narrow track lined with

ferns and blackberry when she realized with a shiver of apprehension that this must be the footpath her attacker had come from. But it was too late now. She kept walking, swaying heavily and grunting with pain. Her face felt three times its normal size and her teeth seemed to bounce in their sockets at every step.

Then she rounded a bend and saw ahead of her a triangle of green bordered by a couple of houses, a church and a pub. She made for the pub.

Dimly aware of the landlord's startled expression, she limped over to the bar and told him who she was. Then her knees buckled, and she crashed down on to the brick floor.

She came to, sitting in a chair with someone's arm supporting her head, and she heard the hollow ringing sound of her own voice as it reiterated, 'I am the Countess Dullingham . . . please telephone Reve 1 and ask for my husband. . . .'

There was a whispered consultation, then the arm was withdrawn and she saw the kindly, worried face of the landlord's wife.

Arthur would cycle to the telephone straight away, she said, and in the meantime Her Ladyship ought to lie down and rest. The best front room was always kept aired and ready for visitors. . . .

Weakly Lizzie concurred, and allowed herself to be led upstairs. She sank on to the big feather bed, and the landlord's wife knelt down and removed her shoes and then helped her to creep under the eiderdown. The room smelt of lavender, and the landlord's wife murmured reverently that there was a chamberpot under the bed if Her Ladyship required it, and then withdrew.

Lizzie slept, and only half woke when the door creaked open and someone tiptoed across to the bed. She felt the springs give as they sat down, then a hand slipped beneath the muffling eiderdown and took her own.

Without opening her eyes she knew who it was. Their fingers clasped and entwined, and she thought how typical of him to know the right thing to do. Other men would have

480

rushed in and made a fuss – roared for doctors and police
and made a great drama – whereas he knew instinctively
that her first need was for peace.

His fingers gently disengaged themselves and felt for her
pulse.

'What hurts?'

'Only my head . . . and my neck a bit.'

'That all? He didn't try anything else?'

She shook her head. 'Everything's all right now.'

She opened her eyes, and there he was bending over her –
tall, broad-shouldered old Dully with iron grey hair and
eyes tilting up at the corners in the old loving smile. She lay
looking at him in silence, and she had forgotten how much
he reminded her of Berry and Tommy.

'Yes,' he said. 'Everything's quite all right now.'

She closed her eyes again and seemed to sleep. It was dark
in the room now and she heard the scrape of a match as he lit
the candle that stood on the bedside cupboard.

'Want to come home?'

She drifted back, and groped for his hand again. 'Let's
stay here. I feel so warm and happy. . . .'

'What about some supper? Could you take a little soup?'

She shook her head. 'Not hungry, just tired.'

'My poor girl.' She felt the touch of his lips on her
forehead.

'You won't go, will you?'

'No, I won't go.'

'Not even for a minute?'

Without answering, he removed his shoes and slid under
the eiderdown with her. They lay side by side and holding
hands, gratefully aware that the healing process – the other
healing process – had begun.

Her face felt very stiff the next morning and she gave a
cry of dismay at her reflection in the dressing-table mirror.
Her neck was bruised and her jaw swollen on one side, but it
was strange how little it mattered. The horror of the attack
had already grown surprisingly dim.

'The police have got the man,' Dully said quietly. 'He
walked to Mildenhall, apparently, and gave himself up.'

481

'Thank God for that.' She shuddered, then turned to him. 'But he was so strange, Dully. I mean, he began by saying he would help me and then he just walked off . . . I don't think he was all there.'

'Another war casualty, it seems. Blown up at Passchendaele and now has a silver plate in his head. He's known locally.'

'Oh, poor *thing*.' She dropped her hands from pinning up her hair. 'They won't send him to prison or anything, will they?'

'I imagine it's more likely to be a mental home.'

She finished doing her hair in silence, then said in a low voice: 'We'll never get away from the war, will we? No one will.'

He kissed her without replying.

Downstairs he briskly settled the bill, thanked everyone again for their kindness and made arrangements for Lizzie's car to be put in the care of a local garage. He drove her home in the big Lagonda, and they had just turned in past the south lodge when he stopped the engine.

'It was her twenty-first birthday,' he said.

'What was?' Lizzie looked blank.

'Miss Brookes'. I only discovered it by accident, and it seemed rather dreadful that no one should be doing anything about it.'

'So you decided you would.'

'I took her out to dinner at the Angel. We had roast duck, I think, and green peas and – '

'Spare me the details.'

'And a rather dreadful pudding with prunes. Miss Brookes threatened to get tight on a thimbleful of sherry, so it didn't seem worth ordering champagne. I had half a bottle of German wine and she had a glass of lemonade. We talked mostly about the girls and the weather and the Empire Exhibition. Which, you may have noticed, is now in its second year.'

'How time flies.'

'We returned returned home at ten-thirty to be assailed by drama. One twin daughter missing and one missing wife returned and steaming at the nostrils.'

482

'She was merely on fire with jealousy. Nothing to worry about.'

'But, oh, why didn't she tell me?'

'Anyone with the smallest grain of sense wouldn't have *needed* telling. Oh, Dully, what an old idiot you are. . . .'

He sighed. 'Ah well, better an old idiot than a vile seducer, I suppose.'

The healing process was completed, and when they arrived at the house he said: 'By the way, I've a present for you.'

The library was deserted, and he handed her a small thin package wrapped in tissue paper and tied with a ribbon.

'Sit down before you open it.'

Wonderingly she obeyed, and the colour fled from her face when she saw the title of the book. *The Collected Poems of Thomas Dullingham. 1912–1916.*

'You had them printed.'

'On the contrary, I submitted them to a publisher and he accepted them.'

She turned the leaves slowly, recognizing some of the early ones that he had written during the holidays from school.

'The war poems are best,' Dully said, without looking at her.

She turned to the last page, to the poem called 'Will I Pass'? and she could hear his voice speaking the words.

Latin and Greek, Geog. and Maths –
And what about Divinity?
Oh God, please help me pass
Your own magisterial test.
I know Genesis and the Prophets –
And the tale of Lot and his wife;
And in the New Book
I know the Betrayal, and how
You tried to go bravely, meekly,
Into the cold steel of hatred.

Latin and Greek, Geog. and Maths –
I know cricket and swimming and

The kiss of the sun.
Please let me pass, God;
Be brave and unheeding, and not
Feel the pain. Let me
Come top in exams
And be known as the chap who went
Smiling and glad on a bright
Summer's day.

It was impossible not to cry, yet the tears at last had a soothing, restorative effect.

'I can accept it if you'll go on helping me.'

'I'll always be here,' he said. They held one another tightly, without moving; two rumpled, crumpled, middle-aged people who had slept in their clothes.

Lizzie had not looked forward to telling Martha that she wanted to relinquish her share in the business.

'I'm letting you down,' she said, in the Portman Square flat. 'I feel I used you and the shop like a crutch to help me over the bad time, and now I . . .' (Now I want to look after the girls and be with Dully because, God help me, I think I'm more in love with him than ever.)

But she couldn't say that aloud. So she mixed them both a cocktail, then added: 'Now I've got to put in a lot of work on the almshouses I started all that time ago, then there's the uncles and aunts; Aunt Minna's far from well – trouble is, they're all getting a bit long in the tooth, and – '

'Don't feel bad,' Martha said. 'I want to give it up too.'

'Martha!'

'Fairford and I are divorcing and I'm going back home.'

Lizzie stared at her incredulously.

'Careful, you're spilling your drink.'

'But, Martha, I'd no idea . . . I mean, well I knew that . . .'

'Seems everybody knew.'

'Oh, I don't mean anything *definite*.'

'No, just the general drift.' Martha leaned back and lit a cigarette. 'As you're aware, Fairford's always had a wandering eye, and now it's finally wandered to a lady he thinks can make him happy ever after. We're parting good friends, but there's nothing much to keep me here now. Is there?'

'You mean Felix?'

'Uh-huh.'

'He wouldn't consider going with you?'

'I dropped a hint that he might care to, but he says his roots are here. And he seems to prefer his own company.'

It was hard to find the right thing to say; something that was cheerful and encouraging and true.

'I want to go back,' Martha said. 'I'm looking forward to it.'

'Funny how you and I started out, isn't it? You were bought and I was caught, as you might say.'

'Only I did the buying, didn't I? And I guess I bought a dud.'

'Perhaps when you go back you might one day meet someone who . . .'

Martha smiled. 'Not on your sweet life. But in the meantime, divorce is all the rage, so pour us another drink, darling, and don't be so stingy with the gin.'

Four months later the hat shop was sold, the divorce made absolute, and all legal matters tidily disposed of. Lizzie and Dully saw Martha off on the *Aquitania*; she was wearing a mink coat and clutching the bouquet of orchids they had sent her. She looked brightly happy.

'Take care of Felix for me!'

'Only until you come back!'

Smiles, and blown kisses; then the deep-throated echo of the ship's siren against the scream of excited gulls.

'Do you think she will come back?' Dully asked as they drove home.

'I don't know. The place where you're born means something special – I have to keep going back to the fens, don't I?'

'Thank God they're not so far away.'

'And Felix told her that his roots are here.' She sat silent for a while. 'But I wish he'd gone with her, all the same. It makes her feel a failure as a mother as well as a wife.'

'Felix senses that he's got to work out his own salvation, and I think he's right.'

'Living in a poky little flat all on his own? It's all so cramped and stingy, Dully, with awful furniture.'

'He can't see it, can he?'

'No, but . . . Anyway, he knows he's got an open invitation to come down to Reve whenever he wants to.'

'Good.'

The divorce had featured in the society gossip columns (Lord Fairford Polperro exchanges American heiress for nightclub hostess), and in the meanwhile Lizzie had also appeared briefly in the headlines (Countess waylaid on country road: desperate struggle on verge).

Her attacker had won the Military Cross at the Second Battle of Ypres and the vicar of his local church spoke movingly on his behalf. The judge in his summing up likened his personality to that of a fair summer's day shaken by thunderstorms, and he was committed to a home for neurasthenics for an indefinite period.

'Can't we do something for him, Dully?'

'Such as?'

'Well, we'd have to ask him what he'd like, I suppose.'

'And the answer would probably be let's undo the past; let's go back to August '14 and proceed in a different direction.'

Inevitably their thoughts returned to the boys, and Lizzie's gaze fell on Tommy's book of poems.

'One thing I've never asked, how did you find them all?'

'The last ones were sent home with the rest of his things and I kept them hidden for a time. The others I'm afraid I filched from your secret room.'

'I sensed you knew about it, but I just couldn't say anything. And I couldn't share it – not even with you.'

'Never mind, it's done its work,' he said.

It still seemed as if the effects of the war would haunt mankind for ever, but with the withdrawal of the last British occupying forces from the Rhineland came a new feeling of confidence and hope. It had, after all, been the war to end all wars.

486

The elder Dullinghams were now becoming truly old.

Aunt Minna, who had spent her final years in her own suite, died in 1926, and Uncle Merton was found one morning by his manservant curled cosy and motionless in his bed like a small hibernating animal. The death certificate said heart failure due to natural causes, and he joined Aunt Netta in her corner of Reve churchyard.

It was typical of the Dullinghams that they should see no reason to dismantle the tree dwelling, or even to remove its contents. Their spacious treasure-house world still had a timeless, dreaming quality that would remain closed to the twentieth century for a little while longer.

Not until the 1970s would the general public park its cars in a roped-off enclosure set about with tastefully designed litter bins, and enter the great hall to buy their admission tickets and guide books. They would file through the vast intercommunicating rooms, glancing at the pictures and porcelain and silver, and peering hungrily at the second Earl's dancing pumps, the third Countess's impassioned letter to Clive of India, and at the room, polished regularly but otherwise untouched, that had been made into a touching little shrine to her dead sons by the ninth Countess, who had died in 1964 aged eighty-five. They would see her full-length portrait hanging in the picture gallery next to that of her husband.

All these things and more would be laid bare, and they would file through the west wing, in which bombé gilt and Constable landscapes lived side by side with terse orders still visible on the walls: *Lights Out 9.30. Matron.* There would still be a few pairs of unclaimed crutches leaning in corners because the Dullinghams had omitted to have them removed, and because it was now felt that they added to the atmosphere. There would be teas in the kitchens, a gift shop in the servants' hall and loos in what used to be the laundry, and Reve would be run with great care and good taste because it was now part of England's Rich Heritage.

But not yet, not yet. There was still a little time left, and with Aunt Miriam vowing creakily to outlive her parrot, and the uncles – gouty, wheezy and occasionally grumpy – relying more and more on the tough-tender ministrations of Bird, the scene was being set for perhaps the most poignant family drama of all.

Because of the grief that in the early years had imposed a voluntary silence on the family, it came as a surprise to Celia to learn that she had had two brothers.

Pam accepted the idea with equanimity, only pausing to ask their names before dismissing the subject as one that needn't greatly concern her, whereas the effect upon Celia was profound and disturbing.

Too young to spare her elders' feelings, she demanded to know what being dead was like, what it really meant. How had they died? Why had they died?

The questions opened up old wounds, and away from Lizzie's hearing Dully tried to explain that being dead meant that Berry and Tommy had gone for ever, that she would understand the how and why when she was older, and that in the meanwhile it was kindest not to pursue the subject too closely.

'Why?'

'Because it causes pain to all of us who remember them.'

'Why?'

'Because we loved them.'

'Would you talk about me if I died?'

'We would feel precisely the same about you and Pam,' Dully said firmly. 'And now, I think we'll change the subject.'

She tried to discuss the momentous disclosure with her sister, and was exasperated to discover that the prosaic Pam was already better informed.

'They died in France when we were fighting the Germans because they invaded Belgium. Lots and lots of men were killed, and a lot more were wounded. That's why Felix is blind.'

Celia stared at her for a moment in silence, then turned on her heel and walked out.

She came upon Uncle Badger snoozing in an armchair in

the library window. She stood contemplating the gentle rise and fall of his moustache as he breathed, then said: 'What was the war like?'

'Awful.' His eyes remained closed.

'Did you fight with the Germans?'

'Too old.'

Questions tumbled through her mind, but his marble stillness and old man's silence told her that it would be a waste of time putting them into words.

Everyone, she discovered, had a self-protective barrier behind which they retired whenever the two brothers' names were mentioned. Mummy was particularly evasive, taking a deep breath and smiling brightly as she nimbly changed the subject, and once when Felix Polperro came to stay, she waylaid him tapping through the rose garden with his stick and asked him what Berry and Tommy had been like.

'Marvellous chaps. The best.'

'Yes, but what were they *like*?'

'Red-haired, brown-eyed. Berry very tall, and a bit of a devil. Tommy quieter – poetic sort of chap.'

'Why did they have to fight the Germans?'

'Sense of duty, I suppose. And in the early days we all thought it would be a bit of a lark.'

'Uncle Badger said it was awful.'

'He's right. It was.'

'And now they're dead they'll never come back, will they?'

'I say,' Felix stopped tapping, and turned his closed eyes towards the sound of her voice, 'you're rather a ghoulish kid, aren't you?'

'Is she being a nuisance?' Pam's clear young voice seemed to slice through the still summer air. She came up to them, a wave of brown hair falling across her forehead.

'Shut up and mind your own business.'

'Oh, buzz off, Cee,' Pam said equably. 'Can't you see that everyone's had enough of the war?'

Celia's mouth tightened with the old small-child instinct to hit out. Then once again she turned on her heel and marched off, while Pam reached up to take Felix's other arm.

'The roses in this bed are all pink,' she said. 'They've got a pink sort of smell, and I know that because I sometimes come out and sniff them with my eyes shut.'

'Why do you do that?' They tapped along a few more paces.

'Because I want to know what it's like being you.'

It was simple for Pam, because she had that kind of temperament. Easy, calm, practical, and loving in an undemonstrative sort of way. Things fell smoothly into perspective for her; there appeared to be no hard edges, no uncomfortably sharp angles. And she never seemed to get on people's nerves the way Celia did.

Celia was a loner, an outsider in the big house with its echoing footsteps and faded flags hanging motionless in the great marble hall. In solitude she rambled the stairways and corridors, no longer frightened by the sense of brooding because now she understood the reason for it. It was the memory of her dead brothers Berry and Tommy hanging on the air, and curiosity about them had reached a point of burning but inarticulate obsession when she discovered the small panelled room set in the embrasure of the central block. The key was in the lock. She turned it and went inside.

And there they were. The quiet, airless room seemed to quiver with their presence and she stood motionless, hands clasped behind her back as her gaze travelled slowly over the photographs and toys – toys that she had never played with – the kid button boots and little sailor suits, the faded College caps and ties that for all their shabbiness still exuded faint whiffs of masculine pomp and circumstance. Girls' boarding schools provided nothing like that.

She fingered through the school books, the bundles of letters from prep school and Eton (Dear Mater and Pater, I'm beginning to like it awfully here . . .) and she cautiously touched the big black service revolver that stood near a cross-shaped thing suspended from a piece of red ribbon. Then she sat down in the window, pulling her short cotton skirt down over her knees and letting her gaze travel once more round the carefully arranged exhibits. The big rocking-horse, and the big pair of riding boots with creases across the toes and heels slightly worn down. They looked too big even for her father and she sensed that they must have belonged to Berry, whom everyone said had been a large chap. Larger than life, some of them said.

She wanted to stay there for a long, long while, absorbing their lost summer world of tennis racquets and cricket bats, the happy picnic faces and ink-blotched schoolboy riddles: Dear Mama, when is a door not a door? Answer: When it's a jar. Ha, ha! All the family's laughter seemed imprisoned in this room, and she knew with a child's penetrating lucidity that no power on earth would set it free to boom and ripple along the corridors and through the rooms and gardens the way it must have done, once. Before They were killed in the war.

She left the room with reluctance, locking the door behind her and telling herself that she would return immediately after luncheon. But at two o'clock the dressmaker arrived to measure her and Pam for new school frocks, and by the time she had made her escape the door was locked and the key had gone.

It was like being shut out of a strange sort of paradise.

Moody, spotty and slouching, she endured boarding school as being neither better nor worse than home, and her form mistress said how extraordinary that twins should be so totally different in character. Nanny and Miss Brookes had said the same thing, of course, and Celia watched with a sardonic eye as Pam was carried shoulder-high from the hockey field, or called to the dais to receive prizes for this and that. It wasn't that Pam was particularly brilliant; she was just practical and sensible and enjoyed work.

Celia could have equalled her performance in most things if only the old tormenting question of *Why*? hadn't constantly impeded her. *Why* learn Latin when it's a dead language? *Why* play lacrosse when it's cold and wet?

'Trouble with you is,' Dully once said, 'you always want to know the engine-driver's name.'

She asked him with a trace of wistfulness if Berry and Tommy had really been absolutely brilliant at everything at school, and he said, 'Good Lord, no – just better at some things than others, like the rest of us.'

She made no reply, and her brooding, pimply face – so much more sensitive than dear old Pam's – made him lean forward and take her hand.

'They were only ordinary, decent chaps, you know.'

'Mmm.'

'I mean, we haven't put them on any sort of pedestal just because they're dead. We were all very cut up at the time, but there's no sense in going *on*, is there?'

'No.'

She wished she could believe him, but most of all she wished she could talk to him about what seemed to lie at the heart of her own difficulties. Imagination and the contents of the secret room had made her put them on a pedestal of her own. They were both dead, but they were shaping her life in some terrible and disturbing way, and she didn't know what was going to happen.

'Help me,' she muttered, her head bent, her hair falling in strands across her face.

'I'll always be here,' he said very quietly and gently, the way he had said it to Lizzie. He released her hand and put his arms round her shoulders in an attempt to hug her close to him, but instinctively she recoiled. Every muscle, every nerve, seemed to tighten.

Dear God, we did her a lot of harm in our grieving selfishness, he thought. And let her go.

Felix Polperro had made a life of sorts out of impenetrable darkness, and had learned to accept appreciatively whatever compensations crossed his path.

The four senses that remained to him were now tuned to an extraordinary degree of sensitivity; his hearing was as sharp as a cat's, he could smell a distant garden bonfire through closed windows, and could distinguish between five proprietory brands of breakfast marmalade by taste alone. Occasionally he would demonstrate these skills, and with a pleasure totally free from bitterness, encourage his audience to laugh and perhaps even to tease him about the supernatural.

A glimpse of another, darker Felix only came if someone inadvertently used the wrong word for sense of touch.

'Your ability to *feel* is absolutely amazing!' they might cry when his fingers had successfully told the difference between real and artificial silk.

'My feelings are my own affair,' he would reply, and they would recoil in embarrassed dismay, abruptly aware that they were after all merely being nice to someone who wasn't quite normal.

Courteous and unerring, he would show them to the door, and then return to his chair to sit slumped and silent in the heart of his imprisoning blackness.

His feelings were his own affair, and there was no one to share them with because he had nothing much else to offer.

He had made his peace with his mother a long while ago, but had resisted her invitations to return with her to Boston because however congenial her company, it was non-essential. He now had difficulty in remembering what she looked like. He was fond of his errant father in the same rather kindly and impersonal fashion, and strangely, had no problem in supplying a face to go with his stepmother's voice. It would be rounded and heavily powdered, with a blobby little nose and summer-blue eyes in whose besotting depths lay only a calculated desire to look after number one. She always called him Sonny, and exhibited in public a motherly flirtatiousness that was not difficult to snub. Occasionally his father tried to borrow money from him, and that too he found easy to resist.

His private income, adequate if not excessive, came of course from his mother. He lived comfortably within his means in a flat in Gloucester Place, and spent his days in listening to the wireless, and in taking long walks, during which he listened to the multifarious voices of London. People were very kind in seeing him across busy roads.

A young lady who lived opposite – he presumed youthfulness because of the pitch of her voice – began passing the

493

time of day with him, and then suggested with becoming diffidence that he might care to visit Kew Gardens with her one day. She helped him up the spiral stairs of an open double-decker bus and he felt the warm gritty London breeze on his face, the touch of the sun on the backs of his hands.

They spent a pleasant afternoon among the trees and shrubs, and he learned that she was very lonely because her father, a widower and ex-precentor of Wells Cathedral, had brought her up very strictly. She didn't greatly care for her job in a solicitor's office either, but hoped one day to meet a Prince Charming with whom she would be able to share the rest of her life.

She invited him back to her flat for coffee. He accepted, touched by her ingenuousness and a little flattered that she should see fit to waste her time on a blind man.

She asked him whether he had been blind from birth, and when he said no, only since the Battle of Jutland, she laid aside her cup and saucer and moved closer to him on the settee. She cradled his face in her hands and began to kiss him; unnerved and deeply embarrassed, he strove to prevent her, and then abruptly capitulated. The female presence of her drove him suddenly mad with desires he had thought crushed and vanquished for ever, and it was only when his tongue became trapped in the gap between her front teeth – a hazard he had naturally been unable to foresee – that his passion died. Deflated and filled with cold self-disgust, he bade her goodnight and tapped rapidly from her presence. It needed little skill to avoid one another thereafter.

The place in which he felt happiest was Reve. The Dullingham boys had been like brothers to him, and he gratefully accepted Aunt Liza's and Uncle Dully's invitations to stay with them. He was always given his old room and treated with the same unflurried geniality that had always made childhood visits so pleasurable. He sensed that in their goodness they even cherished him a little more for having come through the slaughter that had taken their own two sons.

He remembered his way about, and traced unerring perambulations along corridors down which he had once raced with Berry and Tommy, and stroked with sensitive fingers the baluster rails down which they had slid.

Encountering Celia one day, he asked whether she had ever tobogganed downstairs on a teatray. She said, no. Why?

'Your brothers and I used to.' Then sensing another *why?* hanging on the air, he added: 'We did it because it was fun, and also because it was quicker.'

'They enjoyed having fun, didn't they?' For once she seemed disposed to linger in his company.

'*Rather!*' He turned his face in her direction. 'Don't you?'

'I don't know. I'm not really sure how you start.'

'Oh, you poor old thing!' Her elderly tone made him laugh. 'I'll have to buy you a book on it.'

'I think about them a lot, Berry and Tommy I mean. It's so odd the way they're all round the place and yet I never met them.'

They paused by a life-sized statue of the goddess Flora, a calm marble figure with a garland of flowers in her hair. From the open window behind her came the cry of a peacock.

'They don't oppress you, do they? They wouldn't have liked that.'

'Oppress,' she repeated, examining the word. 'When I'm in a bad mood I sometimes feel jealous of them, but mostly I'm just interested in how people who are dead can still be so sort of vigorous.'

'What are you going to do when you leave school?' he asked abruptly.

'I don't know. Why?'

'You ought to do something special. I think you'd be good at helping people in some way.'

'Pam's better at that.' They walked on.

'Pam will make some lucky young chap a wonderful wife, and a wonderful mother for his kids. I can't help feeling that fate has reserved a different role for you.'

'I'm not keen on getting killed off in a war.'

495

'What made you say that?'

'I think about wars a lot. I suppose it's the influence of my brothers.'

'Dear Celia,' he said, and found her hand without fumbling for it. 'Try to be happy and try to have fun. After all, that's what they died for, you know.'

'And why you lost your sight?' He felt her candid gaze on his eyes.

'Oh, no. I lost that because I blundered in the path of an oncoming shell. Serve me right for not looking where I was going.'

He willed her to laugh, but she didn't. The gong for luncheon sounded.

Both girls passed Matriculation at their public school – Pam through slogging and Celia because of a last-minute burst of concentrated energy, during which she slept little and ate next to nothing.

Next year they would be presented at Court. They would share a coming-out ball and be part of the London season, a prospect that Pam viewed philosophically and Celia with ill-concealed distaste.

She pondered Felix's suggestion that she should do something of a philanthropic nature with her life, but didn't know what. She didn't like babies, or the sick, or people from the slums. She didn't even like animals all that much.

So she hung about at home, uninterested and un-committed, restless and moody until shortly after her eighteenth birthday, when once again she found the key in the door of the small panelled room. She went in, but this time she was not alone. Bird, in a green baize apron, was dusting the exhibits and whistling quietly as he did so.

'Oh – I didn't realize. . . .'

'S'or right, Miss. Come in.' He still couldn't quite bring himself to call her Lady Celia.

'I didn't know it was your job to keep it all spick and span.'

'What you might call a laboura love. I do it for the Countess.'

'I see.'

'And for *them*, of course.'

'Of course.'

She watched his bright yellow duster busying over the pair of riding boots; the ones with creases across the toes and slightly worn-down heels.

'Were those Berry's?'

'The Captain's. Yes, Miss.'

'He had big feet, hadn't he?'

'They was in proportion to the rest of him. Very tall he was, with broad shoulders and red hair. Marvellous-coloured red hair.'

'I know. I've been told.' If there was a hint of bitterness in her voice, Bird chose to ignore it.

'Last time I polished 'em – *reely* polished 'em – was in the trenches. Front line on the Somme in '16.'

'I know about that, too.' She moved past him and sat down on the window-seat, where the autumn sun was warm on her back.

She and Bird had had a special relationship ever since the night she had tried to run away; too distant to be called friendly, it had developed into a kind of grudging and rather grim trustfulness that had survived more than one furious skirmish conducted out of family earshot. They both valued it more than they would admit.

'Was that Berry's, too?' She nodded at the service revolver, the Webley .45 that lay near the Victoria Cross.

'No, that was his brother's. The Captain's was lost when he died.'

'In some ways I don't think it could have been all that bad,' Celia said reflectively. 'I mean, to have a short, neat sort of life where you don't have to make any big decisions – it's all done for you. And then after you're dead they make a museum out of all your old vests and boots and things, and everybody worships your memory and you still have to be careful what you say in front of Mummy in case you upset her.'

Her voice began to tremble and she realized that she was on the verge of another fit of jealousy. She hadn't had one for a long time. 'They couldn't even bear to tell us that we'd ever had two brothers.'

Bird returned the boots to their rightful place and then slowly straightened up. His face looked pale.

'How would you like to die now, at your age?'

'Sometimes I think I wouldn't mind all that much. So long as I didn't know the actual minute it was going to happen – and *they* didn't, did they?'

Slowly and pityingly he shook his head. 'You've got it wrong, Miss. They was expecting to die at any minute all the time. They lived with it, day in, day out – we all did – and I always reckoned it was worse for the ejicated ones because they'd bin taught to imagine things better.'

'In that case, death must have been a happy release.' She knew she sounded flippant and defiant, and didn't care. She was in one of those moods.

Bird turned as if to move away, then evidently changed his mind. He jerked his head at the big photograph of Berry on the white pony, with Tommy laughing over his shoulder.

'Do you know how he died?'

'No one's ever told me.'

'No one knows except me. And I tell you, it wasn't like switching off a light.'

'How, then?' Her lips were suddenly dry.

'Let's put it this way. The coffin buried in the nice tidy grave in the war cemetery – the one your Mum and Dad went to the official opening of – doesn't contain all of him. All they could do was shovel up loose arms and legs along with bodies and heads, and make a rough job of sharing 'em out. There wasn't time to do no more. As for how he died, it wasn't all brave and fine and soldierly the way *he* was – he was ripped through with machine-gun fire, but that didn't kill him. He drowned in the mud. He led his men over the top like he always did, and when he fell they just had to run over his body with their hobnail boots even though he was still alive. The mud was like treacle and they fell on top of him – I saw it, I was there – and they drowned in layers and their arms and legs hadn't snapped off nice and clean, they was rotted off by the time we come to dig them out and try to bury them. They was all full of maggots.'

498

Bird choked, and suddenly began to cry. 'It was all so fuckin' *dirty*, that's what gets me.'

Dazed with horror, she could only think, it's still going on for him. He's still living through it and he'll never be rid of it. . . .

She went awkwardly towards him and was appalled and shattered when he put his arms round her and cried hot convulsive tears into her neck. He smelt of sweat and furniture polish.

'Don't cry, Bird . . . please don't.'

'S'or right, Miss.' He wiped his eyes on his duster.

She wanted to say more, but her mouth was dry as paper. White-faced with pain and pity and rage, she only knew that today marked the one great decisive turning point in her life. It was as if the pattern into which it was destined to fall was at last becoming clear.

But the day wasn't ended yet. After dinner the family sat in the library, and when Dully switched on the National programme in search of the nine o'clock news, they all paused and listened in wonderment to a high-pitched voice screaming in German.

'Herr Hitler,' wheezed Uncle Woodstock. 'They say the stupid fella wants to start another war.'

He had become Reich Chancellor on 30 January 1933, an event noted with passing interest by the occupants of Reve. They remained equally unperturbed by Germany's withdrawal from the League of Nations and the Disarmament Conference in the following October, finding it difficult to believe that such a comical little chap could seriously jeopardize world peace.

Mussolini was equally bizarre, and they viewed his invasion of Abyssinia with disapproval. They began to consider the facts of National Socialism and unlike some members of the British aristocracy, found them unpalatable. Not only did fascism seem cruel, pompous and militaristic, its particular brand of thrustful self-assertion appeared to them ridiculous, and they fell into the trap of finding it funny rather than fearful.

'I read somewhere he's only got one testicle.'

'Who?'

'Hitler fella.'

'The way he carries on, you'd think he had four.'

'There can't possibly be another war, can there?' Lizzie asked Dully on the morning after Lord Halifax had met Herr Hitler at Berchtesgaden. 'They seem to have got on quite well together, don't they?'

'It's always difficult to know how much to give in, for the sake of peace and quiet.'

'Remember how the boys used to go on and on about swimming when it was still only March?'

'Perhaps we mollycoddled them. Should have let them swim all the year round.'

They fell silent, hand in hand.

'I cannot agree with the principle of judging people *racially*,' Aunt Miriam thought, feeding Benbow with a piece of apple. 'I was once guilty of it myself because I disliked the Baron von Kassel before troubling to get to know him, although in mitigation I must add that he could never have come high in my estimation for marrying such an extremely tiresome woman. But there, I believe they are both dead now.'

Reve was still calm, still safe, and Aunt Miriam carefully measured two drops of olive oil into Benbow's drinking water because she believed him to be suffering from constipation.

The only person who had no pleasant preoccupations, no comforting nostalgia to snuggle into, was Celia.

On the day after her encounter with Bird in the secret room, he tapped on her sitting room door and asked if he could have a word. Although he bore no sign of previous emotion, there was a tight-lipped intensity about him that made her heart beat faster. She turned her back to him and stared out of the window.

'Yes, Bird?'

'About yesterday, Miss. I'm sorry I told you, very sorry indeed, but what's done's done and can't be undone. Reckon you hit me on the raw a bit.'

500

'Yes. I'm sorry too.'

'But what I want to say's this.' She heard him come further into the room and close the door behind him. She didn't turn round. 'Don't tell the rest of them what I told you. I vowed I'd never tell no one, see, and I mean to stick to that. The Captain wouldn't have wanted it, and it don't do no good, their knowing. They're better off without it.'

'Yes.'

'So you promise? On your solomn God's honour?'

'Yes,' she said in a muffled voice. 'I swear on God's honour.'

It seemed for a moment as if he might say something more; something to the effect that this new secret would deepen their friendship. But he didn't. Perhaps her hitting him on the raw had had the reverse effect.

There again, she might have told him about the pattern of her life beginning to fall into place. It still wasn't quite complete, but the things he had told her were enough for her to start work on. Very shortly it would all make sense and her future would be clear.

In the meanwhile, a child's raw sensitivity coupled with an adult's sickened despair that such things could be, drove her to seek consolation while keeping Bird's secret intact. She tried her father.

'Is there really going to be another war?'

'Difficult to say, but I hope not.'

'Supposing there is, will it be like the last one?'

'Worse, I should think. They say it would be conducted mainly from the air.'

'Can't we do something to make sure it doesn't happen?'

'Such as?' He gave her a melancholy smile.

'Well – all rise up against Hitler, or something. Tell him that we just won't stand for his stupid bossing.'

'I think we would have to be a little more diplomatic than that. He seems an excitable character, and to treat him like a naughty child would only promote further tantrums. And don't forget, he's got a huge army and air force.'

'But it's wrong for him to want Austria and Czecho-slovakia! It's unfair.'

'Not that simple, I'm afraid. In the Treaty of Versailles at the end of the war, they drew up new territorial boundaries so that the old Austro-Hungarian Empire, for instance, disappeared and became Yugoslavia, Hungary, Rumania, Czechoslovakia and Austria. You must have done it at school. And while it was a good idea in some ways, it annoyed a lot of people – such as all the Germans who found themselves stranded in Poland.

'Serve them jolly well right!'

'I dare say, but it hasn't stopped them feeling miffed. And it partly serves us right when some firebrand comes along determined to exploit a situation we rather sanctimoniously created.'

'But if the Germans hadn't started the war in the first place, there'd have been no need for new boundaries and reparations and everything.'

'It depends how far back into history you're prepared to go. Which came first, the chicken or the egg?'

'Oh – you make me cross!' She couldn't share his elderly resignation. 'Your two sons died in the war, but you're not doing anything to help stop another one from breaking out! They said it was the war to end wars, but if the people who are left won't take a bit more interest in what's going on, Berry and Tommy will have died for nothing, won't they?'

Indignation made her tremble. She folded her arms, hugging herself tightly as she tried to suppress the memory of what Bird had told her.

'Dear Celia,' her father said patiently, wearily, 'I have other perplexities, apart from Herr Hitler. So far as I'm concerned, he's merely a rumbling accompaniment to the ever present economic problem. The farms have had three bad seasons in a row – they scarcely pay for themselves these days, let alone make a profit. Having to turn men off isn't a pleasant prospect, but the money's got to come from somewhere. Believe me, cheap imports are a far greater threat to this country than Hitler.'

She turned away, baffled and frustrated that he should set the loss of income against his sons' lives. Because that was how it appeared.

502

She tried other members of the family in the hope that they might display some sense of perturbation about the possibility of war, but none of them seemed to evince the slightest ambition to discuss it, let alone do anything about it.

The uncles feigned sleep, Aunt Miriam replied that we should leave it to our representatives at the League of Nations; to preserve world peace was what they were there for, and no doubt they drew a more than adequate remuneration for doing so.

'In any case, I think you are worrying unnecessarily.' She picked up *The Daily Telegraph* and adjusted her pince-nez: '*Peace for the people of the world, declared Herr Hitler at the New Year Reception given for the Diplomatic Corps, was the aim of his work and that of the Reich Government.* So you see, everyone wants peace.'

'But the papers keep saying the Germans are going to invade Austria and that a lot of Austrians are glad because they're Nazis too – '

'Sheer war mongering,' said Aunt Miriam. 'Now come and help me with the crossword.'

Pam told her to stop being an old grouch and come and see the new Labrador pups, and her mother's reaction was equally inconsequential.

'Charity begins at home,' she said, carefully putting on her hat. 'Come over to the sanctuary with me, they haven't seen you for ages.'

'Who's talking about charity?'

'They'll think you don't care, which would be dreadful.'

'Why?'

'Celia darling, don't be so dense.' Lizzie arranged a curl beneath the hat's brim. 'For us to live at Reve is a privilege, and the very least we can do in return is to look after the people who work here. In particular the poor old ones . . . Mrs Stoddart's dying, by the way.'

'We're all going to die if somebody doesn't do something soon.'

'What about?' Lizzie twirled away from the mirror to face her.

'Hitler.'

'Oh, him. He's nothing to do with us, whereas ole Mrs Stoddart *is*.'

'Oh, why can't you *see*?'

Useless to argue. Useless to try. Everyone was too intent on letting the horse loose in order to bolt the stable door after it.

Hunched and smouldering, she put on her tweed coat and combed her hair back with her fingers while her mother eyed her critically.

'Why don't you use a spot of lipstick and have a nice little perm? You could be lovely, you know.'

I don't want to be lovely, Celia thought. I want to be me, the way I am, but most of all I want people to talk sense. I want them to take me seriously. . . .

She stared back at her mother.

Lizzie at fifty-eight was still slim and still maintained the graceful lilting deportment of the old Gaiety days. She dressed carefully without being a slave to fashion, wearing her skirts longer than was currently in vogue and preferring silk blouses with ruffles at the neck and wrist to the more tailored variety. She had also refused to bob her hair and continued to wear it piled on top of her head, its deep auburn now heavily interlaced with grey. She remained a remarkably good-looking woman, and the years as Countess Dullingham had given her added presence without obliterating previous mannerisms and habits of speech. The occasional broad fenland vowels blended with the light seasoning of Cockney, and the careful refinements of George Edwardes made her a conversational delight – and she still had the gift of lighting even the largest and most sombre room with the sudden warm glow of her smile. Bird, who seldom passed audible comment to anyone, once told Celia that only her mum could have given birth to the Captain.

How did she come to give birth to me? Celia wondered.

'Never mind, you'll just have to come as you are,' Lizzie said.

Briskly she drove them across the estate in her two-

504

seater. The sky was leaden grey, the air full of the cold promise of winter.

'I can remember the days when there'd be more than a dozen beautiful big stacks over there.' Lizzie nodded in the direction of the home farm. 'This year there's only one, and a poor little old thing at that.'

'Mmm.'

They drove out on to the public highway, where the Elizabeth Dullingham Sanctuary stood close by the church and the Dullingham Arms. Now thirty years old, the brick had mellowed and the trees Lizzie had had planted were grown to maturity.

'I want us to build on a couple more bathrooms, but your father says we can't afford it.' She handed Celia a big basket of provisions to carry. 'Take these, there's a duck.'

The front door opened and the matron greeted them with a series of glad little cries. Celia handed her the basket.

'And oh, my word, what have we here, Lady Celia?'

'I don't know,' Celia said lugubriously. 'I haven't looked.'

She didn't mean to be lugubrious; she would have quite liked to sound animated and lovingly concerned, but she could no more emulate her mother's charm than she could emulate her looks.

They were led into the office and given afternoon tea while Lizzie put on her gold-rimmed spectacles and read through the monthly report and statement of accounts. They then discussed each inmate in turn, and gazing at the opposite wall Celia tried dutifully to remember who was incontinent and who was not. The vicar had called to see Mrs Stoddart, who had rallied a little.

They discussed plans for the coming Christmas dinner and the party to follow (Shall we have the Dinky Dots again, or the conjurer?) and the visit ended with a trip round the common room to smile and chat and shake hands with the occupants.

The day had already faded by the time they drove home, and low clouds of starlings were flying in to roost. A new young moon lay poised above the river and they sensed the great park and all its small secret creatures settling for the night's rest. Berry and Tommy must have loved it, once.

'Mother – how can we stop wars?'

'Easy.' Lizzie peered ahead for the first glimpse of Reve's lamplit windows. 'Don't start them.'

'But it's other people, not us, who – '

'Now listen to me.' Lizzie switched off the engine. 'My great-grandmother Bessie Hinton took the law into her own hands during the Ely Bread Riots and ended up being hanged for her trouble.'

'*Hanged*?'

'That's what I said. She joined the other rioters and went out at night with them, setting fire to places and looting and all that because the price of food was too high – bread in particular, I suppose. Anyway, she was caught by the militia and hanged outside Ely Gaol.'

'Gosh. What a wonderful woman.'

'She wasn't a bit wonderful. She was just a damn fool.'

'But if it was something she believed in – '

'No beliefs . . .' Lizzie began to say, then halted. She didn't want to discuss details, and above all had no desire to tell Celia about the family curse (or strange series of coincidences, whichever you chose to call it). While personally maintaining an open mind, she nevertheless preferred to think of Bessie Hinton as little as possible.

So she restarted the car and drove home in silence, unaware that, for Celia, another little chunk of the pattern had just fallen into place.

Worried by her aimlessness and exasperated by her long morose silences, Dully and Lizzie asked Celia what she would like to do. Surely she must want to do *something*?

'Yes,' she said on the spur of the moment, 'I'd like to stay in London for a while.'

'Good heavens.' Her father looked astonished. 'What on earth for?'

She didn't know exactly, then once again inspiration came to the rescue.

'I want to read books.'

506

'Masses of them here in the library, old thing.'

'I don't mean that sort. I want to learn what's going on *now*.'

They looked at her a little dubiously, then remembering that they had raised the subject in the first place, smiled and began to formulate plans. So it was arranged that she should go and stay with Felix for a few days, and in order that the proprieties might be seen to be observed, Pam was to accompany her.

They went by train, sitting on opposite sides of the carriage and smiling little tight sisterly smiles whenever their eyes met. Celia didn't want to stay with Felix, Pam didn't want to stay in London, and neither wanted to stay in company with the other.

'I hope Felix won't behave like a Victorian chaperon,' Celia said. 'I'd hate him following us about all the time.'

'You shouldn't have much trouble giving a blind man the slip.'

'I know, but . . . I wanted to put up at a little hotel somewhere on my own.'

'Well, you can't, so shut up complaining.' Pam rustled in her handbag. 'Here, have a bull's-eye.'

How like the staid, comfortable old Pam to come armed with a bag of sweets. Celia accepted one and crunched it noisily.

They found their way to Gloucester Place, where Felix was waiting for them; his daily help had left a cold lunch on the table in the window, and they discovered that he had given up his double bedroom to them and transferred to the small boxroom at the end of the passage. He greeted them cheerfully, and seemed to be looking forward to their company.

'Tell me what you both look like,' he prompted. 'And what you're wearing.'

His request, coupled with a glass of dry sherry each, dispersed any slight restraint there may have been. Pam started to say, 'She's in a sort of grey-blue and I'm in brown – ' when Celia cut in.

'We're both wearing brown brogues, hairy tweeds and

507

hairslides, and we look as if we're off on a pheasant-shoot.'

'But we both brought our pearls, just in case,' Pam added.

He had known them all their lives, but had never troubled to fit an appearance to them until today. At home, they were merely part of the quiet blissfulness of Reve – two little-girl voices blending with the purring of wood-pigeons, the laughter of Aunt Lizzie and the lilt of piano music spilling from an open window.

But here in his small London flat he could picture them quite vividly: two rather shy, serious country girls with broad shoulders and small waists and squarecut fingernails. Their presence was suddenly striking and positive, and so individual that when he heard a stomach rumble he knew (God knows how) that it was Celia's.

'Pardon me,' she said, as if in corroboration.

'You must be getting hungry.'

He led the way to the table, moving easily and un-hurriedly among the furniture, and when one of them picked up a tablespoon and said, 'Shall I be Mother?' he knew with equal certainty that it was Pam.

It was not only the effect of the sherry that enabled both girls to openly admire Felix's dexterity with the corkscrew, his ability to pour the Graves '32 into each glass without spilling a drop.

'Good old Felix – cheers!'

'Cheers.'

'Honestly, you know, you're just like a brother.'

'We once had two real brothers. . . .'

The voice was Celia's; slightly higher than Pam's, and with a curious quality to which his ear had become instantly attuned.

'Yes. I know.'

'You were great friends with them, weren't you?' This was Pam.

'We were inseparable as kids. No, that's nonsense, of course, because we were constantly separated. We lived in different homes and we went to different schools, but all I know is that I used to long with all my heart to be told that I

508

was going down to Reve for the hols. If I asked to go, there would be ructions – after all, I suppose it's fairly rotten for parents if their kids so obviously long to go and stay with another family – but when they told me that I was going on a certain date, oh Lord, how I counted the days and the hours! Yet I can still remember the awful feeling of terror just before we got to Reve in case it had changed. Bowling along those quiet green roads and getting nearer and nearer to what I thought of as some sort of paradise, I'd suddenly start thinking supposing it's all different? Berry and Tommy mightn't be the same any more. They might have turned priggish or domineering – and I was always afraid that old Tom might have clambered out of reach up some sort of poetic Mount Parnassus, but nothing like that ever happened. They were always the same. They always came rushing to meet me, jabbering away as if we'd never been apart.'

'And then they were killed.' A flat statement by Celia.

'Yes.'

'In what they called the war to end all wars.'

'Oh dry up, Cee.' Pam kicked her sister's foot under the table.

'And now there's probably going to be another one,' Celia returned the kick.

'If there is, there's not much we can do about it,' Felix said.

'But we should *try*.'

'If Hitler's really determined to conquer Europe, we have two alternatives. One is to submit, the other is to fight.' Felix turned his blind eyes in Celia's direction. 'Which would you advocate?'

'I don't know – I don't know. I suppose I'd try and argue with him, try and persuade him not to.'

'And suppose he took no notice of you – just went ahead and invaded your country as planned? What would you do then?'

'What would *you* do?' He heard anger in her voice.

'Fight, I suppose.' He sounded weary. 'Provided I could see the enemy coming.'

'I'd hate them goose-stepping up the avenue at Reve,' Pam said. 'But perhaps old Cee wouldn't mind all that much.'

'Of course I would! I'd want to kill them! But all the time I'd be thinking here it is all over again. We've got ourselves trapped into killing each other and the – all the awfulness of – ' She clamped her lips tight.

'Shall I go and make some coffee?' asked Pam. 'I know where the kitchen is.'

'Dear Celia,' Felix said when she had left the room. 'They would have loved you, you know.' He found her hand and patted it.

'Would they really?'

'Although they'd probably have teased you.'

'Why?'

'Because you take life so seriously.'

'How can anyone not? Especially when you think of how . . .' Once again she suppressed the sudden impulse to tell him about Berry's death. Withdrawing her hand from his, she said, 'Perhaps I ought to go and help Pam.'

They turned to lighter subjects over coffee, and Felix suggested a walk in Regent's Park before the light failed.

Pam said, 'Oh, what a jolly nice idea,' and although Celia also quite wanted to go, something impelled her to say, 'Sorry, I can't. I've got an appointment at the British Museum.'

'An appointment?' Felix looked surprised.

'In the Reading Room.'

'Gosh, Cee, you never said.'

'I made it ages ago,' Celia said. 'So if you'll both excuse me. . . .'

She left them sitting there, still looking surprised, and she put on her hat and coat in the bedroom and let herself quietly out of the flat.

She had no idea in which direction the British Museum lay, but it didn't matter as her appointment was fictional. She didn't know why she had told the lie – she seemed to be telling quite a lot of instant and unpremeditated lies these days. Perhaps it was caused by a need for privacy without the bore of hurting other people's feelings, but there were times when it seemed as if these random, silly lies were all part of the darkly intricate pattern into which she was being drawn. It was strange, being a twin and yet feeling so far apart.

Purely by chance, she began walking in the direction of the West End. She reached Oxford Street and decided to turn right. She came to Marble Arch, and bare trees soaring over budding daffodils tempted her through the gates of Hyde Park.

She had never heard of Speakers' Corner, and curiosity overcame apprehension as she moved from one group to another, listening to the hoarse upraised voices of the chronically indignant. A man mounted on a stepladder urged his audience to renounce the demon drink, while a large loud woman in black exhorted a return to the bosom of Jesus Christ. But mostly the messages were of a political nature and seemed chiefly concerned with getting rid of people. Get rid of Chamberlain – get rid of Churchill – the Royal Family – the Jews – and then at last a small pale man with thin hair ruffled by the wind who said get rid of Hitler.

He spoke without raising his voice, yet the passion of his words seemed to carry far beyond the attentive half-circle of listeners.

'Hitler means war,' he said. 'He means to conquer the world and to spread his evil doctrine in place of all that is kind and good, loving and beautiful. There will be no more justice, no more mercy. Everything we hold most dear will be ground to dust beneath the jackboots of the oppressors . . . we must *fight*!'

'*Peace*!' cried a young woman in horn-rimmed spectacles. 'Join the Peace Pledge Union!'

It was suddenly marvellous to be among people who believed in things, who actually espoused causes, and she listened to them all with passionate attention and dropped sixpences in the collecting boxes of those whom at the time she considered most worthy. She even listened to a group of girls in funny green uniforms who were singing 'My

Saviour is My Loving Friend', but she didn't give them anything.

She was disconcerted when Felix asked how she had fared at the British Museum, yet something prompted her to mutter, 'Oh, fine, thanks.'

The instinct for secrecy seemed to be growing stronger.

The girls' visit proved one of unmitigated pleasure to their host, and after the first two or three days had passed he found himself thinking they must come again. They must come often.

Despite Celia's propensity for going off on her own, the three of them seemed to establish a domestic routine without effort, and now approaching the age of forty-one, Felix's attitude towards them was a happy blend of the brotherly and the avuncular.

By the end of the week he was also a little bit in love with them, and quieted his conscience (elderly blind men have no business falling in love) with the knowledge that it was a mere harmless fantasy. And it was obviously safer to fantasize about two women rather than one.

The idea of their twinship fascinated him, and he would ask how much alike they really were to look at. Were their eyes exactly the same colour, their noses precisely the same shape? Were they both the same height and weight, and if they were dressed alike did Aunt Liza and Uncle Dully really have difficulty in telling one from the other? And the growing love that he was still able to disguise as laughing light-hearted affection seemed to promote in them an answering glow. He could hear it in their voices, catch it in the little woolly draught of their dressing-gowns as they sped soft-slippered from the bath, and sense it lingering on the air after they had left the room.

He never had the slightest trouble in telling one from the other, for he had learned to read physical presence as only the blind can. Pam used a fresh lemony scented face powder, her footsteps were positive and unhurried, and her voice, a half-tone deeper than her sister's, was smilingly matter of fact. It could only belong to the girl who made herself quietly at home in the kitchen without upsetting the daily woman's self-esteem.

He didn't think Celia wore face powder; once, when he inadvertently put out his hand and touched her cheek, he had a quick impression of smooth firm shininess that brought back a memory of sun-flushed apples ready for harvesting in the orchards at Reve. And her footsteps were like her voice – quicker, lighter, less self-assured. They fitted the elusive, private quality of her.

'Tell me about Celia. Do you feel preternaturally close, for instance?'

'I don't believe either of us do. I'm awfully fond of the dear old thing, of course, but I don't think anyone can really get near to her.'

They were strolling in Regent's Park, Felix without his stick and with his arm linked in Pam's. On the lake the ducks were courting.

'And what's this passion for the British Museum?'

'Search me. I only know that she seems to feel things deeply and to brood a lot, but she never really tells us what about. I think she prefers her own company most of the time.'

'In the meanwhile,' Felix said, 'I can smell spring coming.'

'The willows are turning gold, and there's an enormous bed of wallflowers over there. Won't be long before they open and then you'll be able to smell them as well.'

Yes, spring was coming, and three days later on Sunday, 13 March, Hitler entered Vienna, standing up in the car with his right arm outstretched from the shoulder, his pudgy face set in a smile of triumph. Black-uniformed Storm Troopers drove in procession behind him, and Viennese lining the Ringstrasse screamed and cried for joy.

'At any rate, they won't take you,' Pam assured Felix with a matter of factness impossible to resent.

'Not unless they're really desperate.'

'But there won't *be* a war – the Austrians want to *be* Germans and it's no affair of ours!'

The growing tendency to regard war as inevitable increasingly exasperated Celia. Friends of Felix's who dropped in for a drink seemed unable to talk of anything else, while the government spoke of air raid precautions and the possible evacuation of cities in the event of a national emergency. Helpless and fuming, she broke the news to Felix and her sister that she was going to join the Peace Pledge Union, and when Felix said very quietly, 'Much good may it do you, old thing,' she retorted that she was at least doing something positive. People in London were as hopeless as the family at Reve.

She flounced out, and because the afternoon was wet, took herself off to the cinema in Baker Street. The film was an old one but she hadn't seen it before. Its innocuous charm both soothed and bored her, and she fell into a light doze and woke in time for the newsreel.

She didn't understand it at first, and when she did, she couldn't believe it. Elderly Jews were on their hands and knees in a Vienna street, scrubbing the tramlines. The whole cinema was hushed with shock, and a few seats away she heard a woman give an involuntary sob.

A very old Jew in a wide-brimmed hat paused in his labours for a moment and received the full force of a rubber truncheon. His hat rolled off as he doubled up in agony. The camera swung to his assailant, one of a group of uniformed Nazis. He was laughing, and so were the others. Then they all began beating the Jews, seizing them by their collars and raining blows on their heads and faces, then flinging them down like old rags among the overturned buckets. Helpless with terror and pain, the old men lay where they had been thrown, and the grainy flickering film picked out a woman applauding from a nearby pavement.

Dazedly Celia left her seat and fumbled her way out of the auditorium. She didn't know what to think, what to do. It was the first time she had seen the naked face of violence and it seemed to immobilize her senses. Yet the pictures continued to flicker across her mind: old men like Uncle Badger and Uncle Woodstock gasping and grotesque as they sprawled beneath the pounding rubber truncheons.

514

She hurried back to the flat, and Pam looked up from a book and said, 'Gosh, you look as if you've seen a ghost!'

'I have.'

She badly wanted to tell them, to describe what she had seen and to insist that they should go immediately to see it for themselves, but she couldn't. She also wanted to ask for comfort and reassurance, but for some reason that was equally impossible.

'What was it?' asked Felix.

'Oh, nothing.' She gave a quick, tight smile. 'Just a man who tried to follow me, that's all.'

No one said any more, and it was not until Pam went off to the bedroom to change that Celia remembered that they were going out to dinner because it was their last night in London.

She didn't feel like going out, then realized that it would probably take her mind off the newsreel. She wanted to forget it, to wipe all trace of those poor bearded and black-clad old men from her memory because she didn't know what else to do. She was as helpless and hopeless as everyone else.

'Did he really upset you – the man who followed you?' Felix was sitting opposite her with a large book open on his lap.

'What makes you ask?' Her voice was sharp.

'Don't know exactly. A sort of vibration in the finger-tips.' He removed them from the Braille he was reading and held them out to her. 'Come and tell them they're wrong.'

'Oh, Felix.' She darted out of her chair and made an ill-coordinated grab at his hands. For a wild moment she wanted to kiss them, to hold them against her face, but instead she half-squeezed and half-shook them before bolting from the room.

Both sisters changed into the dark silk dresses they had brought for evening; both put on their silk stockings and low-heeled court shoes; both wore their pearl necklaces, and in a sober suit brightened by a red bow tie, Felix escorted them to a small French restaurant in Wigmore Street.

515

'I wish I could see you both.' He was sitting between them at an alcove table.

'We both look utterly divine,' Celia said. 'Pam's painted her nails pink and she's wearing a navy blue frock with buttons down the front in which her pearls get entangled if she's not careful.'

'And what are you wearing?'

'Me? Oh, I'm wearing a bright, bright smile.'

'Yes,' he said, holding his hand close to the sound of her voice. 'I can feel the warmth of it from here.'

'Please do feel privileged,' Pam said. 'She only wears her bright bright smile once every seven years.'

'I like a girl who doesn't fling her bounty to the winds. . . .'

'Oh Felix, I'm so terribly, terribly glad you like me,' Celia said, flapping her eyelashes. 'I do want most awfully to be liked.'

'Shut up, you noodle,' Pam said, but the silly light-hearted banter seemed to be setting the tone for the evening. They ordered the meal – early asparagus flown in from France, then a delicate concoction of fish *en papillote*.

'Isn't that "little butterflies"?'

'No, stupid. Butterflies is *papillons*.'

'Are – not is. Try learning English before you tackle French. . . .'

Schoolgirl banter, sisterly teasing, with Celia's voice clear and bell-like, Pam's a deeper, rather husky chuckle, and sitting close to them Felix thought, Oh God, I do love them. I loved their brothers, and now I love them.

'I don't want you to go,' he said.

'Then come back to Reve with us.'

'Rather short notice for your parents.'

'Oh, they'd be pleased. Reve's a bit quiet these days.'

'Yes,' he said. 'I know.'

After the cheese they ended the meal with Alpine strawberries, and Felix insisted on a light sweet sherry to accompany them.

'Gosh, you aren't half pushing the boat out!'

'Might as well, while there's still time.'

516

'Will you really come back with us, Felix?'

Smiling, he shook his head. 'There are one or two things I must see to in town, but perhaps in a few weeks' time.'

'The flowering cherries will be out then.'

'And Merton's tree will be in leaf.'

'You could come and give a hand with the haymaking.'

'And stay on for the harvest. The farms have to take on casual labour these days, but Dad says when he first inherited there were two hundred estate workers. Do you remember when it was like that, Felix?'

'Yes,' he said. 'Nothing will ever rob me of my child's-eye view of heaven.'

'All your visual memories are a young person's, aren't they?' Pam said meditatively. 'And they ended when you were our age.'

'I sometimes wonder if colours are as bright now as they were then.'

He sensed that something was wrong a split second before Celia said in a small unsteady voice: 'It was just a waste, their being killed and you being blinded because it's going to happen all over again. It was just a stupid wicked waste and I can't bear it. I don't know what to do.'

'You can't do anything.'

'But somebody's *got* to!'

'Shut up, Cee,' Pam admonished in an undertone, 'everyone's staring.'

Felix knew that Celia was crying, although she was managing to do so in silence. He could sense the tears rolling down those smooth apple cheeks and read with his fingertips the hopeless grief that filled her as he surreptitiously tucked a folded handkerchief into her hand.

'I think we'd better go,' Pam said in a low voice, and he signalled the waiter.

They walked home – no longer jauntily arm in arm, with Felix in the middle – but with Celia alone in front, hurrying with bent head and her handbag clutched under her arm.

'I think she got a big squiffy,' Pam said. 'I'll help her to bed as soon as we get back.'

They crossed Baker Street in silence. It was late and the

streets were quiet; Celia had already disappeared round the corner.

They caught up with her outside the house; she was leaning against the railings, with her face uplifted to the lamplight. Her tears had dried and her voice was steady.

'Come on,' she said, 'let's go for a walk round the Inner Circle.'

'What – now?'

'Why not?' She looked suddenly jaunty and defiant. 'As Felix said – we might as well while we still have time.'

Time was also running out at Reve, but in a different sense.

Woodstock was now ninety-four, Badger ninety-two and Aunt Miriam a game eighty-six. Cousin Lavvy had died in Naples two years ago.

It was strange how old they had all seemed to Lizzie when she first arrived at Reve – the uncles could only have been in their forties – but now that she herself was on the verge of sixty she regarded their extreme longevity as unremarkable.

Bird, now tubby and bald, continued to minister to them: tucking in shawls, heating brandy and milk on portable spirit stoves and answering patiently and judiciously each feeble piping request.

And Reve itself seemed palpably older. Bereft of fifty per cent of its indoor staff – there had been no footmen for years – the great rooms seemed lost in sleep, the windows like closed eyes behind the drawn holland blinds. Brocades paled, silks thinned and split, and delicate plum-coloured bloom tinted the polished surfaces of cabinets, commodes and credenzas. Less than half the clocks were kept wound; whether porcelain or ormolu, marble or cloisonné, their voices were silent, their hands marking the last moment before slumber. The calm of old age suffused each corridor and hallway, and only two people struggled to resist its faded and exquisite charm, its invitation to everlasting sleep.

One of them was Edwina Hinton. Dying of cancer at Damperdown Farm, she continued to fight every attempt

518

to move her to Reve. Haggard with strain, Walter at first joined in the effort to persuade her, saying over and over again how nice it was of Lizzie and Dully to want to look after them both and how quickly she would get better once she got away from the fen damp and the old ague-ridden mists, but Edwina remained adamant.

The suggestion that she should go to Reve was the only thing that roused her from the silence of her empty days, and the nurse whom Lizzie had engaged all that while ago would try to restrain her wild arms – so thin and white now, and so unnaturally strong – and curb her hoarse agitation at the mere mention of the place. Perhaps the insidious tendrils of cancer were also invading her brain, yet her mind seemed extraordinarily clear.

'You're not taking me there! I won't go, and God'll see to it that you can't make me! Poor ole Netta was took there against her will – plucked like a daisy out of where she'd took root, and look what happened. The curse of Bessie Hinton followed her, didn't it? She died same as Bessie did – hanged by the neck and they all of them said it was an accident, didn't they? But that wasn't no accident, and the same thing ain't happening to me – nor to him over there. We'll both of us die in our bed same as decent folk. . . .'

Exhausted and choking, she would subside against the pillows stuffed with feathers from their own hens, and the London-trained nurse would think, If only she'd go to her daughter it would all be so much more hygienic. I don't suppose they have to boil the drinking water in a place like that.

Edwina died while the twins were staying with Felix. Lizzie was with her, and watched as the wild fenland sunset coloured the room in a coppery glow and her mother's lips relaxed their pale obdurate line and slowly reassumed something of their bonny country-girl sweetness. She held her hand, and when it was over laid it gently across the folded sheet, then put her arm round her father and led him from the room.

She arranged the funeral, inviting no more than a few nearby fen-dwellers who were her parents' friends, and

519

selecting a site in the churchyard beneath a solitary windblown ash tree.

'Make it a double,' Walter said. 'Don't reckon I'll be so long in follering.'

'Oh, Pa, don't be morbid.'

'It's not morbid to talk common sense. What's the point in paying out for two singles when I'll be along directly?'

'I'd rather hoped you'd come back with me to Reve. . . .'

'Make it a double,' Walter said, side-stepping. 'Me and your Ma bedded together all our lives and it's only sense that we end up in a double same as we always done.'

'But if you came to Reve you could still be buried with Ma when . . .'

'I'll stay here,' Walter said. 'It's where I know, and where I feel most easeful.'

So she paid off the nurse and saw her on to the London train. She filled the larder with tins of food, instructed the daily woman to notify her at Reve should anything go amiss, and left for home. She looked back once, and through the thin tangle of dying fruit trees the house looked like a brave old ship gradually slipping beneath the waves. In a few more years there would be nothing left of it.

She felt deeply tired in mind and body, and for the first time in her life the thought of Bessie Hinton began seriously to preoccupy her.

She still didn't believe in the idea that there was a curse – but neither had her mother until latterly. Poor old Bessie had been hanged, but then, according to the ideas of her day, she had deserved it. And that was that. The subsequent fate of first Johnnie Moon and then Aunt Netta had been mere coincidence.

Hadn't it?

Carefully offhand, she mentioned it to Dully, who reassured her that the three events were obviously un-related as they all sprang from completely different causes. Bessie was hanged because the law demanded it, Aunt Netta was hanged because of a tragic accident, and as for Johnnie Moon, he had hanged himself because the balance of his mind had been disturbed. It was superstitious nonsense to believe that there was any connection between the three.

'Yes,' she said, 'you're right. Of course you are.' And the small dark cloud of unease seemed to disperse. Warmed by the unfolding of spring, she gratefully allowed the beauty of her surroundings to re-envelop her.

And now that Edwina was dead, only Celia remained alert and hostile, and her hostility was based on hard fact.

The two weeks spent in London had had a profound effect on her, and that first impromptu visit to Speakers' Corner had impressed her not only because of the variety of views and theories so passionately expounded, but also because for the first time in her life she had felt part of a great mass of fellow beings, homogenous and yet marvellously diverse. In a life so far composed of Reve and boarding school, she had never rubbed shoulders with the broad mass of humanity and the experience both humbled and exhilarated her.

Walking in solitude through the crowded streets, she had stared into the oncoming faces and tried to imagine what it would be like to be the Prime Minister or the King or the Archbishop of Canterbury: to be someone who had the authority effectively to alter – for good or ill – the myriad anonymous lives flowing past her.

What must it feel like to be Hitler?

Boarding school had not equipped her with social or political awareness – modern history in the Upper Sixth had ended with the Second Reform Bill of 1867 – she knew nothing of the Russian Revolution or the Spanish Civil War except that they were considered regrettable.

The only war of which everyone seemed unanimously to approve was the last one; not for nothing was it officially designated the Great War. Of course, everyone said how dreadful and wasteful it had been, but the pride was there, all the same. In Whitehall she had watched elderly men surreptitiously raise their bowler hats as they passed the Cenotaph, and it brought back memories of the service held each November at the cenotaph on the green at Reve Magna.

521

Watched with sorrowing respect by the villagers, her father always laid the first wreath, and holding Nanny's hand she would spend the ensuing two minutes' silence in carefully reading the names engraved on the smooth white marble. Five Jessop boys, two lots of three brothers – the Watertons and the Carrs – and by the time she was ten she could chant the entire forty-seven names from memory.

Her own brothers were commemorated by a simple plaque inside the south door of the church. Tombs, monuments and memorials to past Dullinghams abounded in rococo exuberance and rhetorical Latin, but Berry's and Tommy's brass tablet bore nothing more than their names, their dates of birth and death, and the words *Pax Vobiscum*. Peace be with you.

But she knew now that there could be no peace; not unless somebody did something. She had known it since that last night in London when the three of them were so happy in the restaurant until the memory of the old Jew's humiliation had become fused in her mind with the squalor of Berry's death. It was all starting again, and she knew with certainty that the pain and the wickedness would grow and grow and ultimately envelop the entire world in an all-devouring conflagration unless somebody did something. Now. Once and for all. Before Hitler invaded Czecho-slovakia and Poland and France and everywhere, and then came over here and joined forces with Oswald Mosley and his Blackshirts and started beating Jews in the streets. She didn't know, but presumed that there must be Jews in England.

Fierce, ignorant, lonely and terribly in earnest, she began to ponder the best means of precipitating the crisis that would result in immediate worldwide action to get rid of Hitler and the Nazis. Impassioned letters to either Chamberlain or the Führer would do no good. Neither would a soap-box at Speakers' Corner or joining the Peace Pledge Union. It was too late for all that.

She remained taut with indecision until she read quite by chance that the Great War had been abruptly ignited by a single pistol-shot fired at a place called Sarajevo. And when she remembered about the courage of her ancestor Bessie Hinton, she knew that the last little fragment of her life's pattern had finally slipped into place.

A knock on the door.

A hasty reshuffle of cushions in the armchair. 'Come in.'

'You ordered afternoon tea, Miss Chester.' The chambermaid was dressed in brown, with *DH* embroidered on her cap and apron.

'Thank you. Leave it on the table.'

'Thank you, Miss Chester. Will that be all?'

'Yes.'

The tray was carefully set down, the silver twinkling in net-curtained sunlight, the milk swinging a white smile on the ceiling.

'Thank you, Miss Chester.'

The chambermaid withdrew, and Celia removed her hand from beneath the cushions where the Webley .45 lay hidden. She was in the penthouse suite of the Dullingham House Hotel, answering to 'Jane Chester', a name of her own invention.

It had all been remarkably easy. A letter written on Reve writing paper, stating that Miss Jane Chester would be a guest of the Countess Dullingham in the family suite for a few days, was presented by Miss Chester to the reception clerk, who presented it to the reception manager, who snapped airy fingers at a brass-buttoned boy to carry away the modest leather suitcase containing Celia's pyjamas and dressing gown, her sponge bag and a change of underwear and another summer frock. It also contained her brother Tommy's service revolver and four live cartridges.

That too had been very easy: a mere matter of waylaying Bird on the morning of the week he always reserved for dusting and polishing the contents of the small panelled room.

'Oh, Bird – sorry. . . .'

' 'soright. Come in, Miss.'

'Lovely day, Bird.'

And you got nuffink better to do with it than mooch

about like a lost dog, thought Bird. His duster licked between the ears of the old rocking-horse. 'Gonna cheer up for the Countess's fête, by the looks of it.'

'Oh, yes. . . .'

She wandered round the big central table stacked with her brothers' memorabilia.

'Which of them did the revolver belong to, Bird?'

'The Lieutenant, Miss. Captain Berry's was never found.'

'Yes. I remember now.' She fingered it. It was of polished black steel with a small wooden butt. 'Is it loaded?'

'No, Miss.' Bird applied a little wax polish to the worn red saddle on the rocking-horse. He buffed it vigorously, then added: 'There was four cartridges went with it, but I keep 'em separate.'

'I see.' She picked it up. It felt cold and heavy. 'Where do the bullets go?'

He glanced at her sharply. 'What you wanna know for?'

She shrugged. 'No particular reason. Just passing interest.'

She laid the revolver down again and Bird finished the rocking-horse in silence. Then he went over to the table and opened the drawer in one end of it. He took out a small box that had once contained Oxo cubes.

'There y'are.' He shook the four cartridges on to the palm of his hand. She came closer to study them.

'An' they go in there, like that. See?' He opened the breech and slipped a cartridge into one of the six chambers.

'I wonder how often he fired it?'

'No meanza knowin', Miss. Prob'ly not at all – he sounds to have bin a very kindly young gent.'

'But the thing holds six, doesn't it?'

'He probably give the other two away,' Bird said, with only a hint of sarcasm. He removed the cartridge and replaced it with the other three in the Oxo box.

'Yes. Probably.' She moved away, as if already bored with the subject. From the tail of her eye she watched him put the little box back in the drawer, then she laid the revolver back in its appointed place.

It was all so easy.

And the next step was equally so. She telephoned Felix at his flat and established during the course of casual conversation that he would be remaining at the flat for the next couple of weeks before coming down to stay at Reve. She then told the family that he had invited her up to stay with him for a few days so that she could go back to the British Museum to check a few facts.

'What facts, dear?' Her parents looked at her with mild surprise.

'Facts connected with what I was studying there. History and stuff.'

They continued to look at her, and sudden nerves prompted her to ask with unnecessary sharpness whether they feared poor old Felix might be tempted to seduce her without Pam as a chaperon.

'Of course not. Don't be silly.'

They asked when she was thinking of going, and she said, Tomorrow, Thursday, and Lizzie reminded her that she had promised to help at her birthday fête on Saturday.

'I'll probably be back by then.'

'Can't you be a little more definite? I'd counted on you to help with the white-elephant stall.'

'What about Pam?'

'Pam's organizing the children's sports.'

'Oh. Well – I'll try.'

'Do,' said Dully. 'We need you, you know.'

Yes, it was all so easy. So simple. And she half-loved and half-despised them for being so gullible.

Nevertheless, here she was on Thursday afternoon, sitting in the hotel that had once been her family's London home, sipping afternoon tea with a gun concealed behind the cushions at her back. Tomorrow she was going to kill someone with it.

On the following morning she left the hotel and took a bus to Liberty's, where she bought a new handbag, a big soft leather one that clipped shut at the top and fitted easily and comfortably under her arm.

She then strolled on down Regent Street, mingling with

the crowds and pausing every now and then to look in shop windows. No one would have taken her for a potential assassin. She crossed Piccadilly Circus and continued down Lower Regent Street to Waterloo Place. At the top of the Duke of York Steps she turned right, and her heartbeats quickened when she saw the three houses number 9, 8 and 7 Carlton House Terrace.

This was where he lived.

She crossed to the opposite side of the quiet little road and leaned against the railings. Plane trees hung over them from the private gardens they enclosed, and the stately cream-painted terrace stared back at her.

She was glad that she had come on reconnaissance because it was going to be more difficult than she had imagined. The place was so quiet, so deserted; only the banner flapping lazily from the balcony of number 8 gave any sign of life, yet she had an uneasy feeling that she was being watched.

She moved on past several large parked cars, trying to look unconcerned while she pondered the best way of approaching her target. Although she had studied the terrace on a map, she had somehow imagined that it would offer more places of concealment while she waited for him to appear. But the classical design admitted no extraneous detail – not even a pillarbox to hide behind – and it was impossible to contemplate climbing over the garden railings in full view of all those windows. Already their implacable stare was beginning to unnerve her.

She turned and walked back, and tried to imprint every fraction of numbers 7, 8 and 9 on her memory while giving them only a casual glance.

She returned to Dullingham House and ordered luncheon to be sent up, and in the meanwhile loaded the revolver the way Bird had shown her and placed it in the new handbag. It fitted beautifully, which was at least something achieved.

She returned to Piccadilly by Underground, carefully carrying the new handbag and its contents. Early afternoon calm lay over the broad expanse of Waterloo Place, and in

Carlton House Terrace sparrows chirped in the gardens behind the railings.

The banner still flapped idly, and as she strolled past, a curtain twitched on the first floor of number 7 and a man glanced down at her. She couldn't tell if it was him or not, but it made her heart thump. She walked to the end of the terrace, turned back and then propped herself against the base of the Duke of York's statue at the head of the steps that led down to the Mall, and began to read the book that had lain in the new handbag next to the gun.

The three houses now formed a very clear picture in her mind. The two at either end of the terrace jutted forward, leaving the centre ones receded behind a paved driveway and railings. Numbers 9 and 8 were the two end ones nearest the Duke of York Steps, and number 7 the first in the row of those set back. Staring blindly into her book, she couldn't for the life of her see any advantage to be gained from the houses' position; two sticking out and one set back didn't help in any way. All she could do was to remain in the vicinity and hope that he would either arrive or depart before long, and that she would have sufficient time to run up and shoot him at point-blank range.

Resettling herself, she tried to concentrate on the book while remaining alert for any signs of activity coming from the terrace. It was a very boring book about a married woman who fell in love with another man, and Celia found it difficult to understand how anyone could take an interest in that kind of soppy tripe when Europe was poised on the brink of another war.

At half-past three a large black limousine drove past her, and automatically her hand sought the gun lying at the bottom of the handbag; but it wasn't him. She knew his face from a photograph in the *Illustrated London News*. The man stared back at her gravely, incuriously, from the back of the car, and she thought, If only you knew, you bastard. If only you knew what's going to happen.

At four o'clock she returned to the hotel, heavy with disappointment and boredom. Nothing much seemed to be happening anywhere; even the West End seemed to be

527

taking it easy before the hectic gaieties of night.

She realized then that she should have planned more; she should have tried to establish his movements so that she wouldn't have to hang around for so long, praying not to be noticed. Going up in the hotel lift, she suddenly remembered the time she had run away from Reve and how Bird had tried to impress upon her the importance of planning. Poor old Bird. She wondered what he would say if he knew.

She kicked off her shoes and lay down on the sofa. The suite had two bedrooms, two bathrooms, and the sitting room was furnished with reproduction Hepplewhite and unobtrusive shades of soft pink and pale tea. She lay thinking about the times she had stayed here with Pam and her parents after trips to the pantomime or the circus or Madame Tussauds. She remembered the night she was smacked for pulling the arm off Pam's teddy bear, and the memory made her smile. This time she was going to kill a human being. How funny, she thought. Bessie Hinton, you're going to be proud of me.

She dozed, lying on her back with her ankles crossed and her hand trailing over the side of the sofa on to the new handbag. She would sleep for half an hour, then have a bath and put on her other frock before going back to Carlton House Terrace.

She was going to shoot him before he went out to dinner.

On the other side of the raked gravel below the south terrace at Reve, the remaining five gardeners were mowing and hoeing. Lilac and newly opened roses scented the air, and through the yew archway that led to the knot garden the male peacock spread its tail with a soft rattle of quills, while its mate plucked daintily at a tuft of grass.

The annual midday dinner and garden fête that celebrated Lizzie's birthday were always held on the huge expanse of greenward bounded by lake, house and woods. In the early days it had been for the sanctuary inmates only, but its scope had widened and now included all the families who lived and worked within the boundaries of the big house, whatever their age or station.

And now the big marquee was erected, its guy ropes taut and its pennant fluttering. The yards of bunting, once so bravely red, white and blue, had faded with the years to gentler tones. Dully and Pam marked the course for the children's races, while Lizzie supervised the stands for the flower show and deck-chairs for the inmates of the sanctuary.

'Can I have that table for the prizes?'

'No darling, it's for the white-elephant stall. Which reminds me, has anyone heard from Celia? She's cutting it a bit fine if she does intend to be here in time.'

'I'm sure she won't let you down.'

'Has anyone remembered about the ice cream?'

'I did,' Pam said. 'Everything's under control.'

The breeze dropped, the evening settled to a calm grey-blue, and down by the lake a heron flew homeward across the dying flush of the sun.

'We're going to have a fine day for it,' Dully observed, taking Lizzie's arm. They said goodnight to the men who had helped to erect the marquee and hang up the bunting, then walked towards the house.

'I do hope Celia won't forget,' Lizzie said.

Celia was positive that he would go out to dinner. Everyone did in London; particularly people in his position.

In a dark dress with a white Peter Pan collar, she returned to Carlton House Terrace at about seven. It was still broad daylight, and the lighted chandeliers in number 7 gave no more than a pale gleam through the closed windows. There was a lamp post outside number 9 and another outside number 8, but they were not yet lit.

She walked to the end of the terrace and it was so quiet that her footsteps sounded painfully loud. Returning, she saw that a large car had arrived in the paved driveway outside number 7. Her spirits rose. It was waiting to take him out to dinner.

She walked to the Duke of York Steps and propped herself against the old familiar ledge at the base of the statue. Lights were now beginning to twinkle in Waterloo

Place. She unclipped the top of the new handbag and her fingers closed round the butt of her brother's revolver. My brother, she thought. Well, someone's going to prove that he didn't die for nothing.

Hitler was now poised to invade Czechoslovakia. Everyone said he was going to. He was going to invade it as Belgium was invaded last time, unless somebody did something. Appeasement was a dirty word when your two brothers had been killed on the Somme. So she was going to do something; she was going to light the match that would set the torch ablaze. She was going to be the means of getting it over and done with now, quickly, before he overran the whole of Europe and then Great Britain.

Restlessly she walked back to the terrace. The lamps were lit outside the houses now and the banner hung motionless in the silver-grey light. The car was also motionless, driverless, and she leaned back against the garden railings, an indistinct blur against the dark trees and shrubs.

' 'evening, Miss.'

She jumped violently.

'Anything wrong?' The policeman looked down at her from beneath his helmet.

'No. I was just – wondering what the time was.'

Without haste, he extended his arm and then bent his elbow to reveal his wristwatch. 'Seven minutes to eight, Miss.'

'Oh. Thank you.'

'Waiting for someone, are you, Miss?'

She shook her head, then tucked the handbag a little more firmly beneath her arm.

'Then I'd get along home if I was you.' He was kindly, fatherly, and for some reason his presence brought her close to tears. She nodded without speaking, and began to walk with bent head in the direction of Waterloo Place. There was nothing else she could do.

Back at the hotel she dialled room service and ordered dinner for one to be brought to the Dullingham Suite.

'Yes, Miss Chester,' they said.

She slept badly, and when she did sleep it was to dream about old, black-clad Jews scrubbing the Duke of York Steps while crowds of people looked on and laughed. In one dream they were laughing at her, too, because she was proving so inept in the role of assassin. You gotta plan, Bird was saying. You gotta make preparations like you wos going to war. . . .

She woke at about five and crept into the sitting room, taking a blanket with her and making up a bed on the sofa. She watched the light strengthening and remembered that the tenants' fête was being held today. She decided to go back to Carlton House Terrace just once more, and if he still didn't appear she would take an early afternoon train home and, like a dutiful daughter, serve on the white-elephant stall.

How jolly appropriate, she thought. If anyone's a white elephant, I am.

She didn't want any breakfast. A drink of water from her tooth glass was sufficient, but she bathed and dressed with a kind of dreary care, took up the Liberty's handbag and went downstairs in the lift.

It was only nine o'clock, but the hotel seemed full of bustle and busyness, the reception hall a mass of hurrying staff and the foyer piled high with baskets of flowers. A giant roll of red carpet stood waiting to be laid and a trollyload of champagne glasses missed her by inches.

She paused, then stopped a page and asked him what was going on.

'A big reception this evening, Miss,' he said. 'The Foreign Secretary and lots of other bigwigs, and one of them's the German Ambassador.'

She dismissed him with a nod then quietly returned to her suite. There was no need to go back to Carlton House Terrace now.

'Bad news,' Dully said at eleven o'clock that morning. 'Miss Barton's been called away to nurse her mother and can't run the home-produce stall, and the vicar's wife's just rung to say she can't come either.'

'Why not?' demanded Lizzie. 'Part of the profits go to her ole man's church, don't they?'

'She appears to have met with a mishap,' Dully said, his eyes slanting with amusement. 'But I couldn't quite catch all she said because she didn't seem able to enunciate clearly.'

Lizzie grunted. 'So now that's three people who've let us down. Which reminds me, where's Celia?'

'Still in town, I presume.'

'Well, she shouldn't be. She should be down here helping.' Hot-faced, Lizzie recommenced shunting the long wooden forms in place before the trestle tables.

'Here, let me.'

'You don't know how I want them.'

'You're getting tired,' he said, 'and a little bit cross.'

'Only because I've too much to do.'

'Then let me *help*.'

'No.' She straightened up, massaging her back. 'If you want to do something useful, go and ring Felix and tell him to pack Celia off by the next train home.'

She was still busy in the big marquee where the dinner would be served when Dully returned, looking puzzled.

'I got hold of Felix, and he didn't know what I was talking about. He hasn't seen Celia since she and Pam stayed there together in March.'

They stood looking at one another in the greenish light.

'He must have done. She's gone to stay with him,' Lizzie said finally.

'It appears she hasn't.'

They remained motionless, searching one another's faces for a possible answer.

'Where else could she be?'

'God,' Lizzie said, 'I hope she hasn't run off with someone.'

'She wouldn't be such an ass.'

'How can we tell? Do any of us really know Celia?'

They found Pam putting the finishing touches to the hoopla stall. She looked mildly surprised, then said 'Poor Felix.'

'Why poor him?'

'Because he'll feel so responsible, won't he?'

'I'd better phone him and tell him not to,' Lizzie said after a slight pause. 'I mean, nothing can have happened to her, can it?'

The man arrived to set up the amplifiers for the music, and Bird came staggering along with a crate of beer. He told Dully that his two old gents were planning to put in an appearance during the afternoon, all being well.

'Splendid,' said Dully. Then on impulse asked Bird whether Lady Celia had said anything to him about her trip to London.

Bird looked surprised. 'No, Me Lord. She never said a word.'

Dully thanked him, and after a moment's consideration walked back to the house. He thought it might be a good idea if he waylaid Lizzie and they both had a stiff drink before the guests began to arrive.

The puzzle of Celia's whereabouts buzzed in his head like a fly.

The reception to be held at the Dullingham House Hotel that evening at seven was being given by the Council for the Promotion of European Fellowship, of which the Foreign Secretary, Lord Halifax, was President, and the guest of honour was to be Doctor Herbert von Dirksen, the German Ambassador.

So there was nothing to do now but wait. The mountain was coming to Mohammed.

She couldn't believe her luck; it was the first decent thing to have happened since her arrival, and now there was nothing left to worry about. All she had to do was to go downstairs and shoot him in the reception hall instead of hanging about the German Embassy in Carlton House Terrace. That was one place on earth she never wanted to see again.

Then triumph died, and for the first time she became filled with fear at the prospect of what she was about to do. To kill someone in cold blood was a terrible thing. She went

533

over to the dressing table and studied her reflection: rather round brown eyes beneath firm eyebrows, a straight nose with narrow little nostrils and a no-nonsense mouth. She swept the fringe of thick dark hair back from her brow and studied the result because she had read somewhere that all murderers had low foreheads. Hers wasn't particularly low, but then she was an assassin, not a murderer.

But whatever she was, her hands were clammy with fear.

Did you feel like this, Bessie Hinton? And what did you actually do – did you kill someone? I suppose you must have done, although Mother's never said. She doesn't seem to like talking about you – I suppose she's ashamed. But I'm not ashamed of you. You had a cause you believed in and you died for it. I'm proud you're my ancestor, Bessie. . . .

But the fear wouldn't go away.

She also felt rather sick, then realized that it was because she had had no breakfast. She still wasn't hungry, but as it was now a little after midday she rang room service for a pot of coffee and some biscuits, then suddenly changed her mind and on impulse cancelled the coffee and ordered a large gin and orange, twenty Craven A and a box of matches.

They arrived on a silver salver, and the chambermaid – one she hadn't seen before – called her Madam instead of Miss.

She had never tasted gin before, and for an incredulous second or two thought she was sipping eau-de-Cologne. Hurriedly she ate a biscuit, then turned her attention to the cigarettes. She had never smoked before either, except for one nauseating puff behind the games pavilion at school.

She lit up cautiously, and took a series of hurried little pecks at it. It didn't seem too bad – not as bad as the gin, anyway – then she realized from the lack of smoke that it had gone out.

'How fucking silly,' she said, remembering the word that Bird had once used.

She ate the biscuits, sitting on the sofa in the sitting room window. From there she could look down into the hotel courtyard, where all the bigwigs would be arriving at seven.

Six and a half hours to go.

Perturbed and unsettled by the two phone calls from Reve, Felix wandered through the Gloucester Place flat, lightly touching doors and pieces of furniture with his fingertips.

Why had Celia used him as an alibi? Why did she need one? What bit of girlish naughtiness was she up to?

He went into the sitting room and sat down by the open window, where a light breeze caressed his face. It was difficult to know what to do because he was uncertain of the gravity of the situation. Girls of almost nineteen were old enough to begin tasting the joys of independence, yet young enough to get into muddles. Neither Pam nor Celia struck him as particularly vulnerable, but it had to be admitted that their upbringing had scarcely fitted either for an early plunge into the outside world.

He sat listening to the tick of the clock and thinking about the time when they had stayed with him, and he remembered the sound of Pam's slow, slightly husky chuckle and Celia's higher, lighter voice with its quick, nervous intonation. He remembered her curious insistence that she should keep an appointment (with whom – what for?) in the Reading Room of the British Museum on that first afternoon, and the sudden suspicion that she had arranged to meet a bloke there instantly became a certainty.

She had often gone out on her own. Had he been remiss in not questioning her a little more closely about her movements? He remembered how edgy and upset she had been on that last evening when she had complained of being accosted. Had she tried to break with him and failed? He became more and more convinced that there was a bloke behind it all.

Restless, worried, and vaguely jealous, he collected his hat and stick from the hall and set off for the British Museum. It seemed a good idea, but by the time he had reached the vast and sonorous building and asked his way to the Reading Room, he realized how ridiculous it was.

Naturally they had no recollection of a young woman called Lady Celia Dullingham-Reve, and were therefore

535

unable to say whether she had ever visited the premises alone or in company with another person.

He thanked them and left, and outside in Great Russell Street a newsboy was shouting, HITLER PLANS AUGUST ATTACK ON CZECHS!

He returned home, and telephoned Reve to see whether Celia had returned. She hadn't.

No matter how hard everyone tried, Lizzie's birthday sit-down dinner and fête was no longer the glorious occasion it had once been.

To begin with, there were fewer guests than there had been in the old days. Several farmhouses remained empty, and despite attempts to modernize their cottages, estate workers preferred the new redbrick council houses on the main road where the bus to Bury St Edmunds passed the door.

And among those who were left and who continued to turn up each year, the atmosphere was subtly different. They enjoyed themselves, and were very civil, but the time-honoured thrill of coconut shies and bowling for a pig and shaking hands with Her Ladyship had worn a little thin by 1938, particularly when *Mutiny on the Bounty* was on at the pictures and you could get in for fourpence on Saturday afternoons.

Kitchen-maids now wore lipstick and had perms, and their small brothers and sisters would have preferred dodgems to donkey rides. Even the music wasn't quite right; no one wanted Gilbert and Sullivan in the age of Henry Hall.

But they made the best of it, and were loyal and good-naturedly indulgent to all of Them because they were mostly ancient now and because they were the end of the line. With the two sons being killed in the war there would be no more Earl Dullinghams, which was a pity but there you are.

Lizzie and Dully sensed how things were, and each year became a little more conscious of playing a part in a charade. Yet it was difficult to call a halt, to announce that

536

from henceforth there would be no more birthday fêtes or Christmas parties, in case it should promote the suspicion of apathy or lack of concern. That was a risk they were unable to contemplate.

'I believe they *are* enjoying it.' Lizzie indicated with a nod of her head the row of comatose old things from the sanctuary. 'And they ate almost as much as the younger ones.'

When I am dy-y-y-ying . . . thought Dully, remembering Uncle Badger's mock-mournful rendering in his old ebullient days. He looked at the dozing profiles, the work-knotted hands folded peacefully over their paunches and knew that it couldn't go on for much longer. We're all reaching the end of the line. . . . He hurried away to organize the tug-of-war.

Over by the fruit and vegetable stall, Lizzie encountered Miss Printemp, who played the church organ and was now manning the white-elephant stall. Miss Printemp told her that the vicar's wife had dropped her dentures in the washbasin that morning. They had broken in three places, which was why she felt unable to attend.

'But it's being a top-hole afternoon,' she added loyally, 'and their Ladyships are wonderful the way they work!'

'One is,' murmured Lizzie, and Miss Printemp gave a small whinny of embarrassment and said: 'But she seems to be everywhere at once, so naturally I concluded that . . .'

'Don't let it worry you,' advised Lizzie, and moved smilingly away. It was her Countess Dullingham smile, and it concealed her increasing disquiet about Celia.

It was a long afternoon, top-hole or not. By half-past five the judging of flowers and cakes and handicrafts had been concluded and the prizes distributed; Matron from the cottage hospital had awarded a five-shilling postal order and a knitted rabbit to the bonniest baby; the tea urns had been drained of their last nectar, and after being thanked by the vicar on behalf of all those present, the Earl and Countess gracefully withdrew. They walked away hand in hand towards the big house, and watching them go, people said what a shame it was that they were the last of the line. It was a shame, but there you are.

Pacing up and down the library, Lizzie said: 'We've got to think where else she can be.'

'There's only one place I can think of,' Pam said, 'and that's Dullingham House. Apart from Felix's flat, it's the only place where she can stay for nothing.'

Dully went over to the telephone, asked for the hotel number and waited. Lizzie sat down tapping her fingers, and then stood up again.

'I see. Very well. Thank you.' He replaced the receiver. 'There's a young woman staying in the suite but her name's Miss Chester. Who she is, I've no idea.'

'I don't know anyone called Chester,' Lizzie said, 'and who gave her permission to – '

'Did Celia have any friends at school called Chester?' Dully asked Pam.

She shook her head. 'She didn't really have any friends at all.'

Her father moved away from the telephone, then paused as Bird knocked on the open door, coughed discreetly and came in.

'Miss Celia – ' He looked pale, almost haggard. 'If she's not come back there's somethink I ought to tell you, Me Lord.'

'She hasn't.'

He told them that the revolver was missing, that it had been there the last time he swept and dusted, but now it was gone. And so were the four cartridges.

They looked at him in silence.

'What on earth would she want with a gun?' Dully said finally. 'She wouldn't even know how to load it.'

'I showed her,' Bird said in a small broken voice.

Lizzie gave a little gasp and Bird started to say something more, but Dully brushed past them both.

'I'm driving straight to the hotel,' he said. 'It's time we knew what's going on.'

Half-past six.

The hotel was warm and quiet and smelled of sweet peas and roses. The small string orchestra engaged to play music

538

of a non-assertive nature had arrived at the staff entrance, and the hotel commissionaire in grey top hat and tailcoat had supervised the placing of No Parking signs in the forecourt.

Doctor Herbert von Dirksen.

Lying on the sofa in her dressing gown, Celia studied the photograph cut from the *Illustrated London News*. A bald head, eyes that protruded slightly behind horn-rimmed spectacles, and a thin mouth dragged down on the left side by what could have been a scar. A cold, correct, bureaucratic face, and his death in an hour's time was going to precipitate the war against Hitlerism. A halt was about to be called to the spineless shirking they called appeasement, and it would all be over in a few weeks' time because all of Europe would rise up and join in instead of cowering about waiting to be invaded, and then America would come in on our side and we would win. And then the whole world would jolly well come to its senses and realize that no one's got the right to boss other people about or try to hog more than their fair share of things.

And Berry and Tommy would not have died in vain, after all.

To give her her due, she was totally devoid of egotism. She had no sense of personal importance and had spent none of the waiting hours in dreams of self-glorification. The idea that she had been chosen by God or Destiny to fulfil a momentous role in history never occurred to her. To assassinate the German Ambassador was merely a job that had to be done, and she had no need of anaesthetizing visions of martyrdom to lend her courage.

The fear and the feeling of sickness she had suffered earlier in the day had left her now. She was cool and purposeful and content to accept whatever punishment fate had in store for her. But she did feel slightly unreal.

She had poured the gin and orange away and deposited the cigarettes in the waste-paper basket. She had eaten nothing since the biscuits, but she had no sense of hunger or thirst, any more than she felt either trepidation or elation. There was merely a task awaiting fulfilment, and in the

539

absence of anyone better qualified or equipped she had decided to take it on.

At six-thirty-five, she went through to the bathroom she had been using and took a shower. She towelled her thick bob of hair then combed it into place so that it would dry neatly. Her two summer frocks lay across the bed and she stood for a moment in her camiknickers, debating which one to wear. She chose the dark one as being the most suitable for the occasion. Her hair was dry now, and she brushed it vigorously with the silver-backed brush that had a *C* inscribed on the back. She had no make-up to put on, but as a final touch fastened her pearls round her neck.

She was ready. The loaded gun was in her handbag. There was nothing left to do now but wait and watch for the arrival of the limousine adorned with the German pennant. And then go downstairs.

At that moment someone knocked briefly on the door, inserted a key in the lock and walked in.

Celia remained by the sitting room window, tense as a coiled spring.

'Oh, beg pardon, Miss – I didn't know – '

Celia stared at her in silence.

'I came to turn your bed down. . . .'

Something about Miss Chester's intense, hypnotic stare slightly unnerved the chambermaid. She hurried into the bedroom, folded back the counterpane and turned down the sheet. She drew the curtains, although it was still daylight, and turned on the bedside lamp.

'There, Miss. All ready for you.' There was no need to be frightened of a harmless young girl, for God's sake.

'Thank you,' Celia said, barely moving her lips. 'You may go now.'

The chambermaid withdrew, and Celia turned back to the window in time to see a slow procession of shining black cars drawing smoothly into the hotel forecourt. One of them was flying the German pennant.

She picked up the handbag and, closing the door of the suite behind her, began to walk slowly downstairs.

It was just six o'clock when Dully drove the Bentley rapidly through Reve Magna and took the road towards Newmarket. At sixty-nine he still handled a car with competence, and the empty country roads sang beneath the tyres.

Newmarket was blessedly quiet, and he swept on to the A323 that led to London. He knew the route very well: Stump Cross, Newport, Bishop's Stortford, Harlow and Epping; he sped through them all without noticing one of them. He only saw Celia – so like Pam and yet so different – and the fear that something was very wrong deepened with every mile.

He approached London through Tottenham, and at Finsbury Park drove into the first traffic jam. He sat hunched over the wheel, his lips tight. After three minutes he blared the horn; a useless gesture, but it relieved his feelings.

Glancing at the dashboard clock again, he saw that it was twenty-five minutes past seven. He had never done the journey faster, but there was no sense of achievement; merely a nagging premonition that time was of paramount importance.

And that he was too late.

At half-past seven the telephone rang in the library at Reve and Pam hurried to answer it.

It was Felix, asking if there was any news.

She told him no.

He asked if he should come down. Was there anything he could do?

Pam relayed the message to her mother, who was sitting huddled in a corner of one of the sofas. She shook her head.

'But thank him for me.'

Pam thanked him.

He rang off.

They continued to wait in a drab and wretched silence.

Celia continued to walk downstairs with the handbag's clasp unfastened beneath her arm. No one passed her.

It was a very grand staircase, with shallow marble steps

which the hotel had covered in royal blue carpet. She could remember peering through the gold-painted wrought-iron balustrade when she was quite small.

Coming to the curve which, once passed, would make her visible to the reception hall, she paused for a moment. Sounds from the string orchestra drifted up through the scent of flowers and mingled with the polite murmur of voices. They had arrived.

She smiled, and continued on her way, taking each step with a quiet deliberation and a calm grace a little at odds with her ingenuous ex-schoolgirl appearance.

No one noticed her, and she was able to stand motionless on the third step from the bottom while her gaze passed unhurriedly among the members of the Council for the Promotion of European Fellowship. They were all men. Most were wearing tails and decorations, but there was also a sprinkling of uniforms. They all seemed elderly, which didn't surprise her.

The Foreign Secretary, Lord Halifax, was standing in a prominent position on the red carpet and he was smiling and shaking hands with a man wearing a lot of gold braid. Her eyes travelled slowly to the right of Lord Halifax, and there he was. Exactly like his photograph: bald, spectacled, and with a thin mouth tugged downwards at the lefthand corner. He was wearing a broad sash across his white waistcoat and he was standing very erect and correct by a large gold basket of flowers.

Her presence continued to remain unnoticed and her right hand moved towards the mouth of the open handbag. It withdrew the revolver and she paused for a moment before raising it.

She fired. The recoil made her stagger and she almost fell backwards, while the noise of the shot all but deafened her. The sound was still hurling itself through the marble pillars when he fell.

She steadied herself. 'That was for Tommy. This one's for Berry – '

She fired again, and the shot ploughed into a waiter's upheld tray of champagne glasses. They exploded in a mad

542

twinkling prism and the roar of voices and the buffeting figures churning this way and that filled her with the first real sense of achievement she had ever known.

'And this one's for Bessie Hinton!'

She fired again, then threw Tommy's revolver aside and walked calmly down the last three steps towards whatever form of retribution lay ahead.

At least, the war would start now.

When they turned the body over, the hole where the bullet had entered the chest was considerably smaller than the place where it had made its exit. The back of his coat was soaked with blood that had flowed, a deeper crimson, on to the celebratory red carpet.

But it wasn't Herbert von Dirksen. Unskilled in the art of marksmanship, Celia had made no allowance for the revolver's kickback and had hit a Foreign Office counsellor instead. He was still breathing as someone with medical knowledge knelt to rip away his white waistcoat and shirt. Miraculously, the other two shots had hit no one.

They seemed extraordinarily slow to notice Celia.

'I did it,' she said for the second time.

Only then did a man with thick white hair stop gesticulating at someone else and turn abruptly to stare at her. '*You* hef *sshhot* him?'

'Yes. I just said so.'

For a second or two they all seemed to stop whatever they were doing in order to focus their attention on her, even the man kneeling by the side of the victim. Then someone rushed forward and grabbed her, and instantly the turmoil broke out all over again. Several more of them attempted to seize her, their faces hot and red with anger, and she felt herself being half-marched and half-dragged over bits of broken glass until they reached a smallish room containing an office desk and some filing cabinets. They thrust her down on a chair and she remained there, drooping and tiredly acquiescent.

She had made a mess of it. She had seen the German Ambassador alive and well and glaring at her as she was

543

hauled past. She didn't know who the man was who was lying on the floor; she only knew that he was the wrong one.

Sick with disappointment, she sat gazing at the floor while they surrounded her and barked questions in a variety of languages.

Wearily she told them her name, and there was a murmur of astonishment that she should be the daughter of Earl Dullingham. They moderated their voices a little and asked her what on earth had possessed her to do such a thing, and she asked them who the man was whom she had shot.

Never mind that, they said, *why* did you do it? What *made* you? Where did you get the gun from? It went on and on, then the police arrived, and then Lord Halifax stood in the doorway and asked if there was anything he could do, if not he would take His Excellency back with him to Downing Street. . . . He seemed the calmest of the lot. Perhaps that was why he was Foreign Secretary.

'God knows what the PM's going to say.'

'Has the ambulance arrived?'

'What about the press? The press *must* be kept out.'

She felt so very tired. Someone was holding her by the shoulder, pushing her against the back of the chair as if she might try to escape. His hand was burning a hot patch through her frock and she grimaced with distaste. She closed her eyes, and the hubbub went on and the hand that was holding her shoulder began shaking it, while a variety of voices kept saying *'Why? Why? You must answer. . . .'*

Then a little silence seemed to fall. She heard a single pair of footsteps advancing towards her, (Mr Chamberlain? The *King*, even?) Unwillingly she opened her eyes and saw her father standing tall and pale and tense with shock.

'What have you done?'

She moistened her lips. 'Shot someone.'

'Who?'

'I don't know.'

'Why?'

She was sick of hearing the word *why*. 'Because of Berry and Tommy.'

He looked as if he wanted to say something, but couldn't

544

find the words. A man in a dark lounge suit touched his arm and said quietly, 'Sorry Sir,' then helped Celia to her feet.

'Come along, Miss,' he said, and propelled her quite gently out of the room.

'May I come too?' she heard her father demand.

'Arrangements will be made for you to see her later, Sir.'

The man she had shot was no longer there, but she saw the dark stain on the carpet. The hall was full of uniformed police now, their boots scrunching over the broken glass. Another man in a dark lounge suit came up to them and showed Celia's escort the revolver. It lay on an outspread white handkerchief on the palm of his hand. Her escort nodded, and led her outside into the strained grey light, where police cars had replaced the earlier cavalcade and where a small knot of curious spectators had already gathered.

'For Christ's sake keep the press out until we hear from the Home Office,' she heard someone say as she was hastily pushed into the back of a big Austin. Her escort climbed in beside her and the car was driven rapidly away.

In a voice that was almost inaudible, she asked where they were going and he told her: Holloway Prison.

She remembered that she had left her pyjamas and dressing gown and her other things back at the hotel, and thought how stupid she had been not to have packed them in readiness. Then she realized that it didn't matter much anyway. She was too tired and too fed up to care.

Her appearance at the magistrate's court on the following morning was brief, the outcome predictable.

She was remanded for a week on a charge of attempted murder, and Dully and Lizzie watched her leave the court between two burly women in uniform. Her dark summer frock was creased and her face very pale, but she seemed quite composed; if she was aware of their presence, she gave no sign. She was driven back to Holloway.

They met Felix outside, and returned with him to Gloucester Place. Numb with confusion, they followed him up to the flat, where he poured them all a brandy, but the

545

ability to speak of what had happened and their fears of what was going to happen, seemed quite beyond them.

Lizzie excused herself and went to the bathroom, where she leaned her head against the cool tiled wall until the waves of sickness passed. She soaked her handkerchief with cold water, squeezed it out and then dabbed at her cheeks with it. She looked old and lifeless in the mirror (what a sad joke, Felix having a mirror), and she stared hard at herself, taking a sudden savage pleasure in the little lines and incipient wrinkles, at the greying auburn hair plastered close to her forehead by the heat and a tight-fitting hat. She was old and ugly now, and life had once more snapped shut on all happiness.

'I know nothing about legal procedure,' Dully was saying to Felix when she returned, 'and I can't imagine what the outcome of all this is going to be. Attempted murder's one thing, but if she's going to insist that she was out to assassinate the official representative of a foreign power – and Germany, of all countries she had to choose – God Almighty, she could end in the Tower!'

'But she didn't kill him.' Felix strove to sound comforting. 'And she didn't actually kill the other bloke either, did she?'

'He could still die.'

'I've a feeling he'll be all right,' Lizzie said in a half-hearted attempt to support Felix. She had never seen Dully look so ill with worry. At least, not since 1916. . . . Hastily her memory shied away.

Felix asked what Pam's reaction had been.

'As dazed and devastated as the rest of us,' Dully replied. 'We left her holding the fort.'

'The worst thing will be when the newspapers get hold of it.'

'No,' Lizzie said. 'The worst thing will be if the man dies.'

They sank into a profound and wretched silence, which Dully finally broke with an effort. 'We'd better be heading for home. Apparently there's nothing we can do at the moment, and they won't let us see her.'

'Can I come back with you?' Felix asked suddenly. 'I might be of some help, if only in a minor way.'

They said they would like that – that they were in need of all the moral support possible, and waited as he left the room to pack a bag.

'Dependable sort of chap,' Dully muttered, pacing the hearthrug.

They drove back to Reve, and Pam hurried across the great hall to meet them. 'Any news?'

They told her that the magistrate's court had been a mere formality, that Celia looked pale but calm and that she had been remanded in custody.

'Where?'

'Holloway.'

Pam shivered, and instinctively caught hold of the nearest hand; the fingers curled protectively round her own and squeezed them reassuringly.

'It's nice you're here, Felix,' she said, trying to steady her voice.

Although none of them was hungry, Lizzie ordered a light luncheon to be served in the summer parlour, and they were discussing the question of Celia's defence when Aunt Miriam appeared.

'Something is wrong, isn't it?' She looked from one to the other.

'Yes,' Dully said. 'You'll have to know sooner or later. Celia took it into her head to go to London and shoot someone.'

'Was it anyone we know?'

He shook his head.

'Did she kill them?'

'He was still alive when we left London.'

'Oh, the stupid girl!' Aunt Miriam sat down abruptly. 'Do we know why she did it?'

'She's saying she wanted to precipitate the next war, so she took a pot-shot at the German Ambassador – '

'According to the newspapers,' snorted Aunt Miriam, 'the next war is well on the way to precipitating itself, without any help from her.' She took out her handkerchief and pressed it to her forehead, then asked for a detailed account of what had happened. Dully told her all he knew.

She seemed slightly less shocked that Celia had attempted to assassinate someone ('As you know, I have never greatly cared for Germans') than she was by the fact that the attempt had been carried out at Dullingham House ('One should never foul one's own nest').

'It's no longer our nest,' Dully pointed out. 'We sold it years ago.'

'It still bears our name,' she replied.

They returned to discussing the larger issues involved, until Aunt Miriam, pale but apparently unruffled, said she would like to go and lie down for a while. Before she left, she asked Dully whether he proposed making some form of official announcement to the household staff. 'It's far better that they should hear it from you, dear, and not from village gossip.'

He did so early that evening in the servants' hall. He told them the facts as he knew them, simply and briefly, and resisted any temptation to make sentimental references to loyalty or old family ties. If they were there, there was no need; if they were not, no words of his could suddenly promote them now.

For their part, they listened in silence; the butler – who since the war had taken the place of the footmen – the maids, the kitchen staff and the three houseboys. Bird stood slightly apart, his gaze fixed unblinkingly on Dully's face, and when he had finished speaking was the first to leave the hall.

The others dispersed slowly, and not one of them had the heart to point out to His Lordship that the news had already broken in the stop-press column of the evening paper.

The next weeks constituted a nightmare that was only matched by the political storm brewing in the world outside.

Hitler's demands for the Sudeten regions of Czechoslovakia, which included all the country's chief fortifications, were becoming ever more insistent and his threats ever more violent. Only those who considered Germany a barrier against Bolshevism argued that Czechoslovakia should be sacrificed, and only those naturally inclined, like Celia, towards over-simplification demanded immediate and decisive action to smash Nazism. The majority of people merely wanted the problem solved quickly and painlessly so that they could get on with the ordinary business of living.

But as each day passed, the feeling of insecurity increased. Householders were asked to join civil defence classes and to consider turning cellars into air-raid shelters. Tension mounted between those who cried, *Make war on Hitler now!* and those who retorted, *What with?* and the word 'appeasement' was tossed back and forth like a shuttlecock. Peace was running out.

In the meanwhile, the Dullingham-Reve drama was the season's great gift to newsmen hungry for a human story to set against the background of international unrest. It had everything: a young girl (dark-haired and passionate in her beliefs): aristocracy (and many interesting parallels were noted between Dullinghams and Mitfords), and then there were the other two great essentials of violence and (with luck) death. All that was missing was sex, and in that respect what was not known was speedily invented.

Reporters swarmed up the great avenues of Reve, and when eventually their progress was barred, found their way without too much trouble through the perimeter walls and fences.

They prowled through the gardens and skulked on the terraces. They importuned the servants, who mostly preserved a tight-lipped silence, and the less they were told the more they fabricated. They discovered a rich vein of romanticism in the Dullingham preference for seclusion, and it wasn't long before they gleefully uncovered the fact that the Countess had been a Gaiety Girl. (*Recluse Earl's runaway romance with chorus beauty.*)

Their victims were spared nothing, either in cheap sensationalism or in the more unctuous impertinences of leader columns. They were stripped bare, and their only consolation lay in the fact that now it had all been said, they might perhaps be left in peace until the trial.

Then the Foreign Office counsellor's last flicker of life dwindled and died, and the charge against Celia became that of murder.

Miss Size, the Deputy Governor of Holloway, broke the news to her.

'Will they hang me?'

'Try to take one day at a time,' replied Miss Size, a noted humanitarian.

Nevertheless, she had to be moved from the comparative comfort of the hospital wing to an ordinary cell, and to begin with she was amazed by its littleness. Nothing in her life so far had prepared her for economy in living space. There was a black iron bedstead, a small wooden chair and table, and a mean window set in the thickness of the cream-painted brick wall. She paced up and down the strip of matting, listening to the harsh echoing clangour of prison life: the crash of iron doors, the rattle of keys, the stamp of feet along the iron galleries. Her short spell in the hospital wing had reminded her of boarding school – in fact, the hospital personnel had been more deferential towards her than the staff of her public school – but instinct told her that it was to be different from now on.

She was allowed to wear her own clothes and was treated with impersonal civility, but something in their eyes constantly warned her that she was remanded on a charge of murder.

Then Sir Peddimore Fowler KC, who had been engaged to conduct her defence, came to see her.

He was a tall and rather foppish man with nice grey eyes and smooth grey hair that looked as if it had been painted on. After the first few moments, he began calling her Celia, and removing a pad of foolscap paper from his attaché case, unscrewed the cap from his fountain pen and told her to explain precisely what had happened.

'Where do you want me to start?'

'From the beginning.'

She sat on the side of the bed with her hands pressed between her knees. 'There's not much to tell, really,' she said finally. 'I decided to shoot the German Ambassador because I think the Germans are going to start another war, so the sooner we get it over and done with the better. But I missed, and shot someone else, for which I'm very sorry. And I suppose that's all there is to it.'

'But why do you want the war to start now, Celia?'

'Well, before everyone's had time to stockpile masses of armaments so that it'll go on and on like the last one.'

He sat contemplating her with his nice grey eyes and asked her to tell him some more about herself.

She found it extraordinarily difficult. The facts had been recited in a couple of sentences; as for the rest, she had never had the slightest inclination to analyse her own feelings, or to indulge in bouts of self-dramatization. Since she was a small child, she had merely done whatever a combination of mood and instinct prompted her to do, and left it at that.

He asked if she was a Communist.

Surprised, she shook her head.

'Are you quite sure?'

'Yes, of course.'

'You see, it's quite possible to associate with people on a purely social basis without knowing anything about their political beliefs until you discover that they've rubbed off on you. Do you go to parties? Or perhaps to pubs with groups of other young people?'

'No. I live out in the country.'

'Ah, but you spent a week in London with a friend last March, didn't you, Celia?'

'You mean Felix Polperro? Yes, my sister and I both went.'

'And I understand that you spent a lot of time going out on your own without the other two. Are you sure you weren't meeting other young friends? All quite harmless, of course – having a drink and listening to their views on politics. Are you quite sure you didn't go to any meetings with them?'

'No – I've just told you.'

'Then what *were* you doing? How did you spend your time, if it wasn't in the company of other people?'

'I just – well, walked about.'

'Is that all?'

'I just looked at things and thought about them.'

Sir Peddimore laid down his pen and folded his arms. 'I'm afraid this isn't getting us very far, is it?'

Her lips tightened. 'In that case, I suggest you leave me in peace.'

Strong words for a girl of her age and in her situation. Very quietly he put the writing pad back in his case and replaced the top of his fountain pen.

'I think you're right. Goodbye, Celia.' He shook her limp hand and departed, wondering whether they might perhaps get away with a plea of diminished responsibility.

A few days before the trial, her parents were given permission to visit her. They were shown into a big bare room and allowed to sit opposite her at a scrubbed wooden table. A wardress sat by the door, gazing at her fingernails, but when Dully tried to grasp the prisoner's hand she noticed, and politely forbade it.

So they sat down in their appointed places with their hands in their laps, and both suddenly realized that during recent weeks they had been too preoccupied by all the worry and confusion to give much serious thought to the actual perpetrator of it all. It was just Celia being naughty again; Celia being an irresponsible idiot and a source of trouble; but now that they had come face to face with her in this harsh and terrible place, the effect was devastating.

It was made even worse by the fact that she still looked like a schoolgirl. Her brown bob of hair was combed smooth and straight, and her round brown eyes were candid and direct. But not so much of a schoolgirl now as an orphan, Dully thought, noting with compassion her prison-starched and crudely ironed summer frock.

They asked her how she was, and she said, Fine, thanks. She moved her lips with slow deliberation, as if she wasn't used to speaking much. She asked how they were and they said, Not too bad, all things considered, then floundered a little because they didn't want her to think that they were cross with her. Not now. Not any more.

They had brought her some books, a mixed bag of Priestley, Edgar Wallace and Pamela Frankau. They had also brought a tin of biscuits – 'Cook baked them specially' – and a few more changes of clothing.

'Not many, because you won't be here for much longer.'

'Won't I?'

'No, of course not.'

A short, helpless silence, during which the wardress shifted her position slightly and they heard the clink of keys.

'How are you getting on with Sir Peddimore?'

'He's okay. A bit bossy.'

'But you *are* helping him all you can, aren't you?'

Celia nodded.

'He's an excellent man. I believe he's hardly ever lost a case.'

'Oh. That's nice.'

Oh God, the indifference in her voice. For the first time they were almost tempted to wonder whether she was quite all there. They tried to smile reassuringly.

'Are you managing to sleep well?'

'Not too bad. Bed's on the hard side.'

'And what's the food like?'

'A bit like school, really.'

Hopefully they searched her face to see whether it was a joke, but there was no give-away twitch of humour.

If only they could have talked about the things that mattered, Dully thought, but it was impossible even to attempt it with the blasted wardress listening to every word. For a second or two he was on the point of trying to exercise whatever authority an earl might have in such a situation, then contented himself with staring hard and meaningfully at her in the hope that she might leave the three of them alone. She refused to meet his eyes.

'The fête went off well,' Lizzie said. 'The weather was better than last year.'

'And we've got four new foals. The latest one was born last night.'

'Did we tell you Felix is staying with us?'

'One of the maids has gone down with chicken-pox, of all things. Hope it doesn't rampage throughout the entire household. . . .'

'I'm afraid time's up,' the wardress said. She rose clinkingly to her feet.

The three Dullinghams sprang up, precipitated by overwrought nerves and a passionate desire not to let the side down.

'Thank you for coming. Goodbye,' Celia said, then suddenly gave a long harsh cry, and Lizzie banged violently against the table leg in her haste to reach her. Like two magnets, mother and daughter flew together, and Lizzie wrapped the shaking, sobbing girl in her arms and rocked her to and fro.

'I've made such a mess of everything – I'm sorry.'

'It's all right darling, it's all right.'

'I'm so frightened.'

'Don't be, my darling, ole Mums is here.'

'But they'll hang me – they're going to *hang* me!'

'They won't! They won't!' Hysterically, Lizzie sought to hold Celia, not only in her arms but with her hands – cupping her head and pressing it close against her breasts, then seizing her shoulders with fingers grown hard and violent with terror. Dully was there too, trying to encompass them both in a futile effort to shield and protect, then the wardress came over and with heavy obdurate movements began to wrench them apart.

It was a ludicrous scene, pitiful in its agony and farcical in its clumsiness. Lizzie and Celia were both screaming, and Dully stopped holding them and tried to pull the wardress away. She was a big woman and she thrust him back against the table so heavily that he almost fell. Above the screaming he heard the sound of running footsteps, then the door burst open and it was all over.

Lizzie and Celia were separated, and Celia was taken away by another wardress. She went with a new, heartrending meekness, her head bent, and the wardress had her arm round her in a kindly fashion. The books, the biscuits and the clothes remained abandoned on the table as Dully, ashen-faced, led his weeping wife away.

And that was when the final horror began.

After almost nineteen years, Celia had at last burst into their lives with a sudden personal impact that shattered them. It was as if that desperate physical contact between mother and daughter – one previously so lukewarm, the other so listless – had ignited a wonderful soul-warming fire that was about to be brutally extinguished.

Made desperate by this abrupt and frenzied contact, Lizzie found herself driven at last into the ghostly presence of Bessie Hinton. She had never really believed in the superstitions that had clung to her throughout the years; she had ignored them, played with them, derided them and fought them, but now she could fight no longer. Johnnie Moon, Aunt Netta, and now Celia.

She knew it was true. She believed now in the power beyond the grave, and in the wicked strength of a curse uttered by a condemned woman.

Back at Reve, she collapsed on her knees by the side of her bed and tried to pray, but the words wouldn't come. She hadn't had enough practice. For her, praying had always been a matter of discreetly mumbled responses at weddings, christenings and funerals. Now she was trying to reach God in a hurry, to grab at the hem of His nightgown and tug it imploringly: It's Lizzie here and I'm sorry, so sorry, I meant to get in touch earlier but somehow there's never been time. (And in any case, I haven't had all that to get chummy about, have I? What about my sons? My two lovely sons aged seventeen and eighteen?)

Not surprisingly, He didn't answer.

She couldn't get the memory of Celia out of her mind: the nape of her neck as she was led away – pale, childlike and vulnerable, with the bobbed hair parted a little as her head sank forward in weary despair. And now she was passing from her as inexorably as the boys had done. The waste of it

555

all – the waste of love and the sheer sad and bloody uselessness of it all made her start sobbing again.

'Mother keeps telling me about her great-grandmother being hanged during some sort of riots at Ely – I'd heard her mention it before, sort of jokingly, but now she's got the idea that she laid a curse on us all from the scaffold.'

'Do you believe it?'

Pam thought for a minute, then said: 'Well, no. I don't see how anyone could, unless they believe in the occult and all that caboodle.'

She and Felix were sitting in deck-chairs on the south lawn. There had been no rain for three weeks and the flower gardens wore a parched, exhausted look. The whole world was parched and exhausted with worry; Celia awaiting trial on a murder charge and Lord Runciman in Prague trying to effect some kind of face-saving agreement between Czechs and Germans over the Sudeten problem. If Hitler invaded Czechoslovakia, Russia and France were formally committed to go to her aid, and if France went to war with Germany, Great Britain was once again formally committed to aiding France. And we weren't ready. Lord Runciman therefore had the task of persuading the Czechs to surrender the Sudetenland while appearing to preserve an air of impartiality.

'I sometimes think it would be nice to believe in something,' Felix remarked.

'Don't you believe in us?'

'You and me, you mean?' It was a relief that he couldn't see her sudden healthy schoolgirl blush. 'Oh, no one could help but believe in *us*! We're real and solid and sensible as a couple of old gateposts. I just wish that the Hitlers and Stalins and Chamberlains were a bit more like us.'

'I believe in Celia,' Pam said. 'Although heaven knows why.'

'It's her cock-eyed integrity. It gets me, too.'

'Oh Felix,' she said abruptly. 'Will they really – I mean. . . ?'

'No one will know until the judge's sentence.'

He heard the slight rustle of her frock as she stood up, and he sensed that restless misery was driving her on another fruitless ramble over the parkland. It was the same for all of them. No one could settle in one place for long.

'Can I come too?'

'Yes, of course.'

'Are we going anywhere in particular?'

'We could go and see the foals, if you like,' she said. Then added: 'Don't bother with your stick, you can take my arm.'

They walked in silence to the home paddocks, and when one of the foals trotted over with its dam, Pam guided Felix's hand to its soft enquiring nose. She described it to him, simply and naturally, and her words seemed to imprint a sudden glowing image on the fathomless darkness of his world.

Celia's trial took place at the Central Criminal Court, otherwise known as the Old Bailey, on Monday 15 August. Because of the extreme seriousness of the indictment, the court was sitting during the long vacation.

The press and the general public were both well in evidence, and Dully hurried Lizzie and Pam past pointing cameras and waving notebooks. They also saw Sir Peddimore for a few minutes, and he told them that Celia had finally promised to co-operate over the vital point of whether she had gone to Dullingham House with the sole intent of shooting the German Ambassador, as opposed to brandishing a gun as a form of intimidation. He hoped for a conviction of manslaughter.

'Try not to worry,' he said.

There was a buzz of interest in the public gallery as the three of them took their seats, Lizzie wearing a black hat with a deep protective brim. She sat between Dully and Pam, and tried hard to pretend that she was at the theatre, watching last-minute preparations before curtain-up. But in this play the male lead was a High Court judge, and playing opposite him was her daughter.

She became conscious that Dully was squeezing her hand

557

as Celia was led up the steps to the dock by a policewoman. She was wearing a navy blue coat that Lizzie couldn't remember seeing before – surely it wasn't her old school coat? – but for the rest she looked neat and tidy, and blank as a glass of water.

The proceedings opened with the indictment read out by the clerk, and when he had finished he looked hard at Celia: 'How say you, guilty or not guilty?'

'Not guilty.' Her voice was barely audible.

The jury was sworn in and the trial began, unrolling itself in stately language honed to a fine legal precision: words biting like scalpels, probing like a lancet, and rising in the still air in carefully controlled, simulated passion. For Lizzie, the black-gowned figures had a curiously birdlike appearance; a field of crows, she thought waiting to peck someone's eyes out. Celia's eyes.

She steeled herself to look at her again, and she couldn't believe that this was really happening. Sheer incredulity made her feel suddenly faint and she closed her eyes. She sensed Pam glancing at her, and tried to give her a little smile of reassurance.

The counsel for the prosecution was a large man with bulldog jaws and gold spectacles balanced on a small rubbery nose. He examined hotel staff from Dullingham House, and they identified Celia as the Miss Chester who had stayed in the Dullingham Suite. Had they not recognized her as Lady Celia Dullingham-Reve? The two chambermaids said no, the suite had not been used by the family during the time they had been employed, and the hotel manager, who normally welcomed them personally upon arrival, had been away on holiday. The reception manager had seen no reason to query the letter presented to him on writing paper bearing the family crest. It was established that Lady Celia had last stayed in the hotel with her family four years ago, when she would have been fourteen years of age.

They then came to the question of the revolver, and Celia's head jerked sharply when she heard Bird's name called. He marched into the witness box, very pale and polished, and took the oath. He admitted that he had shown Celia how to load the Webley, but when charged with dereliction of duty for not keeping an offensive weapon under lock and key while in his care, retorted that the gunroom at Reve bristled with offensive weapons, and that the door was hardly ever locked these days because the family had no interest in killing either things nor people.

He was asked to stand down, and he gave Celia a hard fierce stare of allegiance as he passed.

The court adjourned for lunch, and Dully asked whether they would be allowed to see Celia. They said no, My Lord, very politely and reluctantly, so the three of them took a taxi to a small restaurant in Chancery Lane. Lizzie couldn't eat anything because she kept seeing mental images of Celia being given a lump of bread and some stew in a cell. They began to think that people were staring at them, so they left. They took another taxi, and asked to be driven along the Embankment (or anywhere the driver liked), provided they returned to the court for the afternoon session.

They had thought that it would be over that day, but it wasn't. It dragged on and on, with Celia in the same dark coat and blank expression in the dock, and the jury, all men, sitting in a row and occasionally glancing at each other with what seemed like worrying significance.

The time came for Celia to be called. With large pink hands gripping the front of his gown, counsel for the prosecution began by asking what political organization she belonged to. She shook her head, and the judge stirred into life and asked her to speak up. She said that she didn't belong to any.

Had she ever in the past belonged to any?

No.

He suggested that she had joined a group of Bolsheviks, but before she could reply Sir Peddimore jumped to his feet in protest.

The protest was upheld.

The prosecution switched tactics. 'I believe you had two brothers?'

'Yes.'

'Two brothers whom you never met because they died in the war?'

'Yes.'

'Would it be true to say' – he gazed towards the roof – 'that during the course of your childhood these two brothers – these two brave young men who laid down their lives in what has become known as the war to end all wars – became your heroes?'

Celia made a little movement that was half-nod, half-shrug, and was again requested to speak up.

'Yes. In a way.'

'Yes. In a way.' His gaze remained on the roof. 'And would it be true to say that as you grew older, this hero worship, this simple child's adoration of two by now legendary young men, was beginning to turn from love to envy?'

'No.'

'Because you were by now becoming aware that you were not alone in adoring them. That other people adored them too. Your mother and father, for instance?'

'No. Well, I knew they – '

'And as you grew towards adulthood I suggest that you become filled with the idea that, no matter how hard you tried, you would never quite measure up to them. You were a girl, and not a boy. They were handsome and brave and beyond reproach. You were . . . merely you. They were dead, and you were alive, and subject to criticism.'

'No. . . .'

A rustle of agitation ran through the court. Lizzie sat with her gloved hand pressed tight against her mouth.

'I therefore put it to you that hero worship turned to envy, and that in your jealous desire to compete with your dead brothers you decided to assassinate a public figure coming from the race that had once been your brothers' enemy. In other words Doctor Herbert von Dirksen, the German Ambassador to the Court of St James!'

Celia raised her bent head. She looked across the court and met her father's eyes. Their eyes seemed to lock together, and he dared not blink in case he cut off the beam of courage he was trying to send her.

She looked away; then seemed to settle her shoulders inside the navy blue coat a little before saying in a small clear voice: 'It's not true. I didn't.'

The court adjourned, and while Pam met Felix for a drink and a sandwich, Dully and Lizzie took another taxi ride. He offered her the first nip from his flask of brandy and remonstrated mildly when she took two asprin with it.

'You'll make yourself ill.'

'No, I won't. Oh, but Dully . . .'

'I know, dear. I know.'

Their inconclusive whisperings seemed like a small antidote to the endless thrust and parry of the courtroom.

'But she's bearing up well, isn't she?'

'She'll come through. Just you see.'

'Are you sure, Dully?'

'I'm absolutely certain.'

The taxi drove back over Waterloo Bridge and along the Embankment to Blackfriars. They crossed Ludgate Circus and for a last moment clung speechlessly together in the privacy of the back seat. Then Lizzie straightened her hat, hastily powdered her nose and told herself, Of course she'll be all right. Dully's said she will, and he *knows*.

Although the examination by counsel for the defence was by comparison a far more muted and compassionate affair, Celia seemed to encounter more difficulty in answering. Perhaps, thought Pam, it's because she's always tended to thrive on conflict.

Courteously Sir Peddimore led her through his own romanticized version of the shooting, and when he asked the final question, 'Did you or did you not intend to kill Doctor Herbert von Dirksen?' she remained silent for a long moment.

Scarcely breathing, Lizzie saw her hands gripping the edge of the bar. Then she raised her head and replied wearily: 'No. I didn't intend to kill him.'

It was as if she had just been robbed of her last shred of self-esteem.

The concluding speeches were made to a packed court, and if the prosecution presented Celia as a jealous, embittered and cold-blooded revolutionary ('. . . and in a country that has no place for the callous assassin, I demand a verdict of guilty . . .') – Sir Peddimore seemed equally determined to portray her as a kind of fantasizing half-wit.

'. . . and this young girl, a daughter of one of our oldest and most distinguished families, reared in aristocratic seclusion away from the common rough-and-tumble of the ordinary world, is guilty of no more than a very laudable and natural anxiety relating to the times in which we live. Have *none* of us shared her anxieties relating to our troubled era? Have *none* of us dreamed of finding a solution to the problems that would seem to surround us on all sides? Have *none* of us, even momentarily and in moods of special foreboding, *ever* been tempted to imagine that we alone know the answers to these same problems, and then go one step further and imagine ourselves taking the law into our own hands? Of course we have. But with most of us, these dreams remain securely locked away in the imagination, out of harm's way. It is only in the case of a young girl like Lady Celia Dullingham-Reve, gently born and reared in an atmosphere of exclusiveness, that these dreams can appear capable of fulfilment. Sensitive, lonely, solitary . . . living in a private world of historical beauty, it is only too easy for these dreams to proliferate. . . .'

It sounds as if I've never existed, thought Pam.

Sir Peddimore's golden rhetoric rolled on. He described Celia's dreamlike state as he took her brother's gun to Dullingham House; how she remained there in a solitary, self-induced trance until she heard quite by chance that Doctor Herbert von Dirksen would be attending a function there. He explained that her visits to Carlton House Terrace had all been part of the fantasy, and defied anyone present to swear that at no time in their lives had they ever walked past – nay, even *lingered* outside the house of some particular notable, whether a king or a film star or a politician.

No one answered. No one stirred. Even the London traffic seemed mute.

He described Celia's increasing withdrawal into the world of make-believe. He reminded them that she had eaten nothing for more than twenty-four hours, then led them step by step on the somnambulistic journey downstairs to the hotel foyer. He told them how she had removed the gun from her handbag, and only as her finger closed upon the cold steel did she suddenly awaken to reality. Shocked and confused, her fingers instinctively tightened on the gun and it went off, accidently injuring a Foreign Office official who – let it be clearly understood – was standing some ten feet away from Doctor von Dirksen.

'A bizarre and outlandish accident that ended in tragedy – yes,' Sir Peddimore finally concluded. 'But a deliberate and cold-blooded murder committed by a dangerous and cold-blooded fanatic – no. Never.'

He sat down with the air of a man who has done his very best, and drank a glass of water. The court was adjourned until ten o'clock the following morning.

The judge, who had previously presented a wizened, motionless figure huddled in a red robe, now stirred into life. He arranged and then rearranged the papers in front of him, whispered briefly to his clerk, coughed, and then began the summing-up.

He had presided at many criminal trials, picking a solitary path through forests of conflicting evidence and bogus alibis with an impassive skill. For the past twenty years he had been known as the Graven Image; a soubriquet that didn't entirely displease him.

Now, staring across the court at him, Dully wondered how much his judgement would be influenced – either deliberately or unconsciously – by the political implications involved. He felt sure that the Cabinet must be keeping a close watch on the proceedings, and tried not to imagine that attempts had probably been made to exert a little quiet pressure on the forthcoming verdict.

Nothing had appeared in the press about Doctor von Dirksen's – or any other guest's – reaction to the shooting, but details would almost certainly have reached Germany via the diplomatic bag. Hitler probably knew all about it, and was merely awaiting the outcome of the trial before turning the whole ghastly business to his own political advantage.

God alone knew where it would all end, Dully thought, and continued to stare with haggard intensity at the row of men who held his daughter's life in their hands.

The summing-up took over an hour, and the three Dullinghams strove to read the slightest hint of bias towards guilty ot not guilty in each carefully measured statement that fell from the dry lizard lips. He began by dealing with the law, and impressed upon the jury that they must be sure of the guilt of the accused before they convicted her. He referred to the crime of murder and described how it could be distinguished from manslaughter, and after warning them that their judgement must be swayed neither by sympathy for the accused nor by prejudice against her, led them back over the case step by step. He made reference to the political considerations, while taking care not to go outside the evidence or arguments of counsel, and ended by reminding them of the gravity of the issue they had to decide and the solemnity of the oath they had taken to return a true verdict according to the evidence.

Then the court rose, and although Lizzie tried to catch Celia's eye with a bright and encouraging smile, she stared back as if they were total strangers, before being led from the dock.

The crowds outside the Old Bailey surged forward and police had to clear a pathway through them. White-faced, Lizzie clung to Dully's arm as a girl in a pink frock suddenly darted up to her and asked for her autograph.

They drove to Felix's flat, and Dully tried to persuade Lizzie to eat.

'Come on, you must. Just to please me.'

'I can't, I can't. I think I'm going to faint.'

Felix gave her a brandy while Pam loosened the neck of her blouse and smoothed the thick grey hair from her forehead. Pam had borne up well, but the sight of her parents' bloodless faces and haunted eyes was suddenly too much. She burst into tears, and Felix put his arm round her shoulders and held her close, without saying anything.

He returned with them to the Old Bailey, and during the long wait that ensued, Lizzie and Dully asked repeatedly whether they could see Celia. The request was again refused, and they went on waiting in the small private room furnished with leather chairs and a few copies of *Sporting Life*.

At four o'clock they were given a tray of tea. In numb silence they listened to the muffled sound of traffic in the world outside. The ordinary world, Lizzie thought. We'll never belong to it again, after this. Even Reve itself will never be the same.

They were back in their places as the jury filed in. Celia, with a different policewoman in attendance, stroked her hair down with her hand.

The foreman of the jury wore a blue suit and a stiff collar. His hair shone with brilliantine beneath the wan lights.

On behalf of his fellow jurors, he was asked whether the verdict had been reached. He said that it had. He was asked whether the verdict was guilty or not guilty.

'Guilty,' he said.

That was on 21 August. Application was made to the Court of Criminal Appeal and a temporary stay of execution granted. After that, there was nothing further to be done until the date of the appeal.

They returned to Reve an hour or so before Lord Runciman returned to London from Czechoslovakia. Gentlemanly persuasion had failed, the Sudetens wrecking each tentative approach towards agreement with ever more outrageous demands. Fresh concessions were offered, but on 12 September Hitler made an emotional speech at Nuremberg, during which he promised the Sudetens the support of the German army if their claims were not met in full.

It looked as if war was imminent without any help from Celia, and on the 15th Mr Chamberlain, the Prime

Minister, flew to Berchtesgaden for his first meeting with Hitler. It was also the first time he had been in an aeroplane, and he took his umbrella with him.

In appearance the condemned cell at Holloway Prison was much the same as all the others, except that it was conveniently placed for the execution shed.

It had the same iron bedstead, the same small table and an identical strip of matting. But it had an extra chair, and across the corner by the window a little triangular shelf. On it stood a glass vase of flowers and a photograph of Lizzie and Dully taken with the boys when they were small. Tommy was wearing a sailor suit and Berry an Eton collar and breeches that buttoned below the knee, and they were all facing the camera with expressions of carefully assumed gravity. Sometimes when she lay on her bed looking at it with her cheek on her hand, she could almost hear the suppressed sounds of laughter.

It was a world she had never been able to enter; it had vanished before she was born.

Her parents had been allowed to visit her once, and this time she had not broken down; partly for fear of demolishing her own knife-edge composure, but also because she felt herself to be drawing further and further away from all relationships.

Perhaps she had always loved the boys best – or, at least, her imaginary version of them – and if that was really so, there was no reason for her to fear dying. She didn't believe in heaven; merely in the fact that she would have more in common with them once she was dead.

The prison chaplain visited her and asked if she would like to pray. She said no, not really, thank you, so they got on to the subject of Reve, and he said he had heard it was one of the finest examples of Flitcroft's work in the country. It must be marvellous to live in a house like that.

'Yes,' she said. 'I suppose it was.'

He pulled himself up pretty sharply then, and took her hand.

'My dear,' he said, 'there's still hope.'

566

From suppertime onwards, a wardress used to come and sit with her. Four of them took it in turns and encouraged her to play dominoes and ludo with them, and it was their presence – kindly, lumbering and faintly worried – that somehow brought the full significance of her situation into focus.

Like Bessie Hinton, she was going to be hanged. And in the meanwhile they had removed her own clothes and substituted garments without belts or tapes in case she tried to make a noose and beat the hangman to it. She was not allowed a knife and fork, only a spoon, and whenever she was alone she was constantly aware of an eye watching her through the spyhole in the door.

She didn't particularly mind the thought of dying, but she wished they hadn't persuaded her to deny any intention of killing the German Ambassador. She still wished she had killed him, because of Berry and Tommy.

She couldn't help feeling that she had let them down.

Without telling anyone, Felix typed a letter to the Governor of Holloway asking whether, as an old friend of the family, he might be allowed to visit Celia.

She haunted him. Not merely because of her predicament, but because he had now begun to realize more and more clearly that she didn't really belong anywhere; the sense of lonely alienation must always have been there, and the attempt on von Dirksen's life had been a childish and desperate attempt to establish herself in some kind of role. What happened after that was of little consequence to her because she had always considered herself doomed.

He wanted to talk to her, to try to help her in some way before it was too late.

Although Pam had been more often and more recently in the flat, it was Celia's presence that clung to it. Her voice, her footsteps, her odd sunshine-and-showers personality. He brooded about her using him as an alibi during her stay at Dullingham House; he wanted to believe that it was because she trusted him, but feared that it was no more than the first slapdash scheme that came to hand. Personalities

567

didn't come in to it, although he realized now, of course, that there hadn't been another chap involved. (*Another chap. . . ?*)

Restless with nerves, he remained at the flat, waiting for a reply to his letter. Explaining his disability, he had asked if they would kindly telephone their decision, but the phone remained silent for two days. On the third day the Governor's secretary rang to say that a visit would not be possible.

Although it was the answer he had expected, the chill formality of it made him very angry. He poured himself a double whisky and drank it neat, splashing a little on the front of his shirt. Then he hurried into the bedroom and threw a few essentials into an overnight bag, scribbled a hasty and largely illegible note to his daily woman, and hurried down to the taxi rank. He asked to be taken to Liverpool Street Station, and he arrived at Reve just as the sun was setting.

His appearance caused no surprise. They seemed to have passed beyond all emotion into a state of grey inertia, but Pam took his hand and said that she was glad to see him. Her voice sounded muffled, as if she had a heavy cold, and he knew that she had been crying.

She led him into her own sitting room, scooped a small dog out of her chair and seated him opposite.

She told him that Lizzie was in a state of near collapse and in bed under doctor's orders. Dully spent most of the day with her, and at night slept on a small divan bed that had been brought into her room. Tomorrow the appeal was to be heard and he insisted that he should be the only one to attend.

'I'll go with him,' Felix said.

'You'll have an uphill job to persuade him.'

He asked about the rest of the family and she told him that Aunt Miriam was trying hard to be brave, but the uncles remained in ignorance of the situation.

'They know something's going on, they can sense it, then they go back to sleep and forget all about it. They sleep an awful lot these days.'

'Winter's coming,' he said.

She rang for the butler and asked him to take Mr Felix's case up to the room he normally occupied, and that they would have dinner together in her sitting room. She was marvellously comforting, for one so young.

'By the way, it's our birthday tomorrow,' she said lightly, and he knew instantly that that was why she had been crying.

There was nothing he could say or do. In the silence that followed, the little dog snuffled round his ankles. He bent to pick it up and it snuggled on to his lap.

'Remember Scotus and Eulalie?'

'Practically all versions of them. I remember the boys having a pet pig that used to scuttle across the great hall with a couple of footmen in furious pursuit.'

'It must have been fun in those days.' She sounded wistful.

'It will be again,' he said with an effort. 'We'll all come out of this into another brighter era. Nothing, however awful, goes on for ever.'

'I hope you're right.'

Over dinner, which they could make no more than a pretence of eating, she talked to him about Bessie Hinton again.

'Mother just rambles on about her all the time. She's convinced that if it hadn't been for her, this would never have happened. She keeps saying that it's all part of the pattern – what she calls echoes of violence.'

'Is the doctor giving her sedatives?'

'Yes. Not enough to knock her out, but – '

'But enough to distort her reasoning powers. Poor Aunt Liza, she shouldn't have to put up with additional torment – did her own mother believe in it, by the way?'

'Yes, after Aunt Netta died. So I suppose Mother caught the infection from her.'

They lapsed into silence, and in the deep melancholy that encompassed them it was difficult not to brood on the strangeness of coincidence.

They retired early to bed that night, and Felix leaned out

of his open window inhaling the scents of late summer and listening to the owls calling.

Celia and Pam. Pam and Celia. . . . He wondered whether the ability to see them both side by side, if only for an instant, would deliver him from the pain of being in love with them both as one single individual.

He breakfasted in his room, and the first person he met downstairs was Bird. He recognized the soldierly footsteps before he spoke.

'Morning, Sir. Heard you was arrived.'

'Good morning, Bird.' Then an abrupt halt. What to say next? Aware that Bird was still standing in front of him, Felix decided to say what was in his mind. 'So, today's the day.'

'Yes, Sir.' Bird clenched his lips tight for a moment, then said: 'Reckon she'll git orf?'

'If hoping's got anything to do with it. Whatever happens, we mustn't stop hoping.'

Bird half turned away. His voice sounded muffled. 'It was me what givver the gun. Showed her how to load it and everythink.'

'But how were you to know?'

'I wasn't,' Bird said. 'All the same, I dunnit – didn't I?'

'You mustn't blame yourself,' Felix said, wearied by his own clichés. 'Nobody else has, have they?'

'No, but I gotta live with it, haven't I?' Bird said darkly. He walked off, his shoes squeaking.

In the library the curtains had been opened, the sofa cushions plumped and the tables dusted. The morning papers lay neatly arranged on one of them.

There was a lot about the political crisis. Gloom, resignation and cynicism were expressed after Chamberlain's return from Germany. He had agreed to the German occupation of the Sudetenland, and upon returning to London had signed an Anglo-French agreement to the effect that any area of Czechoslovakia containing a more than fifty per cent German population should be handed over to Hitler. The wisdom of first throwing a small bone to a greedy dog before surrendering the entire carcass was

570

largely lost upon the Czechs. Mr Chamberlain had now flown back to Germany in order to present the agreement to Hitler.

It was also noted that the Dullingham-Reve appeal was to be heard today in the Court of Criminal Appeal.

It was a little before ten o'clock when a chauffeur brought the car round to the drive in front of the south terrace. Felix, who was sitting in a wicker chair, rose to his feet as he heard voices behind him.

'Felix – how nice!' It was Dully, with Pam.

'I do hope you didn't mind my sudden appearance.'

'God, no – *any* time, you know that!' The hand that grasped his was very strong, very hearty. The voice too was very strong and hearty, and Felix read a great deal in its vibrant depths.

'Father's off now – ' Pam began to say.

Quickly Felix stepped in and asked whether he could go with him. It wouldn't take more than a few seconds to change.

'Wouldn't hear of it, my boy! You stay here and look after the family, and tell Nixon to chill some champagne for when I get back.'

Felix promised to do so, and blindness spared him the sight of the gaunt figure in cheerful spongebag checks, a soft brown trilby and a carnation in his buttonhole, running light and long-legged down the steps. It also spared him the ghastly travesty of a smile that accompanied the final wave of his hand as he drove off.

Sensing Pam standing by him, Felix put his arm round her shoulders and held her close. For a moment she stopped being the steady, reliable old Pam and clung to him. He caught the fresh scent of her hair just beneath his chin. With both arms around her, tight and protective, he kissed her forehead, but for the life of him couldn't offer the conventional salutations. During the night he had woken with the memory that Berry had been killed on his nineteenth birthday.

The day was endless, endless. During the morning Pam sat with Lizzie in her room, while Felix wandered stick in hand through the gardens. Reve, more than anywhere else on earth, brought back the memory of being able to see. Colours, shapes, faces, swam through his imagination stimulated by the scent of box and late lavender. Most birds were silent now, but the sudden bitter-sweet song of a robin instantly transported him to soft autumn mornings and speeding over the dew-pearled grass in pursuit of Berry and Tommy while a nursemaid cried, 'Master Felix – your *jacket*, if you please!'

Perhaps he should bury himself in the past more; concentrate on old memories and be grateful for what he had once had. After all, he had been luckier than most.

In the saloon he came across Aunt Miriam.

'I am sitting in a little patch of sunlight,' she called. 'Come and join me.'

She reached for his hand and her fingers felt cold and spiky with age.

'Is Boney with you?'

'He is on the floor, eating a raisin. He will come to me presently.'

'I haven't seen the uncles yet.'

'I saw Bird wheeling them on to the terrace a short while ago. He is a great believer in fresh air, but always pays great attention to wrapping them up.'

'There's quite a chill on the wind this morning.'

They sat in silence, the air heavy with unspoken thoughts. *Celia . . . Celia . . . Celia. . . .* Then Boney finished his raisin and hopped on to Aunt Miriam's outstretched foot. He plodded up her leg on to her lap, and she adjusted the position of her arm so that he could walk up it and reach her shoulder. He nuzzled her cheek with a pleasant clicking sound.

'Dear old fellow,' she said.

It was not until Felix, impelled by restlessness, stood up to go that Aunt Miriam broached the subject in both their minds. 'Today is going to last for a very long while, and all we can do is try to fill it with hope.'

'You're right,' he said.

He rejoined her for luncheon, and halfway through the

meal Pam reappeared. She ate a small sliver of Stilton and some grapes, then suggested that she and Felix should go out for a spin while Aunt Miriam and Lizzie were having a siesta.

They drove with the hood down and the air was crisp as an apple. She handled the little two-seater well, and Felix said he remembered her mother driving him in a dogcart with Berry and Tommy. 'She had a marvellously vivid, vigorous sort of beauty, I remember, and a great mass of auburn hair piled up under a straw hat with roses on it.'

'She's still got her long hair,' Pam said, 'but it's gone grey now. As for being vigorous, well, she always was – until this happened.'

It was the first time they had broached the subject of Celia. He wanted to say something comforting, but found it difficult.

'The chestnut trees are beginning to turn yellow. They're always the first.'

'I used to love the colours of autumn.'

'What do you miss most,' she asked suddenly, 'since you lost your sight?'

Only Pam could ask such a straightforward question without arousing the old resentment that still lay deeply buried.

'Looking at pretty girls,' he said.

'Good job you can't see me. I'm not pretty.'

'Bet you are.'

She shook her head. 'Neither of us takes after Mother in the least bit.'

'Describe yourself to me,' he said. 'Go on.'

She turned down a lane where the trees met overhead in a soaring arc.

'I think I look what I am,' she said finally. 'Sort of serviceable.'

'And how about Celia?' If she could ask straightforward questions, so could he.

'Well, we are identical twins,' she told him, 'but she's got a more private, sort of shut-away look.'

'Yes. I can see it, somehow.'

'And she's shut away all right now, isn't she?'

'For the moment. . . .'

They had driven for some way in silence when Pam said that she thought there was a place nearby where they could have tea. She found it, a comfortably dilapidated farmhouse with a couple of rough wooden tables set out in the orchard under the apple trees. They sat side by side on a bench, and the farmer's wife brought them a tray of tea, bread and butter and fruit cake. She eyed Pam curiously but without discourtesy.

'Come on, Old Serviceable,' Felix said when she had gone. 'Pour us some tea and pass me the jam.'

Suddenly they were hungry. Perhaps it was the fresh air, perhaps it was being away from the waiting silence of Reve. They finished the bread and butter and asked for some more. 'We'll bring old Cee here when it's all over,' Pam said. 'She likes places like this.'

'I wrote to ask if I could visit her,' Felix said abruptly. 'They wouldn't let me.'

He sensed her turn her head to look at him; he caught the scent of raspberry jam on her breath.

'Oh gosh, that was nice.' She turned her head away again, then added: 'You're very fond of her, aren't you?'

'More than fond,' he said. 'I love you both.'

There's love and love, she thought, staring through the trees. But I won't think about that now.

'Have a piece of birthday cake,' she said, passing the plate, and her warm chuckle of laughter prompted him to raise his teacup ceremoniously.

'Many happy returns of the day,' he replied, and having at last been able to utter the trite words, became filled with a strange contentment that he knew she sensed and understood.

They drove back to Reve without saying any more. It was too early for Dully to have returned but the tension seemed to be gathering in the great deserted rooms; it hung on the air like an omen and crushed the fragile bond of happiness between them. Unable to relax, Pam suggested that there might be some advance news on the wireless.

574

She switched it on in her sitting room, and as usual the political situation dominated. Mr Chamberlain had met Herr Hitler at Godesberg and Herr Hitler had indicated that the concessions agreed in the Anglo-French agreement were now insufficient. All military installations in the evacuated Sudeten area were to remain intact, etc., etc. Mr Chamberlain was due to return home tomorrow. In London, decontamination centres were being planned in case of gas attacks and emergency plans were well in hand for the immediate evacuation of children.

There was a slight pause before the well-mannered voice continued with the statement that in the Dullingham-Reve murder case an appeal had been heard by the Lord Chief Justice. No reason had been found for allowing the appeal, and the findings of the court were confirmed.

He then went on to speak about the weather.

Numbly Pam turned it off and went over to the window. 'Does that mean she'll hang?'

'Yes.' He sat with his head in his hands.

Pam gave a great gasping sob, then jerked round as someone tapped on the door.

Without waiting for a reply, Lizzie came in. She was wearing one of her favourite long skirts and a frilled blouse. Her hair was immaculately coiled in place, and the youthfulness of her figure – now that she had lost so much weight – contrasted strangely with her ravaged face.

'I suddenly thought what a mean ole thing I am,' she said, coming into the room. 'Dully's done nothing but run round after me, so here I am all dressed up and best face forward to welcome them home.'

'Them?' Pam said involuntarily.

'They always release prisoners straight away after there's been an appeal,' Lizzie said. Then faltered. She stood looking from one to the other. 'You know something.'

'It was on the news just now.' Pam spoke without looking at her.

'You're telling me . . . it's failed?'

Aware that Pam was incapable of replying, Felix sprang up and went over to the sound of Lizzie's voice. He reached

575

gropingly for her hands and imprisoned them tightly within his own.

'Go on thinking of Dully,' he said urgently. 'Keep thinking about what he must have gone through today, and how he'll be driving home all alone and trying to rehearse breaking the news.'

'He's here now,' Pam said, from over by the window.

'The last prisoner we had in here asked if she could call me Mum,' reflected one of the wardresses. 'I had to tell her things like that weren't allowed.'

Celia made a wordless sound indicative of faint but polite interest.

'Poisoned her hubby so she could claim his insurance.'

'How many days have I got left?' The words were brutally direct.

'They haven't fixed the execution yet, dear.'

Silence. A blank silence which the distant clatter of feet on iron walkways, the clang of doors and the jangle of keys failed to penetrate. Since the appeal had failed, a second wardress had moved into the cell with her. She was never left alone now. It was warm and airless in there, and smelt of Lysol from the toilet arrangements and underarm sweat from one of her companions.

'Fancy another game of brag?'

'No, thank you. Not just now.'

They had taught her all sorts of card games, but didn't seem to know any of those she had played in the nursery with Pam. She didn't want to play games now, and she didn't want their company.

She wanted to be left alone so that she could get used to the idea of being hanged, like Bessie Hinton.

She had imagined that she was already used to it – or had at least accepted it – from the moment she decided to shoot von Dirksen, but she realized now that it had only been like a vague possibility in her mind. It had had no substance, no reality. Now, it was going to happen in a few days' time.

She wished they would tell her when, so that she could start counting. And start getting her courage together.

She couldn't stop thinking about it; wondering how long it would take and how much it would hurt. The wardresses wouldn't discuss it, except to say that she wouldn't know much about it. Did that mean they would give her a sleeping pill or something? They wouldn't tell her, but for their part seemed fascinated by the fact that she was an earl's daughter. They asked if she had a coronet and she replied that if she had, she had never seen it. Yet, like Bird, they seemed reluctant to address her as 'Lady Celia'; it obviously embarrassed them in some way, so they evaded the problem by calling her 'dear'. Which was quite nice of them, in a way.

The only time she could have her thoughts to herself was when they occasionally rambled off into whispered conversations of their own. Then she could sit on the bed with her back propped against the wall and give herself up to daydreams about Berry and Tommy. But although she had only attempted the assassination because of them, she found that they were now becoming curiously thin and insubstantial; however determinedly she fixed her gaze on their photograph, they seemed to be receding from her; withdrawing their presence as if they were disconcerted and perhaps rather shocked by the cheap vulgarity of her gesture.

And their place was being taken by Bessie Hinton, that stealthy shadow on the wall that seemed to be growing hourly in strength and clarity. It was Bessie now with whom she identified, and Bessie who brought her a rough, kindly comfort during the spells of silent, stomach-churning terror: I've been through it and it wasn't too bad because I had the satisfaction of knowing I died for a cause I believed in. And you'll do the same. You'll go out there when the time comes with your head held high and only you will know that I'm right there with you, holding your hand and saying, Come on now, be a brave girl; I was, and you can be the same because we're two of a kind, you see. . . .

Then one morning Miss Size, the Deputy Governor, came in and told her that the date of the execution had been fixed for Monday, 3 October. She told her very gently and quietly, and the two wardresses moved a little closer to Celia in case she might have to be restrained from making a scene.

'What's the date today?' She moistened her lips.

'The twenty-eighth. But there is going to be a final appeal to the Home Secretary.'

'When will we know?'

'That I can't say. The political crisis is taking up a lot of his time.'

Miss Size talked to her for a few more minutes and asked if she would like some more books to read. Celia nodded.

'I will choose them personally,' Miss Size promised. Then she paused by the door. 'I dare say it could be arranged for you to see your parents again, if you wished.'

Celia's fingers were making hidden counting movements against the side of her prison frock. Twenty-eight, twenty-nine, thirty – thirty days hath September – first, second, third . . . only four clear days left to go.

'No, thank you,' she said in a high, clear voice. 'I don't think I'd better.'

'Don't forget the chaplain is always available,' Miss Size told her before leaving. 'He is ready to comfort you all he can.'

He can't do anything, and neither can my parents, she thought. Even the boys have gone. Only four days to go, but at least I've got Bessie. Bessie's the only person I believe in now.

Four days. Then three.

Patient, polite and faintly pathetic, Mr Chamberlain and his umbrella had been to Berchtesgaden, to Godesberg and now finally to Munich. He had been shouted at, stormed at, screamed at, and had tried hard to remain composed in the suffused face of fanaticism.

The whole world knew that the flight to Munich was the last chance. A national state of emergency had now been declared, the British and French fleets were already mobilized, and over a million Czechs were manning their defences on the German border. Peace, and Celia's life, were trickling away together.

Life at Reve had reached total standstill. Regular meals and regular hours of sleep had been abandoned; they catnapped where they sat, and moved dazedly from one tray of cold coffee to another. Tiny tempting sandwiches on silver salvers lay untouched, and the household staff crept about their duties and shrank in silent compassion from the family's presence.

They listened to the news without taking in what was said and stared out of the windows oblivious to either rain or sunshine. Only the uncles displayed any signs of normality, and when awake enquired in piping querulous tones why everyone had become such a bore.

On Friday the thirtieth the silence was shattered by a sudden sharp altercation between Lizzie and Pam.

'For God's sake, Mother,' Felix heard Pam expostulate, 'stop maundering on like some superstitious old peasant!'

'I *am* an ole peasant!' Lizzie stormed back. 'I was born one and, if it's all the same to you, I'll remain one!'

'Well, don't inflict any more of your mumbo-jumbo soothsaying on *me!*'

He heard the slam of a door and the sound of quick and furious footsteps across the great hall. He half-rose to go in search of Pam, then decided against it.

Dully came in, and told him in an undertone that he had telephoned again to Holloway and been told that the prisoner still preferred not to see her parents.

'All you can do now is to respect her wishes,' Felix whispered.

'What are you two mumbling about?' demanded Lizzie. 'Has anyone heard anything?'

'Not yet,' Dully said wearily. 'But we'll tell you the minute we do.'

Felix waited in silence for Pam's return. Luncheon for him was a whisky and soda, and when he said to anyone who might be listening that he was going for a walk, there was no reply.

He tapped his way across the terrace and down the steps to the sweep of carriageway, then decided to walk down the avenue in case Pam had gone out in the two-seater and he could meet her on the way back. He didn't meet her. No sound broke the stillness, and the damp sad smell of autumn began to depress him even more. He returned to the house and went up to his room. He lay on the bed, trapped in his world of impenetrable darkness while the minutes ticked remorselessly away.

She didn't return home until after the lamps had been lit and the curtains drawn. Her father and mother, Aunt Miriam and Felix were all in the library; all sitting on different sofas, all listlessly apart from one another.

She threw open the double doors. Evening rain had dampened her coat and deepened the wave in her hair. She looked extraordinarily bright and brisk and full of purpose.

'It may interest you all to know that I've spent most of the afternoon in the Cambridgeshire Record Office,' she announced. 'I've been through all the newspaper reports and all the legal documents they've got about the Ely Bread Riots that took place in 1816, and nowhere could I find anything about a woman called Elizabeth Hinton. There was no mention of her name among the rioters, let alone among the people who were hanged. So at least I've disposed of that old cock-and-bull story!'

She looked at them expectantly. No one said anything. Only Lizzie opened her mouth and then closed it again. It seemed as if nothing could ever break through their quiescence, their terrible deathly apathy.

'Listen.' She opened her handbag and took out a sheet of paper. Unfolding it, she began to read aloud: 'The trial opened on 17 June 1816 and lasted for a week. Out of the twenty-four men originally sentenced to death, nineteen were reprieved. The names of those condemned and hanged were John Dennis, Thomas South, Isaac Harley, George Crow and William Beamiss. One man was transported for life, five were transported for fourteen years and three for seven years. I got that out of the *Cambridge Quarter Sessions Records*. Then I went all through all the old copies of *The Bury and Norwich Post* as well as the *Cambridge Gazette*, and there wasn't a single thing about a woman called Bessie Hinton. There *were* some women who'd been had up for looting . . . hang on a minute' – she consulted the paper again – 'Hannah Jarvis, Elizabeth King, Amelia Lightharness and a Lucy Rumbelow and an Anne Fuller. But no Bessie Hinton!'

She stared across at her mother, pink-cheeked and shining-eyed. Lizzie made an inarticulate little sound, then turned her head away.

Pam screwed the paper up in a ball and tossed it into the fireplace. She began to unbutton her coat, and although no one said anything they couldn't stop watching her. Even Felix, from the far side of the room, felt the strange new power that seemed to emanate from her.

'And while we're at it,' she said, 'there's something else. In a way it concerns all of you, so you might as well hear me say it.' She peeled off her coat and laid it over the back of a chair. 'Felix,' she said in a loud, defiant voice, 'will you please marry me?'

A sharp intake of breath seemed to come from each sofa. Well, that was better than nothing, she thought.

'*Pamela* . . .' began Lizzie, then faded.

'Really, my dear . . .' Aunt Miriam started to say, then she too faded.

'I think this is hardly an auspicious time to choose for – ' Dully began tersely, but Pam cut across his words.

'Will you, Felix?' She stood looking at him, young, generous and glowing with life.

It was a long while before he answered. 'No, Pam,' he said.

'Please, Felix.'

Felix stood up, smoothing his hair back with both hands. His face was turned towards her and she saw that he was trying hard to smile; to match her own desperate brightness.

'Of course I can't marry you, you silly ass. For one thing I'm far too old, and for another – '

'You're blind. Yes, I know. I've never known you any other way.'

'Pam, for God's sake,' Dully protested.

'I know exactly what I'm doing,' she said in a voice

suddenly reminiscent of Celia's. 'I'm making another crisis, but I'm not making it intentionally because it'll help to take our minds off Cee. I mean every word. It's all true about Bessie Hinton, I searched and *searched*. And it's also true that I want to marry Felix because I've been in love with him ever since I was little, although I don't think anyone ever noticed – and I did the asking because I knew perfectly well he'd never ask me because of all that stuff about being old and blind and everything. So, having got that off my chest . . . what time's dinner?'

Her voice had a slight catch in it towards the end, and it almost seemed as if her wonderful bright-eyed gaiety might let her down.

'I don't think anyone's ordered anything,' Lizzie said in a faint voice. 'I know I haven't. But I don't understand all this about Bessie. . . .'

'I'll tell you tomorrow.' She had to get out of the room before she burst into tears.

'Someone go with her,' Dully said.

Felix went towards the door, threading a slow careful path between the furniture without his stick.

She stood by one of the great heroic statues, watching him in silence. Watching the way he turned his head this way and that to catch the slightest hint of her presence. His grey flannels wanted pressing and one of his shoelaces was coming undone.

'I'm over here.'

He went to her. 'Pam, my dear, I didn't mean to sound so ungracious – '

'Oh, you didn't.'

'I was merely trying to say that the reason why I – '

'Listen,' she said, 'there's only one reason that I'll accept, and that's Celia.'

He shook his head, and it had never ceased to surprise her how much expression there could be in a face with closed eyes. She stood looking at him, careful not to sniff in case he guessed that she was crying.

'I adore you both.'

'Suppose there's – only going to be one of us?'

582

'In that case I'll just have to make do, won't I?' He removed the handkerchief from the top pocket of his sports jacket. 'In the meanwhile, come here, Old Serviceable, and let me dry you.'

He wiped her eyes, then stroked the handkerchief across her forehead and down her cheeks. His touch was tender, and very sure.

'I love you, young Pam,' he said.

Only Dully and Lizzie remained sitting in the library when Bird entered carrying a tray of glasses and decanters.

'Having seen me two ole gents orf to bed I took it upon meself to bring in a little somethink to celebrate the Peace with Honour, Me Lord.'

They looked at him wearily.

'Mr Chamberlain,' Bird explained patiently, 'is back from Munich with a paper signed by him and Adolf to say it's all all right. It's bin on the nooz – I wonder you didn't hear.'

They hadn't heard. He had to explain it again, and he told them how the crowds had surged into Downing Street, laughing and cheering and singing 'For He's a Jolly Good Fellow'. The state of emergency was over. They could stop digging trenches and planning to issue gas masks and evacuate all the kids – it was over. Mr Chamberlain had said so. 'Peace in our time, he called it.'

Dully poured three brandies.

'Oh – ta, Me Lord,' Bird said, and raised his glass above his head. 'And now, here's to Miss Celia!'

Like Pam, he seemed imbued with a strange new vigour; a sudden strong brave optimism. He no longer minded mentioning Celia's name.

They raised their glasses in reply, smiled a little, and managed to say 'To Celia. . . .'

They went to bed that night for the first time for a week, and lay in one another's arms, sleeping, waking, and hoping with a new flicker of confidence.

The confidence was not misplaced.

The prolonged crisis had exacted its measure in many

respects, not the least of them being the backlog of work piled on ministerial desks. On the afternoon following the Prime Minister's return to London, the Secretary of State for Home Affairs remained at work, picking through the welter of letters, reports, statements and agendas.

He was tired. He had had little sleep. His summer holiday had been cancelled, but now it was all over. At least, for the time being. It was very sad about Czechoslovakia being handed over to Germany lock, stock and barrel, and beneath all the cheers and the tears of relief there were strong voices of condemnation. Winston Churchill's was one of them. But a temporary respite had been gained, and provided one was careful to ignore the human element, the right measures had been taken. There was no option but to play for time.

He lit a cigarette, leaning back in his chair and exhaling deeply. Then he read through a letter placed singly in a buff-coloured file, and to prove to himself that he was far from indifferent to the human element, lifted the telephone receiver and spoke to the secretary on duty.

'That damn Dullingham girl,' he said, 'you'd better have me put through to the Governor at Holloway.'

Peace in our time, thought Lizzie. Who could ask for anything more than that? We know it's all bound to change after we've gone, so we'd better make the best of it and be grateful.

She was walking along one of the main first-floor corridors of Reve. Sunlight filtered lazily across faded carpet and old polished furniture, and glimmered on a bowl of pot-pourri. She stirred it with her fingers, awakening the scent of last summer's roses.

Peace in our time. She walked on, her long skirt rustling as she passed closed door after closed door. The rooms were still furnished, but empty of people. The Chinese room, the Admiral's room, the Walpole room; she passed the open doors of the picture gallery and glanced inside. They stared back at her, all those Dullingham-Reves with their long straight noses and eyes tilting in the suspicion of a smile.

Dully had sometimes spoken of having to sell some of the Romneys, but so far they had managed not to do so.

She came to the small panelled room. The door was never locked now, and she was able to contemplate the memorabilia with wistfulness in place of pain.

'You were so lovely,' she said aloud. 'And we were so lucky to have you.'

Her thoughts returned to Bessie Hinton. The black spider trapping one coincidence after another in its web had been briskly swept away by Pam – who else? – and all that remained was the question, *Why*?

Leaning against the doorpost, she remembered the man who had come to Aunt Netta's that hot summer afternoon after lunch. A strange man with dark hair and a pointed nose who pinched her knee and whose sudden appearance had so disconcerted Aunt Netta. She wondered if he had been an old beau, and whether he had made up the story as a particularly spiteful way of paying her back for some misdemeanour. Perhaps she had jilted him. . . .

Suddenly she felt she understood how it could have been. Aunt Netta, young, prim, ignorant, and faced for the first time with young male ardour in all its earthy vigour; how alarming she must have found him.

And poor . . . what was his name? Poor Vernon. Lizzie could imagine the pain of the rebuff turning to anger, to bitterness and the desire for revenge. Who would have imagined the consequences, the echoes and shadows of such a long ago incident reverberating down the years, finally to end today, of all days.

Peace in our time, she thought. Peace for the living and the dead.

At the foot of the main staircase Pam's little dog came bouncing towards her. In a sudden paroxysm of joy it seized the hem of Lizzie's skirt and began tugging it vigorously.

'So you've escaped again,' she said. No one ever succeeded in keeping animals in their rightful place at Reve, and she picked it up in her arms. It licked her face, frantic with love.

Where was everyone?

The great hall was silent, no sound of voices came from the library or the saloon. It was so sleepy and quiet, and she lingered in a patch of sunlight, the little dog now lying quiescent against her shoulder. Peace in our time. Peace before the cold of winter; peace for the little time we have left before we die.

She saw them from across the terrace, a small group of people gathered round the white-clad tea table on the lawn. The uncles were drawn up side by side in their wheelchairs, and Aunt Miriam was wearing a large straw hat with a chiffon scarf tied round the brim. Pam and Felix were sitting on the grass very close together, and Dully, in a deck-chair and wearing his old panama hat, had a folded newspaper on his lap. The October sun, golden and gracious, touched them all with the last of its loving warmth, and she saw Uncle Badger stretch out an indolent hand towards the marchpane slices.

She walked down the terrace steps towards them, and the little dog woke and scrambled from her arms. It ran towards the family, yapping its delight at having found them.

'Here you are!' Dully said. 'I've just been reading another article about us. Or at least, about me.' He unfolded the newspaper and read aloud: ' "The Dullingham case had inevitably brought into focus both the family and the background of this unfortunate girl. Secluded stately homes run by armies of flunkeys have no more reality in this day and age than the crime she tried to commit, and one can scarcely blame Lady Celia for her lack of common sense. Girls brought up within the narrow confines of the *ancien régime* have little chance of becoming acquainted with the harsh facts of the modern world." '

Lizzie poured herself a cup of tea, then sank into the wickerwork chair by Dully's side.

' "We have therefore taken it upon ourselves to investigate the life of the present Earl Dullingham, who is Lady Celia's father and presumed mentor." ' Dully crackled the paper a little, cleared his throat and read on: ' "Our investigation has taken very little time because there has been precious little to investigate. The best schools and a prestigious university college, followed by a wearied sinking back into the arms of the family estate. He inherited the earldom from an uncle when in his late twenties, and so far has not raised the necessary energy even to take his seat in the House of Lords." '

A butterfly hovered over the brim of his panama, settled briefly on the newspaper and then fluttered away.

' "His Lordship displays not the slightest discernible interest in either politics or the humanities, or indeed in any subject which might prove of the slightest benefit to us less privileged mortals. . . ." '

'Jealous, that's his trouble,' observed Lizzie. 'Will someone pass me a scone?'

Someone did.

'But I have to admit there's a great element of truth in it,' Dully said, laying the newspaper aside. 'I haven't exactly proved one of the world's greatest innovators, have I?'

'Isn't being happy and minding your own business enough?' Lizzie asked in a low voice. 'Let alone making other people happy too.'

'Everything is going to be all right now,' Aunt Miriam said. 'Dear little Celia is safe and Mr Chamberlain has dealt most admirably with Herr Hitler.'

Uncle Woodstock, aged ninety-four, awoke from a momentary doze and said: 'I can feel a cold wind on my shoulders.'

'Blood's getting thin,' said Badger, and suddenly raised his voice in a quavering tremolo of mock pathos: ' "*When I am dy-y-y-ing* . . ." '

'We're both dying, you old tomfool.'

Yes, the cold wind would come. Winter would strip the leaves from the trees and whiten the breath of the cattle in the park. Old limbs would creak and sigh, and it was highly probable that the central heating would break down again.

But in the meanwhile, the sun was enfolding them all in its autumn glow, and dear old Martha was coming over from Boston for the wedding. Walter had finally consented to vacate Damperdown and spend his last days at Reve, and tomorrow Lizzie and Dully were going to see Celia. They were going to see her once every fortnight until her release.

Peace in our time, thought Lizzie. And there was old Bessie Hinton over in Australia, after all; lying in peace with her husband the way a good woman should.

She leaned back with her eyes closed and her hand in Dully's.

Peace in our time. What more could you ask?